SPITFIRE
AND THE
OBJECTS
OF
DESIRE

PAUL BAUMAN

FLOWER
CITY PRESS

Spitfire and the Objects of Desire
Les Nouvelles Nymphes: Première Partie
by Paul Bauman

Published by Flower City Press LLC

Copyright © 2024 by Paul Bauman

This is a work of fiction. Names, characters, places, and incidents are either products of the author's imagination or exist in the public domain and are used fictitiously. Any resemblance to actual persons not in the public domain, living or dead, is entirely coincidental.

Cover design by James T. Egan of Bookfly Design

Printed in the United States of America
Paperback ISBN: 978-1-7325465-2-3

LES NOUVELLES NYMPHES:

PREMIÈRE PARTIE

Bonjour, weary traveler. What brings you to the Wild Garden? The lush green shade? The soak of dawn? The purple wildflowers perhaps? Your tour is enjoying the rest of Hermes Hill. Go, be with them. You will miss the view...

Ah, you are like me then, a glutton for nature. Let me guess, you want to see the *real* French Athens. I'm looking for it myself. We can look together if you like. Moulin Rouge? Non, you won't find it at the cabarets. Not today. I have searched. And searched. How I have searched. My name is Jacques. This is Marlène. She would shake hands if she weren't holding up the roof. Don't laugh. She has been loyal company to me for some time now. She says, enchanté.

Why, this competent structure is a nymphaeum. What's a nymphaeum? Why, this. Feast your eyes on the semicircle of beautiful archways. Listen. The water is music to the ears. Oui, those are water lilies. In French, they are called nymphéas. Fitting, don't you think? The ladies? Caryatids. Look how Marlène winks in the dappled light. Her friends are very charming. You would think they are water nymphs, the naiads. An easy mistake. They are maenads, for this arrondissement used to be

1

countryside not so long ago, and this shrine is dedicated to the cult of Dionysus. There is a vineyard close by.

I most certainly do *not* work here.

Tell me, have you ever seen a nymph? Ah, I'd have hoped you'd say yes. Maybe you have seen one and knew not what it was. It's been a while since the last reported sighting. I have met several. They are long-lasting creatures, especially if granted immortality. Non, it wasn't Marlène—she is a sculptor's fancy. Perhaps his girlfriend. Now, she is Jacques's girlfriend.

Yes, I'm sober. Don't believe me? Smell my breath. You barely know me? I barely know you, my friend, and here I am, sharing intimate details.

You see, French Athens once had a great concentration of artistic energy. Artists would channel the muses. The nymphs, in turn, delighted by this play of light on canvas, ink on page, song abreast the air, would come and dance and marvel in our ability to reflect nature through our own unique viewpoints. The creative output was largest here on Hermes Hill, back when the cross-pollination of cultures began to flourish.

Care to hear a story? No one listens to my stories. No one but Marlène. My muse has come, I obey, yet nothing completes the circuit. No listener. The world is too distracted. It grows tiring, this march. What! Maybe I'm not any good? I'll have you know I can spin yarns with the best of them. I am as good as Hugo, better than Balzac, than George putain de Sand! Let me prove it to you. Please, I have very few friends. We can sit by the nymphaeum as the sun comes up. It is a fitting scene, for the story is about a nymph. Two nymphs. Two women.

One mademoiselle desires to disappear from life's problems. The other to find her soul and manifest her identity. They have yet to meet. Sit?

Merci. The first young lady is not fluent in French. Lucky for you, I am a polyglot, you monolingual cretin.

You desire to leave? It is a powerful thing, desire. It can drive people beyond the pale, over the brink. I have seen men die chasing visions. I have seen women fall pursuing pleasures.

Perhaps a stray nymph will visit us during our repose in artistry. Fear not, I will keep you safe. Inhale the moss on the marble, smell the wet stone, and relax as we travel to the German Orient—a colony in the Middle East. Our point of interest, a desert town north of the Persian Gulf, on the Khuzestan Plain, called Jacoma.

Nayla at the Blast

Nayla binti Azmi, a young Fräulein of sixteen, laid out the mecha-sleeves on the workbench and picked up a screwdriver. She envisioned the piston rods working, extending over the arms, as she blew the dust from each slot, revealing little screws that held the cylinders together. The hold was not good enough, it appeared. The screws were loose, the washers missing.

No wonder greasing the pistons didn't work. She removed the end cap and sparked a lighter. Sand had gummed up the sealing rings.

Scheisse. What was Baba thinking? Nayla examined the breastplate. He wasn't. He'd forgotten to secure this cover too. Through the glass, she could see a layer of soot had coated the gears underneath. What about the water tank? The lid was gone. The water, carbon juice. There was a burning coal hearth not four meters from where she stood. Baba couldn't leave the innards exposed to the elements.

She clutched her throat as if she could scrape soot deposits off her windpipe from the outside. Her tongue pushed into the roof of her mouth, unlikely to reach her throat as this machine was to work. Current prognosis: these sleeves couldn't bend pig iron, let alone push a coal car down a track.

Baba must have tinkered with the sleeves while drunk, fell asleep, and suckled from the water tank to quell his headache. This was the opposite of progress. If she succeeded where Baba had failed, it would make him a fortune. Then he wouldn't have to slave so hard and drink so much and make her work at the Blast.

The work shed door slapped open. Cold desert air blew. The hearth flickered. A skull-like face greeted her, painted black, as if night itself had barged in.

"Nayla," Baba's voice thundered. "I need you at the Blast."

She pressed her butt to the table's edge, her filthy hands made filthier on the ash-laden surface. Her feet quaked in her boots. She inhaled, attempting to find the scent of whiskey on his breath or discover it sweating through the clogged pores of his skin, but the old cigar smell of the hearth was too strong and Baba too far.

The whites of his eyes were mottled red from burst capillaries. Caused by alcohol or ejections at the Blast? Black rings encircled his eyes from where his goggles had rested. Whiskers shadowed his chin, his hair disheveled. Did this mean hours dedicated to work or drink? She knew not which.

She tried diplomacy. "Please, Baba. I just cleaned my hair."

"Rent is up." He looked around. "I don't see any suitors coming to take you off my hands."

"Arranging my marriage was your job, or are you planning to wed me to a rishi in exchange for two cows?"

Baba sneered. "You are more valuable to me than two cows, my daughter. The cows can't lift a shovel. I'm going to need you all weekend too."

She stroked her braid for comfort—or to savor its smooth touch before the coke fumes would suffocate it again. "I worked for the rent last weekend."

"Spent it on bus fare."

"To the rathskeller for moonshine." She sniffed the orange blossom on her braid. "How am I responsible?"

He crossed the room like fury unleashed. She dropped her braid. How fast could she put on the broken mecha-sleeves and hold him off? She leapt backward onto the table and postured in defense with a curled boot in the air. The pressure of his grip enclosed her calf. He pulled her toward him deceptively quick—his biceps tied on his bone with wormy strings. He had muscles in there somewhere, for he grabbed her ear and pinched. The stench was cloying. Whiskey.

"You live in my house. I put food on my table for you to eat. You will go to the Blast and support yourself."

"Autsch! You're pulling my earrings," she whined, clambering off the table. A wrench clanged to the floor. The thick lump of rubber and metal rods that made up the sleeves followed.

"I won't pull nothing." He tugged her to the door, her cartilage threatening to rip from her skull. "Go home and get dressed. Be at the Blast by eleven sharp." He squeezed her wrist and drew her watch to her nose. Gears moved under the glass. "Don't give me the excuse that your watch is broken again."

He shoved her hand at her side and prodded her out the door, onto the sandy trail that led to the main thoroughfare.

"Why pay for the shed if we never have rent?" She regretted it the moment she said it. She loved the shed.

"I come here to do my thinking." The door slapped against the frame.

"I wish I had Kameera's baba for a father." Tears wet the corners of her eyes.

The door swung back open. "And I wish your mother stayed in French Athens." He leaned his scrawny body against the doorway. "Where does that leave us? With overdue rent. If I don't see you shoveling scrap into that furnace, you have no home."

"Where will I go?"

"You can ask Ravi to be his daughter. Maybe he'll take you. Fill your head with silly Vedas until you reach enlightenment or starve to death. Whatever happens first."

How dare he make fun of Ravi uncle's teachings. The Vedas were trivialities to her, but their sacred, exclusive nature made her feel special. She placed her hand on her ear to ease the pain, took three paces, and looked back. "You're an Arschloch!"

"Fine, I'm an Arschloch. Watch that dial, Fräulein."

She slogged up to the road in tears, wishing for her shawl, for Maman, to be older so she could escape this trap. She hugged her arms. One look from Maman and Baba's grieving would stop. He would have no reason to drink and all his bad habits would evaporate in the morning sun.

Don't be so naïve. Unrealistic. Maman wasn't coming back from the dead.

Aging herself. That could work. No landlord would rent to a sixteen-year-old, but a twenty-year-old, however.

Nein. She could not pass for twenty in disguise and Kali, the goddess of time, didn't move clocks that quick.

A box, she would live in a box. She didn't care. Whose box? She had seen a nice crate outside of Kameera's from a new majlis sofa Ravi uncle had bought. Their apartment was twice as large and filled with love. Ravi uncle had hired an instructor for Kameera to play the violin and encouraged her to practice every day, dreaming she'd perform in a great concert hall. He didn't pawn her sitar and send her to the Blast to *support herself.*

Adoption, then.

Would Ravi uncle really go for that? A Vaishya adopting a Shudra? They were landowners, she a laborer. It was laughable. However, he had broken the social order more than once. Only Brahmins, Kshatriyas and Vaishyas could study the Vedas, yet here he was of a higher caste, showing her sacred texts and teaching her to read them, teaching only a Brahmin could do. Their friendship itself was frowned upon, and Kameera's. If it was not for Kameera crying a qanat at the bazaar whenever they parted as children and the fondness they shared, they'd have never been allowed to play together.

When Nayla had asked why he was teaching a Shudra, Ravi uncle had said that, although she was born here, they were strangers in a strange land—surrounded by Muslims, controlled by Germans—and he wanted to preserve their culture, even to a Hindu girl who was half-French and a quarter Malay, to which he concluded with a wink and a nod.

Jacoma had shaken things up. Ravi uncle, a landowner, worked at the Blast, but he was no shovel hog. Any more breaches, and she feared the temple would throw him out and their community shun him. Imagine the guilt! It would all be thanks to her!

She ought to run away. But to where? Jacoma was desert on all sides. Walking was impossible. She could save for a ticket on the Orient Express, buy a camel, head to the mountains. Anything. Anywhere but here.

Then who would take care of Baba? He was all she had in this big, cold world.

She rubbed her arms.

Moonlight tinted the golden town in green. Gears kissed behind glass domes on the sides of the buildings she passed—the library, the post office—generating steam for indoor heat. Large, pointed archways reflected the moon off their ceramic columns, the light unable to reach the dark recesses in between. Some lurker might've been watching her from one of these iwans.

Nayla reached for her knife. It was in her purse, back at the shed. She needed protecting. If only she had a man... a hopeless dream. Baba had no property and no dowry for marriage. *You are free to arrange your own*, was Baba's reply. How? She wasn't good enough for anyone robed in silk, and a poor boy couldn't take her out of Jacoma. She had tried and failed. Poverty was all that people from her caste knew. No one left the Sand Pits.

Gas lamps guided her home where she whisked her key into the door of her tenement. She waited for the whir of gears and entered. Dogs barked in the basement. Her boots thumped the grated steps as she climbed to the third floor. The twang of her old sitar reverberated down the hall from Mirza's apartment. She missed her instrument. Had Baba paid the pawnshop on time, Mirza wouldn't have bought it, and the strings would be responding to her touch right now, helping to forget her troubles. From Mirza's hands, the sound was torture.

And so was that smell. Something stunk. It came from her door. She inserted her key, gears whirred, and the door opened upon a faint outline of tubing on the kitchen table, illuminated by the moon coming in behind her from the foyer windows. There were tubes and some kind of oil drum, a large canister the size of a stew pot she could wrap her arms around.

Her fingers brushed the gas light on the wall, feeling for the valve. She pinched the weighty, studded knob, cranked it a full turn, and picked up the lucifer matches from the sill. She raised the match head to the stucco wall and froze. She knew that sour odor anywhere, only this time it was magnified, and it made her nose want to bleed. Something was fermenting. The drum and tubing—it was a distillery. Baba had bought a distillery! The man was verrückt!

Strike the match, Nayla. Vapors had rendered the apartment a powder keg. It could all be over with the flick of a wrist; let the flame consume the air in a flash. *Strike the match.* Baba had thought it was a good idea to squander their money, did he? See if she went to the Blast to recoup the rent. One downward stroke. It was all it would take. Would the fireball char her body into burnt naan or fling her into the street?

Would Baba mourn? Would he miss her? Would he bother to have her cremated, the parts that survived? The thrill of escape roused the hairs on her neck as if she received a shock from the lamp. *Don't strike the match.* This scenario ended like all the others. Who would take care of Baba? If only he'd appreciate her, the burden wouldn't be so heavy. He wouldn't mourn. He'd think, *Gut, more marks for whiskey,* and lose himself in a schniquered haze.

Maman would've cared.

"Nayla," she would have said. "Put down the match. Turn back the knob on the lamp."

Nayla restored both and passed through the Bengal tiger design on their beaded portiere into the living room, where she pulled a lever on the wall. Gears lifted the window and spread the Kashan curtain. Baba was going to complain that she'd let the heat out.

Who cared what he thought? *So long as that contraption spews gas into the apartment, this window must remain open. Imagine if he passed out drunk. He'd have died from the fumes.*

She shook her head as if to free the yoke of parenting from her neck and went to her room. She removed her earrings, set them on the vanity, slid out of her tunic, and bunned up her hair. Why she talced her armpits, she never knew. The steel mill was a rotten egg factory. The stench clung to her skin like sweat and impregnated her clothes. She cinched in her waist with a rope and tucked the tassels into her salwar, draped to her ankles in baggy reams of cotton. She gave herself a final look. No tassels or jewelry loose at the Blast.

The moon outlined her Nataraja statue, Shiva, in one of his many forms, dancing in his sprocket. Moonlight gleamed off her watch. She could make the last omnibus. She grabbed her bag, threw on her embroidered jacket, and locked the apartment.

Sure enough, two blocks over, the omnibus was still there. Nayla scratched behind one of the horse's ears and said "Hallo" to the nice man. He said "Hallo, Fräulein" as she climbed in the cab. The café at the corner was making bastani. She could smell the ice cream through her open window.

"Traveling without an escort again, Nayla?" asked the man across from her, his voice deep and hypnotic like a tambura.

Ravi uncle. A smile crept beneath his handlebar mustache, expanding in kindness with his smoky brown eyes, dignified features on his long, squarish face of medium tone; his eyebrows thick and dark like mountains, glad to see her; his chin showing growth from a lack of shave, and his earrings outshining the soot.

He was dressed for work, with tassels hanging from his vest and fez like always—a uniform mandated by decree of the Blast owner, Herr bin Ramli. To Nayla, the tassels seemed like hazards. She had voiced her concern once. Ravi uncle, balmed in sandalwood, warm and sweet, had sandwiched her hand in calm reassurance and said that crane operators didn't work with anything jagged, and she never brought it up again. But it didn't stop her from thinking the worst. *Nein, Nayla, he is as safe up in the controls as you are traveling alone at night.*

"It's why I carry this." Nayla opened her purse and pulled out a switchblade.

"Wherever did you get that?" he asked.

"Street urchin," she said. "Don't worry. I didn't show Kameera." Nayla shifted in her seat, wanting to assure Ravi that life with Baba wasn't making her a bad influence.

"Just point it away from yourself when you open it." He leaned across the aisle and spun the knife around in her hand.

"Danke."

"It makes for good physical protection." He rubbed his chin. "What about spiritual?"

Nayla had not thought of that. Not seriously. The scriptures gave her hope and put her in a good mood. She had a snuff tin at home filled with quotes from scripture she was proud to own—her Brahman Box—goodies she wrote out with Kameera and brought home from Ravi uncle's—but they weren't something she could actually apply to solve her problems.

"You know, I have a Purana for just this occasion," said Ravi uncle. "The Lord protects everyone, but one who depends completely upon Him is especially looked after by the Lord."

Was he implying what she thought he was?

"So I don't need the knife?" she asked.

"You need absolute conviction the Lord protects you. The Lord in the passage refers to Shiva, another form of Brahman, the universal consciousness that resides in all things. The knife, you can decide for yourself when you're ready."

"Danke, Ravi uncle."

She could reflect on that hairy endeavor some other time.

Right now was the perfect opportunity to learn if she could move in with Kameera. And leave Baba all alone? Ja. There was no hurt in asking. It was only to see. She opened her mouth but the words jammed in her throat. It was too big a favor. She would be an imposition. It was dumm. Baba would find her. Tell the neighborhood she thought she was a Vaishya. It would cause all kinds of trouble. And yet...*Ravi uncle might actually say, Jawohl, Nayla, we'd love to have you.*

"I'll bring you a coffee before shift change," Ravi uncle said, wiggling his mustache. "It is quite late."

"Cardamom spice, please, if they have it."

"The finest in the German Orient." He smiled and winked.

Nayla smiled. Ravi uncle was practically a second father.

By 11 p.m. sharp, she took her position before the charging doors to the open-hearth furnace with a pair of tinted goggles strapped to her head. The furnace doors shined on her lenses in bright orange squares. She drove a shovel into the box of limestone and approached the hot cavity. The port lifted like a guillotine blade. Through a wall that protected her from the fires, she tossed in her powdered rock. Her face sponged heat, the magma frothing, and she backed off for a cooldown and the next man in rotation.

Sweat dampened the insides of her knees and soaked her arms in soggy reservoirs. She didn't know if the caffeine had taken effect. There was something about feeding a sixteen-hundred-degrees centigrade pool of sun that made one highly alert.

The rotten egg stench disappeared by the time her crew moved on to scrap metal. Rather, she'd become accustomed to it. She scooped her shovel into the box of old parts. Bed springs, dented pinions, and escape wheels flung through the charging door. Gears hit the lava, each with a profoundly satisfying splash. Worm gears shaped like cylinders, bevel gears with small tops and fat bottoms, helical gears with angled teeth, chipped and broken. Where did all these parts come from? No matter how many were shoveled in, there always seemed to be more than she knew what to do with, piling up behind her in miniature mountains.

Soon she'd be as broken as these parts. Her joints swelled against the wool padding in her gloves. Pain stemmed from her wrists, though she couldn't blame it all on the Blast. It was partly from the mecha-sleeves. The wrists needed support. All she had managed thus far was to push a carriage in the road. Tried to. The wrists needed their own set of pistons, much smaller than the two that extended from her shoulders to her hands. And her legs? What about the legs? If her arms were going to exert force on a coal car, she needed stability from the legs.

How was Baba going to earn extra marks to buy parts?

She could work every weekend. Then when would she find time to assemble the thing or study human anatomy to build it correctly? The library had diagrams that needed reading. Had only Ravi uncle tutored her like he did Kameera. Kameera could recite all of the bones in the human body. The information was trivial to her. Kameera didn't need to build a mecha-suit to live.

"Right behind you, Nay."

Ojas sent the last of the gears gleaming into the furnace and chucked the tongs in too, if only to spite the Blast. His onyx black hair waved above his goggles as he stepped his lanky frame aside, no more the emblazoned silhouette, and dusted off his hands. His brown skin glowed, as though he received a tan from the hearth. With his height, he reached for a long pole attached to a lever and lowered the door with a grin. Behind the crooked smile, part of her thought he still held their awkward night in the yakhchāl against her, but she could've been mistaken.

If only it had gone smoothly, maybe it could've led to a Gandharva marriage, one based on love with no rituals or family consent—just her and Ojas running away together. Would he still do it? After the night in the yakhchāl, she didn't bother him with these ideas. He wanted more out of life for her, so he had said, while accepting his to be one of drudgery. It was a sound answer, but maybe there was more to it. Maybe the sight of her didn't get his blood pumping hot enough.

Thoughts of anatomy and mechanics faded as her mind went numb. An imposing ladle slid down the track on a traveling crane filled with hot metal from the furnace and poured its contents into a spout next to the charging doors.

She seized the lull in work and uncapped a kidney-shaped pouch strapped to her shoulder. She guzzled; the water always warm, almost boiling. Lava bubbled through the portholes. Respect the flame, and the flame would respect her.

She had three more open hearths to charge. That meant thirty-six more boxes of lime and scrap metal to weigh out and toss in. She had rather not think about it. Her arms were going to fall off. Science decided that it took twelve hours for a hearth to make steel. Why, science? Why?

By the time she arrived home, the first batch would be half complete. And so, it was. Most likely. When the bell rung, steel was the last thing on her mind. Only home and sleep.

Her fingers ached as she lifted the pretzel key into the slot of her building. Dawn spilled through the gold-coated latticework of the temple's tower across the street and splayed upon the stucco façade. She climbed the grated steps, a dead girl walking. Gears purred. She staggered into her apartment.

A new tool set lay inside an open chest on the table. Baba sat on the majlis sofa through the tiger beads, reading the paper.

"What's this?" Nayla asked.

Wrenches, screwdrivers, and drill bits never shone so brightly.

"A gift," said Baba.

"For me?" she asked, wary.

He nodded.

"Where did you earn the money?"

"Sold the mecha-sleeves for scrap."

One of the last good things about her life exploded in her heart like a tiny bomb. Shrapnel penetrated her lungs.

"That was our ticket out of here." Her lips twitched, losing elasticity and the saliva necessary to speak. "I—I had something new to try."

He sat with his knee folded and said, "If I couldn't figure it out, you weren't going to."

She pressed her hand on the wall and parted the tiger curtain. "What do I possibly need with these tools, then?"

"To fix stuff around the house."

"Around the house?" The whites of her eyes showed. "You are a massive Fickkopf."

"What did you say?" He threw the paper onto the cushion and pounced through the beads.

Maman, save me. Nayla put up her hands. *Vishnu, someone.*

Baba grabbed her throat and seized her in a headlock. She plucked a wrench from the tool chest. Her fingers hurt to form a fist, though grasp the wrench she did and swung it at Baba. The tools clattered to the tiles. His hand stopped her before she whacked his collar with a second blow, and he pressed her into the icebox. She couldn't hold back the tears. She was tired. A gust from a vent could flatten her.

"You left the window open," he said, rage brewing in his voice. "Do you know how much heat costs? The price of coal?"

She grabbed his wrist with both hands. "You would have blown yourself up with the fumes." She glanced at the homemade distillery on the table.

The whiskey was stale on his breath, the poison on its way out of him. His hand relaxed around her throat and moved to her shoulder.

"I'm sorry, Nayla. I didn't know you were trying to protect me." The lines on his forehead lifted, wiping the anger from the ridge of his brow.

"Why do you do these things?" she whimpered, rubbing her throat.

"I need some fresh air." He marched into the hall, rubbing his collar, and she crumpled to the floor.

Hot tears drifted over the crust of ash rimming her eyes.

If Baba didn't love her, who possibly could? What was it about her that made her so unlovable? She looked into the gleaming tools scattered on the floor. Was her face too gaunt? Her voice too screechy? Her brain too big, yet stupid? She did everything he asked of her. Everything he demanded.

Why did Kameera get a father who treated her like a princess and a mother to brush her hair and pick out saris with? Why did Kameera get a maang teeka for her upcoming wedding, and Nayla didn't?

She didn't want much. Just a normal life with cooking and sewing and dates for bastani and maybe a maang teeka with a gold chain and a pearl. Even though makeup served no functional purpose, it would be nice to wear every day. She hunched over her fragmented reflection. She was a frog.

She wanted to pitch herself on her bed and cry. First things first though. These boots wanted off. She chucked them on the doormat, their burnt odor trailing behind in invisible tails. Bracing the table, she labored to her feet. The tiger grazed her grimy skin as she passed into the living room. On the iron table, woven as though made of wicker, stood a jar of moonshine. Baba called it medicine.

It was always there for him. Would it work for her?

Her fingers found the lid and twisted. The jar reeked. No worse than the Blast. It would help her sleep, help her forget she was the linchpin to Baba's world. She raised the grooves of the opening to her lips and gulped. Her throat burned like she'd swallowed a cup of lava, like the ones she extracted from the holes in the charging doors for sampling. She set the jar back on the iron filigree.

Now the pain inside her throat matched the bruises on her outside.

No nymphs to report, though I believe we have attracted a song thrush. Non, I won't play games and pretend like Nayla didn't just turn to moonshine. It is merely good to come up for air once in a while. Trust me. The jar leaves me awake, staring at ceilings at nights. Oh, how I can make a career staring at ceilings. That sounded dirty. There's a coffee table book idea for you. Take it, my friend. It's yours.

But to the jar.

Sometimes I wish I could travel back in time and swipe it from her hand. Remove external temptation. C'est la vie. What can I do? Everything happens for a reason. If it weren't that jar of shine, it would have been another or another. Pierre Janet would agree. Ever read him? A psychologist renowned the world over. Used to be. Allow me to summarize: Bad parenting has consequences. That is the intellectual angle. As to the emotional, you must come to realize—if you don't already, for I see you are very keen—that we can't control people in this life. To keep them safe, to keep them from doing stupid things, hurting others, hurting themselves. We both know attempting to intervene for long periods of time tears one apart inside.

Of course, it was Nayla's choice. I don't subscribe to pre-determinism in a way that contradicts free will, but there is psychology to consider. Traumatize any child for a decade or so, and they don't always turn out okay.

Oui, she was a real person. The 1920s? It was 1890. La Belle Époque? Non, non. They didn't call it that until 1940-something, and it was only a beautiful age if you were rich, as any age would be, or if you had a wealthy patron of the arts. We shall label it Le Fin de Siècle, The End of the Century. Decadent, thrilling, haunted, artistic, a spectacular time of myth and mythmaking. Utopian visions painted in the sky. You're sure you won't miss the view? French Athens is magnifique at sunrise, burnished in orange and pink like a beautifully wrapped present. Although, it was très magnifique when the city used to be Guimardized. Hector Guimard, famous architect. Swirling metal, flower-inspired façades, Greek columns abound. It is rather tranquil here. Feel the water. It's cool.

You're what? Waiting for Victor Hugo to arrive! So what, he can tell the story better? Ask Marlène. You will find I am no casual flâneur. I am an expert. Oui, she has read him. Front and back, and seen the musicals. I know I promised nymphs. Who is the curator here? Shh, walk with me before you hurt Marlène's feelings. Nayla's life was about to have a turn of fate. Rock bottom isn't so immediate as we all like to think. Roller coasters come back up after the first hill. Behold, three months later...

IN A CANTINA
(THE WHISKEY DRINKER)

Nayla picked up a bicycle frame with a pair of tongs. Her hands trembled as she dragged it to the furnace. A sip of moonshine could stop the shakes, but it would have to wait until after her shift. Even Baba hadn't dared drink at work. Everyone knew what happened to Khakhar.

Khakhar used to shovel scrap here in the charging bay ten years ago. When his wife ran off with another man, he clocked in drunk and clocked out dead. He had fallen into one of the lava pools. Baba, working in the casting bay, claimed he smelled flesh when he drained the hearth. *That's right*, he'd said. Steel streamed into the ladle and Khakhar's remains floated to the top with the slag. Baba was full of stories.

Nayla hung the tongs on a hook and picked up her shovel while Ojas chucked in the bicycle wheels. In a circle they walked, Nayla, Ojas, Nimit, and Sparsh, like figurines in a cuckoo clock. Into the scrap box, she dug. Over to the door, she marched. Above the lava, she froze. The hearth's orange gleam emblazoned a cylinder at the end of her shovel. She cocked her head. The shovel sat in the air above the pool, jittering. A piston from the mecha-sleeves? She pulled the parts to safety and dumped the contents on the sandy ground.

"Nay, what are ya doin'?" asked Ojas.

"Halt!" She picked up the cylinder by the piston rod, which was warm through her gloves. "Halt! Drop your shovels!"

They set down their charges. The roly-poly Nimit scratched his head.

"My mecha-sleeves I was telling you about." Nayla's knees fell into the sand by Nimit's shovel. The heat glowed on her back. "The parts Baba sold. They're here! Help me look!"

It sounded absurd. They didn't know what to look for. She picked up the other cylinder and made a pile.

"You're going to get the foreman called on us," Sparsh complained, his voice a broken reed.

"There—in the box." She salvaged the water tank. "Praise Shiva. It's a miracle."

"The box has been weighed," said Nimit.

"We can reweigh it," she said, gathering up her parts. "I can put my belongings on the scale and add in what I took."

"Who's going to pay for it?" Sparsh propped his hands on his waist, his body as thin as a shehnai.

"My week's pay," said Nayla. "The Blast can keep it. I take full responsibility."

"Help her get these parts on the scale to swap them out." Ojas pointed. "Oh, don't give me that look, Sparsh. Like we're all not replaceable. We need to charge this hearth before Ravi cranes in the hot ore. Don't mention the missing scrap."

"Oh, danke, danke!" Nayla hobbled the parts over to the scale across the bay.

"What is she, your girlfriend?" asked Sparsh.

Nayla listened for any breath of a chance.

"Den Mund halten, and help me carry." Ojas raised his goggles to his perfect black hair. "We'd do the same for you." He picked from Nayla's pile.

Sparsh shrugged and grabbed a cylinder.

Nayla breathed, too good for two miracles in one day.

The wool sleeves were missing, but everything else was here. If she was bright enough, she could make the sleeves work.

And if no one caught her smuggling scrap, Baba wouldn't ask her where the rent was later. She hugged Ojas dearly. He was so kind to her. Marriage to him did not matter.

"Danke," said Nayla. "I don't deserve it."

"What you don't deserve is to be here," said Ojas. "You're my friend, and no friend of mine is going to be a shovel hog her whole life."

"What about me?" asked Sparsh.

"We're friends?" Ojas smiled.

Nayla smiled too, her tears hidden beneath her lenses.

"Come by the junkyard this weekend," said Ojas. "We'll smash some windows to celebrate."

"I call mirrors," said Nimit.

When Nayla's shift ended, she borrowed a wheelbarrow, loaded up the parts, and went straight to the cantina. Breaking glass was a good way to relieve stress. Drinking beer was better. She wheeled the parts in past the camels and carriages, over the mosaic threshold, and up to the zinc bar. Oriental rugs lined the gold-veneered walls, capturing the festive music from the group that played in the corner. Among them was Mirza, her current neighbor with her former sitar.

He rocked his head back and forth, smiling, his gray beard a pendulum on his boulder frame. The musicians grooved with him, their eyes closed in peaceful melody.

Fingers plucked the strings of the oud. Lungs blew notes from the fluty kaval. Hands banged the dhols to give the belly dancer a rhythm, and her dance gave the hookah-smoking men a show to enjoy.

She was so beautiful with her long plaits and gold coins that jangled on her hip scarf. Maman had one just like it. Nayla wanted to blow the dust off, put on the matching headpiece, and dance along. *Look how the woman mesmerizes the legionnaires like Maman did.* The legionnaires would dance with Maman, which irritated Baba to no end. They'd ask her why she was with an Oriental and not a Frenchman, and this irritated Baba the more. These were words. Once they touched Maman, however innocent the touch, Baba would strike.

German soldiers would break it up, ask Maman what happened, and side with Baba each time. The Germans were the picture of gallantry. The French Foreign Legion recruited killers and thieves. Maman would still thank them for their service and share with Nayla all the stories. Nayla wished a legionnaire would fight over her one day. If only she weren't lacking in the rhythm department.

She placed two five pfennigs on the bar and received a bottle of beer and a dram of whiskey.

"Look at this, Binu," the bartender called the waiter and pointed at Nayla's wheelbarrow. "The Blast has them melting steel at home now!"

"The Blast," replied the curly-haired Binu, "or Naem bin Azmi?"

"Very funny," said Nayla. "Baba isn't that cruel."

Thankfully, he would be tapping hearths all evening. Nayla took a gulp. The whiskey scorched her throat. Plenty of time for her to install these parts in her room and fetch some water from the stepwell.

When she got home, she swept the sand up as best she could and moved her mattress to the floor. The bed could be her workbench. How wonderful to have the mecha-sleeves back in her life. She made a list of parts she needed. Wool for the sleeves and torso. Pistons to steady the wrists. New glass plates to protect the gear train. Some type of brace that retracted to the ground so her feet wouldn't move.

The electric bell sounded. Nayla dashed into the living room. She looked out the window, over her planter of succulents, and spotted a girl at the foyer door holding a violin case. She had a gajra of jasmine flowers crisscrossed around her braid and a clean orange sari, an image Nayla could only hope for in the next life.

"Kameera, my oldest friend." Nayla outstretched her hand. "Kameera, take my key! I have marvelous news!"

The key landed in the lily garden.

"Nayla!" Kameera wiped off the dirt. "I wrote you a song!"

"Well, come up, then!"

"What's this wheelbarrow here for?"

Within moments, Kameera was in the apartment, her head on Nayla's shoulder, studying the heaps of parts on the bed.

"The coal box heats the water by heating up the pipes inside the boiler. The pipes are heated by smoke. The smoke leaves through the stack up here and the steam enters the cylinders on the arms through these tubes. The pistons, housed in the cylinders—the little ones here—extend and apply pressure to my wrists. When the pistons are fully opened, the exhaust steam comes out through these holes where my hips go."

"What do the gears do?"

Nayla picked two of them up. "Control the piston valves." The teeth interlocked when she pressed them together. She rolled one gear across the other to demonstrate, feeling their blocky heft. "Once I push the piston rods back into the cylinders manually, they won't open again unless the valve moves with it."

"It's like a personal locomotive."

"Ja! Except no wheels," said Nayla. "What do you think?"

"I think it's great." Kameera picked up a gear. "I'm so happy you found it. Are you going to stop drinking to finish the job?"

"Oh no, the whiskey is just to stop my hands from shaking. I don't go overboard and get mean like Baba. He's verrückt."

"But you missed my recital." Kameera held up her violin case. "You were passed out. I sent a telegram."

"Es tut mir Leid." Nayla's chest tightened. Kameera had stuck with Nayla in spite of caste, before Maman died. She couldn't lose her over this. "Please, forgive me."

"Don't worry about it, Nay. If you miss my next event though, I'll kill you."

"I won't. What event?"

"A big one." A smile lit up Kameera's round face. "Pradeep and I are getting married in May. Our parents finally set the date."

Nayla leapt at Kameera and squeezed her, braid and all. "Das ist erstaunlich!" She grabbed her hands and hopped up and down into the living room.

"You won't miss it, then?" Kameera beamed.

"Nein! I'll sleep at the temple if I have to."

"Gut!"

They stumbled and fell onto the majlis, giggling.

"You and Pradeep are going to move into a large palace and have lots of babies."

"I'll invite you over to play with them." Kameera pumped Nayla's hand. "I'm going to miss you dearly. We're not staying in Jacoma. Pradeep and I leave for Spanish Cairo in June."

The words made Nayla's heart swell and sink like a gear in the blaze. There would be no easy way to see Kameera. She'd known Kameera would marry Pradeep since she was thirteen, but Egypt... The only way to Cairo was by caravanning across the desert.

Kameera looked apologetic. "Oh, Nay."

A tear ran down Nayla's cheek. Her face must be melting. "If one of us can leave this place, it should be you."

Kameera latched her arms around Nayla.

Nayla held on for dear life. "I'll miss you."

"I'll write every day," said Kameera.

Nayla thought about a letter on a dromedary traveling twenty-six hundred kilometers to reach her.

"Take care of your succulent garden while I'm gone," said Kameera.

Nayla laughed through her tears. The string of pearls wept in the planter. She got up with Kameera to water them.

"Aren't you scared of moving?" Nayla moved the spout around the hens and chicks.

"Terrified." Kameera took Nayla's arm. "But it will be a new experience."

Nayla set the ewer down.

"You'll fix your machine," Kameera whispered, "and be right behind me."

25

"Lend me some courage."

Kameera rubbed her chest. "May Hanuman give us both the courage we need. Here you go." She placed the courage in Nayla's hand.

Nayla held it tenderly and smiled, glancing at the black bindi on Kameera's forehead, soon to be colored red. "Now ask Kamadeva to find me a man."

Kameera cracked a smile. "I have someone in mind." She drew out her helix bow and pointed it like a sword. "Binu."

"The waiter at the cantina?" Nayla slapped her with giddiness.

Kameera slapped her back, snickering. "What's wrong with Binu?"

"I'd wear my rotten egg smell on purpose if Binu ever got the notion."

"I don't know." Kameera unclasped her violin case. "Not everyone needs to smell like jasmine on a spring day. Mama never walked out on my baba, and when he comes home from the Blast he stinks."

Nayla looked at the glass violin. It was different for men. Expected, even. But for a girl to reek, even in Jacoma, wasn't preferable, never mind impressing a man of noble caste like Pradeep.

"If I quit, no smell," Nayla said in a serious tone. "But no marks and no food."

Kameera took the bow in her fist and pressed her thumb to her chin. "I've got it. If you don't have the marks to build your mecha-sleeves after I move, I'll pawn my maang teeka and send you the money."

The idea choked Nayla into a step backward. "I—I couldn't. It would be wasteful."

"Wasteful?" Kameera's eyebrows peaked like crescents.

"Baba couldn't get the sleeves to work. Neither could the man he sold them to."

"Do you believe you can?"

"I—"

"Can you get this machine to push rail cars? Ja oder nein?"

Nayla stared into her bedroom. "Ja, I guess so. But there's no guarantee. It's so much money. I'm not worth the trouble."

"That's your baba talking. You're worth a maang teeka, and you're worth writing a song for."

Kameera tucked the violin under her arm and stepped into the sunbeam from the window. The floral ironwork shadowed her face as she twirled the bow along the strings. Cogs and gears spun within the glass. She absolutely shined.

Nayla ran to the lacquered chest in her room and unlocked the doors. It opened like a cabinet, revealing her most sacred possessions, two items, her Brahman Box, whose sight always warmed her heart, and Maman's headpiece, profoundly more heartwarming. She pulled out the headpiece. The vanity mirror showed her the effect—a golden set of ram horns swooped and curled with a pair of ornamental gears dotted with rubies dangling off each one. She swung back into the music.

Kameera smiled, tapped her foot, and sped up the bow.

Nayla cocked her hips. Her wrists touched overhead as she signed different mudras. She let down her hair and let it fly, gesticulating all about the room. Kameera's gaze made her feel safe, the only one she danced in front of. Everyone else had thought a piece of food was caught in her throat. Maybe Kameera did too, secretly. But the music was so beautiful.

Verwunderlich. She had to finish the mecha-sleeves now. For Kameera, who cared enough to make her a song. The maang teeka, though, was all too much. Nayla had to resist for as long as possible. It was the thought that counted.

The sweet gesture replayed in Nayla's head on her way to the stepwell. She held her pail against her salwar while her clothes aerated, and Kameera kept her company. At the next street, they descended the stepwell, a rectangular hole dug into the ground, tiered in steps like a ghat, with a center the size of a swimming pool. Garlands of marigolds decorated the fence that spanned the perimeter, lending the place some majesty. Nayla and Kameera mingled with the townspeople on the way down. All of Jacoma lived on the qanats beneath its feet, a water system running from aquifers in the distant mountains, accessed by stepwells throughout the desert city.

Kameera grabbed the handle and together they dunked it into the well and carried it up the steps.

"Remember when my baba read us the Bhagavad Gita?" said Kameera.

"Ja," said Nayla, "you found it boring."

"It is, but certain parts spoke to me... Charity given out of duty, without expectation of return, at the proper time and place, and to a worthy person is considered to be in the mode of goodness."

Nayla winced. It was about the maang teeka again.

"If the time ever becomes proper," said Kameera. "Remember those words."

Nayla nodded.

"I know you too well, Nayla binti Azmi."

At the top, they hugged goodbye. Kameera left with her violin. Nayla waited for her to be out of sight and snuck a sip of moonshine from her flask. She picked up the pail and carried the violin melody in her head all the way home.

The apartment felt dull without Kameera there. A new tone had muddied its energy. The moon replaced the sun and cast a pall over the cuckoo clock, the Kashan curtain, the dancing Shiva. Nayla set the bucket down. It was a different place, full of disharmony. Her bedroom door was open. The lamp was on. She walked to the doorway. The whiskey on her breath merged with Baba's.

"What are you doing?" she asked as he stood eyeballing the gears and cylinders laid out on the bed as if it were a person sleeping.

"Where did you get these?" The soot had blended into his ashen face.

"Those are mine. Haven't you heard of privacy?"

"The lease is in my name. It's my house." He scooped up a gear in his hand like a pear. "Did you buy these back from the vendor at the lookout?"

"Never mind where I got them. I got them. This time, they are mine." She unfastened her purse. "You're in one of your moods."

"We can resell these."

Nayla pulled her knife. The blade flicked out.

Baba's eyes widened like a pair of moons. Cautiously, he set the gear on the bed.

"If you touch these parts again," said Nayla, "I cut you." The words stabbed her. Couldn't he see she was trying to save them both? Why did he drive her to such limits? Why couldn't he help her build it like Kameera's baba would have?

Baba tilted his head to one side, searching Nayla's eyes for a bluff.

"You would deny your baba his ability to support his family?"

"You would deny your daughter a better life?" She wanted to include Baba in this better life out loud, but he would only bend her words to entitle himself to the parts. It was a wonder the mecha-sleeves returned to her at all. Fortune wouldn't favor her twice. She raised the blade as a testament to this fact.

"I would never," said Baba. "I didn't know the sleeves meant so much to you."

"There's a wheelbarrow in the entryway." Nayla steadied her voice and the knife. "Scrap that."

She stepped back from the doorway, positioned herself in the bow window, and let Baba through. His boots creaked on the floorboards, carrying little more than bones and muscle. Those muscles, sopping in whiskey, were what made him a spring trap. *Don't leap. Don't leap at her. Hare Krishna.* He picked up his keffiyeh from the end table and covered his head.

"I'm going to the cantina," he said.

"I hate that you make me do this."

"No one made you do anything. We're lucky we're caught up this month."

The tiger beads swayed as he breezed into the kitchen, stumbled into the bucket, and shot out the door with a mechanical tick of the apartment lock. She needed to purchase one for her room.

The knife hung suspended at her naval long after Baba's clumsy footsteps trotted down the stone path by the road. She had to build the sleeves and apply for the patent. The question was, could she complete it before Baba drowned her? It was clear his intention was sabotage. She would leave the city before that happened. Yet she hated the thought of letting Baba fend for himself. Who would roll him on his side when he fell asleep in his own vomit? Who would turn off the oven when he left it on overnight? Who would make him chicken kabsa or chicken shawarma? It was not easy preparing a new dish every day.

Baba used to be the cook. Where did that man go, the one with the warm smile who played dolls with her and hosted tea parties? Who taught her how to play sitar? Who drew pictures of how steel was made? Maman must have wanted the good part of him to stay with her always. Nayla would have liked her to share it.

She looked at the dancing Shiva.

Maybe Nayla had it wrong. Maybe because of her karma, her deeds, from a past life she deserved a drunk Baba and a dead Maman—and all the suffering that came with it. It was because of her karma in a past life that she was born a Shudra, was it not? Could Shiva really protect her from Baba's liquor-fueled tantrums and bandits in the street?

Bäh! Kameera never had to think about any of this.

Nayla closed the knife.

See the toads on the pond? Look! One jumped. You can't see him now. He's swimming beneath the algae. Mon Dieu, will you breathe in that flora? I smell horse chestnuts, reeds, and elderberries! See the ivy coiling up the rail? How the vine swishes back and forth from the ground to our hands? It's made of iron. C'est l'art nouveau. It's a relic of the End of the Century, forged in the German Orient, crafted in French Athens. The Great War killed the style, though it survives here in the Wild Garden. It's very apt, is it not? The lines were inspired by nature. Now it is one with nature, a living trellis. Shh, it will be our little secret before it gets updated like the rest of the city. Oui, it may have come from an ingot at Nayla's Blast. Who knows?

TRIALS AT JACOMA YARDS

Pistons forced the linkage around the wheels on the big locomotive as it chugged past Nayla on the platform. The fireman, covered in soot, glanced from the cab. Balls of smoke chuffed into the air, while each passing gold-plated car rustled her sari, and she inhaled the glorious smell of coal.

"This is it," Nayla whispered to herself. "Act above your caste."

She'd better have scrubbed the hearth fumes thoroughly from her hair. If anybody wafted in egg in such opulent surroundings, she'd be jailed. What was she thinking, listening to Ojas? A fake ticket? He'd heard too many adventure stories. She only wished she had a way of comparing the ticket in her purse to a real one to verify this insanity. She didn't belong on a luxury car. She could never earn 450 marks the ticket implied she could.

The wheels screeched and the train came to a halt.

The conductor lighted onto the black marble platform. "Alle einsteigen! All aboard the Orient Express!"

Nayla raised her chin parallel with the ground. No shoe gazing.

"First class line starts here," said the burly conductor. Clean shaven with a finely groomed mustache, he and his shiny-buttoned tunic approached Nayla with two porters. "Guten Morgen, gnädige Frau. Where to?"

Her bangles rattled as she handed him the fake ticket.

"Constantinople." He squeezed the hole-punch. "We'll arrive in three days' time, Frau Varma." He surveyed the platform, maybe looking for Herr Varma.

"Wunderbar. My husband is running late. See that he makes it to my compartment." She nodded, waving the red bindi between her eyes in the steward's face.

"I'll see to that, Frau Varma, and the luggage." He reached for the handle. "Allow me."

He clasped the large Persian bag and grunted. "What do you have in here?" His voice tensed. "Rocks?"

Nayla's eyes darted to the train car as if what to say was written on the windows. Then a Kameera phrase popped into her mind. "You can take the girl from the desert, der Herr, but you can't take the desert from the girl."

"Well, I'll be." He passed the bag to one of the porters.

His scrawny arms let it sink to his shins. "Right this way, Frau Varma," said the young curly-haired porter.

Nayla followed him onto the magnificent gilt train and through a mahogany hallway. The train was too good for her. She brushed her fingertips on the smooth surface as the porter limped to her compartment.

"Here we are." He set the bag down. "The observation and lounge cars are to the right, restaurant and bar cars are to the left. My name is Khajeer. Enjoy your journey on the Orient Express."

Nayla reached in her purse and tipped Khajeer one mark. He took her hand and raised it to his lips. She had the sudden urge to retrieve it, fearing he would smell rotten egg, which no noble woman would ever let touch her skin. She had hesitated so long, her hand simply went limp.

He gave it a peck and let it fall. "Danke sehr." He stepped away and slid the door shut.

Nayla's reflection gleamed back at her as she locked it. The yellow sari, the bangles, the red bindi on her forehead; she could abandon the mecha-sleeves now and never be seen or heard from again. Start her new life in Swiss Constantinople. A life on the Bosphorus. Married to a Bashi-Bazouk.

That wasn't so hard. Purchase the ticket, hand the nice man your bag, and sit on the train bound for a better life. Not scary at all. Only positively terrifying. Oh, but the velvet cushions were so soft. Why could Baba not make it on his own? Why did he require constant attention?

Nayla tapped her foot. Was Kameera this nervous when she left for Cairo by camel? Leaving behind everything she ever knew? Nayla couldn't fathom. Maman's grave was here. The cantina where Maman danced. Her apartment where Maman lived, where Maman's skin cells still clung to the floor. Kameera didn't have to worry about abandoning the place where her Maman lived or fear the conductor returning with the travel list and her name not being on it!

Nayla unfastened her purse and yanked out gray coveralls. She unpinned her sari, pinned up her braid, and traded outfits with the bag. The mirror in die Toilette revealed the fruits of her labor as she tugged the railroad cap firmly on her head. The stitching was loose in places, but it was natural, right? From all her work on trains.

Hare Krishna. *Move it, Nayla, before the real passenger showed up.*

She pried open the Persian bag and removed the thirty-four-kilogram mecha-sleeves. The boiler sat on the bed with pistons dangling from the arms and legs. She crouched to slip into the sleeves proper and wore the boiler like a pack. Her hands found her gloves and clenched into fists, found the belts and tightened them around her diaphragm, and tightened the piston drills to her hamstrings.

Buckled, she wadded up some paper, and, contorting her arms into zengoula, opened the firebox door behind the small of her back and lit the coals.

Progress. She kicked off her slippers and scrambled for her boots. She buckled the top of the first one when a knock came at the door.

"Frau Varma," said Khajeer, "I believe there's been a mix-up with the rooms. I'm standing with a gentleman bearing a ticket matching this room number who is not Herr Varma."

"I'm changing in the open. My apologies. I'm not decent. If you could have my good man wait in the restaurant car, I'll buy him a meal and we can sort out your error."

Muffled discussion. Nayla slid the window down and mounted a leg. She hunched her back so low in the frame that her stomach touched her thighs.

"Very well," came the reply at the door.

Nayla slid her next leg over the edge. In the blink of an eye, the equipment was weightless before she crashed to her hands and knees on the ground below. Smoke drifted up the funnel on her boiler, up the royal blue train car, past the window, over the gilt roof.

"Frau Varma, are you all right?"

"Perfekt," Nayla hollered into the compartment and ambled away.

She stuck close to the Orient Express, checking her pressure and temperature gauges, walking casually toward the caboose, and broke off at the next wheelset, heading deeper into the golden-fenced switchyard. A switcher uncoupled a log car and waved to the yard pilot manning a small locomotive.

At the risk of others gawking, Nayla stepped over the coupling between two loggers and found a solitary tender brimmed with coal. Sagenhaft. This was her ticket out of the Blast. To rescue old Baba. To never lift a spade again. She lined herself up behind the coal car.

Sand unfurled over the gray flagstones and gathered against the rails. She thumbed the buttons on her index fingers. Rods extended from the pistons on her legs and screwed into her boot calves. They twisted through her heels into hard gravel. Hot wool, the boiler's insulation, pressed into her spine. Sweat dripped down her legs, beaded on her brow under her cap.

The signal tower beamed, a gold sword in the cobalt sky. She hoped no one saw her. With all this activity on the tracks, who would pay her a second glance?

This coal car had a sixty-eight metric ton load.

"Los geht's!"

Nayla pressed her gauntlets to the studded panel. Gears spun inside the living, breathing engine on her chest, sounding like a horse trot. This had to work. It must.

Her arms hung in Vs. The cylinders hummed. Her elbows slowly extended, functioning like two jacks. Her forearm and shoulder muscles burned as the pistons forced them apart. If she calculated wrong, her bones may've snapped, yet the motion, though stressful, was painless.

Wheels squeaked on the coal car. It moved! *Quick!* What should she do!?

Press the rod buttons and step forward. She pressed them. The rods didn't unscrew. She was stuck in place!

"What?"

The gears in her chest should have aided the retraction. They stopped ticking. The leg pistons failed. What about her arms?

She leaned into the coal car, collapsing the pistons on her sleeves home into their cylinders manually as planned. She hit the piston buttons. They failed to redeploy, not as planned. Now the pistons on her legs were stuck out and the ones on her sleeves stuck in.

The problem appeared twofold—the gears and the piston valves. Without the valves, the steam couldn't cycle through for another push. Without the gears, no leg retraction.

She checked her dials. The pressure gauge showed the needle trembling in the red.

She slid the glass plate off her chest and smacked the gears. No give. The boiler. The hopes of her and Baba escaping the Sand

Pits evaporated with each jump in the needle. She grabbed her leg and tried to pry her foot from the ground. The tank rumbled uncontrollably on her back. She covered her ears for the bang. Either the safety valve would pop or the boiler explode. If it killed her, the struggle was over. But in case she survived, she liked the use of her ears.

The safety valve exploded like a pistol shot.

Her ears hummed so loudly she couldn't tell if the entire yard stopped work to locate the disruption. She put her hands around her knee and slowly dragged the spike underfoot from the gravel. When she stood on it, she fell onto her butt. She'd never thought she'd be saying this, but *Shiva help me. Spare me from annihilation.* The sleeves would be confiscated, and Baba would never pay her bail. Trespassing was surely more costly than public drunkenness.

A haggard switcher with a bottle nose circled the car and spotted her.

Her heart nearly exploded. What should she do? *Quick, treat him like one of the shovel hogs.*

"I was testing a new machine for the boss, and the safety cap blew. Mind giving me a hand?"

Nayla reached up for him. He hesitated, scratched his five o'clock shadow, and hoisted her onto her foot.

"My other leg is stuck. If we pull together..." She regripped her leg, the man grabbed her calve, and together, they freed her boot—along with twenty centimeters of auger.

"Danke."

"Gerne. I didn't know we let women work the yard."

Nayla pressed her finger to her lips. "Don't say anything. I'm the boss's daughter. He doesn't think I can invent anything, and I wanted to prove him wrong. It appears he was right."

The switcher looked up to a figure in the tower, raised a fist and made a turning crank signal.

Another switcher approached. The first turned to the second. "Minor mishap. Back to shunting."

The haggard man waved the stocky newcomer to get back to work and walked with him—though not before giving Nayla a wink. "Better scram, kid."

Steam rose from the valve in a feather of smoke, wasted. She took off her boots and walked behind a cargo tank, out of the tower's view, while pebbles kneaded into her soles. Wincing at each step, she found a depot in where servicemen repaired broken train cars. Her heart sank so low at the failure that she didn't care about being captured anymore. She moped through the bustling depot, imagining what Kameera would say.

So many old parts you're using. No wonder it failed. Let me buy you new ones with the maang teeka, bitte.

Nein! She was already beholden to Baba for every pfennig he had spent on her. Kameera would never use kindness as a weapon, but one person to be indebted to was enough. Nayla would examine the parts, unbend the spikes, and replace the safety valve however she could on her own. She looked at the men in gray coveralls skating around on dollies. It would not be so easy to come back here.

This tunnel was her path in life. She could resign herself to hard labor in a desert steel mill—which, she was convinced, must be one of Yama's twenty-eight hells, ruled over by the god of the death and justice himself—or she could build mecha-sleeves. There was no other option. In or out, forward or back. It was a one-way trip on a bed of coals.

The porous rocks dug into her spine through her coveralls, feeling their jagged edges at every bump. She reached for the boiler, heating up in the dark next to her, providing a cocoon of warmth, and palmed one of the piston's smooth cylindrical curves to make sure it didn't run away.

Still there.

Her hearing, however, had vacated as the train beat the rails like jangly bones, marching through the mountain pass. Surrounded by black noise, she could imagine the individual train parts, much like she could the mecha-sleeves. Steam hissed from the pipes—the engineer feeding the boiler more water, a very important feature for any steam-powered machine.

She'd rescued hers in April, tested it in June, saved money in July, and repaired the gears and valves in August. It was September already. This time, she'd be guaranteed success. She understood the basic principles.

Gears were a lot like people. There were drivers, idlers, and followers. When too much tension was placed on the driver gear, its teeth may chip, or in the case of the malfunction at the yard, tear loose of its shaft. It was old and brittle like Baba. The alloy experienced a stress fracture. Baba was a driver. She was a follower. If her life fell apart, Baba would find a cheaper apartment. If his life fell apart, she'd be out on the street.

Ojas had said she was the driver. What an odd boy. She was the driver, he'd explained. She wanted to build the mecha-sleeves. Baba sold them for moonshine. She had dreams to dance like Maman. Baba's life goal was the next dram of whiskey. It was all so unfair. It wasn't Baba's fault Maman died of consumption and left him in this state. If Nayla could sell a working pair of mecha-sleeves to the Blast, she'd get Baba out of hard times, and then Ojas would see the truth. If she was the driver, why did she keep taking Ojas's advice?

Pretend to be rich and ride the Orient Express. Rent a mahari—a lightning-fast camel—and a mule for Ojas because he deserved it for his verrückt plan. Ride to the mountain, climb above the tunnel, and when the train cruised by, hop a coal car. It was the best way. Best for who? Ojas, finding entertaining ways to live out his adventure fantasy? He smoked too much hookah. Why didn't Ojas come with her? Well, you see, he didn't like jail. It was safer if she went alone. He could munch on popped sorghum and watch from a safe distance. Far away. This was her punishment for losing her virginity to him unseductively.

Wasn't that right, Ojas? Nein, Nayla, never. Den Mund halten, Ojas. Did she want to save Baba or not?

Good old youthful Baba must be saved, and new rundown Baba discarded like moldy socks worn for two shifts at the Blast.

Starlight peeked through the smoky blanket gushing from the chimney beyond her head. She rolled over. Coal jabbed her side as she located the buttons on her gloves to feed the boiler more water. The buttons had to be pressed right in a row. One was for steam, the second for water to condense the steam and shoot it back into the boiler. *Click, click.* Water picked up the steam with a quiet hiss. The boiler was happy. Nayla laid her head on her cap. The moon gleamed through the smoke while she nodded off to the gentle, jerky rhythm of the train.

The whistle blared. Her eyes opened. Was she in Jacoma? At the railyard? She peered over the edge at the lanterns hanging around the perimeter. The bell rang to alert the yardmen to open the gate. She ducked as the air brakes squealed. The iron beast lumbered to a stop. She laid perfectly still, waiting for the switcher to uncouple her car from the rest of the tender. She wasn't dumb enough to land in the one nearest the engine. That one stayed with the train. Minutes passed and, as predicted, the other tender pulled away from her with a clank.

She listened. The train chugged off to the service house. Voices grew distant. She lowered her hat to her eyes and pulled the mecha-sleeves close to the ladder on the back of the car. Careful not to bang the hand cranks she had devised for the outside heels, she threw her legs over and sat flush with the boiler. Fingers snug, she strapped in, turned, and climbed down with her back muscles clenched, the heavy boiler always threatening to tip.

Only a few switchers operated on the periphery of the yard. The signal tower was vacant. She uncoupled the car from her tender. Her blood pulsed through her veins under the band of her cap. Her gears clicked like a wound timepiece. Hands firm on the coal car, she set her arms into Vs.

"For Baba."

She thumbed at the buttons. The rods drilled her boots to the gravel. The arm pistons moved out. Wheels squeaked. The car lurched forward.

"Heiliger Strohsack." Her stomach fluttered.

Her gears were still ticking. *Work piston valves, work. Don't fail me now!*

She heaved against the car using her own energy to retract the pistons, kept her shoulders close to the rear panel, and fired the buttons. The pistons were coming once more. It was working. The car rolled again.

Come on, Nayla. Keep the momentum. She triggered the piston drills. The rods unscrewed. She took a step on the wooden ties, planted a foot on solid earth, and pressed the left drill, then right. Bursts of steam shot at the ground from her sides. The rods went down, rods came up, left right, left right, until she was walking with the car.

The pressure was high. *Plink-plunk.* She tapped the steam and water buttons to feed her little boiler. Wait. She pressed them sequentially. No water pickup. Why did the water not pick up the steam? She pushed the car onward, trying to multitask the issue. *The boiler's working too hard.* If the safety valve popped here, she'd have to run.

She let the car roll a few meters on and retracted the augers. The dial on her gauge teetered in the red. The safety valve should have burst. Was that her heart thundering in her ribs, or the boiler on her back? *It needs water. Now.* She tried the steam injector valve again. The lines were clogged. With what? She'd found them at the junkyard. Rust? Nein, nein. She'd tested them.

Water dripped down her thigh. The lines weren't clogged. There was a hole in them. Corrosion. What was that smell?

The air reeked. It smelled like burning hair. She eyed her shoulder. The safety valve was melting to the tank, singing her braid where it poked out from her cap. Frantic, she unstrapped the first belt at her abdomen. The boiler whistled like a tea kettle. Two belts left. She unbuckled the second. The steam flew into a higher pitch, climbing up the scale. She drew the strap through the loop and pinched the tooth out of the stubborn belt by her groin. The boiler absolutely howled. Piston drills. Piston drills. She unstrapped them from her legs and slithered out of the gloves, making sure no one was around. The boiler thudded on the plank, and she ran for her life.

She flung herself behind the coal car she had moved and threw her back on its protective steel. Hands found ears.

A deafening sound cracked the air, cannonball-loud. Bolts and gears flew past the car. Debris tinked against the panels. A cylinder skipped across the gravel and landed close by. Nayla faced the aftermath full on, a ball of rising steam. Wet liquid formed in her eyes. Her hands shook. All her hard work. A year's savings. Five million scoops of lime into hearths and down the drain. *Nayla, how dumm could you be?*

Coal fragments littered the yard. The rails were bent at the epicenter. She stumbled backward. She couldn't pay for this. She might've been able to, had the machine worked. But it had, hadn't it? The mistake was faulty parts, not user error. Her arm bumped into the car's ladder.

Up she climbed. Property destruction. Trespassing. She had to escape. Her boots balanced her on the uneven mound of coal. Hiding was stupid. They'd check the tender for fire and question why it was uncoupled. The fence. The fence was two meters away. Voices in the yard, far off. The fence was two meters away, one meter down, three meters high. She couldn't clear that. And fall four meters onto sand!

She couldn't clear that, she couldn't design mecha-sleeves. Without the sleeves, who was she? What did she have to look forward to? What hope was there? Baba would never change, never accept her, and he was stuck this way forever.

Nein, but the machine worked. Maybe she drank too much during assembly. Overlooked the lines. She stood on the corner of the car, ran the short length of the edge, and leapt.

She slammed into the fence close to the top, hands grasping the rails in awkward positions. Voices called through the smoke. *There you go, Nayla. Pull yourself over.* It was too taxing on the wrists. She fell hard on her schaffouse. She was going to be arrested. No more Blast, no more money.

She tilted her chin. A few meters away revealed a break in the fence. Part of the boiler had blown clean through. She scampered to the bent picket and reached through the bars to grab the protrusion, for it had curved out toward the desert. She used all her strength and wrenched it up.

"Ey! You there!"

Footsteps kicked gravel.

Nayla sunk down and stuck her head through the slot.

"Stoppen!"

She wriggled her shoulders through.

The bars caught her pelvis.

She laid sideways with her midsection bowed, grabbing the bars, kicking off the pebbled earth. Her pelvis squeezed through. Her leg next. Something reeled her back. A yardman had her by the foot. She placed her other one on the exterior of the fence and pushed with all her might, tears dripping from her cheeks.

"Es tut mir Leid. Ich wollte nicht. I'm sorry. I'm sorry." She kicked and kicked and lunged back on the sand, finally free.

The man reached at her, his twisty beard grazing the bar. She scrambled through the sand, a lizard under attack, fumbled to her knees, and fled into the desert.

How could she explain to the man that she wanted to make their lives easier, to make her life easier? If only he'd seen what the mecha-sleeves could do. Aside from self-destruct. She hoped nobody was hurt. There weren't any screams. That was a good sign. *Nayla, shrapnel flew everywhere. It sent a steel plate through a fence.* But the fence was much closer to the explosion than the poor men in the service house. They were safe. They must be safe. *Who was safe when over one hundred parts projected in a sphere at high velocity?*

Oh, if she knew her machine could kill, she would've thrown herself on top of it.

"Maman, save me."

Her breath pumped from her chest as she jogged in a wide arc, the plumes dissipating before the moonlight no different from steam. She wanted the cemetery. To go to Maman's grave and sulk. She knew of a secret hole by Jacoma's west gate to reenter town. Maybe Maman's ghost would return and rent Nayla an apartment so she could pay her own way and answer to no one. Ask Vishnu for forgiveness for all the men she almost maimed. Diminish her karma. Remove it entirely, if at all possible.

She would learn about any injuries in the paper tomorrow, listed alongside her picture. Knowing her luck, the grabby yardman may've gotten a good look for a description. Although, it was dark and her cap was low on her head. Why did she need to think about this? Was Kameera up late at night riding in coal cars, moving coal cars, hiding from Polizei?

Had she accepted Kameera's money, she wouldn't have nearly blown herself to bits. She was worthy of building the sleeves. She'd proven that. There was no risk of squandering donations. Yet those invisible strings of power always seemed to bob overhead. It reminded her of Maman's tales of Napoleon Bonaparte. Napoleon had said the hand that gives is above the hand that takes. Then too, it was a big investment. She couldn't afford to slip up once. Not like this.

Did she really want to work in the Blast another five years? Four years to earn the money for parts, and another year for the time it took to assemble them. At that point, she could threaten to leave Baba, and he'd believe her. She'd be older. Wiser. Why was accepting the maang teeka money so hard? The flaw was in the parts, not in her. *Remember Kameera's quote from the Bhagavad Gita.* It would be charity out of duty on Kameera's part, without expectation of return.

"Ja, ja." The cold tears dried to her face. She would write Kameera. If she survived this horrible event, she would write Kameera at once. "Ja." The money was for a worthy person. She hoped.

"Ja." Ojas sized up Nayla's mecha-sleeves, gleaming, sparkling, shining in the sun. "Can Kameera get me a maang teeka too?" He knocked on the glass encasing the gears.

"Hold on. Let me check." Nayla held her fingers to her forehead and shut her eyes. "Kameera, ja, Ojas would love a spare maang teeka. Do you mind getting married again? Walk around the Agni fire seven more times? You don't mind? Great. He'll be right over."

"You women and your jewelry." Ojas stuffed his hands in his coveralls. "Maang teeka, matha patti, passa jhoomar. Buy a horse." He nodded to the saddlers in the marketplace.

"You cannot wear a horse."

"I'd marry a woman on a horse before one with a maang teeka."

"It symbolizes love and wards off evil spirits."

"She can name the horse Maang Teeka. He will chase more ghouls around the neighborhood than a piece of tin. She'll love him dearly."

Nayla played with one of the rivets on her arm. Would a horse have convinced Ojas to marry her back then? Maybe if she had sailed through the streets on it like Lady Godiva. Even so, there was always that nagging yakhchāl moment to consider... Nein. Her love train with Ojas had left the station long ago. Her gravy train, however, was right on track.

Nimit and Sparsh hobbled down the sidewalk in gray coveralls, holding a steel box on poles like a palanquin. They cut between a bastani vendor and a busker with a monkey and arrived at the meeting place under the cypress tree.

"How are the outfits doing?" asked Nayla. "Anyone need stitches?"

"You," said Sparsh, "when you blow yourself up again."

"That's what the box is for," said Nimit. "When she's about to blow up, we throw her in the box."

"Nein," said Sparsh. "It's for our coffin, when she blows us up like the others."

"Nobody got blown up," said Nayla. "Those were rumors. You think I'd be back here?"

Ojas dragged a hand down his face. "You throw the box on top of the boiler and run like hell. She's counting on us. Right, Nay?"

"Richtig. Any questions?"

Nimit raised his hand. "Is it too late to cut a pee hole?" He tugged at his drawers.

Sparsh punched him.

"Ey, I have to wing off my suspenders and drop my pants."

Beyond the colorful robes of customers picking through clothing stalls, beyond the dyers and the rug weavers, beyond all reason for including the shovel hogs she'll never understand, screamed a train whistle.

"A new load." Ojas stuck out his thumb. "That'll keep the switchers busy. Let's go."

Nayla hit the buttons for her steam injector valve. The water purred like a dream, topping off the boiler. She took a step toward Jacoma Yards. A golden statue of Herr bin Ramli, commemorating him for being one of Jacoma's founders, stood mounted on a spire on the service house. The return to the scene made her heart spring out of her chest.

"If Ramli's statue was any lower," said Ojas, "I'd piss on it."

"He pays our bills," said Nayla.

"Not for my lung infection from inhaling smog. Not when I burned my hand."

"I know," said Nayla, "the pay is Scheisse. Focus."

Bulky switchers left the entrance with their lunch pals.

"Do we look well fed enough to work here?" asked Sparsh.

"Nimit does." Ojas took the lead.

There was no turning back. She was in the tunnel. Somehow, the hogs added a missing comfort. Like she couldn't fail if her boys were there. She tightened the cap on her head, ready to break in her new sleeves.

Ojas led them to a wall with a series of wooden pockets and a giant clock.

"Behind, behind. Heavy load coming in."

Two yardmen stood clear for Nimit and Sparsh and the box Nayla had welded together.

"You boys go 'head," said Ojas, "I'll clock you in."

Nayla walked with the box, imagining Ojas punching four random time cards. She stepped onto the yard. Loggers, passenger cars, and tankers sprawled the rows of rail. The gravel was electric. She glanced at the far end, the scene of her accident. Of course, the fence was repaired. As was the track. It had been a year.

"Ey!"

Nayla jumped.

"Ey," called Ojas. "That box doesn't go over here. It goes over there." He pointed to a loan coal car in the corner of the yard. "I can't believe these dopes get paid more than us," he said, catching up to them.

"More of a reason to do this at the transfer yard," said Nimit. "You mess up there, we damage the Blast's payload."

"And lose our jobs?" Sparsh regripped the poles.

"We get new jobs here."

"Good luck," said Ojas. "These Muslims are tenured in till death." He raised his hand at the rear of the tender. "Halt it."

Nayla exhaled, flexing the balls of her feet, jostling the water in the tank. All this running. She was going to blow herself up again. Nein. She was testing durability.

"Put the box down," said Ojas. "Pretend to be working on something." He turned. "I'd pat you on the back, but I'd likely burn myself. Nayla?"

"What's that?"

"No one makes it out of the Blast. Neither will you."

"If no one makes it out, why are you helping me?"

"Doesn't it make you angry? Being told you can't do something?"

"Angefressen." She narrowed her eyes and raised the gloves to the steel panel.

The drills went down. The pistons glided out. The tender moved forward. The screws came up. The pistons came in. Her feet moved forward. The screws went down. The pistons glided out. The tender moved forward. Time to feed the boiler. She advanced at a clumsy pace. It was too much to think about. So much multitasking. There were nine buttons on her gloves. If only there was a way to keep rhythm. What would Kameera do? Play the violin. No violin. Pick flowers. No flowers. Say a mantra. A mantra! Which one would fit? The Gayatri? Ja, for wisdom.

"Aum bhur bhuva svah." Screws down. Pistons come out. "Tat savitur varenyam." Screws come up and pistons in. "Bhargo devasya dhimahi." One step, two steps, the train makes three. "Dhiyo yo naha prachodayat." Water the boiler every eighth walk.

"Great, she's chanting," Nimit said, a car length behind her. "Chant for all of us. We'll need it."

Her heart skipped rope. It was working. Harmony. She was in harmony.

"Aum bhur bhuva svah-ha. Tat savitur vareeenyam. Bhargo devas ya-dhi-mahi. Dihyo yo nah prachoda-yat."

Ravi uncle had said that mantras were thought to echo the underlying rhythms of Brahman, the one all-encompassing entity. Maybe there was something to it.

"Aum bhur bhuva svah-ha. Tat savitur vareeenyam. Bhargo devas ya-dhi-mahi. Dihyo yo nah prachoda-yat."

She closed her eyes in perfect pace. Her eyelids turned a shade of red from the sun. She savored the moment. The screech of wheels. The train whistle. The clacking, the chugging, uncoupling and the hollering. Footsteps crunched stone behind her. The car made a clunk sound. Her sternum jolted forward and smacked metal. Coal sprinkled down. She staggered back, almost forgetting to retract the drills. Someone grabbed her arm. For a moment, she thought it was the twisty-beard man from a year ago.

"Nay, you just went the whole length of the yard," Ojas said, nodding. "I'd call that a success, wouldn't you?"

Nayla nodded, smiling, giddy, dazzled. "Ja."

The coal car had coupled with the locomotive parked in front.

"Wunderbar." He took her by the hand. "Time we go home."

Nayla followed Ojas back to Nimit and Sparsh, delighted at not blowing herself to smithereens.

"What should we do with the box?" asked Sparsh.

"Leave it," said Nayla. "I got what I came for."

Nimit looked at Sparsh. "No way. Free scrap."

"Ey!" called the signal man up in the tower. "What are you mutts doing down there? Back to work."

"Jawohl!" Nimit waved and made a casual dash for the poles.

Too good to pass up, Sparsh helped with the free steel.

"All right, hogs," said Ojas. "Nice and calm. Let's get the hell out of here."

They walked toward the service house.

"Nay, how's the boiler?" asked Ojas.

She was floating on a cloud made of burning coal. "Stable."

Halfway across the yard, they passed a group of grease-stained men. One of them wore his beard in a twist. Twisty beard man. Nayla held her head straight and emotionless, so as not to arouse suspicion, while presiding over the hovering box.

"Ojas," whispered Nayla. "I saw the man who almost caught me in the fence."

"Keep walking. Where?"

"Over your right shoulder."

Ojas stole a glance, approaching the service house.

"Is he looking?" asked Nayla.

"Oh, ja, he's talking with his friends."

"Let's trap him in the box," said Nimit.

"Ruhig sein. Keep walking," said Ojas.

Nayla entered the shade of the house and traversed the polished floor, passing a caboose brought in for maintenance.

"Good work today, boys," called Ojas. "I'll clock us out." He gathered a handful of time cards and punched them in the machine, waving Nayla to the exit.

Nimit and Sparsh made it through the tunnel as the broad-shouldered man with the twisty beard blocked her path. Nayla's tongue burrowed into her throat.

"Do I know you?" he asked.

Answer normally. He may not suspect a thing.

"I don't believe we've met," she said, imitating a grumbly masculine voice as best she could.

He extended a hand with a knowing look in his eyes. "I'm Farid."

Nayla breathed slow. If she was outed, that was no fly in her gulab. But Ojas. She could not let Ojas go down with her. He'd been so helpful, so kind. Risked his neck. Herr Farid was going to take her hand and not let go. Nayla held up hers in surrender and placed them on Farid's chest. She hit the piston-release buttons, pinning him to the doorway.

"Boah!"

"Please to meet you," said Nayla. "I'm really sorry about this. If you let me go, I'll never bother anyone again."

Farid grabbed the cylinders, taken by surprise.

"Oho," said Ojas. "Are you going to make trouble for us? These pistons will cave in a man's chest."

"I would never," Nayla said.

"Ja, you would."

Farid, a fierce look in his eye, pushed back. Nayla was about to deploy the drills for traction when a commanding voice interrupted.

"Farid, are you mentally ill?" asked a familiar yardman. "That's the boss's daughter."

Ojas and Farid's eyes met Nayla's.

She stole a peek at the yardman, his bottle nose—the man who let her go.

"It's true," she said. "I am the boss's daughter."

Farid's bushy brows went from a V to an M.

Steam hissed at the floor from the mecha-sleeves.

Farid relaxed his grip.

Her lungs decompressed with the cylinders.

"But she—I saw her—she tried to blow up the yard."

"Farid, come to your senses." The switcher confronted him. "Why would she blow up her own father's yard?"

"I was testing an invention to improve transit." Nayla touched her chest plate. "Behave, and I'll let you wear it someday."

"See," said the haggard, bottle-nosed switcher. "Logical explanation."

Ojas pulled Nayla into the tunnel while she explained how the second man had almost caught her the first time. Outside, they rejoined Nimit and Sparsh, camping on the box.

"Thanks for running off," said Ojas.

"Every hog for himself." Sparsh uncrossed his arms and stood. "What did the goat want?"

"Her autograph." Ojas turned to Nayla. "That shave was too close."

"You shave, Ojas?" Nimit asked.

"Ja, your sister likes it smooth."

Nimit went to rap him. Ojas hopped back.

"Danke vielmals," said Nayla, laughing. "I can't thank you all enough." She hugged Nimit and even Sparsh.

"I wasn't helping. I was looking at the choo-choos."

"Sure, Sparsh." Nayla latched onto Ojas.

"Crush me to death, why don't you?"

She nuzzled into his chest. "Danke, danke." It was all right that he didn't wish to marry her. He was still a loyal friend.

"Where you off to now?"

"To share the good news with Baba and Kameera!" She mimicked writing a letter.

"What about the uniforms?" asked Sparsh.

Nayla spun into the street heading for home. "Keep them!"

Nimit and Sparsh high-fived.

The mecha-sleeves had a tough time anchoring Nayla to the ground. She was so happy and buoyant. However, by the time she arrived, her energy was spent and the boiler thankfully cold. It was getting heavy. The machine did ninety percent of the work, but she was still the sardine packed into the thing.

Baba wasn't home. She dragged her mattress over her bed and fell on it, wearing the sleeves. After a short nap, she stirred awake by something tugging on her elbow.

A force yanked at her cylinder. Nayla reached in the darkness and found a wrist. She rose out of bed and shoved the man into the lighted doorway of her room—which she forgot to lock—and identified Baba's outline.

"What are you doing?" Nayla tossed his hand aside.

"Aw, Nayla, we need metal for rent," said Baba. "I thought you were asleep on the floor."

"*You* need money for rent. I paid my share."

"I drank my share," he admitted.

"What about the distillery?" asked Nayla. "Wasn't that supposed to save us?"

"The brew comes out toxic. I can't get it to work." He rubbed his face. "You're not going to cut me, are you?"

She had done it. She had finally tamed Baba. What he needed was to be bossed around like a lost pup. It took her suffering the guilt of drawing a knife on him to figure out that the threat of abandonment was all he responded to. Well, maybe not all.

"Nein, Baba. Our money woes are over." She touched the plackart at her navel. "The mecha-sleeves work!"

"What do you mean, they work?" Baba squinted. "Who helped you?"

"No one." She turned and opened the firebox by her tailbone. "Light me up."

Baba grabbed a lighter off the iron table, opened the cap, and turned the switch. The sparker made a loud snap, enflaming the wick.

"What did you use to ignite the coal?" asked Baba, holding the fire.

"Alcohol from the pharmacy."

"I have just the thing." Baba picked up a tin cup from his chemistry set in the kitchen, splashed the coal, and touched the lighter to it. "How about a refill?" He knocked on the water tank to the steam injector, came back through the beads, and added water from their rinsing bucket.

In minutes the water was boiling, gears ticked, and her back was sweating like a Syrian bear's.

"What should I move?" she asked. "The icebox? The stove? The sofa?"

"Yourself." Baba rolled the red and yellow rug out of the way. "If you can do a hundred push-ups, we know it works."

She smiled. Little did he know, she had just hauled a sixty-eight-ton coal car, but she didn't dare tell Baba more truth than he needed to hear. Instead, she lowered herself to the floor, feeling thirty-four kilograms of equipment crushing her back. She could do twenty on her own and possibly two with this boulder attached. One hundred ought to be convincing.

Baba paced her in circles, clutching his ribs and tapping his chin.

With her palms flat, the pistons extended and contracted her arms. Her body rose and fell again and again. She surpassed twenty, beaming with joy, and hoped it would impress Baba. Did he remember she could only do twenty? Twenty without a weighty pack?

She reached fifty with no sign of slowing down. Baba stopped pacing. He braced his hand on the pointed doorway where the beads hung.

"Scheisse," Baba muttered. "I'll be damned."

Nayla reached seventy-five, counting in her head.

"Seventy-two," said Baba. "Sweet Shiva." He took a swig of his flask.

She decided to go past one hundred so there were no drunken contentions.

The pistons whined as they pushed in and out. *Don't break. Don't break. Don't break.* The water splashed in the boiler.

Sweat dripped from her forehead onto the herringbone floor. Flecks of sand blew into the cracks at her breath.

"One hundred!" declared Baba at 102.

He helped Nayla off the floor and took her head in her arms, bringing her to his chest. Did she do it? Bring out the old Baba? She would treasure this moment always. He braced her by the shoulders. A tear streamed from Baba's eyes and rolled into his whiskers.

"Baba, you're crying."

"So I am." He released her and wiped the tear. "Here's what we do. We go to the bank, show those leeches our invention, and get a business loan. Bin Ramli will approve it for his own selfish gains—he owns the bank and the Blast. Then we buy a workshop—a real workshop, not some back-alley shed. Then, we build more engines and sell them to the highest bidder!"

"What about the Blast?" Nayla pet her hands, smiling an open-tooth grin.

"The Blast? We have to keep up appearances. We keep working at the Blast. Plus, this operation will take time, appointments, meetings, locating parts, you know? We sell our first ten, then we quit the Blast. I promise." He set up two drams on the end table. "Congratulations, my daughter. A toast." He poured the whiskey from his bottle and handed her a glass.

She smiled, over the moon at the sight of Old Baba. He'd finally returned! After eight long years! Giving her the approval she'd always wanted.

"By this time next week, we'll be in business."

Nayla looked at the soot marks on the wall where the cuckoo clock used to hang.

"Prost!" shouted Baba.

They clinked.

Escaping poverty is a powerful motivator. So is pleasing your loved ones. But is it worth it? To be well-received at the cost of one's well-being? If I do not please my father, why, according to this paradigm, it would make me less than who I am, decrease my value, and my father will not be happy. Therefore, if I'm not allowed to fail and my father be unhappy, I must strive for perfection. To fail, however small, would displease my father and mean that I don't deserve to exist. What a trap! For you see, without failure, there is no learning, without learning no growth, without growth no change, but going round and around in circles criticizing yourself, struggling from one goal to the next out of sheer survival, and the learning process made so much less enjoyable and so much more grueling. If the plants in this garden were afraid of sprouting up imperfect, they'd still be seeds, and we'd be standing in a barren field.

The gardener, a perfectionist? Ah-ha, think you can trap old Jacques? The ivy rambling down the stairs and up the trees is natural to the park. As are the shrubs. And the flowers. We are in the Wild Garden, my friend. There is no decorative landscaping here. Nothing was planted by hand. But enough pontificating.

Do you wish to find your tour? Perhaps they have wandered into the museum. Le Musée Hermes Hill. I know the way. You wish to hear more? Ah, now that Jacques is about to relieve you, you want more Jacques. Let us be polite and let them know you won't be returning. I am always polite. Come now, I have treated you like royalty. I never bow to a royal. What do you take me for? A monarchist? All the same, I am glad we will remain companions for the time being, as events in Nayla's life are about to heat up.

JACOMA CITY LIMITS

err bin Ramli sprinkled limestone onto the sand, his arm
held out to avoid staining his cashmere burnoose. He was
part Turkish, part Malay. The frontal strands of pomaded
black hair made him resemble a horned viper. Deep lines
above his lips were permanently creased from 45 years of
smiling or snarling, while the rest of his olive complexion was
smooth. Like the sidewinder, he was quick to bite, though the
snake usually had a placid temperament, a fact comforted by
Ramli's coffee bean eyes, set over his sharp nose that, like a
forked tongue, rumor had it, could sniff out a deal or a waste
of time. When bin Ramli finished with the limestone, he wiped
his hands on a rag supplied by his assistant and returned to
his sorbet.

"Move the boulder to this point," he instructed, a twinkle of
opportunity in his eye, "and I will approve the loan on the spot."

Nayla blocked the setting sun. She paced behind the great
stone for a better look. The glare disappeared and a tingle shot
up her spine at seeing the boulder's uneven surface. It too was
a hybrid. Part sphere, part cube—it had clearly fallen out of
the corner wall that served as the city's defenses. The rock was
three meters tall and three meters wide.

It was a cruel joke. She looked around for the section of railroad track with a coal car on it that Herr bin Ramli had implied would be set up for her in their conversation at the bank. This was a joke, wasn't it? She dared not ask. He might've challenged her to shove the stone back into the wall, in spite of brickwork taking its place, or haul the boulder across the desert back into the mountains from where it had been transported by mules two decades ago.

The descendants of these beasts of burden were rotting on the side of the road. She covered her nose from their stench, glancing from the boulder to the decomposing mules and sad little donkeys who'd been loaded with packs double their weight all their lives when all they wanted to do was gallop in the sun and rest in the shade. She looked at Baba, his head curtained by a keffiyeh to shield the occasional whips of sand.

Herr bin Ramli brushed the pesky grains off his shoulder and nodded at Nayla with encouragement.

There was a reason she never conducted her trials here on the purlieus of Jacoma. The boulder had no wheels and weighed a hell of a lot more than a tender. Her pistons couldn't expend that kind of force. Could they?

"You have it in you, my daughter," Baba said, glancing at the other bankers in finely made tunics.

The comment warmed the cold draft in her heart. His presence alone helped with the nerves, allowed her muscles to relax. Think of all that lost bonding time they could make up for—examining blueprints, building gear trains, welding parts together. Old Baba had come back to her. She only had to move this roundish block to keep him. Fail, and it would all go to smash and the rage return. She could not let that happen.

This was her moment, between the lens of day and veil of night, the period of mercy when the vultures traded shifts with the jackals on the carcass mounds. The sight of scavengers had always made her blood run cold. Now, during their absence, her boiler swaddled her in warmth in lieu of a burnoose, stifling the impending chill and anything that came up against these gloves. All of Jacoma would praise her and she would reward them.

No more Sand Pits. She'd erect a palace of multifoil arches, a courtyard filled with date palms, and a durbar hall adjoined to the factory; hire Sparsh, Nimit, and Ojas away from the horrible Blast. And Ravi uncle too. He could read the Vedas to her all day long, if he didn't mind working for a Shudra. She'd hire Pradeep back from Spanish Cairo. What difference did it make if he sold paper or mecha-sleeves? She missed Kameera! These were all fantastic ideas, right Jacoma?

The city winked in assurance. The ceramics on the red and blue iwans of the mosque glinted in the twilight, and her golden temple with its carved spires radiated brightly, surrounded by many gods. Brahma, the creator, smiled down. Palms scattering the city limits waved in purls of green. Her future was waiting.

She reached for the wind-beaten rock while gears ticked in her chest. The rods screwed her feet to the sand. Was she secure? Keep going. Show full confidence in the machine. If she didn't trust it, how could investors? She leaned into the stone and let the pistons separate her shoulders from her hands. They moved rapidly at first and slowed to a crawl. Her heels sunk. The rods wobbled under the strain. Would the pistons hammer clean through bone? She hit a pair of buttons, kicking steam to the mini-cylinders she had on her wrists for stability. The stone leaned like the minaret in al-Nuri Square. Her diaphragm squeezed against the gear box, her tunic acting as a back brace. Her muscles drew taut. She pushed on the stone, heaved. *Nein, Nayla, Nein. Let the machine do the work.*

The pistons thrust forward, accomplishing their reach. The stone pulled away from her fingertips and toppled over. *Buttons, buttons.* She repositioned her boots, caught the stone on its wobble, and shoved again. *Must keep momentum.* Steam puffed out the exhausts while smoke flurried through the stack. She fed the boiler more water as she regripped the stone and levered it forward. Her legs took a new stance. She couldn't see the white line drawn by Herr bin Ramli, but she estimated at least five more shoves.

Another one down. Baba mimed her pushing gestures. She budged and budged and budged while Herr bin Ramli's eyes grew whiter and whiter and whiter. The rods drilled sand. She forced the piston-return on her arms. They contracted and extended one final time and the boulder lurched across the finish.

"Genial!" Baba cheered.

He ran to Nayla, his arms held wide. It was something she thought would never happen again. Too good to be true. His arms encircled her, and he hugged her tight.

"Ah!" he screamed.

For a second she thought she had done something wrong, that she was poison. "Baba, the water tank!"

"Ja, I remember!" He held his fingers.

Baba was crying again. Never had she seen him cry and this was twice in one week. And so was she! Laughing and crying. Joyous tears. She could dress like a lady and trash this salwar for good. Never smell sulfur again as long as she lived. She'd wear saris made of silk, shoes of embroidered fine leather. They would eat fish like the Nizams of Hyderabad. Persian caviar! No more rice, bread, and cheese. But lamb kebabs and salted walnuts and pickled veggies like Baba promised! She'd recline by her baths and drink single malt whiskey, aged from India, and sharbat-e sekanjabin, letting the chilled vinegar, mint, and honey swirl on her tastebuds, and teh tarik—pulled hot milk tea was so good!

"Herr bin Azmi. Fräulein binti Azmi," said the banker, smiling. "I hereby approve your loan for ten thousand marks."

Nayla's trembling hands grabbed Baba for support.

An associate handed Herr bin Ramli the pen and checkbook and propped a sheepskin box on his arms to provide a surface for his master to commit his name.

Herr bin Ramli held the pen out for Baba. "Sign the contract guaranteeing the Blast first option, and the check is yours."

Baba returned Nayla's hands gently to her sides.

The notary pointed to the proper lines. "Signature here and here."

The moment earned Nayla a look from Baba so tender, so fond, that when it was over it only made her long for more.

"Nayla," Baba said, signing his name, "we will never go hungry again."

Herr bin Ramli handed him the check, which Baba stuffed into his vest.

The notary and banker friends boarded a carriage on the stone sidewalk that necklaced Jacoma. Herr bin Ramli, though, had something different in mind for Baba and Nayla's transportation.

"Azmis, you two must ride with me to the bank to cash your check."

Nayla flitted her hand along the spokes of the front wheel of the offered ride. It looked like two park benches welded to a pair of bicycles with a large battery in the back—an auto-carriage.

"We get to ride it?"

Ramli nodded, his teeth shining like his marvelous carriage. Indigo skies gleamed off the chrome tanks and handles.

Baba looked at his pocket watch. "Nayla, you are due at the Blast in twenty minutes. Work the shift and grab our effects from our lockers."

She twitched at the idea of returning to that horrid place. She had expected she might if the demonstration failed, but now she never wanted to again.

"We want to leave you on good terms," Baba said to Ramli.

"An honorable choice," said Ramli. "We may become your sole customer."

"I'm working the night shift," Baba said to Nayla. "When I leave, I will tell them to find replacements."

One more shift at the Blast wouldn't be so bad, compared to the riches awaiting her on the other side of the clock.

"Come," said Herr bin Ramli, offering a hand up. "I will drop you off on the way!"

He assisted Nayla into the backseat. Baba sat next to her, patting his chest to make sure the check was still on him. Over Nayla's shoulder, one of the bankers grabbed hold of a flywheel on a horizontal axle and spun its wavy spokes. The single-piston engine rattled to life. Gears twirled. Herr bin Ramli pushed the handbrake forward and took hold of the steering crank, mounted on a cane.

Wind licked through Nayla's hair. A smile plastered her face. The tires hugged the milky white streets of the Persian Quarter, while gears kissed in the golden façades of the bakeries, hotels, and offices they past. They cruised by flower beds and green plots, the crust of Baba's miserable veneer crumbling into powder. She had to safeguard the mecha-sleeves for the dream to go on. As Old Baba had emerged, a newly washed statue, she couldn't let any residual trace of him sabotage their progress.

What a time to dwell on such things. She laughed as this grand invention cascaded up and down hills, receiving stares from men in turbans and claps from playing children. She smiled gayly, her bandeau flapping in the wind, as Herr bin Ramli veered around the corner and almost clipped a rickshaw.

"Sorry!" shouted Ramli.

Smog drenched the neighborhood in blue haze. The smell of rotten eggs tainted the air. The great bulging chimneys of the blast furnaces towered over the apartments on Industrial Row. Herr bin Ramli, having a great gas at driving, pulled the lever, and slowed the motorcar to a crawl in front of the gates where the milky streets had long turned black.

"Nayla," said Baba, "leave the sleeves with me. They might get damaged by the Blast."

"They're supposed to be used at the Blast." Nayla stepped out of the auto-carriage. "If they can't handle one grueling shift, they're not going to last a day."

"Very well." Baba looked at Herr bin Ramli. "My daughter is the brains. Longevity should be tested."

"You must be proud," said Ramli. "I have full confidence in you both." He looked at Nayla and waved. "Lebewohl."

Nayla dragged her feet through the iwan, imagining Baba walking back into that magnificent bank with its red vaults, blue pools, and green palms. She had gawked at the ceiling tiles overlaid like a pebbly kaleidoscope while Baba and Herr bin Ramli had discussed business. When she grew up, she would put one in her palace just like it.

She signed her name to her tab, fed it to the time recorder, and yanked the lever to punch in.

"New clothes, Nayla?"

She turned. Ravi uncle leaned on his feet in the forming line.

"Ja. Shh, don't tell anybody, but this is me and Baba's last day at the Blast. We finally got the mecha-sleeves to work. The bank gave him a loan."

"I see. Does this mean he'll be paying back Kameera for the maang teeka I bought her?"

Ravi uncle's sharp eyes sent a jolt through her body. Her stomach pounded under the weight of her gears.

"I didn't realize—Kameera said it was hers to do as she pleased."

"It wasn't." The time clock hammered a stamp into Ravi uncle's card. "I saw the pawn ticket last I visited her and Pradeep." He slipped the ballot into the pouch and faced her. "I knew they didn't spend it. They're living in squalor and have a baby coming."

"Baby?" How wonderful! And horrible! She would never have accepted the jewelry if Kameera had a baby to care for. Kameera promised there were no strings attached, that she was her best friend, that it was all right to ask for help. There was no imposition.

That beautiful line from the Bhagavad Gita. She had let Kameera remove all of her doubts with compliments on her work ethic, the value of her ideas, and her ambition to leave the Blast. To rescue Baba. She hadn't even asked Kameera directly for the money. She'd only written Kameera, scared out of her wits, about how the boiler exploded and German soldiers were possibly looking for her. The ink bled out in squiggles. Her hand had trembled like the pressure gauge's needle, holding the pen.

"Nayla, they need that money."

Kameera, a mother. This was all wrong. It was joyous news. Why did she and Ravi uncle look as far from joyful as possible? Concern creased his eyebrows with severity. He looked as though Kameera had died. The times he'd bought Nayla coffee and treats. The hours teaching her Sanskrit and Pali. Reading the Vedas and Upanishads. The Puranas. They should be hugging each other on the omnibus and laughing. He was an understanding man, not like Baba.

"If we talk to Kameera, she can explain. She brought up the Bhagavad Gita—Charity given out of duty, without expectation of return—."

"I'm familiar. She went behind my back. You and I will resolve this between ourselves." He drew closer. "Is that clear?"

His voice sent a shiver down her spine, fracturing his image of compassion and kindness. She'd always wanted him for a baba. Why was he treating her this way? She tried to think of a passage to bring him to his senses, even though her scriptural knowledge was no match for his.

"What about detachment from all that is material?" She recalled the Purana from out of her Brahman Box. "Everyone considers certain things within the material world most dear to him, and because of attachment to such things one eventually becomes miserable—"

"—One who understands this gives up material possessiveness and attachment and thus achieves unlimited happiness, ja, ja, ja," he replied. "Nayla, I could say the same thing to you. There were diamonds in that headpiece."

Did he not practice what he preached? Did she not either? Nein. She was a student. She was still learning and uncommitted. He'd been through the sacred thread ceremony. She couldn't walk the street without a knife. It was dangerous. As for the mecha-sleeves, to allow some compromise, once she got down to it, they weren't so important to her as keeping Old Baba.

"I'll get the marks for you." Her voice wavered, unraveling words to glue Ravi uncle back to normal. "Baba is on his way to the bank this moment. I'll explain everything to him after work."

"Eh!" shouted Nimit. "I need the clock, Nay. I'm late!"

Nayla scooted over with Ravi uncle. Hearth fires gleamed in his eyes from the corridor.

"Oho!" Nimit punched her arm. "Got the guns on today. Hammer geil!"

Nayla forced a smile. "Danke, Nimit."

Ravi uncle whispered in her ear. "The maang teeka cost two thousand marks."

The pack suddenly became heavy. She braced the wall for balance.

"Kameera only sent me a thousand."

"I know. She was ripped off."

"You know? Then why are you asking for more than I received?"

This wasn't him.

"Pradeep's business isn't doing well. Kameera must have that money."

A vision of Kameera working at the Blast flashed in her mind.

"We'll pay back the full amount. Baba has ten thousand."

"I must see him at once." He untucked his tassels from his pants, turned to the hazy blue sun, and departed.

Two thousand marks was a lot of gold, even for a crane operator's salary. For two thousand, he must've saved for two years. Who was that man? Was he really Kameera's baba? Why not sell his land? Ravi uncle had gone verrückt. She'd warned Kameera that karma would seek her out.

Nein, Nayla, nothing bad will happen. Ja, Kameera, ja. You pick up one strand of Indra's Net—another length was bound to follow.

Nayla stood in the pointed corridor. She ought to run and find Baba and explain things to him so he wasn't caught off guard. But the hearth needed limestone. It needed scrap and molten iron. The hogs would fall behind. It would cost the business money. Upset Ramli. Get Ojas in trouble. The Blast stopped for nothing. And the owners might not purchase her and Baba's mecha-sleeves. Besides, it was not like Baba was going to drink ten thousand marks of moonshine by the time she got home.

She unhooked the shovel from the wall, hoofed through the sand, and helped Sparsh weigh the metal on the scale. Into the charging box it went. Internal gears, rotors, and nails spilled into the container. Nayla and Sparsh hoisted an iron desk up, tossed it on, and set about the limestone. Grime and sweat greased her skin. It didn't discourage her. Today, she could see the light at the end of the tunnel. After today, she was never going to shovel a scoop of lime into a charging box again. Or lower her goggles. Or throw scrap metal from across the Orient into the furnace.

Ojas smiled at her. She could marry anyone now. Maybe catch the eye of a twice-born—those higher caste men who've undergone the sacred thread ceremony and experienced a spiritual birth. Then they could tell her how enlightenment was done, how to liberate herself from illusion, experience moksha. But what did she need moksha for when she had a gold mine?

The positive outlook carried her through her shift and onto the omnibus where she crumpled into the seat. She wanted a nice tall dram of whiskey. The cantina was open, but she had to make sure Baba turned out all right with Ravi uncle.

Gaslights lit the fruit vendors at the bazaar, all of them making last minute deals before their stock rotted. Wood apples, karonda, and tadgola. Now she would be able to afford all the fruit she wanted. She'd buy a camel too. Tie it outside the cantina so he could drink at the trough with the others. A woman in a shawl whizzed by on a bicycle. What fun it would be to own a bicycle! The Sand Pits had bumpy roads, but she could swerve around them, unlike the carts and carriages, until she moved into her palace. Her sore muscles noted each bump as the omnibus horses trotted to the station.

An explosion rumbled the ground. The horses whinnied. Nayla bolted upright.

"Oho, now!" called the driver.

Were those fireworks? Were they under attack?

Nayla stepped through the rear door and climbed the stairs to the roof. Smoke plumed into the sky from the direction of home.

"Baba." Nayla's hand went to her mouth. "Stop the bus!"

"Ohooo!" shouted the driver.

Nayla braced the handrails and thudded down the steps onto the sandy street and ran. She reached into her purse, clutched the knife, and slunk down a back alley to cut through. A baby cried. Dogs barked. A busker strummed a sarod. She jogged out of the alley, the boiler an anchor. Up a block, her apartment was in flames. The distillery!

"Baba!" She limped on with lead feet, using the bottle palms along the route for support, the knife stowed back in her purse.

She arrived at the lily garden. Her third-floor window was shut, the glass blown out. Her fingers stabbed through her matted hair and squeezed her head.

Bang-bang-bang.

Her neighbors rapped on the foyer door. Mirza, another man, three women, and a pair of German shepherds. The gears in the wall must've malfunctioned. They were stuck.

"Nayla," shouted Mirza. "The door is jammed!"

"Where's my baba? Naem bin Azmi! Have you seen him?"

"Not in a few hours," said Mirza.

The woman in the pink sari shook her head.

"Get us out of here!" said the man with the dogs. "Try your key!"

Nayla withdrew the key in her purse and clunked it into the door.

"It turns, but it won't open!" she shouted.

Her neighbors pressed their saris and scarves to their mouths.

"Get low to the floor." Mirza motioned them down. "The firehouse is but three blocks."

The neighbors obeyed as the dogs cowered in the corner by the ironwork.

"Nayla," said Mirza, "grab something to smash the glass!"

"I have it!" said Nayla.

She picked up a piece of flaming debris from the lily garden, opened the firebox to her mecha-sleeves, and chucked it in. Scheisse. It would take five minutes for the water to boil.

"Nayla, dear girl," said Mirza, "we don't need more fire!"

"Nein, we need steam." Nayla reached to check the boiler. "Ah!"

The heat at the Blast must've kept it simmering.

"Get back!" Frantically, she waved them off. "Stand against the walls. I'm going to break the door."

Rods drilled from the pistons on her legs into her boots into the compacted earth. She placed her hands on the door's crossbar and pressed her shoulders close to the glass. The pistons on her arms flexed open from the cylinders while the gears ticked like train on track. Squealing, the big iron door bucked off its hinges and snapped to the tiles.

Black smoke dumped out. Her neighbors stepped on the broken shards, fleeing into the street. Smoke obfuscated the high-ceilinged foyer, the grated stairs, and the landings. One deep inhale and she'd be dead. It didn't matter. Baba was up there. She stepped onto the third step and jerked. A force yanked her down. Arms enveloped her chest.

The mysterious force pulled her outside. Mirza? How was her boiler not burning him? She turned. Fire protective clothing. These were firemen.

"My baba is in there!"

"Hold that girl," called a disembodied voice.

Nayla squirmed under the tangle of arms pinning her to the ground.

A man tightened his black dhoti around his waist and slipped a helmet on his head with a whistle for a mouth. His circular eyes, paned by tic-tac-toe boards, paid her a distant expression before he marched into the building. A small oxygen tank hung from the base of his skull, consumed in smoke.

Firemen uncoiled the hose from the pumper and projected water at the third floor.

"Baba!" Nayla shrieked. She had no leverage, but she extended her pistons, pushing a fireman pathetically half a meter, while the other men braced her shoulders and legs to the sand.

"You see that helmet he was wearing?" asked an incensed fireman. "That's a Vajen Bader helmet. You enter that structure without one, you're kaput."

"Give me a Vajen helmet," Nayla cried.

"You run up there, I got to send a man after you, and I won't like that."

Nayla tilted her head. Smoke poured from the foyer past the curled toes of her boots. Without Baba, she had no one. She couldn't leave the Orient without him. It was too scary. This wasn't happening to her. She was asleep at the Blast. Suffering from heat stroke. It was too much. Good things didn't happen to her. Karma had returned for trying to reach outside her caste.

The brave fireman emerged over the felled door with an emaciated, lifeless figure.

"Baba! Let me go! Oh, please, let me go!"

The firemen released her. She hurried to the Vajen man as he laid Baba on a stretcher and took off the helmet. She held her ear to Baba's coarse fabric and listened for a heartbeat. She found none. No breath. No movement. No flutter of eyes. She contorted every muscle in her face. Snot driveled from her nose. Whimpers jumped from her throat. His chest was warm from the fires. She scrunched his tunic in her fist and inhaled the scent of whiskey and rotten eggs.

Mind the stinging nettle. Care for some? It cures back pain. We are going up a hill. Non, you can't eat them raw. You need to cook them or the hairs will sting you. Coronis would have used nettle in Ancient Greece. She was a nymph—I know, your favorite word. You paid with your time to see nymphs. Where are the nymphs? I want nymphs! Give me nymphs!

Coronis was one of the maenads, the followers of Dionysus, god of wine. She and her nymphy friends nursed him from childhood after he was born from Zeus's thigh. When Dionysus grew up, he instilled in them a divine madness to help the Earth remain fertile and to achieve in others a state of ecstasy.

The moment wine touches a maenad's lips, they sing and dance, engaging in the most raucous debauchery. If they lose control of their senses, they're liable to go berserk and tear a man apart. Man, woman, cow, whatever they encounter.

Now wasn't the best time to bring it up, as we descend down a secluded path to a gate which belongs on a dungeon. We don't want to be cornered by a maenad in this cellar-looking hold. Even a maenad like Coronis.

Very well. In addition to a nurse, she was also a patron. Not a mentor, thank heavens. No seventeen-year-old needs that kind of guidance. Coronis sponsoring Nayla? It would be the drunk leading the drunk. It's a bad look now, and it was a bad look in the summer of 1891. What Coronis sponsored was creativity. A blessing or a curse, I'll leave for you to decide. Oui, the gate opens. The path continues. Never fear. You can't go wrong with Jacques.

PORTRAIT
OF A NYMPH

N ayla clocked in abnormally happy. It was the same feeling as the day Baba had died, after demonstrating the mecha-sleeves to the bankers. How promising the future had looked then. Two weeks had passed and not a second longer. The light at the end of the tunnel appeared in the corridor in the shape of the hearth fires. Ravi uncle was behind her at the time recorder.

"I hate to trouble you in mourning." He wrung his hands. "When Naem passed, he still owed me the two thousand marks."

Nayla raised her eyebrows. Her mouth fell open. Outings to local festivals, dining in restaurants, shopping with Kameera, hours of study—was it all an act? How could this man who treated her like a second daughter be so insensitive?

"Did you not see him before the fire?" she asked.

Ravi uncle shook his head with downcast eyes. "Nein."

She owed Jacoma Bank ten thousand marks. What was another two? Her and Baba's last paycheck was spent on Baba's cremation.

Nayla stood in the pointed arch that led to the charging bay. An orange glow waxed her face. "The banker cashed the check, but there's nothing in our account. No money found in the debris of the fire, either. It's gone. Why are you pressing the issue? My baba is dead."

"Kameera is having a baby."

Nayla knew all too well. Kameera had written her offering to come live in Spanish Cairo with her and Pradeep. It would be an imposition and a half, where if Nayla had accepted, Ravi uncle would pop out later to ask for room and board. Ravi uncle hadn't told Kameera about the maang teeka fiasco, and Nayla hadn't brought up Ravi uncle's shake down. It would've created a rift between father and daughter.

"Kameera gave me the money as a gift," said Nayla. "I didn't ask her for it. Why—"

Nayla searched the fires in his eyes. Was Ravi uncle living beyond his means? Kameera had always said they were well off. They were Vaishyas. Why wouldn't they be? Was Ravi uncle lying to the family? How did he afford the maang teeka and the violin and a large wedding? Pradeep was a struggling paper merchant. Ravi uncle was lying—and possibly involved in something illegal.

"Why what?" he asked.

"Your land in Jacoma. Do you still own it?"

"Technically, ja." Ravi uncle dodged her gaze. "The bank has it. I put it up as collateral for a personal loan to pay for the wedding."

It didn't matter now. Nothing mattered.

"I will turn our apartment upside down," Nayla assured him. "What's left of it."

"You still live there?"

"Until the end of the month."

"Then what?"

Now he pretends to care. She took his hand in hers. "I'll have the money for you by tomorrow."

"Wundervoll."

Nayla walked into the charging bay, her chin held high. She pulled her goggles down, ready for her face to be painted with soot. There was no reason to worry about anything. Baba had no life insurance. She was ruined. It would take her until the age of forty to pay everything back. They'd throw her on a work farm before that happened. She'd hoped life would've been kinder. There was the Sand Pits and there was whiskey, but no Baba to guide her, old or new. Moksha was a pipe-dream. Ravi uncle was the only one brazen enough to teach a Shudra, but he could not teach something he could not find. The whole concept might've been fake. She may as well have been lost in the desert. Nobody cared about her in a way that she wasn't expected to provide something in return. Except for Kameera and Ojas. How much could she inconvenience them?

Dirty sunlight that never seemed to reach her filtered through the skylight in the lofty ceiling. She unscrewed her flask and gulped the burning liquid, wishing it could warm the furnace of her heart. Her hand found the knife in the ropes of her waist, should anyone stop her. She retrieved the shovel from the wall and entered rotation.

"How you holding up, Nay?" asked Ojas.

"I feel great." She pulled him in for a long hug. "Danke for helping me at the train station."

"Uh, ja. I couldn't let you blow yourself to pieces. You all right?"

"Ja, never better."

He tilted his head to study her and found the next scoop of metal.

She dug in with him. Her adrenal glands sent a fresh jolt of energy into her body every time she approached the hearth. Heat rippled up her arms. In went a toy train. Steel shavings. Rusty bolts. Lava bubbled in the hot square of the charging door. It sounded like noodles boiling. She wouldn't feel it. Did a gnat feel its body go squish when a camel switched it with his tail? The unpleasant sensation would be over fast. Next time she approached, she'd do it. Next time, she'd get her inside to match her outside.

Sparsh threw his load into the open door. Then Nimit. Nayla scooped up a pair of rusty faucets and motor parts. Then Ojas went. Nayla was up, a meter from the fires and closing. Would it burn her embroidered vest before it got to her flesh? She would soon find out, take her chances with the next transition, and shelter herself from the horrors of this world.

Her shovel dropped to the sand.

She bolted headlong for the door.

"Nayla!" cried Sparsh.

A flash blinded her to a skidding stop. She put her hands out and caught herself on the sharp square frame. Lava dripped in trickles of light from the head and shoulders of a figure inside the hearth. She had fallen in. It was her. She was having an out-of-body experience. She had to be.

"Nayla," shouted Ojas, "bist du verdammt verrückt geworden?"

The figure loomed toward her as if wading through water. It did not wish to remain unrecognized. It placed a glowing white hand upon the frame of the charging door as Nayla stumbled back and fell. She landed hard on the shovel, bludgeoning her butt.

Nimit and Sparsh crowded, pointing in fright at the emerging shape.

"Khakhar's ghost!" Nimit cried.

"Khakhar's ghost?" Nayla asked, glued to the sandy floor.

Nimit and Sparsh ran for their lives. Ojas tugged on Nayla's arm. She didn't budge. She was too transfixed.

Ravi uncle climbed down from the crane ladder and hurdled the piles of scrap, headed for the exit.

The ghost put its foot through the hole.

Nayla scrambled backward. "Don't come any closer!" She pulled her switchblade from her waist. "Stay back! I'll stab you, Khakhar!" The blade shot out toward her navel. "I mean it!" She turned the sharp side at the ghost climbing through the hole.

Ojas picked up Nayla's shovel.

The hot figure advanced, walking slowly—slowly enough for Nayla to spring to her wobbly feet and shake the knife in her hand.

"Khakhar, I'm warning you. I will kill you! Your ghost!"

The figure, in a deep voice, said, "Don't be afraid, Nayla."

"Oh my Vishnu, it spoke to me!" Beneath her goggles, Nayla's eyes grew to the size of macaroons.

"Nay," said Ojas, "if you don't run, I'm going to knock your lights out and carry you."

She dropped the knife and hobbled over the heap of limestone to escape the building. Powder sloughed off her salwar as she approached the corridor. *Run,* she repeated. *Run.* If anyone was clocking in, she would bowl them over. She was being haunted by a rakshasa. No other explanation.

Ojas sprinted over the mound and through the corridor.

Green lightning flashed in Nayla's peripherals, igniting the doorway like a gas ring. A beautiful, pale face strobed past her, wearing a headscarf. Nayla's footsteps landed in echoes, the cushion of sand lost. Her lungs inflated with the scent of clean-burning oil, a shock in the absence of sulfur. The air was cool on her skin. Her stubborn heart beat hurriedly as she stumbled into a cave. Whoever that face belonged to was gone.

She lifted her goggles to her temples. A ramp eased her onto an expansive floor that sucked in light from the walls, fragmented in shards, the effect of being trapped inside a dark prism. Some planes were black as charcoal, others blue as ultramarine and green like jade. The rockface glowed, reflecting, refracting light from a river of blue fire that serpentined along a trough through the cavern's center.

Something glass shattered on the ground. The ceiling, vaulted as high as the trusses in the charging bay, revealed a female form strung up like a bird in the butcher shop. She had wings, cinched to her ribs in a mangled knot by gossamer thread. Her hair dangled like a tassel. Cobwebs stretched in the corners like hammocks. The ceiling was dark as pitch. The glass at Nayla's foot glinted blue in the flame.

She picked it up and noted the embossed symbol of a mint leaf on one side and a peacock feather on another. There were four of these little glyphs.

She had to leave this place. The ghosts might be harming Ojas. She set down the glass and turned up the ramp to go, her knife in hand. At the top stretched a hallway with a deadend. She touched the barefaced rock, the angled stone smooth on her palm.

"Ojas?" she called.

He hadn't passed through the strange lightning, only she had. On second thought, she would stay here. Anything was better than the Blast. Unless she were dead? Was this Naraka—and if so, which one of the twenty-eight hells was it? Śūkara. She must be in Śūkara, the hell for drinkers. *Do not panic, Nayla.* According to the Puranas, hell was only temporary.

She pressed on down the ramp and across a bridge that arced over the fire. Ten meters before her stood a pair of doors as big as an iwan.

This was not any German architecture she'd ever seen. Nor Malay, Indian, or Persian. It was Greek. They had fluted pillars bracing a pediment. The frieze displayed symbols of a hammer, lightning bolt, and sword. An inscription read: *την αίθουσα με μυθικά αντικείμενα.* Gibberish.

No wait. She walked closer. The writing shifted.

The Hall of Fabled Objects

"The Hall of Fabled Objects." She recognized the lettering's style in newspapers from the fatherland—Jugendstil.

The fluted columns faded into carved pillars flaked with gold, and the gray portico into golden fronds forming a dome like a cabbage. Gorgons, gears, and geometric patterns decorated the exterior. These doors looked enchanted.

Goose pimples covered Nayla's skin. *Remain calm.* She must have been trapped in samsara, she was sure now, in some lower realm, somewhere between the cycle of life and death. She found herself recalling stories in the Mahabharata, the lessons in the Vedas, having nothing else to turn to for answers.

She might've been in Yama's kingdom. She had the distinct feeling of being watched.

Something moved in the dark. Squishy feet trudged overhead in the crevices as if their boots were filled with mud. Nayla flung her gaze at the ceiling. A spider as big as a Blast ladle dropped toward her. Fangs, eyes, hair. She crouched fast, head covered, knife raised.

Green electricity encircled her feet and the floor gave way to bright sand.

"Boah!"

Hot wind breezed through her greasy hair, lifting her vest into a sail. She was outside, in a dream, in the desert, in freefall.

"Oof!"

Sandy ground struck her chest. Her canteen bonked against her hip. She rolled onto her back next to a slanted wall. It was a ziggurat, forty kilometers from Jacoma. Fate was playing a cruel joke. Whatever hole she had dropped out of had vanished.

"We don't want to damage her, Hecate." The ghost from the hearth. Its voice changed mid-sentence from deep to shallow, male to female.

"Damage her?" came a second disembodied voice, another woman. "She was about to dive into a furnace and swim laps."

"Well, I didn't expect her to stroll into Hades," replied the first.

Nayla found her knife in the sand and pointed it toward these ghostly intruders. The sunlight blinded her momentarily. When her eyes adjusted, she was met by a woman with an orange sari and a curled braid strung with gold coins. Eyes stared back at her, nonjudgmental brown almonds. The woman's nose was short and slant like the ziggurat. She had a rounded chin that followed the contour of her headpiece. Rings adorned her dainty hands with gears for charms. She was warm and inviting.

Nayla lowered her knife. "Maman?" Was she reincarnated? Sent to save her?

"I'm sorry, Nayla. I'm not your mother, though I am with you in the home. My name is Hestia, virgin goddess of the hearth."

"Nein, nein. There must be a mistake. That is Agneya."

She bowed. "If you wish."

When she raised her eyes, her bronze skin changed to a deep red. An extra pair of arms emerged from her sari, and a second head delved from her cheek.

Was this a glimpse of the afterlife? Was she the same goddess? What culture influenced which here?

"Better?" asked Hestia-Agneya.

Nayla nodded, her eyes stretched to her ears. The goddess was a shapeshifter. "Why do you appear Greek?"

"As creators, we are attracted to those who create. When artists create, they channel the very life force of this world. It energizes them, revitalizes our beings. When artists congregate, they form a crucible. It stimulates competition with the self—voices and visions are in the air. The atmosphere is electric. In this era, French Athens burns brightest, therefore we translate accordingly."

Nayla nodded, unsure if any Veda she'd ever read explained this.

"You don't want a passing brigand to identify us, do you, sweetheart?" replied the second voice.

Green electricity burned a hole in the sky, producing the pale-faced woman Nayla had seen on her way into the cave. The woman wore a purple headscarf and a seven-pointed crown, and she searched Nayla with the fiercest of eyes. The woman's bangles jingled on her wrists. Purple chiffon flowed above and below her exposed abdomen. Her belly was as slim as her face was angular.

Nayla raised the knife.

Hecate's nose ring rose with a sneer. "Mortal weapon."

A cobra darted out from under Hecate's arm and snatched the blade in his fangs.

"Scheisse!" said Nayla.

Hecate took the knife and pet the snake on the head. "Good baby." She turned to Nayla and bowed in mock ceremony. "My name is Hecate, goddess of the moon, doorways, and long hair. You like it?"

"She is not," said Hestia, returned to human form.

Nayla eyed the locks streaming down Hecate's back. "How many of you are there?"

"How many are here to meet you or how many exist in the pantheon?"

Sweet Shiva, there were more to meet her? "How many gods exist in the pantheon?" This would solve the riddle once and for all. Were they Greek or Hindu?

"Oh, a test!" said Hecate. "I love a test. She is sharp."

"How many gods?" Nayla repeated. If they said thirty-three like in the Vedas or three hundred and thirty million like after the Upanishads were recorded, they were liable to be impostors, as these numbers only represented the truth.

"We are the many manifestations of Brahman," said Hestia. "The one supreme being."

"What you call the universe," said Hecate.

"That's cheating," said Nayla. "I am Brahman."

"Then you should know we all have our functions," said Hecate. "You got a natural occurrence, there's a god for it."

Real. Nayla touched her head. Everything Ravi uncle read to her was real.

"You're Hindu gods," said Nayla, stupefied. "All right. Why are you dressed like you live in the German Orient?"

"It's all Greek to me." Hecate flipped her hair.

"We have to appear somewhat normal," said Hestia.

"Walking through fire is somewhat normal?" asked Nayla.

Flames licked up from Hestia's palms as she smiled hopelessly. "It can be."

"Did you hurt Ojas? Was I in one of the lower realms? Sūkara? Pūyavāha?" She winced, hopeful. "I am dead, richtig? What was the spider?"

Hecate laid a hand on her hip as the snake coiled around her shoulders. "Nein, ja, nein, nein, and nein, and that was Arachne, mistress of the loom."

Nayla exhaled. She was lost. "Ja to lower realm, then?"

"Ja," said Hecate.

Puh! They hadn't hurt Ojas. Good. "And those grand doors?" She had to know.

"That, my dear," said Hecate, "is the Hall of Fabled Objects. You know, Apollo's Lyre, the Cap of Hades, the Golden Fleece."

"Nein."

"Right. German Orient."

"What about Baba? Have you seen him? Don't turn Baba into a fly. He did the best he could. Maybe a hoopoe bird. Oh, a tiger. He always liked tigers. Is Maman here? She used to be Christian. She meant well."

"Look, I lead the dead. I don't determine what happens to them."

"Really, Hecate," said Hestia, snuffing her flames, "don't tell her such trivia. We're about to give her the power of the gods."

"If she can keep it," Hecate said in a huff.

"I get to be a god?" said Nayla, dumbfounded.

"A nymph," Hestia amended.

"A new nymph." Hecate dropped her chin.

"What's a nymph?" asked Nayla.

"I am," called a third voice, a woman standing in an open ring of green lightning. Roped in gold chains with bedlah like a belly dancer, she had a red cutaway skirt and red hair. She stepped into the sands, speaking beneath a veil. "Coronis. Maenad. Take my card."

Nayla extended her hand. Coronis set down a silver chalice of wine. Nayla hesitated to drink it, but if they were going to kill her, they wouldn't have saved her life. She sipped. The juiciest fermented grapes of some unknown region touched her tongue, swished in her mouth.

"That's my girl," said Coronis, snatching her cup. "A nymph is mortal, has eternal youth until death, can travel anywhere she pleases, and is loyal to"—she hiccupped—"one god or other."

"Coronis is partly responsible for us being here," said Hestia.

"I was sauntering by and heard the most loveliest song," said Coronis, "by your friend, Kameera. I followed her, found you, and saw you working on a refrigerator."

"Mecha-sleeves," said Nayla.

"Whatever."

How peculiar. To think these creatures had been watching her. It sent a shiver up her spine. Yet it was oddly comforting. Maybe she wasn't as alone as she'd thought.

"Coronis told Dionysus," Hecate explained, "knowing he wanted to impress this unattainable lady to my left."

"Are you impressed?" Nayla asked Hestia.

"By a contraption forged in a hearth that carries a hearth? Ja. But not as much as Hephaestus was when I shared the news of your creation with him."

"Hephaestus?"

"You know him as Vishwakarma," said Hestia, "the craftsman of weapons and chariots for the gods." She brimmed her hand to the horizon. "Here he comes."

Heat waves flared in the distance, out of which labored the mirage of a man. He was a hatchet-faced ogre, his girth as wide as the boulder she'd toppled on the city limits. He looked nothing like Vishwakarma—a grandfatherly, four-armed god in orange robes. This rock with legs had a blacksmith apron and tunic. Maybe he was so impressed by her invention that he wanted to purchase it from her. Juhu! They were here to help with her money troubles.

The ground trembled as Hephaestus's shadow touched her, in spite of the man it belonged to being ten meters away.

He could kill her by sitting down.

Were her legs shaking out of fear or from the vibrations?

"The asking price is twelve thousand marks, Mein Herr," Nayla quailed.

Hecate put her hand to her chin and laughed. Her cobra hissed with her. Hephaestus chuckled, deep and guttural. Nayla suddenly felt self-conscious and dirty, surrounded by all these freshly bathed women and the well-groomed rock.

"We're not here to buy it from you," said the giant. "We're here to reward you for it. I'm Hephaestus. Guten nachmittag."

His hand was a saddle. "Guten nachmittag."

Nayla stared dumbly. She was shaking hands with a rock.

Hestia opened her hand and revealed a thin glass bottle with a stopper. "We offer you the chance to become a new nymph."

"It's kind of like a regular nymph, but with more flavor," said Hecate, "and minus eternal youth."

The elixir bore an embossed symbol like on the glass that fell in the cave. That woman dangling like a bat was a new nymph. Maybe this bottle was part of a sacrifice ritual, and Nayla was their next victim, and they meant to kill her after all! They were manifestations of Brahman, yet so were killers and thieves, and no one in recent memory had seen one of these gods outside of a shrine.

"I'm not drinking that!" said Nayla.

"All right, let's go." Hecate turned.

"Wait, Hecate," Hestia scolded.

"If I drink that, I'll be a fly kebab for that spider creature!" Nayla cried.

Coronis sipped her wine. "And they say *I'm* a moody drunk."

"What did you see in there?" asked Hestia.

Hecate shut her eyes and pinched the bridge of her nose. "Arachne guards the Hall of Fabled Objects. I don't know how that new nymph got down there, but she was likely trying to break in, and Arachne doesn't take kindly to strangers."

"Her bottle had a peacock feather and a sprig of mint," Nayla explained.

"Now she's sprig of dead." Coronis laughed hysterically.

"She had consumed the aura of Minthe the nymph." Hestia snapped her fingers in recognition. "Minthe was an associate of Hades. That's how she knew about the objects."

"Associate." Hecate waved. "He slept with her."

Nayla had no idea how to verify what they were saying. However, their actions told her they wanted her around.

Hephaestus gazed at her with a soft smile. "Why did you try to kill yourself?"

Nayla's lips quivered. "Baba is dead. The money is gone. My choices were live out my days at the Blast or enter the next realm. I wanted to escape my parents' karma. My own."

"And now it has found you." Hephaestus tinked against her boiler. "We have something that can help you on your path to escape life's problems."

Hestia held the vial between her thumb and forefinger. "This is a mixis."

"Pieces of yourself have drawn us to you, crystallized in one remarkable act—your invention of mecha-sleeves." Hecate held her hand over the bottle and sent a blue gas into its contents. "This potion can be where the crossroads of your life join together." The emblem of a key appeared next to one of a flame.

"What will being a new nymph do for me?" Nayla pointed.

"Benefit life," said Hephaestus. "Fortune. Freedom. Cross the threshold and find out." He tapped the bottle. A hammer symbol appeared on the glass.

"If I die," said Nayla, "will my next life be better?"

"Why think about the next life," asked Hephaestus, "when there's a lot left to learn about this one?"

"Take it from someone who's never died," said Hestia. "Life is what you make it."

"Besides"—Coronis belched—"karma follows you wherever you go."

"She has to say that," said Hecate. "If I ran around telling everyone the next life was paradise, they'd commit suicide en masse."

"Good or bad," said Hestia, "they'd miss out on the beauty hidden in plain sight."

"Beauty," said Nayla, "among all this suffering?"

"What do you desire?" Coronis danced around the group in a circle, banging a tambourine.

"For karma to stop chasing me," said Nayla, doubting that suicide would've helped. "To escape all suffering."

"Enlightenment." Coronis giggled. "Moksha. To be one with Brahman. I will give you a fair shot." Coronis rolled her belly and lifted her hand to the vial. "In exchange for loyalty. That's right, there's always a catch."

"Drinking the mixis means taking an oath," said Hecate. "Endanger the pantheon's integrity, and you face the wrath of Nemesis."

"Meaning," continued Hephaestus, "if the uninitiated identify you exercising your powers and disrupting the status quo, a winged goddess will come and restore it."

"How? Murder?"

Hephaestus nodded. "Secrecy is paramount."

"Is Ojas safe? He saw Hestia. Everyone did."

"They didn't see me," said Hestia. "They saw Khakhar."

"So don't despair." Coronis touched the bottle. A magenta haze engulfed the glass and faded, leaving behind her ivy stamp of approval.

"When you drink this vial," said Hephaestus, "you will become a new nymph."

"Yet still mortal," Coronis qualified, "in the physical sense of the word."

"When you celebrate life," Hephaestus continued, "you will become immortal."

"As in, becoming one with Brahman immortal?" asked Nayla.

Hephaestus nodded.

The crushing weight of wearing the pack for so long, the splendor of being in the presence of these divinities, it was all too much. Why her? Why now?

"Why didn't you save Baba?" She looked at Hecate. "You could've saved him through a magic hole." She looked at Hestia. "Or walked through flames." She fell to her knees and cried.

Hestia crouched and met her eyes. "Nayla, we didn't know. We can't predict the future."

"Well," said Hecate, "I can."

Hestia glared at her.

"I was there in spirit through every barking dog."

How helpful had that been?

The cobra showed its fangs as if it could read Nayla's mind.

"Silence, Jerome," said Hecate.

"Get up." Hephaestus raised her by the boiler. "You're a craftswoman, not a quitter."

Nayla felt her legs suspended off the ground for a moment before resettling.

"Destiny led us here to you." He handed her the mixis. "Not to your baba."

Her fingertips traced the outlines as she gazed at the red and blue luminescent vial. If she didn't drink it, would she be thrown into the hearth? Dropped from the sky? Fed to the spider? If they'd been watching her, you'd think they'd have evaluated the odds she'd accept. Vetted her properly. Would they really let her walk away after witnessing their divine wonders?

"What if I say nein?"

Coronis stopped banging her riqq.

Hestia lowered her head. "I return you to the hearth." She looked up. "The mixis is a second chance at life."

Nayla staggered back. So, it was life or death!

"The choice is yours," Hecate reminded her.

Nayla had tried death, and Hestia had intervened. Maybe she would try life. She could be loyal to the Hindu beings who saved her. She could keep their secret in exchange for a chance to escape karma, join with Brahman, and gain immortality.

Nayla uncorked the stopper.

"To life."

Coronis clinked the mixis with her cup. "Prost."

The rim touched Nayla's lips. The warm liquid pulsed in her mouth, one flavor after another: butter naan that Maman used to bake, chocolate bastani, strawberry wine, roast chicken. She guzzled the transformative contents and felt reenergized.

"Did it work?" she asked.

"You tell me," said Hecate, stepping back into her portal. "Wave goodbye, Jerome."

The cobra bobbed its large bowl of a head. Nayla waved back. Perhaps she had ingested a hallucinogenic.

"Don't do anything I would do." Coronis disappeared into a green ring. Nayla recognized the ironmonger's shop in the background. Jacoma.

"Wait!" Nayla ran to her, but she was gone. "Hestia." She turned. "It's forty degrees out. The heat is sweltering. How do I get home?"

Hestia pressed her hands together. "You have everything you need." She vanished in a teardrop of fire.

"Hephaestus." Nayla touched his hairy arm. "I could use a lift." She proceeded to mount his back.

"Consider it a trial by fire." He plucked her off and rotated toward the horizon.

"Please!" She clung to his arm. "I'm going to die of thirst in this climate. I don't need more fire!"

"Call Poseidon."

"Can he fly? Do I have wings like the nymph in that horrible cave?"

"You can find out."

"Am I immortal?"

"Nein."

"How do I celebrate life?"

"You tell me. Viel Glück." He went up in a fireball.

Nayla shielded her eyes.

Vishwakarma was a warm and hideous and frightening man.

Nayla walked in a circle. What on Earth was she going to do? She had a water pouch, a flask of whiskey, and an empty mixis. She pocketed the mixis. Its only purpose was to prove this really happened. All these years of doubt. *Heilige Scheiße.* Moksha was real.

Why couldn't Coronis take her back to Jacoma? She was going that way anyhow. Which way was Jacoma? The ziggurat. She would climb to the top and look for it. Maybe she could jump off and sprout wings, or make a doorway, or burst into flames, or drink herself silly.

She trekked to the foot of the ramp alongside the ziggurat. Could she truly sprout wings? Jumping off the top might be deadly. Perishing in a hearth was more preferable to broken legs and heat exhaustion. This height might be a good place to test her wing theory.

Ja. She laid her vest on the ramp and got ready to leap. *Nein, nein, nein.* What if her shirt got in the way? She lowered her goggles and panned from hazy horizon to hazy horizon. Not a soul was in sight. No one to judge or be embarrassed by. Only Jacoma on the horizon, forty kilometers out, and the hazy mountain range beyond.

She pulled her tunic overhead and laid it upon her vest. At the edge of the ramp, enveloped by the sun's warmth, she stood naked. If she grew wings, she could fly back up quickly and recover her clothes. *One, two—you're verrückt, Nayla—three!*

With a tight bend and hard spring, she launched herself into the desert air. Feeling no rush of wind, she thought for a split second she had done it, before collapsing face down in a sand dune. She sprang up, looking around. With her luck, a camel merchant would see her. But not until she got dressed. She sprinted back up the ramp and donned her clothes. Dripping in sweat, she guzzled water from her pouch.

She dragged her heels up the ramp to the plateau, found the next ramp, and reached the top. To the northwest glimmered the shining city of gold and gears. She cupped her hands to her mouth, begrudging the deadly walk.

"Hephaestus!"

No answer.

"Hephaestus!"

A gust of wind blew a wave of sand across the landscape. Celebrate life. Become immortal. Did she need a tambourine? Maybe this flask would do. She unscrewed the cap. Would celebrating life come at the same time as becoming immortal? Becoming one with Brahman would certainly be cause for celebration, but she supposed that was putting the cart before the horse.

"Here's to life."

She threw back half the whiskey, burning her gullet. She came up for air in a coughing fit, grasping her throat. This was not how she pictured the day going. Drinking on top of a ziggurat. Might as well get her money's worth. She polished off the flask and stood up in a head rush. Better get out of this sun before it killed her. She wiped the sweat off her forehead as she turned to the citadel and found the temple's entrance.

No doors, but a tunnel. She sheltered inside the cool, shady alcove. She pressed her back to the wall, slid down the stone, and tucked her forehead in her palms.

Why did Maman have to die of consumption? Why did Baba have to die from a bomb? They'd left her alone, and she couldn't even kill herself properly. She had to see visions. Wait until Kameera heard about this. What would she say about the nature of how these deities saved Nayla? A suicide attempt required explanation. Kameera would be so ashamed. She wouldn't get it. She wouldn't see it as a solution. Her shame for Nayla would make Nayla feel shame.

Nayla sighed.

She couldn't tell Kameera anyway because Nemesis would come for her life. Now Nayla felt worse for being denied someone to talk to about her feelings. She'd have to bottle it up. It was not worth provoking Nemesis. With what powers could she fight back? The sweat pouring off her face? Oh, keine Ursache, they're tears.

Come on, Nayla, do something worthwhile. She earned the blessing of the gods, and wiped her eyes and sulked. Maybe focusing on the task at hand would help.

It would be easier to travel at night. Maybe the ziggurat had supplies hidden within its gloomy passages. She lit her hand on fire to see. The tunnel walls glowed inside the opening.

Lit her hand on fire?

"Oho! My hand's on fire!" She swatted it with her other hand. "Boah! They're both on fire!"

She held them away from her body, glanced down, and noticed her hair, draped on her collar, saturated with red pigment. The red was bright, too lively for blood. Her chest heaved. *Slow breaths, Nayla, slow.* She had burned herself at the Blast countless times. This was not that. Her mitts flamed like torches. Something strange was occurring. Nayla stepped outside into the light. The sun, her hands—they didn't feel hot. She wondered if she could set her whole body alight, then second-guessed it. Her clothes weren't flame retardant.

If she could get these fires back in her skin to avoid being seen, she could voyage across the desert like this. She imagined turning down the gas jets in her apartment. *There.* The mantles, those silk mesh sacks affixed to the lamps in her home, burned softly now. *Wunderbar.* She looked out at Jacoma and back down at her hands.

Was she immortal now? No more immortal than the dead nymph in Arachne's Cave. The dead nymph had wings, and therefore, powers. Even so, for a mere mortal, this new gift was a lot to take in. Limitless possibilities came with a lot of decisions. That meant treading into uncharted territory. What if Nayla chose the wrong path? It was all too scary. Living in her scorched home and continuing work at the Blast seemed the most stable choice. It would give her a chance to catch her bearings, get a handle on her powers before seeking moksha. She left the alcove and sauntered down the ziggurat ramp while the sun massaged her neck.

What does one do when confronted by a band of gods who gives one preternatural powers? How do they work? What are they for? Why do they come about when Nayla drinks? You can't very well ask around. No, sir. You must listen to Hecate's warning. Hecate with her seven-pointed crown. When Bartholdi's Enlightening the World steps off her pedestal and tells you to keep a secret, you listen. Or else Nemesis will come for you!

How do you like me up here? It's what I call dramatic effect. Hop on. I will push you. It's where Renoir painted *La Balançoire*. The original swing? My stars, no. It'd be older than you are. Oui, I will take your photo. Perhaps I should stand with the woods in the background so it can match the painting. *Fromaaage*. Come. Now that your friends are informed of your whereabouts, we are free to explore. I give you Renoir Gardens. Walk with me under the arbors. Across the courtyard is Café Renoir. It does kind of resemble a miniature hot house. And the frame has that bouquiniste green color.

You would buy me a book? Shall I read it to you? I am already reading you a book. It is all up here. We mustn't start two at once. I'll settle for tea and a scone. Speaking of twos, there is the matter of that second nymph I mentioned. Un nouvelle nymphe, oui. Our young French Athenian woman—although not a nymph yet. This would be a good time to introduce her. Café tables. String lights. Rose of Sharon. It is the perfect setting. Then food later.

If you must toss a centime into the pool, I will wait. The pool is an ordinary circle, not as fancy as Marlène's pool, but she would be proud. There, it is done.

Now then, as to our French Athenian, for we must let her catch up. She is stuck in July 1887, at Hôtel Marchand at the corner of boulevard de Courcelles and boulevard Malsherbes. Hôtel in this case means large house, one she could not so easily check out of. Let me see your map. Here. Behind it is Parc Monceau, but it was not the park that impacted her life most greatly.

Come, my friend, there is a forgotten world to explore, a world inside of which moves the botanical lines of art nouveau and a girl who struggles to appear.

HÔTEL MARCHAND

E veryone had a secret to keep. Céleste Marchand was sure of it, though none were quite like hers. A young mademoiselle of fourteen such as she couldn't possibly go around saying their deepest darkest thoughts. How would others react? Squeamishly? With pity? What if you told someone the worst thing that had ever happened to you? Would you feel ashamed? Would they believe you? Help you? There was no where to turn. Not when it involved a family member.

She squeezed the bellows over the clothes iron and breathed life into the coals. When the heat was sufficient, she closed the lid, hooked the flower knob to latch it shut, and set the iron onto the bodice of her tutu. Her performance was in one hour. She had to hurry, being ever so careful not to spill soot onto the white fabric. Nice and easy, she pushed the curvy weight of the iron forward and back, forward and back.

Footsteps clicked in the great hall.

"You better not be using that fireplace in there!" shouted Maman.

Céleste's shoulders rose to her ears.

"It's hot as bricks out." Maman stormed into the salon. Her white bustle skirt, tiered like a wedding cake, buoyed up her backside. The glint of diamonds shone on her necklace, her emerald eyes set ablaze. "Did you find your costume?"

"Oui, Maman."

No thanks to you.

It had been wadded under a mountain of underwear in the drawing room. That was all the drawing room was—little mountains of clothing, like the French Alps.

"I would have done the ironing earlier," said Maman. "I forgot your little show was tonight, dear. No one told me."

"Oui, Maman."

She had known for a month.

"You have a schmutz." Maman pointed.

Céleste reached for her cheek.

"Other cheek. I'll get it." Maman descended on her at the ironing table in a cloud of fancy perfume. "Hold still, would you? You grew inside me, you know."

Céleste's nostrils flared as she fought the urge to run.

"Oui, Maman."

Her toes curled in her shoes.

Don't make waves. Don't capsize the ship. Spoil the party. But to fall into her old role—*oui, Maman, oui, Maman*—Was Céleste absolutely *folle*? She certainly was crazy to endure this behavior. But she couldn't miss her performance, and had to get to the Folies by whatever means necessary. If it meant being the perfect little girl, she would not provoke Maman. *Give monosyllabic answers and cautious nods.*

Yet there was no telling what could set Maman off. Sadness begat Maman's rage. Happiness begat Maman's rage. Any emotion was a losing battle. Céleste had better fight the war carefully and at least pretend to be grateful, but while her mind had one plan, her body had another. She felt herself leaning further and further back, her cheek kneaded raw by Maman's thumb and forefinger. The smile, frozen to Céleste's face, twitched in revulsion as she jerked away.

"Oh, leave it then," Maman snapped. "You're not that pretty anyway."

Céleste clenched her fists, arms shaking, neck tense. She wanted to shout, call Maman ugly, grotesque—an eye for an eye—even though she knew Maman was gorgeous. She had a perfect heart-face and perfect blonde hair piled loosely atop her perfect head in a perfect bun with perfect long parted bangs. To criticize her looks was asinine, but all the pain from all the years came flooding back and Céleste needed somewhere to put it! She took a step forward and shoved Maman. "Get away from me!"

Maman found her step and lurched forward. "How dare you?"

"How dare I? How dare I!" Céleste pointed two fingers to her chest. "You lost my white tutu and did nothing to help me! You knew my show was tonight! You've been salivating over it since I was born!"

"Oh come now. You're a young woman. You can help yourself."

"You're the mother. You're supposed to be there for me like the other girls' mamans. Instead, you do nothing all day but gamble the family inheritance and lounge about dressed like Catherine de' Medici!"

"Keep it down," Maman scolded. "You're distracting your father from his work."

Papa. Céleste had almost forgot he was there in the next room. His bold stripe pants and windowpane coat blended Papa right into the divan, colored like roast coffee. Were it not for his pallid complexion, he would have been totally disguised, and unless Maman draped one of her stoles on the sofa back, his Van Dyke beard and ash blond hair also compromised the effect of total disappearance.

He sat on the edge of the circular hall as if the floor design had blown him under the stairs—a giant leaf mosaic fanned out like a pinwheel. Papa flipped through file cards, planning the order in which the Folies acts would appear for the next show; the same task he did every Thursday night.

Who should come first, the charmers of pigeons or parakeets? Who the finale—the wolf tamer or werewolves? And where to stick the thaumaturgist, Count Patrizio of Castiglione? Likely before Le Spectre de Paganini.

How could Papa block out Maman's theatrics like he did? Sit there dreaming like the man in the fresco that covered the walls? The man in the river scene had his floating maidens to preoccupy him. Some played lyres; others gazed down at their sedate dreamer who was lost in their supple shapes enfolded in chiffon, half-nude; One maiden kneeled at the man's side on the river bank and tenderly caressed his back to keep him entranced—not rouse him from it like Maman did Papa.

"Éd! Éd! Isn't Céleste distracting you?" Maman bellowed.

Papa sat up, flashing his blue eyes to life. "I was doing fine until you called me directly. I can't think straight with you two shouting at the tops of your lungs!"

"You heard him." Maman whirled. "The man needs to think. How do you expect him to provide a roof over your head. Lazy, good for nothing, waste of space," she spoke under her breath.

No wonder Céleste didn't tell Papa about her secret. It would've been a big mistake. Papa couldn't even protect her from Maman. Why would he do anything to save her from Théo? His own best friend? Théo wasn't leering at you, Papa would say. Those creaks in the hall at night weren't Théo. Théo wasn't making advances. Théo would never. *We grew up together.* That made him a member of the family. He didn't reach for your chest the other day.

The sober Théo they knew and loved didn't, non. It was an intoxicated Théo, muddled on beer. It transformed him into someone else. If she told Papa the truth, he'd deny it, dismiss it, become indifferent.

"Céleste, are you ready yet?" Papa slid in his chair. "You're to perform in forty-five minutes."

"Papa, do you hear this woman?" asked Céleste.

"You honor thy parents, young lady," said Maman. "You live in my house."

"*My house, my house.*" Céleste threw up her arms. "Grand-mère and Grand-père gave us this house. It's all of ours."

"Is that what you think, sweet child?"

"Oui, I know. Tell her, Papa!"

"The Allemands gave us this house." Papa braced his head and stuck his beak in his programmes.

"See," said Céleste.

"The deed is in my name," Maman assured her.

"There's no time for bickering." Papa slapped his papers on his knee and waved for Théo, stationed at the front door, busy reading a periodical.

Please God, let Théo be sober.

"Is there someplace important I should be?" said Maman. "I think I'll stay home in my house."

"So quick to claim ownership," said Céleste, "except when it comes to cleaning the place. Towers of dirty dishes, clogged drains from pouring soup down them, stacks of newspapers floor to ceiling, toys I no longer play with you refuse to throw away. We have receipts from the Second Empire and enough santons lying around to start their own country, if they could escape their boxes."

"Oui," said Papa, "tidying the house wouldn't be a bad idea, Berthe." His voice made it to the salon like a shuffle of drapes. "I can hire servants."

"Oh, you two are ganging up on me!" Maman spun to the far-off Papa. "I don't want servants touching my things!"

"Quand même..." Théo tossed his newspaper on the pile and straightened his grey sack suit's thin lapels. Would he intervene on Papa's behalf with clumsiness or with grace? Would he show a sign he was not the well-to-do family member Papa took him for? Was he drunk or sober?

His cheeks were too naturally ruddy to tell from this distance if a slip-up would occur and his gait too measured as he closed the gap into the salon, his bulky figure plodding up to Maman while he scratched the misplaced eyebrow on his upper lip, Maman completely unaffected by his approach.

She turned to Céleste. "You want me to tidy the house, we can start with your dog's shedding."

"It's not Nougat's fault," said Céleste. "It's in his nature."

"Well, I'm tired of finding hair on the carpet. Get rid of him."

"Why, Bertie," said Théo, entering the salon, "he's just a friendly Airedale." He scratched Nougat's head.

That was the chummy Théo she remembered. The one with the husky voice. The Théo that would take her to the races every weekend in the Bois de Boulogne. They'd ride a steamboat down the Seine to Longchamp Racecourse where he'd imitate the people walking by and make up funny words, like *Taites affention*. He planned on building his own small track one day. Perhaps he still would, if he could stay civilized. How could Maman and Papa not detect his new turn? Somehow he even had Nougat fooled.

"That dog is a nuisance," said Maman.

Nougat followed Théo to the ironing table where Céleste crouched to safeguard him.

"Nougat is my friend."

"You don't need friends," Maman retorted.

"Like you?" Céleste rose.

"What I don't need is some pre-pubescent child telling me how to live my life. Do you hear yourself? Your voice is so screechy."

And hers was like the bells of Notre-Dame—beautiful—another impenetrable subject for rebuttal—and Céleste was well past giving compliments that never stuck anyway—*Oui, Maman, Oui Maman. Hmph.*

Théo checked his pocket watch, raised his caterpillars for eyebrows, not counting the third, and took up the iron.

Bon, let him. His breath was stale. He hadn't been drinking today. Céleste could divert more of her energy into fighting Maman. God knew, she would need it.

She stared at the diamonds on Maman's shoes, her voice aquiver. "I know more about friends and ke-keeping a house and owning a theater than you." Her voice found confidence as her eyes met Maman's on this new tack.

"You, running a business? That's rich."

"You don't understand the first thing about the Folies," said Céleste, "other than how to spend its money. Tell her, Papa."

"Your mother doesn't need to run the Folies," said Édouard. "Her place is in the home."

"Where?" Céleste demanded. She stood clear of Théo's tremors and waved her hands frantically. "With all this trash, there's barely room for us. The amber glass transoms, the lobelia chandeliers—she's taken a masterpiece and destroyed it, like she does everything."

"Ooo." Maman went so red her face matched the stairs. "Make her stop, Éd!"

"Leave your mother alone."

Céleste wagered another step forward. "You don't deserve this mansion."

"After all I do for you," said Maman, spittle forming on her mouth. "Selfish, ungrateful snot."

"You are a burden on our family and a leech on Papa's purse strings—"

"You don't know the value of a franc."

"What a funny thing to say. Does your croupier repeat that when raking in your chips?"

"Foolish girl." Maman's green eyes pierced Céleste with such bile and contempt. "I brought you into this world, I can take you out of it."

"Oh oui? I wish you were dead."

Maman growled, knuckles white.

Céleste wanted to take it back the moment it left her lips. Théo spluttered into his. She kept one eye on him for any uncertain movements, but was torn away by a motion before her.

"Why wasn't I blessed with a good daughter!" Maman stepped to the wall and bashed her head against it several times. Her blonde locks unbound from her bun. Plaster of Athens sprinkled to the floor.

"Maman, non! Arrête!" Céleste reached out for her and stopped short, fearing Maman may've lashed out in her volatile state.

"Bertie!" Théo abandoned the iron.

In the commotion he'd wiggled it too hard and gotten ash on Céleste's tutu.

She had bigger problems than dancing. "What are you doing to yourself?"

She had seen Maman punch the wall with her fist before, never with her skull. Why did Maman have to take things so far? Céleste shouldn't have wished Maman's death. What a horrible thing she'd done. She had only wanted a Maman who could iron a tutu and say nice things and cheer her on without trying to own her—a safe place to go, someone to confide in and reveal Théo was twofaced. That was all.

Papa stood in the doorway to the salon, Théo as near as the doll cabinet, his blue eyes bulging out of his round head.

Maman held the wall. "Get her away from me," she whimpered, her voice full of scorn, aimed at Céleste. "Remove her, Théo."

Papa shot Théo a glance.

"Right," said Théo, motioning to Céleste. "What say we head to the Folies before St. Bartholomew's Day repeats itself?"

"Chut, Théo," said Maman, teary-eyed.

"Quand même..." said Théo.

"You've ruined my tutu," Céleste remarked, her face numb. It was better off wrinkled. "What am I to dance in now?"

"Don't worry about it. We improvise." Théo picked up the iron and shook ash all over the costume, smudging some here and smearing some there. When he was done, he picked up the piebald tutu and placed his heavy hands on Céleste's shoulders.

Céleste jumped. She pressed her molars together until his grip relaxed. He wouldn't dare try anything in front of Papa or Maman. He was sober and just as nervous about them finding out about his creepy behavior as she was. He had made her promise not to tell. He'd said he was trying to do better not to drop his defenses. That he was sorry. That he never knew what came over him. To give him another chance. It was a sober Théo pleading for help. His motive for keeping his behavior secret was selfish, hers to spare her parents from seeing Théo's true colors, from imagining the terror he caused her, but also because her parents would let her down. It was every man for himself.

"Am I supposed to be a cow?" she asked.

"Leave it for the audience to interpret," said Théo.

He picked up her pointe shoes by the ribbons and, under his weight, guided her through the salon. She wished to shake his skeevy fingers off her collar and wash the area several times repeatedly—passing Papa who offered a look that begged her forgiveness.

Oui, Papa, I forgive you for marrying this woman and befriending a reprobate. They tricked you as much as they tricked me.

Papa directed his attention to Maman. He reached out to console her and stopped, just like Céleste had, just like Théo, as if an invisible bubble prevented the act, should he burn his hands on her wrathful being.

Céleste crossed the mosaic in the great hall, the air smothered by Théo's presence. She could not tell Théo to leave or have her parents get him to leave without a good reason, a reason he couldn't talk his way out of. Dance was the only thing in her life she seemed able to control. She touched her cheek where Maman had squished it, when she suddenly remembered, "I have to do my makeup."

She broke their line to the foyer and headed for the water closet. When she reached for the stemmy handle, footsteps came thundering from behind her. Théo on the attack? The hairs on her neck bolted upright. *Non, he was sober.*

"I was just about to use the toilet," Maman shouted. Her delicate hand seized the knob, and she barreled in with her wobbly bustle. "I have incontinence."

"That's not fair." Céleste pounded the door, rattling the stained glass, heart thumping in her ears. "I have to do my makeup."

"Life's not fair," she said through the wood.

"You were only going to use the closet because I was."

"Come on, beautiful," said Théo. "Do it at the Folies."

The compliment made her stomach turn. "I don't have my bag." To think how special *beautiful* had once made her feel.

The door slunk open. Maman waved the bag through the crack.

Céleste grabbed it like a life preserver.

"Good luck at the show tonight, mon poussin." Maman closed the door with a weak smile.

Céleste took a step back, her mouth parted. After all the rage, a word of kindness had shined through, a ray of light in a thunderstorm, something a mother would say to a daughter and not to a lady in waiting, which was how she'd been treated lately.

The door cracked again. Maman leaned into the narrow space. "Are you sure I can't see you on your big night? Remember how I used to do your makeup and iron your costume?"

Céleste's throat tingled. *Don't fall for it.* She went tight in the chest. She knew Maman's tricks.

"After all the time and energy I invested," Maman continued.

It would be wrong not to allow Maman to come. All the other girls' mamans were going.

Was this not the nurturing mother she'd always wanted, to soothe her pain and wish her well? *Come now, Céleste.* This good luck was not for her. It was for Maman.

A few years ago, Céleste would have taken the bait and savored any crumb of attention, back when she had started dance, when Maman had doled out money for lessons, before Céleste had figured out that Maman wanted her to become a famous ballerina and live vicariously through her, as though Céleste was one of Maman's arms or legs or the furnace she slapped around when it didn't work to her liking. When Céleste danced well, Maman lavished on praise. When she misstepped, Maman berated her. But Maman's plan had backfired.

"Non, Maman," Céleste said, quietly.

"Eh bien, va te faire foutre alors!" Maman slammed the door.

Tears welled in Céleste's eyes.

She had wanted Maman to come. Really, she had. But not when she was like this. Not when Céleste never knew what to expect.

"She'll get over it," Théo whispered. "Always does." He prompted Céleste forward. "We're going to be late."

Céleste walked down the marble steps into the foyer, opened the heavy door, and went out into the dusk wearing nothing but her chemise and slippers.

The orange sun deepened the purple hues of the wisteria facades on the surrounding houses. The oriel windows on hers glowed.

"That's Bertie for you." Théo popped on his derby hat. "It was nothing you did."

His frock coat fell on Céleste's collar, a cocoon of soft wool she wanted to toss off and escape from, though kept it on for propriety's sake.

"Quand même..." Théo shrugged.

He walked to the carriage, a walnut on wheels led by two brown horses, Clemence and Claudette, and held the door.

"Mademoiselle Marchand."

"Don't Mademoiselle me," said Céleste. "Your breath stinks. Are you well?"

"Drank last night," Théo confessed, "which is why I didn't come home till morning. To avoid you. See, I'm trying to fight the urges."

"Why do you do it?"

"To blunt the dark thoughts... It makes me feel better for awhile. Then more come out to play."

"And now?"

"Don't worry about it. I'm a fried egg. You'll have no monkey business from me."

"Where do the thoughts come from?"

"I don't know." He looked at the glistening sidewalk. "I don't know what comes over me."

"We can call a doctor."

"Non. This is our little secret, se souvenir?" He narrowed his eyes. "If you tell, no one will believe you."

Then when would it end? When she was old enough to move out?

This was not her Théo.

"Who are you?" asked Céleste.

"I'll make it right," said Théo. "I'll make it right."

Céleste lowered her head and stepped into the green velvet interior with her ruined tutu, her pointe shoes, and her problems. Théo shut her in. He was always one step behind her.

After a moment, the Percherons stamped their hooves on the flagstones, she closed the drapes and tapped her knees.

Quand même? So easy for Théo to dismiss everything, from his degenerate behavior to the event with Maman. Little wonder. He wasn't on the receiving end. He wasn't being terrorized by his chaperone. It wasn't his mother that bashed her head into the wall. Céleste dispensed with Théo's coat. She smelled her skin, baked in his woody scent. Cedar.

He very well wasn't going to try anything while the carriage was in motion. She unlaced her chemise and crawled out of it, one leg at a time.

Quand même indeed. Did Sarah Bernhardt deploy the phrase with equal disregard? She had lived on rue Fortuny, right down the street. Céleste would've asked her in person if the Divine Sarah hadn't moved.

Bien sûr, Sarah wouldn't have moved if her son and lover hadn't drove her into debt.

Gambling debt, you say?

Quand même. All the same.

My lion cub destroyed my hotel room?

Quand même. Nevertheless.

My pet alligator died drinking too much milk and champagne?

Quand même. Even so.

My portrayal of Ophelia was a flop?

Quand même. Despite everything.

I was a courtesan once.

Quand même. Anyway.

I made love in a coffin a time or two.

You know the rest.

Sarah had the words engraved on her revolver.

Was this the sort of behavior Maman expected of Céleste? To engage in wild antics to contribute to her publicity? To build her legend so that gentlemen could obsess over her like Théo did Sarah? She preferred not. Maman could keep her fame.

Céleste stepped into the skirt of her tutu and drew her arms through the bodice. Black and white—really! The title of the piece was *Light as a Feather*. The white was supposed to symbolize purity. Now she would be prancing around like a cow on stage. On the other hand, the piece did feature a theme from Swan Lake. Perhaps she could pass for some amalgamation of Odette, the white swan, and Odile, the black.

The horses whinnied as if to disagree.

Céleste fell forward and caught herself on the seat opposite. What had spooked her beautiful babies? Had Théo been stealing sips at the reins? Was this his time to strike? She'd sic Claudette and Clemence on him so fast.

The door flung open. Céleste jumped. They'd stopped at the Folies entrance on rue Richer.

"Why aren't we at the stage door?" she asked.

"Too many carriages blocking the street." Théo lent a hand. "Five minutes."

It was bad form to let the audience see a dancer before a show, let alone entering the theater in a tutu, but you have to keep people in suspense, especially when the audience competed with performers for attention, the demi-monde and aristocracy abound. They were no less living pictures than the tableaux vivants onstage. Why, one may cast a lorgnette over the entire army of Athen's high gallantry if one wished!

Céleste wrapped herself in Théo's coat, grabbed her make-up bag, shoes, and welcomed the escort for the sake of dance, holding hands with a reptile, dragging his worsted wool over the shepherdess mosaic on the sidewalk as she hurried toward the glittering factory that was the Folies Bergère.

Théo uttered "Pardon" and "Excusez moi" as he guided her through the crowd to the theatre's checkered windows, through the open door past the ticket barrier.

The ticket seller waved them on, into the winter garden, a rectangular room with an arcade of columns wrapping both floors, where a lawn of green carpet stretched out before them to the grand double staircase. Céleste followed Théo between the stairs and into the promenoir, the circular promenade that ringed the auditorium, colored in faded reds and tarnished golds, while she breathed in acrid dust, like the kind that comes from carpets and chairs when you beat them, and bounced off a woman's breasts thrust out over her corset.

"Pardon moi," murmured Céleste, inhaling balsamic vanilla, as the woman rejoined her train, prancing by like wooden horses on a merry-go-round, their spicy scent on parade.

The heavy curtain swept the planks, revealing Céleste's corps de ballet lying onstage, their tutus white, knee-length, their heads lying on pillows like sleeping angels. One pillow in the center had no angel.

"Théo, mon Dieu!" Céleste cried.

The oboe's bittersweet notes struggled out of the orchestra pit, drilling Tchaikovsky's Swan Theme into the dimly gas-lit air with a harp as the angels alighted. If only there was some way to tell the conductor to wait! Monsieur Desormes, this was an emergency!

Théo took Céleste by the wrist and led her down one of the bends, through clouds of cigar smoke blown from café tables by men watching the show with their painted ladies. One monsieur with a big mustache ordered a drink at the west bar—Monsieur de Maupassant.

"Arrête!" Céleste cried.

She wriggled free of Théo and mounted the nearest barstool.

"Hé!" cried Théo. "Your show!"

"I'm not dancing barefoot and makeup-less." She tossed him his coat and kicked off her slippers. Was he going to Quand même this action too? He would perhaps if his job didn't depend on getting her from point A to point B prepared and on time.

She placed her pointe shoe on the neighboring stool and thrust her foot into the toe box.

"Look at you," said Maupassant, "ripening on the vine before my very eyes."

"I'm not here for a drink," said Céleste, tying her ribbons around her ankles. "I'm here for wardrobe."

"Perchance too many tannins." He threw back his gin daisy.

She unfastened her makeup bag and opened the powder tin. The girl in the bar mirror looked back, her reflection flickering in the smoke, as she applied white powder liberally to her face. The lighting was awful. How she wished Maman would've helped her.

A woman with a blue jacket and strawberry-blonde hair stepped in frame.

"Suzon!"

"Allow me, ma chérie?" She blew one of her bangs out of her eyes, smiled softly, rosy-cheeked, and reached for the brush.

"S'il te plait." Céleste relinquished it. "I'm late as mustard after dinner."

"I know." Suzon glanced over Céleste's shoulder. The trombones and tuba joined the melody and the bass drum's boom vibrated the stool. "Hold steady." Suzon rested her elbows on the marble top. The strings carried the horns into the next transition. "I'll have you on stage in no time. Close your eyes now. There we are." She rummaged in Céleste's bag and pulled out some black for the eyes and the chin and the forehead and the—

"Suzon!" said Céleste.

"Hold still. Don't you want to match your tutu?"

Céleste pulled a face. The horrid cow tutu hung to her bones like a blight. However, with the makeup, she *would* look more unified. "Suzon,"—Céleste smiled—"you're a genius."

"I took lessons from Manet."

Maupassant leaned in. "What else did he teach you?" He winked at Suzon.

"Not to speak with debauched men." She winked back and wiped her fingers on a rag. "Off you go, Céleste."

On stage, through the pilasters dividing the promenoir from the audience, ballerinas spun as if through molasses, their movements falling heavy, while the bassoons eased the rest of the orchestra into silence. She was past the three-minute mark on a six-minute piece. She had thirty seconds to get her body on that stage and gracefully cut in.

Céleste hopped off the stool and made a mad dash down the promenoir. She overtook Théo charging for the ornamental trellis at the end of the hall. A pewter lotus had bloomed amidst the blossoms, which Céleste turned like a knob. The wall gave way, a secret door opening into the bottom of a stairwell. On the other side, a door to stage right, whereby awaited Madame Mariquita.

Decked in black bloomers, she stood in erect posture, able to thrust out a kick at a moment's notice. Even with her elfin appearance—her messy hair in a bun, the strands covering her round head like stone crop—she always looked imposing, and tonight was no exception—She came armed with a lorgnette and a fan to cool her French Algerian temper should her voice become too shrill.

"Tu es en retard," Mariquita said sternly. "You. Are. Late." She looked pointedly at Théo. "Too drunk to find the place?"

"It was Bertie's doing," said Théo. "She had a tantrum."

Mariquita creased her brow. "She's not here, is she?"

Théo hesitated. Perhaps Maman had followed them, or perhaps he was too weary to *taites affention*. Mariquita rolled up her sleeves, paced upstage, and scanned the audience.

Thank God for Mariquita. If it weren't for her advice not to dance in Maman's presence again, Céleste's life would've been completely under Maman's reign. There'd have been nowhere to hide.

It would be just like Maman to show up. One time she had snuck into rehearsal. When Mariquita had spotted her, she stopped the production.

Please, Madame Mariquita, Maman wept her crocodile tears, *she is the apple of my eye. I only wish to see my daughter dance.*

Madame Marchand, you're overbearing presence is forcing my pupil to overthink. You may be the owner, but I am the ballet mistress and this is my court. With all due respect, you may leave.

Mariquita had known a thing or two about dance when it came to monarchs. When the Sun King had revived ballet in the 17th century, his courtiers were so busy learning steps, they didn't have time to plot against him. But the deceived courtiers did not have Mariquita as instructor, and her ability to see through manipulations.

If only Mariquita could see through Théo's.

It would create rifts in Céleste's family, to be sure, but if Mariquita revealed the secret, perhaps it would lessen the guilt for Céleste. She'd felt enough guilt distancing herself from Maman. She knew of Maman's games and still felt guilty. It made no sense. Other girls' mamans didn't act like this. Why was it that if Céleste didn't jeté properly, she was a bad person? Her eyes wandered to her fellow ballerinas.

Was she really a bad daughter for not treating Maman how the other girls treated their mothers? *Non, Céleste, non.* Parce que...parce que...because those mothers adored their daughters. Maman had said she cared, but did things that went against it.

"The look on your face, child." Mariquita touched Céleste.

"She makes me feel so guilty." Céleste cringed.

"Ep ep ep." Mariquita patted Céleste's hands, while Théo's shook like leaves.

"Don't worry about Bertie," he said, recovering. "Left her in the toilette."

"You, mon chou," Mariquita said to Céleste, "are not in charge of controlling her emotions. You are safe here at the Folies. See out there? There is no one judging you out there." She studied Céleste's spotty tutu and leveled her crow's feet eyes at Théo. "Can I blame you for this blunder?"

"Quand même..." Théo murmured.

"Nevertheless,"—Mariquita touched Céleste on the back—"the show must go on." She leaned into her ear. "Make it look easy." She nudged her on.

The ballerinas formed a circle around the pillows, following each other making large, expansive jumps—sissonnes, jetés, and pas de chats—guided by the brass horns, clarinets, and piccolo. A gap appeared in the circle where Céleste belonged.

She inhaled deeply, placed her feet in the fifth position, and sprung high, bounding across the floor in a grand allegro to the hauntingly powerful music. Maman was nowhere in sight and Mariquita kept Théo at bay, unyoking her from all the shame and guilt in her life so she could be free, a surrender from her war on many fronts and a reprieve from her threats that fatigued her. Who cared about being the best? On the stage she was untouchable, dancing inside an uncrossable boundary, where she could enjoy herself in peace; feel alive.

The other girls appeared stoic as the strings lifted them to new heights and great falls, grabbing their pillows, where they laid in an oval, all eyes on Céleste.

If fame came for her it wouldn't be for any publicity stunt. It would be for the art of dance. Sarah Bernhardt may've once owned a baby alligator named Ali-Gaga, but when Sarah was on stage, when she played Theodora and Phèdre and La Dame Aux Camelias, even she enjoyed her art form.

To Sarah, the artist's personality must be left in her dressing-room; her soul must be denuded of its own sensations and clothed with the base or noble qualities she is called upon to exhibit. She must leave behind the cares and vexations of her life, throw aside her personality for several hours, and move in the dream of another, forgetting everything.

Céleste kept her body at the center of gravity with great aplomb, calling down celestial bodies so to be in harmony with the world. She bounced across the void, exhibiting fine l'adresse and dexterity, power in her calves, thrusting her airborne, legs together in assemblés, apart, back to fifth, up again, hanging in the air, arms and legs in opposition, perfectly balanced.

Her tutu breathed across the stage like a jellyfish, the tulle rising and falling, with her widening port de bras and the enchanting melody, opening her heart to all French Athens. She launched into a pirouette, feeling her own existence, graduating to a fouetté, whipping one leg out to the side, à la seconde, back in to a passé, forming a triangle, foot to knee, over and over, as she came on and off the tips of her toes on her opposite foot in one relevé after another, one revolution and another, the world blurring, blending, bowdlerizing as she captured the south bar in the back of the house with each turn to stifle dizziness. When she lowered her arms, bras bas, when the notes of the woodwind section faded, when the spotlight narrowed and the world ceased to spin, the bowler-hatted, bustle-wearing, blaspheming crowd leapt to their feet with stupendous applause.

Canes struck the floorboards. Fingers made whistles. The reaction made Céleste's heart flutter. This type of ovation was unheard of at the Folies. She touched her sternum, her chest, her face flushed.

Suzon clapped by the mirror, way back in the promenoir. Monsieur Maupassant whistled. Stage right, Mariquita bowed graciously next to a grinning Théo. *Forget him.*

Céleste took Mariquita's cue and bowed a dainty bow to her admirers. These people—these were people who earnestly enjoyed her dancing without trying to own her, without trying to fill her being with their thoughts and emotions like Maman did, without duplicity like her chaperone, Théo. Céleste reached out for her other girls, formed a line, and bowed together, smiling bright, her makeup running with tears of joy.

Céleste's dilemma reminds me of a certain passage, a passage in the nautical and literal sense, from Homer, about the Strait of Messina, where two monsters lived. Sea monsters. Scylla and Charybdis. These plastic forks will be the reptilian creature, Scylla. It had six heads, and lived in the rocky shoal off the coast of mainland Italy. Quite fearsome in this side of the pool, non? By Sicily, dwelled Charybdis, a worm with a bottomless pit and a mouthful of teeth like a set of buzz saws. With his deep inhalations, he created deadly whirlpools. This stick will serve as our current. Now then, the ship.

A ship deck bears a striking resemblance to a stage, does it not? Our safe passage, if we can remain afloat. Take this cork, my friend. Toothpick. Empty sugar packet. For your sail, admiral. Lastly, we shall tie a shoelace to the ship. Stand over here. When I begin stirring, try to get through. Ready? Go.

Ha-haaa. There you are landing on the rocks. Oh, taking your chances closer to the tide? That won't save you. Of course people are staring. It's a catastrophe! Don't abandon ship over a wet sleeve. You are doing so well. Oui, it's built to scale. The width of the strait is but three kilometers, which puts these devils smack on top of each other, a Venn diagram from hell.

Ah, throwing the handle after the ax, I see. You are right to quit. I give you, the proverbial rock and a hard place.

I don't know about you, but all this doom and gloom has worked me up an appetite. Time for the café?

Super. Can you order in French? Without pointing to the menu? Check out these cute wicker chairs and these handsome rattan lights. Oh, oui. To order, say, *Je voudrais un thé et un scone*. Don't worry if you mispronounce something.

You can only study a thing so much in private. You've got to take it out in the streets to see what you can do. That's what Nayla did. She spent the summer of 1891 rediscovering herself. Rather, discovering her new self, out in the Jacoma salt flats, where the average high of forty-five degrees centigrade felt like room temperature. Summer. L'été, très bien. Who cares if people laugh? Jacques will handle them. We're up.

SPUCKFEUER

N
ayla lobbed fireballs off the top of the ziggurat. They splayed around Jacoma, which stood out like a gold coin on a dusty table, and made little divots in the sand below. The corners of her mouth curved into a rewarding grin. It reminded her of the times she and Kameera would chuck mud cakes at the city wall in the park. The fire was even squishy like mud. If Kameera hadn't learned how to be a lady and moved to Cairo, they'd be hurling mud cakes to this very day. Maybe Nayla ought to try for an overhand?

She glanced at the Vajen Bader helmet tied onto her salwar and debated whether putting it on. The horizon was a clean slate, absent of brigands and caravans. The only brigand around was her. She felt horrible about stealing the helmet from the stationhouse, but she didn't want to be identified and have this Nemesis creature tearing after her. The helmet was indifferent to guilt or a change in ownership. The expressionless eyes looked up from her hip as if to say, *You don't need my permission. I'm an unwilling participant.* These eyes had seen Baba carried from their home.

She wound back her hand and let her rip. A shaft of flame launched from her hand like a javelin. It bounded to the sky and splashed to the ground, where it smoldered for a moment, before the flame died off and left discolored sand.

"Tolle!"

She couldn't throw fireballs yesterday. Only set parts of her body on fire. Her arms. Her legs. She was too afraid to light the whole kabob. What had changed? She had celebrated these flaming appendages by swilling half a jar of moonshine last night. Her headache was gone, and now she could chuck fire. If she drank more what else might she accomplish? Maybe she ought to tap her full potential in this state first. It was like exploring a new body. Like puberty. Hair growing in embarrassing places. The softness of breast in her hands. Changes she wanted to ignore but couldn't.

To hell with it. She stepped back from the edge of the manmade plateau and untied her salwar. The tassels dropped to the stone floor with her drawers, revealing the lower half of her union suit. She untied her tunic from the back and peeled it off. What if her hair caught fire? Would it grow back? Why was it red like someone had dyed it with henna? Was it protective? Some of her hair was still black. These questions went unanswered as she stepped out of her underwear and stood naked before the lukewarm sun.

The sun, be it Surya Dev or Helios, shined on her chest, supplied her hips their lines, streamed light onto her legs, and poured at her blackened feet. Her boots were far enough away so they wouldn't catch. She reached to the sky, wondering if she was being silly. Fire expanded from her navel like a broken gas jet and went rollicking up her arms and down her legs in waves. It was though she had dunked herself in kerosene and lit a match.

Her braid retained its black-and-red color as she burned like a pyre. The freedom was incredible. To be in a constant state of combustion. Was this moksha? Had she escaped the cycle of death and rebirth? Had she escaped all suffering? She squeezed her hands into fists and panned from left to right, spraying flame through her arms into bright balloons, embodying the fire-god, Agni Dev. She didn't want it to end. She had celebrated life with drink like Coronis had said. If only Kameera could see her now.

Nayla pictured her fingers on the knob of the gas lamp in her apartment and slowly turned down the flame. She arched her back and spread her arms wide. What a rush! Her skin hadn't melted, and she hadn't singed her scalp. She dressed and walked home, beaming, plugging the holes of her mind where shame might seep through.

She slid the pretzel key into the slot of her building, climbed the grated steps, and stood the door aside where it had blasted off the hinges. The kitchen was scorched, the bead curtain charred. She pressed her back to the living room wall and sank to the floor. This couldn't be moksha. Everywhere she looked, there was dukha in plain sight—suffering. The majlis couch was burned up, the hens and chicks in her planter roasted. Nothing had survived but the chamber pot and her chest with Maman's headdress.

Her life in the desert, being a nymph—was it all a pretty distraction? Her home was destroyed, she owed the bank ten thousand marks plus interest, and Baba was gone. At least being a nymph cheered her up for part of the day. She held a candle to her thumb and lit the end, inhaling the smell of burnt lacquer and yeast. Somehow, it gave her an edge, like she could better cope with her problems by having something to fall back on to relieve stress. Maybe it was a taste of moksha. Maybe the mixis was a stepping stone to becoming one with Brahman. Where to step next, she had not a clue. How did one escape suffering? How did one escape reincarnation? Where was the next foothold? Relying on the afterlife was out of the question, or Hestia wouldn't have saved her. Nayla was boxed into this life now.

Box. Her Brahman Box. Filled with wonderful quotes from the scriptures. She ran to Maman's chest and pulled out the old German snuff tin. The strips of paper were still intact. She covetously brought the quotes to the living room floor and withdrew one.

"In Ordnung," she said. "Just as the spider creates and withdraws its web, just as trees are born on the earth, just as hairs on the head, and the body grow from a living person, in the same manner, the universe is born here out of Brahman. Right. Everything is Brahman, but how to tap in?"

To think what she had once heard as interesting fairytales, her life now depended on. What was that Purana about the lamp? She sifted through her pile.

"When the mind is thus completely freed from all material contamination and detached from material objectives, it is just like the flame of a lamp." She snapped her fingers. "Ja, the mind is one with Brahman." She looked around. "I've lost nearly everything. Did the text mean physically detached or mentally?" She rubbed her chin. "It said the mind has to be freed, not the body. How did one go about that?"

There was a Upanishad quote on the tip of her tongue. She fanned out the papers to find the one she was looking for. *Fand es!*

"All is change in the world of the senses," she read, "but changeless is the supreme Lord of Love. Meditate on him, be absorbed by him, wake up from this dream of separateness." She leaned forward. "Natürlich. Meditation was the answer." She reached for a burnt pillow and sat upon it, her spine erect. A mantra would help to clear her mind. She closed her eyes. "Om mani padme hum." *Detach from memories, from karma—deeds and actions.* "Om mani padme hum." *Detach from all desire.*

Think you can escape our caste? Baba's voice shouted in her head.

Nayla's eyes flashed open.

She sat there pitifully with a woebegone face. Something deep down made her feel unworthy. Baba had sensed it. That's why he hadn't bothered teaching her about boys, why he'd sold her belongings, never arranged her marriage. It was why Maman hadn't spent enough time with her. But Maman was always out dancing to support the family. It wasn't fair. None of this was fair. Maybe Baba had killed himself to escape her, to really make her suffer, and was having a great big laugh. They had the loan for the mecha-sleeves. He didn't need the distillery anymore, unless to drink his own profits.

If she couldn't find the money, she would have to leave Jacoma, leave the place where Baba and Maman had started a life, started *her* life. Where was the money? Stolen. Stolen after death. Baba had opened an account but never made the deposit. She had turned the old shed upside down. Maybe it was the fireman who carried his body. Nein. She only accused the fireman because she stole his mask. Who, then? The landlord? He was being awfully nice not to evict her. Maybe he was saying thank you. The place was a dump in need of remodeling. Now the landlord's insurance would cover the cost. The explosion did him a favor. Would he honestly resort to murder to fix his property?

Maybe it was Herr Mirza. He may've killed Baba and taken his money for cannabis, then blown up the apartment and feigned victim. Nayla piled the quotes in her snuff box and sealed the tin. Brahman could wait.

Carefully, she hid the knife in her pants, walked down the foyer hall, and knocked on his door. Music played behind the thick wooden slab. It swung in. Herr Mirza's bloodshot eyes jumped at the sight of her.

"Hallo. Nayla, poor girl. How are you?" A hookah burned on the table where a phonograph played. "I'm sorry about what happened to Naem."

"Danke, Mirza." She rested her hands on her stomach. "I'm not so good. New phonograph?"

"Ja. I just picked it up. Come in, I will show you." Mirza bumbled back into his apartment and held up the case the wax cylinder had come in. "I had it printed in the Persian Quarter. It's of me and my band."

He stuck the hookah tip in his mouth. Guilty pains stabbed Nayla. He was so bald and fat and jolly, she instantly regretted bringing her switchblade.

"Lovely." She sat down and examined the newspaper next to the horn. A drawing of a flaming ghost with big circular eyes spanned the front page.

"Have you read it?" Smoke hissed between his teeth. "Some urchin spotted a demon out in the desert and described the image to a journalist. Spuckfeuer, they're calling it."

Nayla bit her lip. "Makes for an interesting read."

"I wonder what was in the urchin's pipe." Mirza set the stem down. "Maybe the Blast fumes have finally gone to our heads. Would you like tea? I have ginger."

"Tea would be great." Nayla spotted her sitar on a stand in the corner among the leafy plants.

Mirza's wispy hair flailed as he turned his coconut head to meet the object of her gaze.

"Ah, come to buy it back?" He bopped off to the kitchen, calling over the music, "I'll sell it to you."

"I haven't the money." The mijwiz solo smothered her voice. "I spent it on the funeral!"

He dispensed the tea from the samovar. "Naem didn't leave an insurance policy?"

"Nein."

"Pity." He returned with some teacups.

"Did you notice what time he came in that day?"

Mirza rubbed his chin as if polishing an apple. "Why yes, I passed him on the grating around three. About an hour—nein, forty-five minutes later, I heard you two arguing."

"That can't be right." She looked up from stirring. "I was at the Blast. What were the voices saying? Did you hear?"

"It was muffled. You know these walls." He took a seat in an arm chair and leaned forward. "I did recall the event ending with a loud thud."

"Was it our apartment door?" Nayla crept to the edge of her seat.

He shook his head, lifting the brim to his lips. "It wasn't a door slam."

"And you didn't run for police?"

"Nayla, dear, I can't be hollering for the police at every creak and pop, can I?" He gave her a knowing look.

"Nein, Herr Mirza. Nein." She traced the diamond patterns of the Persian rug.

"I did skip out to get the mail from my box around five. The foyer reeked to high hell with yeast. Another experiment of his, I imagined."

The tea wobbled in her hands. Baba had arrived home from the bank and turned on his distillery. Ravi uncle confronted Baba. They argued. Baba collapsed. The thud. Ravi uncle took the money. Not two thousand marks. All of it. Baba woke up sometime after five. He struck a match to see. It stole his life. Ravi uncle had the gall to ask her for two thousand marks after he caused Baba's death. Ravi uncle, Kameera's baba, who did nice things for her, like give her Kameera's old clothes to sew and keep, bought her succulents, and read her scripture.

"I must be going. Thank you for tea." Nayla swallowed the cup in one gulp. It burned, it burned. She stifled the urge to activate her powers. Red hair and red eyes would frighten Mirza out of town—and Nemesis into it. "Something needs my attention at the Blast." She rose from the chair and lit off.

"Left an iron in the fire?"

Spoons rattled as Nayla bumped the table.

"Well, all right, child. Watch out for Spuckfeuer!"

Her knobby legs carried her out the door and down the grated stairs, the knife pressed between her cords and her hip. Blood rushed to her brain. She walked the same old streets of the Pits, seeing them through a fever. Had Ravi uncle really lied? This was Kameera's baba, after all. Of course he lied. Baba refused him the two thousand. Did Ravi uncle see the wad of cash and want more? Did the maang teeka even cost two thousand?

She shuffled past the produce vendors, skipping a ride on the bus, so inconsolable as she was. He'd better explain himself, or she'd choke the confession out of him. No fire, no blade would need to harm Ravi uncle. Her hands would suffice. If Kameera knew what he'd done, she'd be so ashamed. Maybe Kameera's perfect Vaishya life wasn't as perfect as Nayla thought. Nayla raised her flask to her lips, running past the stepwell, where a mother chased a naked boy going for a swim.

Kameera's kindness and good luck husband hunting was because she was raised right, Nayla had thought. She didn't know what to think. For all she knew, Ravi uncle was a filthy liar—

Bicycles whizzed by. Camels tied to hitching posts did their business in the street. A woman in a yellow sari sold white roses. Nayla followed in the footsteps of her ghosts, walking to work, clocking in with dread, clocking out exhausted, ambling home when Baba spent her bus fare. She slammed another gulp of moonshine down her throat. Her eyes watered. Her stomach burned. Her feet stamped prints in the ground, blown away daily by the desert tide. Nayla walked here. Then she didn't. This time, her imprints were spaced farther apart.

Smog infected the clean air and clung to the ground. Rotten eggs never smelled so pleasant. It meant she was one step closer to demanding answers. Baba's fading smile pushed her forward. Was this the gods responding to her wishes of having Ravi uncle for a father? Were they making it come true? Is that why Hestia had not intervened to save Baba's life? It was too much speculation. *Ravi uncle wasn't going to adopt you. Stick to facts.* Ravi uncle was the last one to see Baba alive, and he was operating his crane as if nothing had happened, as if he hadn't cost Baba his life, as if he didn't care.

The iwan towered through red mist, the archway that permitted her entry to the Blast. She arrived in hell on Earth. Into the gate, into the iwan, down the corridor that held the time clock. Her shift wasn't until nightfall. She bypassed the line of men in dhotis and blank faces and walked into the charging bay. Shovel hogs chased their tails, dumping lime into one of the hearths. Round and round they went, oblivious to her tripping behind the mounds of scrap and powdered stone. At the next hearth, one hog recognized her. Rumor had spread that she was haunted by a bhoot. He nudged his friends.

Ahead, halfway up the rust-stained wall, Ravi uncle sat stationed at the electric crane, guiding the ladle of molten iron down the suspended track. If it weren't for him, Baba would be in the casting bay right now, tapping a hearth. Nayla placed a hand on the ladder and climbed. The spiraled grooves in the rungs impressed upon her skin as she ascended five meters to the controls. Her head sprang up to a view of Ravi uncle's shoes. There was barely enough room for two people to stand on the platform. Nayla could easily lose her balance and fall, so she remained stuck to the ladder, climbing to meet Ravi uncle at eye level.

He monitored the ladle, drawn to the open hearth before him, and turned his head.

"What did you do to Baba?" Nayla's voice cracked, betraying her resolve to be as menacing as possible.

"What are you doing here?" Ravi uncle glanced at her. "What are you talking about?"

"The day you went to see Baba to ask for money. You robbed him." She grabbed his arm. "Why?"

He traced his mustache with his thumb and forefinger. "Listen to me, Nayla. You are smart, practical, and reliable. Naem was a drunk. You're turning into one yourself."

She was taken aback at these compliments and criticisms.

Ravi uncle pushed a lever forward. Molten iron poured into the spout on the wall of the hearth.

"Why did you rob him and ask me for money after? To make it look as though you'd never stopped by our apartment? Why didn't you sit with Baba until he woke up?"

"When he woke up, he'd have fought me again," said Ravi uncle, slowly tilting the vessel.

"Again?" Nerves fluttered in her chest at his admission. He knocked Baba out. She knew he had been there. This confirmed it.

"I didn't know he'd blow himself up," said Ravi uncle. "This is not the right time to be talking about this. I never meant to harm him. I'll return the difference in marks."

"I don't want the money! I want my Baba!" Nayla shouted. "I'm reporting you."

"No! Wait!" Ravi uncle grabbed her arm and held her on the ladder.

A white flash blinked in the vast room. An explosion crackled like a giant had laid a horse on a skillet. Sparks ejected from a point on the floor by the hearth, sending a tide of lava rolling up toward them. Nayla raised her arm so fast she didn't know why. It was partly to shade her eyes from the glare or shield herself from the gushing liquid. Fire rushed out from her feet and rolled into a sphere before her face.

The tidal wave of viscous goo coated her body with a heat equivalent to dunking her head in a steam bath. Screams of horror erupted from Ravi uncle's windpipe. The sharp succession of notes made Nayla's hair rise like iron filings on a magnet. Ravi slumped back in the chair, shaking uncontrollably, his flesh displayed in the glow of Nayla's fire and the gleam of the receding tide.

The stench churned her stomach. The number *fifteen hundred degrees centigrade* flashed in her head. She lowered her hand. The half-sphere faded in the dark. Shovel hogs squealed to the exit. The ladle had moved back from the hearth and dumped its contents on the steel floor by the spout. Nayla stepped onto the platform and grabbed hold of the lever. It was caught on Ravi's tassel. She unwound it and pushed the ladle forward over the spout. It was too late. The vessel was empty, the controls fried.

"Hold on, Ravi uncle. We'll get you help." She pressed her hands to her chest to stop them from shaking. "Shiva, Shiva. Kameera will hate me forever. Oh, Kameera." She placed a hand on the ladder to descend. "Ravi uncle, stay with me. Ah!"

Green lightning crackled opposite the ladder, producing a ring with a view of Arachne's Cave floating alongside the platform. Nayla clung for dear life at the fear of being sucked in.

"Hecate?" she said, uneasy.

A birdlike silhouette swooped out of the portal and cut across the smoky charging bay, obstructing the sunbeams from the skylight.

"Oh, nein. Nemesis." Nayla returned to the platform, ill-prepared for the fight of her life. "I'll get you help, Ravi uncle."

She had to. *Forget Nemesis. Ravi uncle is dying.*

"He's dead," said a deep voice.

On the scaffolding crouched a male figure with enormous wings, the wings of a raven. Nayla hesitated. Nemesis was a woman. This was a man.

"Nein, we can save him." Nayla stepped down a rung.

"He's dead," called the voice again.

"How do you know?" Nayla cried, examining Ravi uncle's face, stuck in a terrorized grimace.

"Because I'm here." He stood to full height, wearing a turban.

"Yama?" She cringed.

"Thanatos. God of death. Not many can see me. Or the doorways. Are you a new nymph?"

Nayla nodded, befuddled.

"Hecate must've granted you a taste of her powers in your mixis. Well, duty calls." He dropped onto Ravi uncle, lost shape, and engulfed the platform in shadow.

Ravi uncle's soul glowed white, flame-like, his Atma plucked from his chest by Thanatos's shadowy hand. Secure, Thanatos whisked Ravi uncle's soul through the electric void in a diaphanous plume. Arachne's Cave lingered in the gateway as the cloud subsided. The webs shone green in the light.

Looking into the underworld, Nayla had never felt so insignificant. So small. She told Kameera she didn't deserve the maang teeka. The karmic link of that event picked up the link of this one. She just wanted the suffering to end. To escape karma. To escape reaping everything she had sown, that her past lives had sown for her. Moksha was a carrot dangled in front of a donkey.

Ravi uncle's body smoldered in the chair while his soul traveled to the unknown. The Hall of Fabled Objects dominated the far wall in Greco-German Jugendstil, visible for another moment before the electric ring shrank and the view crackled shut. Could any of the items hidden within that vault be of help? They might be carrots she could reach. Not carrots. Stepping stones. Her powers could help her take the next step in that direction. She could have researched these objects at the library, but she didn't think she'd ever travel to Hades again without Hecate. She hadn't known that death opened doors.

If she entered now, without knowing what she was after, with no help to fight Arachne, she would end up trapped like a fly, like that dead nymph. The barrier of fire she had made couldn't stand up to molten iron. How would it do against a mystical weaver?

"Boah, someone's up there with him!" called one of the shovel hogs.

Scheisse. Nayla attached herself to the ladder and climbed. The only way to go was up, past the scaffolding, toward the rafters.

The hearths glowed in the bottom of the bay, their square charging doors shedding light onto men carefully reentering the Blast. If she slipped and fell, she would accept it. Anything but facing Kameera or herself. Mirrors were her new enemy. Ravi uncle had spilled his ladle because she distracted him. Had she not approached, had he not stolen the money from Baba, had Kameera not given her a loan, had she not told Kameera about the mecha-sleeves, had she not had the overpowering desire to escape her position in life, had Maman not died of consumption and changed Baba into a drunk, none of this would have ever happened.

She pulled the chained pin on the ceiling hatch and shoved it open. Fog hung over the Blast like a red miasma. Smokestacks poked out from large cylindrical stoves. Skip cars chugged up tracks leaned against the mouths of each blast furnace, depositing coke into hoppers at their summits before sliding back down. Tuberous pipes bent every which way through fumes that filtered the city in rose gold.

Nayla climbed onto the roof, kicked the hatch shut, and ran beside the plexiglass skylight. Over her shoulder, a man was perched in the crow's nest by the blast furnace, checking on skip cars. The fire escape on the side of the charging bay was too close to the man. She would be recognized. They'd blame her for Ravi uncle's death. It was her fault, though, wasn't it? Nein, she didn't tell Ravi uncle to spill lava on the floor. But if she hadn't distracted him, he'd still be alive. Him? What about her? He disrupted her life by causing Baba's death.

She uncapped her flask and bottomsed up. The burn. The stink. What was she celebrating? She didn't know anymore. She wanted off this roof. Out of samsara. Without dukha. No more rebirth, no more suffering. At six stories up, the fall would kill her. If she turned back, a shovel hog may identify her as someone who projected flame from their body—on top of being arrested. All she knew was the more she drank, the more creative was her fire. First it was setting her body alight, then throwing projectiles, then making barriers. When oh when would she sprout wings like the dead nymph in the cave?

"Maman, help me."

Her boots smacked the padded roof as she stepped onto the ledge and leapt into the haze. She flapped her arms and stuck them in front of her, bracing for a fall ten meters out. Her hair whipped in the wind straight up and then straight down, changing from black to red as a geyser of flame exploded from her hands. The spire of flames cratered the soot-covered sand. Nayla fell to the ground, cushioned by her collapsing funnel.

Not dead. She was not dead. She dragged her fingers through the soot and sat on her knees. A fence on the outskirts of the property barred her way. She placed her hands on the piles, forgetting the mecha-sleeves were at her apartment, and squeezed. The bars glowed red, brightened to orange, and sizzled to white hot temperatures, snapping forward in her grip like saffron brittle.

She stuffed her body through the slot into an alley. The fear of being caught fizzled out. The guilt of Ravi uncle's death flared up. She wanted to find somewhere to sulk.

"Kameera," she whimpered.

Her oldest friend.

Pass the cream, s'il vous plait. Merci. Kameera made the trip home for Ravi's funeral, naturally. Nayla attended unseen, perched on a rooftop. I know. It's not the reunion we'd have hoped for. When something happens in your life that comes with a lot of guilt, you go numb inside. You feel less than yourself. The last thing you want to do is face those you've hurt.

Kameera was unaware Nayla was involved in Ravi's accident, which may give us an idea of how guilty Nayla felt not to show up. One look from Kameera would've flattened her. Nayla had wanted to go. What she didn't want was to be coddled or told it wasn't her fault. Or inform Kameera that her father lived beyond his means, and the maang teeka—something Kameera ensured would be all right to accept—led to both their fathers' deaths. Non. Nayla would rather face Kameera fully healed, psychologically armored, in a state of moksha. That was the answer!

While Nayla was avoidant of Kameera in 1891, Céleste was ambivalent toward Théo in 1887. The man was Jekyll and Hyde. Thankfully the good Dr. Jekyll had been choosing to give Mr. Hyde sick leave, but for how long? Céleste's plan as it stood was to outgrow the situation. An adult did not need a chaperone.

The logic was there, but the time span glacial. One could not remain adrift in the Strait of Messina forever. Even the crafty Odysseus had to choose. To keep Théo's advances secret or lay waste to her family dynamic as she knew it and free herself? Our Scylla and Charybdis. A heavy burden. Too much weight for a young lady's shoulders to bear.

INCIDENT

"Papa, we must see Pierre. Think of how lonely he is. All by himself in his cage."

"I'm planning next week's show, princesse." He looked up from the posters sprawled on his lap and the divan. "Théo, would you mind taking her?"

Théo added the old newspaper to the stack. "Oy, not at all."

Céleste retreated inside of herself. "Papa," she said, "you promised we'd spend time together after my performance."

"We will, we will." He licked his fingers and flipped through his note cards. "Very soon. Weekend after next. I promise."

But now was the perfect time without Maman around. Weekend after next... Maman would be back from the Greek Riviera by then, and their house likely in the hands of Monte Carlo.

"Please, Papa."

He sandwiched Chang the Chinese Giant between the Griffiths and the Leopolds. "Two clown acts in a row." He shook his head. "What was I thinking?" He looked at Céleste. "I'm working, ma choupinette," he said, mildly irritated.

To support a wife with an insatiable gambling addiction, she wanted to add, but didn't. It would've only led to argument.

"Enjoy the zoo." He lightened up. "Tell Pierre I say salut."
Théo shrugged and opened his mouth.

"Quand même," Céleste filled in the blank for him, "oui."

"I'll get the carriage." He walked by leaving the air's rose fragrance undisturbed.

Sober. He was sober. Not even groggy. He shuffled down to the foyer and out the door. He shouldn't be any trouble. But just in case...

Her skirt wobbled as she descended into the chamber. At the mirror she examined her hat—a tapered red number with a tall crown and narrow brim turned up at the front—a stunning flowerpot. She plucked a rose from the vase on the table, cut the stem, and tucked it into the band. From the table drawer, she withdrew a long hatpin, fifteen centimeters in length, and its mate, their pinheads ladybugs on twisting leaves—her favorites—and skewered the buckram hat material to her locks.

Céleste, you're overreacting. Hatpins... What was she going to do? Poke Théo in the ribs? Stab his heart? She wasn't a violent person. Could she really live with herself knowing she caused someone physical harm? Death?

She shivered as she stepped onto the sunny boulevard de Malesherbes surrounded by its purple stonework and green iron—a wisteria wonderland.

She ought to just enjoy her day at the zoo. Let the hatpins give her peace of mind. There was nothing to worry about anyway. Théo was sober and seemed to be working hard at avoiding her when he wasn't. Maman was out of town. If anything this was a vacation. She could've invited Annette and the ballet girls over if the house didn't look so lived in. *Your mess is why I can't have friends over*, she'd say to Maman. *You don't need friends,* was always the response. Céleste could've tidied up, but Maman would've pitched a fit when she returned. *Where are all my papers! I knew where everything was!*

Everything was everywhere. The horses had more gumption.

Clemence and Claudette rounded the corner and stopped. She raised her hand to Clemence, who bowed, kind-eyed, so she could scratch behind his ears.

"There's a good boy. Did you eat a carrot today? Did Théo feed you a carrot?"

"Ay, that he did," said Théo.

"Bon garçon. Oh, I didn't forget you, Claudette." Céleste stepped into the street and scratched her mane too. "There's my girl. You want to go to the zoo and see your friend, Pierre? You want to pull my walnut carriage? I knew you did. You love giving me rides."

Théo held the door. She glided her fingers along the smooth shell and hopped in, collapsing her chimney bustle as she sat.

Théo smiled the same way he had in his dryer days and lightly closed her in. The horses strode the flagstones and, in moments, they left Elysium for Hermes Hill, where the wisteria gave way to dappled green light speckling rue Saint-Vincent, the leaves an explosion of green confetti, real nature amongst the architectural mimicry—a segment of French Athens known as the Wild Garden, a wilderness of hidden glades and stone pools.

But why were they so far up on the hill? La Ménagerie du Jardin des Plantes was along the Seine by the Sorbonne.

She opened the communicating slot to find out.

"Em, Théo, what are we doing here?"

"Apologies, Céleste." Théo looked over his tweed shoulder. "Left my accordion behind the other day picnicking with a lady in the Wild Garden. Figured I collect it and play some tunes at the zoo. Here we are."

He stopped the coupé.

An auburn-haired, stout-bodied, gingham-wearing, freck-le-faced woman stood on the forest's edge and approached with his instrument, meaning business. There was a whispered exchange mixed with street noise, and she stepped back into view stuffing something in her bosom. The woman smirked at Céleste and waved, tickling the air. Céleste waved back, unable to place her, and the woman disappeared into the forest.

"Onto the zoo," announced Théo. He flicked the reins.

The window replaced her view of the Wild Garden with rows of apartments and a pedestrian street, set on an incline, layered by steps. A jungle of silver lace vines engulfed the buildings—They were the buildings, as she snaked her way to the top of the hill, and the vines peeled away like a curtain to reveal Sacré-Coeur, an immaculate work of frosted glass, the triple-portico unfurling its white stone in watery fronds, with a dome in the center guarded by scaffolding, flanked by two domes on the outside, erupting in frozen showers of gelatin, the cathedral owing its appearance to snow fungus, a jelly mushroom, similar to coral—a parasite on her life that Maman dispensed with glee.

You will wake up and go to church, young lady.

Non, I'm tired.

You should be obedient to your parents in all things, she'd say, high and mighty, leaving the room.

Céleste would turn in bed with the covers.

Swiftly they'd be yanked off, and Céleste greeted by a cup of ice water.

The shock would numb her face. She'd wipe her eyes.

Now come to church, Maman would say, *for it is well-pleasing to the Lord.*

Vile woman, Céleste would snap. *If Jesus were here, he'd send you to hell.*

What did you say?!

At that point, Céleste would leap from her bed and Maman would chase her around the house.

You have many sins against your mother you need to confess, child.

Maman thought that going to church was all that was required to make her a good person. That any bad deed could be forgiven and forgotten, swept under the rug with a Hail Mary or Our Father at the confessional, but the only thing reconciled was that she was free to sin again, carte blanche—against her own daughter! Religion was a cage for Maman, no different than the scaffolding around the dome, a cage she sometimes used as a weapon to trap Céleste in too.

Still, even Céleste could not resist the portico's finished glory. The statue of Jesus, standing in the pediment's niche, arms wide in second position, welcoming all of French Athens to his embrace, his robes white like her dress when she received first communion at Notre Dame, so cheerful was Maman and Papa on her happy day.

Jesus, why do I have an ogre for a mother?

Why did you choose her?

Please make her normal like me.

Please don't send her to hell.

Céleste touched the crucifix in the niche of her neck.

Make Théo go back to normal too. Make him stop drinking.

Make Papa stop them from hurting me.

Thank you for my formidable dancing last Thursday. Athens said it was a tour de force.

And bless Mariquita.

Amen.

He appeared to be listening, though his eyes were clearly on Athens, perhaps watching over the foundations of La Tour Eiffel, golden feet of the letter A in filigree. The window afforded her one final glimpse of the flowering city as her walnut turned the corner, and Théo steered her to the boulevard de Magenta, the neighborhood's walls populated by orchids, the bricks in the shape of their vertebrae-like petals, leading her invariably to the Pont d'Austerlitz and ultimately the zoo.

Gargoyle elephants guarded each side of the main entrance, hyena heads protruded from the arch, and polar bears stood sentinel on the roof, the whole affair colored aqua, coming to a stop with the carriage.

Pierre would be so excited to see her.

Céleste's chimney bustle sprung back into shape as she rose and opened the door, and Théo helped her down without a hint of his devious countenance. She'd only just been here in June, but everything was aglow with girlhood. It was like she'd stepped back in time to the late seventies, when Maman was more tame and Papa less timid, Théo was a trusted guardian, and the pretty green trees were right where she'd left them on Quai Saint-Bernard as saplings.

Théo hitched Claudette and Clemence to a post and grabbed his accordion off the driver's seat. While he warmed up his instrument, Céleste withdrew two apples from a cupboard in the side of the carriage. She met her babies and held her palms flat for them to bow and eat, their lips wet on her skin.

She followed Théo, keeping him in her sight, as he paid the ticket man two francs at the window and walked through the mammoth arch.

Théo's tunes carried her through the exhibits, playing Camille Saint-Saëns's Le Carnival des Animaux. He squeezed the accordion's diaphragm, hitting the treble buttons for the aviary, the scales rising and falling to emulate birdsong, capturing the cuckoo's emergence after each climb with a C note and A-flat. The lion enclosure provoked the bass buttons, the song regal and majestic, teasing a smile from Céleste, for the entertainment was a welcomed delight. This was Théo.

He smiled back, transitioning to Mary had a Little Lamb, while children holding their mothers pointed, encircled by cheery pink faces. One bold girl frolicked over with her younger sister, as brave as Tamer Seeth and his Menelik Lions, ignoring the beasts in the cage completely, as they danced haloes around Théo.

Théo hammered on the bass buttons, relaxed the bellows and forced air through the grill, taking lumbering, surefooted strides, toward the elephant house. The big ham.

Céleste laughed, rapping Théo on the arm, as the children emulated the trusted melody in their own step. She followed him under the weeping willows, the mothers lazing behind in veiled hats, all the way until the canopy released her to the elephant house, a holy sight resembling a mosque, its fish-scale domes enameled in green, outlined against the blue sky.

Céleste jumped up and down, beaming, sparkling, taking in the glazed ceramic heads of hippos, rhinos, and elephants ringing each dome. She skipped under the archway's bull elephant mascaron. Children darted around her in their dresses and sailor suits, footsteps pattering, bodies tumbling against the cage, where she pressed her hands to the curled bars.

"Pierre!" Céleste shouted, inhaling the odor of a stable.

Pierre flapped his ears, gnawing on grass, nonchalantly. He reached up for his bale of breakfast hanging from the ceiling in a net and continued to munch while Théo continued his refrain marching into the palace.

Pierre looked at her with his amber eyes, as if to say, *where have you been?*

Oh, Pierre, I should have been here sooner, but Papa doesn't believe in breaks. He was working harder than the Percherons and faster than Maman could spend.

"Well, are you going to neglect me too?" Céleste pointed at the ground at her feet. "Viens ici."

Pierre galumphed to the bars. Céleste stuck her hand through and rubbed his pearly tusk, then caught hold of his trunk. She slid her hand along the furrows.

"The zookeeper doesn't show you any affection, does he?"

One of the girl's tugged at Céleste. "Can I pet him?"

"Of course, you can. Don't be afraid." Céleste lifted her up, hair falling onto her lace collar. "He won't bite. C'est bon."

The girl pet the elephant and smiled. Emboldened, she kissed her own hand and pressed it to Pierre's trunk. "A bisou for me and a bisou for you."

Céleste set the girl down. "I think he likes you."

"How can you tell?" asked the girl.

Céleste smiled knowingly at Pierre. "We have a special understanding."

"Does he like it in his cage?"

"Non." Her smile faded. "I'm afraid not."

If only there was something she could do.

"At least he has yummy grass and a big palace to live in." The girl galloped back to her mother. "Did you see me, Maman! I touched the elephant!"

Théo serenaded Pierre's home with a series of falling notes to symbolize a descent into an aquarium.

"Eh bien, Théo," said Céleste, "I know where you want to go next."

She waved goodbye to Pierre and followed Théo out of the palace, onto the cobbles, the accordion's melody conjuring images of Captain James and Miss Lorli, famous aquatic acrobats, until they dove into their tank. Then they were Fish Man and Fish Woman!

Ahead, beneath the willows, a tin statuette of Hermes was on his tiptoes in relevé, waving a flag from the peak of a tin can, a câlin—a fountain strapped to a vendor's back. A feather breezed in his hat. She recognized that plumage anywhere. The coco man!

"Coco! Coco on a hot day!" he called.

Children trailing behind her broke from their procession to ring around him, the boys digging in their pockets to hand him their sous. Théo noticed he'd lost his crowd and shrugged his quand même shrug while the coco man, a big-jawed Alphonse, collected money and unfastened tin cups from his straps to make drinks. He held the cup under the spickets extending from the tank on his back like the arms of a chair.

"Théo, we must have some coco." Céleste held out her palm. "I'm awfully parched."

"The show had to end sometime." He forked over the sou.

"One coco." Céleste paid the man.

"Pleasure, mademoiselle." He retrieved a returned cup, wiped it clean with a handkerchief, and refilled it for Céleste.

She pressed the metal to her lips. Licorice, lemon, and water serenaded her tongue with visions of Grand-mère and Grand-père's business they used to own in French Corinth, a wonderful yellow estaminet with teal shutters that sold coffee, candy, cigars, and soft drinks.

"Add more licorice to mine, s'il vous plait." Théo turned to Céleste. "Stuff is sweet."

The coco man filled Théo's order and winked at him, good-naturedly. Théo gulped it down in a blink.

"Still dangerous." He returned the cup. "Right we go."

Théo squeezed the bellows and walked toward the aquarium. He hit the treble buttons, setting loose a torrent of notes. This was no longer the Carnival of Animals, but La Danse Macabre. Hauntingly beautiful, it reminded her of all the spiritualists who purchased ad space in the programmes at the Folies—Indian cartomancers, ladies who claimed to be palmists, and soothsayers who told fortunes using coffee grounds.

"Hungry?" asked Théo.

"Famished."

"What say we escape in the style of the English and go somewhere new?"

"Where do you have mind?"

"A bistro just opened up on boulevard de Clichy,"—He smiled with mock mischief—"Cabaret du Néant. The waitstaff are dressed like undertakers and they put on magic shows."

"What fun!" Céleste clapped.

They made for the exit under the stone polar bears, guarded by mandrills, and the melody brought her to Clemence and Claudette. Clemence neighed and snorted as though he'd been wounded.

"Easy, boy." Théo set his accordion on the sidewalk and took the reins. "What's spooked him?"

Céleste shrugged, sizing up the carriage. The horse's unease made her uneasy. If she stepped into that walnut, she was basically a traveling hostage. She took a slight step back. Non. Théo couldn't possibly deceive her after the glorious day they'd had. She tipped her head to the side.

"Théo, I think now would be a good time for my driving lesson." She swallowed.

"We just started you on horseback two weeks ago. Not sure you're ready for carriage driving."

"If you intend to build a racecourse, how am I to get to it?"

He shot her an ironic look. "Very well Bonne idée." He climbed into the driver's seat with his accordion and offered his hand.

She sighed. How silly she'd been. He was on good behavior. But now at least they were in the open, in the public eye. She mounted the leather-cracked bench.

"It'll be just like riding a horse, but from a meter behind the saddle." He handed her the reins and Perpignan—a long pole with a whip.

"Take the reins between your middle and ring fingers," he continued. "Like this." He slipped them in. "The loop comes between the index and thumb. There we are." He demonstrated by pantomime. "Rotate the hand back for a left turn, and forward for a right turn. If you like, angle the reins so they're aligned with the direction you want. For left, angle right. For right, angle left."

"So opposite from saddle riding?" asked Céleste.

"Oui."

"How do you make them go?" asked Céleste.

"Relax the reins."

Céleste did so. Clemence and Claudette clopped their hooves, and they advanced with a tingle in her stomach.

"Signal left with your whip. Like this." Théo wrapped his arm around her and raised her right arm high, pointing the whip to the left at 180 degrees.

He snaked out from behind her, while her eyes darted around the cobbles, mindful of other carriages and passing drays loaded with casks.

"Don't tense on the reins or they'll stop. Keep the reins relaxed. Not too slack. There we are." He leaned back. "The horses can feel your heartbeat through the material."

"Can they tell I'm a first-timer?"

"Oui, it's why they're being good."

Steel girders representing lily of the valley led her down the garden path, approaching the Pont de l'Archevêché.

"How do you signal right?" she asked.

"Wave the whip out to the right and point." He reached for her, getting too handsy.

"I'm driving." She scooted over. "Don't touch me."

"Don't worry about it. Just keep your eyes on the road."

Céleste took quick breaths. Sweat formed on the whip, the reins, as she bounced her knee.

"Keep good posture," said Théo. "If the horses stop suddenly, you'll go shooting over the dashboard."

"I'm driving." She rotated her hand forward and angled the reins to the left, sticking out her whip like a flag.

The turn properly executed, she crossed the bridge under the arbors of climbing roses, detecting movement from Théo out of the corner of her eye, glancing at her chest.

In an effort to avoid being trapped, she was stuck driving the carriage, right where he'd wanted her. *Non, Céleste.* Nothing was going to happen. She was in public. There were people about everywhere, from the chestnut-seller by the boulangerie to the boot blacks at the corner. She rounded Ile de la Cité fighting to control her breaths. Théo didn't drink. She was fine.

But why did Clemence jump? He must've seen a squirrel. And Théo was not looking at her chest. He was watching the whip and reins. His life was in her hands as much as she was in his. Why, she could strike her babies into a gallop, jerk back the reins, and send Théo flying.

Beneath orbs of fennel on gables, around sheaves of larkspur on gutters, as night melted the blue day into pink, she drove through Place Pigalle, where Greek columns supported flowers mythified by antiquity, and the Cabaret of the Void bloomed on her right like a black hellebore. By some court of miracles, she'd managed to arrive.

She tightened the reins and commanded her babies to, "Arrête!"

They obeyed, Dieu merci!

Her hands shook with fright as Théo took the reins.

"There now, we made it."

He climbed backwards to the ground and reached for Claudette to tie her off. She shied back.

"What's gotten into you, girl?" He seized the rope and hitched her to a fluted post.

First Clemence, then Claudette. It could be the foreboding façade of black windows and white trim, or the funky character actress coming out to greet the queue. She had pigtails and wore a top hat, split down the middle in a high contrast of black and white like the building. Le Spectre de Pagani might come out next, or Count Patrizio, or Okill the Ventriloquist.

The top-hatted woman cracked a joke at the crowd, earning her a laugh. Céleste stepped down with the whip. If only she could carry it in with her. Théo reached out. She jumped.

"Waouh." Théo raised his hands in supplication. "Don't think the other diners will like us herding them by whip."

What a goose she was being. She eased her grip and relinquished the weapon. Théo left it in the carriage, she scratched her neck, and they got in line.

Her pulse quickened as the people advanced past the black cerements, into the void, and she was up.

"Have fun, macchabées," the female clown cooed in Céleste's ear.

Macchabée? Who was she calling a stiff? Céleste had a beating heart and breathing lungs—and before she had time to protest, the clown nudged her in.

The black curtains parted to the interior of a coffin, where black stained glass served as panels and wainscot, set into mahogany frames. Burning sage, taxidermied birds, and other weird smells laid stagnant in the air.

"Bonsoir," said a waiter, his eyeball dangling from its socket.

Céleste covered her mouth.

"Is my hair crooked?" asked the waiter, raking his fingers through his greased cut.

"Just a bit of wax." Théo laughed. "Une table pour deux personnes, s'il vous plait."

"Certainly." The waiter led them into a large room with a fibula chandelier and tibia candelabras. "Like the fixtures?" He caught Céleste's eye. "It took us four grown macchabées to make those."

"Beurk!" said Céleste.

He gestured them to a black table—a closed casket—and pulled out a chair, also made of bones. "We had some left over." He set the menus on the box.

Théo tossed his hat on the rack behind her near an umbrella stand and took his seat.

"Two skulls of dropsy," he said, "s'il vous plait."

The waiter called to the bartender, "Two skulls of dropsy with a pinch of diphtheria!"

The bartender busied himself, removing bottles from the pipe organ façade behind him.

"Théo," said Céleste, "are those beverages alcoholic?"

"Course not," said Théo, "they're like coco."

Céleste leaned back in her seat. Bien sûr. They had to be soft drinks. She was having one. He ordered two.

In a moment, the waiter returned with their drinks, presented in a pair of human skulls. "Nothing goes to waste. May I take your order?"

Céleste perused the menu. "Tender bone oysters and Scared and stiff greens."

"And I'll have Grumpy Truffles from Philippe Ricord," said Théo.

"Trés bon." Frankenstein's waiter slid his pen in his apron and stalked off to the kitchen.

Céleste lifted the skull to her lips and drank the strange fluid. It tasted like pineapples with a sting of rum that snuck up on her. When she lowered her cup, Théo had turned his upside down on the casket.

She cast hers onto the table. "Théo! What is wrong with you? This is not coco. It's poison."

"Should hope so." Théo chuckled. "We're in the Room of Intoxication."

He turned to the bartender and hollered for another.

"Théo, non." Céleste reached to grab his arm and failed. "You are a good person. You don't need to drink."

"Can too, as much as I like." He shooed her off. "Read the print." He pointed to the menu.

The posthumous is required, to drive guests back to their last home.

"That means you," said Théo. "Aren't you glad I taught you how to drive?"

Céleste sunk her head. "You were doing so well."

"Appears the coco man spiked my coco."

Céleste's lip curled.

If Théo tried anything those hatpins were coming out... Plan. She needed a plan.

"Go on," said Théo, "drink up."

She wouldn't. She couldn't. But if she didn't, Théo would change more and more into a grotesque version of his former self. Into a monster.

She picked up her skull and sipped.

When he turned to face the waiter returning with their meals, she dumped the rest into the pelvis of the umbrella stand.

The waiter placed the fresh drinks on the table. "Bon appétit," he said, the eyeball dancing on his cheek as he left.

Théo emptied his skull. She reached for hers, catching her finger on the jaw, as he plucked it up.

"I'll take this."

Had he seen her dump the other one? She fidgeted in the chair.

"Théo, you're scaring me."

He looked at her with cold dead eyes, unresponsive. They flashed green by the light of a lantern, carried high by the playing card clown.

"Hear that, macchabées?" She asked the diners at large. "A bell in a graveyard rings. A man has been buried alive. Down this tunnel. Come, come, we may saveth him anon." She roused the men and women from their anatomical chairs and conducted them into the tunnel. "Follow me hither, into the Vault of Trespasses, and henceforth to the Cave of Ghosts."

"Time for an illusion," said Théo.

Plan plan plan. She needed a plan. She could escape him and drive the carriage herself, alone. Out the front door? Non. He would follow to quickly. He was always one step behind her. She could escape through the back. The actors must have had some way in which they came and went—a door that led onto the street. Oui, she could slip away during the magic.

She rose from her chair.

"After you," said Théo, taking his hat and gesturing to the tunnel.

Céleste swallowed. Why take his hat if he was going to return? They hadn't been served their meals. She walked to the toxic light, his heavy footsteps falling behind her. The tunnel was ticking. Clocks and bones had been encrusted into the walls of the corridor, ticking cruelly, and blasting shadows onto faces, as she followed a man in a sack suit and mustache, guided by the marshy glow.

The party filed into a claustrophobic chamber with a narrow stage on which stood an upright coffin. Stage left was a door, the exit into the next illusion. The clown woman hooked out her lantern.

"O macchabées, I request a hot-blooded donor from—"

Maintenant! Céleste silently broke off from the group, disappearing behind the clown as she turned to hang the lantern. The hallway was robed in black, sloping downward, absorbing the clown's voice.

"O macchabée, beautiful, breathing mortal, pulsating with warmth and the richness of life, thou art now in the grasp of death! Compose thy soul for the end!"

They don't know you're gone, Céleste. Keep going!

She stumbled through the hall and ran face-first into a curtain. She peeled it open. Her footsteps echoed. Dim candles burned on the sconces. This was a bigger room—the Cave of Ghosts apparently. Rows of benches occupied the room, made of stone, backless like the benches in a cemetery, and set before a stage with a ratty curtain.

"Where are you, my macadam flower?" Théo's baritone whisper reverberated off the walls.

Céleste's hairs stood high. She breathed in, breathed out. *Chut, Céleste, he could hear you breathing.*

He? Who was he? It was not her Théo, but the monster inside.

She took cover behind a pillar to this charnel house.

Had the monster been testing her limits the whole time?

He had called her names—shrimp, street mud, milk cow.

She didn't tell.

He had approached her room at night.

She still didn't tell.

He had reached for her chest.

She didn't tell even then.

"Come out, my half-salted butter. We're missing the illusion."

Céleste froze.

He was waiting until he knew she wouldn't tell, until he confirmed he'd put her in an impossible situation, cornered in a basement, with nothing to stop him but a hatpin.

Her knees nearly buckled.

She reached for her hat, hand trembling, and withdrew a pin, the grace and finesse she displayed on stage gone. Where was the exit? It had to be stage right like the one in the Vault of Trespasses. She could only presume it would lead up to the street, or back into the Room of Intoxication—She'd settle for that. Her leg muscles went taut. She made a fist around the pin like the handle of a knife. On three she would run to the right side of the stage and hope beyond hope there was a door there. *Un, deux...*

"Céleste," Théo called, "help me."

Je suis désolée, Théo...trois!

She raced through the murky room toward some approximation of stage right. A hand grabbed her arm. She turned and stabbed the needle into his, another into his tweed-coated belly. A shove sent her backwards, bruising her calves on the bench, her spine thudding flat on stone. Wind escaped her lungs. Her bustle snapped. The pin clanked on the floor. The second pin. She reached for it, her arm intercepted by Théo tearing at her collar, engulfed by his cedar cologne, ripping free her necklace, knocking off her hat, renting her dress apart at her bosom, dethreading her chemise, lying bare her chest.

God, help me.

He pinned his weight on her legs and reached for her chest with his claw. The room flickered to a darker shade of black, and suddenly she was standing next to the bench as a spectator, Théo's eyes obsidian as he cut into her like she had no skin, like it wasn't there, her flesh bloodless. He glommed onto something housed between her rib cage, something bright—the tool that kept everything sacred, the weapon that shielded her from darkness—a white flame. He pulled it loose, stripping her of its power.

He said nothing.

She said nothing.

I think we can let go now. We're okay.

Non, Théo was not Thanatos. The god only collected souls off the dead. Oui, the white flame was Céleste's soul. To remove one from the living is theft. Though it was not a crime punishable by the gods. To them, it was life. C'est la vie. You and I, however, are not so dismissive, not so forgiving. Where do we go from here? Do we seek vengeance? Justice? Let us catch our bearings first.

We must come up for air, surface the whirlpool, and seek refuge in the library.

Meditate.

You see, my friend, moksha is about being one with Brahman. Brahman is in everything. You. Me. This coffee cup. Therefore, this amazingly complex network we call life is actually quite simple. You are everything, and everything is you. You can't have a character without a setting or a setting without a character. Ah, Aristotle says different, but I disagree. Poetics nothing. The two are joined. We can't exist without setting. We are drinking coffee that came from the ground, sitting on chairs that came from the ground, bathing in sunlight that helped these things grow out of the ground, a ground that we need to stop us from floating away. Does it scare you? That I am you, and you are me?

Fear not. There is nothing wrong with being Jacques! Oh, there is? Lucky for you, each person has their own identity, and they are part of a whole system called Brahman. You want to speak fluent French? Does it aggravate you at times, your practice? When my countrymen say things that you cannot understand? Embrace where you are in your learning now. Do not cling to the outcome and you will enjoy the journey.

However, should you cling to something you want and force the desire, you will suffer. To be one with Brahman is to detach from everything you want. What Nayla desired was to be one with Brahman. But she desired it in a clinging way. Do you see the paradox? What she needed was an assist.

Bonbon?

THE CAP OF HADES

I f the gods in the Vedas pretended to be Greek, information on the objects in the fabled hall had to be in Homer, Hesiod, and Pindar. These editions had such lovely illustrations. Nayla flipped the pages and took notes.

The cap, which looked like a helmet, made the wearer invisible. The Cyclops had given it to Hades to fight the Titans during the Titanomachy. Athena used it to help Diomedes fight the Trojans. Hermes put it on to fight the giant, Hippolytus, during the Gigantomachy, when giants attacked Mount Olympus. And Perseus, the last to use the relic, wore it to escape the two Gorgons after cutting the head off their sister, Medusa. It brought success to whomever wore it. Why couldn't it work for her?

It would be the perfect catalyst to enlightenment, the power to become one with the universe and open her eyes permanently. What better way to perceive herself as her surroundings than to optically become them? She leaned back in the library light, staring up at the golden candelabra. It was funny. As a girl, the way Ravi uncle had presented enlightenment was like a bedtime story. It was make-believe. Impossible for her to comprehend. To see yourself as a rock and see the rock as you. Her and Kameera had tried for a week seeing themselves as each other and gave up when nothing happened.

Nayla had squinted really hard, sat in meditation, tried chanting, and talked to a temple pūjari in the bazaar. Now, after a visit from real gods, there was physical proof that enlightenment was real. Moksha. But how to achieve it? When she drank to celebrate life, she would become immortal. Drinking gave her powers, yet immortality did not come. Case in point, the dead nymph in the cave. There had to be some intermediary step.

Her gods told her about the Cap of Hades—showed her where it was located—and gave her powers that could take her there. Everything pointed in that direction. Imagine meditating with the Cap of Hades on her head? How complete she would feel?

She leaned over the Vivekachudamani and read teacher Adi Shankara's description.

"The knower catches in the ecstasy of his heart the full light of that Brahman, that Divine Essence, which is indescribable—all pure bliss, incomparable, transcending time, ever free, beyond desire."

Brahman was something she wanted to shrink inside of, then turn out the light, as if Brahman was missing a piece of itself it wanted returning, and she was it. To feel lightness of heart, transcend time. It would be as though she were never born a Shudra. It would be as if she were born lovable. To not have to impress anybody, to not care about the approval of others, to not have confidence one day and feel like disappearing the next, to not be ashamed for having feelings, to not be called a whore when asking about the male persuasion, to not have to parent her baba. He would have treated her so much differently.

She had experienced enough suffering to fill the average lives of ten men. She was ready to remove it and live out the rest of her days in a hovel, spiritually at peace, knowing when she died, she would not to be reborn into a person, plant, or animal according to her actions, but free herself from the cycle of life, from attachment and suffering, and return to Brahman forever.

The one being who stood in her way was Arachne. Nayla pulled Ovid's text to the table's edge. Arachne had declared that her weaving skills were naturally occurring and not a gift from the gods. Apparently, it had angered Athena enough to disguise herself as an old woman and arrive at Arachne's loom to confirm her claim. When Arachne had doubled down, Athena challenged her to a weaving contest. Athena's tapestry portrayed the gods punishing insolent mortals. Arachne's depicted Zeus abusing his powers, deceiving women in the form of bulls and flies and other creatures. Arachne's needlework was far superior. Enraged, Athena destroyed it and transformed Arachne into a spider, as she loved weaving so much.

It would seem Arachne was mortal. She was not goddess of the loom or some such title. Neither of her parents were gods. She could be defeated. But what about her cave? Nayla flipped through her books. There were no sources on the hall, or Arachne's reason for guarding it. Maybe it was recent history.

Judging from the dead nymph caught in her web, fighting Arachne alone would prove unsuccessful. She did not want a repeat of her early trials at the yard. Finding help the first time was all right by her. Ideally, what she needed was another nymph, but she couldn't exactly go asking around. What qualified as compromising the pantheon's integrity, anyway?

The shovel hogs had witnessed a supernatural phenomenon. Nimit and Sparsh thought she was haunted. Ojas knew better, though not by much. He believed a divine anomaly had taken place to stop Nayla from making a "dumm" decision. So long as no one identified her as a nymph or pinned any of these occurrences on an earthly origin with a name and a face, she ought to be fine.

That was her working theory, which meant when it came to recruiting, the shovel hogs were out. They knew her too well. Ojas might connect the dots should anything else ethereal happen. They'd been in the Blast together when Hestia showed up. Nayla was running behind him. Then she wasn't.

One connection between her and weird transpirings had been made. She preferred the connection remain loose.

As for getting to the underworld, she needed a door. It appeared Hecate could open and close doorways at will, yet they only appeared to Nayla when someone died. And two of the few doorways she had seen led to Arachne's Cave. That would be her entry. Finding death shouldn't be too hard in a blistering desert. She could try the hospital. So gruesome to think of.

What about the Hall of Fabled Objects and that fantastic door? Nayla smiled. The mecha-sleeves should force it. And she didn't need the firebox. She *was* the firebox. She just needed someone to divert the spider's attention. Someone brave. Someone verrückt. Lucky for her, Jacoma was crawling with soldiers. Would a German soldier help? What about a French legionnaire?

Maman had told her how the legionnaires fought with bravery at Camarón, Mexico, led by Captain Jean Danjou. It was sixty-two legionnaires versus two thousand Mexicans. The legion was completely surrounded. Instead of surrender, the legionnaires decided to fight to the death. Danjou, with his wooden hand, was slain early. When the last five legionnaires ran out of ammo, they fixed their bayonets and charged. Two were shot and killed. The Mexican colonel ordered a ceasefire. The three survivors were brought to the Mexicans' commanding officer, where he declared, *These are not men, they are devils!* That was Maman's favorite part. Then she would poke Nayla with a prop hand made of broken castanets.

Nayla had to enlist one of these devils. She could wear the Vajen Bader helmet to keep her identity secret. It would have to do until she could trade up for the helmet of Hades. Where to find the right soldier was easy. How to choose him would be tough. She got up from her desk chair...

...and sat down at a bar stool in the cantina.

"Binu," she said to the waiter while he counted his tips, "I am looking for a husband."

"Really?" he said exuberantly.

"Ja, a soldier."

"Oh." He returned to counting.

"The manliest soldier that ever set foot in the cantina. I need your help to find out who that man is." She slid over her entire week's pay. "Eavesdrop at their tables. Probe them hard for military exploits. When I say manly, I mean bravest."

"Interesting request. Why not ask yourself?"

"They will be more candid around their friends. And he must be a legionnaire."

"Why?"

"They are the most verrückt."

Binu scooped her money into his tips. "Give me a week."

She let a week pass, meditating her life away.

"Well?" she asked when she sought out Binu.

"I found an interesting candidate. Capitaine Beauvais. He is part of a detachment that got off the train this morning. He is thirty-five years old, speaks French, and fought in West Africa on the Ivory Coast against the Wassoulou Empire. He claims he is the best soldier the legion has, that shipping him across the desert to Indo-China is a grave injustice. Then he slammed a knife into the table, threatened to kill anyone who said different, and ordered the kale pache. I told him kale pache was sheepshead and animal hooves. He told me, kiss my ass, curly."

"He's perfekt."

"Oh, gut. Shall I book your bridal shower?"

"Ja." Nayla laughed. "When he comes in next, give him this." She passed Binu a sealed envelope. "I doubt he will appreciate someone tampering with his mail."

"Nein, I won't read it. For a small fee."

"The letter is in French."

"Maybe I should read it and correct your grammar. For a large fee."

She slid over a silver mark. "I'll send it as is." She didn't want an open letter to alarm Beauvais that others might ambush the two of them—assuming he accepted their meeting and didn't think the proposal was an ambush to begin with.

When she stepped outside, her eyes adjusted to the evening sun around the lanky frame of Ojas.

"Ghost hunting, Nay?"

"Husband hunting."

"Not Binu."

Nayla held up her hands. "Nein. He's helping me search. Does this mean you're not mad at me?"

"I still think what you did was dumm, but I get it. You lost your parents." He placed his hands on her shoulders. "It was hard for me to believe the girl jumping into the furnace was the same girl I was rooting for in the train yard." Nayla looked at his shoes. "I think Brahman saved you so you can find that person again."

"The one fighting to survive?" asked Nayla.

"The one who believes in herself. Maybe a husband isn't such a bad idea. He may teach you how. Or buy you time away from the Blast to figure it out."

Nayla hung off his arms. "Danke. Ojas, you are the best shovel hog a girl could ask for."

"Don't you forget it." He hugged her. "Now, who is matchmaker Binu betrothing you to?"

"A soldier. A Frenchman."

"I hope he likes Hindus."

Nayla hoped he liked anybody.

He was more charming when he was sober, I promise you. Welcome to the vineyard. This one happens to be inside of a clos, a walled in, sloping corner of Hermes Hill. Something like a fort. See how the posts stand like soldiers at attention in viny rows. Over there is the Wild Garden. You accuse me of bringing you here on cue to discuss alcohol? Perhaps Jacques will surprise you and choose another topic.

Demons. What else could drive a man like Théo to that level of hatred? To attack the daughter of your best friend? With no regard of how it would affect her? Who was to blame? The demon is the obvious party. Théo another. Or was it Hades's fault for allowing it? If Plato were here, he would say that responsibility—also known as αἰτία, that is, guilt—lies with the one who chooses. The god is not responsible. The god is ἀναίτιος, not guilty. But Céleste was in no mood for Plato. There was a demon afoot and it had left its mark. In the Cave of Ghosts, she had blacked out and Théo had fled. We are seven days A. I.—After Incident.

QUAND MÊME

Nobody spoke much anymore. No comment on Maman's overcooked roast, buried under so much seasoning the house nearly caught fire. Not a peep on Papa's failure to remove the mold on the bathroom ceiling that *he's been meaning to get to*. No word about Maman digging through the trash to rescue old papers. Nobody knew what to say. No one had prepped them.

Céleste sat there, eating green beans with her ivy-leafed fork.

Maman chewed and gnawed and gnashed her teeth on a slice of roast.

Papa chomped on a cob of corn he spun in his mouth, kernels flying.

Céleste flinched at every crunch, every smack of lips, tightening the squeeze on her legs, if only to prevent herself from covering her ears. She wanted to yell *stop chewing so loudly!* but she didn't want to open up a conversation.

The Incident had eclipsed even one of Maman's proverbs— *If Maman isn't happy, nobody's happy*. Now it was they who depended on Céleste's mood.

They wanted her to speak. And there was nothing to say. Not even something innocuous, like pass the salt, to which she'd have to get up and hand it to either of them, they were spaced so far apart. Instead they washed down their food with dark Cahors and began anew.

She could have throttled them both, but a wave of emptiness sapped the anger right out of her.

She bowed her head.

The turtle-shell bowl of pistachios sat on the table. Beyond it, a vacant chair, where Théo used to sit and eat with them. If he were here, he might suggest she eat in the garden or play his accordion to block out the noise. Arguments were twice as bad on soup night. Or in all likelihood, after an apéritif, he might've put his gruff hands on her collar and given her a flush. She set down her jittery fork. Would everything she did remind her of him?

She grabbed her neck.

She didn't hate him for what he did. She hated him for what he did to her family—What the demon inside him did to her family—Maman and Papa looking at her with pity, unable to voice it—trying to move forward while she was left in the past. The way Théo had glared at her with those unnatural black eyes...Why the demon targeted her, she might never know, but it had got what it came for.

Céleste pushed forward her plate and back her chair. She screwed her collar to the base of her skull as she crossed the threshold into the great hall, preparing for a word of protest. *We sit as a family. Do not leave this table until everyone is finished. No dessert until you finish your mutton.* But no word came. They had left her frozen, weak, and lost, with nowhere to turn for compassion but the animals.

"Viens ici, Nougat," she called.

He caught up to her at the spiral mosaic and climbed the stairs, stopping to look at the dining room with his beard through the wiry struts in the rail. Céleste didn't risk a backwards glance. She past the dreaming man in the fresco on the riverbank and walked on water, rounding the stairs, below the flying maidens. Surely, a miracle had taken place for Maman and Papa to let her leave undisturbed. Or perhaps they sensed an unspoken change in her.

The creamy domed ceiling gazed down with its blue flowers dotting the plaster like blood vessels, growing smaller the closer they gravitated to the chandelier, a cluster of sapphires, one large pupil to the creamy-eyed dome. Her toes dug into the tuft of carpet as a draft swept through the house. But it was July. Where did it blow in from? The space between her ribs throbbed. She reached for her chest, her cotton tea gown soft on her fingertips. It wasn't a bad heart. What was it?

Nougat whimpered, nestling his head against her leg.

"You feel it to?" she asked.

She gripped the railing. It was like someone had taken her glass of sunshine and emptied it to the last dregs. Emptiness. Exactly in the spot where Théo's demon had trespassed. A shiver planted her to the floor. She drew her mouth into a straight line and bit her lip while icy winds crackled against the walls of some interior cavern, howling, aggravated, begging—for what?

Nougat bowed his head, looking up.

The white flame.

Her grip on the banister had loosened into a tap. She beat a staccato and rocked in place. There came a voice from within the cave:

I am nothing, I am nothing, I am nothing.

Her eyes widened. It sounded as though multiple voices had spoken at once, broken yet unified, indecipherable, encased delicately with a gloss of her own silvery timbre. An urge compelled her arms to reach for something, someone, anything to make the winds stop, the voice. She crouched and hugged Nougat.

"Oh Nougat," she whispered, "what's happened to me?"

He licked her cheek.

"It's all a horrible nightmare."

The maidens floated at her side strumming their lyres in the world of the painting. Song.

Song and dance. Dancing would clear this whole thing right up.

She fled into her bedroom and ran to her commode where her music box lounged, as if resting in sweet woodruff. She hurriedly cranked the handle and flicked the switch.

The cylinder, covered in braille, rotated, the pins striking different notes along the comb, filling the mossy hollow of her room with Carmen's Habanera while she found third position and eased into an adagio, painting the air with her hands and her feet, chasing Bizet's music, unable to catch it, taunted by the melody of a Delilah's perspective on love being rendered into twinkling mirth, the music box outpacing her feet as a frown hung over her chin—an ocean of happiness engulfed the void inside her chest, so close, and far off, the cavity impenetrable, forming a hum around her body, as her smooth enfolding lines, once executed with great skill, without effort, a beautiful sequence of motion that inspired awe in hearts and minds, was now a discord between arms and legs—a disharmonic train wreck unworthy of Mariquita or the stage.

Non! Non! Non!

That demonic monster did not take one of her last joys she had in this world.

She launched into an arabesque penchée, failing to resonate.

She tried a développé to the front, losing the rhythm.

She gritted her teeth.

Whether her leg went into a standing split behind or in front of her did not matter. Her body and the music were severed. Her link was broken. She could not feel it.

Tears wet her eyes as she crumpled to the floor and held the room to stop it from imploding.

The music box clicked off. The heavenly strings fled the air, allowing the woodwinds to open up—her sulky alto flute of a voice bursting from her pipes in a wavering cry.

The white flame. It was her soul.

What else could it have been?

The voice telling her she was nothing was buried in the same place her soul was kept.

"Oh Nougat." She grabbed him and fell to her side, pressing her cheek into his fur.

She rolled onto her back. The topaz light of the stained glass above the door set her bed canopy aglow, the veils draped like Spanish moss, catching voices in their sails.

Céleste crawled into the hall and stopped at the railing. Her arms sunk into the velvet. Through the profusion of wires, past the riverbank fresco, off the splashy mosaic spiral, words traveled up the stairs.

"She was lucky to have survived," Papa said at low decibel.

"To what end?" Maman asked in a snide tone.

Céleste hadn't thought about it. She was dealing with supernatural forces. She had encountered a demon and it let her live. How did she survive? And for what purpose? It wasn't to lead a life of dance, evidently.

"The light has gone out of her, Éd."

So they did sense it.

Nougat walked up to the rail. Céleste pulled him low.

"It's a bout of melancholia," said Papa. "I'll call for the doctor."

"It's too late," Maman lamented. "Who will want her now? No one. They'll all run."

There must've been someone to treat her.

"Dr. Moreau is on call," said Papa. "What on Earth are you talking about?"

"I was so looking forward to being a grandmother," said Maman, "but you didn't stop to think about that, did you, when you hired Théo, that we'd have a spinster for a daughter?"

Spinster? Her life had been dance dance dance. Children were the last thing on her mind. What was Maman talking about?

"I think you're being overdramatic," said Papa.

"She's tainted, Éd, and it's your fault. You. You let a degenerate get close to our family."

They'll all run—Suitors. Boys. *Men will all run.* That was what she had meant. It couldn't be true, Maman. Papa, tell her it wasn't true. She was mistaken. A bald-faced lie. It would mean the demon had damaged her more irreparably than she'd thought. Why did it have to possess Théo? Did it take him unaware or did he welcome it in?

"I've known him my whole life," Papa defended. "We went to school together. There was no way I could know—"

"The man was a tippler and a suiveur. He made it a practice to follow women and so he did. Ours. Now my little girl is deflowered."

Céleste gasped. Her face burned. She wanted to melt into the floor. Théo had taken away her light to such an extent that Maman and Papa feared the worst. Was it Théo or the demon who'd taken her power? Both of them? She didn't know. She flipped onto her back, a hollow gourd, cracked open, seeds gutted. Her chin quivered, arms slack. Her stomach tingled. Tears escaped down the sides of her face. Why did God let this happen? What had she done to deserve this?

She couldn't dance *and* couldn't find a partner, *ever?* She had tested the first, though couldn't confirm the second. *Please, don't let it be so.* The price was already too dear. She wanted to have babies one day, a family.

Surely, Maman was wrong. But Maman had the ability to detect any change in emotion, however subtle, however nuanced. Maman had said outlandish things, but never had she made a claim like that, something that affected her future as well as Céleste's. Why, Maman valued Céleste as if she were an arm or a leg.

"If I could go back in time," said Papa, "I would. I didn't see you do anything about it."

"You're the man of the house," snapped Maman.

The blue chandelier, the eye of the dome, peeked at Céleste from behind the rail as she lied in her incumbent state.

"Théo was always at hand when I needed him," Papa continued. "He might have sometimes charmed the fleas, but he showed up."

"He stole from the bar."

"So what if he took ten or twenty francs of wine a week. We can afford it."

How long had that monster been inside him? Was it four months, from when the advances started, or Céleste's whole life? Perhaps he was concealing it the entire time.

"Do you hear yourself?" asked Maman. "The man was a thief!"

He *was* a thief. He'd stolen her soul.

"He was reliable," said Papa. "He put in sixty hours a week. Tell me, who else would be willing to do that?"

"You should have fired him."

"I'll hire someone new," said Papa. "If Théo shows his face again, he pays."

"He better," said Maman. "To think he's out there right now doing God knows what to God knows who."

Preying on others? The demon was still in him. How many others must suffer? How many had come before?

Céleste's hands trembled as the void in her chest pounded on every wall, sending out electric shocks, her heart palpitating furiously next door. *I am nothing, I am nothing, I am nothing. Make it stop!*

An invisible weight pinned her to the carpet. She braced her sternum, taking long sluggish breaths. Saliva drained from her mouth.

Could she reverse what had happened? Return her soul to its throne?

She swallowed hard.

She had been so close to outgrowing Maman and Théo's supervision. There were only a few short years before a marriage proposal came along, before she could be a star ballerina, before she could help Papa run the Folies, before she could live on her own. Her life had once held such promise. What was there to look forward to now?

Her light at the end of the tunnel, out of Maman's clutches and out of Théo's, into a world of freedom, had been sealed and replaced by her white flame. Her only options were to recover the flame or dwell in misery—unartistic, unrelenting, unforgiving misery.

"Make the interview more than, *Do you have a pulse?*" Maman instructed.

Céleste checked her pulse.

"Oui, chérie," said Papa.

Alive—Why had the demon left her alive?

She touched her neck—Her missing crucifix, pinging onto the floor of the du Néant. Had God spared her?

"Make it more than *Do you have a brain cell?*" Maman continued. *"That was a trick question. You don't need one. You're hired. Get in there."*

"I will vet thoroughly."

The cave in which her soul-throne stood vibrated its walls, boomed against the ceiling, shook the stalagmites, each tremor declaring once more, *I am nothing, I am nothing, I am nothing.*

She needed her white flame. Now.

Théo had it—his demon. But where was he? And if Papa did not know, who would?

The freckled woman in the Wild Garden. Her coy smile. Her ironic wave. She would know. She could take her to him.

And then what, Céleste, kindly ask for her soul back?

She wiped her eyes.

If the demon hated her crucifix, it should hate holy water.

She leapt to her feet and scurried into her bower-like room, straight to her armoire, where she opened the doors and felt behind her dresses for the cut-glass bottle. The holy water shined in the green shades of her lamps.

I am nothing, I am nothing, I am nothing.

Nothing without her soul. Céleste itched her neck as the indigo light of dusk painted the windows. Maman and Papa would never let her out at this hour. She dropped the holy water into a chatelaine bag, along with some hatpins, looped her belt through it, buckled it around her waist, let the chains droop as she pulled the Spanish moss off the pergola over her bed in reams, tied them together, and opened her window in like a door, leaving nothing between her and the intersection of boulevard de Courcelles and boulevard Malesherbes but a viny grille, ankle-height.

She tied a corner of the fabric to the window grille and tossed the rest off the ledge, where it brushed the sidewalk, six meters down. She put an ear on her bedroom door and waited. No footsteps. No sound. If Maman or Papa were standing in the salon, they'd have seen the bedding and come running up the stairs. The silence encouraged her to put on her slippers.

D'accord, Céleste. Quand même. Against all odds. Her heart surged in her chest as she gripped the ironwork tight and climbed over, placing her body in mortal danger of the concrete. She entwined the organza in her legs, heart in throat, and shinnied to the salon windows. *Dieu Merci.* The blinds were drawn. She hurried, sliding, and touched her foot to solid ground, her chest aflutter. *Check the vial.* She felt the bag, the vile protected in velvet, a soft lump in her fingers.

Did anyone see her? A horse and cart filled with coal trotted the flagstones. The lit windows, girded by wisteria carvings, showed no silhouettes of bemused neighbors, that she could tell. Twilight pinks and purples glinted off the unlit windows. It was getting dark. To hail a cab into Hermes Hill unescorted might not've been the best idea. She needed a chaperone, someone big and scary who loved her.

Clemence. She ran along her house, past the walled-in garden, and to the stable, a stone enclosure, embossed in ryegrass, its door locked. In her chatelaine, she found the key, shoved it in, and swung out the door. Clemence and Claudette gaped at her, gnawing on hay in stalls divided by posts decorated with spikes of barley.

Céleste crept inside, inhaling hay and horse dung. The door swayed shut as she approached Clemence and opened his gate, shrinking inside at the sheer size of him. Her head didn't even reach his withers and she was planning to mount his back? Without Théo's help?

Oui, she decided. For her soul, she would ride a cheetah.

"Salut, Clemence." She picked up the stool and placed it beside him. "I need your help."

He looked at her with a sorry eye.

"I know," she said. "I should've listened to you." She stood next to him with the bridle in hand. "Will you help me? I'm listening now."

He lowered his head.

"Merci."

She had seen Théo do this hundreds of times. Top of bridle in right hand, the bit in her left.

"Open your mouth. S'il te plait, don't bite me." She stuck her thumb into the corner of his lips, let him take the bit and put the band over his ears. "Good boy." She fixed his hair and rubbed her fingers, still attached to her.

What came next? She threw on the blanket and picked up his saddle, heavy as a stage curtain. With a grunt, she flopped the saddle onto his back in a single motion. The girth hung down, which she grabbed and secured. If she mounted him now, she'd have to get back down once outside to lock the stable and have nothing to remount him from. The stool. It would have to come with her.

Leading Clemence by the reins, she walked him out of his stall, the reins in one hand, stool in the other, earning a snort from Claudette.

"I can't very well ride both of you, can I?"

Claudette whinnied.

"Chut." Céleste pressed a finger to her lips, the rein touching her chin. "You're going to alert Papa."

Claudette bowed.

"Don't feel too bad, ma cocotte. You'll be safer here." All the more so by locking the stable.

She walked Clemence outside, set the stool down, and locked the door while she clung to his reins.

"D'accord." She put the key in her chatelaine and hopped onto the stool.

This was a bad idea. What was she doing? Riding a horse to the Wild Garden? With only two lessons under her belt? It was pure folle. She ought to get back to her room before Papa discovered her missing. Crawl into the safety of her covers. Listen to her music box and sleep.

Her soul-cave shook, sending a tremor up her spine, accompanied by those same nagging words:

I am nothing, I am nothing, I am nothing.

There was no safety in her house. Nor in sleep. The voice in the void could not be silenced. It had to be sated, to be filled—with her soul. She put her foot in the stirrup and threw the other one over Clemence, heart beating fast. Surely, he could tell how nervous she was.

Her knees trembled against his sides. "Be brave for me. We're hunting the diabolical."

She relaxed the reins, sat up straight, and squeezed his sides with her heels.

Clemence set foot onto boulevard Malesherbes, trotting into a violet-skied, amber-lanterned, wisteria-curtained evening, and approached the intersection, bouncing furiously, the moss canopy to her bed breezing from her window.

"Right, Clemence, right. Aller à droite."

She pulled right, applying pressure.

"You're turning too far." She pulled left and tightened his reins. "Hue!"

He trotted across the sidewalk onto boulevard de Courcelles, clipping the corner, back onto the street. Maple leaves indented the buildings, the gutters internal, their spouts protruding at their bottoms like spigots.

She was bouncing too much. What had Théo told her? She had to stand up and sit down in rhythm with the horse. *Up, down, up, down.* Heels down. Toes up. There. Now she had it. Sort of.

Clemence worked hard beneath her legs, one thousand kilograms of muscle and bone, driving onto rue Caulaincourt, keeping his trot, veering circuitously around Hermes Hill, the iron lamps sprouting up like yarrow, umbrella-shaped glass made of lemon quartz, *I am nothing, I am nothing,* echoing in her soul-cave, while she bounced on his back more than she liked.

"Faster, Clemence."

She sat up straight and kicked him with her right heel. A burst of energy launched her backwards. *Don't pull back on the reins or he'll stop. Lean forward. Into the motion. Stop posting. Hands over his neck. Oui, this is how you canter*, just like Théo had showed her—*I am nothing*—the brute having served her the pain and the skill to reach the cure. Did Théo teach her to ride to save him from his demon? Perhaps. Perhaps not. It would've been too much foresight on his end, but everything happened for a reason.

She had survived last week in order to climb Hermes Hill today, for what purpose, she did not know, sailing through wind, rigid, as she pulled right, ready to fly off, *eyes up,* up the rear of the hill, to the fringe of the Wild Garden on rue St. Vincent, where the iron cattails crossed, forming an arch, one of many entrances to the garden and its glades, allowing her to search for the freckled lady. The woman had approached her carriage near this very spot.

Céleste tightened her grip on Clemence and pulled back, slowing to a walk, and pulled left, stalking into the wilderness, into its long shadows, spilling onto each other from the velvet sunset.

She was going to be bruised and sore from all the bouncing, though her body nothing in comparison with the state of her spirit.

In the twilight haze, she guided Clemence up the stairs around a pond, each dirt-packed step a new platform. The crown of a miniature Greek temple peeked over the crest of the hill. Céleste pulled on the reins, bringing Clemence to a stop. A woman sat on its base—the freckled lady!

Don't look this way.

"Shhh." Céleste scratched Clemence's neck.

The lady was looking at something far off in the glade, behind the trees. Clemence's walk hadn't alerted her. But the woman was spooked, fidgety. She arose from her marble seat, staring into the distance.

Théo would come out from hiding any moment.

Céleste clung to Clemence, as her heart took off at a gallop. Suddenly she had the lungs of a small bird, barely able to supply herself with air, her breaths were so soft and so weightless. She clutched the holy water in her chatelaine.

The freckled lady sat down. Sighing. She was sighing.

A man approached from stage right—sandy-haired, straw-hatted, in a white shirt with his sleeves rolled up. He sat beside her and must've told a joke, for the woman laughed into her hands.

D'accord, Céleste. Walk up and ask where Théo is.

Wait.

The man was still talking.

The lady creased her brow.

He leaned in.

Slapped him. She slapped him.

His eyes, locked on some statue holding up the roof of the small structure, found their mark again, as he turned his chin back to hers.

She recoiled, claws out, eyes wide.

"What is wrong with you!" The lady shouted.

Was she dealing with a demon? Was it the same one that possessed Théo, but now in a different body?

Could the demon lead her to Théo?

To her soul?

If she couldn't retrieve it, she could stop a monster from stealing someone else's.

"Ouais, Clemence." Céleste dug her heel into his side.

He took off like a cannon, thundering into the glade, straight for the sandy-haired man and the freckled lady at the Greek pavilion and its shallow pool. Céleste let up on the pressure, stopping before the couple. The man whirled at Céleste's intrusion, his eyes black—just like Théo's! His throat issued a low growl. Clemence, whinnying, alighted to his hind legs. Céleste toppled off his rump and struck the ground. Something splashed in the water.

Céleste pressed her fingers into the sod and crooked her neck. The freckled lady had escaped into the pool, evading clumsily. Her dress was soaked through. The demon-possessed man watched his prey throw herself over the pool's outer edge and flee into the woods.

Céleste fumbled at her chatelaine. The man turned to her full-on, revealing his snipe nose, high cheekbones, and puffy lips.

Céleste flinched, sensing the same dread and foreboding as she had with Théo, as if the creature swallowed up any ray of hope in its vicinity, sucking energy greedily through its pores. She dug into her bag, scrambling away on her butt, and groped at the cut-glass bottle while he advanced. She pulled the stopper and held the water to threaten him.

He stopped.

She brandished the liquid.

He looked at something behind her.

There was another presence. A breath. A scent.

Lilies.

If she took her eyes off this demon, she was mincemeat.

"What a brave young girl," remarked a wispy voice.

Céleste turned on instinct.

Two woman stood side by side, one in a pink bustle dress, the other in blue. They were beautiful. Alarmingly beautiful. More pretty than Maman.

The woman in blue had a round porcelain face, apricot in color, large nurturing eyes and a nose that sloped out of her forehead without any bridge. Brown hair fell in curly locks onto her collar; a golden tiara of olive branches adorned her head; her dress a combination of the bustle and an Ancient Greek peplos; the skirt pleated, the bodice draped off her shoulders.

The woman in pink had the hips of a seductress and the face to prove it; her complexion spotless, glazed in a warm hue, each feature stunning on its own, while complimenting, non, amplifying all the rest—her cleft chin, her cobalt eyes, her ice blonde hair—parted in the center and cascading to her arms—her heart-shaped lips, her thin eyebrows—what a painting!—her body deceivingly athletic, ornamented in gold—rings, necklace, armlets, bracelets of olive leaves—her head crowned with lily of the valley tucked into her diadem to present her face before the world.

Something told Céleste these weren't the nightly denizens of Hermes Hill, but from one of the wealthier arrondissements, like Temple-Bourbon or Quartier de Passy.

"Taking her eyes off the enemy," said the woman in pink, in a more grounded tone. "She is brave."

"Well, it can't steal what's not there." The blue woman held out her palm in a stop gesture.

"Only maul her to pomace," the pink woman retorted.

A white glow engulfed the sandy-haired man and froze in him in place.

"Are you angels?" asked Céleste.

"Oh, aren't you sweet?" The pink woman swooned.

"We are your patrons," said the blue woman, "if you so choose. You may know me as Psyche."

"Psyche? The Greek goddess?"

"Splendid to meet you."

Greek goddesses. Céleste's lips quivered. "Then you are the embodiment of soul." *Non, they couldn't be.* They weren't in any Bible story she'd ever read. Yet here they stood. "Wait. Are *you* my soul? Do you know where it is?"

The pink lady tittered. "She is goddess of the soul, Céleste Marchand, not yours specifically."

"How did you know my—"

"Don't worry," said the pink lady. "I'll set you right. I am Aphrodite. Your dancing attracted us."

"Attracted Asteria," corrected Psyche, "who attracted us."

"Here she is now," said Aphrodite.

Meteor showers lit up the night. One fell into the glade, shaking the earth. Sod and smoke flung into the air. A slender woman emerged from the haze with milky white skin and a twinkling robe.

"You said you were going to wait for me," said Asteria.

"How was I to know she'd go putting herself in danger so soon?" said Aphrodite.

"Where's our nymph?" asked Asteria.

"Nymph?" asked Céleste.

"Oui," said Asteria. "To make a nouvelle nymphe, we need a nymph for the mixis." She looked at Psyche. "Did you not tell her about the mixis?"

"We were getting there." Aphrodite withdrew a thin vial from her bosom and held it in the cup of her hands. The vial glowed pink. When she held it out, it bore the embossed stamp of a heart.

"It's a potion for you to drink to help you find your soul," said Psyche.

"And grant you god-like powers," said Asteria, touching the vial. "No small thing." A shooting star emblem appeared. "Where is our nymph?"

"She is here." Aphrodite removed a seed from her chatelaine. She dropped it in the ground, sprouting a woman with magenta skin, her eyes viridescent globes, her figure covered in flower garlands, carrying the intense aroma of irises and peonies.

"Who is this sad flower?" The nymph sized up Céleste.

"She is our nouvelle nymphe, Chloris," said Aphrodite. "Assuming she can keep our pantheon a secret."

"Ah, yes," said Chloris, languorously. "Do not tell anybody you have powers or Nemesis will come and lop off your head like a dandelion's." She tapped the vial, branding it with a flowerhead. "That goes for anyone who discovers you."

"What if I just want my soul," asked Céleste, "without becoming a new nymph or getting powers or being decapitated?"

"Then we, mademoiselle," said Asteria, "are wasting our time."

"Now, Asteria, we mustn't pressure her," said Aphrodite. "The choice is hers. If she doesn't want our powers, we can set this cacodemon loose and be on our way."

"Set it loose?" asked Céleste, looking at the sandy-haired man's puffy face.

"Oui," said Aphrodite, "as if we never intervened. Like you don't need our help."

"Too bad," said Chloris. "Razor sharp claws. Lizard skin. Wings of bat. Nasty creatures. My powers could've helped her fight them."

"Is that what they look like?" asked Céleste. "The demons? Inside the people they possess?"

"An ugly exhibit," Chloris confirmed.

Céleste's holy water glinted in the moonlight. It should exorcise the demon in the name of Jesus Christ. Should it not? Not unless... unless Jesus was not real and the heavens were populated by Greeks.

"Do you know Jesus?" asked Céleste.

"After our time," said Psyche.

"He was there from the beginning." Céleste held her arm.

"Before our time," said Aphrodite. "We've not met such a man. Though you could ask Chaos. He is very old."

"And very busy," supplied Asteria. "The mixis, if we could. I hate slowing down for so long. I need action."

Céleste pressed her temple.

"What power did you contribute?" Chloris turned to Asteria. "Impulsivity?"

"Non, she's already got it," said Asteria.

"A world without Jesus," Céleste whispered. Entertaining the idea hurt her heart. If Jesus wasn't real, did demons not exist either? Something had taken her soul.

"Is a cacodemon like a Biblical demon?" she asked.

"When a man is capable of evil," said Psyche, "he might be possessed by a cacodemon. When a man does good, he might be under the guidance of a eudemon. One can loosen the soul from the body, the other secure the binds."

The possessed man stood, spine erect, surrounded by a white glow, his eyeballs black, his mouth contorted into a grimace.

"Is he the one who stole my soul?" asked Céleste.

"Non," said Psyche. "I can point you in the right direction. But, not without commitment to the pantheon."

It was blasphemy. To join them would forsake the one true God. It would forsake Jesus, Jesus who was the Father, and the Father was Him. *Non, Céleste, don't do it.* Your holy water could vanquish the demon. You didn't need help from these women, these goddesses, this nymph.

But where was God in the Cabaret du Néant? Where was God when Papa let Théo go unchecked? Where was God when Théo had straddled her, hungry for soul, and that dirty, blackguard demon ripped it from the seat of her universe so hard she had felt the snap? It was there. It was gone. Two parts separated. Taken by a sorgueur—a thief in the night.

God was an invisible man, while these specimens of Greek antiquity were beside her in the flesh, here to put the brakes on this demon from ravaging her. *Non, Céleste, you love Jesus and Jesus loves you.*

Then where was he!

She bowed her head. "Nobody loves me."

Did she say that out loud?

Who cared?

She knelt in the grass with her holy water, crying.

Fingers held Céleste by the chin—Aphrodite tilting up her head. "Stand, child."

If she did not drink the potion, they would allow the fight to continue.

The slender, square vial glowed in Psyche's hand as she imposed a butterfly onto the glass.

"When you find love," said Psyche, "you will become immortal."

She placed the vial in Céleste's hand.

One held the mixis, the other holy water.

Her soul-cave zapped her with a shock to her system:

I am nothing, I am nothing, I am nothing.

Her trembling hands unstoppered the mixis, and she put the rim to her lips. The bottle lingered there, and she drank. She drank the taste of cotton candy and burnt sage.

Psyche held out her palm and clenched her fist. The white glow surrounding the sandy-haired man squeezed a black mist from his mouth, swirling into a figure she'd not seen in all the years of her life.

The poor host slumped to the ground, unconscious, while his parasite manifested on three-toed feet. It glared at Céleste—a black-skinned, iguana-headed, spade-tailed reptile. Smog hung on its body like shredded clothing. Bat wings hinged off its spine as Chloris had described. It raised its hand and cut a slice through the air into another dimension. The vertical rip doubled in size, wide enough for the lizard to fit through.

It took one fleeting glance at Psyche and leapt into the smoky portal.

"What is that place?" Céleste peered inside.

"A shadow room," said Psyche, "one of many gateways to the underworld."

"Pardon moi." Asteria aimed her palm at the demon in the gate. "Make a wish." A yellow light pulsed from her hand, giving her elbow kickback as it launched at the demon, and turned him to ash as he fled.

Something familiar called to Céleste from deep within that realm. She touched her chest.

"My soul is in there."

"If you go in," said Psyche, "you won't come out."

Aphrodite folded her arms. "You did."

Psyche gave a lopsided grin. "I had help."

"Please, tell me how," said Céleste. "I just want to feel complete."

The smoke ring closed, returning her view of the tree line.

Perhaps she could reopen it. She held out her palm.

"I don't understand," said Céleste. "What powers do I have?"

"Ours," said Asteria.

"How am I in any better position?"

"Now you have hope," said Chloris.

"Find love, I become immortal, is that right?" asked Céleste. Aphrodite nodded.

"But my soul is already immortal," said Céleste. "Is the immortality for my body?"

"Listen, Céleste," said Aphrodite, "we are patrons, not prophets. Finding things takes time. The more of it you have, the more answers will reveal themselves to you."

"D'accord," she said, unsatisfied. "How do I get into the underworld?"

Psyche looked at Aphrodite. "I told you she was brave."

"Thank Zeus she has something to defend herself with." Asteria shot into the sky, a blazing meteor.

"Look out for Nemesis," said Chloris, "or we'll both catch the scythe." She withered to the ground.

Céleste cringed at the disappearance and turned to Aphrodite, not wanting her to vanish too.

"Be glad," said Aphrodite, "you saved a woman from a horrible fate. The man's soul, I'm afraid, was stolen long ago."

"Oui," said Céleste, the freckled lady and sandy-haired man now a distant memory, "but, please, don't leave."

The moon shined on Aphrodite's matted shoes.

"The separation will only be physical," she said. "Do you feel our energy, you and I? We have resonance."

Psyche touched Céleste on the shoulder. "Don't get in your own way."

A flash illuminated the night and both Aphrodite and Psyche were gone.

Bullfrogs and katydids played their nocturne.

Get in her own way—They were a lot of help. How was she supposed to find her soul without access to a shadow room?

She sighed, tears hot on her face.

The Greeks might've abandoned her, but at least they'd showed up.

She chucked the holy water into the temple's pool, wincing when she heard the splash.

You think the holy water is still there? Over one-hundred years later? How I love your whimsy! Look past the trees. The closest I can deliver is a water tower and the domes of Sacré-Coeur. Perhaps Céleste will find her way there again one day, though we won't hold our breaths. It is a sad thing. Nayla's intervention bolstered her faith, but Céleste's challenged hers. If we are to accept the Greek deities at face value, they were no different than an imperialist country, but colonizing people instead of places. Did the colonizers hurt or help? Were the Greek gods friends or foes?

Have a seat on the barrel under the ivy pavilion. Our canopy is fit for a wedding. You and I aren't getting married. Ah-ha, you accuse me again of stage direction. Maybe these scenes remind me of important details for our interludes. The marriage of cultures was not always so peaceful as a child mixing paints. What began with Britain establishing ports in other countries for trade in the 1700s exploded into competition in the 1800s among rivaling nations to secure not only transport of resources, but lands that provided them.

These brutalities are best forgotten with drink and best remembered with living relics of the past. We cannot erase an account of erasure, can we? If we are to learn from our mistakes, that is. True. I did say hurt or help. Perhaps expansion was a good thing. New technology, improved farming methods, plumbing, railroads, harbors, schools, hospitals. So many pros, so many cons.

Ah, my friend, I'm not advocating devils. Humanity is often messy. Non, we need not follow the herd. Spoken like a true artist. For that was the loose thread in Capitaine Beauvais's stitching, the only chance for Nayla to unbind him from a life of servitude—if she could pull it the right way.

Come. Let us visit the gift shop in the museum. They sell wine from this very vineyard. I see you eyeing the vines for grapes. You won't find any. Harvest is in late summer through l'automne. October is when the season ends, but in Jacoma, October is still summer, even back in 1891, and the next leg of the journey is just beginning.

NYMPH
IN THE
YAKHCHĀL

Moondrops funneled through the hole in the roof, illuminating the bricks of the yakhchāl, defining the many ridges of its beehive-shaped structure, as if hollowed out by thumbprints. A candle burned on the ice table. Nayla's butt warmed the ice chair. Through the crossbars of her eyeholes, she studied the arched doorway for the arrival of her guest. It was the only way in, besides the roof, and she wanted to appear harmless, seated opposite the rim, across the chasm of chopped ice.

Quit tapping your feet, Nayla. There's no reason to be nervous. You are in disguise. You are Spuckfeuer, and Spuckfeuer doesn't have to be nervous. The soldier wasn't going to judge. Why did she care about being well-received? She needed his help. She wasn't trying to actually marry the man. Why the anxiety? Ojas, that was why. For failing to pleasure him in this very yakhchāl. If only she could have aroused him, shame would not keep rearing its ugly head.

A muzzle thrust through the door.

Nayla sat up straight, hoping the soldier wouldn't shoot.

"Capitaine Beauvais," she said hurriedly, clear as crystal. She had removed the lower part of her mask, so as not to appear or sound so alien.

The rifle preceded a man in a blue coat that fell to his knees. He had white pants and white ear flaps over his cap that popped in the moonlight.

"J'ai besoin de tu aide," she began.

"You speak French like a Spanish cow." His rugged voice bristled on the ice. He stood across the chamber, gun raised, radiating masculine energies.

"Do you speak German?" asked Nayla, closing her translation book.

"Half the Legion Étrangère is German."

"I don't understand. Why is that?"

"Frenchmen can't join the legion."

"But you're French."

"And you are a young Oriental." He lowered the gun to his chest. "Why are you in a mask?"

"To lie about my identity. Isn't that how you joined the legion?" she guessed.

"Yes."

"Will you have a drink with me, Capitaine?" She gestured to the ice cups she had shaped with her hands like a potter at a wheel.

He slunk around the circle, drawing closer. His gun moved uncertainly. "Your letter mentioned a proposal. I am not a mercenary."

"Then why are you here?" She felt her pulse under the table.

"The spectral nature of the mission you wrote of."

She nodded to the chair. "Sit down, and I'll tell you."

"Hands above the table."

"Sorry."

Beauvais sat with the rifle across his lap. His whiskered face came into the light. He had a broad chin, a sharp nose, and blue eyes she could feel penetrate her Vajen Bader stare. He was both handsome and frightening. He saw the cup of wine she had procured just for him, being French, and dumped the contents on the floor. He smacked it on the table, unscrewed a flask, and poured his own drink.

"I'm listening," he said.

"First, what are your credentials?"

"Credentials?"

"What happened in West Africa?"

"Oh, you're a spy."

"When drunken soldiers talk, I hardly call that spying." She sipped her cup.

Beauvais blew into his lips. "We were attacked at Dabadougou and Kankan."

"The French dance?" Her bobbles shook on her headdress.

"A small village surrounded by field and jungle. We lost. They're still fighting. I've been reassigned. Rumor is the French want Laos from Siam. As punishment, they're shipping me the scenic route. Through a godforsaken desert." He looked around the yakhchāl. "It's summer by day and winter by night. Is it ever fall here?"

Nayla shook her head.

"Of course not," he said.

"Pardon my intrusion, but you don't seem happy."

"All of this conquest. I just want to make art on Hermes Hill."

"Where is that?" She'd heard Maman mention it.

"French Athens." He chuckled. "Look at me blathering on about far-off places. You probably never gave it much thought. How old are you?"

Eighteen. "Ancient."

"Right." He took out a long pipe.

"That's a chibouk. Where did you get it?"

"French Algiers."

"But it's Turkish." She marveled at the pipe.

"The place is Babel." He took out his pouch. "A little of everyone. Spahis, Zouaves, Bedouins, Arabs, Jews, gentiles. Kind of like this place."

"What do you mean?"

"Hindus and Muslims. There must be friction."

"They stay out of our temple. We stay out of their mosque. We're too busy working to otherwise care."

"So, you are from here?" He packed the pipe.

She winced, regretting having said it, forgetting who she was. But no more.

"I blend in as a local. Allow me." A flame ensconced the end of her finger.

Beauvais's eyes widened as she brought it to the pipe. Dumbly, he sucked in the flame, if only to catch his breath.

"Sacré bleu!" He removed the tip from his mouth and pointed. "You're one of them."

"One of who?" She gawked up at the shaft to see if Nemesis would fly down and kill them to restore the status quo.

"I knew I was right to come." He rose from the table.

"One of who?" she repeated, rising too.

"Will-o'-the-wisps and wild green fairies. Creatures I've seen out of the corners of my eyes. Maybe you are what I left home for."

"Were you afraid? Leaving home?" she asked.

Beauvais seemed taken aback by the question. "Momentarily, oui. Although, after I stepped on the ship and the shore receded, I let go of the past. Are you the one I read of in the local newspaper? Spuckfeuer."

She nodded bashfully.

"How came you to this little oasis?"

"Jacoma? The city was built to make steel."

"Are you Jacoma's guardian? Did you inspire the location? The construction?"

"It is the crossroads for the ingredients. The limestone is from Malaysia, the iron ore Persia, and the coal from India. It was founded by entrepreneurs. There is nothing supernatural about it."

He waved off the subject. "The proposition. What is it you want?"

In his excitement, his hand had gripped the pistol in his holster, leaving her unsure if he was going to hear her out or blow her away.

She raised her hands. "I want an object inside of a secret vault. The entrance is protected by a giant spider. If you shoot the spider, I will give you something in return. Maybe one of the objects will interest you." She tripped over her words, backing away from the table. "There is a lyre that can telekinetically move stones. There is a conch shell that can stir the ocean if you blow into it. There is a fleece that makes you fly."

"Fly."

"Ja, fly." It ought to be in there.

"I want to see you fly."

"Me, fly?" She was not expecting that.

"Oui. You see, I am an artist. I left French Athens for adventure. For material. All of my friends have found their creative fires and have made something of themselves. Meanwhile, I am still on the ramparts, in the battlefields, making war so that I can make love. My art is a labor of love. I have penned one story thus far. Expelled it in one great burst. Le Figaro published it last week to good reviews. They call it a masterpiece. I fear it was a fluke. Now that I have met you, I can finally create genius."

"Me?"

"You have chosen me, have you not?"

"Well, ja, but—"

"Do you not see? You are my muse."

"That sounds like a lot of responsibility."

"None whatsoever. I am the artist, you are the art. I only want to see you fly."

She glanced at his hand white-knuckling the holstered side arm. "Are you going to shoot me?"

"Nein, nein." He raised his hands, matching hers. The brim of his cap blocked his eyes as he took in the ice sculpture table and chairs she had made. "I will help you fight the giant spider. However, I must see you fly. I don't think you quite understand what the legion does to people. In my effort to seek out my muse to express my individuality, the legion has broken it down. I feel you can revive it, ma chère."

"The thing is..." Nayla began and stopped. The dead nymph in the cave had wings, but Nayla? Fly? She had much preferred to win him one of Arachne's trinkets. She couldn't back out now, though. He was a willing participant. "I'll do it. But it has to be from a tall height. Like this yakhchāl."

"Whatever you need. It is all I ask."

"Follow me." Nayla blew out the candle in the ice jar on the table and led Beauvais around the diameter of Jacoma's ice supply.

She heard him pick up the rifle and tensed, preparing for a shot in the back. The moon showed him sling it around his shoulder at rest. To be someone's muse. How odd. How flattering. What wonderful art might he create once he saw her fly? Or splatter on the side of a yakhchāl. It was six stories high. She ducked through the doorway and stepped out to examine the summit. Narrow steps spiraled the mountainous beehive all the way up, ones that would require the legs of an ibex to climb.

"Stand back and behold your muse."

It felt good to say. It gave her courage as she found the stairs. Moonlight drenched the starting side in cool white. The steps were mere centimeters wider than her feet, narrow to the point she had to hug the hive wall. It was made of sarooj, a heat-resistant compound to maintain the ice therein and permit her to burst into flames to see as she reached the hive's dark side.

Beauvais goggled up at her. If she backed out, perhaps this spectacle was enough to satisfy. Round and round the yakhchāl she went, carefully, methodically. At the top, the moon shined down the front of her, reflecting off the pool at the bottom, which fed water to the yakhchāl from the qanat.

Do it for Hades's helmet, Nayla. The catalyst to moksha. She took a swig from her flask to steady the nerves and felt the breeze in her hair. Sweet, sweet Shiva. This was a long way up. She'd break her legs on the slope, then fall to her death. She was more afraid to die when she didn't want to. *Show bravery, Nayla, courage.* Was a bird anxious when it dove from a tree?

No fire rescue this time. She held her arms at her sides and looked at the desert. Her lungs struggled for the air to lend her a breath as blood raced through her body, and she jumped. Soft fabric tickled her back. Extra limbs burst from her spine with great force. The fall turned horizontal. Desert palms fluttered in the breeze below as she cleared the yakhchāl. When she realized the fall should have happened by now, her heart skipped around her chest and ejected from her throat as her moonlit silhouette emerged onto the landscape.

Wings. She had wings. Red, feathered wings, bright with fiery glare. Whips flailed past her feet. Tail feathers. She had tail feathers. It was absurd. She could fly! The motion was similar to swimming, like when she and Kameera would jump in the stepwell as children. She spotted Beauvais and swung low, climbed out of the air and shed herself of flame, tripping over her own feet.

Beauvais caught her.

"Pass me the thread," he said in stupefied wonder. "Fantastique!"

Unexpectedly, he wrapped his arms around her and kissed her on each side of the face.

"This visitation will spark many great works."

"You will help me, then?" she asked.

"Oui, come, we will strategize. I may need others."

"Others?"

"Oui. How big is this spider?"

You think the gate handle is cute? A petite wine bottle that turns like so. Welcome to another of Renoir's gardens. There are three. We have already visited the first by the café. Those grand leafy plants are called philodendrons. Over there is a trellis-style gazebo. We can walk in it for fun. Oui, spin around. Not many come to this place.

Call me a dénicheur, an old-fashioned term to describe people such as moi who unearth curiosities. Take the French Athens Salon of 1884 for example. A painting was put on display there of a Madame Virginie Gautreau. She was confident, alluring, and portrayed in a low-cut black dress by the artist, John Singer Sargent.

But here was the kerfuffle. One of the chain straps holding up her dress was shown to have fallen off her right shoulder. Being a woman of Athenian high society, a scandal ensued. Sargent grew fearful of his reputation and repainted the shoulder strap, thus covering the original underneath.

In painting and literature, we call this pentimento, an alteration to the canvas or text that covers up a portion of the old. Pentimento is Italian for *repentance*, though we need not be pressured to change by some moral wrongdoing. The change could be simply to better reflect our personal expression and depict said expression more accurately. We are all pentimenti in a way. Ah oui, Jacques is getting fancy with his plurals. Cactus, cacti. We are walking pluralities. The self is ever-shifting, our realities ever-changing. Do not be discouraged. To thrive in change depends on one thing—Where is your center?

ᑫENTIMEᑎTO

Trumpets, French horns, and trombones circled high in the air, as the young conductor—Céleste's future husband—fought off his own orchestra. A flutist chucked his instrument straight at her beloved's head. He abandoned the trumpet and caught the flute, dispatching the brass into the percussion section where it smacked into a bass drum and toppled a pair of cymbals. This was no ordinary conductor, hopping up and down in a bright orange suit, wavy hair abounce, but so happened to be Antoine Hanlon—This, according to the programme, Papa's ledger and Céleste's future marriage certificate. Antoine was the youngest of his brothers—Céleste's future groomsmen who would be standing behind him at the altar, but for now they were his musicians furiously lobbing instruments at him, aimed to kill.

Antoine beamed confidence, so self-assured and heroic that he was. His handsome jaw, thin eyebrows, and masculine contours of his body communicated little love pulses with every leap and bound, not to mention his beautiful brown eyes that glanced at her in the balcony for encouragement. Where else could he have been looking?

They had so much in common. His pantomime acrobatics were practically cousins with pantomime ballet, each gravity-defying stunt more uplifting than the one that preceded, intensified by Monsieur Desormes' real orchestra blasting Wagner from the pit, crescendoing rises and silencing falls the same way Desormes would for a pas de deux.

Do Mi Sol Do was daffier than the Hanlon-Lees other numbers, different than their macabre performances like where Pierrot sold coffins and killed a man for declining to purchase one, or where Pierrot lopped off the heads of his lover's parents, to which he carefully glue them back on.

All of Antoine's talent, all of his skill, he flexed it like a muscle to impress only her. Her? What her? He didn't know it yet, but now there was only *us*. Perhaps she had spoken too soon. Perhaps he did know. He sent her a wink as he volleyed a bomb with a lit fuse into the strings, blowing cellos and violas to bits.

Antoine was in love with her. They'd get married and have little baby clown jugglers. But first, she would need to get his attention, in the name of her unborn children. His autograph. She would get his autograph. *Non, Céleste, that was silly.* She would have Papa introduce them. *Non, too formal. Simply walk back there and introduce yourself.*

When the orchestra was thoroughly destroyed and the musicians incapacitated, Antoine took his bow, closing out the curtain and the show.

Céleste shed herself of the programme in her private box and walked the sloping hall to the end, where she was met by a trellis and a dial. The coast was clear. She turned the dial, a lotus blossom, and fled into the hidden stairwell, dark and dusty like an old hat box, without a clue on how to approach Antoine. *Hé, I see you like to juggle. I also like to juggle.*

At the bottom, she spun the lotus, pressed her body against the wall and came out behind the curtain. The crew had begun clearing the set. Floodlights lit the stage. Some of the Hanlon-Lees had departed; one iced their shoulder stage right and another was doing stretches, but where was Antoine?

Talking to Geneviève upstage. An ache consumed Céleste, squeezing her ribs against her lungs. Geneviève had not even bothered to change out of her tutu, so eager she was to speak with Antoine. Geneviève was older, seventeen, the same age as Antoine. How could Céleste compete? Black spots filled the room, raining from the rafters in dark haloes. She held her stomach.

Him talking to a ballerina should be good news. It meant he was interested in dancers. *Show him, you're interested in acrobats*. If he didn't notice her, she'd throw a tuba.

She picked up three tambourines, latching onto them like life preservers, and tossed them airborne. She caught one and nothing further, cringing as the second crashed to the floor. The third one hit a music stand.

The clatter seized Geneviève and Antoine's attention.

"Céleste?" said Geneviève. "Are you all right?"

"Fine. I'm fine." Her cheeks went hot. "Just clowning around."

Antoine turned to Geneviève. "A friend of yours?" His voice was lotion.

"Oui, that is Édouard's daughter. She's a peach. I'll see you tomorrow."

"A bientôt." Antoine walked mid-stage toward Céleste. "Not so easy as it looks, eh?"

"Non," said Céleste. "I suppose not."

"May I teach you?" Antoine waited for a reply. "I am very qualified, an entortilationist."

"Sounds made up."

"Because it is. To seize the passerby's attention on the poster in the street and get them to come closer."

"I don't know entortilation, but *entortillage* means twist."

"Allow me to define it." Antoine smiled. "An entortilationist is a slapstick comic, a tumbler, and juggler rolled into one." He gathered the tambourines and made them dance. "Toss me another."

Céleste found a fourth and threw it underhand.

Antoine snatched it low and added it to his collection. "Another."

Céleste found a fifth. Look at them. They were already a team.

It was them against the world.

He recaptured the five tambourines in his arms. "Your turn."

Céleste held out her hands.

Antoine smiled, passing the tambourines to a stagehand. "Not with real objects." He came up behind her. "First let's get the motion down." He reached for her hands. "May I?"

She nodded, inhaling his odor of sweat and magic.

He enclosed her hands in his and lifted. "Move up and down at a slight angle with a slight flick in the wrists. You're throwing rings. Not too far out. Keep the rings vertical with your body. Just like that." He stepped away, gazing somewhere at her back. "Keep going. Don't stop. Very good."

His voice came near. "D'accord. Let's add some objects again."

She smiled over her shoulder. "I think the tambourines walked off."

"Why not triangles?" He made one chime.

"Why not?"

He handed her three of them. "One revolution." He held up his index finger. "Give me one successful revolution."

She took the cold steel in her hands and exhaled. *Don't botch it, Céleste. Redeem yourself.* One in the left hand, two in the right, she tossed the triangles in gentle flicks, eyes darting as she caught first, sent the third, caught the second, sent the first, and dropped them all, clanging to the floor.

"So close," said Antoine.

She sighed. He wasn't mad. He still liked her.

"I think I need more lessons."

"An apprenticeship?"

Her heart thumped so loud she feared he might hear it. Did she really want him to see her for who she really was? If he couldn't detect her heartbeat, he could surely hear the voice inside her void booming *I am nothing, I am nothing, I am nothing.*

Even so, how could she pass him up? He was something, he was something, he was something! But how to let him know it without being humiliated? More humiliated. Double-entendre. She would use double-entendre. If he didn't pick it up, her intent would remain safely hidden. If he did pick it up and didn't respond, she could always deny any double meaning. Genius.

"We could try somewhere less noisy," she offered.

"A floor with a carpet, eh?"

She smiled, growing more emboldened. "My box." She pointed at the closed curtain.

"Tomorrow night during intermission." He gave her his hand. "Je m'appelles Antoine."

"Céleste."

"Like the instrument." His eyes lit up and shot to the pianolike device.

"Oui." She braved a step hither, placed her fingers on the keys, and hesitated. "Is this a real celeste or one of those prop pianos your brothers dive into?"

"*Soirée in Black Tie.* You've seen it?" He looked impressed.

"Oui, he came crashing out by the foot pedals." She felt the bottom panel to check for thickness.

Antoine chuckled. "This one's real." He gestured to the keys for her.

"I only know one song," said Céleste. Notes of the Sugar Plum Fairy twinkled on the air.

"Are you a ballerina?" he asked.

"Oui. Dancing was my life. Is my life."

"Was your life?"

She froze. He was getting too close. It wasn't safe. He would use it as ammunition against her. But this man was her future husband. Perhaps she could test the waters and gauge his reaction.

"It appears I lost my spark."

"Stage fright?"

"Non."

"Distraction?"

"You could say that."

"Injury?"

"Getting warmer."

"I think I know."

She shied back. *Too fast, too fast!* Could he see through her? There was no way he could know.

"I won't divulge it now," he said. "It will give us something to talk about later." He walked stage right. "It's like our mentor, John Lees, had said. Always leave your audience wanting more... I'll see you."

She did see him—together in holy matrimony, if it were not for her soul-cave getting in the way. How would he treat her if she revealed her true self? He might hide his face, or wince, or say, *What is wrong with you, I knew something was off, Normal people don't act like that. You don't deserve me.*

These thoughts drummed in her head for the rest of the day and into the next, following her up to the balcony where she waited for him, listening to Monsieur Desormes's orchestra practice, and it was all a big mistake.

What had Psyche told her? *Don't get in your own way.* She ought not to let these thoughts cloud her desires. She wanted Antoine. Antoine wanted her. That was it. There was no need to overthink anything. He seemed helpful enough so far. He might even be here to save her, in fact.

She clasped her hands. She would wait for him and he would rescue her from the horrible voice in the void. But that was the future. Presently, she was on pins and needles to hear his diagnosis.

"Bon après-midi, Céleste." Antoine appeared in the doorway.

"Salut, Antoine. I'm surprised you're using the door. I thought you were going to fly in via trapeze."

Antoine chuckled. "That is a zampillaërostation where I come from."

"Mars?"

"Snorfblat." He sat down beside her. "Interesting place. You should see it sometime."

"You can tell me all about it. But first, how did I lose my spark, doctor?"

"Ah." Antoine held up a finger. "The problem,"—he leaned forward—"is spiritual."

Céleste clenched up. "How did you know?" Could he sense the emptiness within? Feel the echo in her organs?

"Because," he said, "something happened to me where I lost my spark. There was a trick my brother Thomas used to do called the Perilous Ladder. The ladder was shaped like a plateau. It hung horizontally from the proscenium. He would leap underneath it from the first rung to the last—and in between, like he was on the uneven bars.

"To end the act, he would leap for a rope six meters away, held in position by Georges and Guillaume, and then descend the rope safely to the stage. He called it his Leap for Life. We were in Finnish Cincinnati the last time Thomas leapt for the rope. I held my breath. Something went wrong. A miscalculation. His hands were badly blistered from performing the stunt at prior engagements. It impaired his abilities. He fell twelve meters to the ground onto a footlight. He survived, but the bone splinters in his brain destroyed his sanity. It was all very strange. He was fine at first. Then something happened one day. He would clap at shadows, had trouble forming sentences, needed help eating. He was a different person."

"I'm so sorry. Does he still come to your shows?"

Antoine shook his head. "He was put in a hospital to keep him safe. They put him in a cell where he tried to slice his throat with a piece of dinner plate. When he tried to hang himself, they gave him a new cell. It had a steam pipe running along the wall by the floor with a connecting brass bolt. It took Thomas about twelve jumps. He would start from the cell door, spring into the air, and, gathering himself, turn a half somersault each time, and come down full force, driving his head onto the sharp nut. Attendants found him on the floor, his skull entirely broken."

"That is absolutely dreadful."

"It was his choice."

Maman had said those who committed suicide were going to the Lake of Fire, but Céleste didn't say that out loud, or how Maman had said that life was a gift and it was considered a sin against God to take the life God gave you. But God didn't show up for Céleste like Aphrodite and Psyche did, and who was Maman to judge the suffering Thomas? Céleste certainly couldn't judge. Her soul was in hell.

"Why didn't you use a safety net?" she asked.

"We hadn't invented it yet."

"We?"

"My brother Guillaume. After Thomas died, Guillaume wanted to prevent it from ever happening again, and so, the safety net." Antoine caught his breath. "Accepting that Thomas had to do what he had to do helped me grieve. I usually don't share, but it looked like it might help you. Please, tell me you didn't experience anything as bad as that, eh?"

"There was... a loss." Her cheeks burned.

If he was to rescue her, he needed to know what from. But how to explain her soul-theft without bringing Nemesis to her door?

"My chaperone... He did something to me. Something unspeakable."

"Dear God. When? Where?"

Perhaps this was all a mistake. Maman was right. No man would want her. He was going to run. Well, she had already started. If he reacted favorably, then it meant he accepted her. If he shied away in disgust, then she deserved it. The buildup was too much, this anticipation of judgment bubbling under the surface. Just get it all out. One shot. Firehose.

"It was at one of the cabarets when no one was watching," she said. "He was sneaky. It began as small incidents, seeing what he could get away with. Time would go by. I wouldn't tell.

Then something new would happen. I swore to take the secret to the grave. Then the big incident happened. After that, the damage was too big to hide."

Céleste winced for the backlash, the ocean of shame.

"Is he still around?" he asked.

Question. He asked a question. He expressed interest. He didn't run.

"Non," she said, "he left and never came back."

"I don't understand. Why didn't you say anything sooner?"

"It was impossible. I was too ashamed and too trapped... I didn't want my parents to picture me in that situation, and Papa is, we'll say, nonconfrontational. He wouldn't have done anything even if he believed me. My chaperone was his best friend, and my chaperone knew it." A lightbulb went on. "Théo knew it. He exploited my family's weaknesses."

"I'm sorry."

He was pitying her. It made her feel less than. Not on his footing. "Don't be sorry," she said. "It was something that happened to me. He's gone now and"—after scrubbing the skin off her bones with carbolic soap—"the crisis is over."

"Is it?" he asked.

The carpet threads stared at her from beneath her feet.

"Non," she admitted. "I am not who I was."

"Nor am I."

"Things people say and do remind me of what happened."

"Thomas is everywhere I go."

"To be perfectly frank, I thought you were going to jump off the balcony the moment I told you."

Antoine smiled, weakly. "Georges does the balcony stunts."

It was like Antoine had a magnet inside him getting stronger and stronger at every declaration. What was this pull? Was his soul missing too? Perhaps a demon robbed him of it, though it would be foolish to ask, and it might've been something else. Perhaps he didn't have a tight grip on it at birth. Or he missed his ensoulment altogether, and it was tacked onto his body as an afterthought. *Non, non, non.* It was all so simple. His brother

Thomas's death had jarred it loose. Whatever the reason, she was hooked.

"What about you?" she asked. *Go on, this was your chance. Initiate. Try it.* Her soul was gone. What else did she have to lose? She touched his leg. "Do you do any balcony stunts?"

"Not without a net."

He didn't get her double entendre. But he'd gotten it earlier, didn't he? Double-down.

"I can be your net," she said. "Will you be mine to catch me?"

"Seeing as your father is my boss, the question is how close to the sun do you want to fly, eh?"

He did get it. She dove into his arms.

They were lean arms with twitching muscles that he used to juggle with.

She undid a button on his shirt like flipping a coin. Little coins flipping while her heart palpitated, until it must've grown too much for him, for he rid his limber frame of its shirt, revealing his tight abdomen that helped him tuck and roll.

Go on, Céleste, place your hand upon it. Feel his skin. Warm. He was warm. She flushed. She could feel his pulse through his stomach. Or was it hers? She touched her chest, her heart. It was dancing a gargouillade. Her patrons' words repeated in her head—Psyche, Aphrodite—*Find your love and you will become immortal.* She exhaled. *This was your love, Céleste. You found it, now take it.*

She rode the shooting star out of the Wild Garden and up into the vast cosmos, heading straight for the rod-like flower of a cigar plant someone had flipped into the heavens with a long green stem; a floral flute, and like a hummingbird to nectar, she pierced the opening, collecting sweetness, and rushed into the green tunnel of the stem while the trumpet keys moved up and down, trilling portholes, serenading her with sound that shook her body.

Out of the mouthpiece, she emerged, her lips against his. The orchestra fell to silence, clearing a tonal path for a French horn solo as a petunia revolved at her like a planet—a massive bell, its orbit inescapable, to which her star said, *oui, oui,* before funneling into a choice aroma, fragrance in her face—admission through a winding green tunnel, a dizzying network of greased chlorophyll, that intoxicated her senses and threw her head in a fog. Playful measures coursed through the oily valves in a never-ending labyrinth of ethereal delights she wanted to stay lost in—yet the exit lied ahead.

Not the exit!

Through the mouthpiece, his lips had gone slack, the notes losing power, which she tightened up with a nibble.

Upon the vista of her galaxy, a new horn appeared from below—the bell of an angel's trumpet—the green stem tortuous, beautiful, and toxic—a single touch was all it took—and the meteor she rode, dripping in white light—plunged in—flashing into a kaleidoscope, nerve endings left, right, and pleasure center—Who was she?—An emotion in time—bliss.

A light flickered within the cave of her soul, dimly, brightly, progressing into a glow, the glow stagnant, illuminating the dark, sweeping around its columns and into its crannies.

She fell onto the musty Folies carpet with an almost imperceptible smile. Whole. This was what she'd been missing. Chasing. She felt whole.

Antoine leaned over her ear and whispered. "Wasn't I suppose to teach you juggling?"

She smiled, eyes closed. "You did."

"Then the lesson is over, eh?" He touched her arm. "I'm leaving before your father shows up."

A pang of abandonment grazed her heart like a bullet. "Don't be afraid of him."

"If it pleases you, I'll tell you I'm not, but I am. I don't want him to find us in this state."

Her eyes flashed open. "Oh, go if you must." The glow in her cave washed over her again and again. "I'll see you later, eh?"

"Are you stealing my *ehs* now?"

It had just slipped out. "Oui." She blushed. "I hope that's all right."

"Bien sûr."

He shoved his legs through his trousers, buttoned his shirt crookedly in his haste, the buttons too high, and left.

Dust motes floated in the chandelier's light.

Dust motes. So carefree.

She reached out to touch one.

Somehow her movement grew heavy, as if underwater.

Her finger disintegrated before her eyes—eyes wide as oysters.

What was happening?

It wasn't stopping. Her fingers flaked away, and thumb, the back of her hand. She brought it to her face, a stump.

The smell. It smelled of petunias and pastry, caramel and cream, like croquembouche. Pollen. She was turning into pollen.

Her elbows vanished. Arms gone. She was the Venus de Milo. Aphrodite had cursed her!

Legs, her legs had abandoned her to dust. She would never dance again!

She held her breath. No use. She was powder.

The gold brocades and red curtains swirled into the chairs, twisting into the private box, blending into ribbons, unblending into brushstrokes. Over the balcony, the auditorium were dabs of paint depicting lines on water, the orchestra little springs effervescing with light and color.

A full-body portrait of Papa peered into the box. Papa! She swam out over the balcony. Swimming! She was swimming! Or rather telling her body to swim. She swam back.

Papa was looking right at her, though couldn't see her, she was too dispersed. This was her life, among the dust motes now. He shook his head. At what? What was so disagreeable? *I'm the pollen storm, Papa, not you.*

Oh non! He couldn't see her clothes on the floor, could he? *Non, not a chance. Stay where you are, Papa.* Please don't walk around the seats and spot her clothes!

He hesitated, hesitating, hesitatingly. *Please, Papa, no more hesitation.* He stuck his hands in his pockets, mercifully, a good place for them, and strolled down the hall.

She sighed, out of danger, out of danger stuck in a gaseous state.

Wait a minute. The mixis.

When you find love you will become immortal.

This was it. Immortality!

She had found love in Antoine and changed into, into a cloud.

What good was being immortal if she was a cloud?

Her thoughts seemed to control her movements. Perhaps a thought had metamorphosed her. She had been thinking of dust motes, her head in dreamland. Perhaps thinking about dust motes again would cause a reversion.

Dust motes. Nothing happened. *Dust motes.* Nothing. *Dust motes dust motes dust motes.*

Hmmm.

Perhaps thinking the opposite. Something solid. Like, *je ne sais pas*, a bass drum.

Pollen jolted her back into shape a meter above the floor. The impressionistic world focused to photorealism. Her hands flung out to catch her, too late, as she hit the carpet stark naked.

She giggled, holding her head. Immortal. She giggled louder. She was immortal! The mixis flowed through her arteries, back through her veins, her heart circulating this immense power. She flexed her muscles.

"Merci, Chloris."

She could kiss the confectionary pollen right off that magenta nymph's cheek, she was in such glory.

What else might she be capable of?

At ballet practice the following week, Céleste spun piqué turns around the stage as yellow feathers bobbed off her tutu.

Mariquita slapped her fan against her palm. "Piqué, two, three, four. Châiné, two, three, four. Piqué, two, three, four."

Céleste alternated between turns, bending her leg to her knee for her piqués and spinning with both toes close to the floor for her châinés, the whole time her soul-cave droning *I am nothing, two, three, four.*

Oh non. The voice was back, muffled but present, the light in her cave dying and the effects of her love with Antoine fading fast. Why couldn't it have been permanent? Where was Antoine? He must've been on a lunch break with his brothers.

Mariquita pointed at Geneviève, feathered in orange and blue. "Allez, Geneviève. Chase the wagtail." She sent her after Céleste. "You are the kingfisher in love."

Geneviève obeyed, and together she and Céleste spun in unison.

"Arrête!" cried Mariquita. "Céleste. Come here."

Céleste flinched. Her knees shook as she found safety under Mariquita's wing off in the corner, downstage. "Did I do something wrong?"

Mariquita hissed through her teeth and furrowed her brow. "Your technique is there, mon chou, but your body has nothing to say." She eyed Céleste with her lorgnette and lowered her voice. "I am sorry I could not protect you from Théo. Truly. I didn't know. I had detected something amiss, but I didn't know. It was not my place to pry."

"You would have done something if you could," Céleste consoled her.

Mariquita touched Céleste's back and nodded. "I can only protect you on the stage. In all things on the stage. Even if it means protecting you from delivering a mediocre performance."

"What are you saying?"

"It pains me to do this, but I'm switching your roles with Geneviève. She will be the wagtail and you the kingfisher for the pantomime."

A demotion. Unheard of. Céleste nodded, forcing herself to remain perfectly still, fighting the urge to smash something. This was Mariquita. She was doing the right thing. Céleste's head spun. Unbelievable.

"I'm telling you, Antoine,"—Céleste regaled him up in the box—"She demoted me. Me! My grandparents own the place."

"My brothers did the same thing to me in *A Trip to Switzerland*." He looked down at the firebreathers practicing on stage. "I was to play Finsbury Parker, the bride's husband-to-be, but I was out of step over Thomas. They made me a servant that crashed through ceilings."

Whatever he'd done in the interval, he was clearly back to top billing in *Do-Mi-Sol-Do*. She ignored Les Dante belching fire below and edged closer to Antoine, thirsty for his secret knowledge. "How did you relight your spark?"

"My brothers. They helped face my fears. We have dream sessions."

"Dream sessions, eh?" she asked.

"Oui," he said, gruffly, "you think these macabre shows come out of nowhere?"

Céleste chafed at his tone, oddly familiar as it was. "How am I to know?"

"Je suis désolé. Forgive me. You don't hate me, do you?"

He must've thought he was talking to his brothers. They probably got on his nerves to no end.

"Non."

"Bon," he continued. "You are the center of my world, you know."

"So are you." She kissed him, her lips wet on his. "About these dreams."

"Of course. We mine our dreams for material and hold weekly chats. After Thomas, many of them were nightmares." He sighed. "Maybe if you had someone to talk to..."

"I'm an only child. That's why I have you."

"Your net."

She snuggled up close. "And such a nice net it is."

I am nothing, I am nothing, I am nothing. Her soul-cave was going ballistic. She needed light, distraction, his love, to quiet this voice which had regained its clarity.

She unfastened his shirt button and slid her hand onto his chest. He touched her neck, his flesh hot on hers. Within moments, she was lost in time and space, falling through ceilings in a hallucinogenic phantasmagoria. Through the floor, out a ceiling, over and over. Lips parted, breath stolen, her nerves spun pirouettes.

Les Dante were still exhaling their fire in thick whooshing sounds by the time Antoine changed and left.

She slipped into her tutu, preened her blue and orange feathers, and moved the chairs aside. *Face your fears.* How was she going to do that? Find Théo? Highly doubtful. Perhaps her dancing had improved some, now that she was more fulfilled and the light back in her cavern, artificial though it may be.

She danced in her box, uncertain of Mariquita's ruling.

Her pliés were perfect, her lines nimble. Look how she extended her hands, her fingers tense to represent the kingfisher's needlelike beak.

What was that glowing? She retrieved her hand from the pose. Balls of light were stuck under the pads of her fingers, in her palm, beneath her skin.

"Putain de merde." She shook out her hand. A ball came out her fingertip and whizzed at the stage.

She held her breath. The thing had a tail. It arced over one of Les Dante, the pair dancing around in their bat costumes, and spangled the stage with sparks. Les Dante covered their heads as Céleste ducked and clamped her hands in her armpits.

Oh non, she was dead. There was no hiding that. Nemesis was going to cut everyone's throat. Everyone's but hers, seeing as she was immortal. But Les Dante did nothing wrong. It wasn't fair!

"Where did that come from?" asked the monotone Les Dante.

"Some kind of pyrotechnic display," said the strident one.

"For whose act?"

Footsteps joined them. "Anyone hurt?" asked the surly voice of a stagehand.

"Non," Les Dante said together.

"Leave it to the Hanlon-Lees," said the surly newcomer. "The place is wired to blow every night. I'll have you break so we can check for more bombs. Can't have these going off willy-nilly."

Céleste's breathing returned. Oui, a check. Trés bon. She examined her hands. The glow had vanished. If she didn't know any better, that was a shooting star. *D'accord.* She could shoot stars. Like Asteria. She was going to calmly walk out of here with her hands glued to her legs. If she saw a Greek goddess try and stop her, she'd calmly open fire.

Céleste laughed nervously. Walk? Why walk when she could pollinate? Pollinate... she liked that. If Antoine could make up stupid words, so could she.

And all she must do to pollinate was think light and airy thoughts.

Cobwebs occupied the corners of her box. For some reason, Papa did not believe in feather dusters.

Cobweb feathers.

She disappeared into the haze—

—And reappeared backstage the following week.

Ballet class stopped for nothing, not even nouvelle nymphes bestowed with magical powers.

Céleste, relax. Take it easy. You will be the best kingfisher the Folies had ever seen or blast everyone to kingdom come. No extraneous tension and her limbs should abide.

Mariquita directed a yellow-feathered Geneviève to the stage.

Desormes conducted a melody of curious clarinets.

Mariquita waved her fan at Céleste. Her cue.

Céleste stepped daintily, maintaining a level head while moving her body like the kingfisher did, gifted with neck tendons, and swept down at the yellow wagtail like she would a fish. Geneviève leapt away right before the clasp.

Behind Céleste, the pink lotus entwined her arm, which she broke from with a rond-de-jambe and hopped clear with a jeté.

"Arrête, Céleste," said Mariquita. "Where is the playful-ness? Where is the magic?" She marched toward her. "Where is the soul?"

Got your magic right here. Céleste flounced out her hand and clamped it to her mouth. *Do not lose control.* Keep a lid on it. She locked her hands together. "All great questions."

Mariquita spoke into her ear. "I love you, mon chou. Trust me when I say, you may be better suited as the pink lotus, who is in love with the kingfisher."

The voice in the void choked out a garbled *I am nothing.*

Céleste put a cork in it, and let it fly at Antoine's face later in the box.

"Pink lotus! Pink lotus! Any more demotions I'll be punch-ing tickets!"

"Mariquita said she loves you."

"But not my dancing. How is that possible? Who else is doing the steps? Are my feet not part of me? Are they sentient beings? My family pays the woman's bills!"

"You want to talk money problems. My family went into debt buying a Pullman that splits in two. The contractor we commissioned charged us double and took the rest."

"Do you not hear me?"

"Oui, I hear you. You want nepotism over talent."

"Whose side are you on?" She clenched her fists.

"Yours, ma chérie," said Antoine. "You're rather attractive when you're mad. I didn't offend you, did I? I can speak to Mariquita if you like."

"I don't like. Your job is to listen, not solve my problems for me."

"I am listening. Are you?" He moved to the door to leave.

I am nothing, I am nothing.

"Oh, don't leave me alone." She clung to his arm. "Some-thing about a train."

He walked back in and sat down. "The Pullman was a key scene where Finsbury Parker's friends have to stop the evil

Popperton from consummating his marriage with Julia. We ate potatoes for a year waiting for the show to open."

"I don't know poverty."

"And you never will with me around."

Her heart rate fell to a normal pace. His words had a calming effect she couldn't do without. They'd be married one day and have acro-dancer children.

"Did this fear of consummating a marriage come from one of your dreams?" she asked, touching his hand.

"Guillaume's." His lips pressed into her neck, arousing the fervor of Aphrodite herself.

"Too bad for Guillaume."

He dragged the sleeve of her tutu off her shoulder. She cradled his head in her arm and left the Gare du Nord riding a star in a perfumed frenzy, darting through several tunnels, and reached her destination with a quick pulse in her neck, helium in her chest, and light back in her soul-cave.

What new ability had she unearthed? She might've been able to shoot stars from her eyes or grow as tall as a tree, make vines spring from the ground or control meteors. Antoine was gone so fast she barely noticed him leave. She could not risk another spectacle, even in the privacy of her box, so she put on her tutu and ran to the lavatories to see what marvelous power she could perform next. Better to take the scenic route, eh?

Oxygen.

The world burst into that of an impressionist painter.

Down the double staircase she swam, into the Winter Garden, through a door to the parlor, down a hallway, and into the ladies room, empty this midday hour and the majority of the time, for it was a recently installed novelty, detested by those Second Empire women for permitting bystanders to see them go in and thus invite dissolute imaginings. Céleste checked the monkey closets, sifting through cracks and hinges of each one. Not a soul, not even hers. Only chains dangling from sisterns.

Lead.

She rebirthed herself standing on the parquet floor.

How to get her powers out?

She did jumping jacks, flicked her nose, waved her arms, spun in circles, clicked her tongue, held her eyelids. Perhaps Aphrodite and friends had only given her the two abilities. An instruction manual would've been nice. The mixis! The bottle it came in, perhaps that was what the symbols were for. She could picture it in a velvet-lined drawer in her vanity where she had placed it for safekeeping. It had a flower, butterfly wings, a star, and a heart.

She spluttered into her lips. She better not have to live in a cocoon for a month. Chrysalis. What have you.

The ladies' room door creaked open down the hall, in the parlor.

Don't interrupt now! Couldn't this person see she was trying to—Pollen sprayed out from her skin, discharging a maroon cloud throughout the room. She covered her mouth.

Que diable?

Coughing erupted in the short hall. Footsteps beat a hasty retreat, slapping the parlor door opened again.

That poor woman.

Céleste chanced a breath. It didn't seem to affect her. What had it done to that lady?

Céleste pollinated through a vent, floated into the Winter Garden, and tread the air as though it was water. A black-bustled woman stumbled out of the parlor and hung off an iron post, touching her chest, her eyes bloodshot. Mariquita!

Céleste flutter-kicked behind a marble planter with a frosty fern, checked if the coast was clear below, around, and above, before pollinating into shape and running to Mariquita's aid.

"Mariquita!"

Mariquita held up her lorgnette revealing the eyes of a wino. "Stay out of the privy, mon chou. Someone sprayed perfume. I think I'm allergic."

Céleste's stomach turned. She would hate herself forever if the effects were permanent. "I'll get you some water."

"Please do. And put out whatever skunk fire that can-can dancer decided to varnish herself with."

Céleste grabbed an empty carafe off a nearby table and ran into the ladies room for some tap water. The cloud had dissipated. *Thank goodness.* She filled the tap and returned.

"To health," said Mariquita, facetiously. She was alive enough to make jokes. She had to turn out all right. She just had to.

Céleste would never use her powers at the Folies again. It was much too dangerous. She was just glad she hadn't killed anyone, by her own hand, or through Nemesis. Mariquita could demote Céleste as much as she liked.

But not really!

A week later, Céleste performed her glissades—jumping from side to side and landing in fifth—along the reeds and mossy boulders surrounding the stage, while she chased the peppy kingfisher, and the water lily chased her. She turned, her flower pedal skirt opening on the pond with increasing speed.

"Arrête!" Mariquita cried to Céleste.

"Demoted to water lily!" Céleste cried to Antoine up in her box. "I don't know how to get my spark back!"

D'accord. That was a lie. Her soul's return would do it. But there was no point in demon-hunting before she'd met Antoine and found love. She'd have been defenseless. She could not engulf a man in white light and squeeze the evil out of him like toothpaste the way Psyche had.

"I don't see you doing anything to work through it," said Antoine.

She wasn't! How could she? *I am nothing* had whispered in her chest whenever she was apart from him for too long. And seeing as their time together silenced the voice in the void, what was the rush? She had an eternity to search, after all, since she could live forever, being immortal.

"Be grateful you don't have to wear an ape costume," Antoine continued, "and do somersaults in it."

"What was the name of that one?" asked Céleste.

"*Apes and Bathers.* We escaped the zoo and went to the beach."

She leaned over the seat and kissed Antoine, charming herself into an interstellar beach ride upon a shooting star, the cotton skirt of her swimwear billowing in the rush, her legs tight around the conveyance as though hugging Clemence's sides to encourage speed. Monkey bathers in striped linen roamed from their striped tents onto the shoreline, instinctual, animal, restless.

Céleste detached herself from Antoine in a sweat to cool off, content as the light refilled her soul-cave. She fell back into the blankets of her private box, knowing Antoine was going to leave again. But he didn't.

She opened an eye in his direction. "You're not leaving?" she asked.

"You flinch whenever I do." He lied down and cuddled with her.

She nestled into his chest. Now was a fine time for him to stay, when there might've been new powers brewing inside her itching to break free.

You can go if you like," she said. "I'll behave."

"Non, non, ma chérie. I want to stay. I feel like I won the jackpot at Monte Carlo when I'm around you."

"What about Papa?"

"I'll face the consequences. I love you."

Suddenly the room shrunk in size. His hand was a weight upon her hip, his arm a vice. She felt smothered, like he wanted to capture and suck the life from her, what life there was left. Had her love for him vanished? Was it him she wanted or the feelings that came with him?

She brought this question home with her and paced the bedroom floor. No new abilities had endowed her body. None. She had reached her apex. The butterfly symbol on her mixis must've been metaphorical—a transformation to immortality.

She shut the drawer and glanced away from the Hanlon-Lees poster.

Antoine. The sight of him made her sick. While she was over here racking up powers physically, she had given away too much of herself emotionally. To him. She'd let him handle her emotions too freely. *Here is rage, deal with my rage. Here is ennui, deal with my boredom. Here is my sadness. Turn it to happiness.*

"You've been distant lately," he asked her a few days later in the box. "I was hoping you could teach me some ballet."

"You want to learn ballet?" she asked.

"Oui, it'd be genial. I could incorporate it into my shows."

Feelings of endearment and revulsion tied her chest in a knot. The idea of him invading her life. The stage was her sphere. Her love for him was fading—she was sure of it—and only the love of acquiring powers remained, but even that was a dead-end now. How to cut ties? She couldn't hurt his feelings and cause him pain. It was too mean.

"D'accord," she said. "We'll start by watching my rehearsal of *Fleurs et Plumes.*"

Sure enough, at rehearsal time, Antoine had taken his seat in the auditorium.

Mariquita smacked her fan in her palm. "Un, deux, trois, Céleste, pas de bourrée—plié, step to the side, back to the front—Good!—pirouette renversé!"

Céleste in a white pancake tutu performed the requisite pirouette renversé, bending her body toward the raised leg as it traveled backwards high in the air in a grand rond de jambe. She skipped and chased the pink lotus around the lakeside as the dragonflies rose from the trees, and her heart wasn't in it.

"Céleste," said Mariquita, "what am I to do with you? It will get better, mon chou, I promise, but for now, you are going to play a dragonfly."

Céleste dropped her arms to her side, frowning. "Dragonfly, oui."

She couldn't dance right without her soul. To get her soul she needed powers. To get powers she needed Antoine. And if she spent half her time with Antoine and the other half dancing poorly, she could not spare a minute to even look. It wasn't fair.

And Antoine watching didn't help. There must've been something wrong with him. For him to be in love with her, a soulless body, a half-person with a soul-throne chanting *I am nothing* every week—it was plain folle.

Antoine bounded up the stairs stage left. Céleste walked stage right. If she walked fast enough she could beat him to the exit without seeing him.

"Céleste!"

Too late. He caught up.

"Antoine," Céleste began.

A decision had to be made. *Antoine or your soul.*

Her voice cracked. "Antoine, I don't wish to see you anymore."

"Nonsense."

"Non, I mean it."

"But, I need you." He knitted his eyebrows and took her hands, limp in his. "You complete me."

"I thought I did," said Céleste, "and I thought you completed me for awhile," but only her soul could do that.

"Please," said Antoine, "I've been so happy lately. I'm nothing without you."

Onstage he had his life together. Deep down, he was in shambles.

A lightbulb went on again.

Antoine was too much like Papa.

Did that mean she was too much like Maman?

The thought stung her heart.

Maman was right. The boys would all run. It was better Céleste ran from them before they had a chance to run from her.

Tears welled in her eyes as she took back her hands. "Non, Antoine. I mean it."

She fled around the curtain into her secret stairwell, locked the door and sat in the dark, losing a part of herself, the part of her she filled with his thoughts and emotions. The part of him she filled herself with. She could barely articulate it. The anger she handed him, the doubt—he soothed her. She was the emotion, he the soother, the job of one person assigned to two.

She buried her head between her knees and clasped her ankles.

Antoine had grieved Thomas's death and regained his stage presence—Perhaps it meant there was a chance for her to without her soul—Because Antoine was a half-person, like her—and she had sliced them in two! A Siamese twin cut down the middle. Amputation. Torn asunder. Why did it hurt so bad! Why could she not have seen it!

It appeared it took more than a stolen soul to make someone half of who they were. Any tragedy could do the same.

Why, there must've been half-people everywhere—at the bakery, at the grocer's, *Les Halles*, these lost and broken demi-gens, that made them cling to other demi-gens like molecules, merging, hoping to be complete. They were a tribe of dysfunction, caroming into and off each other, creating Frankenstein's monsters by forming relationships, disconnected from their parts and their sums.

She could've found her soul by now. She would've started looking had she not been so attached. Aphrodite, Psyche—they'd told her where it was. Inside the shadow room—and she had the arsenal too attempt such a foray.

To open the door she had to exorcise a demon and shepherd him to hell. A glimmer of hope shined in her bloody hack of a wound. She was free. Incomplete, unbearably alone, but free to try.

What was she saying?

Who could hunt demons at a time like this?

Now Antoine was going to love Geneviève instead! Céleste wiped her nose on her arm, blubbering. Geneviève could have him. Céleste didn't deserve anyone. No one cared. Papa hadn't even noticed she'd been sulking for an hour in the dark.

The dancers had probably gone home.

And where was Maman?

Cooking a roast a flambé. She wouldn't notice if Céleste came home again.

Her name was Berthe. Mamans cared about their daughters. Berthe did not.

"Oui, Berthe." The person who was supposed to love her most was the person she most needed to protect herself from.

Look at her. She had become the thing she feared. Céleste fell onto her side, crying. Berthe had filled her with thoughts and emotions and now Céleste had done it to Antoine. Was Berthe under demonic possession to be so angry all the time? Or did she too have her soul stolen in a past life? What else could have made her a half-person?

Was Céleste being too harsh? She couldn't trust herself to pick the right boy, how could she trust herself to judge Maman correctly, a woman who tried to gobble her up?

Psyche, Aphrodite! Would someone make this pain stop! Free her from this snare!

If she were to heal first, if she were to reunite with her soul, then she could feel complete and find a husband. Not before. Never before. She could not pass on this scramble for affection to her future children. She did not trust herself in this soulless state. She would inhale her babies, absorb them, try to use their souls as replacements for hers. How could she live with herself—to believe she was a good mother while a voice in the void said different.

On that day, when body found soul, she would be truly free.

Something shoved Céleste onto her feet, piercing her in the back. She reached between her shoulder blades and found something furry protruding from her spine. Was it? Could it be? She reached out and felt the soft, scaly texture of wings. Her wings! And her wings could feel her fingertips, no different than how hair felt a brush—her wings were brushing the walls they were so big.

"Incroyable!"

Her heart fluttered.

She wished she could get a look at these embroideries.

How to get them back in?

To think, she had been so normal once, eh?

The relationship was real to Céleste, though its lack of authenticity didn't make her parting with Antoine any less painful. If anything, more, because they had merged. There is codependence and there is interdependence.

Tell me, have you ever had your heart broken? Then you have come to the right place. French Athens draws many to our city—those who have conquered love, and those whom love has conquered. Love always plays a role, I promise you, for this is no place for the heartless. If we are not loving, we are trying. Juggling.

Not juggling partners! Juggling our hearts outside of our bodies. Dear me. Perhaps we have lingered inside the gazebo too long. The flowery smells have gone to our heads, the sweets to our stomachs. Renoir's Gardens can sometimes have that effect.

I doubt Pierre Loti would've written of this place, though it is magical just the same. Perhaps he saw a nymph too. He was in the navy. He traveled the world, to France's colonies and beyond. What started as scribblings in his diaries developed into novels. He has a café named after him, just like Monsieur Renoir. It is in Istanbul. Non, it's not Swiss Constantinople anymore. Or is it?

He and Beauvais would have been friends.

Come. We shall climb the steps, burn off some calories, and I will juggle the narrative and tell you of his scheme to dispatch Arachne. You see, the legionnaires were loyal to the legion, not to France. They must take orders from le capitaine, and le capitaine so happened to be inspired by his muse. However, there was a snag.

ANANSI

egionnaires gathered around the brick table in the old caravanserai—an inn on the northern edge of town. The sun beat into the courtyard where the men stood in a circle, their eyes protected by the brims of their kepis, fading from white to beige. Some men lingered in the arches to the open-air rooms that splayed the outer ring, absent of sojourning travelers. Nayla stayed alert. She listened for the bells of any approaching caravan and watched for birdlike shadows as she divulged her plot. Senegalese soldiers nodded along to her talk of portals, death, and mythical objects. They grimaced when she got to the spider.

"It is Anansi," said the broad-shouldered Khoumag, Beauvais's right-hand man.

Nayla was glad of Khoumag's concern. The less soldiers willing to risk their lives for her to experience moksha, the better. She couldn't bear the idea of any more people suffering on her account. Then again, if she didn't have enough soldiers to subdue Arachne, harm could befall the number she did bring. What a quandary. She was better off with as many soldiers as possible. Nayla was about to correct Khoumag, but she didn't want to provoke Nemesis with names and faces. If they wanted Arachne to be Anansi, so it was.

Beauvais puffed thoughtfully on his meter-long pipe. "Who is Anansi?" he asked.

"A selfish spider," said Khoumag. "It is the story of stories."

"Story of stories, richtig," said Nayla.

If a camel could speak, she decided, it would sound like Khoumag.

"How stories came to be," Khoumag continued. "The people of Earth wanted something to occupy themselves, so Anansi climbed a web up to the heavens to visit the sky-god, Nyame. Nyame said he would share all the stories he had if Anansi was able to accomplish four impossible tasks. He must capture a python, a leopard, the Mmoboro hornets, and the fairy Mmoatia."

"Well," said Nayla, "my spider can't be Anansi if Anansi is a man, because my spider is female." Nayla at least wanted to keep the threat alive. "She is dangerous."

Khoumag spoke with his fellow Africans in Senegalese and turned to Nayla. "You are deceived. Anansi is a shapeshifter. What are you after in this vault?"

"It is Anansi's scrolls," replied a legionnaire.

"Nein," said Nayla, "it is a helmet."

"What does it do?" asked Khoumag.

"It makes the wearer invisible. It will lead me to moksha."

Khoumag spoke with his group. Was Beauvais able to understand them? He looked queerly at the lot—or perhaps the look was directed at her. To him, moksha was probably just Hindu flummery.

While the men discussed, Beauvais eyed something over Nayla's head. She turned to see what it was. An inscription on one of the arches—

Oh Hafiz, seeking an end to strife,
Hold fast in thy mind what the wise have writ:
"If at last thou attain the desire of thy life
Cast the world aside, yea, abandon it!"

It would prove difficult for Nayla to abandon the world when her desire was to merge with it. Surely, there was a safe way to negotiate both desire and world and herself. How selfish to think otherwise. These men were her responsibility.

"Capitaine," said Khoumag, "you want us to help this creature to make your art? We will help."

"Super," said Beauvais.

That made thirteen men.

"We need to find someone on their deathbed," said Nayla, "to access the portal."

It shook her conscience to think of it—exploiting death—but death would occur with or without her present.

"How do we escape the cave?" asked Khoumag.

"Another death." Nayla winced.

"Naturally," said Beauvais, "we'll have to kill the spider."

"What if we cannot?" asked Khoumag. "How about bringing a sacrifice to get us out?"

He whispered something in Beauvais's ear.

"The spider will do," said Beauvais.

Ach nein. Nayla did not like whatever Khoumag had suggested. She hoped Beauvais had her best interest at heart.

"No sacrifice to get out," said Nayla, queasy. "To get in, we scout the hospital."

"Armed with Kropatscheks?" Khoumag nudged his rifle.

"Ja, and we have to try to save the person first," said Nayla. "It's the right thing to do."

"Does the portal open for surviving?" Khoumag said snidely.

Beauvais pointed his chibouk at an unwitting soldier. "Put Eugène in a leg splint. We shall pay him a visit."

"Nein, wait," said Nayla. "How will I get in?" She gestured to the curtain. "I need my machine to open the vault. Wearing it in the open will look conspicuous."

Beauvais exhaled. "Khoumag, Eugène, strap the boiler onto Spuckfeuer. Eugène will play doctor, and you—" He addressed her directly. "You shall hide under the sheet on a stretcher."

The two men harnessed her into the mecha-sleeves while two more laid her conveyance on the table. It wasn't quite a palanquin, though it would have to do. She climbed up and sat on her hip. Beauvais rested his foot on the table and his arm on his knee.

"Comfortable?"

"Nein."

He waved his pipe like a wand, and they sheeted her. The men fell into a column. The hospital was two streets away. Boys selling papers shouted on the corner. A woman begged for Khoumag to hear his fortune. Another asked for an evening with the capitaine.

Nayla heard a man walk in a three-legged gait. The man had a cane. They were near the hospital. Gears ticked in glass domes on the exterior walls. Beauvais led the charge into the reception area. Footsteps and the splash of a beaded curtain.

"Herr Captain?"

"I have a wounded soldier. We have our own doctor. We just need a room."

Nayla heard the tinkle of coins in a bag.

"Install us next to the operating room."

She moaned for effect.

The doctor pocketed the marks. "Right this way."

She felt the men shift her weight and reposition their grip as her feet listed toward her head. They were traveling up a staircase! She clung to the rods for dear life, moving upward in a spiral. At the top, she evened out, and the men picked up the pace. Boots slapped the floor as they hurried down the hall. Another swish of a portiere. They turned a corner and the legionnaires filed in.

"Danke, Herr Doktor," said Beauvais to their escort.

Nayla's stretcher lowered to the bed.

"Call me if you need assistance," said the doctor.

"We should manage," said Beauvais. "But some of us are still green to the smell of death. Tell me, how often does someone perish in this hospital?"

"Every day."

"Great. I mean, horrible."

"How long should I expect your stay?"

"Two nights."

"The charge will be double after that. Don't disturb the other patients." The doctor left the room.

Beauvais whisked the sheet off her. Overcrowded, the soldiers had unwound in chairs, leaned on walls, and sat on window sills.

Moans echoed in the hall. The soldiers exchanged hopeful looks. The moaning faded.

"Not dead," declared Khoumag.

Beauvais looked at Nayla. "Care for a tour of the premises?"

"Please."

"To gather our surroundings," Beauvais said to Khoumag. "We need a closer look at the operating room."

Beauvais peeked into the hall before letting Nayla out. The antiseptic was strong and clear, bothering her nose as he parked her in front of the operating room. The windows revealed polished tools and clean table. He pulled her in, treading on a beautiful mosaic that adorned the floor.

"I don't understand Khoumag's resistance," said Nayla. "Aren't you the capitaine? Cannot you order them into battle?"

"I could," said Beauvais, "though I prefer not. It is all right if I die for my art. If anyone else does it will be by volunteer."

"I don't want anyone to die."

"That's why we need willing numbers."

"Why are they helping?"

"Like me, they have also seen strange things. They think you are Mmoatia."

"The fairy from Khoumag's story?"

"Oui. They are going to give you up to Anansi in return for the tales in his vault and safe passage back to Jacoma. There, they will sell the tales for profit."

"I never said the vault was filled with tales."

"They drew that conclusion on their own. They know I am a writer in search of stories. They don't believe I've already experienced the art in you. They think the art is behind closed doors, secreted away in a spider's vault. Not out in the open for all to see."

"Even so, my spider can't give them safe passage back. Someone needs to die to open a—" Nayla clutched her heart. "They mean to kill me."

Beauvais hesitated, almost apologetic. "Oui."

"Beauvais! What's going to happen when we get down there?"

"They'll learn your spider is hostile and shoot it when I command them. Now, what is all this moksha helmet business?"

"The helmet will let me be one with Brahman. It means many lifetimes of suffering fulfilled and a break in samsara—reincarnation."

"Reincarnation?"

"Ja, so my karma doesn't follow me into the next life. If I do good deeds, I am bound in chains of gold. If I do bad deeds, I am bound in chains of iron. When I attain moksha, I will be released from the chains entirely." She glanced at her reflections in the neat array of scalpels. "I must've done something terrible in my previous form to deserve all this."

"Spuckfeuer"—Beauvais's eyes searched hers from left to right—"are you a human?"

As in, of this earthly realm?

She sucked in her breath. "Nein."

"Go tell that to Dache."

"Who is Dache?"

"The Zouaves' wigmaker. It means I don't believe you."

Clunk.

"What was that?" Her eyes darted to the ceiling. She fled to the window and looked three floors down at the sandy lot. Suddenly, a large bird disembarked the roof above her. The wingspan was incredible, the body feminine.

"You hear that ticking?" asked Beauvais.

"It sounds like a gear train."

"It's a bomb," said Beauvais.

The bird—Nemesis. Restoring the status quo.

Shiva, nein. She had revealed too much.

Tonics shattered on the mosaic as Nayla shoved a cart out of the way, lunging for the door. Beauvais instinctively pulled his bolt action, cocking a round into the chamber. Nayla tore into the hallway, shouting at the room of legionnaires.

"Get out of there!"

Three blue coats scurried into the corridor, followed by a large explosion. Shockwaves flung a fourth against the wall and slapped at her eardrums. A high-pitched whine obscured Beauvais's voice. Smoke billowed from the room and changed course, following the path of least resistance through a hole where the windows displayed the grounds.

Unbothered by smoke, Nayla stepped into the room. Men in red-stained uniforms lay strewn on the floor. This was all her fault. Something grabbed her ankle from under the flipped bed. Nayla jumped. It was a hand. She gripped the iron footboard and lifted the veins right out of her neck raising the heavy bed—made heavier by the rubble. Beauvais appeared with a cloth on his mouth and yanked the soldier from the ruins. It was Khoumag.

Nayla recoiled in horror. Why did she have to get so personal? She had only wanted the legion to know her motives were pure. Her pursuit of a karma-free existence wasn't meant to be a blank check to spend however much she wanted. The goal was to shed the layers. The more she added, the harder it became to live with herself. Curse this guilt. She was wholly responsible for these soldier's lives, no matter what Beauvais said.

Khoumag scrambled to the missing wall for air.

Beauvais tapped Nayla. "Where is the portal?"

How was he so calm? A bomb just went off.

"Portal," he repeated.

Portal, portal. She could wallow and brood later. Where *was* the portal? Thanatos should be collecting their Atmas. Where was he?

A turban materialized in the smoke, gathered three soul-flames at once from the dead men lying on the floor, and ferreted through the gaping hole in the wall.

"Did you see that?" asked Nayla.

"I see nothing but smoke," Beauvais grumbled.

She peered over the ledge. A green electric ring hovered below, as if someone had laid a picture of Arachne's Cave on the ground.

"Do you see the ring?" Nayla asked.

"Non," said Beauvais, looking out.

Only she could see the ring. "It's there. I would greatly appreciate if you followed me, but if you choose not to, I understand. Truth be told, I don't deserve it."

"Maybe not, but you are my muse." He held his rifle in the ready position. "Take me with you."

Nayla took him round the waist, sprouted wings, and leapt, clumsily flapping until the bright day phased into the cool night of the cave. She flew over a large web netted across four stakes at the bottom and landed with Beauvais on the glossy tile. Khoumag's shout dissipated as he landed in the net with three surviving legionnaires—the ones that had sought cover in the hall—they came back. They really didn't leave a man behind.

Khoumag's large body kicked and flailed in a fight to get free. Nayla touched the threads. Her flame traveled the latticework and burnt it up. Khoumag, Eugène, and the other two men fell a meter onto their butts.

"Anansi's lair." Khoumag grunted. He crawled to his feet and surveyed the dark shine of the cave. "This place is real."

"The vault door," said Nayla.

The doors to the Hall of Fabled Objects stood in gold-flecked glory across the blue-flame river. Beauvais led the legionnaires over the bridge while Nayla eyed the ceiling, listening for spongy feet, hurrying behind. They regrouped by the doors. Beauvais appeared like a toy soldier beside the Greek column, three times his height.

"Ouvre les portes," he commanded.

The men heaved their bodies against the stone doors.

Water burbled inside Nayla's boiler. She set her hands on the door, hoping this sucker opened in and not out. Her elbows hung in Vs. She thumbed the buttons on her gloves.

"Please work."

Rods drilled from her legs to her boots and from her boots, screwed to the ground, cracking the polished floor like a vase. Steam sprayed from her hips. The pistons on her arms expanded the gap between her hands and her shoulders and froze. The door budged a centimeter and no more. Steam hissed. The boiler shook. The cylinders applied force to the gloves, force to her body.

Two legionnaires wedged their guns into the opening and snapped their bayonets.

"Formez un cercle," Beauvais ordered.

The men encircled Nayla, defending her work on the door. She glanced over her shoulder. "The green ring just closed."

"Is there an exit through there?" Beauvais nodded at the doors.

"Je ne sais pas," said Nayla.

"Feed Mmoatia to the spider," said Khoumag. "That will open them."

"I don't think Mmoatia warned you of a bomb so you can feed her to a spider," said Beauvais.

"My name is Spuckfeuer."

Gossamer threads crept onto a soldier's coat. His white boots snapped off the ground. Beauvais aimed at the ceiling and fired. Khoumag repeated the message. Eugène took aim while Beauvais slid bullets from his pouch into his breech loader. He cocked the bolt and fired with his corporal.

The shots made Nayla deaf. Black-powder smoke ballooned around their company. The abducted soldier fell by Nayla's foot. Green light outlined the shard-like walls as Thanatos flew in and recovered the dead legionnaire. What was he doing? Their souls were already in the underworld. Oh—he was sending the bodies back to Earth. The portal of the desert-image closed. Another opened nearby.

"I see it," said Eugène. "The green portal."

Nayla quickly counted their party. Beauvais, Khoumag, Eugène, the fourth soldier, and herself. No one else had died.

"I thought we couldn't see it," said Beauvais. "It's beautiful."

"Haunting," said Khoumag.

Eugène ran headlong into the desert picture and failed to pass through. He was stuck to it like it was a piece of tapestry. The image enfolded on him and his body rose up the cave in a sack.

"Arachne," Nayla whispered.

"An illusion," said Beauvais, firing at the ceiling.

"The apparitions are threads." Nayla trembled.

Steam spat on the floor. Her cylinders struggled to open. The gears within her placard rattled like those on a clock trying to count the next unceasing minute.

Screams pierced Nayla's ears like a slaughtered goat. Karma. *No more karma, please.* Vishnu, preserve her, wake her from this nightmare.

"Anansi," said Khoumag.

Nayla glanced at the gore. The spider's legs rotated Eugène's body like a pig on a spit. Its fangs had sunk into the gauze, producing another heart-wrenching shriek.

Beauvais pulled his trigger. The chamber clicked. "God damn hand-me-down Chassepot."

"Ananseee!" Khoumag cocked his bolt and fired again and again. "I've got a story for you."

Guilt sapped all feeling from Nayla's senses. She hadn't even learned all their names.

"You," Nayla cried over the gunfire to the unnamed soldier. "What is your name?"

"Hans."

"Danke for helping me."

Hans brushed off her maudlin behavior.

Focus on your task, Nayla. You are only distracting them.

Beauvais picked up a fallen brother's rifle, pushed his bolt forward to the side and squeezed the trigger. An explosive force rushed from the gun barrel. Arachne jumped to the floor. Her legs bristled as her feet hobbled their wet, marshy steps. Gun smoke blocked the approaching target. Beauvais's muzzle barked eight times, blaring in Nayla's head. The next shot came not from him but from the clear.

Sandaled feet walked casually out of the dark. Bare breasted, Arachne had assumed a womanly shape with flowing black hair pinned with desert blossoms and a trigger-happy trigger-finger, unloading the gun in loud bangs until it clicked. Hans fell at Nayla's side.

"You bring earthly men and earthly weapons into my domain, nymph? What skulduggery is this?" Arachne breathed her raspy words across the narrowing space between them and chucked her gun toward the blue-flame river. A train of chiffon dragged on the floor as Arachne advanced, the skirt clipped to her waist by a string of medallions.

"So Spuckfeuer is a nymph," said Khoumag, "not a fairy. And that is not Anansi."

"It's Arachne." Nayla shifted her gaze from the spider to Thanatos, walking through the portal for the most recent victim of her hare-brained scheme.

"The doorway is open," said Nayla.

"It's our last ticket out of here," Beauvais surmised.

"For Camarón?" asked Khoumag, shooting away at Arachne.

Beauvais hugged him with a slap to the back, wild eyed and bellicose. "For Jean Danjou."

Water gurgled in the boiler. Brute force was futile. Nayla released the rods from the floor and leveled her achy joints toward Arachne. She wound back her fist and thrust it forward to unleash a geyser of flame... but none came. Nothing happened.

"My powers..." She looked desperately at Beauvais. "They're gone."

Beauvais closed his eyes in meditation, leaving her to wonder what he was thinking.

"Forgive me, my muse."

Without warning, he shoved her forward through the portal. She spun and fell onto the sand. Beauvais raised his weapon and aimed it above her head.

"Come with me!" Nayla shouted.

"One thing about the legion." He kept his target in his sights. "We never leave our dead behind."

"But Thanatos has already taken them!" she cried, but too late.

The painting of Beauvais and the Hall of Fabled Objects, hung on the open air of the desert, collapsed into its frame. Around her, by the ziggurat, laid the bodies of Eugène and Hans and their fallen brother. She wished it were her lying there.

A shadowy figure protruded from the ziggurat's umbra stretching across the desert floor. Nayla spun onto her butt to look.

High on the plateau towered a woman. Cascades of auburn hair rolled off her head in tresses. A blue cloak flowed at her back. Leather straps secured sandals to her feet and a cloth to her loins. She wore silver plates over her arms and shins, imprinted with eagles. A gold-plated bird covered her buxom chest, its tail drawing stiff over her navel. Large wings issued from her back, like those of a dove.

"Nemesis," Nayla blurted.

The goddess raised a sword to the sky, encompassed by golden flame. Tip pointed, she sailed toward Nayla and landed right next to her with a bend of her knees.

Nayla trembled as she rose to confront this goddess.

A blindfold fluttered from her heart-shaped face, an indifferent expression drawn across her lips. She pointed the talwar's sharp edge to Nayla's throat.

"I was just doing what I thought was right," said Nayla, "The helmet..."

"I don't care about that," Nemesis's voice warbled. "I care about the secrecy of the pantheon. The separation of godly beings from earthly beings in the minds of the masses. Today, you receive a warning. All who saw you are confined to the underworld. Don't let it happen again." She peeled up her blindfold.

Underneath the blue silk was a pair of closed eyes with the distinctive feature of unlimited sight, for tiny holes had been cut into her eyelids so that her pupils were visible when her eyes were shut.

"I'm watching you."

The words, the image struck Nayla with a terror that cut straight to her Atma. Nemesis blinked and soared to the skies. Nayla crumpled to her knees, branded in the mind by a sight she could not unsee. She rubbed her eyelids, wondering what became of Beauvais and Khoumag, wanting to see Baba, to see Maman, to save Ravi uncle, to hug Kameera, to outpace that horrible monster, to die for the legionnaires, to regain her powers if that were even possible, and—most of all—to find Brahman.

Nayla could not fly. She could not throw flame, set her body on fire, see doorways, rien. She had done too much celebrating, shall we say, and experienced burnout. Watch your head on the lamp in the corridor. Non, we won't be going in the house. Simply passing through the outdoor hall cut into its center. Ah, here we are in the final Renoir Jardin.

He painted *Jardin de la rue Cortot* on this very site. I doubt the flowers are original. They are beautiful, though. See the red poppies along the wall beyond that planter that looks like a birdbath? The purple flowers are bindweed. I am not sure what tree this is, but look how it leans handsomely on this iron pedestal. Look at the pink roses climbing the arbors.

If there was one thing Beauvais had shown Nayla, it was that he saw beauty within her which she may have overlooked. To be a muse, you are the content, the spice of life, the ingredients to the artist's vision. For a martyr like Nayla to accept this claim, examine it with a magnifying glass, turn it over in her head like a piece for a different puzzle, it was unlikely to stick. But it gave her a jolt of confidence to carry on and formulate a new plan.

What she needed was another nymph to take down Arachne and get through the door. Now, we know better than to think

Nemesis—the creature with hole-punched eyelids, beurk—would appreciate Nayla asking around for other nymphs. Ah, but Hermes Hill. She could ask around for that. Beauvais and Hestia had both said French Athens was a cultural hub, a magnet for artists and muses alike.

I think it is time we take a jaunt through the gallery. Oui, a museum. I will buy your ticket. They have paintings, artifacts, and an atelier. Renoir did *Bal du moulin de la Galette* here. Ah, you've heard of that one! How exciting! Let us take a trip back in time, to October 1892. Five soulless years have passed and Céleste was 19 years old, out of touch but in her element, contemplating life in her plush box at a certain music hall own by her grandparents where Papa directed, where the show started every evening at eight o'clock—tous les soirs à huit heures, as the posters say—at 32 rue Richer. Where else?

LES FOLIES BERGÈRE

When it came to one's sense of self, everyone but Céleste knew who they were.

Maybelle Stuart, the woman on stage, knew she was Maybelle Stuart, matinée performer, swirling large flags of silk around with each motion of her arms. She was an American with rosy cheeks and a yellow bun and yellow curls pinned over her yellow forehead, who danced a serpentine dance, accompanied by an orchestra and spotlighted in multicolor by weeping bells in the corners of the stage, the border decorated by acanthus leaves, a combination of maple leaf and curled parsley, a real Ancient Greek affair, with the flower stems chasing each other to the floor in a pair of iron twirls.

The people of French Athens knew who they were, crammed into the green auditorium on a Sunday afternoon. Ladies in puffy gigot sleeves swaddled together like sheep, wearing fine-blooming hats, their frizzy bangs escaping onto their men in ditto suits whose shoulders they leaned on, or clasped in children's hands anchored to their mothers' hips. They were the audience, and they paid three francs to be entertained for a couple of hours—four francs for a seat close to the stage, two for the

promenoir and garden, and twenty—*non, thirty*—for a box—
Papa's updated figures.

A courtesan or two had squirmed past Gustave's eye on
the promenoir—they knew who they were, even at this young
hour. They enjoyed sex. They enjoyed selling it. They enjoyed
selling it discreetly, gaining admittance to the Folies via red
cards issued every two weeks by Gustave to keep out the tramps,
so long as they kept to the promenoir—an area demarcated by
window frames without windows partitioning the back of the
house from a semicircle hallway where men and women could
promenade, sit at tables, and order drinks. One could even sit
at a bar in the Winter Garden, the lobby outside the promenoir,
and stare at himself for one franc and fifty centimes a beer. She
had tried to probe her reflection there without success.

Everyone knew who they were except her. She fanned the
part of her that was in the auditorium wondering why Papa had
paid for her dance lessons when the woman on stage merely
waved her arms and spun in a circle, while the other part of
her was lost in the shadow world of Hades.

Did Théo know he had deprived her of motherhood when
he stole her soul? Did the demon that possessed him give it any
consideration? Did they want to dump a broken half-woman
onto a broken half-husband to raise half-children in one chaotic
half-family, thinking she would really let that happen? Non.

When she tied Étienne's booties, her future son would not
worry about Maman's distress or be fearful she may abandon
him on a whim. When she danced with Eulalie, the child would
not need to store love in her heart like a squirrel hoarding nuts.
Céleste had their full, undivided love and attentions. You had
enough love for Maman, and Maman had enough love for you,
she would tell them. As did Maman for your Papa. Her husband
wouldn't be just any man, but a man of worth, and a man of
worth did not want a soulless wife. Whither did it wander?

The spirit world hurt to think about. It couldn't be in-
tellectualized. She could only intuit the goings on there. She

should've asked Psyche the specifics when she had the chance. The questions you think of when the moment's over, eh?

Céleste adjusted her field glasses. A woman sat alone in the back of the house. This old girl looked like she was having a moment now. A cold sweat beaded on the woman's cherub face—an aged cherub of about thirty, hair curled in ribbons, her body stout and pasty. Céleste wanted to lend her a fan. They had electric ones installed downstairs, but that wouldn't be enough. The adult cherub was likely the poor waif set to audition after Maybelle's act. Papa sandwiched all auditions between the matinée and the main revues.

Did this newcomer juggle? She would have to outdo Cinquévalli, King of the Jugglers, for his spot—Antoine Hanlon, long deposed. Or was it magic? No one could beat the Isola Brothers. They shot apples off each other's heads with a rifle. *Hmm.* Maybe she was going to shoot an apple off her own head, or that of the austere man next to her in the top hat. Or do something with animals. She might play with snakes like Nala Damajanti, who was so pretty. She might even pick up a horse like Iron Jack, and the jockey too, while Jack flew on a trapeze. What Céleste really wanted to see was the cherub woman box a kangaroo. There were never enough kangaroo boxers in this mad world.

But then why was woman so tense? Maybelle waved her wands in corkscrews, upset her drapes by the self-made wind. The campanula flowers colored her billowy figure in rainbow light until her hands speared the sky in a finishing pose. The audience applauded. Children hollered. And the Folies Bergère's cherubic guest laid her palms on her knees, quite relaxed.

The tasseled curtain swept the planks, and the cherub alighted to prepare backstage.

Mentally, Céleste ran down her list of what streets to prowl that evening while the habitués shuffled out of the auditorium, chatting about the show. There were twenty arrondissements to choose from. Each night, she had ventured into a new one, hoping to attract the evils of man and expel their demons.

How many shadow rooms must she race into? They were nothing but antechambers preventing her from entering the full realm of Hades. But the demons had to get home somehow. Through a second door somewhere. Stubborn creatures. One of them would yield her access eventually.

Hermes Hill—that was where she would try tonight, arrondissement number eighteen. After this lovely performance, of course.

The cherub stepped out from the drawn curtains in her dress, presided over by the gentleman in the top hat. She spoke with Papa and Mariquita in the front row.

"Mr. Stein," said the cherub woman in clear American English, "please ask Monsieur Marchand why he has engaged a woman who gives a feeble copy of my dances, after you wrote to him from Indian Berlin to propose that he talks with me."

Oh! This Mr. Stein was her agent, and the dance was stolen!

"We could be polite," Mr. Stein replied. "He's probably already heard the Opéra turned you down earlier today."

"That doesn't matter," griped the cherub woman. "Put the question to him. Besides, this man doesn't know anything. If I spoke French, I'd ask him myself."

Céleste smiled so wide at the faux pas, she covered her mouth to contain herself. Mariquita must've chuckled inside too. *Wait until the cherub woman finds out that Papa speaks English.*

"I hired a serpentine dancer to compete with the Olympia," Papa said in French for Stein to translate. "My audience has been underwhelmed by Miss Stuart."

Stein turned to his client and set the words to English.

She snorted. "Of course they're not impressed. She's horrible."

"If Miss Loïe Fuller would be so kind as to show me how the dance is really performed, she may have the stage," Papa said in his best English.

Loïe's face went scarlet. She nodded obsequiously and ducked between the curtain folds. In the five-minute interlude, Mr. Stein took a seat near Papa.

The curtain wiggled and spread to a black stage. Shaded in the center, behind a layer of darkness, rose a mountain of white fabric. The weeping bells glowed blue, shining a beam of pollenous light onto the mass of silk. Loïe raised a hand and gave the silk a short twirl. Maybelle's wands had the silk tied on like two flagpoles. Loïe's were completely wrapped, extensions of her arms, sprawling into tendrils.

Wagner played on the lone violin from the orchestra pit, guiding the fabric's movements, radiating pink in the light, malleable to the dancer's twists and spins—green, blue, red—the vanishing dancer left only the figure of a shapeshifting canna lily. Her cherubic face appeared, reminding Céleste there was a human on stage, wiped clear again by a tongue of flame. Ripples coursed through her silken tides like the struts on a seashell, washing out to shore at the edge of space three meters off her body in every direction. The petals folded and refolded, opened and closed, playing spring and autumn all in a heartbeat.

The apparition showed Papa her side profile in reptile green and spun her arms forward and back. Piles of silk tipped overhead, splashed at the ground behind her, and slithered back up. Now *this* was a serpentine dance. The second the waves faded at her feet, new ones appeared from on high. The glum woman's beauty had blossomed like the flower into a butterfly. Rotations. Revolutions. She waved her hands in figure eights, making wings tumble over and soar, her beauty worthy of Aphrodite.

Maybe she *was* Aphrodite, incarnated into this cherub woman. What supernatural force. The butterfly turned pink. Could this dancer be Céleste's patron goddess, returned in disguise? What message was she trying to send about love? About the immortality they had granted her? Psyche and Aphrodite's words flickered in Céleste's mind as the arc lamps flickered onstage at the electric fée, lulling her into a state of hypnosis. *When you find love, you will become immortal.*

The fée spun round. Antoine's face flashed in her mind—his wavy black hair, his boyish features. The fée lowered and raised her batons at even heights to make the zigzag pattern of a basket, herself in the center, drenched in amber light.

In a final spin, her dress unfurled like the rings of Saturn around her orbit and settled on the floor in perfect black. The last note of the fiddle hung in the air with the shroud upon the stage. Who was this goddess? Who was Loïe Fuller? Papa and Madame Mariquita left their seats in the empty theater and hurried backstage with Mr. Stein to find out. Whoever she was, she was Maybelle times one hundred.

Céleste rose from the green velvet box and walked the iron-vined halls to investigate. She'd made it to the orchestra pit when Mariquita reappeared from the wings.

"Who is she?" asked Céleste.

Mariquita turned up the corner of her mouth. "An American. Her ex-husband funded a dance company that toured the Caribbean, and she worked at the Gaiety Theatre in Japanese London. She failed both. Do you like her?" She raised the lorgnette to her face.

Céleste opened the side door and leaned on the rail. Seeing as the performance had little to no ballet, this might be a test of loyalty.

"I love her," Céleste confessed.

"Yes, well, don't get any ideas. One serpentine dance is too many. It hurts my heart."

"You didn't like the dance?"

"It hurt my eyes."

"Well, the costume was beautiful."

"It will hurt my laundress."

Céleste mounted the steps. "Where are they?"

"Dressing room."

She and Mariquita turned the corner into the bowels of the wings, toward the elephant cage and the stagehands that fed them.

"Salut, Pierre." Céleste caressed his trunk through the bars.

Pierre glanced at her and ate his grass.

"Pierre wants me to be a sheet dancer."

Mariquita donned her lorgnette to check Pierre's reaction and turned back to Céleste. "I catch you in one of those, mon chou, I drown you in a well."

"So lucky I have your advice at my disposal."

"And it's lucky for me drawn wells are seldom dry," said Mariquita. "Practice your fouetté, and I'll make a star ballerina out of you yet."

Mariquita rapped on the dressing room door with her fan, but Céleste barged right in. Loïe Fuller stood in her chemise, unruffling her massive dress, which she had placed on a mannequin, the fée-like figure on the stage replaced by a woman in spectacles. Papa sat on a vanity, playing with his mustache. He looked up at Céleste.

She marched past Papa and Mr. Stein, right up to Loïe and shook hands. "Salut! My name's Céleste. Big admirer."

"My overzealous daughter," added Papa.

Loïe's plump face spread wide with a glistening smile. "Merci."

"You were much better than Maybelle," said Céleste.

"About the same," said Mariquita, shaking hands.

"I had met Maybelle in Italian New York," Loïe said to Céleste. "I performed it in February. I loaned her five dollars."

"Small world," said Céleste.

"It's clear to me," said Papa, "you inspired Maybelle, but, if I may ask, what inspired you?"

"I did a show last year called *Quack M.D.* I had to stitch together a flowy dress to play a hypnotized patient. I stepped into the projector light, and what do you know? Magic. All by accident."

"Quack M.D.," said Mariquita. "I don't recall that one."

"Perhaps," said Céleste defensively, "it was off-off-off Broadway."

"Was it in a subway tunnel?" asked Mariquita.

"The show flopped," Loïe conceded, "but I got nice reviews."

"So you weren't inspired by Greek mythology or anything?" Céleste gritted her teeth, coming dangerously close to having Nemesis smash through the side of the theater and kill everyone but her. "Pink butterflies, maybe?"

"Ah, that was to add some local flavor. I understand there's been some fairy sightings. What was her name? Fleur d'Étoile... Starflower."

Céleste was flattered. Loïe's inspiration made sense. Artists attracted nymphs, nymphs served as muses, artists made more art. It still felt like Miss Serpentine Dance Loïe Fuller was guarding something, something Aphrodisiac-related—as in, she was Aphrodite in disguise.

"Well," said Papa. "I'm sold. We change out acts every two weeks. Something tells me you'll stick around longer. How does ten thousand francs a month sound?"

Céleste clapped at the fantastic news. She was in the midst of an admirer, and so was Loïe.

Loïe plopped onto the stool, uprooting its ivy legs from the floor as she slid back in disbelief.

"You'll get the full forty-piece orchestra," Papa added, "conducted by Monsieur Desormes, and you can dance your own choreography. It doesn't appear like you need help. Does she, Mariquita?"

"No," Mariquita said pertly. "She's perfect."

Papa looked eagerly at Loïe, waiting for the blush to leave her face.

"Miss Fuller, the dancer usually responds."

"She'll take it," Stein cut in.

"Mama will be so happy." Loïe teared. "Where do I sign?"

"I'll have Gustave arrange the contract." Papa got off the vanity and leaned back on his heels. "There is one small detail. I've already told the public that Maybelle is to dance the first two shows at the end of October. The ads are posted. The public will kill me if I don't give them Maybelle."

"You want me to wait the extra week?" asked Loïe.

"God, no. I want you to perform the Serpentine Dance as Maybelle performing her version of your Serpentine Dance. And do it wearing a blonde wig. Maybelle's a blonde."

"Papa," said Céleste, "that's a lot to ask. I don't think she traveled all this way from America to pose like her imitator."

"It will be dark," said Mariquita. "It can be anyone up there. You, me, anyone."

Loïe glanced at her ghostly dress and eyed Papa. "I'll do it."

"Génial." Papa clapped. "I'll leave you to change. Gustave will be in shortly."

He gestured Céleste into the wing with a hand upon her back. When Mariquita walked through, he silently shut the door.

"Mariquita, you have to sack Maybelle."

She gasped, all too familiar with Papa's fear of confrontation. "Édouard..."

"I can't," he preempted. "She'll hate me. Say I'll pay for the two remaining nights."

"Papa, it's showbiz," Céleste said, frustrated. It was this same fear that had kept Théo in her life for so long. "People get sacked all the time."

"Not by me, they don't."

"Non," said Céleste, "by me and Mariquita—and I think Carl sacked a dancer last week."

"Carl?" asked Mariquita.

"The clown who smashes plates," said Céleste.

"Oh, that imbecile."

"He's a genius."

"At being an imbecile."

"Just sack her this one time," said Papa.

"Once is all it takes," said Céleste.

Mariquita fanned herself. "Perhaps we shall teach Pierre to hand out walking papers."

Céleste smiled. "We shall tell Maybelle, 'The elephant requests your presence.'"

"He desires to see you in his pen."

"He was very disenchanted with your performance."

"Perhaps I shall have him post the callback sheets next."

"Hush, you two," said Papa, wheeling on Céleste. "Take her to dinner. Maxim's."

"Papa, she's been caught red-handed, stealing Loïe's dance."

"Don't order wine."

Céleste didn't get how Papa had survived without her—his Folies run, six years and counting. Everyone liked him for his untarnished reputation, but to appear spotless before the world had consequences. She was just glad she was old enough to do something about it, and grateful that Papa was acknowledging his foibles enough to *let* others do something about it, even if this acknowledgement was in a low-key way that skirted all responsibility and came with dirty work.

Céleste sighed.

She hated being so hard on Papa. In spite of his shortcomings, he must've been doing something right. The man had built an empire. The Folies rivaled the Olympia and the Casino de Athènes, and he was starting to attract the haute bourgeoisie. He scouted talent like she hunted demons—by knowing what to look for, from experience. He'd found some duds—to be sure—but his success was owed to the hires that didn't take advantage of him, like Mariquita, and the Barrison Sisters, masterly upholding the Folies brand of vulgar elegance. When it came to something he cared about, Papa had gone out and made opportunities. Like father, like daughter.

"I'll ring Maybelle for tonight." Céleste could eat and sneak off to hunt demons.

"Formidable. Gustave will chauffeur."

"Oui, oui, Gustave."

"No running off to café concerts. Do not leave Gustave's side."

Mariquita bowed out of this father-daughter bonding time and stalked down the wings. Pierre let out a trumpet horn.

Mariquita rapped the cage. "Not now, Pierre."

Céleste smiled up at Papa. "There is simply nothing to worry about."

"When Gustave is on duty, I don't."
"Oui, Papa."
"You let Gustave chaperone."
"Oui, Papa."

A BAR
AT THE
FOLIES BERGÈRE

Céleste walked into the porcelain light of the Winter Garden. As her eyes adjusted from the shadow of the auditorium, Gustave shoved his handsome face in her ear like a nosy usher, the brim of his top hat resting momentarily on her head. Any closer, and she would've felt his mustache.

"Wait at the center bar," he said in a tone that both spooked and aroused her. "I have to talk with Édouard."

She looked down his coat, which revealed just enough of his Breton striped shirt to evoke menace to boulevardiers and bystanders in the street. He had long since dispensed with the cravat, two of three trademarks of Les Apaches—a gang of muggers who dressed like dandies. They were very fashionable and very dangerous. Céleste advanced her gaze lower into Gustave's waist for a peek at the group's third trademark, a brass knuckle revolver with a folding knife mounted to the drum in lieu of a barrel.

Was it the fact Gustave was a former Apache that scared her periodically, or was it because he reminded her too much of Théo when he popped out like that? She typically found Gustave's past thrilling. It wasn't his fault he occupied the same position as her old chaperone. Gustave had nothing to do with the Incident. Perhaps the fear was an admixture of the two; Gustave's gang activities plus the Incident, painted over by a layer of passion as she inhaled his oaky aftershave.

"I love it when you tell me what to do." She went to nibble his earlobe.

"Not here, Céleri," he scolded.

While Gustave departed into the theater door behind the grand staircase, Suzon, the barmaid, spotted Céleste's approach and rested her welcoming arms on the marble top before a bowl of oranges. Her strawberry-blonde hair showed threads of gray, tied back and trailing on the lace of her midnight blue jacket with a posy of red carnations pinned to her bosom.

"What'll it be, princess?" she asked warmly.

Céleste climbed onto the lily pad stool. "La Tour Eiffel."

Suzon clanked the phone onto the bar, decorated in licorice plant, shaped like the Eiffel Tower. Céleste lifted the receiver from the cradle and tucked it underhead while she cranked the handle.

"Salut, Castel Béranger," she told the operator. "Can I have Maybelle Stuart? Suite 406. Yes, I'll hold."

Suzon grabbed some champagne bottles off the bar and buried them in the ice chest. Céleste traced the smooth coins of licorice with the pads of her thumbs.

"Maybelle speaking."

"Bonsoir, Maybelle. It's Céleste." She played with the frosted pewter on the phone's base. "You know how sometimes in life we hit a dead end, artistically?"

"I suppose."

Céleste put herself in Maybelle's shoes. If she were getting the sack, she'd like to be told right away, not buttered up over lobster and sent packing. But Maybelle had been with the Folies for a couple months now. Maybe she deserved an in-person send-off. Could Céleste do that again? Look an employee in the eyes and crush her hopes and dreams? It was like letting go of a family member. It was a dirty job that shouldn't have been hers, but someone had to do it.

Céleste braced the stick against her head with both hands. "Maybelle, I hate to be the one to tell you, but we have to let you go."

"What? Why? Was it my act?"

"Sort of. An acquaintance of yours came by. Loïe Fuller. Papa hired her."

The tink of bar glasses filled the silence. Céleste pulled a face, expecting Maybelle to telepathically strangle her with the cloth cord of the phone. Instead, Maybelle answered sullenly, "It was only a matter of time."

"Think of the Folies as a stepping stone." Céleste coiled the cord around her fingers. "There's the Menus-Plaisirs, Ambassadeurs, El Dorado. Reinvent your act, and you'll find somewhere else."

"Tell it to my heart." Her voice split in two. "I can't stop it from sinking."

"Je suis désolée, Maybelle. Really, I am. Wait at your apartment. I'll bring you some fine wine, on the house."

"Why didn't you say the Olympia?" She sniffled.

"Too big. I'm starting small, myself."

"That's true. You are a figurante, aren't you? An extra?"

"Oui, but I dance really close to the star."

"In divertissements."

She was really laying it on thick. Star ballerinas only danced the divertissements. They were numbers that diverted from the plot. In opera, the star ballerina would play the lead for the whole show. Here, the lead was reserved for celebrities, and Papa was batting around the notion to cast courtesans. Guest dancers were rarely classically trained, so Mariquita included divertissements to keep real ballet onstage.

Céleste used to be a star, she wanted to say, in Mariquita's children numbers, though she decided not to defend her rank if it meant helping Maybelle feel better.

"Oui," Céleste conceded, "I'm an extra for one dance a show. These music halls are cutthroat." If only she could dance like she had in her remarkable act that would teach Maybelle, but that was in happier times. "Do you want the juice or not?"

"Merci, Céleste." She sobbed. "Top shelf, s'il te plait." The line went dead.

Céleste set down the licorice stick. She had ruined someone's life. It was true that Maybelle had stolen Loïe's act, but that didn't make firing her any less difficult. No wonder Papa avoided it like the plague. He would actually prefer the plague. He was not the impresario to fire pistol shots and smash chairs to heighten each orchestra's climax like Philippe Musard had at the Opéra. Papa was subtle, bordering on invisible.

Céleste breathed a sigh of relief. The hard part was over.

Maybelle knew who she was: a discount Loïe Fuller. And Loïe knew who she was: a discount Maybelle Stuart. One by flattery, the other by incentive, at least for the last Friday and Saturday in October. Is that all a person was? An actress made up of the people in her life? Like attracted like, did it not? Couldn't you tell a lot about someone by who they associated with? Were they so interchangeable? What about their differences? There had better be differences. How could anyone stomach a world full of mindless puppets simply copying one another?

It was as terrifying as looking into the mirror and not seeing your reflection look back. Suzon blew a lock of her strawberry bangs out of her eyes while she sliced limes and oranges on her cutting board. She was to the left. On the right sat Monsieur Desormes, the bearded and mustachioed composer of fifty-two years of age with slicked back hair and a thin head, reading the *Journal d'Athènes.*

Directly in front, the Louis XV mirror failed to display the woman at the phone, her hair frizzy blonde, her chignon at the back, the curls on her sides, her violet day dress by Doucet with the big gigot sleeves, her oval head, her rosy cheeks, her eyes perpetually happy like a sea otter's to perpetually betray her heart, her dragonfly pendant by Lalique, the insect's wings an interlocking arabesque, her short-brimmed hat with fresh gardenias, her skin touched by the sun from a recent trip to the

Greek Riviera, her button nose, her fleshy lips parted open to wonder where she was, and her blue-green eyes—the windows to the soul—remote from the rest of her.

She would've loved to say the mirror was haunted.

It wasn't.

She was.

She only saw the Winter Garden.

Dichondra, a plant with leaves made of tiny platelets, showered from the fluted columns of the arcades like silver francs, each column braced at their feet by spires of wormwood—*Artemisia absinthium*—Its leaves resembled snowflakes, but green like the beet drink and gray like frosted glass. The metallic spires and showering stems swooped into whiplashes and attached to the second story, another level of arches with railings, where silver ragwort sprouted on the posts of the balustrade.

The ceiling was tent-like, iron-framed white glass, germinating chandeliers of lunaria, the silver dollar plant, its seed pods transposed into stained glass and lit by electric bulbs to brighten the coins and the muted daylight pouring in from the sky. Beneath the center fixture rose an impressive fountain modeled on the one in Square Louvois and remodeled by Papa with some readily accepted creative input.

Céleste had the four women posing between the water dishes sculptured after her patron gods: Psyche, goddess of the soul; Aphrodite, goddess of love; Asteria, goddess of the stars; and Chloris, a flower nymph. They had chosen her. Not Apollo or Athena or somebody. These four. Somehow, through her mixis they had become a part of her.

Psyche, in her milky patina, in windswept robes, stared through the raindrops into the mirror exactly where Céleste sat. Was this flat-faced beauty meant to fill the void or guide her to the genuine article by butterfly wing? Was it having a purpose that breathed life into the soul, or merely being present? She dwelled on the past and hoped for a future—and being immortal, this could go on indefinitely. Dwelling and hoping was a chore. It was difficult for her to stand out.

Her purpose was at the whim of Mariquita. Maybe Céleste would stumble upon her essence like Loïe Fuller did for her serpentine dance—by accident. It was that thing that made Loïe feel alive, the ability to change her identity into a flower and a serpent and a hurricane and be at peace with herself, assuming she was.

Gustave leaned over Desormes. "Any rumblings of revolution?"

"Pénis, couilles, seins," Desormes blurted. "No sign of the next Georges Boulanger, if that's what you're asking."

"Well, have your pen ready."

"I'll compose another—merde, baise, pisse—Boulanger March."

"I'm as upset as you are." Gustave removed his top hat. "Isn't that right, Céleri?"

Céleste turned to Gustave. "Et alors?"

"So what?" Gustave said, indignant.

"Oui. Politics is arguing how you think the world should be run. With so many voices to shout over, et alors?"

"Because this godless city is outlawing Christ," said Gustave, growing impassioned. "Priests are no longer allowed on charity boards or in public administration. Any woman on the street can work side by side with nuns in hospitals. Why, I am old enough to remember religion class taught in school before they banned it."

"Gustave, mon cher"—she touched his arm—"what difference can I possibly make? I am a nineteen-year-old woman."

He smiled. "So was Jeanne d'Arc."

Céleste closed her mouth. Maybe she wasn't so powerless as she thought. But diplomacy? Politics?

"Georges Boulanger was a full-grown man," she finally said. "He didn't take back Alsace-Lorraine from the Prussians or stage his coup and oust the Republic."

"He didn't have the prunes." Gustave waved the coward's name out of the air with his hand.

Desormes repeated the action. "He wanted an election. That's not how you revolt."

"Mark my words," said Gustave, "the right man will come along and restore the monarchy. Then the Catholic Church can replant our morals."

"I'm not so sure Catholicism has the answers," said Céleste.

"Ah-ha," said Desormes. "She is a Republican. Sound La Marseillaise."

Gustave set his hands on the bar and spoke authoritatively, solemnly. "Christ is the handbrake to the decadence that consumes us all."

Suzon continued wiping a glass. "You should join a seminary, Gustave."

"He would miss all his favorite women," Céleste teased.

"Je ne sais pas," said Gustave. "As priest, I could hear your confessions, my child."

"Depends if I'm in the mood."

"In the mood for Maxim's, like your father insisted?"

"I am in the mood"—Céleste leaned toward Suzon—"for a Bordeaux."

"One glass or two?" Suzon propped an elbow on the counter.

"The whole bottle."

"I hope Maybelle likes Sauvignon Blanc." She stood the pin on the marble.

"How did you know about Maybelle?"

"Overheard you on the phone."

"Vagin, chatte, con." Desormes took up his cocktail. "Barmaids hear all."

"Céleste?" asked Suzon. "When your father fires me, can I have the Alsace Riesling '68?"

"The older vintage. Pre-phylloxera," said Gustave. "Smart girl."

"What do you say, Céleste?" asked Suzon. "Do you agree to my terms?"

Céleste bit her lip. "So long as you go quietly."

"Sack Suzon?" said Desormes. "She makes the best brandy crustas in the city."

Suzon folded her arms. "After ten years, I better make something right."

"Don't worry." Céleste grabbed the bottle. "You've got tenure. Manet painted you."

"So that's why your father relocated me from the promenoir." Suzon winked. "I'm a permanent attraction."

Desormes lifted his glass to Suzon's reflection. "Santé."

Céleste winked back and headed for the exit, feeling as if the copper Psyche was watching her. Before Céleste reached the door, Gustave caught up.

"Where to, Céleri?"

"Castel Béranger. In the Aeneid. Maybelle needs a parting gift."

"And then Maxim's?"

"If you're good."

"Shh," he scolded, walking past the ticket counter. "We can't do that again."

She flicked her eyes at him and tugged on his coat sleeve. "'Shh'? That's what you said last time."

"I can't betray Édouard's trust, and it would be un-Christian-like."

"You said that last time too."

They walked out of the Folies Bergère, through the cowslip-framed door, and into the iron blossom of the city. Vines sprang from the concrete to form apartments five-stories high, topped with garrets, grown on every side of the road to make the four streets resemble wide-cut floral hallways. Céleste found herself on a slab of tile illustrating the meadow of a pastoral scene.

"This time I won't let you out of my sight." Gustave stood on a lamb tile.

Céleste touched his cheek. "Then how are you going to bring the coach around while I wait here?"

He walked across the shepherdess chiseled next to the lambs and said, "Don't move."

Céleste awaited his return, holding the bottle like a newborn babe, her parasol open to guard its complexion from the sun. Within moments, an acorn on wheels drawn by Clemence and Claudette drove around the corner onto rue Richer. Gustave dismounted from the driver's seat and fetched the carriage door. The Folies' insignia of Orpheus's lyre swung out.

"You covered for me last week," Céleste reminded, putting her bottle on the seat.

"That was last week." He held out his hand. "No gallivanting."

Céleste took it. "He's not going to fire you."

He smiled. "No, *you* will."

She looked at the brim of her hat, displeased. Gustave helped her into the carriage, shut the door, and hopped in the driver's seat. The horses clopped along at an even pace. Purple velour comforted Céleste's bottom as her carriage jounced along rue Royal in the 8th arrondissement, a neighborhood characterized by the gentle curlicues of the pea plant sashaying from buildings in ferrovitreous poetry, as if Viollet-le-Duc and Gregor Mendel's sister had fancied each other hard enough to produce a family of architects for Céleste to enjoy their work while riding in style that made her feel like a bonafide member of Aphrodite's cult of the beautiful buttocks.

Céleste could hear Gustave sigh through the acorn walls as they passed Maxim's. If only he could understand that she needed wings tonight there would be less formality. If he but knew there was a voice in her chest whispering, *I am nothing, I am nothing, I am nothing*, there would be no resistance. She had danced around his ethics and morals—and they were very worthy ideals to strive for—but now it was time to finish the song. When a girl had to fly, she had to fly, and the hunger be fed.

Clemence and Claudette trotted into the tunnel of thorns on Athenian Boulevard along the Seine. Céleste loved this street. It was like they had shrunken into chipmunks inside of a rose garden, their little hollowed acorn steered by two field mice, each building's girders jutting above the thoroughfare sharpened into stems and blooms. Céleste slid open the mini-door to speak with her top-hatted fellow mouse.

"Gustave, there's a nice park behind Castel Béranger. Go there."

The reply came in hoofbeats on the brick-laden boulevard. No voice. He must've been contemplating. Go to the park? In the back? Whatever for? You know exactly what for, Gustave. But how do you know of this park? Who else have you been there with? No one, Gustave. Starflower only patrolled the whole city. And it's really a courtyard. Since when are you jealous? Answer already!

"D'accord," came a response other than street noise.

"Thanks, doudou."

Gustave broke off the boulevard and snaked into the Aeneid arrondissement. They rolled by the façade of Castel Béranger. The fluted pillars listed at opposite sides of the main doors. Whimsical climbing plants squiggled their way up the gate. Bowed windows impressed upon the sky from the edifice on a diagonal, one floor at a time, like a staircase, leading Céleste around to the half-enclosed courtyard, where Gustave parked the acorn under a tree in the afterglow.

Céleste reached all around the white interior to draw the blinds and smiled, giddy inside, as Gustave opened the carriage and climbed in. She turned on the bench, her back to him, with her come-get-me smile, her lust-for-flight smile. A kiss touched her neck beneath the lobe of her ear, leaving a fresh dew upon her skin, and another. Gustave began unlacing her bodice in earnest. She felt the pulls and tugs of his fingers, these pleasure-makers, sensitive digits, brushing against her spine until the top of her dress opened like a bearded iris.

He gripped her shoulders and guided her to face him.

"This isn't a *this for that* situation," he said, firmly. "I won't cover for you running about to all the caf'concs in town."

"You think I'm buying your silence? Au contraire, Gustave. I think a woman can make love to you for your handsome face alone."

She placed her hat on the cushion.

"I know you too well. You're not a schoolgirl anymore. After this, we are going into that apartment to give Maybelle her wine."

"Who will watch the horses?"

"The horses shall watch themselves." He eyed the front of the coach. "Honestly, Cél. Édouard may detest conflict, but push the man to the edge, he will lash out." He looked her up and down. "I can't have his most prized possession damaged."

"It is a misprint." She slid out of the tulip dress, feeling the sack with her costume in it stored in the pleat. Holy Aphrodite, how she missed bustles.

"His most prized possession is Les Folies Bergère." She turned and did a little hop. "It's his escape from family responsibility."

"I care not to test that theory." He unclasped her corset.

"He'd be working every day, every night if we had one strong man or ten."

"Fine. It's Les Folies Bergère he treasures most. We work for the Folies. Therefore, my original statement rings true. I can't damage the goods."

"Then don't be so rough with me." She stepped out of her bottoms and went for his shirt.

He kissed her full on the lips. Pink, delicate skin joined together. His mustache bristled her nose, and he pushed her back.

She gasped in the sweetly perfumed space.

"A flower grows best when exposed to the elements," he said, as if giving himself permission.

She was well aware that any resolution to him covering for her or not covering for her had slipped through the cracks.

He sat across from her while she unbuttoned his pants and spun around, feeling the heat of his pistil caress her well of petals. The scent of nectar flooded the compartment and carried her off to a distant place, somewhere beyond the carriage skylight. She reached up through the red-leafed tree, plucked a star fastened to the firmament, and pressed it to her body to illumine the empty seat of her soul.

She saw grassy hills and meadows and trees on hilltops, homely nooks under wooden bridges that she wanted to get lost in just for fun. All the while, nebulas pulsated in her chamber, bone deep. The glow burned hot and warm and hot and warm, a charming interplay within a once-enchanted hollow. Golden suns brightened her walls, calming the chaos left behind by a night trapped in the basement of the Cabaret du Néant.

The star exploded, titillating all senses, her head swimming. Starbeams blasted through the skylight, her chin locked on the heavens while her soul-throne captured the slow-dying flash, and she was content. The world was well. Her nerves stopped clamoring and basked in the radiance.

She turned to Gustave, touched him on the cheek, and kissed him over her shoulder. As her hand drifted to his neck, it caught on a thin gold chain with a pendant.

"What's this?" she asked, breathing heavily.

He sat her across his lap. "A miraculous medal."

She inspected the oval in the gleam. It was an image of the Virgin Mary, her arms open before her, like how Manet had posed Suzon.

"What's it say?"

Gustave held his chin high for her to read. *Ô Marie, conçue sans péché, priez pour nous qui avons recours à vous.*

"O Mary," said Gustave, "conceived without sin, pray for us who have recourse to thee. Remember the tale?"

The story tugged at her childhood, though some of it she'd forgotten. "It's hazy."

"Sister Catherine Labouré," said Gustave, "had witnessed a Marian apparition in a convent on the rue de Bac in 1830. Our Lady charged the nun to have a medal struck and appeared as the image you see on the mold—Mary standing on a sphere, crushing a serpent. The bright rays of light shining from her hands are the graces she grants to those who ask her."

"Why are there gaps in the rays?"

"They are the graces for the people who do not ask."

It was hard to reconcile Jesus and Mary with these Greek deities who'd invaded her life. There were no nymphs in the Bible, only demons.

"Does it work?" she asked, unsure.

"If it's worn with confidence." He ran a hand down her back. "There was a cholera epidemic two years later. It killed twenty thousand Athenians. Those who were ill and wore the medal survived."

"Oh Gustave, you're such a chaste pervert. I love you."

"And you're an honest liar." He kissed her on the forehead. "You're sure you won't come with me?"

"Well, not in there." She laughed, handing him the bottle. "Tell Maybelle I say, bonne chance."

"Very well." He got dressed and closed the carriage door without a fuss.

Céleste put on her hat. "That was easy, eh?"

She raised the blinds and watched Gustave walk the stone path to the courtyard entrance, the back as lavish as the front. An electric arc lamp lit his way. She would wait three minutes and go. Tonight could be the night she found a cacodemon and forced him to reveal his cache of stolen keepsakes—namely, hers. Then she could return her pearl to her shell. All she had to do was slip past Gustave. She pulled the door handle down and pushed out. It didn't give. What? It was locked!

She bounced to the other door. Locked too!

"Gustave, you blackguard swine." He had seen a locksmith.

C'était bien. She hopped to the other bench. C'était bien. If he came back and found her gone, he would need a reason for her vanishing act other than magic. Oh, génial. It was an illusion. *You see, Gustave, when you opened the door, what you saw was a mirror, and your captive slipped away undetected.* Oui, she learned it from the Isola Brothers. Where did the mirror come from? She clapped her hands together. Excellent question. She pointed her pressed fingers to her chin, looking around for an alternative.

Skylight. She pulled the lever and opened the hatch. It was thirty centimeters across. And a thumb. Could she even fit through this thing? Of course she could. *Can't you see, Gustave?* She had wriggled through the opening like a gommeuse épileptique. Oui, an epileptic gummy, the singers you see onstage that tremble and gyrate and lose their minds. She had a waspy waist like Polaire. Not quite like Polaire, but close enough to Polaire to fit through that chute with some imagination. Super.

She had her excuse. All that was left to do was think airy thoughts.

Soap suds.

Her dress flaked off her body and crumbled into grainy particles. Her skin, her hair, her bones all crumbled to dust. The acorn's velour benches, the white polished wood, the windows—they dispersed into the brush strokes of an impressionist painter. Her world dissolved into an underwater experience with Vincent van Gogh, who must have been visited by her patron nymph, Chloris, to serve as his muse. Céleste's body composition—made entirely of pollen—sifted through the narrow skylight and emerged into the courtyard where she floated above the trees to think dense thoughts.

Pierre the Elephant.

Her pollen rushed into position, accumulating into her lithe figure, her limbs poised back, fluttering with the aid of butterfly wings over Castel Béranger and its creeping jenny-styled roof. Instantly, she fluttered in a circle to keep aloft, perceiving a tremendous sense of ballon—the feeling of being suspended in the air at the height of a jump—times one hundred, her big, sheeted wings pumping open and closed in figure eights, the soft scales patterned like that of a monarch's, pink and white and black. Floodlights set the Eiffel Tower ablaze in amber, more beautiful than the Folies' bar telephone, fashioned like a fleur-de-lis. Over the iron, shrub-topped rooves, past the tower, lay Hermes Hill. Sacré Coeur, the grand cathedral, dominated the summit.

A chill traveled up Céleste's tailbone, out to her hind wings, up her spine to her fore, and onward where the frisson settled in her neck and perked up her blonde hairs, which had been let down to flail in the autumn wind. Her soul called to her from somewhere on the butte. It was a spiritual connection, one shared between lovers, the body and the soul. It was silly, but it was as though her soul called to her from the depths of the underworld through its demonic gates. Which demon would be her ticket down?

Well, her pink dress was on, her purple one slung around her shoulder in a sack. *What say she find out?*

FLEUR D'ÉTOILE

Chaotically, she fluttered, the breeze on her open toes, twirling through her hair, antennae bouncing on her head as she followed the Seine above the bark-coated garrets, flew north and wound up on the back slant of the butte. Her sandals touched down in an alleyway. She placed her hand on the roughshod wall and poked her head out on rue des Saules at the Nimble Rabbit Cabaret. Men in newsboy caps smoked rolled cigarettes by picnic tables. Accordion music rang through the green shuttered windows of the little house and echoed into her plaster alley, resurrecting visions of Théo's Carnival of Animals.

Should one of these men be possessed by a demon, she might lure him from the party to follow her. Should they glance down the street at her now, they'd see a girl in a carnival mask. She would have to fix that.

Her wings folded through the embroidered slits on her bodice and into her spine. *Think light thoughts.*

Dandelion clock.

The opening of the alley, framed by its narrow walls, showed a fence across the street; diffused into wavy lines as she dematerialized into pollen, clothing and all.

Anvil.

She rematerialized wearing her purple dress, the pink one tucked behind her butt under the bell of her skirt. Now she was in business. She walked the shorn brick path, feeling the eyes of the artists look her way as she sauntered by. Some of them were sozzled on absinthe, waiting for their muse to return, but even drunk men had morals. Women too. It would take a demon to follow her around the corner and down the street.

When she neared the edge of a neighborhood vineyard, a horse and cart trotted by, and she turned. The orange lamp at the Nimble Rabbit, shining on its curvy fence, captured no silhouettes in the street. Nobody had followed. The gardenia on her hat wilted in the moonlight. It was just as well. If an unescorted woman didn't provoke a demon, then the street was demon-free.

She would cut through the Wild Garden into Renoir's backyard and come out on the next crossing. Where was that entrance? *There.* She stepped out of the trench of buildings with their sinuous girders and into the woods they emulated. Black locust trees, sycamore, and tall maples played tricks on her as she wandered the brambles uphill. At the end of a short wall of stacked rocks, a light caught her eye. She looked again. It was gone. She stepped backward. Her shoe crunched twigs. There it was again. The woods—formless, shapeless—displayed the moon on a mirror on the earthy floor.

A wooden fence surrounded a pond, letting the moon appear and disappear as she trekked onto a path with compacted steps and a railing, leading up to a small glade haunted by the trickle of running water. Marble nymphs supported a pergola over a rectangular pool, as if this very spot let her commune with her goddesses. She peered over the edge hoping to see a glint of moon on glass or perhaps her long lost holy water and found nothing but a bum note in her heart. Someone must've fished out the vial of holy water years ago. Were the marble nymphs judging her for checking? She couldn't tell.

Leaves fractured the moonlight and obscured their faces in shadow. Their hidden eyes watched her stare at them, then she looked up at the sky, at the crows in the trees. *Focus, Céleste.* The nymphaeum was her marker. There was another path leading down—if she could remember where she left it.

She backtracked to the opening of the glade and saw the path had a fork. Her heels stamped divots into the soil, progressing into clicks. Slabs of stone led her down a mossy stairwell—the same by which the freckled lady had once fled—with an arched doorway at the bottom, barred by a gate. Paint chips on the lateral bar stuck to her palm as she pushed on the door. Hinges shrieked. She stood erect, feeling foreign eyes drill into her skull. Quickly, she threw her chin at her shoulder. Wind rustled the leaves at the top of the stairs. Ivy crackled against stone.

She stepped through the gate, off the slab and onto leaves. Somebody was breathing behind her. She stood deathly still. Her pupils fled to the corners of their sockets. She spun. A man in a smock and cap watched her. His gaze was intense. He seemed to be a part of the masonry, until he lunged from the archway. Hands pressed her shoulders with such force she launched onto her back. The thud choked a grunt from her throat. Before she could react, he crawled to the ground and sat astride her body.

Mon Dieu! Breathe. Breathe. She took slow, obstructed breaths, fighting the urge to let her mind escape her body. His freezing hands tore at her bodice. He must've been watching her the entire time, fantasizing about her soul, anticipating when to strike. Her brain hurried to catch up. This was no time to dissociate.

Stay present, she told herself, or else she'd be sucked into the past through her old wound. If she could smell, it meant she was still here. She expanded her lungs, the inhale sweeping up cloves and cedar and sweat. The scent of alcohol and linseed oil permeated the air around the man, unintended fuel that kept her lucid in her own time period. The odor was sharp and overwhelmed her perfume.

He ripped the fabric on her chest and plunged his fingertips into her skin. Deeper they sank until he buried his wrist and squeezed.

"Where is your soul?" The question rattled out of his windpipe like nails in a tin can.

His voice wheeled the image of a casket into her mind and opened the lid. Inside lay her waxen bust. The ice had preserved her beauty, and an artist had applied his bronze, giving the illusion of her natural color.

The stars moved above the branches, circling Polaris. A flashback fired—dread, pain, and loss hurled toward her from that unknown place emotions come from, raw as the day they had first invaded. Le Sorgueur. The Thief. The demon. Théophile. Non. *Stay back.* It wasn't her fault. Not. Her. Fault. Not real. She dug into the soil at her sides, clinging to whatever scrap of reality she could grab hold of.

Deep breath in. Deep breath out. It was no use. Memories leaked into her mind's eye against her will. The scene of a basement began to manifest out of her exhale, which dissipated before her into the hazily defining room. Unable to move, she found herself pinned to a stone bench, her deathbed, shedding silent screams, the arc of her spine on a slab, waiting for the Thief to reach in with his ghostly hand and steal her soul.

It wasn't Théo, she tried to console herself. Her old chaperone would never do such a thing. It was the cacodemon who possessed him. But why did Théo bring her here, to the Cabaret du Néant? He was the town dipsomaniac—and he welcomed the demon inside him—prying, clawing, groping for her sweet, juicy soul.

Non-non-non, she refused to go there, refused to stay trapped in that time, struggled to latch on to something, anything. *O Mary, conceived without sin, pray for us who have recourse to thee.* Her fist brimmed with light. The man's inkwell-eyes narrowed.

"Where is your soul?" asked the man.

She opened her palm, blinding him. "That's what I'd like to know."

Goose feathers.

The outline of the man in the smock fragmentized into swirls. His ears, nose, mouth, and eyes enlarged into black pits that she penetrated on all points. In the misty tunnels of the artist's body, she swam, swam an ocean around his heart to the middle of his rib cage, and pried the demonic claw off his empty soul-throne. Her tendrils mingled with the black smoke and flutter-kicked to the surface. Ambient starlight brushed the wild-stemmed, iron gate in blue strokes as she emerged.

Wrecking ball.

Céleste reconstituted herself as Fleur d'Étoile, carnival mask on, hands thrust out, glowing yellow. The man hit the ground a sack of potatoes. Black, reptilian, slimy, the emerged demon swiped a rip in the canvas of her world, creating a portal, to which it gathered its spindly limbs and weaseled through. Light absorbent, the smoke hole dimmed her yellow flares while the demon shied inside the pocket to escape their spiritual power.

This was it, a chance to reclaim her soul. She didn't get her hopes up, but she dove in nonetheless. She barely had time to react when the demon's tail lashed out like a whip, cracking her around the wrist and proceeded to throw her into the lichen poking from the walls.

Hot air balloon.

The dilapidated chateau masonry spreading the perimeter swirled into an abstract painting and sharpened starkly.

Grand piano.

She appeared behind the demon's back, its spine plated like a stegosaurus, and she unleashed a volley of shooting stars from the heels of her palms. Blue projectiles shrieked at its gangly body at close range and exploded on impact in a burst of sparks.

Bo-bo-boum!

The bombardment knocked the beast onto its belly. Smoke rose from the inky floor like seaweed. The sky was dome shaped, extending into a sphere on all sides, forming an arena about the size of a stage. It was a shadow room, all right. Occupancy: two. And only one of them was leaving here alive.

"Take me to the shadowlands," she demanded.

"Leave me alone," croaked the demon.

"Leave *you* alone?" Céleste put her palms together. "You tried to steal my soul! Who knows how many you robbed before I showed up?"

His guttural voice died to a whisper. "Six."

This poor, dangerous creature. "Why do you have to steal?"

"It gives me power." It dragged its claws along the floor, skating around to face her.

She tilted her head. "Why did you possess that man?"

"Because he let me."

Her eyes widened. Perhaps Théo really had let his demon consume him. *Wake up, Céleste, this was no time for cold weather.*

"Where do you hide the souls you steal?" she asked.

The demon lifted its head, snooty, too good for the question.

"Open a hole into that godforsaken place," she said, "or I won't be so nice."

"Come over here, and I'll tell you where your soul is."

Céleste looked both ways, as if crossing the street, and marched up to the demon, stopping within biting distance of its snout. She turned her ear toward him.

"I'm listening," she said quietly.

The beast hissed in her ear, exhaling his rotten garbage breath.

"Die, nymph."

Cotton candy.

Her particles whisked through his teeth as his jaw snapped shut. Bright light intruded upon him from behind—orange bands of paint smattering her portrait of the lizard among the ruins.

Watermelon.

Céleste shielded her eyes from the fire, stomaching the squeals of roasted demon as it disintegrated to ash. The flames spumed out from a pair of hands attached to a lanky Gentoo woman. When the demon was nothing but a scorch mark indistinguishable from the rest of the floor, the woman lowered her cannons and turned. Where had this yak-horned, black-braided, belly-dancing automaton come from? Was she with the lizard?

Céleste aimed her fire-arms. "Move, and I shoot."

The woman raised her goggles, revealing two incandescent red irises. She let out a long sigh. "Je suis une nouvelle nymphe." She let her gob hang open, as if she couldn't believe her eyes. "You don't know the hours I counted looking for someone like me."

EREBUS ROOM

For so long, Nayla had wanted to fly down and introduce herself. Now here she was, being inspected by Fleur d'Étoile. The nymph's eyes were glazed over in her mask like gulab jamuns, and her lips wore a contented smile. The woman loved pink. She had a pink bodice, a gladiator skirt with strips fashioned to resemble flower petals, and black sandals with thongs laced around her ankles. The most striking thing about her was her hair. Pink strands of spaghetti cascaded hurly-burly through her blonde with a mind of their own. She was beautiful.

"Who are you?" asked Fleur d'Étoile. Her wings unfolded in giant screens.

"Nayla binti Azmi," she said, relieved. "I come from the German Orient. I mean you no harm."

"You're very bold to go throwing your name around to complete strangers, eh? If I were an ordinary person—"

"Nemesis." Nayla flashed the name like a hundred-gold-mark bill. "I know. I found out firsthand by saying much less than my name. Yours is Céleste Marchand. You like to see shows at the Folies Bergère."

"You little sneak." Céleste abruptly looked at the floor and leveled her pink marble eyes at Nayla. "Who did you tell?" She stepped forward.

Nayla stepped back, fearing a face-full of Bengal fire. "No one. I would never jeopardize your life so carelessly."

Céleste smiled. "Oh, Nemesis can't kill me. I'm immortal. It's the people in my life I'm worried about."

Immortal? How could she have achieved such a feat? Was she one with Brahman? Did she drink to celebrate life? So many questions. *Better stick to the plan, Nayla.*

"If you know I'm Starflower," Céleste continued, "do you think anyone else does?"

"A man called your name inside of your carriage. But he said, '*Céleste, don't stop.*' Not 'Starflower.' No one else was around when you went poof. I saw you from the sky." Phoenix wings burst from Nayla's back to prove it.

"That's creepy."

"The wings?"

Céleste blushed. "That you heard me in my carriage."

"Not you. The man, Gustave."

Céleste covered half her face. "How many days have you followed me for?"

Nayla bit her lip. Gray clouds floated across the crystal-ball hemisphere.

"You're not my first spy," said Céleste.

"Other nymphs tracked you down?"

"Men."

"Must be nice," Nayla muttered. Was the attention similar to the flattery bestowed her by the late Capitaine Beauvais?

"How long have you been watching?"

"Long enough to see you help people in need," said Nayla, "even if it means using yourself as bait."

This was as good an opener as any. Nayla moved her mouth to speak again but stopped.

Beauvais shrieked in the caverns of her mind, laying prone with his men, run through by Arachne. *Bang. Bang. Bang.* Ravi uncle, Kameera, Baba—she could not involve more lives. Céleste was a good person. She didn't deserve to become a spider snack. It was too much guilt to live with.

Isn't that why you are here, Nayla? To escape the cycle of life and rebirth? To become one with Brahman? To end your lifetimes of suffering? Céleste was no ordinary girl. She could fly and shoot Bengal fire and poof into smoke. She had drunk a mixis. She was a new nymph, for Shiva's sake. And immortal! She fought hell spawn for a living. So long as all the facts were presented up front, the decision and responsibility would fall on her.

"I am someone in need," Nayla continued.

"Do you have a demon that needs exorcising?"

"Nein."

Céleste braced her hip. "Is your soul lost in the shadowlands of Hades?"

Nayla dragged her foot on the ground. "Nein." She held her arm. "And, er, it's a land that has shadows, but it is not called 'shadowland.' It's called Erebus. It's a part of Hades where the dead pass immediately after death. Right now, we're in an Erebus Room, one of thousands of connecting chambers accessed only by cacodemons."

"Have you been to Erebus?" Céleste asked excitedly. "Do you know how to get in?"

Nayla shook her head. "Why do you want to get there so badly?" She squeezed the bridge of her nose and waved aside the question. "Your soul is there."

Céleste frowned. "Oui."

"I wish to find a mythological item," Nayla confessed. "The Cap of Hades."

"So, what are you going to do? Yank it off his head?"

Nayla folded her arms. "It's not on his head. It is in a vault called the Hall of Fabled Objects. By the Phlegethon River."

"Phlegethon..."

Had Céleste not done any research? She just got her powers, and up and became immortal? Boah. "There are five rivers in Hades. It's the one on fire. I'm surprised you don't know. French Athens has libraries."

"I'm sure we do." Céleste's wings slowly fanned open and closed.

"The door is guarded by Arachne. If we bop her on the head, you can poof inside the vault and collect the helmet."

"And what do I get?"

"You help me," she said, "and I will help you find your soul." Céleste stared.

"Please," Nayla said, "I've come all this way. I can't beat Arachne on my own. I need another new nymph."

"You don't know what I'm up against," said Céleste. "These demons..." She rubbed her chest by her heart. "They cut holes in victims' bodies, committing partial murders. My vase is fractured in so many pieces I want to lie in a bed of broken glass to try to reglue them. I'm not dead, nor am I alive. I remember what the vase looked like before the demon smashed it, sort of. There is a voice..." She concentrated on the floor. "It tells me I am nothing." She checked over her shoulder. "In the place where my soul should go. Somedays, I feel this is the day I silence the voice once and for all, this is the day I rejoin my soul and feel complete, feel love emanating from my own being, and know another soul can love me in return. Then somedays, I feel doomed to search forever."

Feel complete... Feel love... "You are seeking the divine," said Nayla.

"Oui, you could put it like that. My soul, it appeared like a—"

"—white flame."

Céleste knitted her brow and tilted her head.

"I see Thanatos take them off the dead," Nayla answered. "He is god of death."

"Are you toying with me? You don't have your soul either, do you?"

If Nayla said nein, Céleste would help her, having removed some personal danger, but lying made Nayla feel guilty and Céleste might've been able to tell.

"Ja, I do."

Céleste shook her head. "I can't let other people feel like this. That goes for you and everyone else. I am the only nymph that I know of in French Athens who fights these vampires."

Nayla took all this in, feeling very sorry, while searching for another verbal inroad that might appeal—if only she could find the courage to bare all.

"It's too much," said Céleste. She raised her palm to the dome and closed one eye for aim. "It was nice to meet you, Nayla."

An energy beam shot through the room's barrier, reopening a hole in the park where they had entered.

"Don't let me catch you spying on me," she added.

Nayla couldn't let her last chance fly away. She had traveled too far, sacrificed too much, acquired too little.

"Please." She grabbed hold of the snake bracelet that entwined itself around Céleste's arm. "I don't want to feel like this anymore."

"Feel like what?" Céleste hopped to the side, sylph-like, anchored to the floor.

"Like I don't want to be in my own shoes. My friend Kameera loaned me some money. Her baba wanted it back. So I told him my baba could pay him. They met, and there was an argument, and my baba died. If I didn't tell Ravi uncle about the money, he would never have gone to my apartment, and Baba would still be alive. No matter how hard I say, 'Nayla, don't blame yourself,' I do anyway." She sniffled. "Je suis désolée. I know you don't know who these people are."

Fluid covered the hole in the sky and solidified to glass.

"You came through a smoke hole and set fire to a demon to ask for my help?" said Céleste. "You poor idiot. Let me hug you."

Nayla leaned her cheek on Céleste's bare shoulder.

"The Cap of Hades grants invisibility, does it not?" asked Céleste. "How will it help?"

"Oh, you see, it will help me visualize Indra's Net, the interconnectedness of all things, and I will become one with

Brahman. I will be complete. Don't you see? We both seek the divine. You want Brahman in you and I want to be in Brahman."

Nayla paused to see if Céleste knew what Brahman was. The attentive gaze implied she did not. "Brahman is absolute reality. It is everything you see and everything you can't. It is the essence of all things living and nonliving. To be one with Brahman is to be free. It's called moksha. I desire moksha. It's kind of like nirvana."

"Nirvana, d'accord," said Céleste. "That's from the Hindu religion."

"It's not quite a religion," said Nayla. "It is a practice. Did the gods not promise you a chance to reach moksha?"

"They promised immortality. You're looking at it."

Nayla hesitated. "Immortal in the same body forever?"

Céleste nodded. "What other kind is there?"

"Becoming one with Brahman," said Nayla. "My gods told me it was possible. If I reach it in this lifetime, I will be fulfilled and, when I die, my spirit will reunite with my creator in the unphysical reality."

"Death doesn't sound so immortal."

"Oh, but it will be beautiful," Nayla continued, feeling good to talk to someone. "He dwells in everything. That means I am everything, and everything is me. I am the earth we stand on, the air we breathe, the water we drink. I am you. I cannot exist without my environment or other people to compare myself to, or how would I know who I am? We're made of the same stuff. I've read the Vedas as a child, and the Upanishads, though I must feel it. I must feel Brahman. I just need the cap for a little boost."

Céleste touched her hand. "Well, if they told you moksha is possible, perhaps your version of immortality is different than mine."

"Maybe." Nayla withdrew her hand. "I—I don't know if I can help you find your soul, but I want to... in exchange for your help to poof inside the vault."

Céleste jerked her head. "I pollinate. I don't poof."

"It looks like a poof."

"How will you help me, exactly?"

"My services, ah. There are other ways into Hades than chasing demons. When someone dies around me, it opens a portal into Hades. To Arachne's Cave, to be exact. It's the same spot every time, by the Phlegethon River and the Hall of Fabled Objects. I believe it's in Tartarus."

"Have you been outside of the cave? Do you know the way into Erebus?"

"Nein. What we need is a psychopomp, a guide to the underworld, a chthonic deity."

"How?"

"From what I can gather, the gods are attracted to artistry. If we can attract a specific god, we can ask him or her to be our guide."

Céleste eyed Nayla's headpiece. "Do you dance?"

"I try. I play sitar."

"We'll need one hell of a masterpiece. I haven't seen any of the major pantheon since my patrons offered me my mixis."

"Nor have I. Only Thanatos and Nemesis."

"What did you do to eek her out?"

"I enlisted a group of legionnaires to fight Arachne. I may have let on that I lived too earthly an existence."

"That must've been rough." Céleste put a hand on Nayla's arm as if to stop her heart from sinking. "It's not your fault, though. You didn't know. There's a lot they don't tell us."

"The attracting a god angle is pretty sour then, huh?"

"Well, I do like the concept. It gives me some ideas." Céleste put a hand on her hip. "We may not find the cap."

"We may not find your soul."

"Have we been dealt a bad hand or what?"

"Ja, a horrible one."

"Your French is quite good for a German."

"Oh, it is nothing."

"Don't belittle it. It takes hard work to learn a language."

Nayla's neck receded like a turtle's. "Eight months of intense study."

"See."

"And my maman was French. She danced at the cabarets."

"French blood, dancer in the family, *and* a nouvelle nymphe. It appears we have more than one thing in common. I have a feeling an alliance might be a nice change."

"I feel..." Nayla's eyelids hung half closed. Her lips quietly spread across her narrow jaw. "Stoned." She walked as if through water. "What is this sensation?"

"Hypnosis. We're between life and death here." Céleste had the same placid expression. "In limbo." She managed a smirk. "Your textbooks don't tell you about feelings, eh?"

"Nein," said Nayla. "I guess not."

"You get used to it." Céleste aimed her palms at the overcast ceiling. "We need to hash this out. Meet me tomorrow at Cabaret de L'Enfer." A yellow light flashed on her hand, preceding a rocket that struck their crystal ball and made a white-powdered smoke hole. "Six p.m.," said Céleste. "Before the drunks show up."

"The drunks?"

"Oui, I hate drunks."

"Me too. Why?"

"They're so unpredictable."

"Right. I'll be there. Danke, Céleste. I don't deserve this."

"Says who?" Céleste winked.

Her wings touched and unfurled in the softest of claps as she fluttered through the smoke in a straight shot.

Nayla glanced at the scorch mark on the ground where the demon had burned, lowered her goggles, and soared into the French Athenian night.

There you are. I nearly lost you. It appears the game is up. You have no doubt discovered these paintings form the very story I am telling. Don't say it. I know what you are thinking. Did the paintings inspire my story, or did the story inspire the paintings? Ah, not so easy with Jacques, is it?

There are some blanks to fill in, of course. May I interest you in the particulars of Nayla adopting French dress, renting a garret, and acquiring a seamstress position at the local workshop?

I thought not. Perhaps some French lessons will rivet you to the orange tiling? We can rehash Nayla's studies.

I suppose you could sleep standing up, although you may bonk your head and damage the artwork.

When we are young, we believe ourselves invincible. Much like Céleste. Add immortality to the mix, combined with her—something bad happened to me, it can't get worse, quand même and et alors—and it only exacerbates the feeling. You wonder how she can live without a soul? Look no further than Ancient Greek philosopher, Parmenides, which is looking pretty far back, if you ask me. To Parmenides, even the dead man has feeling and sensation, deserted by the warm fires of life and given over to the cold, dark, silence. That's right. Perception, emotion, and thought are exercised by our soma, the body, not our psyche, the soul. That is how the Greeks explain it in Homer.

The soul sleeps when we are awake, and is awake when we dream. The only time it is active during our waking hours is when we are in a state of flow, in the act of creation.

I see this photograph has caught your eye. The burnt sienna wall it's hung on was intentional, to enhance the mood. In Fin de Siècle Athens, there were many themed cabarets, ranging from prison to Japan, heaven and hell. Some came with a twist of Greek myth. Here is the waitstaff in this photo. Ah, but were they actors or mystical beings? Nayla would say actors, though Céleste might be inclined to say more. She chose the locale to inspire the plan. You need reality to cultivate fantasy, and a plan is but a dream before action can bring it to life.

Come, we will journey together. See you in hell, my friend.

CABARET DE L'ENFER

éleste parked her Sirius bicycle in the alleyway on boulevard de Clichy and found Nayla beneath the mushroom column, staring at posters for the Folies Bergère. Of all of Jules Chéret's art, it was not Captain Costenténus, the bearded Greek with 320 animal tattoos, or Little Titch, the British dwarf with baggy pants, or even Douroff the clown, who caught Nayla's eye, but Loïe Fuller, front and center. The image showed a pyre burst from Loïe's feet, as if standing on a brazier, while she reached for the typeface.

"You want to see her?" asked Céleste. "I can get you tickets. On the house."

"On the house?" Nayla stopped gawping at the image and blushed, radically transformed from the other night by her gray dress and leg of mutton sleeves.

"My papa is the director."

Nayla gawped wider. "Your family owns it?"

"Oui, my grandparents, but Papa runs everything." She pointed in the direction of the theater, when a carriage swerved around an omnibus. The carriage had a lyre insignia. Quickly, Céleste dove behind the column, stiff against the poster of Little Titch and his oversized shoes.

"What are you doing?" asked Nayla.

"Shh. Pretend to look at the posters."

"I am looking at the posters."

"Non, you're looking at me."

"Now I'm looking at the man on the carriage going by, looking at me. Top hat. Waxed mustache. Dark hair. Cute face."

"Gustave!" Céleste bit her lip and pressed her fingers into the paper. "Glare at him."

Nayla gazed at the street, her pointed chin following the trot, her immense black eyes, ringed by charcoal, set into her Salome-like face, sure to drive him off. When the hoof beats faded, she chewed on her cheek and threw her lightbulbs at Céleste.

"My chaperone," Céleste explained, "looking to horse-whip me."

"He horse-whips you?"

"Whoever grabs it first." Céleste kinked a shoulder and detached herself from the mushroom. "How do you like Athens?"

"It makes me dizzy," said Nayla. "If it were just the buildings, I could bear it. But it's the furniture, the fixtures... There is no refuge."

"It's what you Germans call Gesamtkunstwerk, a total work of art."

"I'll pass. Keep everything but the cabarets. We don't have cantinas like this in the Orient. What adventure!" She faced Cabaret du Ciel and, right next to it, Cabaret de L'Enfer.

At the Cabaret of Heaven, statues of the Olympians posed triumphant on clouds in cold blue light. At the Cabaret of Hell, Cerberus—the large, three-headed pit bull—guarded the balcony above the entrance. Hobgoblins poked their heads out of grilles, trapped in their crannies with writhing female nudes.

"You'll get used to it," said Céleste. "You're already gentrified." She glanced at the rings riding up Nayla's ears and nose. "Somewhat." Céleste gestured to the fangs protruding from the craggy doorway of Hell Cabaret. "Shall we?"

Nayla withdrew a rolled cigarette from between her breasts and struck a match on Loïe's poster. "We shall."

Céleste approached the entrance, doused in crimson.

Steam burst through the nostrils of Cerberus overhead. Nayla jumped and dropped her cigarette. While she ducked in the fog, Céleste read a sign explaining that, should the temperature of this inferno make one thirsty, innumerable beers might be had at sixty-five centimes apiece.

"Enter and be damned! The evil one awaits you!" growled a man with yellowed eyes, judging their party from the hollow of a cloak. "Ah, ah, ah! Still, they come!" He pointed at the forming line. "Oh, how they will roast!" He brushed aside the great lolling tongue from the doorway and called into the fanged beast. "Hist, ye infernal whelps! Stir well the coals and heat red the prods, for this is where we take our revenge on earthly saintliness!"

He stomped the pole of his oar on the ground and raised his jaundiced finger to the group. "One, three, seven. Ten souls for the pit! Follow me hither." He pointed at himself. "I, Charon, will help thee."

Céleste led Nayla into the monster's throat. Streams of silver ran through the volcanic walls. Flames crackled to life in the clefts. Golden ale poured from barrels, spilling toward a hallway which opened into a massive room where tables glowed red and cauldron fires dotted the partitions.

Très bon. Céleste clapped. They still had novelty games set up in each corner, with the bar dead in the center. Weaving in and out of these festivities were red dwarves, the waiters of the place. Charon conducted their group inside the threshold, pivoted, and raised his oar.

"Nymphs, satyrs, welcome to Tartarus!"

A dwarf tugged on Céleste's hand and led her to a table with a mysterious glow that shined on Nayla's chin as she sat.

"Order, s'il vous plait," said the dwarf in devil horns.

Nayla tossed down the menu. "Three coffees, black, with cognac."

"Three?" asked Céleste.

"So I don't have to bother him again."

Their dwarf hollered at the barman, "Three seething bumpers of molten sins with a dash of brimstone intensifier!"

While he scampered off, Céleste took in the spectacular goings on. Taking up the section behind her was a boulder on a sloping track presided over by a tall, bearded man in a loin cloth with bulging muscles. A sign hailed him as Sisyphus. His punishment, to push a boulder uphill.

"Want to play games while we wait for our drinks?" asked Céleste.

"I don't mean to rush," said Nayla, exhaling spiced tobacco, "but whereas you may live forever, I'm a bit strapped for time. I don't care to relearn everything in my next life, accrue more suffering, and seek the cap all over again. Odds are, I will only become"—she spun her head for eavesdroppers—"a nymph in this lifetime."

"Maybe you were a nymph in all of them."

"I doubt it," said Nayla. "As for the plan..."

"Are there nymphs in Hinduism?" Céleste interrupted. "What's the equivalent over there?"

"A nymph is an apsara, who is very good at dancing. You know, that thing you can do to attract a guide to the underworld."

My, she's antsy. "That was my remarkable act."

"Your what?"

"How I attracted my gods. I danced to a packed house in the last days before my soul was stolen. The audience gave me a standing ovation. How about you? What did you do?"

"I built a machine you wear on your back. It moves train cars and almost opens doors."

"The clock thing you wore in the Erebus Room?"

"Ja." Nayla smiled. "Glad you used the proper name."

"Naturally. Do you still have your powers to invent?"

"Ja, but what's the use?"

"Perhaps none in this case. And there's no use for me to create either. Without my soul, I can't dance the same. But my ballet corps can."

"Well enough to attract a god?"

"Je ne sais pas. The most I've seen are nymphs and satyrs lurking in the mezzanine. Perhaps if we all danced at once. Who do recommend we attract?"

Nayla looked at the master of ceremonies as he conducted newcomers into the cabaret. "We could use Charon. He ferries the dead."

"I'm only half dead. He will take me half way. How about Hecate?"

"She told me explicitly to stay out of Arachne's Cave. She's one of my patrons."

"Do tell. Who are your patrons?"

"Hephaestus, Hestia, Hecate, and Coronis—she's a maenad. She is madcap. Who is your nymph? You have four sponsors, correct? I assume one must be a nymph."

"Chloris."

"Is she an oread, a dryad, or a naiad?"

"Who can keep them all straight?" Céleste threw up her hands. "Her skin was magenta. She had large green eyes, full lips, and flowing green hair. Oh, she was beautiful. Her body was covered in nothing but exotic flora, and her breath smelled like roses."

"A limoniad," said Nayla.

"No lemonade," said the waiter.

Nayla jumped.

"Only brimstone intensifiers!" he continued.

The little bugger had snuck up on them.

"This will season your intestines," he informed, "and render them invulnerable, for a time at least, to the tortures of melted iron that will be soon poured down your throats." The mini amphoras glowed in phosphorescent light. "Three francs seventy-five, s'il vous plaît, not counting me. Make it four francs."

"I'm a seamstress," Nayla blurted. "I can't afford—"

Céleste paid the man.

"Thank you well," said their dwarf. "Remember, though hell is hot, there are cold drinks if you want them."

He scampered off again.

Nayla felt her heart. "I meant limo-niad. Chloris's life must be attached to a meadow somewhere. The meadow dies, she dies."

"There was a meadow when I received my mixis. In the Wild Garden. It's the same park we leapt into that smoke hole from last night. Lucky for me, my life isn't attached to a landmark."

"You should defeat Arachne no problem then. She is mortal." Nayla pulled her drink close. "But to have the full picture, who are your other patrons?"

"Aphrodite, Psyche, and Asteria."

Nayla braced the table. "So, you don't acquire your powers from alcohol?"

"You do?" Céleste tensed. "That explains it." She relaxed.

"What do you do? Something with love?"

"Oui, Vidocq," said Céleste. "I make love."

"Love." Nayla peered into her drink. "What was your riddle? Did the gods give you a riddle?"

Céleste nodded, arms at her side. "When you find love, you will become immortal. Et toi?"

"When you celebrate life, you will become immortal. I need to drink to gain powers." Nayla quailed. "After four binges, I burn out and lose them."

"Well, if alcohol gets you off, you don't have to act prim and proper around me. You won't get intoxicated off two brandies."

Nayla dumped a drink down her gullet and wiped her chin with the back of her hand.

"What did you celebrate?" asked Céleste.

Nayla offered an answer with a nervous flip of her hand. "Our meeting."

"Did you celebrate when you first got your mixis?"

"Ja."

Céleste fanned her arms. "Then you are immortal."

"Oh, that settles that, then."

"Oui, all nouvelles nymphes can be immortal quite easily."

"How many have you met?"

Céleste looked around and smiled. "One."

Nayla pinched the bridge of her nose. "So, you drank the mixis, made love, and showed off some powers?"

Céleste nodded at each declaration.

"And that qualifies you as immortal?"

"You doubt my claim, Vidocq?"

"I do. I saw a nouvelle nymphe strung up in Arachne's Cave. Who is this Vidocq you speak of?"

"A famous French detective from a long time ago." Céleste sipped her drink. "Maybe your nymph didn't get her powers yet."

"She had wings."

"Maybe she wasn't a nouvelle nymphe."

"The empty mixis she carried almost hit me in the head."

"Maybe she faked her death."

"With broken limbs?"

"Who knows?"

"I'm not so sure you're immortal," said Nayla. "We better tread carefully."

"Or," said Céleste, "you are immortal too and don't really need the Cap of Hades."

"Oh, nein, I may cycle through lives for eternity, but I need that cap to escape suffering."

"Escape suffering? In this world? Impossible."

"Not if I become one with Brahman. Then I'll be a waterdrop returned to the ocean. I'll be content forever."

"Won't you lose your individuality? How dreadful. Here I am, fighting to be alive, and you're off to lose yourself, to be completely indecipherable from the whole."

"It will destroy the illusion that we are separate from it."

"Destroy." Céleste pointed. "As in, erase? I told you how it feels."

"This is different."

"And what does celebrating life have to do with Brahman?"

"It is the ultimate celebration. It's why my drinking is only a stepping stone, much like making love may be for you."

"Look at you, coming to Athens, trying to smash up my life."

"I'm sorry. I don't mean to. I'm just solving a puzzle, moving pieces around. Maybe I'm wrong. I'm not in Jacoma anymore. People piss in the streets there."

Céleste sighed. "People piss in the streets here, my pet."

"Well"—Nayla followed something over Céleste's shoulder—"do you love Gustave? He's coming this way."

Céleste slouched to the table. "Merde."

The essence of oak intermingled with her perfume. A hand rested on her collar.

"Thought I wouldn't find you in hell?" said Gustave. "These are my old stomping grounds."

"Who were you stomping?" Céleste touched her cheek.

"No one I haven't repented my sins for." Gustave looked at Nayla. "You are?"

"Nayla," said Céleste. "Foreign exchange student. Nayla, Gustave—stagecoach driver."

"Chaperone," Gustave corrected.

"Charming to meet you."

"Oh, you ordered one for me." Gustave wet his mustache with spiked coffee.

"Ja." Nayla scanned the room. "These games look fun."

"Eh, they do." Céleste turned in her seat to choose the perfect pointless task. "Gustave, I bet you can't keep the boulder at the top of that hill."

"Can't I?" He threw a leg on a chair and braced his hip.

"What do you think it's made of?" asked Nayla.

"Papier-mâché." Gustave took off his jacket and rolled up his sleeves. "Don't leave my sight, ladies." He eyed them suspiciously. "No tricks."

"Leave your sight?" Céleste pawed his arm. "I wouldn't miss this event for the world. We'll behave."

Nayla nodded agreeably.

Gustave stretched his arms and left the table. Instantly, Céleste and Nayla hunkered their chins to the glowing surface amid their amphoras.

"It occurred to me," said Nayla. "How do you use Catholicism to explain the pantheon?"

"I don't," said Céleste. "They say they're Greek. I take their word for it."

"I thought you were Catholic."

"I was." She bowed her head. "I was taught by nuns. I wore my crucifix all the time. My spirit kind of... faded."

"But you want your soul back in you. That's Brahman. Brahman made the soul. How do the Greeks explain that?"

"Psyche is goddess of the soul. Perhaps she sits at a cobbler's bench in a workshop somewhere nailing them together all day. Je ne sais pas. How do you not believe them?"

"I do. They appeared to me as Hindu gods. That is who they are."

Nayla was entitled to believe whatever she liked. They could shapeshift into all sorts of things. Meteors. Seeds.

"Did you believe before seeing them?" Céleste asked.

"I... I didn't know they were real," Nayla admitted. "I needed to see to believe."

"Psyche is who I saw," said Céleste. "She mentioned someone helped her through the underworld."

"Eros," said Nayla, "her husband."

Husband... exactly what Céleste needed to find upon her return. Perhaps it was a sign. "If I hadn't thought of that last night, I may not've accepted your help."

"I'm glad you did." Nayla smiled. "I believe Brahman has brought us together."

Céleste wasn't so sure. Although, she had to admit, last night, fighting her attacker, she had regained composure at the exact moment she recited the miraculous medal's prayer. So many people could believe without seeing. Why couldn't she? It defied logic.

"I am King of Hermes Hill." Gustave marched back to the table to which Céleste and Nayla arose like ostriches. "I told you I could do it. Did you see me?"

Céleste clapped. "Incroyable."

"That takes care of strength," Nayla said to Gustave. "What about accuracy?"

Nayla pointed to another corner where Tantalus sat in his dunk tank with a crown askew on his head. Should he reach for the delicious fruit, the branches would rise. Should he stoop to quench his thirst, the water would sink. Or you could chuck a crab apple at the target and put him in the water.

Gustave arched an eyebrow. "It looks..."

"Tantalizing?" guessed Nayla.

"Oui." Gustave unbuttoned his vest. "I'll go two for two. When you're hot, you're hot."

He took another slug of brimstone and got in line to fling apples. Nayla and Céleste curled up to the table once more.

"That's it," said Nayla. "Hermes can be our psychopomp. He will know the way into Erebus."

Céleste was dubious. "How do you suggest we grab his attention?"

"Something eye catching... colorful... ephemeral." She raised a finger. "A poster."

"A poster for the ballet?"

Nayla nodded.

"Wait." Céleste smiled her wide-faced grin. "I've got it. Not just a ballet. A massive variety show at the Folies Bergère."

"The whole show?"

"A Gesamtkunstwerk—a total work of art. The ballet corps alone won't do. But all the best acts. That could do. If we can really attract Hermes, he can lead us to my soul. Then we'll return to Athens, and I'll come with you to get your cap."

"Why not get my cap, then find your soul?"

"Because you asked for my help."

"Your soul is more important." Nayla fixated on the table setting. "More than Hades's cap, I suppose. I don't know one hundred percent that it will work."

"Don't be so down on yourself." Céleste touched her hand. "We'll get them both." She sipped her drink. "But soul first. Also, if we see anyone notable down there, I wouldn't tell them we're breaking into the bank of Hades."

Down there... Céleste scoffed at herself, speaking as though any of this were at all possible. She'd gone soulless for five years. To think, there was a chance at a normal life right before her eyes, a chance to be complete and deal with problems as they naturally came, to sooth her emotions without letting them undo her and reach the summit of an insurmountable Monte Blanc.

Her future daughter would never have to ask, *Does Maman love me?*

What do I wear today? would be a question more in line with the loving family Céleste wanted to have. Eulalie. Étienne. Proud wife. Loving husband. It was all so enticing.

Tantalus climbed out of his pool onto the plank.

"Good arm, Gustave!" Céleste shouted as he reconvened.

"If I beat three games, I get a free drink."

"A free drink in French Athens? They must be rigged."

"Which one ought I try?" Gustave propped a hand on his waist and sipped his brimstone.

Céleste examined the remaining two. The Danaides gathered in a pool around a cauldron handing out buckets. Contestants had to fill the cauldron to the brim using pool water. The catch was that the cauldron had a hole in the bottom. The sign read, *The 49 Danaides (the husband-killers)*, but employing 49 women for a carnival game would've been expensive, so L'Enfer settled for three, and they all clapped and cheered at each contestant's abysmal failure.

"What a frustrating waste of time," appraised Gustave.

"Nayla, we could do it together."

"Ja, but I want to see Gustave on the wheel."

Students turned the crank while their friend vertically spun round. Ixion commanded them to stop after ten spins. When this was accomplished, he let the cad go, free to stumble around and vomit in a barrel to jeers and jocund faces.

"They say Ixion lusted after Zeus's wife, Hera," said Nayla. "Ixion even made love to a copy of Hera made of clouds."

"Are you implying something about our man, Gustave?"

"Sadists, all of you." Gustave emptied his drink, slammed it on the glass table, and set off for his punishment. "No dallying, ladies. I need someone to crank."

Céleste and Nayla traded smiles and followed him to the contest, Nayla bumping into chairs and stepping on Charon's foot.

He shook his oar. "You'll hang for that, sinner!"

"Je suis désolée!"

Ixion, the man with white lipstick smeared on his face, received his due and directed Gustave to the wheel. Gustave placed his top hat on Céleste for safekeeping and stepped right up. Ixion secured his binds. Céleste gathered by the crank next to Nayla, unsure of when to start.

"Ah, you!" Ixion cried down to Céleste. "Why do you tremble? How many men have you sent hither to damnation with those beautiful eyes"—he winked—"and those rosy, tempting lips? Ah, for that, you have found a sufficient hell on earth. But you"—he turned fiercely on Gustave—"you will have the most profound torture. For hanging upon the witching glances and oily words of women, you have filled all hell with fuel for your roasting."

Céleste wondered if Gustave wasn't a little afraid.

"You credit them too much," he replied.

"Start the crank, girls. Ten times around." Ixion laughed maniacally.

Céleste clapped, Nayla spit in her hands, and together they assaulted the crank as the boisterous, roisterous crowd gazed on.

"I'll ask my father to plan the production," Céleste spoke softly, "and to commission the poster. We need his approval."

"You can't do it alone?"

"Nayla..." Céleste shook her head. "We are talking about attracting a god. To stage the greatest show in France, we need the greatest impresario."

"You grew up in a theater," Nayla acquiesced. "I trust your judgment."

"Stop the crank!" rasped Ixion. He freed Gustave from his binds and watched him step off the wooden platform onto the floor.

Gustave braced one hand on Céleste's shoulder and the other on his solar plexus. Onlookers froze. Ixion's smile faded. Gustave found his resolve and struck a Herculean pose, victorious. The crowd cheered, and a red devil passed him a free brimstone.

Céleste pulled Gustave's ear to her mouth as he drank. "Arrange a dinner at Maxim's with Papa. I've got an idea."

"You're joining a convent?"

Céleste laughed and replaced his top hat. "And put you out of the job?" She pecked him on the cheek.

"I'm very disappointed in the lot of you!" Charon mounted the bar. "I have mingled with you miscreants and have found that most of your companions are distinguished gentlemen of learning and ability, who, knowing their duty in life, failed to perform it." He tut-tutted. "Hades would like a word." He pointed his oar at the stairs. "To the hot room, posthaste! Don't forget to pay the boatman!"

MAXIM'S

Nayla tripped over the curb on rue Royale and caught herself on a Morris column, coming face to face with an elephant stamped with the words *Folies Bergère*. The eye of the beast stared back at her.

"Ganesha?"

She steadied herself on her feet.

"I beg your pardon, Herr Ganesha, but why have you, the remover of obstacles, put a mushroom in my path to dinner?"

She looked from the elephant to a monkey dangling from a tree, brushing his teeth, then back to the elephant.

"Oho, no response? Cat got your tongue?"

Her eyes lingered on the column, wishing there was a poster of Maman dancing for a show. What Nayla wouldn't give for a front row seat. She'd raid her garret for Maman's headpiece and the mecha-sleeves and hand them over for a ticket without a second thought.

It was silly. Even Ganesha knew it was silly.

"Well, tell your friends, goodbye."

Nayla didn't mean to drink so much. Starflower was going to kill her. Where was that nouvelle nymphe?

A yellow banner blurred into focus. It was the awning of Maxim's, under which green spears of arborvitaes alternated between café tables, the whole ensemble emblazoned by amber and ruby glows within the oaken restaurant.

Oho! Céleste was partaking in a new adventure without her. Each brasserie and wineshop were a thrill compared to the old cantina. The cantina did not sport a hat boy in a spiffy red uniform.

He opened the door, glass that Nayla mistook for the sheen of a bubble. Her hands reached the doorway for support, and her feet stepped into the heart of a tree. *Careful, Nayla, don't trip.*

Fabulous bulbs in the shape of chestnut leaves shined roseate light from the crevices. How quaint. They were modeled after the trees on the boulevard. *Don't trip on your dress. One foot out, then the other.* She followed the curvilinear veins to the reception desk, where sprites stood holding flowers to provide lamplight for the maître d'hôtel. *Hare Krishna.* It was a restaurant for squirrels. She was not a squirrel. The maître d' looked up from his reservation book.

"Marchand," said Nayla.

The maître d' pointed Nayla into a ventricle. Woody vines overlapped the mirrors on the walls and sepia pond scenes of women lazing in tall grass. The ceiling resembled a trellis, diffusing emerald light through its grid onto the table below, falling upon Céleste's frizzy bangs, Gustave's slicked back hair, and Édouard's wrinkled brow, bewitching them all in a spell.

"There you are." Céleste's face lit up. "Papa, this is Nayla. Nayla, Papa."

"Enchanté, Papa." Nayla shook hands.

"Édouard will do." He gestured across from him.

"Ja, Papa Édouard."

Nayla gingerly pulled out the vine-backed chair, checked its position twice to orient herself, and sat. Gustave lifted his head at the behavior. Oh no. Did she do something wrong? Did he know she was drunk? Did she breach an unwritten contract de rigueur? She had told Céleste she wasn't good at meeting new people. Unless she were Spuckfeuer. That always helped. But a disguise couldn't bury her anxiety here. She really didn't mean to drink so much.

Céleste stirred her bowl of consommé. "I was telling Papa how grand the circuses are in the Orient."

"Oh, ja," said Nayla. "They have flying creatures zipping around on wires, actors play out war scenes from the Mahabharata and there's a monkey that brushes his teeth to Beethoven."

"Monkey brushing his teeth?" asked a stupefied Édouard.

"The Orients must have poor dental hygiene," Gustave supplied.

"They can thank the fatherland for that."

"We have tooth powder," said Nayla, feeling the hole with her tongue where a molar used to be. "We've given Germany far more than they've given us."

"Like what?" asked Gustave.

"Their language. Germanic tribal languages came from India. It's called Indo-Germanic." She picked up the menu. "Guess what? French came from India too."

"Yes, well," said Gustave, "the Greeks influenced your people through the Indo-Greek Empire, Orient."

"And the Hindu gods influenced the Greek, Occident." Nayla smiled crookedly.

"Gustave was an accident," said Céleste.

"The accident," said Gustave, "would be in mistaking those gods for mine."

"This grand circus," said Édouard, "where is it?"

"Jacoma," said Nayla, surprised the top of the menu didn't read *Plant Fertilizer*. Maybe her vision was impaired. Perhaps she was perusing a list of different types of nuts. However, the aroma that drifted in when the kitchen door opened said otherwise. Creamy delicacies, caramelized legumes, and glazed victuals filled the hollow.

"Traveling or permanent?" Édouard clasped his hands.

"The what?" asked Nayla.

"The grand circus in Jacoma."

"Oh. Traveling."

"How many seats?"

"Three thousand."

"That's nearly double the Folies."

Nayla pointed at the wine bottle and waved out her glass. Céleste drew back.

"Hold it still, would you?" Gustave poured her a thimble.

"The show is absolutely wondrous." Nayla toasted the ceiling in a jerky motion.

Céleste lurched back again with a look of fright.

"What's it called?" asked Édouard.

"The Theater," said Nayla.

"Yes, what its name?"

"That's it. Just The Theater."

"Rather bland." Édouard turned to Gustave. "You've checked this place out?"

Gustave glanced at Céleste. "Oui. Apparently they grant all their public buildings unoriginal names. I hear whispers they are to perform a show in French Athens."

"Those damn Germans," said Édouard. "First, they take Alsace-Lorraine, then they open a rival theater company and try to compete with us? Ça alors, this will not do."

A server appeared at the table, wearing a sport coat and long apron. "Is something the matter?"

"My reputation," said Édouard.

"So long as it isn't ours," said the clean-shaven server. "Are you ready to order?"

"I'll have the lamb kidney, skewered, with meadow greens."

"Normandy sole fillet," said Gustave.

"Ladies?" The server turned to Céleste.

"I would like the veal chop with the vegetables casserole."

Nayla scanned the blurry menu and found a kabob, like the type she and Baba were going to celebrate their new investment with. "Special Indian chicken curry, skewered. Oh! And a side of matchstick potatoes."

The server eyed Céleste. "Another melon cocktail?"

"One is enough for me, s'il vous plait."

"Very good." The server departed.

"Céleste," said Nayla in a loud whisper, "who is Alsace-Lorraine?"

"The spoils of the Franco-Prussian War," said Gustave. "Of course, they wouldn't teach it that way in the Orient."

"I didn't realize the Folies was political," said Nayla.

"We held rallies in the '70s," said Céleste, as if she had gone.

"And now we'll hold a variety show so large it will scare off our German competitors," said Édouard. "It pains me to live up to the name *folies*—a whim resulting in crazy expenses—but beat the Germans, we must! Céleste, you will dance in the new pantomime, Le Miroir."

"Moi? But if I am on stage, who will search the crowd for the—the German theater spy?"

"Me." Nayla hiccupped.

"You?"

"Who else?"

"I know it may not be as grand as your Oriental Theater," said Céleste, "but the Folies is too big for one person to look."

"Céleri," Gustave interrupted. "Et alors? We don't need to find the spy. Word travels fast. The German Orient Theater will hear of our show and think twice about coming to Athens."

"Céleri?" asked Nayla. "Like the vegetable?"

"Like wild celery," Gustave explained. "It's a flower. They look rather like baby's breath, but they are shaped like umbrellas. It grows between sidewalk cracks."

"Oh, I just call her Star—"

Nayla looked down and found Céleste's hand clamped to her mouth.

"Would you excuse us? Nayla and I have to use les toilettes."

Céleste placed her warm hand around Nayla's and led her through the lavish thicket into the women's room. Inside the cramped space with three toilet stalls, it was though a hornbeam tree had taken over, securing the mirrors to the cavity.

"Have you gone mad?" Céleste faced her.

"It just happened. I didn't mean to."

"You want Nemesis here? I don't."

"It won't happen again. I promise."

"What good is a drunken promise?"

"I'm not that drunk."

"You are drunk like Robespierre's donkey." Céleste rubbed her temples in between her curls. "I was wrong. You're not immortal. You don't celebrate anything. You drink to get drunk. Three sheets to the wind." She shook her head. "Tell me you're better than this."

Nayla looked around, at the multiple hers struggling to reply, to the multiple Célestes waiting for answer.

"You weren't drunk when you built your machine," Céleste continued, "were you?"

Nayla put her finger to her lip. She had drunk moonshine after work while finding parts, but not during assembly. "Nein."

"Well then, I suggest you take finding Hermes as seriously as you did your clock."

"I will, Céleste, I promise." Nayla wanted to hug her. She hesitated. "Céleste?"

"What?"

Nayla saw the stalls were empty. "Why did Aphrodite and Psyche appear to you in the Wild Garden?"

"I tried to exorcise a demon from a man possessed. He was following a woman through the park."

"But if you weren't a nymph yet, how were you going to exorcise it?"

"Holy water. Would it have worked? Je ne sais pas. The man leapt out, and the gods showed up. It's a good thing they did. The man's demon would have killed me. What about you? Would you have died had your gods not interceded?"

"Ja." Nayla couldn't dare reveal she went running head first into a hearth. Céleste would think less of her. "There was an accident at the Blast. I almost fell in the hearth." She had to get off this subject. "I'm sorry I drank too much. I'm nervous around new people, remember?"

"Papa is harmless."

"He's judging me. I'm from the German Orient."

"He doesn't hate *you*. Just Germans. He likes to complain about things outside of his control. Trust me, he avoids conflict at all costs."

"Then what's wrong with dancing in his show? You're his pride and joy."

"Oui, he's proud of me onstage. He ignores me the rest of the time." Céleste touched one of the mirrors in the corner. "Two of us looking for Hermes will be quicker than one. We have an entire theater to search."

Nayla checked her purple dress in the mirror and met her own gaze. "I can do it. I'll find him."

Céleste searched Nayla's reflection. "Sober?"

"Ja, sober."

"Honest?"

"I swear it."

"You better."

"Now I know why you hate drunks," said Nayla. "We blabber."

"That's not why." Céleste glanced at her. "Théo was a drunk—the man under possession who stole my soul. He was my chaperone, before Gustave."

"I thought it was a demon who stole it, technically?"

"It's hard for my brain to separate the two." Céleste touched Nayla on the elbow. "You look for Hermes. I dance. Just watch your flailing arms."

"Flailing arms, rechts."

Céleste grabbed the door and muttered, "The struggles of the demi-gens."

"Who?"

"The half-people. Us."

"I have my soul right here."

"There are other forms of trauma than losing your soul, my pet."

"What about being born?"

"Absolutely not. Something tragic must've happened."

"It did. In a past life."

"Prove it."

"My proof is that I was born a Shudra."

Céleste chewed on her cheek and pressed the door.

Nayla followed the green dress, spooked by the challenge. No one had ever contested her before. Céleste was born a Vaishya, with less karmic debt from her past life, so it made sense her soul-theft made her a half-person, but was Nayla a half-person like Céleste? If being one with Brahman were to make Nayla feel whole, it would imply she was currently not. She was merely a piece of Brahman, separate, walking alone in a storm of suffering. Ja, a half-person, one of the demi-gens, surrounded by whole-people, free of tragedies in their lives, present or former, like Gustave and Édouard chatting over caviar, perfectly at ease.

"I have resolved to dance in Le Miroir for the big show," said Céleste upon return to her seat.

"Mirifique," said Édouard.

"Super," Céleste agreed. "For the next order of business, commissioning the poster..."

"I have already commissioned a poster for Le Miroir."

"I mean a unique poster for the whole event," said Céleste. "Une affiche artistique. I would like a picture of Hermes on it."

"Hermes does not appear in the entirety of the show."

"He can be symbolic of Hermes Hill."

"But we are not in that arrondissement."

It was true. The Folies was in Elysium.

"Tourists don't know the difference," replied Céleste. "I'd like to work with the artist directly."

Édouard sighed. "Who do you have in mind?"

"Monsieur Chéret."

"I have full confidence in Jules Chéret. He doesn't need input."

"But he's very easygoing. He won't mind."

"I've already assigned him Le Miroir."

"He can do more than one. I have full confidence."

"Do you? I don't think he'll want a client perched on his shoulder. He demands total creative control."

"He's not exactly a rule-follower," said Céleste. "He's having an affair with the wife of his employee."

Nayla opened her mouth and preceded to point at Gustave. "Kind of like—"

Gustave snatched her hand. "I think our friend needs some water. And where is our food? Our server is off playing hide and seek with the manager. We shall find them. Mademoiselle, if you would accompany me, please." He squeezed Nayla's hand until she stood. "Posters." He shrugged. "All the rage now."

He led her into a woody atrium and through a pulmonary valve.

"You are a loose cannon," he whispered sternly.

Floor-to-ceiling mirrors on the stairwell reflected her apologetic face in orange from the glow of the leafy fixtures.

Her shoes tripped on the carpet. Gustave braced her jelly-like body as he escorted her into the bar area on the second floor and parked her by a statue of Eros, bearing a pendulous bloom of light.

Gustave spoke in ear, over the music. "I don't know why Céleste would entrust a sozzled Orient with sensitive information involving me and her, but here we are. You need to sober up." He raised his head. "Barman, two waters."

"I didn't mean to," Nayla quailed. "I only wanted to contribute to the conversation."

He rubbed his maw. "Not like that."

The barman placed two kylixes on the wood top.

"Are the waters for us?" asked Nayla.

"They're for you." Gustave touched her back as he handed her one. "Drink."

Nayla obeyed the brute, watching the musician work the keys on the grand piano, the instrument styled like a massive wooden beetle.

"That music," said Nayla. "So beautiful."

"Debussy." Gustave tilted his head. "What is this grande attraction Céleste is pushing for, anyway?"

Nayla came up for air. "Art for art's sake."

Gustave gave a short, false laugh. "Sure. Did someone piss her off at the Olympia? Don't answer. Keep drinking." He handed her round two.

She felt she was drowning and swam to the surface. "Céleste wants to be a star ballerina."

"Oh, that's what you were about to call her."

Nayla let the water restore some of her nerve cells and thought of a good excuse. "The show will draw talent scouts from the Olympia and the Casino. If they see how well she dances, it'll give her clout when she auditions with them. Then Édouard will have no choice but to make her a star ballerina at the Folies and she will win her father's love."

"Ah, that's what she's after." Gustave tilted the kylix back to Nayla's lips.

The thing was like a cat bowl.

She lowered the brim. "Ja. That is why Céleste pretended she didn't want to dance in Le Miroir."

"Sly." Gustave took her glass and returned it to the bar. "Let's go see what other damage she's caused."

"I don't need help walking, danke."

"Oh, but you do." Gustave gripped her shoulder. "Consider me your ange gardien and try to show some savoir faire."

He delivered her out of the dreamy music and into her seat under the green aura in the dining room downstairs.

"It's a bad time of the month for me," said Céleste to her father. "Can't it be the week before, or the week after?"

"There's no better time than Noël," said Édouard. "Gustave, remember how busy it was last year between Christmas and New Year's?"

"Don't remind me. Cocottes and coxcombs abound."

Nayla stared at the swoosh of the table lamp and its pink snail shade.

"December 30 is the date going on the poster," said Édouard. "End of story."

"D'accord, Papa," said Céleste.

"You can put a hippopotamus on it, for all I care, but that date does not change. Friday, December 30."

"Oui, Papa."

"What's wrong with the date?" asked Nayla, waterlogged.

"Oh, many things," said Céleste. "Many things will be closed that day."

"And the Folies will be opened," said Édouard, buttering his bread. "I'll set the appointment for you and Jules for this week. Where are our meals? Gustave, what did they say?"

"I—uh."

"Look"—Céleste pointed—"Loïe Fuller. She just walked by."

Édouard's head swiveled. Gustave drank his wine, indifferent.

Nayla turned in her chair.

"I must speak to her." Céleste rose from the table and walked out of the ventricle.

"I didn't see anyone," appraised Édouard. "Gustave. Follow her."

Gustave eyed Édouard and glared at Nayla.

Silence, declared his slatey eyes, as he slowly left the table.

Nayla was alone to guard her own mouth now. She had to be super, extra, shut-up careful not to say anything revealing.

The server planted his folding stand with his tray and presented her dinner. She breathed in the chicken curry kabob, inhaling spices emanating from the grilled chicken that lay across her plate. She looked at the empty chairs as if Baba was about to meet her to indulge in their success. It didn't feel right to eat without him. *For the sake of Vishnu, Nayla, it's a kabob. Why are you crying?*

"Is everything all right, mademoiselle?" asked the waiter. "Is the curry too strong?"

"Nein," said Nayla, wiping her eyes. "It's just right."

"She'll come over it." Édouard pardoned the waiter.

"I'm sorry, Monsieur Marchand," said Nayla. "It was—my baba and I planned to celebrate our change in fortune before he—he died. We were going to eat kabobs together at a nice restaurant."

"Would it be all right if I filled in temporarily?" Édouard offered a sympathetic smile.

Nayla swallowed hard and nodded.

Édouard got up and sat next to her. "If I may..." He took a knife and slid half the chicken off the skewer onto his plate. "I'll trade you for some of my lamb kidney. Would that be all right?"

Nayla nodded again.

"It's brave of you. Céleste hates it. Though I'm sure you've tried far more interesting plates in the Orient."

Nayla gave an encouraging smile. "Plenty."

She picked up a fork and hesitated while Édouard chewed his first bite. Why was Céleste so hard on the man? He simply wanted to avoid all the negativity in the world and escape into the fantasy of the Folies Bergère—hiring artists, hiring acts, and choosing what order they appeared in so they unfolded like a symphony. In the Folies Bergère, no one could hurt him, Monsieur Marchand, this great, behind-the-scenes showman. There was nothing wrong with detesting conflict—detesting sadness, rage, or despair.

She brought the chicken to her tongue, chewed the garlic and ginger, and ate in the quietude of the wood heart, assuring herself she'd be more sober in the future, as difficult as it would seem. Potations made the food taste better.

IMPRIMERIE CHAIX

P ierrot, white and moony; Harlequin, checkered and troublesome; and Columbine, the yellow and sensible one, danced in the mural at the top of Chaix Printing along with their friends, the fleeting red Scapino and the gossipy green Ruffiana, all at the building's summit, structured like a headboard. They were stock characters, Céleste explained to Nayla, from Italian comedies called the commedia dell'arte, a favorite of Monsieur Chéret's. He transformed them into his own unique style, making each figure look as though made of flame—Columbine's dress, Ruffiana's tutu, dastardly Scapino's feathered cap. These were the clowns Mariquita preferred in her pantomimes, so they showed up frequently on Folies posters throughout French Athens.

"Would you two stop woolgathering?" Gustave tied Clemence and Claudette to a post on the Folies' namesake, the rue Bergère. "Something tells me we'll be here all day."

"Why, Gustave"—Céleste took her eyes off the rainbow of clowns—"don't you know how art works? I have to gather wool to knit a sweater."

"You knit?" asked Nayla.

"Not like Monsieur Chéret does." Céleste skipped after Gustave. "Nothing to fear about meeting Chéret." She turned to Nayla. "He likes everyone."

Céleste passed between the cyclamens holding up the door with their dart feather-like petals and entered a warehouse with lofts and awnings on the outer rim. A bulky steam-powered printing press occupied the middle. Cylinders rolled paper over inked stones that moved back forth in the printing bed, whereby the operator received the finished paper from the rear of the machine, delivered by a comb of metal spikes. The drums were powered by thick belts that stretched like clotheslines to the flywheel of the engine and traveled up vertically to a pulley system, at the top which spun two metal balls.

Nayla's eyes lit up. "Those balls are the centrifugal governor. They regulate steam."

"I knew you'd like it here." Céleste touched her shoulder, noting the circles on her eyes. "You're not steep, are you?"

"A bit foggy," Nayla admitted. "Yesterday was rough."

"Génial. Sober enough to enjoy the gears."

Chéret's assistants worked diligently. One monitored the steam, while others prepared their limestone slabs with smelly chemicals. But where was the man himself? She scanned the premises looking for the printer with a bushy mustache and side-parted brown hair. There he was, drawing on a stone with a grease pen.

"Monsieur Chéret!" declared Céleste, inhaling turpentine.

Gustave halted his march to the studio and doublebacked.

Jules Chéret lifted his boxy head with a twinkle in his eyes. "Mademoiselle Marchand, comment ça va?"

She greeted him with a kiss on each cheek.

"Oh, good, you brought a friend." He turned with Céleste to see Nayla inspecting the press.

Nayla shook his hand with trepidation. "Nayla binti Azmi."

"An Orient. Jules Chéret, at your service." He spun toward the back of the house. "Follow me! To the drafting table! Édouard tells me you are in need of a poster."

She followed the tall, picturesque Chéret, his hands stuck in his pockets, who seemed as though he struck a pose with each step. Gustave and Nayla joined the march, passing a lithographer dusting his stone with French chalk and another pouring a bottle over his that read "Arabic gum." The loud belts they passed vibrated in a rhythm capped by a hiss of steam. *Hum-hum-tssss. Hum-hum-tsss.*

Boys in aprons smeared with ink clipped Loïe Fuller's unfinished image on a line. One proof showed her silks in green, another her torso in red, her feet in yellow, and a black outline of her figure on a fourth. The multicolored composite hung at the end—the design etched out of fire, fire Chéret had captured on a brush to paint with colored flames.

"Monsieur Chéret"—Nayla roused from her stupor—"what inspired you to draw like this? The flaming garments? The elemental lines?"

He turned, walking backward. "You wouldn't believe it, but I saw a fairy in flaming ribbons dashing through the sky. I thought maybe the nitric oxide fumes finally did me in, but not this print devil. I squeezed my eyes shut like this and opened them like this, wide as can be, and there she was, sailing."

Céleste followed Chéret into a partitioned area behind the press, to his toadstool next to a drawing table.

"You must think I'm crazy," he said.

"Oui," said Gustave, "and your sister."

"Good," said Chéret. "It's why I have a fancy printing press and you don't, my fair philistine."

"I believe you, Monsieur Chéret," said Nayla, gaining confidence in her voice. "When did you see your wild red fairy?"

"March, about. I was leaving the press."

Nayla flashed Céleste a glance of recognition. That was when Nayla had spied on Céleste at the Folies Bergère down the street. Spuckfeuer being Chéret's muse would've been no different than Fleur d'Étoile being Loïe's.

Except Chéret didn't ask invasive questions like Loïe had at Maxim's. *Why are you a figurante in a ballet run by your* tent that Céleste could feel the stare land sharply on the crystal mountain that once throned her soul. All Céleste could muster, exposed in her spiritual nudity, was that Papa disliked nepotism.

"Are these your muses too?" Nayla picked up a pair of happy and sad masks. "Thalia and Melpomene."

"My still life references," said Chéret.

Knick-knacks and curios cluttered the tables. There was a distaff and spindle, a yellow umbrella, a red scarf, a toy bugle, wine bottles, cymbals, fans, a rocking horse, and a mannequin with men's clothing as chic as Chéret had on.

"We may need a reference for your Hermes poster," he continued. "What do you have in mind?"

"Hmmm." Céleste tapped her chin.

The only word that came to mind was perfection. The poster had to be so perfect it drained all creativity from his blood.

"You must have some idea." Chéret plucked up his pen. "Shall I draw Hermes as a clown, a lover, or a villain?"

"Ummm. Hmmm."

"Is there an act with Hermes in it?"

"Non." That was the point. To keep Hermes in suspense. He'd eagerly await the act with his likeness and when it didn't come... Well, Nayla would've found him by then.

"Then," said Chéret, "there is nothing else to do but wait for inspiration to strike." He sat on his toadstool and stared at the blank sheet on the table. "Everyone, stare with me."

Céleste exchanged looks with Nayla and Gustave. Chéret gestured to the table.

Gustave smiled. "You expect us to stand here all day?"

"Until inspiration hits, oui," Chéret said calmly. "Let me know when it does. We don't want to miss it."

Gustave blew into his lips.

"Patience, my good sloth."

"Oui, Gustave," said Céleste, grabbing a spare stool. "The man is a genius. You can't rush art."

"We can sure as hell try."

"Shhh," said Céleste. "If you keep talking, it won't happen."

Gustave checked his pocket watch and tapped his foot. "I am waiting for the art. Where is the art? When is it coming? Where are you, art?"

Chéret sat wide eyed, fully engrossed in the paper's white void. Nayla perused the prop collection.

Céleste turned to Gustave. "Are you late for a tryst in the Bois de Boulogne?"

"Édouard has a strict timetable," said Gustave. "I am sure even Monsieur Chéret has appointments to keep."

"I will cancel them all in the name of art," said Chéret.

"And when you fail to make rent?"

"Hang myself from the rafters." Chéret pointed to the main beam.

Nayla smiled through her fog.

"Now," Chéret said to Gustave, "we can hang together, my gentle troglodyte, or you can wait outside so that we may focus on the incoming epiphany."

"It's all right, Gustave." Céleste touched his arm. "We won't run off."

His eyes latched onto hers, searching for distrust, and let her pass. "I'll see if the horses thought of anything. I return in one hour."

He muscled around a print devil and left the studio.

"Monsieur Chéret," said Céleste, "I don't think it's working."

"You're not staring hard enough." Chéret looked up from his trance at Céleste's raised brow. "You know what? New approach."

"Hourra!" Céleste clapped.

"The problem is that we're not committed." Chéret handed out pens and paper. "Sometimes the inspiration comes after we commit to finding it. Set your brains to creativity and start drawing."

Nayla moved her pen with a dazed look in her eyes.

Céleste let her grease pen doodle in circles, and formed a person with a helmet and wings, and shoes with wings, and the Folies lyre.

Chéret strutted the room and peered over Nayla's shoulder. "Pencils down." He scooped up the papers and presented them. "We have... Baby Hermes stealing cattle in the Orient."

"De rien," said Nayla, indifferent.

"Adult Hermes flying over the Folies with a message, done by moi. And Hermes with a lyre by Céleste. No good, no good, no good—none of it."

Céleste frowned and raised her hand. "If I may be so bold, I find creativity usually comes when I'm doing something else. Something spontaneous."

"Quite right." Chéret reached for the props table.

"Drinking might help," said Nayla. "Is there wine in those bottles?"

"Non, ma chére, but I have these." He slipped on a fencing helmet and thrust a pommel into her hand.

"Oh, please, don't," cried Nayla, holding the drooping blade. "Allez!"

He swung his blade. Nayla lunged off her stool and raised the weapon. They sparred back and forth, tearing at each other over the drawing table, stirring up dust in the frowsy room.

"This will get the neurons firing," said Chéret.

"Please, can we stop?"

"Do what he says," called Céleste. "He's the father of the modern poster."

"He's the verrückt father of crazy." Nayla took off into the printery with Chéret chasing her. She ducked behind a slab.

"You can't hide from me there, mademoiselle."

"You're a crazy man!" Nayla shrieked, dodging the tip. She held up her blade simply to protect her face and rushed to the clothesline of proofs. "You're going to put my eyes out!"

"Oui, Monsieur Chéret." Céleste met the action, heart pounding. "Watch her face!"

Chéret slashed at the partial Loïe Fullers, aiming for Nayla's head. His art was inspired by Spuckfeuer, and he was about to decapitate her!

"Eep!" Nayla ducked.

Shredded lithographs crumpled to the floor.

If Gustave were here, he'd pull his gun.

Nayla darted to the print devils operating the press. Human shields.

"They won't save you!" called Chéret.

Nayla swung wildly at him over one assistant's head. The blades scraped, withdrew, and scraped again. The crew's general lack of alarm implied they were no strangers to Chéret's creative process, save for the poor devil below the flashing sabers.

Nayla followed the belt and ran to the steam engine. Chéret pivoted, about to chase, when Nayla raised the blade to the sky, brought it level, and threatened to ram it into the wheels.

"Not a step closer." She panted. "I'll do it." She menaced the sword with a mad glint in her eye.

Chéret raised his helmet and his hands. "Je me rends. I surrender."

Nayla exhaled hard. "It's not the first time a Frenchman's said that to a German."

"Ah, but you are from the Orient. My pride is not so crushed."

"Hand Céleste the weapon," demanded Nayla.

Chéret handed it over.

Céleste tried it on for size. "I hope everyone has some brilliant ideas brewing." She led the party to the drafting room.

"If not"—Nayla pointed her blade at Chéret's throat—"we shall do something less stabby."

He gestured to a table, set up with two rows of playing cards. "Bezique?"

"Nein," said Nayla, "I've got it."

"Got what?" asked Céleste.

"The poster."

"Yes, yes..." Chéret waited excitedly, teasing the concept from Nayla's mind with pincer hand motions.

"Are you familiar with the Greek story of Hermes and Argus?" she asked.

Céleste shook her head, while Chéret spun onto his toadstool and sketched.

"Recite it for us," he said, doffing an imaginary cap.

"It has to do with Hera and Zeus"—Nayla scratched her arm—"Hera had almost caught him trying to have his way with the nymph Io, but before catching him in the act, Zeus transformed Io into a white cow."

Chéret's pen danced along the paper, and he flapped his hand. "Then what happened?"

"Hera feigned ignorance and asked for the cow as a gift. Zeus, of course, gave in, to save his neck. Why wouldn't he?" Nayla scratched her head. "Then what? Let me think."

"Please keep going," said Céleste, wanting to ring the air. "It's important. Cursed absinthe clouds."

"Hera," Nayla continued, looking sour, "Hera put Argus in charge of watching Io. Now, Argus, Argus was a giant with a thousand eyes." She opened her palms. "He kept watch over the pastures on a mountaintop. So, Io was stuck as a cow guarded by a monster. Zeus felt guilty for her and sent Hermes to stage a rescue. Hermes came, he saw, he saved."

"A la bonne heure!" said Chéret. "Well done!"

Céleste exhaled hard. "So glad you remembered the rest."

"Honestly, Cél, the library is walking distance."

"That's what I have you for." She side-hugged Nayla and inspected Chéret's work.

The vantage point of the poster was Hermes onstage looking out at the audience, an audience that represented Argus and his one thousand eyes.

Chéret wiped his hand across the surface. "Every eye in Athens will be on the Folies that night."

Nayla nudged Céleste and tapped on the image. "Why don't you put Io in one of the box seats?"

The boxes. D'accord. This way, Hermes would know where to find Nayla—in theory. *Look for the endangered nymph.*

"Brilliant," said Céleste.

"Danke."

"A cow at the theater?" Chéret shrugged. "Why not?"

"It wouldn't be the first time." Céleste leaned over him. "No, not that line there!"

He flinched.

"Put that stroke a quarter centimeter to the right. My right. Much better."

Chéret picked up his colored pens to bring the sketch to life. This poster had to be perfect. Not a single mistake.

If it didn't stun Hermes in his airy tracks, she could kiss her soul goodbye forever. She would never function, feel content with one man, get married, or raise children. Not without passing on the same half-person malady. Her soulless body would try to absorb them.

Every color had to gel.

Étienne and Eulalie depended on it, depended on her. This poster had to end her nightmares, end time travel, secure her to her own body. She could demand nothing less than a masterpiece.

Céleste followed Chéret's hand to the top of the sketch. "No, don't write Folies there. Put it in the center."

"The text never goes in the center. The image goes in the center. The text goes at the top and bottom."

"But it will look so good there." She tapped on Hermes's back. "Are you sure?"

"Non, I've only done four hundred posters."

He added "December 30" below the stage. Céleste winced. She was sure to be on her period that week. Which meant Hermes better wait for her to stop bleeding. She wasn't going to hell powerless. There would be demons and goblins and all matter of creatures that went bump in the night.

"What are you drawing now?" she asked. "A feather?"

"It looks like one," said Nayla. "After Hermes slayed the giant, Hera collected its eyes and placed them in the feathers of her favorite bird, the peacock."

"Well, don't make it so big," said Céleste.

"Really, Céleste," said Chéret, "I ought to cut off my hand and give it to you."

The sudden twang of strings interrupted them. Nayla had swapped out the blade for a sitar. She strummed the narrow fretboard, sitting on the props table with her feet on a stool.

"I don't mean to be a pest," said Nayla, "but you ought to let the man work his magic." She flicked the sitar. "Imagine if he were barking in your ear telling you how to dance."

Perhaps Nayla had a point. Céleste was getting in the way of natural talent. She wasn't helping art. She was overthinking it. But it was so hard to let go when her soul's recovery hinged on this poster. She gritted her teeth. *Trust the man, Céleste. Trust him and his idiosyncratic ways.* She relaxed and looked apologetically at Nayla. "I've never heard you play before."

Nayla smiled modestly. She plucked and plucked and made fast music.

"Hé!" Chéret clapped and started doing an oriental jig. His hands arched overhead. "Ommm. Ommm." He touched his index fingers to his thumbs.

Nayla laughed. "Are you Hindu too?"

"Not at all."

Chéret didn't care. No inhibitions. He stomped his polished shoes and did a pirouette. "I was in Japanese London last year. All I heard was *om mani padme hum.*"

"Ah, from the Buddhists." Nayla sped up the music even faster, too fast for Chéret to keep pace.

When she gave the strings a final tickle, Céleste applauded.

"So that's what you do with that thing," Chéret said.

"The Buddhists didn't teach you?" asked Nayla.

"No desire to learn," he confessed, "but they did teach me about desire."

"To achieve satori?" Nayla turned to Céleste. "It's like nirvana."

"I see."

"Tell us more," said Nayla.

"They said to be happy I must eliminate my attachment to earthly desires," said Chéret. "It doesn't mean don't desire. It means not to attach myself to the outcome, pass or fail."

Perhaps that was what Céleste was doing wrong. Attaching herself to the outcome of this poster. How could she not? It had to attract Hermes.

"Any advice on dukha?" Nayla asked.

Chéret rubbed his forehead. "Dukha, suffering, oui. The friendly monk I met shared with me a wonderful lesson. When we experience emotional pain, it's like being struck by an arrow. Embrace it. Accept it. Let it be. Do not dwell on it. The same goes for dwelling on the pain of say, a bad poster—"

"—we better not," warned Céleste.

"If we dwell on the first arrow, we prolong the pain, and it becomes misery. The Buddha said, 'In life, we can't always control the first arrow. However, the second arrow is our reaction to the first. The second arrow is optional.' It did wonders when my mistress's husband charged me with adultery. I had to pay a large fine and apologize to him in court."

"No sitar lessons then, eh?" Céleste smiled.

"Non, but it makes me look eclectic, don't you think?"

Nayla allowed a wan smile. "Fabelhaft." She returned the sitar to the props table.

"Take it," said Chéret. "It's yours."

"Are you sure?" Nayla's voice cracked. "I don't want to deprive you."

"Positif." Chéret handed it to her. "You can do far more with it than I."

Nayla held it close to her chest. "Danke, danke."

"Well, I believe that concludes our appointment. Once I finish the poster, my afficheurs will plaster the Morris columns with them."

"Monsieur Chéret," Céleste wondered aloud, "you know those bronze posts surrounding Athens with the heads of Hermes?"

"The herms, bien sûr. There is a head on his shoulders and one for his, uh—"

"His quéquette. The very same. Have your afficheurs paste our lithos on the herms." That ought to get the god's attention. "Hermes is the god of travelers and fertility and tricks. It will make a fine publicity stunt."

"Oui, sex sells."

Your eyes don't deceive you, my friend. Those are bona fide ticket stubs to la Grande Attraction at the Folies Bergère on December 30, 1892. Look on the next wall. The olive green one. There. The very poster Chéret designed with Céleste and Nayla. This copy has yellowed some, but it is still in one piece. An image is worth a thousand words, that is true, though it won't tell you what happened in the intervening weeks from when our ladies left Imprimerie Chaix to opening night. That is what Jacques is for.

In terms of their readiness, Mariquita had drilled Céleste hard for the pantomime *Le Miroir*. Her legs were mush from assemblés and pliés, and what a relevé it was over, eh? As she had so nicely phrased it. That being said, she was right to fear the date. The wild red fairy had paid her a visit, shall we say, and I don't mean Spitfire. Thankfully, Nayla had revived after a week of burnout and was back off the wagon, if we are to root for public drunkenness. We don't want her unarmed, do we? That takes care of the physicalities.

Mentally, they were as excited and insecure as the whiplash line that climbed our buildings, splashed our walls, and construed our furniture. The endeavor had swept the pair into a state of electromagnetism for the task at hand. Live wires they were, coursing between the spiritual and the material, amplified by the Fin de Siècle's terrifying rate of change and uncertain future—erratic and erotic like art nouveau. You heard right. The approaching event at the Folies was like seeing a lover for the first time, their emotions waffling between anxiety and arousal. Anxiety that Hermes wouldn't appear. Arousal that he would. Their psyche and soma had never felt so close to completion.

Before, the outlook was grim. Now, there was hope. Suzon poured the drinks. Desormes ran his songs. Gustave fine-tuned the details. And Loïe Fuller. La Loïe Fuller created a new dance. She had devised a red glass plate built into the stage floor that illuminated from below. When she stood atop the surface, she would appear like fire. Édouard had seen to it that on this night, only a fool would dream to rival the Folies Bergère, and he didn't mean Pierrot from the commedia dell'arte—for that fool was part of the act. The clowns, the acrobats, and dancers had tirelessly pulled out all the stops. The stage was set for a shockwave to reverberate through the annals of French Athenian history. But did it attract a god? For that, Jacques will give you a front row seat.

LA DANSE DU FEU
(THE FIRE DANCE)

anterns diffused through the foggy street. The clop of hooves and passing murmurs drowned Nayla's quiet steps as she felt her way between the hedge maze of buildings with her eyes, sifting the abyss from under a hood, until at last, through the gloom, light splashed upon the frontispiece of the Folies Bergère. Over the archway to the entrance stood a massive roulette wheel planted in a wedding cake, studded with rubies. On its upper rim read the words "Folies" and "Bergère"—the words divided by comedy and tragedy masks. Above the circle, the building was fitted with a magnificent tiara out of whose center rose a tower.

Everything was so much larger than life. Jacoma's Theater entrance was a beaded curtain. Part the beads, pay a mark, you were in. The fact that Céleste's family owned this place lent it far more gravitas than before. Back then, in the weeks Nayla had spent watching Céleste's comings and goings from this glamorously dark pastry, she'd thought Céleste was in the working class, not the merchant. Although her last name, Marchand, should have been a hint. If Céleste had lived in Jacoma, she would've been in a whole caste above Nayla. Had it not been for their initiation into the world of nymphs, it was unlikely that a Vaishya, a business owner, would ever befriend a Shudra, a laborer. Kameera had broken the mold, but two Vaishyas? Sweet Shiva. Maybe in another universe where Baba owned a mecha-sleeve factory.

Nayla, you are nervous and talking verrückt. You and Céleste are friends now. Who cares about hypotheticals? She hunkered into her pelisse and lit a rolled cigarette off her shaky thumb, wishing Pushan would show up already. Or Hermes, or whoever he chose to appear as. That was the good thing about Hecate and Hestia. They had sprung on her unannounced with no time for overthinking and anticipation. No suspense! Would Hermes show up wearing a burnoose and dhoti, or would he be in French attire and sandals because they were in Athens? Would he treat her like camel dung for being a nouvelle nymphe and not a mighty immortal? Clearly, they had their own caste system ingrained into them, playing Greek and all.

That's why we have to be on our best behavior, Céleste had said. *No alcohol. Promise me, Nayla. Promise me. Celebrate after. You can, can't you?*

What a joke. They were only planning to ambush a supernatural deity. After, she could toast to how she was a stammering wreck who couldn't get a word out for fear of it being a negative representation of herself which could be judged harshly and punitively. *Monsieur Hermes, Herr Pushan, pu-pu-please help me, s'il vous plaît.* His reply would be a swift bop on the head with his caduceus. *Be silent, bleating mortal.*

The tobacco smoke warmed her throat and spiced her lungs. She wished it were absinthe, exhaling into the damp weather as a coachman unloaded nobles onto the sidewalk. She filed into the Folies cake and handed the doorman her ticket. Thirty francs. Box seat. He pointed up the grand staircase at the other end of the Winter Garden.

Tulip dresses spun and whirled as ladies spoke to their neighbors, accepting Nayla into the garden by power of conveyance. The usherettes in red and yellow jester skirts handed out programmes from their baskets. Nayla received a pamphlet and studied it carefully, making it hard to untangle her nerves from the excitement of the spectacle. Strong man, Jack de Fer; trapeze artist, Leona Dare; and the firebreathers, Les Dante. How wonderful these acts would be. What would make them even better was enjoying them with a glass of Bordeaux. Like the kind Suzon was pouring at the center bar.

Nein, Nayla. Think of Monsieur Chéret's advice. Remain unattached to the outcome of your desire.

She desired to meet Hermes and desired him to be their guide, and she shouldn't be nervous of the outcome? How did one do that, exactly? She didn't know, but she thought it best to forestall drinking at this time, and crossed on the Aphrodite side of the fountain, between the trickle of water and the women who sat at café tables lining the arcade in a profusion of aromatic flowers. Roses and irises and those big pom-pom ones called peonies fragranced the room from their hats.

Gustave peered down from the second-story arcade in a neat black suit. Had Céleste sent him to look after her? What was she to do? Her hand flittered in what passed for a wave. He nodded soberly. Gustave was much friendlier when pushing boulders and chucking apples. She bowed her head and hurried to the thick-carpeted double staircase. Her hand caressed the velvet railing, molded into lamb's ear, and, making sure not to trip on her dress blending in with the green carpet, she let the fuzzy metal rail support her up the steps to the right.

At the top, she rounded the corner of the trellised hall of interlaced vines and let the slope carry her to her box. The doorway, styled like an upside-down lyre, allowed her an opulent entry. There were five seats in her little nook, all to herself. Awaiting her by the ledge was Céleste's pair of field glasses. When the curtain opened, it transformed Nayla into a hypervigilant owl. Up in the balcony. Down in the audience. Hermes could've been anywhere. She reached for her hip flask several times and each time remembered Starflower had pollinated the object out of her garret a few days ago as Céleste's dying act, before her period stole her powers. Nayla had been too obedient to buy another.

She set the glasses in the next chair and took measured breaths. In. Out. Les Sisters Barrison appeared on stage, five cuties in pointy bonnets and pinafores. Céleste had told her they were Danish but advertised themselves as American. Maybe Céleste was right. Maybe you could be anyone you wanted to in French Athens. If only Nayla's mind were as fluid as these curly blondes in rainbow pastels and white frou-frou. The butter faced Barrison Sisters sang loud and proud, their voices squeaky and infectious as they danced from side to side.

"I love my little cat, I do
With soft black silky hair
It comes with me each day to school
And sits upon the chair
When teacher says, 'why do you bring
That little pet of yours?'
I tell her that I bring my cat
Along with me to show..."

Slowly, they lifted their skirts from their shins to their knees.

"Would you like to see my puss-see? Puss-see?
Would you like to see my puss-see? Puss-see?
I've got a little cat
And I'm very fond of that
I like to show my meow-meow
Meow-meow
Meow-meow..."

The skirts rose to their loins and fell to gasps and applause. Nayla laughed at the frivolity. She had never heard it called that before. She looked to her left as if Céleste were there to join in. She only saw Gustave, over the tortuous rail, in the upper box, with a top hat and a bird's eye view of her. A ball knotted in her throat. Knotted in her chest. Cigarettes out, she hunched below his sightline and pressed her thumb to light one. What did he want? She couldn't possibly find Hermes now with Gustave hawking over her.

"I'll be so glad when I get old
To do just as I 'likes'
I'll keep a parrot and at least
A half a dozen tykes
But now I've got a tiny pet
I kiss the little thing
I put it in its little cot
And on to it I sing…"

They addressed and teased the audience.

"Would you like to see my puss-see? Puss-see?
Would you like to see my puss-see? Puss-see?
I've got a little cat
And I'm very fond of that
I'd like to show my meow-meow now."

The quintet threw up their petticoats and revealed live kittens sewn into their underwear, looking indifferently as cats do.

The theater erupted in hysterics. "Vive les Americaines!"

Girls Nayla's age giggled below, throwing up each other's dresses. It was rather comical. The Barrisons, the Wickedest Girls in the World, indeed.

Nayla opened her programme. Les Sisters Barrison were the last act under the section titled *Première Partie*. Next was intermission, right after the Barrisons finished taking their bows. Then La Danse du Feu and Le Miroir. This was it. Her chance to calm her nerves, ease the tension, dim her wits. How could she remain unattached to the outcome when her goal in life was oneness with Brahman? Her very immortality was at stake. Chéret had said to remain unattached to earthly desires, ja. But Hades's helmet was unearthly. Maybe she could remain a little attached.

The orchestra cued the curtain to close on the Barrisons, allowing the audience to stretch and vacate their seats. Electric lights brightened the house. Nayla stayed glued to the programme until the French language turned to glyphs on the page. Her foot tattooed the carpet. Her heart drummed in her chest. People shuffled the aisles, heading into the promenoir out of view. She dared a look at Gustave. His box was empty. Well, Hermes wasn't going to prowl the music hall when there was nothing on stage to attract him. She stubbed her cigarette in a seashell and left through the lyre-door.

In the trellised hall, she lifted her skirt, nowhere near as high as the Barrisons, and hurried uphill to the double staircase of the Winter Garden. Intermission was fifteen minutes. She stopped at the frosted rail overlooking the alcohol-fueled scene. Suzon and the other barmaids poured drinks at their counters. Men in homburg hats and squat top cahills slapped the bar in raucous conversation. Women laughed in feathered aigrettes and polka dot veils. Bejeweled princes in pink turbans from the Orient legged the nearest bar side by side with Turkish officers in plumed helmets.

Nayla high-kneed it down the left staircase, drinking in the festive atmosphere. Can-can dancers passed her in their ruffled petticoats, sweating from their pores by vice of the gallop infernal, while Nayla made her way to the middle bar. Water droplets fell before Psyche's copper-green complexion, across from which Nayla parked on a lily pad stool. Suzon rattled ice cubes into a mixer over the wooden counter. A wine glass perched within reach. Full.

"Ep!" Suzon snatched it away. "I'm to deny you. Mademoiselle's orders." She squinted with her mouth, the left-hand corner rising slightly above the right. "No hard feelings." Nayla looked at Suzon's colleagues—the two barmaids adjacent. "You're welcome to try."

Gustave squeezed through the crowd and took an empty stool in front of the bowl of oranges.

The cacophony of chatter, laughter, and music comingled in Nayla's ears.

"A glass of absinthe, s'il te plait," Gustave said over the noise. Suzon's face went slack.

"Ah, now the scene is complete." He framed her with his fingers. "That is how Manet painted you. With that exact look on your face. Wait." He slid the orange bowl further into frame. "Oranger means orange tree," he said casually to Nayla, "which meant 'breasts' where Manet came from."

"Where was that?" asked Nayla.

"The same place as Gustave." Suzon lowered his hands. "The gutter. Except one of them had talent."

"And syphilis," added Gustave.

"There's time for you yet." She eyed him hard, her expression marmoreal. "I don't care if you think you are God's gift to women. If I serve her"—she tipped her head—"it's you who answers to Céleste."

"Don't be obtuse." Gustave smiled. "Women are God's gift to me. And make it a triple, ma chère."

"You'll get the guillotine."

Gustave nodded austerely.

"Go on, then," said Suzon. "Put your head out the window." She set up the glass, the slotted spoon, the sugar cube, and poured water over the top to dilute the dram of green liquid already pooled at the bottom. She slid the concoction to Nayla.

Just one drink. She would need it to speak carefree to Hermes. One drink was enough. Nayla would never forgive herself if she ruined Céleste's shot at finding her soul. The rim touched her lips. Licorice dominated her mouth. The river burned her gullet. She returned the glass to the bar and found her reflection in the mirror—her lovely green dress, her hair curled and braided, her brown eyes staring back at her.

The chandeliers flashed.

Her image strobed in the looking glass, without eyes or tongue or throat, the interior of her skull hollow. She jumped. The chandeliers resumed their glow.

"Why so startled?" Gustave caught her arm.

"The mirror—" She braved a second look. It was her, in the flesh, in one piece, her mouth contorted in bewilderment.

Was Céleste right? Was the mirror haunted? Or were the people who saw things in it haunted instead?

"I think I drank too much," Nayla confessed.

"Nonsense," said Gustave. "Suzon, one more for the road."

"Nein." Nayla covered her mouth. "No more."

"You heard the girl," said Suzon.

"A single," he haggled.

Intermission was almost up.

"All right," Nayla caved.

Gustave grabbed the drink from a reluctant Suzon. Nayla stood, experiencing a sudden blood rush. She held Gustave's shoulder for support, waiting for her brain to recalibrate walking. When it did, he escorted her into the dissipating crowd. She was tipsy. Her hand followed the strip of lamb's ear back upstairs and into her box, where Gustave deposited her into the chair.

"If I didn't know any better, Occident," said Nayla. "I'd say you're plying me with drink."

"When wine sinks, words swim."

"I warn you, I can imbibe enough absinthe to kill a camel before I say anything unwarranted."

He rolled his eyes and sat beside her on her programme.

She popped a cigarette in her mouth and fumbled with her hands. "Sacré scheisse. I lost my matches."

Gustave struck one for her and set down her drink at a cute brass table held up by a satyr.

"I think we took a wrong step somewhere, Nayla. I'm going to ask you once more. What is Céleste into? What is the reason for this?"

"I already told you." She took a drag. "For Édouard to make her a star ballerina."

"By means of competition." He traced his mustache. "So you have said."

"Ja, to win her father's love."

"I reflected on your sentiment." He leaned forward. "She knows that ship sailed long ago. The man will likely never utter the words." He handed her the absinthe. "Pray tell, what's she after?"

She welcomed the challenge. "Why do you care?"

"Édouard is my employer."

"Listen, Herr Gustave, she is here. She's safe. This seems to go beyond the duties of a chaperone."

Gustave relaxed his jaw. "The gutter Suzon referred to wasn't far off. I've lived an insalubrious life of crime and feel called to redeem myself, if you must know."

"You love her," she guessed.

"Oui, but it's not a sexual love."

Her mouth dropped. That was doubtful.

He rolled his eyes again and trained them on hers. "It's more of a love between a protector and someone who needs protecting. She's been through trauma, Nayla. On occasion, she becomes her own worst enemy. Please, I want to make sure this is not one of those times."

Poor Gustave. He really did care about Céleste, truly. The plea on his brow faded as the house lights dimmed. This absinthe was hitting her harder than she thought. It was his fault. The heavy curtain swept open. Monsieur Desormes roused the orchestra. Nayla swung her head toward the stage.

"Are they going to sing the pussy song again?"

"Let's hope not."

She leaned toward him, struggling to hold it together, asking with concern, "Are you trying to save her or you?"

"Both," he replied. "Call it a mutual salvation."

Anxiously, the strings hummed. The flutes perked up in a panic. Then came the trumpets like a freight train. Wagner, "Ride of the Valkyries." The pane of glass supporting Loïe Fuller burned a vibrant red. She lifted the wands attached inside her silk and twirled ceaselessly. Kameera would've loved it.

Loïe stood in blazing embers and did not burn. She exuded light, was herself a flame. Erect in her brazier, she smiled, and her smile was the rictus of a mask under the red veil that enveloped her and which shook and waved like a flame along her lava-nakedness. There was something mysterious about her. It was like she was Hestia incarnate. Inside of the furnace.

Nayla's eyes blurred. She refocused them, catching sight of a pair of winged ankles dangling below the top of the stage, below the ornate wedding cake fleurets. Ankles with wings? She absentmindedly inhaled another puff.

Hermes! He was up in the fly loft!

Nayla snapped to her feet. Head rush. "Gustave. I must use the powder room. My bladder is full."

"Well, don't set the theater on fire over it." He picked up her cigarette and smothered it.

"I'll be right back. I promise."

She spilled out of the box and struck out for the hallway. *Dun-dun-dahhh-dun. Dun-dun-dahhh-dun.* She hooked a left, ran past the next box, all the way to the dead end. *Dun-dun-dahhh-dun. Dun-dun-dun-dahhh.* A lotus blossom hung fastened to the trellis. She turned it, opening a concealed stairwell. It was so dark that she smacked into the banister. *Nayla, light your thumb candle.* Too dangerous. Staggering, limping, hopping, she reached the bottom of the well. Nein, there was one more step. Now she was at the bottom. On her thigh. She could restitch her dress later.

Her fingers reached for the metal flower on the wall. She spun the wheel. The panel opened against her weight. She emerged stage left. Loïe manipulated her cloaks in yellow rays. Nayla tilted back her head. Yellow lights silhouetted the catwalks. Now green. Loïe was green. Green lenses had revolved over the spotlights. Hermes was lurking somewhere on high, and this ladder was Nayla's ticket up.

The metal rungs were cold on her palms. Upward she climbed, dragging her dress along the bars, inhaling fusty theater smell. Loïe changed blue. Backdrops swayed. Nayla put her foot onto the catwalk grid and pulled herself up, knocking into one of the technicians perched in the rafters.

"Oh, sorry."

He fell backward, landing on his platform. The blue light had jostled off Loïe as she turned violet. Quickly, Nayla moved to correct the error by commandeering the light. She aimed at Loïe and cycled the lenses by crank. But she was cranking too fast. Red. Orange. Yellow. Green. Blue. Violet. Red. Oh no! She missed it again. She had wanted violet. She had to catch up!

Frantically, she turned the crank like a jack-in-the-box dousing Loïe in kaleidoscopic rays. Nayla might've been drunk. No matter what color she hit Loïe with, the left side of her still lit up violet. How was that possible? Nayla blinked. Never mind. Now it matched the cycle. But the cycle didn't match the colors of the other beams. She was still off. Loïe's curly hair flung back. A furious glint flashed in the pan of her face in Nayla's direction. Nayla shied away and kept cranking.

"Let me have that." The technician in the newsboy cap manned the crank and gently cycled to red. "Who let you up here?" he whispered. "The tower's interdit." He jerked his thumb at the ladder.

Nayla took a hopeless look around for any shadows with winged shoes and couldn't make out a thing. How would she entice Hermes in the dark, with all these people around? All this planning, the commitment. Céleste was going to be so disappointed. Nayla had seen the god, and he'd vanished. She hung her head low, turned and climbed down the ladder, barely caring if a foot slipped a rung.

Dejected, she returned through the secret passage, walked up the stairs, came out in the hall, and meandered up to her box. She breathed deep as she rounded the lyre-door, saw no one, and exhaled. Gustave had left, possibly to deal with shenanigans in the promenoir. Or maybe he went for a leak too.

The "Ride of the Valkyries" halted its gallop in a final note. The stage went black. The audience thundered applause. Nayla took her seat, lungs deflated, and picked up the programme. When the applause subsided, the next act began. She had ten more acts to think of something.

Pierrot, a white-painted clown with a black skull cap, stood in a cool blue column of light, smoking an invisible cigarette, trying to blow Os without flicking his cheek. It was enough invitation for Nayla. She pulled one from her and sparked it off her thumb. She blew real Os, while Desormes opened up the string section. Pierrot twitched his face and mimed each note in nervous tics, blinking until he sneezed.

She trained her field glasses at the top of the stage, scanning back and forth between the weeping bells. No sign of any winged ankles.

Determined, Pierrot rolled up his cuffs, spit into his hands, raised an objecting finger, then shoved it up his nose! And ear! He was a wild clown. Again, he tried to keep up with the music until he went verrückt. Then he hurled himself from the platform, grabbed an imaginary woman and air-kissed her to a symbol crash. He melted his whole being into her, this airy nothing.

What Nayla ought to do was search the promenoir.

The pretend woman vanished, sifted through Pierrot's fingers, to his ultimate misery. He crouched fetal and bared his head in pain. It conjured up old feelings of the times Nayla woke from dreams and discovered she'd only embraced her tasseled pillow. She felt Pierrot's pain, reversed when the orchestra suddenly roused him into a triumphant pose, sword thrusted, fist up.

She mused at the clown in the fading blue light and raised her elbow on her leg to support her chin. Maman had spoken of an invisible string that tied each man's gaze to the show. Several things could snap the string. Sloppy dancing. Bad acting. Confusing story. No style. The preface was enough to keep Nayla invested, but would it hold Hermes? And if so, where?

"Looking for me?" a polished whisper tickled her ears.

She turned in her seat. Over the back of the chair next to her head hung a pair of crossed ankles. Wings protruded from the dress shoes and dissolved into clouds. Behind her sat a man in a tight-fitting suit, hard and lean, his legs up in repose. Her hair stood on her neck.

His was up in a coif as if perpetually capturing wind. His eyes were large, framed in by eyebrows that resembled bat wings, brushed onto a face weathered by the gale of flight.

"Hermes?" she whispered, frozen.

His cobalt saucers bore into her soul. "The nymph, Io, I presume." He unrolled the lithograph and pointed at the cow.

"Spuckfeuer. Nouvelle nymphe." She dumbly shook his hand.

"Hermes, messenger god. To what do I owe the pleasure?"

She moved her lips to speak and froze, tongue tied.

"Shh." He pointed at the stage. "The first tableau."

Footlights illuminated a backdrop of hills at sunset on a French seaside, dotted with starry flowers of yellow gorse. Oboes and violins played pastoral music. A woman named Nivette in the programme danced into the foreground.

It was so hard for Nayla to concentrate. Hermes was right behind her! And he smelled like egg batter!

Miserably, Nivette collapsed in the middle of the field with her distaff and spindle, her auburn hair thrown over her lip-sticked face. She wore a red dress, black bodice, and blue apron with yellow trim—she was wearing too many clothes. When Maman would lose an audience member, she would dance up to the man and retie the string with her schaffouse.

"Am I allowed to speak now?" Nayla asked.

"Wait, who's this?" Hermes peered.

Captain Scaramouche entered with his soldiers. Instead of asking Nivette why she was sad, they pointed to a distant spot on the canvas. They were looking for directions. Scaramouche guzzled a bottle and pointed again. He was looking for a place to drink. Nayla required no further invitation. She picked up her absinthe from the satyr table.

Hermes fidgeted. "What are you celebrating, Nayla binti Azmi?"

Scheisse. He knew her name!

"Finding you." It was as good an answer as any.

"You were drunk when I arrived." His voice was sickly sweet.

She swallowed the licorice flavor, thinking of how it drowned all her sorrows, all the pain of Baba failing her—and her failing him. Mourning Ravi uncle. Avoiding Kameera. Regretting ever enlisting Captain Beauvais. It was a wonder she found reason to keep going.

"It distracts me from existing," she confessed.

"Ah, you're onto something."

Apparently not. Being vulnerable hurt. Her nerves weren't blunted enough. *Find your courage, Nayla. Speak.*

"What do you desire from me?" Hermes prompted her.

Wake up, Nayla.

If Brahman was in everyone, it meant that a part of her was in Hermes, and there was no reason to be afraid of herself, was there?

"My friend and I..." she began. "Another nouvelle nymphe... We need a guide to take us to the underworld. To go to—"

Tartarus. Say Tartarus, Nayla. Céleste's soul could wait. You want the Cap of Hades first. Hades's Cap was your raison d'être to be one with Brahman. To be twice-born. To experience a spiritual birth to make you lovable, as if you had always been lovable. Explain it to Céleste later, that it will not be this *Nayla helping her. It will be future Nayla.* Nayla with the Cap of Hades, Nayla who had conquered the universe, who had side-stepped her way around the cosmic rules of this world, Nayla at peace. She would be capable of anything then. Retrieving a soul would be no problem.

"Out with it, woman," said Hermes, laid back.

"We wish to go to Erebus."

Céleste's soul was so much more important, and Nayla was the one who asked her for help. At least Nayla wasn't selfish. She had put herself first with Beauvais and look where that had gotten her. Plus, she couldn't exactly flaunt the desire to rob the Hall of Fabled Objects for a cap Hermes used to wear.

"We are looking for a lost soul," Nayla continued. "Stolen, technically."

"I am to guide you in exchange for...?"

Nayla spread her arm across the vista of the stage. "La grande attraction."

Through the glory of gesture, Nivette choked on her sobs. Her fingers were tangled in her distaff, a stick that was coated in wool and not cotton candy. Bagpipes sounded from the orchestra. Nein, it was a musette, which transitioned to other woodwinds in a song of desire and tenderness, preceding the arrival of Pierrot. He was a carefree traveling musician, a clown, and musette player. He skipped in the air with a flutter of his feet. After failing to woo Nivette with a bouquet of gorse, Pierrot produced a two-cent mirror from his baggy pocket.

"What do you think?" asked Nayla.

"I'm considering. Something has drawn me here."

Nivette looked and faltered with emotion. Pierrot withdrew the mirror, to which she chased him across the meadow, hands clasped, pleading to see herself again. Finally, she captured the clown and nuzzled up to his chest. They held the mirror together. In it, she fussed at her hair and prettied herself. When she was done, she arched provocatively, and they swooned in each other's arms.

"I don't wish to frighten you," said Nayla, "but my friend, Gustave, may drop in on us any moment."

"Shh. The second tableau. Have you no respect for art?"

"But—"

"Shh."

She took in the new scene of marble stairs, tendril rails, and silk canopies that filtered dazzling light onto Princess Nivette as she smelled the live roses that festooned the Greek columns. Her ladies in waiting darted out from behind them like antelope. There was Céleste. She was covered in so much white marechal powder, Nayla barely recognized her.

"Oh là là." Hermes lurched forward and pointed. "Who is that?"

"Fleur d'Étoile," Nayla whispered, fearing Gustave's approach.

The ladies danced to the symphony, offering the audience the most sumptuous curtsies. It was a dance lesson. Given by Mariquita! The short, middled-aged woman led the troupe before Nivette and danced with the best of them.

"Tell me about her," said Hermes. "Fleur d'Étoile."

"She's a ballerina. Her soul is missing."

The ballet corps leapt like gazelles around the palace, spinning, catching each other's taut bodies. How beautiful they were. How they commanded the space around them while looking so dainty and delicate.

"Is there a special someone in her life?" asked Hermes. "A satyr? A sybil?"

"Um." Why was he so interested? "Are you smitten, Herr Pushan?"

"Conceivably. Can she cook?"

Powerful lunges. Energetic thrusts. What had Céleste told her? Dancing was painting with your hands and your feet. Nayla wished she could dance like Céleste and Maman. If she had talent like that, she would never let it go and covet it like Nivette coveted her mirror.

"There is an entrance close by," Hermes instructed. "Tell her to bake some honey cakes. Be sure to add drowsy essences and bring the sop for Cerberus. Meet me at 34 boulevard de Clichy tomorrow night at eight o'clock."

"Do we have to drug the poor doggy?"

"Ah, an animal lover." Hermes gazed fixedly on Céleste. "Here are your options, my little nouvelle nymphe. You can choke him into submission like Heracles. Feed him the sop

329

like Aeneas and Psyche. Or play the lyre like Orpheus. Choose humanely."

Nayla tapped her chin and looked at Hermes. "Will a sitar work?"

"If you become the music." He pressed his finger to his heart-shaped lips. "Don't tell her I'm interested. We don't want her turning into a tree like Daphne did for Apollo."

Nivette hugged her reflection like a talisman, hiding it from unwelcome eyes by the opposite pillar.

When Nayla looked over, Hermes was gone.

CABARET du NÉANT

id Hermes have to choose the very place she refused to visit these five years—the one place she hadn't looked? Not returned to? Not in the flesh, at least. In her mind, she went back again every time she saw Théo's features on another man, on a poster in the street—his derby hat, his blue eyes, his round ruddy face, his jowls, his caterpillar eyebrows and mustache. Or when she whiffed his Houbigant cologne that smelled like an old cedar chest. Or if some demon rushed at her in the same drunken gait as the one who comprised her Thief—that would transport her too.

It was not a walk in the park but a living nightmare preceded by fast breath and mangled nerves. Time travel taxed the body like you wouldn't believe. It was best to avoid if at all possible. Yet here she was in La Nouvelle Athènes, the 9th arrondissement, on New Year's Eve, destined for the Cabaret of the Void, powerless.

"Nay-Nay," said Céleste. "Go inside. Tell Hermes to change the rendezvous by place and date."

"I can't do that. We should count our blessings he showed his face. Don't worry. I have my sitar." She patted the instrument slung around her shoulder. "A demon won't steal your soul twice."

Céleste's heart beat in her chest at a rhythm incongruent with her footsteps as she headed west into the six-point intersection of Place Pigalle. Snow dusted her shoes and formed vignettes on storefront windows. Columns grew into swirling flowers to support their buildings' porticos, each one representing a nymph from antiquity. Hyacinth did something. Heliotrope did something else. The closer she neared the center of the horseshoe-shaped square, the more the columns matured into trees—olive, frankincense, and laurel.

Bracketing du Néant were two poplars, their leaves jagged medallions, black on one face, white on another. The entrance in between was draped with black cerements and white trimmings. Above the door, two iron lamps molded into flower cups of arum lilies, throwing ghastly light onto passing Athenians, reanimating them in sickly rays to resemble corpses. An oval sheen floated outside of the dead-black shutters, under the lights, a swaying top hat on a macabre female form.

Céleste froze. "Mon Dieu, non." She squeezed Nayla's palm, swallowing a tiny amount of air fit for the lungs of a mouse. "You can go first. Tell Hermes to take you to Tartarus. You're the one with the problems."

"You're talking irrational. I can't exactly ask for a tour of the Hall of Fabled Objects. Plus, I would need your help to fight Arachne."

"Ask Hermes."

"To steal his brother's stuff?" Nayla rubbed her chin. "He won't go for it. Hermes has worn the cap before."

"He has?"

Nayla nodded. "During the Gigantomachy—the war of the gods against the giants."

"My presence would be redundant then, eh? And I can live forever. It's only been five years. I can wait. But you. You have already waited many long human lifespans."

"Ah, but I am in possession of my Atma, whereas attaining your soul is a much worthier cause." Nayla pumped Céleste's hand. "It's all right. Odysseus himself was afraid of the underworld."

"It's not just Erebus that scares me. It's the way in." Céleste looked back at the square's ghostly hub, wishing Gustave were here for once. To stop the meeting. Or at least for a skip in the acorn to empower her. She had checked her doily belt this evening and the observatory was reopened. Too late.

"Melinoë is standing right at the putain door," Céleste continued.

"Goddess of ghosts, nightmares, and madness? That Melinoë?"

"The very same." Céleste nodded, incredulous.

"That," said Nayla, "is a character actress."

"I'm not so sure."

The aspiring actress lifted her chin. Light the color of quince leaked onto her face. Her hair was frizzed, parted in the center beneath the rakish hat, her makeup a contrast of black and white. Splatter ringed her eye and ran down her cheek as if inked by a fountain pen. Her split lip appeared to bleed when she spoke.

"Enter, mortal of this sinful world, enter into the mists and shadows of eternity."

"She's no actress," Céleste whispered, squeezing Nayla's hand white.

"Think of your children," Nayla whispered back. "Of all the despair and anxiety they'll be saddled with if you can't teach them it's all right to be themselves. They'll never be content in their own skins if you're not content in yours. They'll grow into adults and turn to sex to feel alive. Isn't that what you told me?"

Céleste nodded in pain. "Oui. I'll take the hits, so they don't have to."

"I don't mean to sound harsh," said Nayla. "Your husband can always raise them."

Céleste shook her head. "I won't be able to find a husband until I heal. Not a good one. Half a person can only half love, which means they'll try to merge with me and I with them. To keep a whole person, I need to *be* a whole person."

The Incident hadn't driven her mad yet. The day-mares might glue her to the floor, steal her breath, embarrass her to no end, and send her back to July 1887, but they couldn't kill her. She was immortal.

She clutched her basket of honey cakes laced with laudanum and thought of the children she wanted to bear. Dear Étienne. Sweet Eulalie. Mes choux. The suffering she must endure for this painless future... She pretended she was in a pantomime, walking into the gloom with the sensation of falling into a chasm. It was the only way to move her feet.

Melinoë drew open the heavy curtain and gestured to the foreboding hole.

The cabaret had been updated, the surroundings changed, making less room for the familiar and more for the unknown.

Céleste's heart crossed the threshold and palpitated wildly.

Light from wax tapers and a large chandelier devised of human remains entranced the Room of Intoxication. Wooden coffins resting on biers served as tables, skulls and bones on the walls as décor. Wrought iron curved up the corners and blossomed into dead posies with black stained glass and iron webs spun onto the ceiling. This was no room. This was a rib cage. Suffocating. Smaller than she remembered.

"Select your bier," said Melinoë.

Céleste jumped at the split face on her shoulder.

"Fit yourself comfortably to it," Melinoë continued, "and repose in the solemnity and tranquility of death. May the Fates have mercy on your *soul*."

Céleste didn't like the way she said *soul*. It scratched her wound. Further exposure to these familiar surroundings might just launch a psychic attack. Les gendarmes would come and lock her up in Salpêtrière or Saint-Lazare. What else would these bar patrons make of her writhing on the floor? She could not speculate. She was glad they were here, members of society, the uninitiated who would prevent anything sudden and supernatural from occurring. She hoped.

She searched the bar installed on the side, shaped like an organ, its pipes cut to hold the bartender's liqueurs. The stools were furnished from bones. Théo must've camped there on his nights off and drank until he was red in the face.

Céleste took refuge at an empty chair and sank her chin against the coffin lid. Nayla filled the seat opposite.

"Bonsoir, macchabée!" called the waiter, dressed like an undertaker.

Céleste sure felt like a macchabée, the name Athenian soldiers gave to cadavers found floating in the Seine, she had come to learn. It also meant "drunk." Perhaps Nayla could relate in a moment.

The waiter, masked in impeccable zombie makeup, pointed to the drink menu and asked what cold sweat from a dying man's brow she would like to consume tonight.

"Cherries à l'eau-de-vie," Céleste replied, after a glance at the menu.

Nayla raised her eyes from the print. "Mind if I indulge?"

Nayla's body was more important than her mind at this juncture. She was fresh off a recovery phase and was their only defense, assuming Hermes would stand idly by if Cerberus turned them into chew toys. Céleste couldn't taste death, but she could still feel pain. Cerby better like her cooking, in case Nayla was too drunk to play sitar. Céleste had hoped bringing honey cakes wouldn't hurt Nayla's feelings, but she seemed to understand.

"Two beers and a crème de menthe," sung Nayla's clarinet voice.

"Two microbes of Asiatic cholera from the last corpse," their zombie called to the bartender, "one leg of a lively cancer, and one sample of our consumption germ!"

Women at neighboring coffins tittered. Others shuddered. Céleste wanted to hide underneath. Instead, she thrummed the lid.

"I was afraid you were going to limit me," Nayla exulted.

"You need projectiles," said Céleste, nodding to the sitar case, "and we packed your costume for a reason."

"I packed yours, too."

Céleste sat up at the notion.

"I was being hopeful," Nayla explained. "It's not too late." She eyed the waiter. "Maybe one of the zombies. I mean, if you want to."

"I know." Céleste read it as flattery. "My soul may be crawling with demons."

"Maybe your soul will restore your powers permanently," Nayla encouraged.

"One can hope." All those dead-end Erebus Rooms... Part of her didn't believe Hermes could even take her there.

When their zombie returned, Céleste tried to picture him without makeup.

"Drink, macchabées," he proclaimed. "Drink these noxious potions, containing the vilest and deadliest poisons." He placed the cluster of drinks on the coffin and departed dearly.

"For moi?" Hermes was upon them like a gust of wind. "How considerate." He picked up one of Nayla's drinks, a glass stemmed with finger bones, and sipped.

His body was agile and sinewed under his waistcoat. His face was a masterfully designed rudder with fuzzy hair that he wore like a flag. He may've been in his late twenties or three thousand twenties, and he smelled like a patisserie.

Nayla choked the introductions, so he finished them and took his seat, eyeing Céleste with fierce intensity.

She grabbed hold of the glass skull and sipped the brandied cherries, leaving a red mark on her lips. "I understand you can guide me to my soul."

"You understand well."

"In exchange for?"

"I simply wanted to meet you. You're a magnificent dancer."

"What's all this talk about Daphne and Apollo?"

Nayla fidgeted.

"I felt an instant connection the moment I saw you," he confessed without recrimination, "as strong as Apollo did for Daphne."

Céleste smiled politely. "Thanks for the compliment." *And the upper hand.* "Where is my soul? The precise location." She assumed she would sense it upon arrival, but she wanted to know for certain.

"In time, I will show you."

"And you know where it is?" she persisted.

He set his arm on the table and leaned in. "If every guide told you the way, there wouldn't be much use for guides then, would there?"

Nayla piped up. "You can get us home too, right?"

He examined her.

"Hecate is one of my patrons," Nayla hurriedly explained. "Portals open to Tartarus when someone around me dies. If I step through, the only way back on my own is for someone to die again, someone whom I bring with me."

"What an unpleasant way to travel," Hermes concluded. "Fear not. I can provide safe charter to and fro, provided you brought the sops."

"And a sitar," Nayla added.

"Where is your mechanized contraption?" Hermes checked under the table. "Shame. You could've subdued the beast like Heracles."

"No harm will befall the dog and—you've been reading my mail!" Nayla accused.

"Hephaestus was very proud." Hermes directed his sharp eyes on Céleste. "Same for you. Aphrodite admired the way you danced, heart and soul. As did Psyche."

I am nothing.

Céleste shifted. "Can we please not mention that here?"

She prepared for the whirlpool, an overflow of darkness from the voice in the void, but none came. It was just one bad intrusive thought. Like a hiccup. Nipped in the bud.

Hermes scanned the room. "I assure you no one is listening."

"It's not that. It's... This is where my soul was stolen. It's what sent me prowling the streets. To save other people so they wouldn't have to experience what I live through daily. A demon almost took my life the first time I intervened for someone else's. Then Aphrodite and Psyche intervened for me."

Hermes extended a caring hand.

Hesitantly, she clasped it.

"What happened here, my flower?"

Flower? The god was clearly enamored. Maybe it would prove useful, but it left her with a decision. Ought she to share her deep, dark secret? Fork over a part of herself? It could backfire with criticism. And, usually, when courting desire, the less the other person knew, the better. Love had information. Lust knew very little. If Hermes was drawn to her purely for lust, revelation would lead to disinterest. She got the sense that he had mounted her on a pedestal somewhere in the Greek temple of his mind. Perhaps sharing would throw him into a posture of rescue.

"My old chaperone was a man named Théophile Deveaux. He was heavyset, handsome, and very much possessed by a demon. He snuck me into this cabaret for a drink and drank often, against Papa's wishes. Papa never protested. He shirked his responsibility as a family man and left the role for other people to take care of for fear of conflict and being disliked. So what if his fourteen-year-old daughter was sneaking out to bars? The fault was Théo's. Papa did the best he could, which is the lie he tells himself."

The candle tossed light from Hermes's cheeks to the ridge of his brow, shading the region in between.

"We're in the Salle d'Intoxication," said Céleste. "The next room is La Grotte des Trespasses. The last is an area in the basement with a magic show called Caveau les Spectres. I had ran ahead from La Grotte to escape. It was there in the catacomb, in Le Caveau, before the bar patrons arrived, when Théo attacked. He threw me onto a stone bench, reached his hand into my ribs, and wrenched my soul from its bolt."

"Did you fight back?" Hermes asked.

Céleste squeezed his hand. "With every fiber."

Nayla knitted her brow. "How horrible. It reminds me what these demons are capable of..."

"Yes," said Hermes, removing his hand. "Dreadful."

I am nothing.

Céleste touched her chest.

Oh non. Keep it together. You are something.

Whatever Hermes's opinion of her, speaking about the Incident made her squeamish, as if the walls had ears and she were summoning the event to reoccur. Du Néant was space on a plot of land. Nothing more. But who was she fooling? Even the air knew the truth. Spiritually, if the whole boulevard returned to nature, she bet she could've still located the exact spot where it happened.

She ordered cardoons from the stove to distract her from sitting in her least favorite place in the world, while Hermes preceded to reveal his whole life story. His mother Maia was a mountain nymph, oldest of the seven Pleiades, and had abused him heinously by neglect.

Nayla nodded along to confirm these tales and drained her first bock like a blacksmith off duty. She set the hollowed femur down and ordered another round for herself.

After ample time for guests to finish their meals, a bell rang on the ceiling—a graveyard bell, the last hope for those mistakenly buried alive to save themselves. Melinoë answered the call with a lantern raised above her head, shining on her top hat. Her arms, silk worms, glistened green. The funerary candles in the bony chandeliers joined her lantern in blasting shadows into the cobweb encased vault, casting a spell over diners to follow her into La Grotte des Trespasses so long as she was their loyal psychopomp.

"Is that the real Melinoë?" Céleste whispered to Hermes as they decamped the table.

He nodded gravely.

Céleste gave Nayla an I-told-you-so look, glad they'd chosen him instead for the poster.

The visitors filed into a narrow passage, trailing behind Melinoë's green rays.

"Ladies first." Hermes gestured. "This brief leg of the journey I leave to her."

Nayla offered Céleste her free hand. Céleste took it and walked. Yellow and green revolving light danced on her arms as she ran her fingers on the bumpy walls—over polished skulls, paraffin wax skin, and the peaks and troughs of bones—making sure not to lose her party.

She looked back at Hermes, gliding along, light on his feet, and looked forward, where Nayla's darkened eye was checking to see if a ghoul had nabbed her. Not this macchabée. She was still dancing.

"O macchabées," moaned Melinoë by a dungeon gate, "we have arrived at the Vault of Trespasses. Enter into eternity, whence none ever return." She clanked in the key and swung open the door.

Céleste entered with the group and took her seat upon the cemetery benches, between Nayla and Hermes, the basket of honey cakes stowed underneath, facing a stage. Two candles diffused their feeble light by a coffin-shaped hole stationed in the center. This time she would not run ahead.

Melinoë took the stage and stood by the vacant upright. "O macchabées..." The script replayed a chorus on Céleste's memory of when Théo had brought her here. "...I request a hot-blooded donor from our pool who is prepared to die."

Céleste's fingers went numb in Nayla's relaxed hand. Sweat dewed on Céleste's forehead. She wiped it with her sleeve.

I am nothing, I am nothing.

Her house was haunted. They'd come too far to turn back. She kept quiet. She had to suffer the ghost alone.

"I'll volunteer." Nayla slowly stood.

What? What had gotten into her? Practicing courage? Perhaps having Hecate as a patron steeled her against Hades's other proprietors. Or she was drunk.

Céleste clapped, distracted by her own thoughts, her applause soon accompanied by the rest of their cramped little chamber.

Melinoë assisted Nayla into the reclined cushion within the coffin frame, fit her snugly with a white shroud that covered her from the bust down, and passed silently out of view. Nayla gave a sheepish grin. It tickled Hermes pink and provoked laughter from their small audience. Céleste detected the vertical half of Melinoë's white gown lurking in the corner and reached for Hermes's hand for something to hold on to.

"O macchabée, beautiful, breathing mortal, pulsating with warmth and the richness of life, thou art now in the grasp of death! Compose thy soul for the end!"

Nayla's face petrified to a shade of white—her eyes sank, her lips tightened across her teeth, her cheeks took on the hollowness of death. The skin decomposed into violet and black. Her once dark-ringed eyes shrank into their gangrenous sockets. Her beautiful raven hair fell away, starting with the coiled braid. Her angular nose melted into a putrid hole. The face became a semi-liquid mass of corruption—her poor friend. Céleste turned away.

"Is this an illusion?" she asked Hermes. She had snuck out before this part. "Is it real?"

"Observe."

She forced herself to bear witness.

A skull gleamed in lieu of Nayla's head, her velvet lips replaced by a toothy grin. The shroud slowly vanished, revealing her skeleton. This couldn't have been what Nayla wanted. Was this what being one with Brahman looked like? To sidestep out of reality?

"Ah, ah, macchabée!" Melinoë wailed. "Thou hast reached the last stage of dissolution so dreadful to mortals. The work that follows death is complete. But despair not, for death is not the end of all. The power is given to those who merit it, not only to return to life, but to return in any form and station preferred to the old. So return if thou deservedst and desirest."

Was that how the script went five years ago? Or was the goddess playing on Nayla's belief in reincarnation?

With a slowness equal to that of the dissolution, the bones became covered with flesh and cerements, and all the ghastly steps were reversed. Gradually, the sparkle of eyes shone through the abyss, and Melinoë helped Nayla out of the recess to soft applause and Céleste's utter relief. She brushed her hand across Nayla's leg as soon as she sat down. Still in one piece. She barely got comfortable when Melinoë roused the group to another door.

"Come, macchabées, to your final stop—le Caveau les Spectres"—the Cave of Ghosts.

Melinoë relit her lantern and guided the visitors into another passageway.

"Nothing to fear," whispered Hermes, tugging Céleste to rise.

They filtered into the sloping hall. The tunnel expanded to archways similar to those of an underground mausoleum. It was too much. Théo. Her Thief. Her soul. Erebus. The moment she sat upon the stone, her heart would tumble up her throat and spill out her mouth. The bowler hat on the man in front of her blurred into the shadow.

I am nothing, I am nothing, I am nothing.

"I can't do this." She stopped.

The aperture at the end of the hall pulsated a violent echo, reverberating through her chest cavity. With no soul to absorb the tremor and ground the current, she felt as though she were a hollow log, a mannequin on display in a funhouse.

I am nothing, I am nothing, I am nothing.

"I'm having trouble existing right now."

Nayla was at her side. "Isn't that why we're here?" She turned to Hermes. "Is there another entrance somewhere in Athens?"

"Several. Though it won't do. Melinoë is expecting us."

"What will it be, macchabées?" asked Melinoë, propping open the door at the end of the passage.

Céleste studied her whereabouts. Melinoë was ensconced in her green aura. The crowd had long since pushed through into the next chamber.

Céleste touched her bosom. A shiver hurtled over the discs in her spine. She had to keep going, for her children and their well-bred futures. Étienne. Eulalie. Her unnamed husband who loved her, who was waiting for her to heal so he could meet her and see how special she was. She took a step toward the toxic light.

I am nothing, I am nothing, I am nothing.

Don't stop. Keep moving. One foot at a time.

The arts had attracted a greater presence to French Athens than she ever felt possible. It was Melinoë standing there, for the love of God. Céleste's hairs rose as she passed the goddess, the black eyes viewing her, the bicolored lips smirking.

Céleste staggered into the charnel house theater followed by Hermes, Nayla, and Nayla's hefty sitar case. The door creaked shut, locked by the scrape and thump of a rusty latch. Guests had taken their seats, awaiting the act. The confined stage was but a ratty maroon curtain strung across the archway to a mausoleum. No exit door stage right. Running from Théo... She wouldn't have made it.

"The Lesser Mysteries are near upon us." Melinoë handed Céleste and Nayla two slender potions. "Drink."

"What is it?" Céleste whispered, seeing that other patrons were already wetting their whistles.

"It's a kykeon"—Melinoë pressed her cheek to hers—"which is French for ergotized beer—made from rye smut. Drink, Fleur d'Étoile, and I will guarantee thee safe passage."

Céleste shivered at the sound of her name. She sniffed the brew. Her nose hairs recoiled from the odor. She looked at Nayla. She hadn't touched her drink either.

"If you desire the chance to reunite with your soul, I suggest you get quaffing," said Melinoë. "I shan't repeat myself again." She hung the lantern and made her way to the stage. "O, macchabées..."

Céleste probed the liquid with her tongue. It peeled back into her mouth, capturing the taste of burnt garbage.

"It has to be drank in one gulp," said Nayla. "Plug your nose."

"I'll plug my whole face." With luck, it would take her mind off sitting on one of those slabs.

"Come, ladies, to our seats." Hermes took the initiative and sat in the back row.

Céleste and Nayla exchanged looks and clinked femurs.

"Prost."

"À la tienne, Étienne."

She knocked back the unspeakable mixture and pulled the femur away as if she had submerged her head in a sewer. The only saving grace were a couple fruity notes played at the finale. Nauseous vinegar. She wiped her lips.

Hermes lured them to their seats with a glare.

"Is it the same bench?" asked Nayla.

"Non, thank goodness." She touched the seat, expecting it to undo her. No ice bath sensation came. She was too busy smacking her lips, getting used to the rancid taste in her mouth.

Where was this so-called entrance? Behind the curtain?

Melinoë parted the fold. "Persephone lies deep beyond the veil. I require three macchabées from the audience to fetch her and return with the season of spring by Février's end. Lo, the journey is dangerous, you must be swift. You have been warned."

Was this part of the act? February's end? Would her soul take two months to find? Mercy.

"You three." She pointed to Céleste, Nayla, and Hermes. "Come hither."

Céleste tightened her grip on the basket and stood. The sloshed audience looked on amusedly as she walked the aisle, closer to the scene of her Incident in which an old lady now sat with a dead bird on her toque, watching her—*I am nothing, I am nothing, I am nothing*. Céleste gripped her basket tighter.

"Don't look at the spot," Nayla whispered.

She squeezed Céleste's arm to keep going and led her to the mausoleum steps, legs wobbling as she embarked.

Behind the curtain was an empty niche. There was nothing there, but it didn't stop Melinoë from shooing them in, where she displayed them before the crowd.

"Return with Persephone to Eleusis by Février's end at the time of our Lesser Mysteries and humanity shall be graced by an abundant harvest. Adieu."

The Athenian crowd vanished as Melinoë shut the curtain. Darkness. Quickly, Hermes whirled Céleste and Nayla around to face a growing smoke hole. He stepped through. Blindly, Céleste followed, emerging into the familiar domed arena she had chased countless demons into a countless many times. Maybe this was where the demon that possessed Théo had originally escaped from.

Gray clouds precipitated overhead in the hemisphere. Smoke crawled on the ground like snakes. The crumbling ruins of a chateau and outbuildings littered the plane. The old tranquility of existing in between realms lifted her lips into a hypnotic grin. Hairs tendrilled out from her head in vines.

Hermes pressed on with a spring in his step as the smoke hole closed behind them.

"I'll never get used to these rooms." Nayla held her stomach.

Céleste was glad to be out of du Néant, though she reserved her sigh of relief. "Keep the home fires burning."

Nayla raised her free hand. "Demon?"

Céleste grew tense in the neck, expecting a lizard to get the drop on her, though much preferring physical threat to the mental pitfalls of the cabaret. "Je ne sais pas."

Hermes glanced back at them. "Worry not, my flower. No demons to speak of. *I* punctured the fabric to the underworld."

Nayla lowered her fist. "Does it snow in Erebus?"

Nayla really disliked cold weather and said nervous things.

Hermes knelt to a cellar door and pulled it open. "See for yourself." He smiled, trancelike, and descended into the shadowy bowels of the void.

Have you ever looked deep inside yourself and wondered what the hell is wrong with you? I mean, gazed into your bathroom mirror until you frightened yourself? How about the mirror at the bar at the Folies Bergère?

Céleste and Nayla had. Oui, Jacques too. We're looking at it this very moment.

Excusez-moi, my friend. I should have known. I assume too much. For you—you accept both the positive and negative aspects of yourself. Bravo and brava. For those without self-worth, you must understand, it is very difficult to come by.

We tend to seek outside of ourselves. Some look for male attention. Others find alcohol, to name a few. Once in a while, though, we discover that if we achieve this one thing, all our problems will be solved. Money. Career. Relationship. Health. We just need the Cap of Hades. Our very soul. The panacea, the cure-all, the Advance to GO card. These objects represented a better life. To kickstart self-love from the outside in.

And why not? Nayla believed she was born to suffer based on the karmic debt of past lives. There was nothing she could do about it, save for moksha. Céleste—she had determined she was born normal, and that something bad had happened to her. The Incident. Her soul-theft. If she could not retrieve it, she would be doomed to walk the Earth a half-person forever.

You hear that voice? The one saying you're garbage and always will be? That you have no hope. No future. No chance. I know you don't, my friend. You are a well-rounded individual. But some, left to their own devices, call this voice your inner critic, or Baba. Some even call it the voice in the void. And it reinforces your self-image.

How to contend with this unruly creature? And what is it guarding from you? Dare you challenge fear incarnate? To quiet his snarl, his gnashing teeth... Do you choke him to death? Do you feed him a honey cake? Could you play him a lullaby? If his name is Cerberus, these options are at your disposal.

Hades was not a stroll in a theme park. This was a plunge into the unconscious. Ah, you did not know. Jacques will inform. Homeric Hades is a physical location, oui, but Platonic Hades is a journey into the mind. For all intents and purposes, they are one in the same, both corporeal and ethereal—existing in the outer world of the body and the inner world of the mind, where the seen and unseen blur.

To pursue one of these miracle objects was a dangerous undertaking. For good reason. The underworld did things to people. No matter the motive, if you were there, you were in the muck and mire with everyone who'd crossed its gates, trying to find something, to run from something, or simply lost.

D'accord. What you say makes perfect sense. Perhaps they needed a buddy system to take the leap of faith into the great unknown. They gave each other accountability, because now they had a shoulder to lean on. They had someone who understood chaos.

Now they had their mirrors.

A SOP FOR CERBERUS

Nayla slipped off the sitar case, unbuckled it on the floor of the Erebus Room, and tuned her instrument.

"Get your honey cakes ready," she said.

Céleste creased her brow, clutching her basket. "You think Cerberus is in there?"

Nayla stared into the abyss. "I'm not taking any chances." She strummed her chords, feeling high from the effects of the room—or maybe from the drink Melinoë had served, or the other drinks she'd guzzled down.

Céleste tucked her hand under the basket's linen while Nayla led the way into blackness.

Shadows enveloped her in a rush of nerves, the stone beneath her feet the only thing she was certain of as she plodded down the cellar steps. "Hermes?" Her voice waivered.

"Mind the corner." His voice came on a breeze.

She found a landing and looped around it to more stairs, now leading back up. A pair of stairs that led to the same level?

"You won't need those yet." Hermes glanced at the sitar and basket of cakes.

A cellar door parted to gray skies, the silhouette of Hermes's slim frame between her and what lied beyond. She breathed. Breathed and walked up. Into the very Erebus Room they'd left.

"Is this a cruel joke?" she asked.

"No joke," said Hermes.

"Something feels different," said Céleste.

"It looks identical," said Nayla. "There are the castle ruins, the weird smoldering lines on the floor."

"The trance is different," said Céleste. "Do you feel it? Before it was a convex feeling. This one is concave." She spoke with her hand, sensing correctly that Nayla wasn't getting it. "It's like if someone were to ask you how you feel, you would say, like a deck of cards with one missing or like you have a shoe with a pebble in it. Something is horribly wrong, but it sounds like two dust mites colliding when you say it out loud. Anxiety sets in. Panic."

Something *was* off. Like Nayla'd had some bad cactus juice. She turned to Hermes as he met the wall of the hemisphere. Instantly, she knew. They were elsewhere. In Hades. "Are you going to help us with Cerberus?"

"You are the traveler. I am the guide. I elaborate, elucidate, illuminate. I can't make decisions for you." His hand rotated like a fan until a smoke hole opened in the glass dome. "But I can administer direction."

He walked through the smoky wreath. Nayla checked behind her for Céleste and followed Hermes, coming through the other side of the hole into a stone niche. He yanked aside the tattered curtain.

"The Cabaret du Néant?" asked Nayla.

"Not again." Céleste clung to her arm.

The rows of seats were vacant, the room, dark. Hermes loped off the stage and drifted down the center aisle. Nayla tightened her grip on the sitar while Céleste clung to her back.

"There!" Céleste nearly smacked Nayla on the chin pointing to one of the benches.

A phantom in a bowler hat and jowls straddled a young woman, his fingers digging into her chest. A long needle fell to the floor—a hatpin. He grabbed the crucifix around her neck in the scuffle and ripped the chain. The image flickered and was gone.

"Did you see...?" Céleste's eyes went goggle-wide.

Nayla nodded.

"I never want to see that again." Céleste's voice cracked. "Not outside my own mind." She turned. "Why did you show me that?" She lobbed the blame at Hermes, standing with his back to her.

"I would do no such thing."

Something was happening to Céleste, to her face, as if a light inside struggled to turn on. "I can't sense my soul," she said suddenly. "Like everything is underwater."

Slowly, Hermes turned. Beneath his chiseled exterior glowed his skull in phosphorescent light. "Welcome to Hades." His jaw was visible. His cheekbones burned orange-violet as he moved, the twin holes for his nose, his brow, the light growing and fading depending on his movements. "You'll get used to it."

Nayla thought not. Céleste's vertebrae was greenish-pink, along with her eye sockets. She could see the molars in her cheeks diminish like embers.

She kept her eyes locked on Cél and dared a look at her own hands. Fragile bones glowed vibrant yellow, claw like, blinding red, through her skin. It was like she'd removed a panel to a piece of machinery to see all the moving parts. In glimpses. Coming and going. The glow appeared to respond to some strange miasma that hung in the air.

"The rye smut beer," said Céleste. "We're hallucinating."

"Are you?" asked Hermes, waving them on. "Ready your cakes and song." He picked up the lantern by the corridor. Sparks shot from it like fireflies.

"You're not being very elucidating," Nayla observed. "What was in that drink?"

"The price of admission."

Nayla swallowed. She had bigger problems. Cerberus. "Has anyone ever not made it?"

"He's a three-headed Rottweiler who will tear your head off." Hermes undid the rusty latch.

"Not my head," Céleste said. "I'm immortal."

"Of course, my flower." He framed her face with a gesture of his hand. "I would never let anything befall you. If I have the choice, that is." He bounced into the tunnel on the balls of his feet. "You must face Cerberus without me and hope he's receptive, for the sake of your mortal friend."

Céleste is mortal too! Nayla wanted to scream. But she bit her tongue, not wanting to torment Céleste more than their surroundings already were.

Hermes's suit glowed green, lit by his bones, looping through La Grotte des Trespasses where Nayla had volunteered for the optical illusion. She snaked through another bumpy hall and out into the Salle d'Intoxication. The air was speckled with luminous pollen. It floated over the bar and tables. Vines weaved the walls throughout the room. Nayla rapped at one, expecting the solid knock of iron, encountering instead the pad of soft wood. Not lumber—the tree itself. A flower had blossomed on the floor as tall as her, violet and pleated like an upside-down skirt.

"It's a corpse flower," said Céleste.

Nayla peered closer.

"The window!" Céleste shouted, pointing at a large, distorted shadow lumbering by the cob-webbed stained glass. "It's him. It's Cerberus."

Those shutters were closed in Athens.

"The most I can do is open the door." Hermes reached for the handle.

Nayla's heartrate quickened.

"Zut alors!" Céleste reached for her basket. "Should I throw him a sop?"

Ja, she could start with this guy. He was no help at all.

"Two sops," continued Céleste, when Nayla had failed to reply.

Nayla wet her lips. "Cerberus may be a supernatural creature, but he is still an animal with feelings like us."

A giant black pretzel smudged the glass on the front door. It sniffed loud, repeatedly, hyperventilating like her lungs. The growl was low and guttural, vibrating the pane. Nayla shied back. Cerberus was not going to give her a warm reception.

Céleste tightened her fist on the basket and Nayla's leg of mutton sleeve.

Had Céleste hugged anyone goodbye, in case they were never seen or heard from again? She probably wouldn't have as an *immortal*. Nayla had at least said goodbye to her French acquaintances at the workshop. Writing Kameera was out of the question. Touching the pen to paper filled her with too much guilt, but she'd written Ojas—her first sign of life since leaving for French Athens. She couldn't exactly use the word "goodbye," though she told him about her job as a seamstress, the café concerts, and the asymmetrical absurdity of the place. Or so she'd thought. This was much crazier. In Erebus, the damn architecture was alive.

"You're sure he likes Oriental music?" asked Céleste.

"I could try dancing." Nayla raised a hopeful brow.

"Nay, I say this from a place of love. Go baltering around out there, and you'll get your entrails ripped out."

Nayla bowed her head. It was tough criticism. Yet true. But when she danced, she felt closer to Maman. It was weird. If she accepted her musical gifts, in a twisted way, she'd reject her longing to dance and sever the connection with Maman. Although, Céleste was a professional giving her this painful advice, and her misguided *immortal* life was on the line. In this instant, it was wiser to do what came naturally.

"Everybody ready?" Hermes asked, hand firmly on the latch.

Nayla plucked at the strings, playing a melody she had first composed at the stepwell. Children had gathered around while the women collected water. She pretended as though she were stirring their enjoyment once more. She had to be as good a sitarist as Orpheus was a lyrist, and according to myth, he was one of the best in the ancient world.

Nayla gulped. "Ready."

Céleste released her grip.

Hermes swung in.

Cap of Hades. Cap of Hades. Moksha. Freedom from suffering.

Nayla's fingers massaged the strings, drawing and releasing tension, as she sucked in a breath and stepped through the door. Three pairs of eyes set in three ferocious heads glared at her in low rumbles. Drool leaked onto her foot from the center head, his breath stinking of horse carcass. Cerberus provided no room to move. His body took up the street. Was it a street or a jungle? His leg was as tall as she was. She could fit in his muzzle and be gobbled up in one bite. *Play, Nayla, play.*

She lulled her head side to side and strummed.

What are you going to do with that? Play fetch?—Baba's voice sounded clear as day.

Don't hesitate, Nayla. Cerberus was on top of her.

Céleste had set her basket down and was rocking her hips like a crankshaft on a train. Her arms swooped overhead, a belly-dance without a belly, fully dressed in a gray gown.

You can't play worth mung dal, said Baba.

"You're lying!" said Nayla, dragging the notes.

"Hein?" asked Céleste.

Cut out that racket. I'm sleeping.

"If you're always sleeping," said Nayla, "when will I have time to practice?"

Cerberus growled and let out a thunderous series of barks.

"Gah." Céleste winced, touching her chest. "Nay, don't stop playing. Who are you talking to?"

"Baba. Don't you hear him?"

"Non, only the voice in the void. My soul-cave. It's getting louder." She kept dancing, rocking side to side.

Why do you think I sold it? asked Baba. *To spare me the headache!*

"den Mund halten!" Nayla shouted.

Cerberus barked louder, roared.

Mirza can play better. Go get him.

"I am a good sitarist," said Nayla.

It's your fault I'm dead.

"I'm sorry, Baba. I didn't mean to tell Ravi uncle. Just tell me, why did you have to turn on the distillery?"

Céleste held her chest as though it were on fire. "Nayla, there's no one there. Don't stop playing." Her dance was getting sloppy.

Cerberus lifted his paw and crushed the basket of treats.

"We had the money," said Nayla. "Did you not trust the mecha-sleeves? Did you not trust me?"

Cerberus barked incessantly, drool raining down, eyes ferocious.

"Nay!" Céleste knelt to the ground, covering her chest. "The voice is booming. The dog is aggravating it. Make it stop!"

Something sharp lay nearby—a sword, left by some poor soul.

Céleste picked it up.

A knife had made Baba stop. But so did showing him that the mecha-sleeves worked. It was an act of love. Shouting only made it worse.

Céleste hurried to Cerberus's leg, raising the sword like a bat.

"Céleste, don't!" cried Nayla. "Think of Nougat. You wouldn't hurt Nougat, would you?"

Céleste hesitated. "Non, but, it's not Nougat. It's Cerberus."

"There is Brahman inside that dog." Nayla plucked her notes, somewhat distracting him.

"He's guarding Hades." Céleste froze.

Baba's warnings. His need for perfection. They protected Nayla from failure—from making Baba look like a failure—but how else was she to learn without failing? Without taking a chance? The whole time she practiced sitar she'd felt humiliated. Every single bad chord and dull note brought down buckets of shame. But if she didn't cling to the outcome... if it was all right to fail... if her survival didn't depend on Baba's mood, the unknown process of learning would've been more enjoyable and not so scary. If she could only apply that murky process to grow throughout life she—

"He's not guarding Hades!" said Nayla.

Céleste screwed up her face.

"Not in this situation," Nayla clarified, holding the twang. "He knows we're nymphs. He's protecting us from Hades!"

"Even if it means devouring us?"

"Ja. He is that terrified of us venturing in. We have to tell him we'll be all right. Show him there's no reason to fear for our safety."

"But I am afraid."

"Then he'll never let us pass."

"Nay."

Nayla lulled her head once more. The dog heads lulled too. Trancelike, calm, collected, she drew out her notes. The sounds resonated in the air, the pattern alternating from silence to noise with each strum, creating melody, like riding in a caravan to Cairo, trekking across the ripples in the dunes, the desert floor no different from the ocean's. Another stage for the universal audience. Kameera and Pradeep floated on saddles like boats over sand, crafted by Brahman, who understood the love language of song.

Céleste dropped the sword and danced moving her hips.

Cerberus backed onto the boulevard and lied in the lichen, his bulk the size of an omnibus. Trees had replaced columns in maintaining the structure of the swampy trench that became his crib. Feathery vines draped from ash to oak. Mystic blue colors emblazoned the bizarre forest of apartments, blending into the low-lying fog that crawled along the mossy stones on which thumped Cerberus's wagging tail.

"He needs comfort," said Nayla. "Tell him you're not ashamed to see what's in Hades."

"What?" Céleste knitted her brow.

He howled at the sky and rested on his paws, the outside heads nestled on his main. Animals could sense fear. *Be fearless, Nayla. You wouldn't pet an animal you're afraid of, would you?* She hung the sitar off her back and approached the beast. In many ways, he was no different from a camel. She raised her hand. Her heart worked vehemently. Farther she rose, found fur, and scratched behind his ear, her purple dress full against his ruff.

"Who's a handsome boy?" Nayla whispered. "You are. You're so handsome. Such a pretty baby, protecting me from the big bad underworld. Are you afraid to show us the skeletons? You did a good job defending me, Herr Cerberus, but I have lots of firepower and bravery and there's nothing that can hurt me in there anymore. Maman will be all right. Will you be good for Maman?"

Cerberus whimpered.

"Cerberus, you'll have to trust that I'll make it through in one piece or we'll be locked in a standoff forever." Or until he ate her. "Do you want Maman to move forward or stagnate? You want Maman to grow, don't you? To be lovable? Ja. You want her to reach moksha. Ja, you do. Om mani padme hum. See, I'll make it. Nothing to worry about."

A great tongue like a pendulum snuck out and licked her.

Every muscle in Céleste's neck went tense, her lower lip stretched, her eyebrows shaped like a yakhchāl. "Nay, get over here."

Nayla walked casually to her. "What?"

"You're drunk," she scolded.

"You think I'd do this sober?" Nayla kept scratching. "Tell him you'll face your demons, and mean it."

"Are you—I—"

"It's been five years, Cél."

"I know." Céleste breathed. "I know."

"From the heart. As if he were no different than Nougat."

Cerberus raised his center head at her approach. Céleste held out her hand. He sniffed it and turned aside. Céleste scratched him.

"Thank you for helping me survive. You did your part. It's up to me now. I don't have my powers, but I have immortality and I won't ever give up. The emptiness hurts me, Chouchou. You have to let me fill it. It's the only way I'll start a healthy family. Doesn't that sound nice?" She reached behind his ear. "A nice family that cares for each other?"

The left head wanted scratching too, which Céleste obliged.

His tail stopped wagging, and he shifted his heads and nodded off to sleep.

Céleste swallowed a hard gulp. She straightened her dress and turned to Nayla. "Good job, Vidocq."

"Danke." Nayla swelled with relief and pride at having found some courage.

"How did you know what to do? History book?"

"Nein. I felt it out. Baba needed soothing."

Céleste nodded. "Well, judging from the sleeping canine, I say you are an excellent sitar player."

"Danke," said Nayla.

Perhaps music was her true calling when it came to the arts. Didn't Coronis, her patron nymph, bang on a tambourine? That had to have meant something. Was Nayla meant to celebrate through music or liquor? She didn't know, but liquor worked.

"Where is Hermes?" Nayla continued. The door to du Néant had shut. "Waiting for us to die?"

"If only," said Céleste. "I see what you now mean. He's completely besotted. I have an idea." She waved her in close. "Offer to put in a good word to me on his behalf, say you'll elevate him in my eyes, in exchange for information on the Hall of Fabled Objects."

"I thought discussing that was verboten?" Nayla slung the sitar on her back. "He'll tell Hades."

"Not if he gets what he wants."

"You're going to have a lark?"

"I have to go poof, don't I, if I am to fight demons?"

"Not necessarily. I can protect you. Then we'll return to the surface where you can love Gustave in the interim before we go on to the heist in Tartarus."

"What if we go directly to the Hall without leaving Hades?"

It was so tempting. The enchanted door Nayla had only managed to budge stood between her and moksha, and Céleste wanted to reach it sooner. What a foolish errand, though. A beeline to the cap was a bad idea. But the desperation in Céleste's voice—it was clear she wanted powers to calm her mind and may not take no for an answer, in spite of her sweet talk to Cerberus. Nayla buried her objection, so as not to stall the journey. "How do I get Hermes alone?"

"We'll see if the opportunity presents itself."

Zigs and zags of purple-green pollen crossed her face, creating an ambience of haunted serenity. The boulevard was a mixture of stone and marshland. Knotty trees sent their toxic light into the fogs pervading the horizon.

Nayla looked at Cerberus to make sure he was still asleep. "If an opportunity doesn't appear?"

"We'll make one."

Hinges creaked. Du Néant's door stole open. Hermes slid out, wings on his heels, floating over the ground. He saw Cerberus and grinned at their success.

That's right, not dog food. Where to?

He raised a finger to his lips and pointed up the street. Nothing about this place made sense, but Nayla traversed the sedgy marsh and lichened stones without comment in order to put distance on Cerberus, should her liquid courage wear off.

They'd made it two blocks when Hermes said, "So happy he didn't hurt you, my flower."

"Glad I had you to open the door," Céleste remarked, giving him something to sink his teeth into.

"Céleste," said Nayla, "why does Erebus look like Athens?"

"Je ne sais pas. Care to enlighten us, Hermes?"

"You ask the wrong question. It should be, why does Athens look like Erebus?"

He levitated onward, leaving Nayla to puzzle over this quagmire. Before she gained traction, the boulevard opened into a square. Not so much a square as a dark glade cut into a forest.

"Ha! Ah! Vive les Quat'z'Arts!" A random shout froze Nayla stiff.

"Are there other people here?" she implored Hermes.

"Yes." He glanced back. "They are the artists nobody feted, the ones who will soon be forgotten."

"Where are we?" Nayla turned to Céleste.

A green and pink glow danced upon her face, belonging to a windmill by the hedgerow of the square. The façade lit up in a blaze of electric lights and colored lanterns, where the revolving wings of the mill flamed across the sky and illuminated the root-filled landscape.

"The Place Blanche?" Céleste replied uncertainly.

"Au Moulin Rouge—en route!" called the previous disembodied voice.

Céleste's mouth formed a small O. "I think it's the Four Arts Ball."

BAL DES QUAT'Z'ARTS

lectric pastels streaked each blade of the windmill as if the night were smeared with gelatin. Aquamarine, lilac, and goldenrod rippled through the air. Henri de Toulouse-Lautrec's muse must have paid this place a visit to convey him the scenery. *Mon Dieu!* Could every architect have been influenced by their muse to make Athens look like the underworld? *Je ne sais pas.* Perhaps Erebus and Athens were dance partners.

Even the parties were the same. Revelers rallied around the café tables costumed as Cherokee Indians, Scottish highlanders, and Roman statesmen in all their regal splendor. The woodland square yielded up their dead from nooks and hollows. Medieval knights and Adams and Eves amassed under the mill bubbling with merriment and mischief.

"What's the Four Arts Ball?" asked Nayla. Robust colors shifted on her transparent chin, her mandible, acid green.

"It's a costume party thrown by the École des Beaux-Arts," said Céleste. "The four art schools compete for prizes. Painting, sculpting, architecture, and engraving. No song or dance. A crime, I know." She touched Hermes on the leg. "Is my soul here?"

"Non," he admitted, "just a detour to get you away from that hound. If you would be so kind, I hoped we might partake in the festivities."

"Then to my soul?"

"Yes, my dear."

Nayla agreed with a tip of her head.

"All right," Céleste affirmed.

Hermes set his heels on the moist stone. "To get in, we must adhere to the dress code. Our costumes must be conspicuous in merit, or we risk being conducted to the door."

Nayla unbuckled a pouch in the sitar case and produced their costumes. Céleste grabbed her petal skirt and bodice, and frowned at the idea of changing the old-fashioned way. No pollinating. Just disrobing behind a tree root. She pointed at her back.

"A little help."

Nayla unlaced her back and piled the grey fabric on the ground. Hermes hovered casually, pretending not to look. Céleste didn't bother with modesty, if only to keep the messenger god baited.

She slid on her pinks, her blacks, and struggled with her sandals. Nayla laced her up while Céleste dabbed her carnival mask with glue and pressed it to her face for the big soirée.

Voilà. Fleur d'Étoile. She braced her hips and inspected Nayla. It was her turn. Céleste pulled out Nayla's floaty pants and skimpy top. Gold coins and paillettes abound.

"Don't forget your goggles!" said Céleste. "Do you need goggles? Ah, here are the almighty yak horns!"

"Maman's headpiece," Nayla corrected.

Hermes treated her transformation with indifference and whirled in an airborne pirouette. The suit tornadoed into a cloak, his chiton spread from his knees to his waist. His messenger bag swung to his hip. Of course, the costume wouldn't complete without his splendid winged helmet.

"The classic look," said Céleste, smiling. "I like it."

"Mademoiselles..." His winged feet touched the stone and he hooked out his elbows. "The ball awaits."

Nayla looked regretfully at her sitar.

"Leave it," said Hermes. "Its purpose is fulfilled."

She closed her eyes. Nayla really loved her sitar, but they were after objects more valuable.

Céleste linked Hermes's bare arm and resolved to buy Nayla some new strings when they returned home. Monsieur Desormes must know of a good dealer.

I am nothing, I am nothing, I am nothing.

Céleste shuddered. If she made it back in one piece.

Walking in Erebus had intensified her soul-throne, pounding harder in her chest here than it did on Earth. Her costume did it's best to boost her confidence, but even with her arm linked to a god who worshipped her, the monarch spots couldn't outwit the nagging void. It was the nature of Erebus—a whirlpool sensation that refused to dry up, not dissimilar to pollinating. But with pollinating, she felt buoyant underwater. Here, she sank like a rock, a strange effect, to say the least. On the order of drowning. The scenery didn't help.

The trees in the square were like striped fish she and Gustave had seen at the aquarium. The ones with the glowing lines. Neon tetras.

She looked up, on approach, as the fish swam into the Lautreckian pastels of the windmill. Inside the vestibule a tribune had been erected—a long bar—behind which sat the massiers representing each of the four arts, checking for tickets and vetting costumes. A sign read: *None in civilian dress may pass.* Doubt crept in through Céleste's eyeholes. Was her costume good enough? Hermes produced three golden invitations. The inspector scanned their party and nodded with satisfaction. Merci. Evidently it was.

She parted the curtains and entered a dazzling dream of rich color and reckless abandon. The floor was imbued with saffron, the walls a blur of green. Her skin took on a chalky pallor, china doll white, beneath her serpent bracelet. Nayla's face was white too, her complexion porcelain with turquoise grading her forehead.

Kings and queens gathered at the bar. Courtiers in silk, naked gladiators, and nymphs rounded the tables. Rose perfume thickened the air. Shouts, laughter, and the silvery clink of glasses spun into a whirling mass of life and death bewildering Céleste in a maze of tangled visions, cozy and confused in the soft yellow cloud that filled the vast hall. There was no dream of the morrow.

Each corner had a different lodge, little tents set up with their own themes to mark the four arts. Hermes suggested they seat themselves near the Grecian temple. Céleste knew what he was after. A watermelon dress sashayed onto the ruddy-orange canvas. A lemon tutu. Kiwi petticoat. The great hall swarmed with the din of merry voices all around them as Céleste gamboled through and found a table. She had to think of an excuse to leave so Nayla had time to extract information.

The champagne chilling in the bucket—if they finished it, Céleste could take it upon herself to procure another. She plucked a glass and poured.

"Do these artists know they're dead?" she asked, making small talk.

Hermes nodded. "Even Hades holds the arts in high regard. Creators who failed to attract divine attention in life are honored at least once in death."

"Why did they fail?" asked Nayla.

Hermes raised his hand. "They didn't pique the interest of any wandering muse to call theirs." He dropped it. "Unfortunate."

"I wouldn't say they're failures." Céleste handed Nayla the first drink and began pouring the second. "Isn't the whole point of art to play with the universe?"

"How hard were they playing?" replied Hermes. "How often? Could it be they didn't put enough energy behind their dreams? Believe in the divine strongly enough?"

As the patron god of Hermes Hill, he would know. It was the art capital of the world. Then again, Athens titled the arrondissement in his honor because he was the god of commerce, and Hermes Hill was originally populated by laborers. Maybe the godly wisdom had gone to his head, and he overlooked artistic intention.

Céleste slid Hermes a glass. "So, their goal was fame?"

"A lack thereof implies they are forgotten."

The statement repulsed her.

Was she offended because she hadn't made it? Surely fame wasn't everyone's goal. "What about hobbyists? The penniless and devoted Bohemian? The street musician?"

"Failures."

Hermes touched her hand. "Fret not, my flower. A ballerina of your caliber won't end up in a place like this, with croutons like these."

If not for immortality, she certainly would. What an ugly revelation. Her technique had improved steadily after the Incident, but technique wasn't life force. No matter how much work she put in she was a so-called crouton—gifted, oui, though not to the pedestal Hermes saw her from.

"Are you sure my dancing was first rate?" she asked. "And not hollow?"

"It was stupendous," said Hermes.

"So, if I was mortal, I wouldn't end up here?"

"Never. These are imitators, their styles plagiarized from teachers and peers. You imitate no one."

Zut alors! Her dancing was an imitation of Mariquita's. Much like Maybelle's was of Loïe's. She had fully absorbed the drills, but they hadn't bonded and crystallized into a personal style. How could they? There was no soul to bond to.

"It helped put Cerberus to sleep." Nayla patted her hand. "My sitar alone couldn't have done it."

How very true. Some visual proof. Although, a three-head Rottweiler and a god with rose-tinted glasses weren't the best arbiters. She placed herself above average. It was too bad. If she had her soul, she would never be in doubt. In spite of the ego boost, she felt lost and upset, and animated the degree as she left the table. "I need to spend some time with my people."

As Hermes went to stand, Nayla jerked him back. "Give her space."

Céleste had made it to the band when a cry went up.

"La cavalcade! Le grand cortège!"

The call ceased all dance. Emerging from the gardens through the open glass door was the vanguard of a great procession. The orchestra struck up the "Victor's March," and a great cry of welcome rang out.

First came a band of yelling Cherokees dancing in, waving their spears and tomahawks, cleaving a path for the parade. A roar filled the glass-domed hall when the floats appeared. Borne upon the shoulders of Indians was a gorgeous bed of fresh flowers and trailing vines. Reclined in this bed were four models lying on their backs, head-to-head, their legs upraised to support a circular tablet of gold.

Upon this tablet, high in the air, proud and superb, was the semi-famous model Sarah Brown in all her peerless beauty of face and form, dressed like Cleopatra. Rumor had it, she was notorious for kicking over easels and fleeing from studios when she modeled for life drawings, but Céleste hadn't realized she was dead. Perhaps there was no obituary. It would explain her presence here among the forgotten, nothing left of her on Earth but her image and her ashes. Céleste made it a point to enjoy Sarah's swan song for sake of brevity—the crown of jewels glowing in her reddish golden hair, the flashing girdle of electric bulbs around her slender waist, the porcelain whiteness of her skin, the delicate green tones and shadows highlighting the contour of her figure.

The crowd was spellbound, sans Hermes, whom Céleste could feel penetrating the back of her head with his gaze. She shuffled behind an asparagus fern, helpless but to watch the model surf in. What she wouldn't give to think airy thoughts and eavesdrop. How would Nayla broach the conversation and navigate herself through the Hall of Fabled Objects' verbal boo-bytraps? Would she flat out say she wanted the helmet? What reason would she give for asking? How tightly was Hermes wrapped around Céleste's fingers? Tight enough to stop him from alerting Hades of Nayla's machinations?

Get ahold of yourself, Céleste. Come to your senses. She needed to think of something other than herself to distract her mind.

In walked a magnificent lot of brawny fellows clothed in leopard print, bearing an immense float made of tree branches and weighted down with strong naked women and children of a prehistoric age. Behind them entered Egyptian mummies dragging their sarcophagi, each containing an Athenian model, too alive and sensuous to be dead. Eggs of heroic size entered, from which as many girls—as chicks—were breaking their way to freedom. By the time the gang of troubadours stepped onto the scene, Nayla had appeared at her side.

"Good news," Nayla said. "Hephaestus built the door to the Hall of Fabled Objects. Only those with a password can enter."

"Did Hermes say what it was?"

"The password is 'Odyssey.'" Nayla smiled. "Isn't that great? Now you don't have to make love to him. I'll let him down easy and say talking him up to you didn't work."

I am nothing, I am nothing, I am nothing.

Céleste grabbed hold of Nayla for support. "Oui, fan-tastique," she said lamely. "What about my powers to fight demons?"

"I can protect you."

"Bien sûr."

Céleste's void sapped the energy out of her limbs. Unsteady, she tried to right herself.

"Too much to drink?" asked Nayla.

Céleste shook her head. She only lived on bread and cheese and kisses and was now deprived.

"You just have to keep him dangling," said Nayla, "until we retrieve your soul, and he brings us back to the surface."

Céleste couldn't wait that long. She needed to feel whole now, even if the feeling was temporary. The fog of Erebus was closing in. She needed to push back. And how wonderful she'd feel. Hermes wasn't all bad. He was a god.

"Did you let on that we're in cahoots?" Céleste asked.

"Nein, he thinks I'm favoring him as we speak."

"Good. To be quite honest, I really would like to go poof." She searched Nayla's face for chastisement.

"You're sure about this? He seems very enamored. It might not bode well."

"Oui, but he's clean shaven. I like clean-shaven men."

"Gustave has a mustache."

"Sometimes they have a mustache," Céleste allowed. "Hermes is nothing I can't handle. Besides, I so happen to be immortal. Any objection?"

"Nein," she said meekly.

The grand cortège had paraded the hall several times and disbanded. A new procession began past the tribune, wherein the wise judges sat, for the costume contest. The inscription on the table read, *Death to Tyrants*. Beneath, a row of ghastly severed heads.

"I won't be long." Céleste left Nayla and rejoined Hermes at their table.

"My flower." He kissed her hand. "I apologize for upsetting you. I don't make the rules about creativity."

"I understand." She didn't know what an artist was supposed to amount to, but she knew she was happy whenever she lost herself in dance, imitation or non.

"Have you taken in the sights?"

In marched dozens of waiters loaded with cases of champagne, plates of creamy soup, roasts, salads, cheeses, cakes, ices, charcuteries—a Dionysian last meal to satisfy Bohemian glut.

"I have," Céleste replied.

"There is another sight to show you."

"Where is that?"

He rose from the table casually as a model sprang upon it, sending crockery and glassware crashing to the floor with her dainty foot.

"Upstairs," said Hermes. "Would you like to see the windmill up close?" He led Céleste under popping corks and foamy sprays to the hazy green wall and pushed on a panel. The hidden door gave, opening into stairs that spiraled around the interior of the windmill. Blue stems scurried up the amber walls as Hermes took flight. Céleste patted her sweaty palms on her skirt, the petals splitting at each conquered step to make way for her knees, climbing around the mast. At the ceiling, Hermes flung aside a trapdoor.

Gracefully, he flew. Céleste poked her head into the slot, met by a red boudoir in the peak. Against the wall stood a bed, an L couch in the corner, and a vanity dead ahead where a bundle of scrolls was piled high—messages. Next to it, a tall Greek vase sat on the floor. Hermes had spent some time here. She walked to the window, obstructed by sails, brushed in aquamarine intervals, and looked out to the Place Blanche, where glowworms oscillated in the dark.

Lips grazed her neck below her ear and pressed in. A kiss. Gently, his tongue slipped out as if wetting a stamp. He undid the lace Nayla had so attentively tied. She slid off her costume, turned and ran her palm on the plane of his chest, down the mountain range of his abdominal, and into the fabric of his chiton to find the answer to her problem.

Found.

The heavy oaken turnstile creaked deep within the mill as sailcloths rippled outside. The vanes swelled to fingers, her arm the tower, and window her palm, reaching up from the grave to fire a nova into the void of night. The bright sun bolted, on a pleasure cruise, as Hermes sent messages written in the stars. A heart constellation twinkled pink, a love letter from Aphrodite, pierced by the homemade sun. Upward the missile soared, pinning a blue butterfly to the dead of space. Psychic poetry. The rocket darted to the Pleiades, reconfigured to a seven-pointed star, and whooshed through in a vortex of dust. Telegram received loud and clear. Asteria, don't -(STOP)- Her comet zipped higher, hitting the apex of the starlight ride, and exploded in a blast of fizzling debris, a chrysanthemum mandala that Chloris would be proud of.

The void dutifully absorbed the booming light in sidereal bliss.

The voice fell silent.

Céleste fell onto the sheets—sweaty, dazed, masked, euphoric, whole.

Somewhere below, a grist stone had ground wheat into flour.

"I had dreamed of this moment when I saw you dance," Hermes confided, panting. He lay back in bed. "I will erect a shrine in your honor."

"A shrine?" Who could talk serious? She swam in a nebulous haze of Grecian delight. He couldn't be serious. She rolled to her side. "Is that necessary?"

"Bien sûr, ma fleur. Everywhere you step is sacred ground. The world will know our love. We will live on Mount Olympus for all eternity."

His words were an icy hand on a hot throat.

"What about my soul?" She didn't feel as strongly about obtaining it as she had a half hour ago, but she knew her ecstasy was temporary.

"I was going to take you across the River Styx with the gold Louis in that vase. Given this new intimacy, however, I feel compelled to fetch your soul myself."

"Hermes"—Céleste sat up—"really. I think it's been handled enough without my permission."

"It's heavily guarded."

"By what? Cacodemons?"

"All manner of spooks. I may not prevail. If I can't, you won't."

"I'll take my chances."

"Suit yourself." Hermes pointed a lazy finger. "Retrieve two coins from the vase to pay Charon, and I promise we depart at once."

Céleste crawled off the bed and up to the two-handled vase, an amphora as tall as her navel. Orange and black, it bore a frieze of Hermes guiding Orpheus into the underworld. She could tell it was Orpheus by his lyre. She reached in, clawed for coins, grabbed nothing. The gold shined at the bottom. She tried again, stretching hard, her armpit on the rim. It was beyond her grasp. She tried slowly tipping the vase but it didn't budge.

"I can't reach," she complained.

"I've guided too many travelers. I'll have to replenish soon. Fish one out. Let's go."

The vase was about shoulder width. If she pollinated inside the container, she could grab the coins in bodily form and pollinate out. Génial!

Dandelion seeds.

The room—bed, couch, desk, window—went from Toulouse-Lautrec to Vincent van Gogh, swirling in fine strokes as she funneled into the vase. Her surroundings faded mostly to black, with a wavy circle of red above, her light source shining onto the coins below.

Stagecoach.

She reaccumulated into solid mass, cramped inside the chamber, and grabbed a handful of coin. *Thump.* Someone turned out the light.

"Don't go anywhere, my flower," said Hermes's muffled voice. "I will return shortly with your lost soul."

It was stolen, not lost.

Was he serious? She couldn't really be trapped.

"Hermes! You let me out! Hermes!"

Hot air balloon.

She burst into pollen inside the cavity and flutter-kicked in every direction, searching for cracks, a hairline fracture, anything! She traced along the rim, trying to force her sands through the lid. She was trapped.

"À bientôt!" Hermes called.

Céleste rematerialized to get the last word.

"See you soon indeed, my eye!"

The filthy scapegrace.

NYMPH IN THE AMPHORA

Nayla poured the last drop of champagne into her flute and drank, surrounded by mayhem. The floor was slippery with wine and dangerous from broken glass. Dancing and the cutting of capers proceeded without abatement. Her increasing buzz made her want to mingle. She felt sufficiently drunk enough to create firewalls and other flammable barriers and the like, but remained seated, even while the orchestra played the "Victor's March" with a great flourish and the forgotten artists stumbled forth through the exit, signaling the end of the ball and her opportunity to join the glamorous yellow party.

She couldn't partake in the festivities with Céleste unaccounted for.

An empty chair rested on Nayla's right. On her left, another. Céleste should've been back by now. It had been long enough. What if Hermes took her somewhere and Nayla was trapped here forever? The artists around her were already dead. There'd be no Hecate doorway to transport her home.

Céleste and Hermes had disappeared behind an armless statue positioned by the wall. Nayla got up to investigate, passing women with their hair notched up like Hindu temples among the ceaseless throng of artists making their way to the exit. Her fingers caressed the green scribbles on the wall. She swore Hermes had pushed on it somewhere. Here. Open sesame.

Blue iron twisted up a spiral staircase. She hoped she wasn't disrupting anything. The orange wallpaper hypnotized her with visions of cheddar cheese until she reached a door in the ceiling. She drew her ear to the wood.

"Céleste," she called.

She sounded four knocks.

"Cél, the artists are leaving. The party is over."

The silence terrified her. She didn't care what she was disrupting, she just wanted her friend. She pushed hard. The door didn't give.

"Odyssey," she whispered on a whim. No effect. There could've been a dresser placed over the compartment for all she knew.

A response came, muffled and nearly indiscernible. "Aide-moi!" *Help me.*

Céleste?

Cherry dye streamed through Nayla's braid as she flattened her hand. A blade of fire appeared around her fingers. She hacked at the door in a karate chop motion, slicing all four grooves in the wood, and let the door drop to the stairs. No one protested the intrusion.

"Céleste?" she tried.

"Nay!" came the reply, less muffled. "Help, I'm stuck!"

Nayla stood on the red-carpeted door that had fallen on the stairwell, giving her a bit of additional height. She crouched, flung herself at the opening, and latched on. Her forearms dug into the plush red carpet on the level above, her legs dangling from the hole of which the floor's trapdoor had been orphaned. She dragged herself carelessly through and climbed to her knees. It appeared to be some kind of seraglio.

"Are you in?" came Céleste's muted voice.

The amphora stood like a woman with her hands on her hips.

"Ja," said Nayla. "What are you doing in the vase?"

"Hermes trapped me. Take the lid off."

"Can you go poof?"

"I can go poof, but the vase is hermetically sealed."

A moment of clarity shined through her intoxication. "If the vase is airtight, how can you breathe?"

"There must be some air left in here. Don't worry, if I pass out, I won't die. I'm immortal."

The answer sent a shiver down Nayla's spine.

Céleste must not have been in there long.

Nayla's fingers curled around the finial top. She pulled. No give. She grunted and pulled again. "It won't budge!" She lowered her mouth to the lid. "Odyssey." No effect. She pulled, doubting if Odyssey was the password to anything, including the vault.

Hermes—the trickster god. She shouldn't have let Céleste make love to him, but Nayla didn't like it when people were mad at her. That idiot Hermes must've thought Céleste was immortal too, unless he meant to kill her. Or assumed she would remain safe in pollen form, a potentially correct assumption if Céleste maintained that state.

Nayla took a step back and raised her hands. "If you go poof, I can shatter the vase with fireballs."

"I'll end up with third-degree burns when I rematerialize."

Nayla examined the room, inhaling sage and musk. "The window. I can push the vase out the window. You go poof before it shatters in the square below."

"The vase won't move. I couldn't tip it."

Nayla leaned her weight on the pottery. The vase really wouldn't budge. "All right. Go poof and rematerialize, but do it by extending your limbs horizontally so that the matter of your body exceeds the space within the container."

"Have you gone folle? I may knock myself out and break my arms and legs."

"But you're immortal."

"D'accord. Get behind the bed."

Nayla took cover. She peeked over the disheveled sheets. Nothing happened. "Céleste?"

"Give me a minute."

"Do it. Real quick."

Labored breaths emitted from the amphora—Céleste working herself into a panic—running out of air. Nayla blinked. Particles burst from the vase, transforming into cells, rolling into four limbs and a head. The sudden expansion of matter blew shards into the walls. Céleste crashed to her belly. Coins strewed across the floor.

"Boah!" Nayla rushed to her side. "Are you all right?"

Céleste lurched to her knees. Nude. Her hand came away from her bangs. Blood. "I'll live."

"What happened?" Nayla found a peignoir and draped it over Céleste's shoulders.

"Hermes wants to possess me, and not the demonic way. He tricked me into the vase. He wanted me to gather coins to pay Charon to paddle the River Styx and claim my soul."

Nayla picked up one of the coins. A bald man with a wig was embossed on one side, an olive wreath the other. "Where is Hermes now?"

"I assume flying over the Styx to get my soul for me." Céleste pointed at the window, nipples exposed. "Can you fly yet?"

Nayla eyed the floor. "After one more night of merrymaking, ja."

"Then we have to ride Charon's boat across."

"Across to where?"

Céleste leveled her eyes at the floor for an answer and jerked her head up. "Charon will know. He is a psychopomp too."

It was Céleste's fault they were in need of a new guide, but Nayla bit her lip. "He may prove untrustworthy like Hermes. And if Hermes returns to the Moulin Rouge with your soul and sees you are gone, what then?"

"He may not return," said Céleste. "He expressed doubt whether retrieving my soul is even possible. If he can't reach it, he'll slam his head against a brick wall continuously in the name of love."

If what she said was true, without Nayla, Céleste could've been trapped in that vase for eternity. Her lifeless body, anyway.

"According to Hermes," Céleste continued, "my soul is heavily guarded."

"If a god can't retrieve it, what hope do we have?"

"Our hope is that my soul belongs to me and only me."

"Let's say Hermes gives up and finds us. Do we try to over-power him?"

"I'll make some concessions to get back on his good side."

"Concessions? Is that slang for more lovemaking?"

"Oui," said Céleste, reluctant.

No matter what happened, Nayla could not trust Hermes. The god was verrückt.

"Where is the River Styx?" she asked.

"Erebus is a mirror of French Athens." Céleste rose to her feet and cast off the loose-hanging garment. "The Seine. The Styx is the Seine."

"Are we sure?"

Céleste looked out the window, where a stream of artists flooded into the glowing woods. "Le Bal des Quat'z'Arts parades to the Seine." She picked her costume off the floor, burst into pollen, and emerged from the air fully dressed. "The artists should lead us there."

"We have to catch up with them."

Céleste picked up two coins and inspected one. "Louis XVI... French money. It's got to be the Seine all right."

She made a fist over the coins and hopped through the hole in the floor. She stuck the landing. Nayla, properly soz-zled, crawled on her chest and lowered her legs. She dropped, toppling backward into Céleste's arms. Recalibrated, Nayla tackled the staircase. Round and round the orange cylinder she went, ringing the mast, and falling upon the wall's hidden door at the bottom.

"We get your soul," said Nayla, "and escape through Cabaret du Néant, the same way we came in."

"What about Cerberus?"

"We'll tell him what a good boy he was letting us face the underworld, show him how we emerged unscathed, that there's nothing scary to protect us from anymore. If he gets belligerent, you bait him while I make a run for du Néant. Then pollinate before he takes a bite." She opened the panel to the hall's dying fanfare. "I just thought of something important."

Céleste listened closely, braced in the doorway.

"If Hermes's obsession with you isn't as strong as we think, he may descend on us during the march to the Styx."

"What do you suggest?"

"We remain inconspicuous." Nayla tiptoed around the broken glass, across the ochre floor, and met their old table by the Grecian temple. Hermes's messenger bag was slung over the chair. She found the bag empty, took off Maman's headpiece, and stowed it inside. Next, she uncapped her flask and dumped the liquor into a salad bowl. She spanked the flask's bottom and held it out. "Get in."

"Pollinate in there?"

"Ja. He'll never find you."

"Keep the cap loose."

"I don't want it to come off."

"What if you lose your senses? I'll be trapped."

"Like in Hermes's amphora?" asked Nayla, brow raised. "How far is the Seine from here in Athens?"

"A forty-minute walk—or a two-hour stagger."

"You can't trust me for an hour? You trusted Hermes."

Céleste looked dead at her. Nayla thought about backpedaling, but she held firm. She was in the right.

"D'accord," Céleste conceded and burst into pollen. Her specs whirled into the flask, whereupon Nayla screwed the cap.

"En cavalcade! En cavalcade!" shouted the straggling artists, pulling Nayla playfully toward the door.

Out in the Place Blanche, she joined the rear of the costumed procession under black skies. She looked up at the windmill, the sails now motionless. Onward, she staggered and swayed and plunged down Hermes Hill or wherever she was.

The boggy rue Blanche echoed the wild yells and songs of revelers as they marched through the urban forest. Nayla turned to a troubadour, his arm hooked to a gay vedette.

"Where are we going?" asked Nayla.

"Following the herd," said the troubadour.

The reply was self-evident, even to her drunken state.

At the Place de l'Opéra, hundreds of artists swarmed up the broad stairs of the Palais Garnier like colored ants, climbed upon lampposts, and clustered around the groups of statuary adorning the fane. The musical band from the Moulin Rouge had followed the herd too, for they took up position on the steps while artists danced ring-around-the-rosy.

Nayla scanned the dreary night for any winged gods with helmets. She clutched her flask. No sign of him.

After their fill, the cavalcade reformed and marched down the Avenue de l'Opéra, or something like it, and encountered a large squad of street sweepers washing the stone. In an instant, the squad had been routed, and the revelers, taking hoses and brooms, fell to and cleaned an entire block of moss, making the masonry shine as it had never shone before.

Nayla seriously ought to partake in the festivities. *Look how much fun they are having!*

Cabs were captured, and dances executed on the tops of vehicles. One artist, with enormous India-rubber shoes, took delight in permitting cabs to run over his feet, while he howled in agony that turned the hair of the ghastly drivers white.

Nayla reached for her flask for a sip. Nein, Céleste was in there. *She's trusting you. Hare Krishna. Fight the urge to lose control.*

The immense cavalcade filed through the narrow arches of the Louvre's courtyard like a medieval army returning to its citadel after a victorious campaign. The flags, spears, and battle-axes of their costumes were given a fine setting by the noble architecture of the Pavillon de Rohan. Within the court of the Louvre was drawn up a regiment of the Garde Municipale, going through a drill, and they looked quite formidable with their evolutions and bayonet charges. But the mob of Greek warriors flung themselves bodily upon the ranks of the guard, ousted the officers, and assumed command.

All the rigid military dignity of the scene disappeared, and the drill faded into something farcical. The officers, furious at first, could not resist the spirit of pure fun that filled the mob, and they took their revenge by kissing the models and making them dance. The girls too achieved their fair share of conquering, pinning flowers to military coats and coyly putting their lips where they were in danger. Tall, electric masts in the court were scaled by adventurous artists, who attached brilliant flags, banners, and crests to the mastheads far above the crowd.

An adjacent flag was raised on the edge of the courtyard. This of a crypt keeper, a jolly roger, white on black. The mast stood over the water. It had to have belonged to a ship. Charon?

Nayla squirmed through the masses, eased her gaze down the flagpole, and caught sight of Charon's boat. This was not the rowboat of her imagination, but a two-storied ship with a paddlewheel and canopy—like those laundry boats she had seen on the Seine, refashioned into a luxury cruise, steam powered, with smokestacks and polished decks, from which extended a pair of gangplanks and touched the shores of the Styx, where unknown artists such as herself waited to embark.

LE BATEAU LAVOIR

O il stains in a dark basement. Jet black gems in a covered well. Flies in tar. These observable nightly shades coalesced in the confines of her new home, Nayla's flask. *Talk about cramped.* She was ready to move. Had five minutes passed, or fifty? Would Nayla release her on Charon's boat or at her soul? She'd better do it on the boat. Her soul was surrounded by an army of lizards. Dare she think the worst? That Nayla ran back to the Cabaret du Néant, up the hidey hole, and back to Athens? She'd prefer Nayla land flat on her face and sleep it off than to part from the very world that imprisoned her joie de vivre.

This was her punishment. For letting Hermes dupe her into that vase. It was she who had him on a leash. What went wrong? She knew what. They'd both gotten what they'd wanted, and they both wanted more! Marriage to Hermes on Olympus. Really. That would get old so fast. He would agree with every-thing she said, do everything she wanted. There'd be no debate. No conflict. Just groveling and worship. If only she'd have held out longer, he would've taken her straight to her soul. Erebus made her choke. Every second her soul-cave went without light was excruciating torture. Her void needed flare. Too much darkness, and she'd tear herself inside out from that accursed voice—a group of voices she couldn't parse out that rang as one.

Hermes was a stepping stone, that was all. Something to tide her over until she crossed the river. And she was still going strong. Her soul-throne was brighter than being in the flask. She took it back. Nayla had unscrewed the cap. Luminescent brushstrokes leaked into the spout. She sifted through the opening to a panorama bearing a sharper impression. Nayla stood next to a man she presumed was Charon. It was time to pay the boatman.

Aphrodite's Rock.

"Here's our little stowaway!" Charon loomed over her, wearing a long tusk on the brow of his head, an appendage sewn onto the hood. His pants were fish-scale black, shiny in the gloom. His jacket wrapped his broad chest, cracked open to reveal his white muscles, something like porpoise skin. This was not the acteur at Cabaret de L'Enfer. This was no frail reaper. Here was a man who ate his potatoes at mealtime. He held out his beefy arm to introduce himself and spoke with a hoarse voice. "Who is this exquisite nymph?"

"Fleur d'Étoile," said Céleste, getting a good look at this oily-haired, eagle-nosed, cribbage-faced captain. Next to his body, his eyes were his defining feature. Perhaps the tusk as well. "Are you a unicorn?"

"You never seen a narwhal before?" He seemed flustered. "We keep the party going to the other side. Think of a costume, and it's yours." He turned to face the line stretching back to the Louvre's courtyard.

The Pont du Carrousel should be here. Where did all the bridges go? Nothing but black waters on a promontory, the Styx much wider than the Seine. She couldn't see the other bank.

"Put the money in the box." Charon tapped on the wood. "I'm saving up to buy a yacht."

The forgotten artists reimagined their costumes, parted the seaweed curtains on deck, and ventured into a room with colored lights.

"Here's our Louis." Nayla handed him the coins.

"Two coins? Wait a minute." He bounced his dreamy eyes from Nayla to Céleste. "You two are not dead. Something's off. Yes, yes, you are *half* dead. For you, my lovely, fair creatures, I will charge ye half price."

Céleste blushed.

"Perfekt." Nayla, swaying on her feet, slapped a coin onto the box. "How did you know we were nymphs?"

"All nouvelle nymphes got something wrong with 'em," said Charon. "Bats in their belfries. Sense it a league away."

Was that an insult or a fact? If it were fact, she kind of liked Charon's frankness. Perhaps the gods only chose people in dire need of help to offer a mixis to, saving them from imminent death. However, if the comment was an insult—

"One must not remind people of their infirmities," said Céleste. "Though since you bring it up, regarding my half-dead predicament, if I wanted my soul, where ought I look?"

"The Well of Lost Souls."

"My soul is in a well?" She drew the bridge of her finger to her lip. "Can you take us?"

"I would love to, but you see—" He pointed to a map, highlighting only river stops, a ring over the heart of Erebus. "Not on my route."

"Can you—can you tell me where it's located?"

"I can tell ye where it's not. On the rivers." Charon touched her arm. "As much as I'd like to help a pretty nymph such as yourself, land is out of my jurisdiction. All right, now. This isn't a guided tour. Come one, come all, and join the party!"

He shooed her and Nayla into the seaweed curtains, where colored lights played on a large, covered deck. Mermaid statues bookended the barman. The bar itself rested on a fish tank. Cards flipped at gaming tables. The artists' costumes transformed from cowboys and Indians to squids and clamshells. Nayla tapped Céleste on the shoulder. Her floaty clothing had changed into stiff coral. Céleste looked down. Her petal skirt changed to jellyfish arms, though her top was more translucent than she'd have hoped. How immodest.

They should find a table. Nayla walked with a slope over the white sand sprinkled on the floor and tripped. Céleste caught her. Nayla was tired. She needed sleep. Céleste found a corner booth and crawled in below a crab net draped on the ceiling. Nayla crawled opposite and wedged her head between Céleste's shoulder and the padded wall.

"Wake me up when we dock," Nayla murmured. "Do not leave me here."

Céleste took her hand. "I would never."

When the aspirant artists filled the booths and café tables, the planks rumbled underfoot from a paddlewheel churned at the rear. Bon voyage. The boat pushed away from the shore. The Louvre pulled out of sight. The Well of Lost Souls rested somewhere beyond the horizon. A subterranean pit in the underworld sounded ominous, but Théo's demon wasn't going to bring her soul to a happy place. Her imagination had pictured far worse locales—in a cemetery, the middle of the sun, Cabaret du Néant. She shivered.

Perhaps she'd encounter something nasty in this well. Perhaps someone guarded it, like Arachne did the Hall of Fabled Objects. But those objects were valuable to a lot of people. Her soul was only valuable to her. Gustave hadn't known her before its theft, and Papa didn't seem to miss it. Then there was the obvious quibble. If her soul was stolen, why was it in a well of *lost* souls? Was it filed incorrectly in the wrong well? Where was this well, anyhow? Must she remain so in the dark? The ship was captained by a psychopomp, and he'd just sat down at the bar with a group of models.

This was her chance. March up to Charon and ask him. *If you don't know the well's location, who does?* But that seemed horribly easy. She had to do something to set her apart. To guarantee an honest answer. There was a difference between asking for attention and winning it. The orchestra could help. The conductor wasn't Monsieur Desormes, but she hoped he could play Edvard Grieg. She let Nayla's cheek slide onto the cushioned booth and slunk across the dance floor to the ten-piece orchestra, where she whispered to the man in the lobster hat if he knew any Grieg. Oh, he did. Bien. How about "Dance of the Mountain King's Daughter"? Très bien.

Artists waltzed and two-stepped around the cheap ballroom. Céleste planted herself in the center. If others were impressed, they'd grant her more space. Simple. Her hands formed a hoop overhead in fifth position.

The cello established the song. Flutes guided her pointed toes in small jumps. Drums advanced her powerful steps into the expanding floor. Her arms froze with each strike of the mallets, spurred to motion again by the xylophone's frantic keys. The percussion escalated her steps into grand jetés, leaps so large they carried her out to sea.

She spun into a pirouette, the party a zoetrope going round on an axis, forming pictures between the slats of spectators—Charon turned on his turtle stool, walked to the crowd's edge, and looked at her amusedly—his hand went to his hip, the other clamped to a tiny umbrella drink. The room grabbed hold of her and ground her to a stop. Artists cheered and clapped, many secretly wondering, Céleste hoped, if she were on the right ship after all.

"Superb dancing," said Charon. "Maybe I was too harsh on nouvelles nymphes. Join me for a drink?"

Céleste glanced at Nayla, sleeping soundly in their booth, and let Charon escort her to the bar, where he layered question upon compliment.

Where did you learn to dance? How old were you? How long did it take ye to get that good? Great costume, by the way. The pink goes well with your hair. I could see why the gods chose to initiate you. Did anyone ever say you have beautiful eyes? Aphrodite, I knew it. She's a classy lady. Oh, the mixis was for a dance you did at age fourteen. Plenty more where that came from. Your dad should make ye star ballerina anyway.

Céleste bubbled inside. Why did talking to the ferryman feel so natural? Make her feel so understood? He was not Eros, god of passionate love, or the sexy Apollo. He was Charon the boatman, and he'd crawled out from under a rock. He must've been lifting them; his muscles were so bulbous. And he was fun to be around.

"You'll find your soul and marry a keeper," said Charon. "Have those mômes of yours. Étienne. Eulalie. They will be as divine as their mother."

"You really think so!?"

"I know it."

"It's because you know someone who knows where the well is, don't you?" she asked. "The next step in my journey!"

"Aye." Charon tickled his chin. "Hades knows. His palace is on the water. Hades Island."

"Can you take me?" asked Céleste.

"After I dump the artists, I've got to pick up those dead before their time, then the heartsick, deaths from famine... I've got a schedule to keep."

"You're sure you don't know where the well is?"

"Honest," said Charon. "I know people more than places. I'm a people person."

If he knew people, maybe she could do some sleuthing for Nayla. "Are you familiar with Arachne?"

"Aye, she guards the Hall of Fabled Objects on the Phlege-thon River."

"Why?"

"To break Athena's curse and live out the rest of her mortal life in peace."

"Why must the objects be guarded?"

"The Oracle of Delphi sees a war coming. Something on the scale of the Titanomachy and Gigantomachy. When? Where?" Charon shrugged. "Beats me. But the objects in that yonder vault can be used against the gods. Zeus ordered Hermes to collect them. Hephaestus built the door. Arachne's been guarding it for a century. Zeus will grant her freedom when he feels the threat is passed."

"When is that supposed to be?" asked Céleste. "Tuesday, if it's hot?"

"You know what..." Charon took her hand. "Why don't you ask him?"

"Zeus or Hades?"

"Hades."

"You'll take me?"

Charon scratched behind his ear. "It's a huge gift—to ferry a passenger, and a half live one at that, through me stops and drop her on Hades Island. I can make it happen, sure enough, but it raises new problems. It's best not to hang around the dead too long. The mind"—he tapped his hood—"it starts to dwell on the macabre. What the mind concentrates on, the universe delivers."

"What should I do?"

"The wise solution would be to stay in my cabin."

"What about my friend?" She looked at Nayla, fast asleep.

"She has her soul. She merely wants to lose her body from what you described. It's ye I'm more worried about."

"Promise she'll be safe."

"She won't leave the ship. You can visit any time. Come, I'll show ye the captain's quarters, no strings attached."

She followed Charon from the bar, letting the narwhal horn lead the way. She and this deity clicked so well it was hard to believe. Could a nymph ever have a chance with a son of the gods? Erebus was his father, Nyx his mother. He wanted to introduce her sometime. She had to admit, it was all a bit fast, but these gods, they knew what they wanted.

Through the dangling seaweed, she stepped onto the deck, contemplating what life on Charon's boat would feel like. His narwhal nose skipped across the awning strakes along the cabins. The water was black sludge. The ebony light made it no more pleasant to look at. Any man cast overboard would drown instantly. At the stern, Charon gestured to the paddlewheel plowing up goo.

"How does the water not gum up the wheel?" she asked.

"Powerful engine." Charon patted his baby.

"Is there drinking water available?"

"There's a cistern in the hull. Food is stocked in the galley. I'll get more provisions when we land." He pointed south.

Céleste glossed over the rocky shoreline. The rocks harbored a grotto with an opening supported by silver columns. A woman emerged from the pool, her skin dyed black by the waters, her stature the height of a Santon figurine at this distance.

"Who is that?" asked Céleste.

Charon bandied his hand. "Nobody of note."

He mounted the spiral staircase. Céleste regretted not having brought her field glasses and resumed pursuit of the narwhal. To think, this man might actually complete her. Such high chemistry. Sky-high attraction. He left her head buzzing. He walked nonchalantly to his cabin door and put his thumb on the codfish handle.

"Welcome to your temporary home." He smiled and pushed the door into an undersea enchantment. A glass pavilion capped the room, filtering dark outdoor light into aqua blue. But that wasn't all. Charon had some intricate home décor. The walls faded to green and the floor was tiled yellow like a sandy bottom.

He picked up the trident poker and walked to the creamy mantle, propped up by two oceanids, and readjusted a log. Céleste's jelly skirt fluttered as she crossed the room to meet him. She moved in for a kiss. He rested the poker between the breasts of an oceanid. She pulled him close, her lips devouring his like an unfed rose.

Her hand reached into his open jacket and caressed his ribs. "This room is beautiful." Seahorse sconces. Coral chandeliers. Sand dollar lamps. "Breathtaking."

"Merci," said Charon. "Thought of it yesterday while brushing my teeth."

"Perhaps you qualify as a forgotten artist."

"Oh, but they haven't forgotten me—and I doubt you will either."

"We shall see about that." She grabbed the narwhal horn and pushed it off his head.

His lips suctioned to hers like a barnacle.

She fell into the ocean, spread her arms to the headboard, modeled after a seashell, and felt the lush, alabaster waves roll over.

Pearls shined in the mouths of oysters up on the sea floor—the ocean's stars. She walked the underbelly of the boat, while zappy anglers swam by. Knees bent, she sprang from the keel into the great blue. Schools of neon tetra corkscrewed around her.

Into an undersea cavern she swam, clear through a hole in the rock. A shaft of light beamed upon a sunken ship resting in the sands. She flutter-kicked down the light's shaft, into the cargo hold, where the beam spread upon a treasure chest. She grabbed hold of the locks and secured her feet to the wood ceiling. Upside down, she opened the chest. Glowing inside was a ball of white fire, spectacular. Her soul.

She palmed the starry treasure and embraced it so tightly that it faded into her, from one chest to another. Finally, she could breathe, her hunger sated.

She could shoot stars and she could breathe. Had this god healed her?

Charon cupped her face, kissed her full on the lips and leaned back.

"I'm going to release the art community into the haunts of Erebus." He tossed a key on the bed. "Lock it if you leave."

Pants appeared on his legs, his coat on his torso, and he shoved off. The oaken door clicked behind him.

Moments later came a knock.

Céleste imagined her Starflower attire and answered. Nayla.

"The boat is docking," said Nayla. "We have to go."

"Go?" Céleste was in disbelief. "We can't. Charon's taking us to Hades Island. Hades lives there. He knows where to find the Well of Lost Souls. And chew on this. Zeus stored the fabled objects in the hall to prevent a war that hasn't happened yet."

"Does Charon know if it opens by password?" Hammocks of skin drooped beneath Nayla's eyes.

"I can't make it obvious we're going to rob the place." Céleste pulled Nayla into the cabin. "Have some water."

"Hades Island, then?" Nayla drank from the pitcher on the crab table. "Charon is taking us in exchange for what? I have one coin left."

"He and I sort of fit well together. I've never felt so alive. I feel like I have my soul back."

"Suzon's mirror at the Folies Bergère says different."

"You believe the mirror now?"

"I saw something spooky, ja. My reflection with no organs. Eyeless. Tongueless. Frightening." Nayla took a seat in the tentacle chair.

"When were you going to tell me?"

"When you weren't in a nervous state about du Néant. Like now. I didn't wish to make it worse." She set the glass down and crossed her legs. "So, are you starting a new life with Charon or what?"

"Perhaps. After I get my soul, of course. I really feel he might be someone special."

"A relationship?"

"Possibly."

"I thought you wanted to feel complete first, to refill your soul-cave with love."

"I do feel complete."

"Like how you feel complete whenever you make love?"

"This is different."

"Different than Antoine?"

Céleste shouldn't have told Nayla about him. It still felt so fresh. Used to. "Charon is no Antoine."

The devil himself returned through the door. "All right, party's over. Next stop, death by consumption. Better keep to the cabin for this one. I can't have a corpse up and damage your set of pipes." He kissed Céleste.

"Be careful yourself." She trailed her fingers down his chest.

"How far until Hades Island?" Nayla broke in.

Charon looked at her. "End of the route." He left for the bridge.

"Please tell me you saw that." Nayla turned to Céleste.

"Saw what?"

"Charon's eyes," Nayla whispered. "When he looked at you, they turned to spirals like a mollusk shell. Black and white."

"Are you saying I'm under hypnosis?" Céleste laughed.

"Are you aware of how you're acting?" asked Nayla. "It's like someone flipped a switch and made you verrückt for Charon. If you had just kept Hermes in line, we'd be making better progress."

"You didn't have a problem at the ball."

"I didn't want to upset you."

"So, you trade my anger now for yours before?"

"Ja, it would appear so. What's the difference? It's still true. Hermes could be returning with your soul this very minute."

"We don't know that."

"We would if you didn't make love to him, because he would be with us. Your lovemaking with Hermes and your misadventure with Charon. They are pointless endeavors. Inconveniences that interrupt our quest. You are getting in your own way."

The words struck like lightning. Céleste snarled. That was what Psyche had said, how Gustave treated her. It was an insult, a critique on her character.

"Ahem," Céleste continued. "It's to help you break into the Hall of Fabled Objects."

"Regaining your powers could have waited until we returned to Athens."

"Ahem. What about fighting the lizards that guard my soul?"

"You have me. And you had Hermes. This is a waste of time. Charon could be deceiving us about the hall for all I know."

"Then let's not ask anyone anything. It sounds like you don't need my help anymore."

"I do, Cél. I just hate wasting time."

"Oui, let's drink ourselves to death instead. Sabotage it all."

"You know my background," said Nayla. "I can't help it. I try to. It's hard." She filled a glass of water and drank. "What do you even see in Charon?"

Céleste smiled. "He makes me feel whole."

THE RIVER STYX

Céleste had met Charon yesterday. Yesterday! Nayla didn't want to be judgmental—she was no prize herself—but the man seemed a tad hideous. Whatever Céleste saw in him had to live beneath the surface. The two were both missing something to resonate so strongly with each other. Somehow, he'd felt Céleste swirling around in the flask. Nayla should never have let her out.

It was dangerous the way Céleste was talking. If she felt complete, what purpose was there to obtain her soul? There wasn't one. She could not distinguish a brief feeling of wholeness now versus a permanent state of completion later.

Nayla lowered her head on the bar. When she was drunk, she got the same way. Felt whole, a part of the background. She was everything and everything was a blur.

She tapped at the seashells beneath the plate glass bar in the party room.

When she was intoxicated beyond all reason, she didn't care about oneness with Brahman or the cycle of death and rebirth or how much suffering she accrued. The same part of her that clung to absinthe was the same part of Céleste that attracted her to Charon. They were slaves to the treatment, therefore slaves to more pain. It gave them powers, but no cure.

What was Nayla to do? What would Céleste do if the sandal were on the other foot? The same thing Céleste did when Nayla was fall-down drunk at Maxim's. Céleste had lectured and cajoled and straightened her out. Ja, so Cél better not complain when Nayla returned the favor. It was her turn to play wet nurse. She had to keep a clear head to monitor Céleste and herself, but the only way off the ship was to fly. She'd rather find the Well of Lost Souls without asking Hades for directions. He was Yama, the god of death and justice, in the flesh. What a scary enterprise. Zur Hölle damit. One more night of fun and she'd grow wings, grab Céleste, and blow this joint.

Behind her, a violinist tuned his bow. He was dressed like a sepoy, a redcoat with short pants and a wide-brimmed hat from India. Kameera would've enjoyed the music. Or maybe she'd be too busy with Céleste. Nayla never had to baby Kameera like this. Had the gods chosen Kameera, would she be here, on the Styx, right now? Or was the quest only for Nayla to undertake? Charon had declared all nouvelle nymphes crazy. If he was right, Kameera wouldn't be here. Her belfry was batless. She was perfekt.

The engines ceased. Le Bateau Lavoir coasted to the docks. Nayla could forego the drinking and escape with Céleste on foot. Would Charon allow her to walk so easy? He might order the crew after them. Nayla couldn't picture this burly bartender, the musicians, and deckhands chasing her across Erebus. But she couldn't picture Charon as a narwhal either, and that happened. Drinking to get wings were better odds, though running for her life would make a good Plan B.

The crew moored the ship for new passengers to file in. These men were soldiers. One man with a pith helmet had a bullet wound clean through his chest. Another wore a polar bear coat covered in blood. A third, a Chinaman, had a blue uniform and white shin coverings. They must've died in skirmishes or from disease. Some filled the empty tables. Some danced. Others circled around the bar for a drink.

Nayla found herself surrounded by men in blue greatcoats, white kepis, haversacks, and gaiters. She recognized the uniform instantly. They were legionnaires. Hair stood on her neck like pins. She examined the gentleman next to her, his blond coif escaping his kepi, falling into his youthful and lurid face. Her hands trembled at this familiar sight.

"Eugène?"

The youth turned to her. The light of his skull shifted yellow to green. "Spuckfeuer?"

A tear bolted from Nayla's eye. "Ja."

"Arachne killed you too?"

Nayla rose from the stool and hugged him. Her composure shattered. "I'm so sorry. Je suis désolée. I can't tell you how much grief... There is no apology I can give to take back my asking you for help."

"Chut!" said Eugène, a finger on his lips. "If I didn't perish in Jacoma, it would've been Indo-China."

Her nerves were so agitated that her hands and feet went numb. She had to sit back down.

"We died for art," said a baritone voice, "a worthier cause than nations competing for resources."

The voice, it was Khoumag, the Senegalese. She'd hoped not to see him. She had dreams at night that he and Beauvais had slayed Arachne. Khoumag without a doubt hated her. She did not care. She hugged him anyway, unrepelled by his glowing blue-green brow or the fact he'd wanted to feed her to the spider.

Khoumag pressed his hand into her back. "Mmoatia. Does your mind torment you still?"

"Torment her?" asked Eugène. "She's passed on with the rest of us."

Khoumag shook his head. "A portal opened into the desert and le capitaine pushed her out."

She wanted to avoid revealing this so badly. She would have been more comfortable dead than to face these fallen soldiers alive. It gave her anxiety. Survivor's guilt. She was the one who'd proposed the whole idea.

"I'm sorry. I'm sorry," she repeated. "Es tut mir Leid."

"Mademoiselle," said Eugène. "This is a good thing. Now you can find him."

"Find him?" Nayla was dumbstruck.

"Le capitaine is not among us," said Eugène.

"When I died," said Khoumag, "he was fighting like a hell-cat."

Nayla counted the legionnaires, reposed on the stools and camped around the bar. Thirteen of them had come with her. She could never forget that number. Only twelve were currently present, their bones fluorescing in their uniforms. Capitaine Beauvais was indeed not here. A pitiful ray of hope shined in her gut. A second chance. A glimmer. Maybe he'd slayed Arachne after all. She cried. Beauvais was out there, wandering the underworld, and it was up to her to find him.

Hold your camels, Nayla. Beauvais might've been injured or taken captive. But no matter where he was, the trail to find him began at Arachne's Cave.

"You are connected to the underworld," said Khoumag. "That is clear now."

"The Hindu gods asked if I wanted to be a nymph. I said ja."

"Charon is Greek," said Eugène.

"They style their appearance to our era's hotbed of creativity—French Athens."

"He's coming this way."

"There she is." Charon wrapped his arm casually around Nayla. "Good, you've made friends." He turned to Céleste, draped on his arm. "See, Nayla is well behaved, well fed, and well supplied of alcohol."

"If only you could provide directions to the Well of Lost Souls, we'd be in business." Nayla squinted at Céleste.

"In good time." Charon's mitts landed on Eugène and Khoumag. "Have as much as ye like, boys. The drinks are on me. Am I a host or what?"

"Charon," said Nayla, "these men died in October 1891."

"And?"

"It's January 1893."

"Tell it to the engraver. You think I measure time down here?"

"What took them so long to cross?"

"At the Blast, I'm sure people do whatever they want willy-nilly, pell-mell, topsy-turvy. We, on the other hand, have something called processing."

"Processing, richtig." She nodded, wondering what else Céleste had shared of her personal life.

Charon was all smiles. "Makes the world go round." He whispered something to make Céleste laugh like a whale and addressed the legion. "Excusez-moi, gents. I must tend to my other guests. Thank ye for yer service."

"Flippant and charming, that one," said Eugène.

"Infectious," said Khoumag, "and full of himself."

Nayla scooted closer to the bar and ordered a spiced whiskey for old time's sake.

Khoumag shared a tale of the French attack on the Tukulor fortress of Kundian on the Niger, while Nayla's mind drifted toward strategy.

She could enlist the legionnaires to break Céleste from Charon's spell, but trifling with the boatman would land them overboard, and the River of Hatred did not look swimmable. What was more, the legionnaires were without rifles. She didn't even like entertaining the idea of involving them. She had asked her favor once, and they had paid the ultimate price. To disrupt their afterlife... She knew in her bones she would never live with herself again.

She opted to continue Plan A. Drink and wait for wings.

Laughing and chatting with her legionnaires made time fly. Eugène bragged about a French Algerian lover whom Khoumag identified as a prostitute. The band played bugle calls and marches. The drummer boy spun his instrument and rapped it with sticks. By her seventh drink, Nayla could feel her feathers tickling through her skin. Jippi! She could produce wings if only she willed the bird out of its cage. She excused herself to the toilet and bid her legionnaires farewell, should she not return.

It was a less-than-ideal goodbye for a less-than-ideal meeting, though she couldn't have let Charon take his revenge out on her friends.

She parted the seaweed curtains and hitched a right on the gallery toward the bow of the ship. Four meters from the water, she hopped the rail and fell. Phoenix wings stemmed from her spine and angled into the wind. This was a stealth maneuver. Flame was verboten. She traveled toward the shore somewhere in the darkness, gained elevation, and circled to the stern by the paddlewheel. The blue pyramid glowed on the second-story roof. It was Charon's cabin.

She landed gently with an extra skip, hoping the paddlewheel's hum would drown her racket. Carefully, she tiptoed along the roof and hunkered next to the blue glass. She peered in. Charon was speaking.

"You really dazzled the guests with your sparkling conversation."

"I didn't know that was my job," said Céleste. "I thought I wasn't supposed to interact with the dead."

"As the captain's mistress, it wouldn't be a bad idea. You should work on your dancing too."

"I thought you liked my dancing, bébé."

"I do, but you came in with the tide of forgotten artists. That's not a coincidence. That Mariquita woman you mentioned. Hasn't she taught ye how to make her moves yer own?"

"I said I might have copied her. It's not translating right. I need my soul."

"I was saving up for a new yacht. Now I gotta pay for dance lessons. You better pull your weight around here. Even the dead won't do something for nothing. Disgusting."

Were the dead disgusting, or was he disgusted by Céleste?

"I'll do better," she whimpered, "I—I promise."

"You are nothing, you are nothing, you are nothing."

Nayla gasped. Céleste had told him about the voice in the void and now he was using it against her! Nayla pitied to see her in such a state. It broke her heart. Charon was a monster. Before, he was being amicable. Now, the mask was off.

"I know, bébé, I know."

Céleste had succumbed! All her years of resiliency flushed away.

"Think about how you might contribute around here. I want a handwritten list by the time I get back." He slammed the door.

Céleste crawled into the fetal position on the bed. All right. Nayla had seen enough. She set her palms on the glass and burned the silicon to liquid. Glass oozed into the room. The pane was clear. She retracted her wings, pencil dived through, and sprang them out to break the landing. Céleste lifted her head, teary eyed.

"What are you doing?" she asked.

Nayla strode toward her. "We're leaving."

Céleste hopped to her bare feet, dressed in her peignoir. "Are we at Hades Island?"

"Hades Island can wait. Charon is a bad egg. We have to get you away from him."

"He's really not so bad. You overheard us?"

Nayla nodded.

"It's not how he is. He's really warm and understanding. He makes me laugh."

"Céleste, you're crying. You're not laughing."

"I must have done something to bring out his bad side. If I behave, the old Charon will come out again. You'll see."

Nayla shuddered, standing in quicksand. Old Charon? Like Old Baba?

She felt the structure of her identity slipping back on its foundation. Her whole being, her whole world, was based on how Baba treated her. If Baba thought she was trash, she was trash. If Baba thought she was good, she was good. Her waking days were spent making sure Baba was in a good mood. Then she could be in a good mood.

Charon's vomit wasn't true. Céleste was a great dancer. But it didn't matter what Nayla thought. Céleste believed she was trash because Charon had said it, because the voice in the void kept chipping away at her and Charon delivered the kill-shot. Her father only owned a theater. Her dancing only attracted a god. And on *two separate* occasions. Charon's criticisms were unfounded lies.

Did this mean Baba had lied too? And if Nayla wasn't trash, who was she?

She needed to think. When did Old Baba come out—the good Baba? Before Maman's death, sometimes on payday, whenever Nayla stood up to him, and again when she perfected the mecha-sleeves. Old Baba only came out when he wanted something, or when he was naughty. Maman usually scolded him to keep him in line. Much like Nayla did at knifepoint. When Old Baba was nice, he treated her like a machine who ran on compliments and attention.

Who was real? Old Baba or regular Baba?

Her throat ran dry. She wet her lips to speak. "Old Charon is an illusion. He only wanted to hook you in. He's shown his true colors."

"You don't get it," said Céleste. "I haven't felt so complete since losing my soul. Not from dancing, Papa, or Gustave. Now this man comes along, and you want me to leave him?"

Hare Krishna. This was going to be harder than she thought. Charon had a serious grip, like a tapeworm in a host. Why were there so many mirrors in this room?

"He is in love with his own reflection," said Nayla. "Like Narcissus." She examined herself in the mirrors framed by stags of coral. "His reflection is not real. He does not love himself. He loves an illusion."

"He loves me."

Nayla shook her head. She didn't know if Baba didn't love her because she was unlovable, but she knew for certain now that Baba did not love himself. "He sees you as a reflection of him. We are not their reflections."

"Easy for you to say. I don't have one."

"All right," said Nayla. "I tried diplomacy." She lunged at Céleste and wrangled her, arm over collar. Nayla flapped her wings for lift.

"Have you gone"—Céleste struggled—"mad!"

"Don't you want your life?" Nayla soared to the skylight.

"Charon is my life." Céleste exploded into pollen.

Nayla banged her head on the pane. She smashed into the crab table and watched the pink spores repositing next to the fireplace.

Céleste aimed her finger at Nayla. "Don't make me shoot."

Nayla had never considered fighting her, not at their first meeting in the Erebus Room, not ever. She hadn't worked out the mechanics. How could she overpower someone who could turn into a cloud? It didn't occur to her she'd have to. She had to resort to words.

"Your remarkable act," said Nayla. "You weren't making love when you danced to Swan Lake at the Folies, or when you approached a demon in the Wild Garden and saved a woman's life."

"Don't."

"If you weren't there, Aphrodite and Psyche would not have showed up and saved two lives from evil. The possessed man's and the freckled lady's."

"Just the woman's life was saved. Possessed men have no souls. The demons steal them first before moving in."

"He was alive when you left, wasn't he? It's still an accomplishment."

Céleste nodded. "I have done Aphrodite proud. Finding love made me immortal."

"But it's not all you are—someone who makes love. By staying with Charon, you tell the world that it is—that you are a piece of meat."

"Did I not say I'm immortal?" Céleste raised her voice. "I have a lifetime to fight demons and save people."

"Start with yourself. To me, an immortal would have everything they want. Yet, here you are, searching for healing."

"Perhaps I have found it."

"From a boat captain on the River of Hatred?"

"Oui."

"He is a half-person. Now you are two demi-gens merged and incomplete."

Céleste shook her head in disgust. "So judgmental."

"You're picking up Charon's mannerisms."

Nayla gave her wings a shake and tucked them in to bypass the window on her flight out. She circled the ship high and wide, so as not to be spotted. She would have to rip Céleste away by her petals to pry her from Charon. Words would not work. They couldn't. What a tangled web.

She arced low, flying parallel with the laving river, and re-approached the ship, fanning her wings to slow down. Perfekt. No sailors nearby. Her hands clung to the outside rails while her boots found purchase on the edge of the gallery. She went to throw a leg over as her feathers squeezed into her spine when a force yanked her back and she fell.

"Ooph."

She expected to slap water. Instead, it received her like a baby easing into a basin. The river's black residue coiled over her stomach, arms, and legs. It was thick, dense, and warm. Molasses that moved like water.

"Don't resist," a fluty voice said in her ear. "I won't hurt you." The voice was female.

"Who are you?" asked Nayla, as the black liquid crept toward her mouth.

"Shh. Keep your head up. You're fine. Breathe and float."

Frantically, Nayla searched for a face and got one. A young woman with dripping black hair and skin as oily as the river.

"No peeking."

"Are you going to drown me?"

"Not in my river."

"Your river?"

"I am the nymph Styx, you are a nouvelle nymphe, and your friend is Charon's victim."

"How do you know?" Nayla felt a slippery hand on the base of her skull.

Styx propped Nayla's head up to keep her ears dry. "I saw them."

Nayla shivered at the touch. "Wha-what do you want in re-return?"

"Satisfaction. He discarded me like a passenger on his boat. Like a child would a toy he was tired of playing with. No one does that to me."

"Why not sink the ship?"

"Hades would not approve, and Charon would threaten to tell my husband."

Nayla remembered her studies. "Pallas."

"Very good."

"How do I break Charon's spell?"

"Silence him. My waters take away voice."

"Vishnu, help me." Nayla struggled at this revelation. It splashed in her mouth, tasting of bile. She spat.

"Keep still." Styx braced Nayla's head high. "Save the next gulp for Charon."

The waters raised Nayla over the rail and onto the deck, the wave staining the boat. Sweet Shiva. How on earth was she going to get Charon to drink that scheisse? She checked her arms for sludge and found Styx had spared her a new tattoo. The nymph, with her lamp-oil eyes and black tiara, sank into the tarry river with a finger on her lips. Above the canopy, the smokestacks puffed silently in the night.

Counterfeit love. It is no different from a counterfeit bill. However, it fools the unaware, especially if counterfeit bills are all one has ever seen. Some may think it's love, though it is surface. Hollow. Valuable to the deceived, and valueless to you and me. Oh, you don't want to include Jacques in that assertion? I know a thing or two about love. I will prove it. Kiss me.

Ho-ho, that is a test. It would prove nothing. I will use words instead.

Love is the heart palpitations you get when you a meet a highly attractive someone who thinks you are highly attractive too. Electricity. Magnetism. Sparks fly. Ah, ah, but love is when your lover, she grows fat and you do not leave her. Love is when your man loses all his money and becomes destitute, and the wife, she does not leave him. She can be thin again. The man has not lost his earning power. Love can build a ship strong enough to ride the waves of reality.

Love is behavioral. Charon was never taught how. He was never taught how to be himself. If you cannot be yourself, you cannot love yourself. As an infant, his mother did not like his true self, and so Charon locked it away forever. The real him, bound and gagged, created a false self to navigate life with. This false self made mommy happy. Mommy was satisfied filling her son with egotism and low self-worth. Inside, Charon is a child. Can we blame him? Or his parents, Erebus and Nyx?

Pardon my soliloquy. Welcome to the map room. The walls do remind me of honey Dijon. Stop, you're making me hungry. In the center. This 3D map table is of the Seine ribboned across Athens. Le Bateau Lavoir picked up Céleste and Nayla here at the Louvre. They've paddled the Styx in a giant loop, counter clockwise, back to the start. Almost the start. They are here, on the Styx, circling Île de la Cité. City Island. Oui, that is Notre Dame. A temple stood there in ancient times, dedicated to Zeus. In Erebus, it is Hades Palace. Call it brotherly spite.

First, the minor detail—Nayla must serve up a glass of mud. Until that happens, Charon has voice. With voice, it is easy to manipulate. With voice, it is harder to see actions for what they are. Nayla must palm the counterfeit bill and heat the ink.

HADES ISLAND

Black sands on the shore drifted by through the stained-glass window of a blue-green mermaid. A rock shaped like a skull sat up on a knoll. They had passed it three times. She was sure of it. They were circling Hades Island. But there was no harbor, nowhere to dock.

She walked outside Charon's cabin to the second-story gallery and breathed in the greasy air. She caught a whiff of rotten apples. A black wave lapped into the side of the boat. Droplets splashed her hand. She examined the black speckles, marks that took hours to fade. What a wonderful river. Charon must've grown up here as a boy.

A clunk of footsteps approached, and Charon came into view, her soulmate returned. Charon's face was handsome, collecting spray from the dark waves, slick on his dolphin-white skin.

"Don't move," said Céleste. "I want to savor this picture in my head."

"No need. You'll see it every day for eternity."

Finding her soul seemed a fading memory. "What about Hades Island?" She pointed at the timbered shore beyond the sands. "Aren't we going there?"

"At what port?" He laughed playfully. "This is where I circle to restart my route."

"Oh." Céleste mournfully lowered her finger.

"Who do you need, Hades or me?" He raised his arms, his long robes draped on the deck. "We have food, water, love. Clean air." He sniffed. "All ye could ask for is on the ship."

Céleste lifted her hopeful face and smiled. "You're right." She traced the piping around his robe and hugged his muscular frame.

Charon did not hug back. He'd withheld his affection ever since she fell for him. If she were nicer, maybe she could coax it out. She ran her fingers up his cheek and through his sailor hair. He seized her hand and discarded it.

"Not now, waif. I've got a boat to captain." He set off for the bridge.

I am nothing, I am nothing, I am nothing.

The rejection blocked the sun from her soul-throne, projecting shadows throughout its cavern walls. She must get the light to come back.

"Charon, please. Does steering the ship around in a circle require your expert guidance? Your shipmates can handle it, can't they?"

He turned at the hatch to the bridge. "And spend more time with you?"

"Oui. I love you."

"Thank you, it feels good to be loved." He disappeared inside.

Her head spasmed from the sting. Her eyelids shook as tears streamed past. It felt good to be loved. That was something. She wished it were more. The bed called her name, and she responded by returning to the cabin and curling up under the covers. Her soul-cave had collapsed, the rays of light twinkled beneath the rubble.

I am nothing, I am nothing, I am nothing.

She stared up at the ceiling for hours, numb, defeated, insignificant. What had she done wrong? She was kind to the guests, showered Charon with compliments, and loved him right. But it was oh so wrong. Nothing pleased him. These thoughts cast a pall over the room like cerements on a bier. Only the ceiling's blue capstone glowed in soft light.

That thing had almost landed her in trouble. She had re-imagined the melted pane before Charon had seen it. Céleste wished now to have left it broken. It would be easier to blame Nayla for Charon's attitude. Now Céleste could only blame herself.

Nayla had no idea what she was talking about. Charon was not an illusion. He was not a half-person. Charon was the sun. When he smiled, light cascaded into the cave of her soul. Compliments had warmed her icy walls. Now, but a glance of recognition would make candlelight seem like the sun, though it appeared Charon lounging in the bridge was worthier of his attention.

Céleste felt the ship ebbing in a circle, on the same course. The windows revealed no change of shore. Charon had gone to the bridge to get away from her. She waited anxiously for him to return. When he finally did, she pounced on every word for a crumb of validation.

"I'm sorry I mentioned Hades before," said Charon. A sorry! He was sorry! Sweet relief. "You were never good enough to see him."

Céleste lowered her eyes and sunk back into the sheets.

"Move over. I'm tired."

Charon changed into his pajamas by magic and lay down on his side of the bed. The lights dimmed and went out. Céleste edged closer and cuddled up against his back.

"Why so close? I'm trying to sleep." He pushed her away.

"I'm trying to cuddle you, bébé."

"If I want a cuddle, I'll ask for it."

She scurried to her side of the bed, where he promptly relieved her of the covers. Tears dripped onto her sheets in the dark. He'd had a long day. He would be different in the morning. That was all. How stupid of her to think Hades would see her.

Tell her about the Well of Lost Souls. Charon was much closer than any well. He could reignite her flame.

Snoring. He was snoring. That meant he was at peace and happy to be around her. How could he sleep soundly if he truly despised her?

She lay awake, listening to the rise and fall of his chest, to his pleasurable snores, each gush of wind from his mouth saying, *I'm content with you here. I may be harsh at times, but I love you.* There was still hope. She scrunched the pillow in her hand. The outline of Charon's body moved up and down minutely in the dark.

Something fizzled outside her room and kerplunked faintly in the water. What could that be? While Charon bobbed like driftwood, Céleste slid her legs to the floor and crept out of bed. She opened the accessway to the deck and shut it behind her. Something was burning in the river. It looked to be, oui, a floating garbage can. On fire. What was Nayla up to?

Deckhands below watched a wave engulf the flames. They chattered about whether or not to alert the captain and decided the display was preparation for the Eleusinian Mysteries. The ritual was to take place on the island. Melinoë had mentioned the Lesser Mysteries. But that was due in February. It couldn't be already. How long had the ship been circling?

It felt like a day had passed, though it could've been over a month. She couldn't tell. The flight of time didn't matter to her immortal sensibilities, but she would miss the lives of her loved ones back home should she continue in this vortex. If she tried twice as hard to please Charon, he would chart a course to friendlier waters. First, she must deal with the source of that burning can. It stunk like another of Nayla's plots to *rescue* her. Perhaps if she gave Nayla up to Charon, it would restore his old self. She ought to start by checking the roof.

Mushroom spores.

Black night swirled into variations of orange from the conch shell lanterns dotting the ship's galleries and the green aurora in the sky. She floated over the rail, above the awning, and onto the roof. A figure squatted next to the pyramid skylight.

Cannonball.

Pollen reshaped Céleste, hand up, finger pointed in the same manner that crack-shot Ira Paine aimed his gun at his third wife's head on Saturday nights. Whereas he aimed at glass balls that burst with feathers, Céleste aimed at the intruder's nose. The closer she stepped, the more the night colored in the details. Pipework and a kitchen pot gleamed in Nayla's hands. The device bubbled and purred.

She had made a small boiler and welded it to a pipe, sealed at the end by a rubber gasket, that protruded from the window. It was blowing vapors into the room by fan.

"What is that?"

"Your freedom."

Somebody coughed inside. Charon.

"You're killing him with smoke." Céleste aimed her finger at the window. Her eyes lit up.

A wall of fire rose between her and the skylight. Céleste stumbled back, pondering whether or not to pollinate through flame. She would be horribly disfigured when she rematerialized. It would kill any attraction Charon still had for her.

"What are you doing to him?" she demanded. "Charon, wake up! Wake up!" A blue star screamed off her fingertip, wired the air, and burst into sparks against the thick curtain of flame.

Glass shattered. The flame wall remained constant, embroiling the roof in a ring around the skylight. She could pollinate over the top once it began to dissipate. Until then, she raised her palms, wondering if shooting stars could smother fire. She hesitated, walking back and forth, not wanting to damage the ship, when suddenly the wall died to her knees. The skylight was blown out. Nayla had gone.

Hot air rises, Céleste. Whatever smoke Nayla pumped in had escaped the room. It was safe to enter. *Hold on, bébé. Your nymph is coming!*

Cottonwood seeds.

The dying flames swirled into minnows of light. The solar winds turned clockwise. She swam the air in breaststrokes, down over the canopy and up to her bedroom door, so fast that when she—*ship anchor*—reappeared, she dropped half a meter to the deck before gripping the codfish handle and tossing open the door.

There was no mist, no smoke. The air was clear.

Charon stood by the bed, gazing at the firelight through the broken panes above. He opened his mouth to speak. No words came out. Oh non. Her bébé. What was wrong with him? He used his hands to project his voice, and spoke only like a mime in the street. He couldn't utter a word. He touched his throat.

She ran to his side to console whatever Nayla had done to him. Céleste coddled and rubbed. Charon scowled and spun, throwing her to the bed.

"What happened?" she cried.

He pointed at his open mouth as if instructing a fisherman where a hook should go.

"You can't speak?" Her voice cracked.

He bobbled his head in big nods.

"Oh, bébé, ma bambochino. What can I do to help?" She reached for his arm.

He brushed her off and stormed out to the gallery, scanning the dark horizon. He gripped the rails with white knuckles and grimaced at some unseen enemy he could not articulate. Céleste dared not say her friend was the culprit. Céleste would receive the punishment. Charon snarled and grabbed one of his deckhands, scampering over with a hose. He took him by the nape and shot a finger at the awning.

"There's a fire on the roof," Céleste supplied.

The sailors hurried to contend with it while Charon stalked the gallery to the bridge. She reached for his hand. He snapped it from her. This was bad. Very bad. What else could she do? What cured laryngitis? Or was it sore throat?

"Don't worry, bébé. I'll get you fixed up."

He swatted her statement to the four winds and rounded the corner.

Was there a medic onboard? There was a galley. If Nayla could jury-rig a contraption out of kitchen parts to silence Charon, Céleste could find something to help. She hurried in the opposite direction, down the spiral stair by the sloshing paddlewheel, to the first story, and into the companionway that led to the galley.

Chef Maurice turned from his stove with his one good eye. Half his face had blown off in a gunpowder accident in the 1700s. But Charon hated times and dates. Make that some unspecified time in the past. *Let's see, what can I use?* Maman had taught her a few things on her good days. Red elm bark helped with sore throat. She could boil it and have Charon gulp the contents.

"Chef Maurice."

"Blahp?"

"Do you have any red elm bark?"

"Blahp." He bonked his head against a pantry.

"Merci."

She found some bark, lit a match, and got to boiling. As it stood, she was a lousy homemaker. She'd always thought her soul would enable her to learn how to keep house. Now that Charon completed her, she could start learning. She would need to work hard for him and Étienne and Eulalie, and rely on the crew to smooth out her rough spots.

When the bark was good and sweaty, she poured the water into a teacup and placed the teacup on a cart with the rest of the antidotes she'd collected.

"Chef Maurice, if you'd be so kind."

"Blahp."

She stepped into the service elevator. Maurice pushed the little cart in behind her. On the second floor, she led the charge to the bridge, where she met Charon on his captain chair. He rolled his eyes.

"Bébé, I know you're upset. I brought you some things to help." She held up a platter. "Throat lozenge?"

He slapped it out of her hands. It clanged to the ground, the candies raining onto his first mate.

"I'm only trying to help you!" She tried for the tea. "I boiled red elm bark."

He blocked his mouth and protested.

"Lower your hand and drink." She tried to pry his hand loose.

He was being a petulant child.

She plugged his nose. When he removed his hand to breathe, she forced the teacup brim to his lips and poured.

"I knew you could do it." She pulled away. "Now swallow."

He spat the tea on the floor.

"I'm doing my best, Char-Bear. How about a throat massage?" She walked up behind him and reached for his collar, but he blocked her and pushed away.

"Please, Charon. Throat exercises will loosen your vocal cords. I tried them on Maurice."

"Blahp."

Charon seized her by the wrist, led her to the door, and shut it in her face.

Why didn't he care about her anymore? Where was his empathy?

She fell to her knees and cried. How could she have let him in to torture her so? She struggled to her feet and moped along the railing. Why couldn't she please him? What was wrong with her?

Dust bunnies.

Her world distorted and recrystallized on the roof, sitting on the canopy's edge. She stared in a daze at the trees on Hades Island. They had wooden trumpet horns for branches, reminding her of how bizarre this all was. The last ray of hope for Charon had died in her soul's chamber. There was nothing she could do to return him to his former self. Whatever person she had fallen in love with was a ghost, a nonentity. An actor. He was made up. What had caused him to pretend like that? Surely, he must have some good in him to mimic that persona?

Was Nayla right? Was he in love with his reflection? Céleste tried to remember how she was before Charon. She had liked parts of herself before. Dancing. Being immortal. Being Starflower. She wanted a husband who loved her completely, someone to raise children with and love them enough to teach them to love themselves. Charon knew this. He was mimicking what she wanted to find in a man. He was mirroring her! The slippery charlatan.

The sky transposed the green aurora into midnight blue. She had done all she could. He did not appreciate her or her efforts.

Charon climbed onto the canopy from an access ladder. She jumped a little. What did he want? The question was soon answered as he ambled over and gave her a hug. The sun refused to shine. Her arms hung limp. Charon pressed her hand over his heart. She felt nothing. The heartbeat was absent. He released her hand, and it fell to the canvas roof. He turned her chin to look him in the eyes.

Mon Dieu! She could see it. The black and white spirals. She felt nothing but revulsion. Disgust contorted Charon's brow, mouth, and eyes. Was he mirroring her disgust or did it originate with him? Could it be he was disgusted by his own reflection that he saw in her?

At this point, who cared? Et alors?

Furiously, he got up and stomped around, fuming mad, splenetic, as though she'd injured his pride. She looked out at the lights flickering in the windows of Hades's dark fairy castle, visible from this side of the island. Perhaps she could leverage Charon with attention in order to take her there, as she should've done for Hermes. But Charon was cut from a different cloth, and the only place she wanted to be was away from him. He was too conceited. Suddenly, she received a boot to the back and she was airborne.

She put out her hands as she fell toward the Styx.
Think airy thoughts. Something. Anything!
Kite!

The air grew so dense, and her body so light, that it was like plunging into water, meters above the actual water. Lanterns spiraled under awnings on the laundry boat. Windows spiraled, blots in the far distance. Kicked her. Charon had kicked her. With his foot! There was no turning back. Where could she turn?

Flames burst overhead, fanning into the shape of two wings. Nayla? Would she accept her? Only moments ago, Céleste had contemplated turning her over to Charon for a morsel of attention. Nayla had been right the whole time. How did Céleste not see it sooner? Charon was a half-person. Would Nayla ever forgive her?

Nayla's fire kicked on and off, a warning beacon. Oui. *Approach*, it said, and she'd cut the flame so as not to burn her.

Nayla glided in a straight line, unscrewing the flask that swung on her hip. Céleste didn't care if Nayla trapped her in there. She deserved it. She only wanted to be away from Charon and his nightmarish boat. Dismissing her soul, the entire quest, her five-year journey. How stupid was she? How could she fall for a bratty child? Charon was three thousand years old and acted like he was three. As if his paltry attention could ever replace her sense of self. Thank God for Nayla. Thank God she didn't abandon her.

How was Céleste going to explain herself? She wished she could blame the entire episode on hypnosis, but then she would have to explain why she was idiotic enough to swallow it. She didn't want to face Nayla at all. She'd rather be trapped in here alone with her humiliation. Humiliation in a Bottle. That's what she was. Nayla could brand it. Sell it in an Oriental bazaar.

The buyer would think Céleste was a genie, but instead of three wishes, she'd mope around, eat all their food, and cry a lot.

HADES PALACE

Nayla flew along the surface, breathing a sigh of relief. The life preserver had been cast, and Céleste had grabbed hold. She could have been Charon's victim for eternity. If Nayla ever saw Styx again, she would hug her tight, black tar and all.

Over the black sand shore, across the hedgerow, stretched a parade field upon which stood two lines of maidens in white silken robes. They faced each other holding bare branches, aglow in makeshift archways. A violet-haired woman in a black dress stood at one end of the aisle. At the other, green electricity flashed and formed a ring. Nayla's heart clapped in her head. Hecate was coming. Nayla swooped low to the goopy river.

One glance and Hecate would know immediately what Nayla was up to. The violet-haired woman. That was Persephone, Hades's wife. Those maidens were the lampades, torch-bearing nymphs who accompanied Hecate. Their lights could drive a man to madness. This ritual was the Lesser Mysteries that Melinoë had spoken of. It involved Persephone returning to her mother, Demeter, on Earth, as part of the agreement with Hades, so winter could pass into spring.

This annual event began when Hades had visited Earth to investigate a volcanic eruption. Upon viewing the volcano from the land of Nysa, his attention was captured by a young maiden singing in the valley. This was Persephone. While Hades watched her, Eros watched him. Eros, god of passion, flexed his bow and fired. The love bolt struck. Hades fell in love with Persephone and stole her to the underworld where she fell in love with him.

For retribution, Demeter, goddess of harvest, made the lands infertile. To Zeus, this would not do. He sent Hermes to guide Demeter to the underworld. So long as Persephone did not eat any fruit here, she'd be able to return. But Persephone did eat. Pomegranate seeds taken from the orchards. At learning the news, Demeter became distraught, and a deal was made. Persephone would spend part of the year in the underworld, September to February and part of the year on Earth, February to September.

Was it spring already? Surely, it could not be February so soon. Had Nayla and Céleste been wandering Hades for two months?

Nayla didn't want to interrupt the ceremony to find out. She soared past the shoreline, arced over the trombone trees, and glided into a sprawling orchard, staying far to the right, clear of the parade field. Spires lanced the sky, metallic and reflective. The chateau was made of purples and blues, turrets and parapets. A rounded doorway provided access at the bottom of the wall. Sehr gut.

Land. Sneak in. Ask Hades for directions. Good plan—if Hades was home. There was only one way to find out. Her curled shoes pedaled the air like a bicycle as she came in for a landing. She touched down between two rows of trees, collapsed her wings, and rolled, collecting grass stains on her harem pants.

"Sorry, Cél. Hope you're not dizzy in there."

Did she need Céleste for this? Céleste would cause a lot less damage in the flask than out. Nayla palmed the wet grass and lurched to her feet, sore. Something about keeping Céleste prisoner didn't sit right. It said, *I don't trust you.* It would make her no different from Charon. What kind of friend was that? Did Céleste holler for police when Nayla was too ploughed to walk? Nein. Did Céleste stop her from drunkenly volunteering at Cabaret du Néant? Nein. Did Céleste ever deprive her of drink by force? Well, there was that one time. Céleste had taken Nayla's flask from her garret and told Suzon not to serve her. Look how that turned out. She got drunk anyway. Nayla could've told Gustave *nein*, but the offer was too tempting.

Céleste could not protect Nayla from Nayla any more than Nayla could protect Céleste from Céleste. If Céleste wanted to interact with the world in a way that caused self-harm, that was her prerogative. Charon had abused her horribly. *Who knows?* Maybe she would think twice next time and listen to the people who love her.

Nayla unscrewed the flask. Nothing came out. Where was the nebula? The poof?

Nayla closed one eye and peered inside. Swirling pollen. She was there all right.

"Are you going to be shy around me?" Nayla asked. "You know how many embarrassing things I've done in my life?" She tipped the flask upside down. "I know you can hear me." Nothing spilled out. "Fine, leave me in the spooky forest alone. I'm only looking for your soul, for Shiva's sake."

Pollen teased out of the spout and retreated.

"All right. The cap's going back on." Nayla brought the top to the screw threads.

Pressure knocked her hand away as pollen streamed from the bottle. The dust filled in Céleste's figure, hunched over, her eyes wet and downcast.

"Please forgive me, Nay."

Nayla crept to Céleste, unsure of how she would be received. Céleste weakly opened her arms in invitation. Nayla held her wobbly frame.

"I should've listened to you." Céleste blubbered. "I couldn't see. I was so attached. I was—in a fog. I—I'm sure you hate me."

"I don't hate you," said Nayla.

"Well, I'm not proud of myself. I feel like un morceau de merde."

The statement launched Nayla back to all the times Baba made her feel like a piece of scheisse. What was worse? Choosing your tormentor, or being born at the mercy of one? At least Cél could unglue herself. It was a wonder she had. Maman hadn't been so fortunate. The merge was too strong for her to leave. Hairs on Nayla's arms electrified. The epiphany shocked her. Was that how Maman wound up with Baba? How had Maman coped? Dancing? Dancing at the cantina while Baba worked the Blast. They never saw each other. Nein, they worked to support their family. Or had they worked to escape contact?

"Don't talk me out of it or anything," said Céleste.

"Es tut mir Leid. I was lost in thought. If that's how you feel, that's how you feel. But it's not my estimate of you. You are valuable. Don't listen to Charon's voice in your head."

How frightening. Nayla wished she could take the same advice. If only she could separate the karma from her past life from Baba's appraisal of her. Did they not align? Was not his appraisal accurate? Her kismet—her destiny—was rubbish because of her karma. If her kismet was positive, why was she born to parents who avoided one another?

"The fact you want to be talked out of it," Nayla continued, "leaves room for doubt."

Was there room for Nayla to doubt her own esteem? She sighed. Her karmic influence was too powerful.

"Charon was a liar," Nayla asserted. "He is exactly how my baba was."

But with less alcohol and more laundry boat. Thankfully, Baba wasn't in charge of anything but her tenement. Scheisse. Had they started a mecha-sleeves company, the power would have gone to his head. He was a barely functioning employee tapping hearths. Imagine him barking orders to their staff like Charon did to his crew. And the clients. Baba would have schmoozed with clients as obnoxiously as Charon did passengers.

"I didn't realize." Céleste peeled herself off Nayla and met her eyes. "How did you break free?"

"I didn't."

"But he's dead."

"I know." Nayla looked at the grass. "It's a minefield of emotion. One false step. Kablammo." She raised her head. "I can't make it across without moksha. Then my karma will evaporate, Baba's criticisms will stop."

"If Charon was lying about me, perhaps Baba was lying about you."

Nayla shook her head. "I did not choose Baba. Karma did."

"That would mean you were born a half-person," Céleste pleaded. "How can that be? You need trauma to occur for that."

The desperation in Céleste's eyes. Like it was a mantra she was trying to convince herself of. She'd angrily mentioned the same thing at Maxim's. Nayla got the sense it was less of an attack on her beliefs and more of a fear Céleste had about her own life. What was there to be afraid of? Céleste was a Vaishya, born with substantially less karmic debt.

Before Céleste's Incident, she was normal. Although, the tale of her mother bashing her head against a wall to relieve stress did not seem so normal. In Jacoma, a few years ago, it might have been, though not now. And there it was. The rub. Céleste's fear. She was afraid that she wasn't born normal. But she need not have worried. She was not born a half-person like Nayla was. A bad homelife only meant trauma occurred for Céleste at some earlier date, pre-Incident, and that healing was still entirely possible by retrieving her soul.

"What's true for you isn't true for me," said Nayla. "But one thing is for sure. Baba did not love himself."

Céleste nodded, relaxing her posture. "Neither did Charon. With so many mirrors placed everywhere, how could he? Him reflecting me to lure me in, me reflecting him so I hate myself. Oh, Nayla, you were so right." Céleste embraced her. "I hope your moksha helps you." She palmed Nayla's shoulders. "Thank you for not giving up on me. I'm sorry you had to see me like that." She wiped her eyes.

"I've seen worse." Nayla hoped it didn't sound like a competition.

Céleste wiped her eyes without argument. "I wish we never got on that wretched boat."

"We can't change that."

"Non." Céleste looked up. "What's that glow in the sky?"

"Hecate's blaze." Nayla relayed the sights of when she landed. "There's a door where the orchard meets the chateau."

"Génial." Céleste looked at a tree and reached for an apple. "So hungry."

"Don't eat that," croaked a male voice.

Nayla flamed her hands at the intrusion.

"Snuff those candles. You'll set the orchard on fire." An old man in a spiffy suit limped out of the shadows. His long, stringy hair swayed like a spider web as he reached into the tree by Céleste. "That one's not ripe. Eat this one." He plucked an apple and offered it to her.

"Céleste"—Nayla pointed—"that apple is blue. I don't think it would be prudent to eat fruit in a foreign land."

"You can try the pomegranate instead," said the miser, reaching across the row.

"Nein," said Nayla. "That one makes you bride of Hades. Céleste, eat the blue apple."

"Persephone only became his bride," said the man, "because I tattled on her. Where did that get me? Hades let Demeter turn me into an owl." He flapped his arms. "Loyalty. It's for the birds." He squinted at Céleste, inspecting the fruit. "Go on. It's quite delectable, I assure you. See if I tell anyone anything now. Eat whatever you like."

Céleste munched on the apple.

"Who are you?" asked Nayla. "Aside from a disgruntled employee."

"I am Ascalaphus. I overheard your conversation. Think you two know misery, humph."

"You claim your woe is more profound than ours?" asked Céleste, chewing.

"Before I was an owl, Demeter buried me under a rock, so yes."

Nayla decided to let him win. He'd been through a lot. "That is quite miserable."

"Too tart." Céleste tossed the core. "Where is Hades?"

"He's in the castle, doing what I'm doing. Staying far away from his vile mother-in-law."

"Demeter?" asked Céleste.

"The witch. Thank Hades she visits but two days a year. Spring, autumn. That's plenty. She's taking Persephone with her. Good riddance. My queen turned me into a gecko. It's a vacation when she leaves. The apple didn't fall far from the tree. Like mother, like daughter, changing people into critters, burying 'em under rocks. Can you believe that family? I'm the fucking gardener. What did I do?"

"You deserve better," said Céleste. "Can you bring us to Hades? I'll put in a good word."

"Who are you?" asked Ascalaphus.

"Les nouvelles nymphes."

"Nymphs, sure. A little low on the hierarchy, but worth a whirl. Follow me." He trod through the orchard, heading north to the castle, its wall fifty meters high. "At least a nymph can grow wings," he grumbled. "I'd like owl wings. No. I turn into the whole damn bird."

Tagging along behind him, Céleste leaned over to Nayla and whispered, "What a helpful man."

"Misery loves company," she whispered back.

At the orchard's edge, they came upon a door, the arch made of dead flowers. The surrounding wall gleamed violet and blue like stacked cabochons. The bricks were made of glass and filled with what appeared to be solid ink.

Ascalaphus placed his hand on the glass handle. "Touch anything. Get your smudgy fingerprints all over the goods. I don't care." He opened the glass door on its glass hinges, welcoming them to a glazier's paradise.

A crystal statue of Cerberus dominated the checkered floor of the antechamber. How lifelike. He was bigger than a horse, as big as the real Cerberus.

"Last I left Hades, he was polishing his collection. Right this way." Ascalaphus led Nayla and Céleste down a hall filled with arches covered by brocade curtains. He parted one and admitted them into a study.

Shelves of glass figurines and iridescent vases lined the walls in rows. Individual pedestals scattered the room, displaying goddesses in statuary. In the corner towered a man in a dark suit, his lanky frame accented in violet, and his paunch adorned by silver chains and a pocket watch. His long black hair draped his head, resembling a corpse at a late funeral, on which sat an expensive set of jeweler's headgear. He rotated the lens, examining a figurine of Artemis. Maybe to view the crystalline structure of Artemis's bow.

"Pardon my disturbance, Lord Hades. These fine nymphs desire an audience."

Hades raised the headband, revealing a round face and round chin, with a straight nose and strong brow. His complexion was pallid and leather-cracked, his eyes ringed by anemic shadows, portals from where he viewed the world through his golden irises.

"Come in, my lovelies. Don't be shy. I'll give you a tour."

Ascalaphus bowed sarcastically and left.

Nayla walked on tiptoe with Céleste to meet him.

He stuck out a hand. "Lord Hades, King of the Underworld."

"Fleur d'Étoile, Princess of the Folies Bergère." Céleste shook hands.

Nayla rolled her eyes. "Spuckfeuer, Maharani of the Sand Pits."

"Pleasure." He brought them to a display stand. "Here we have a Tiffany lamp. Bronze base. Wisteria design. Favrile glass. The metallic oxides seeped into the silicon to give it a lustrous effect. Over here." He lumbered to another lamp. "An electric bulb candelabra. Magnolia shades. We gave this one to the Daum Brothers."

"Gave it to them?" asked Nayla.

"A gift. You know—gather, sort, deliver?" Hades waited patiently for Nayla, but she had nothing. "You don't know?" He put his hands together and fluttered his fingers. "The nymphs gather reality perceived by the unconscious minds of the artists, sort the materials, and deliver the idea into hands capable of transposing the work."

"What about dancers?" asked Céleste.

"Performance art, same method." Hades flipped his hand. "Now, you must see this crackled glass by Émile Gallé. He has the ability to create two-colored pieces in one."

"Do the nymphs give every artist a chance?" Céleste interrupted.

"They do. Though most nymphs are drawn to innate talent. The nymphs feed them small ideas for their works until, little by little, these creators gain experience and develop a mastery the level of producing this iridescent phänomen glass, courtesy of Johann Loetz and one of the naiads."

Nayla marveled at the blues and greens and purples.

"When it comes to prodigies," said Hades, "the nymphs swarm. However, if the artist receives a big idea too early, it means a nymph had made a mistake, a fluke, and the novice must wait for their talent to catch up."

"Oui," said Céleste, "what else about beginners?"

"Beginners? Not in my collection. Beginners must trip and stumble without a muse till they hone their skills enough to attract one. Then, if they create something original in their own style, I might feel inclined to include them, like this beauty." He leaned his arm on a shelf with a green jug and twirling spout.

It looked like a hookah.

"Can the nine muses help someone?" Céleste wrung her hands. "Asking for a friend."

"The nine muses determine the medium. The performance is up to your friend. Practice hard, and inspiration will come."

"What if my friend is missing her soul?"

Hades smiled knowingly. "That would be problematic. Superior dance requires heart and soul."

Nayla was about to shout the question already. *Where is the Well of Lost Souls?* But something in the museum caught her eye. On a pedestal stood a rod, and on the rod stood a helmet. The Cap of Hades. A glass replica. Nayla saw her eyes widen in its blue reflection.

"Tell me about this piece," Nayla said a bit too eager.

"My very own. Note the almond shaped eyeholes, the flared cheeks, the nose guard. The black plume is made of horse hair, the entire piece modeled on a Corinthian helmet, of course. You like?"

"I love." She wiped her mouth to make sure she wasn't drooling. "Why isn't the real one on display?"

"On loan to another museum."

"Did they take it from you?"

"Oh, I can check it out if I wish. Us Olympians have a borrowing system in place. By membership only, I'm afraid."

Borrowing system? She could do that. The helmet was a catalyst for moksha. She didn't need to keep it indefinitely. She was teetering awfully close on the brink of being found out, but she must know. "How does one become a member?"

He chuckled. "Don't call us, we'll call you."

"Monsieur Hades"—Céleste made eyes at him—"I hope the Well of Lost Souls isn't as exclusive."

Hades glanced at the bust of Persephone and settled his gaze on Céleste. "Depends on what you're offering."

Nayla winced. Not again.

Hades crossed the small distance between himself and Céleste and held her chin in his hand to make clear the type of offer he'd accept.

Nayla had to avert disaster. "She has a Tiffany vase she's willing to donate."

"A what?" asked Céleste.

"Ja, from your collection." Nayla took her hand. "We must discuss which one to offer in private."

Hades smiled coyly. "Whatever you like." He lowered the magnifiers and resumed his study of the Artemis crystal.

Nayla dragged Céleste to a statue of Hermes so she could hash it out. "Is gaining the power to make a barrier important?"

"Oui," Céleste whispered. "I have to cleanse the palate. Get Charon out of my system."

Nayla looked from side to side. "Making love with Hades isn't going to heal past wounds. It's not like an amnesiac getting bopped on the head twice to restore memory."

"Are you sure?"

"What are you implying?"

"Look, you drink after you grow wings, do you not?"

"Ja, but—"

"Wings are the terminal power. There are no further abilities. What I'm saying is, I need it, with or without powers. You don't know how it feels for me, being here. It's like the walls are constantly closing in. *I am nothing, I am nothing,* blathering away."

Nayla wasn't going to win this argument with logic. Maybe if she took a moral stance.

"Hades is different from Charon," said Nayla.

"I know. He's a king."

As if value were conferred through making love.

"I mean," said Nayla, "he is married. Aren't you Catholic?"

"Nayla, really."

"Aren't you?"

"Well... *He's* not."

Nayla thought about this. "He's had affairs with other nymphs. Minthe and Leuce. Guess where they are? Minthe is a leaf. Leuce is a tree. Maybe he will turn you into a starflower."

"Are you finished?"

"There has to be another way."

"There isn't."

"We'll see about that." Nayla pulled Céleste back across the gallery.

"What are you going to say?" Céleste muttered.

Nayla's hands trembled. Her feet went numb. Mouth dry, as she plucked up the courage to speak while Hades raised his eyewear. Sweet Shiva, she was verrückt. "Does Fleur d'Étoile have to trade sex for information?"

Céleste winced at the pronouncement.

Hades touched his chest, appalled. "Who do you think you're talking to? The Well of Lost Souls is at 32 rue Richer. Good luck and Godspeed."

Why did that address seem familiar?

Céleste's face dropped. "It's the Folies Bergère." She touched her cheek.

"Reality is the theater of our unconscious." Hades touched his brow.

Céleste turned to Nayla. "Spuckfeuer, let me chat with Lord Hades alone. Perhaps there's a minibar to occupy so you don't get bored. Tipple some camphor."

Hades raised a slender eyebrow. "In the grand foyer. Down the hall, third door on the left."

Nayla would be twice as verrückt to leave Céleste with Hades. Nayla was about to regret unscrewing her flask again and stopped herself. She couldn't control Céleste any more than she could control Baba. She could act cheery, do favors, use reason—it didn't matter. Desire did not negotiate. Making a scene before the King of the Underworld was out of the question. If Céleste crashed, Nayla'd have to wait in the wings to pick up the pieces. She inhaled the sterilized air, gritted her teeth, and walked into the hall.

Exactly as instructed, she found the bar recessed into the wall of a round room with a grand staircase twining up the side. If Céleste wanted to engage in time-wasting behavior, she could too. *Throw everything out the window, why don't they?* She grabbed a bottle of Greek wine and poured some into an iridescent glass. A phänomen, Loetz glass. She may as well retain some knowledge on this tour to nowhere. *Can't stop drinking after wings*—Nayla would show her. If everyone was doing what they want, she may as well enjoy her time in Lord Hades's chateau.

Ja, why not act like her Dionysian forebearer and climb one drink at a time to ekstasis, to be outside herself, out of body? Prost!

After swilling a krater of wine, she stumbled back down the hall and halted at the third door on the right. She half expected to see two writhing bodies on the cold museum floor, yet the showroom was vacant. Ah, the Cap of Hades. She ought to try it on, just to see if it fit. As she walked the checkered tiles, a Upanishad played in her head.

So long as the drop remains separate from the ocean, it is small and weak; but when it is one with the ocean, then it has all the strength of the ocean... so long as man believes himself to be separate from the Whole, he is helpless; but when he identifies himself with It, then he transcends all weakness and partakes of Its omnipotent qualities.

Nayla took off Maman's headpiece and set it on the floor. The helmet shined, magnetic. Hands outstretched, she lifted the mighty glass off its stand. Her ticket to a painless existence. She rotated the piece and lowered it on her head.

She could picture it. The museum blending into her body, and her body the museum. Who was who? She was everything. A fire flashed in her mind.

The work shed door slapped open. Warm desert air blew. The hearth flickered. A glowing face greeted her, painted bronze, as if day itself had tiptoed in. He was dressed in a blue kurta and beige pajama, looking very debonair.

"Baba?" asked Nayla. "Do you need me at the Blast?"

"Nein, Nayla. I was checking in to see how you were doing. Work on your mecha-sleeves."

"I'll get them to push a coal car, just you wait!"

He walked to the bench and held her face in his hands—his own face full, his cheeks clean cut, his hair neatly parted, his head small and wide, his nose a honey apple without blemish, his eyes brown kanche without rings.

"You don't have to impress me, daughter. You don't need to do a thing. You are enough." He kissed her on the forehead.

The flame died in a flash. Tears were in her eyes. She had done it. She had felt it. Brahman. It was so unglaublich. As if she were born lovable. She touched her mouth. God is love. She nodded. Divine love—Bhakti. Unconditional. Ascending to samadhi—Bliss. Real. It was real. No childish fancy. But childlike. She had it, and she had lost it. She wanted to get back there, to an alternate reality where she lived in the Persian Quarter and Baba had arranged a suitor. To remain always in Brahman's embrace. Imagine what the real helmet could do.

Suddenly, the gravity of the situation hit her. She was being foolish. Trying on Hades's prized glass collection in the heart of the underworld. If she were caught, what could she say? The game would be up. She had to get this thing off. She placed her hands on the smooth hulk of the cap and lifted. It rubbed against her sweat. Twisting would work. She stuck her arms out like amphora handles and spun, knocking into something hard.

Glass shattered on the floor. Nayla removed the helmet and hurriedly put it back on the stand. *What broke?* The bust of Persephone. She waited in silence. She was probably safe. Never mind. Something was coming. The flapping of wings. Butterfly? Couldn't be.

An owl soared into the room and, in a puff of photography smoke, turned into an old man. Ascalaphus.

"The witches are coming," he warned. "Where is Lord Hades?"

"I—uh—bedroom."

Ascalaphus puffed back into an owl and took off down the hall. Phoenix wings burst from Nayla's back, sans flame. She flew after him. *Down the hall, hang a left, second door, nein, third.* Braid whipping, cherry lowlights out, she soared up the grand foyer's grand staircase, over the balustrade, into another hall, her wingtips brushing the brocades.

The owl landed in front of a fancy mahogany door laden with floral patterns made of glass. In a magnesium flash, he was back to normal. Nayla sheathed her wings, subcutaneous. A quiet fire burned on her shoulders, a loud one on her hands. She exhaled and drove her fingers right through the crease in the jamb. Scraps of metal clinked to the tiles, white hot. She pushed the door.

Céleste leapt off Hades under the sheets of the canopied bed.

"What is it?" Hades demanded, impervious to voyeurism.

"Sire, the witches are coming. I mean, *hoot-hoot.*" Having shared too much, Ascalaphus puffed into an owl and fled before being turned into anything else.

"Who?" asked Hades.

"Per... Perthephone," Nayla explained, the last dram of wine hitting her hard.

"Get out." Hades rose and opened a tall stained-glass window outward on its hinge.

Floor-to-ceiling, Nayla could fit through easily. She unscrewed the flask and extended the ride to Céleste.

She blew the frizzy bang out of her eye, cinched her peignoir, and exploded into pollen. In three heartbeats, the miniature pink sandstorm funneled into the flask. Hades sighed. The pink petal skirt was on the bed. Sandals strew the floor. He gathered up Céleste's costume in a pillowcase and shoved it into Nayla's arms. Cap on, goggles down, she stepped up to the ledge. She ejected her feathers against the exterior glass bricks and jumped.

What side of the castle was she on? She blinked at where she thought the orchard was and saw a tennis court. She was on the north side, flying toward the shore, toward the side of Erebus that harbored the Cabaret du Néant, the Moulin Rouge, and the Folies Bergère—the Right Bank. The hedgerow ringing the island was a thing of the past, the black sands barely visible, merging into the River Styx. She was over the water.

On the horizon paddled Charon's Bateau Lavoir.

Flashes erupted on deck. Were they shooting at her? Nein. Tentacles of light sprawled the sky. Signal flares. They flickered over the boat. A white flag rippled from a smokestack in the glow. In the flag's center, a pink monarch butterfly.

Nayla squeezed her flask. *Not this time.* She thrust out her fist and spurted a gob of fire at the flag, dashing Charon's hopes to cinders.

THE WELL OF LOST SOULS
(TRIPTYCH, PANEL #1)

A somersault flung Céleste into the corners of the flask. Was Nayla flying a loop-de-loop? A metallic thunk slammed her into the cap. What was happening out there? The cap unscrewed. Phosphorescent hairs raced into her canvas. She shot from the flask like water from a blowhole. A black snout smiled its sharp incisors and received a faceful of heat, attacked by a firebird.

Tombstone.

Céleste reformed, standing on blue masonry and grout made of glowworms, the trough-like street braced in by six-story abodes made of wilderness. The demon dug his nails into Nayla's back as she soared up to the canopy, the beast clinging to her front. Her fists poured flame on his torso, sending him screaming into a plant-like receptacle on the side of the building. The thing looked alien—a translucent yellow squash that cupped a pool of acid, a solution that ate the lizard alive. It was a pitcher plant, with an umbilical cord for a tail attached to the building, though she'd never seen any that large in a conservatory she'd ever visited.

Nayla circled around, arcing over a façade at the end of the street with a tuba horn above a marquis. Where Céleste expected to see the words FOLIES BERGÈRE on the outside rim, she read:

THE ꞶⱻⱩⱠ OF ⱠOꞄT ꞄOUⱠꞄ

Her heart beat a little faster. Between *of* and *lost*, the happy and sad masks had been altered to manic and melancholic expressions. Spiraling above the building loomed dozens of lizards, their pterodactyl wings gliding the dense atmosphere like webby reptilian kites. She could smell their rot from here.

"Salut, Fleur d'Étoile, our old friend."

Céleste turned, palm ready, and fired before aiming. A shooting star lit up Erebus in a flash, exploding in sparks on the demon's iguana-sack for a neck.

Atout!

The beast howled, clutching the wound with one of its three fingered claws. Its black lizard scales made it hard to see.

Evading, Céleste took a backstep and another and anon. She froze to the ground. Stuck. She was stuck. Was her leg broken? Non, Dieu merci. Her femur pulsated through her leg, solid, in one piece. That wasn't the problem. Tiny clear globules set on red prongs had adhered to her ankle. The prongs were attached to... *what are these? Round green lollipops?* They were some kind leaves. They looked like round-leaved sundew. And the street was littered with them.

Hé, there was her costume. She bent to pick it up, barely able to reach.

Got it.

Slashing nails glinted in electric blue light.

Dust bunnies.

The claw sliced through her pollen in swirling paint strokes.

A second demon crawled out of a sewer, and a third sprang out of a doorway grown from tree roots. The pair came at her from opposite sides, taking care to avoid the carnivorous plants. The demon she had shot with a star was back on the hunt too, bleeding oil. That made three. If she could use the ecosystem to her advantage...

She traveled to a clearing, meters away, surrounded by sticky globules. Thinking dense thoughts—*Eiffel Tower*—she resumed shape, costume on, with a sting at her ankle. All of her pollen hadn't made it. Exposed flesh showed where the plant had latched on and peeled off a layer of skin. More unnerving were the demons charging to her encampment. She raised her palms in defense.

Nayla flew high above, battling a flock of her own. *Don't count on help this time, Céleste.* She had been fighting these monsters her whole adult life, but always one on one. Never had she seen so many.

The bloody-necked demon leapt over the patch of sticker plants, bent on revenge. She drew her thumbs together and ejected a shining beacon of light. Bright red, it flashed. The demon pummeled the ground, shrieking until his open chest cavity siphoned the remaining air being used for his voice box, smoke rising from the wound in a stench of burning garbage.

"How dare you enter our dominion," the demon gasped.

Out of morbid curiosity, she sometimes inspected their bodies, but a lounge of these lizards would be upon her in seconds.

She dug in her heels and flared out her wrists. Her fingertips lit up, all ten of them, in blue orbs, starting softly beneath the skin and growing to the size of golf balls.

Another demon leapt the lawn of probing filaments. Three more.

The heat and sound intensified on her fingertips. The odd spatial hum increased to a whine as the protostars zipped free, weaving haphazardly at the encroaching lizards, piercing arms and throats like mortars. One blast struck a building. One severed a plant head. Another knocked a demon onto the gel-like tips of the sundews, and there he writhed.

Céleste, out of standing room, stood on his belly and shot him in the snout with her finger gun.

A claw swiped at her bicep, leaving a nasty gouge. She turned at the grabby beast and unloaded her six-shooters. Black smoke. Flecks of blood. Reptilian screams. Mephitic breath. The spongy touch of the sundews. Anything that moved, she shot. A claw reached for her ankle. She looked down to take care of it, when something knocked the wind out of her, sending her sprawling eyeball-first at one of the plant's clear beaded combs.

Dried leaves.

She rushed around the stickers, diverting as much of herself as she could before they claimed a whole pound of flesh. No doubt she'd reappear with more nicks and cuts. It was unsafe fighting in such close quarters, so she flutter-kicked to higher ground. The demons in her former clearing flapped their wings in a frenzy. That was what had slapped her. A wing.

She swam to the T-shaped intersection where rue de la Boule Rouge met rue Richer, or in her case, rue Crazy met rue Insane, dominated by the Well of Lost Souls at the end. There was the Folies.

Where was Nayla?

Adjacent to their destination, flaming through the air. She was bound for a platform supported by a single pole, wearing a demon for a necklace. The monster was strangling her. Céleste front-crawled up to the lookout, but she need not have hurried. Red-hot eyes burned through Nayla's goggles with the ferocity of a perturbed bull. She hammered her fists together and let flame unspool from her body like ribbon. Her fires entwined the lizard choking her neck. Sizzling, he backed away, loped between the spikes fencing the platform, and leapt off in a posture of flight. His wings, badly damaged—the webby canvas scorched—failed to capture wind.

He dropped like a—

—Brick.

Céleste rematerialized on the uneven platform. Her arms and legs stung to high hell. The sundew had grazed her, as predicted. Better her limbs than her face. She took a step, felt a scrape on the sole of her foot, right through her sandal, and stomached the shooting pain in order to deal with the task at hand. She could fit her entire bedroom on this topsy, pink-carpeted terrace. The demons were no longer attacking. Nayla killed her fire.

"I apologize for the rude awakening," she said. "I had to let you out. Why are they letting up?"

"Je ne sais pas." Céleste observed the demons spiraling into the heavens. The nearest flyby had a smile on his snout. "What broke in Hades Palace?"

"The Bust of Persephone."

"Super. Probably a wedding gift. If you weren't poached, you wouldn't have alarmed her."

"If I wasn't—you were making love to her husband!"

"It just happened."

"Oh, gut, just happened. Your brain had no say in the matter whatsoever."

"I think you'd be glad I can make barriers. Look at all the demons we have to battle." Her hand swept across the neighborhood and fell on Nayla. "You broke the statue on purpose."

"I most certainly did not." Nayla sneered. "But if you must know, it was worth it. When I put on the helmet, I had a spiritual experience."

"You put on the replica?" Céleste creased her brow.

"Ja. For one divine minute, I had fully merged with Brahman. But go ahead, say I was mistaken. That I was drunk. If you hadn't run off with Hades, I wouldn't have drank to pass the time."

Céleste wanted to lash out. "I wish you could feel what this place does to me."

"What?"

"It makes me feel outside myself."

"Even now? After your tryst with Hades?"

"Non. After Hades, it felt like somebody glued a shattered vase back together. Like I finished bathing in the sun on the Riviera."

"I hope it satisfies you for the duration of our visit." Nayla panted. "Know this. I would never deliberately put us in harm's way."

The platform creased under Céleste. The center was caving in. The outside came up in two sections, as if the boggy platform was on a hinge. Green spikes poked out from the folds as they begged to embrace.

Céleste flung her hands at the moist walls.

Think airy thoughts.

Non, non, non. She mustn't pollinate. It would leave Nayla to hold the walls alone. She wouldn't have the strength. Céleste didn't even know if they could bear the weight together, but she had to stay. Besides, she was immortal. The flytrap's acid would fail to dissolve her completely.

Veins stuck out of Nayla's neck from the strain. "Go poof."

"This... is no time... for martyrdom." There was so much force sandwiched against them, and Nayla was playing less-than-thou. Thinking low of herself all the time was getting annoying. *Own the space you occupy, Nay.* She deserved to live no more than the next person. If only she'd celebrated life properly, she'd live forever, immortal, and they could just let this flytrap crush them. Wait a moment...

"Do... you... think feeling... Brahman made you... immortal?" asked Céleste.

"Nein."

Nayla's phosphorescent skull vacillated blue and green as if to proclaim her very mortality.

"I'm glad you... got to... feel it."

Nayla nodded, face tense. "Go poof. I have an idea."

"And... if... it doesn't work?"

"Then it doesn't work."

Pink spikes protruded from the walls, bisecting Céleste's view of Nayla.

"Do it," Nayla urged, "and get far away."

The girl was folle.

Paper glider.

Céleste's vision swirled. Nayla cupped her ears as pink blended with blue. Céleste fled the plant's mouth through its teeth. Soundwaves erupted in the air like a detonated sea mine. A sudden intrusion of heat and light thrust her faster to safety. The glowworm street lay below. To her side, the tuba horn façade of the Folies. Behind, a chunk of flytrap stood disemboweled, the middle segment vaporized. Glowing chlorophyl dripped from the wound. It was like a bomb went off. But where was Nayla? *Please let her be all right.*

Phoenix wings flared in the sky. Mon Dieu! The girl was folle indeed. She flashed her bright colors on and off, swooped around the flytrap, and pointed to the tuba's funnel. The cone provided entry, though it was so far away. Céleste waded mid-air as Nayla flew to meet her while opening the flask. Céleste focused her gaze at the narrow aperture and leaned into it. She poured inside. The cap doused her in darkness.

She hadn't felt so close to her soul in five years. Though her intuition couldn't detect it, she knew in her heart it was in this eerie lair, waiting for her in desperate anticipation.

THE WELL OF LOST SOULS
(TRIPTYCH, PANEL #2)

D emons gathered at Suzon's bar. Nayla twitched her wing muscles and swooped into the upper arcade, ducking one of many thorny vines that garlanded the room and landing safely in the gallery behind a column. It could hardly be called a Winter Garden. None of the metal here was frosted. The original Winter Garden wasn't a real hot house either, but there was nothing wintery about this. Red and green prehistoric leaves exuded from every nook and cranny, composing the plasticity of her surroundings. What plants, only Céleste could name. She should let her out. Nein. Nayla ought to clear the room of demons first. She had never expected to see them conversing after hours.

What were they saying?

"Look at these clowns at their circus," croaked a mean lizard, flipping his hand at the mirror.

"What's happening?" One lizard sashayed in from the promenoir with a wiggle in his legs. "Did I miss anything?"

"Noy, the band leader and that schoolmarm instructor are moping around. Barmaid is closing up shop."

"Fleur d'Étoile show up yet?" asked a third, scrawnier lizard.

"Noy, she's gone."

Maybe it would be a good idea to let Céleste in on the trans-pirings. Nayla unscrewed the flask and pressed her finger to her lips as the pink sands leaked out and observed her.

Céleste remolded, taking cover behind a planter on the railing.

Nayla pecked her finger at the goings on.

"I haven't seen Fleur d'Étoile in ages," said the mean lizard.

"She's not in any of the Erebus Rooms."

"Hubert thought he smelled croquembouche and petunias the other night, but he was hunting souls next to a bakery."

"Wish I coulda been there to whiff it. I know that nymph's perfume cloud anywhere. Anywhere, I tells you."

"Maybe she's dead."

Céleste cringed.

"She ain't dead. Thanatos woulda collected her soul. Silly thing's still down there."

"Oy, remember when Gergely yanked it free? Loosest con-nection he'd ever sawn."

"Was it gobbed on with toothpaste?"

"Took nothin' but a little elbow grease to dislodge, said he. Only one looser was her butler's. Dangling by a thread, that one. Fleur d'Étoile's was low hanging fruit after that."

Céleste bit her lip and turned to Nayla in a whisper. "It's not true. I wasn't vulnerable before the Incident."

"They're old braggarts," Nayla whispered in reply. "Dumb blowhards. Don't worry." She reached for some comforting words. "You're immortal."

"Don't patronize me," said Céleste. "I know you think I'm not."

"You believe you are," Nayla recovered. "What does it matter if you were vulnerable before?"

"It would mean I attracted those leeches. It would mean I was born weak and unlovable, and my soul-theft made it worse. That's why Aphrodite wanted me to search for love."

"But you found love. It made you immortal, richtig?"

"Oui, but not invulnerable. Did you hear those lizards? If what they say is true, I'm afraid that once I retrieve my soul, I'll still feel like this. I'll feel how I did before it was stolen, but worse, because I'll be aware of it and know there's nothing I can do."

"Let's not jump to conclusions."

There was no way to know how Céleste would feel until the moment arrived. If the moment arrived. The place was crawling with demons. What if reuniting with her soul left her a nervous wreck? Nayla thought about how to deal with this. If Céleste believed she was born an unlovable half-person, Nayla could explain that she was a Vaishya and that it wasn't so, but Nayla didn't like foisting reality on people. Maybe Céleste's reunion with her soul would leave her in a better state. Maybe she would feel divine love like Nayla had. It would be a start. Céleste needed her Atma, her eternal soul. Then she could realize her connection to Paramatma, the universe, and be one with Brahman.

But Nayla didn't want to get ahead of herself. Feelings came out of the unknown so mysteriously, she couldn't predict how she'd feel about Céleste reuniting with her soul, let alone how Céleste would feel. The best thing to do was wait and see.

All she could do at the moment was encourage. "You're not unlovable," said Nayla.

"You're right. I'm not." Céleste clenched her fists and hopped to the railing.

Nayla reached to pull her down, but Céleste withdrew her hand. She placed it on the viny, stone column with chipped thorns as the blood dried on her calves.

Below, the demon continued his mockery. "Her soul was a tasty scoop of peanut butter on a broken mouse trap."

"Liars!" Céleste called down.

The demons craned their heads at the arcade.

"Fleur d'Étoile, who let you in?"

The scraggly demon fanned out his wings and barred his teeth. "Kill it. Soulless nymph."

Céleste leapt from the rail—arms out, knee up, skirt petals afloat, launching Bengal fire like it was Diwali—before bursting into pollen so as not to break her legs. Nayla knifed out her wings and dove into the melee, scooping up the demon like the peanut butter in his story. She tackled him into the next bar, where she let out a glass-shattering scream. He'd swiped her thigh with his claw. His nails, razor sharp, dripped with blood. How fast these demons grew uncivilized. She feinted back and set him ablaze while shooting stars whizzed overhead.

"Take it back!" Céleste shouted, standing on a demon's throat by the fountain. "I was not born weak. I was born normal."

The demon's eyes bugged out of his skull, indifferent to the comment. The scrawny one lay hunched on the bar, already dead, disintegrating to stardust.

Lips pursed at the end of the last one's snout. "Fine, *you* tell me why your soul is here."

Céleste pointed a finger at his head and fired, sparing countless souls in the process.

"Do you know Céleste?" asked Gustave. His voice echoed from somewhere close by.

"Gustave!" Céleste whirled around, smiling so wide that she lost a tear. "Did you hear him, Nay? Am I dreaming? Where is he?"

"The mirror." Nayla pointed, approaching the center bar.

"Present tense," replied a soft-spoken voice. "What strong faith. You believe she's alive."

Nayla recognized the timbre instantly. "Hermes."

He stood in the Folies where she stood in Erebus. Céleste leaned tensely on the bar where Gustave sat. He tucked in his necklace.

"She is alive somewhere," said Gustave. "Who are you?"

"I saw her the night of la Grande Attraction, the night she disappeared. I can take you to her."

"Don't go with him, Gustave," cried Céleste. She cocked her head at Nayla, helpless. "He's going to kill him."

Hermes was plenty capable. The god was jealous and rife with anxieties.

Céleste hurtled the bar and placed her hands on the mirror.

Gustave looked at the impeccably dressed Hermes, his gray eyes full of bravery and distrust.

"That was two months ago," said Gustave. "To the day."

"I know," Hermes said quietly. "Do you want to see her or don't you?"

"Show me."

"Non, Gustave! Non!" Céleste slapped the mirror. "Don't go with him!"

Gustave rose from the stool.

Céleste pounded on the surface. "I'm fine! I'm all right! Don't go with him!" She picked up a champagne bottle.

Nayla winced as it shattered. Foam drenched the mirror. The picture held firm.

Hermes crossed from right to left toward the exit. Gustave let him take the lead, patted his coat, and followed.

"Don't go! Il va te tuer!" Céleste raised her palms.

Nayla blinked as Bengal fire sparked on the glass.

When her eyes readjusted, Gustave and Hermes were gone. The only image that remained was Céleste, streaked with dripping champagne.

"Cél, your reflection," Nayla said timidly. "Can you see it?"

"I don't care." She crouched into the fetal position on the floor. "I don't care," she whimpered. "I don't care."

Nayla peered over the edge. "Cél, you're lying in broken glass."

"Et alors?" Mucus leaked from her nose. "It's not worth it."

"What did you say?"

"My soul." Her chest heaved. "It's not worth a curse."

Nayla knew Céleste. If her soul could make her immortal, maybe then she could fight Hermes—but not before. And she was going to want to.

"We are in the middle of Erebus." Nayla scanned the tropical Winter Garden to make sure it was clear of any threats. "Hermes is on a vendetta, Charon wants to own you, and Persephone must be furious. We are past the point of no return."

"I can't go on." Céleste peeked up at Nayla. "Can you find my soul for me?"

Nayla didn't know if they were labeled or catalogued or what, and she was a bit inebriated—and furthermore, repossessing one's soul appeared to be a personal venture.

"Cél, I believe there is a reason Hermes could not retrieve your soul. It's not his to manage."

"You know me better. You do it."

Nayla was about to convey the problems with this theory when a faint light crept in from the curtain to the promenoir, located between the double staircase. Ghostly white bands, tinged blue, undulated into the Winter Garden. Doubtful that the anomaly would rouse Céleste, Nayla set the flask on the bar as a last resort.

"Climb in. Can you climb in?"

Céleste raised her head at the container. There was a grave chance she may never want out, but it was better than lying on the cold floor with fresh wounds and wet hair.

"I'll take you to your soul," said Nayla. "Climb in. Go on."

"Don't let me out unless it's good news." Céleste transitioned to pollen and spilled into the flask on the bar.

Nayla put the cap on and lit a cigarette. She inhaled deeply, held, and exhaled the flavor of spiced tobacco. An empty champagne flute taunted her next to the flask. She uncorked herself a bottle and poured it to reclaim lost ground. She'd have to have her mainbrace well-spliced to walk into that light show. The first drink polished off quick. She poured herself another and took a leisurely walk across the Winter Garden as if the curtain was about to rise. Who knew? Maybe it was.

The parted curtain, outlined in light, gave way in a push. Café tables surrounded the promenoir, the layout in a horseshoe, the inside rim partitioning the orchestra level seats by viny pillars which splayed the light emitted from the stage. Nayla downed her flute and set it on a table as she approached the edge of the promenoir. Onstage was—what was she doing here?

"La Loïe?"

Loïe Fuller danced in white flowing robes, a white splotch on a black canvas. Several Loïes manifested around the original like apparitions. The ghostly shroud, the spectral light, her movements. This woman was not human. Boah! The anomaly Nayla had seen while up on the catwalk at the Folies Bergère wasn't a drunken delusion at all. When she had shined a rainbow at Loïe and Loïe remained violet, it was because the light source came from within. Loïe *was* light. She moved like the white figures in the Lesser Mysteries. She was one of the lampades, a nymph of the underworld. How many of her were there?

Nayla took a step into the aisle for a closer look. The floor sloped into a precipitous drop. Her heart leapt into her throat as she caught herself on a pillar. The seats curved downward like a funnel, leading directly into a pit. The sinkhole was massive. She couldn't see the bottom. She could see the stage more clearly, however, from this vantage. There was one Loïe, repeated six times by use of mirrored panels.

The strap with Nayla's flask slipped off her shoulder toward the chasm.

Scheisse!

She fumbled with her cigarette, let it drop, and palmed the leather cord, falling back from the edge. She held the flask tight against her chest. Puh! Close one. As defeated as Céleste was, Nayla did not want the responsibility of keeping her from peril. She unscrewed the cap.

Céleste drifted out and remained pollen.

"That's right," said Nayla. "Giant well. Loïe the Lampad is performing. I need your help."

The nebula floated, deliberating.

"Don't hold me in suspense," said Nayla.

Céleste whisked into human form. "Well, where is my soul?"

"Down there. Go get it."

Céleste leaned over the side. "How prodigious. I'm in a nightmare."

"It gets better." Nayla pointed at the stage.

Loïe disappeared in a puff of smoke.

Three mirrors on the left showed Aphrodite making love to Ares in a white satin bed. Hephaestus loomed above them with a golden net. He cast it down, trapping the lovers. Other gods sprang out to jeer.

Three mirrors on the right showed Psyche walking in the dark by the light of an oil lamp, her long, curled locks bobbing in the glow. She stopped at her bedside and allowed the light to settle on her husband's face. Hot oil dripped from the lamp, scalding his skin. Eros shot out of bed. He chided Psyche and leapt out the window, leaving her behind, distraught and alone.

All six mirrors flashed.

Aphrodite and Psyche appeared side by side in a glade, Psyche causing a man with tawny hair to levitate, his body enchanted by a white glow. The goddess Asteria, her skin white as cream, and the magenta-skinned Chloris, green tresses, green eyes, looked on.

A young Céleste knelt in the grass of the Wild Garden, crying. Aphrodite held Céleste by her chin and bid her to stand while Psyche handed her a slender, square vial—her mixis.

Young Céleste unstoppered the vial while adult Céleste looked on, bedraggled and wide eyed.

Céleste's image drank, Pscyhe exorcised the demon, it ran into an Erebus Room, and Asteria demolished the beast.

"When you find love," said Psyche, "you will become immortal."

"Did you see that?" asked Nayla.

"Oui, I was holding my holy water."

"Not that. The part about finding love. It was Psyche who said it. Not Aphrodite."

Sweet Shiva. It was Hephaestus who'd told Nayla to celebrate life, the god of metalworking, not Coronis the drunken Maenad. Hey Bhagwan! Had she been going about this all wrong? Was Hephaestus talking about reaching Brahman by means of building more inventions and drinking to that?

"What's the difference?" asked Céleste. "All four make up the mixis."

Nayla didn't want to hurt her friend's feelings in such an unguarded state, but she couldn't keep it to herself. "I don't think you're supposed to find sexual love."

"What kind then, Vidocq?"

"Sexual love is part of it, but—I don't know. Pure love. Divine love."

"Like moksha?"

"I don't know."

"If I wasn't supposed to make love, then why does it give me powers?"

"I don't know," Nayla said honestly.

How did one drink to metalworking? Or was it inventing? Building an invention took a long time. Maybe it was work in general, but as a nymph, she drank to the Blast after each shift and that hadn't made her immortal.

The mirrors went blank in a puff of smoke, signaling the reemergence of Loïe. She floated over the stage, over the orchestra pit, and over the colossal well.

Nayla threw up her fists, Céleste her palms, wary of danger.

"Were you spying on me?" asked Céleste. "Did the demons send you?"

"I sent myself," said Loïe, "to become immortal."

"You're immortal?" asked Céleste.

"Yes, thanks to your father's theater and a deal worked out with Hades."

"Do you mean 'live forever' immortal?"

"What other kind is there? Surely not to live on through my art?"

Céleste creased her brow.

"Paint fades, Céleste. Books rot. Buildings crumble. Don't get me started on dance... so untransferable, unrecordable."

"Dance lives on in those it stirred while watching. If the audience felt something, it shaped their lives in ways big or small."

"Oh, a life was shaped," said Loïe. "Mine. I gained my immortality when I used my powers in public using my own name without attracting Nemesis. The critics may say I'm not of this world, but the audience knows better. They can see my face when I dance. See my electricians. My chemically salted robes. And they all love me. Tell me, how many lives have you shaped?"

The round-faced nymph looked at Céleste, supplied an impish smile, and hovered straight down into the well. Her white-blue light illuminated the well's striations on her descent and a ramp that spiraled the outer rim.

"Where is the bottom?" Nayla dropped to her chest and stuck out her head. "It just keeps going."

"Can you fly down?" asked Céleste.

"She must be one kilometer deep. I'll need to stop and rest on the ramp." Nayla observed Loïe's light decrease to a pinpoint. "We have no food. And sleeping will delay the journey." She rolled onto her back.

"How do visitors get down?"

"I don't think they get visitors."

A flare pulsated in Céleste's hand. She tossed it in and squinted really hard at something. "Look."

Nayla rolled over for a peek. The flare burned up on the ramp next to some very round footprints.

"Elephant tracks," Céleste declared. "Come on. There's a hidden door to the stage at the end of the promenoir. I bet you Pierre's in his pen." She hustled down the corridor.

"Cél"—Nayla stood up and hurried—"I doubt it's really Pierre the Elephant."

She caught up with Céleste at the dead end where a lotus blossom rested on a decorative trellis. She spun the flower and opened the hatch.

Nayla followed her onto the planks of stage right, to the back wings. Dressing rooms lined one side of the hall, the other, a large cage, inside of which glowed the large mammal's skeleton. When the phosphorescent glow shined in his skull, Nayla noticed a hole in the center of his forehead like a cyclops. It was where his trunk connected.

"Let's go, Pierre. Miss me?" Céleste unlocked the cage and opened the door.

Pierre let out a trumpet sound.

Céleste pet his belly, over his slow-flashing rib cage. He turned and touched his trunk to her shoulder.

"I know, boy." She held his nose. "We've seen better days. My friend Nayla and I need your help."

Nayla outstretched her hand. The elephant shook guten Tag. This wasn't Pierre. One of his tusks was severed.

Was it? Could it be?

"Ganesha?" she whispered.

The elephant winked. Nayla's hairs rose. She smiled. He was the god of prosperity. He would bless their journey with good fortune.

Céleste disappeared and reappeared atop Ganesha.

"A little help?" Nayla asked, her hands up.

Ganesha coiled his trunk around her waist and lifted her overhead to his back.

"I'm driving, eh?" Céleste pollinated in front of Nayla. "Hue, Pierre, hue!"

Nayla hugged Céleste as Ganesha trekked out of the wing and onto the shining planks of the stage. He approached a ramp leading around the orchestra pit, and together they sloped into the well.

THE WELL OF LOST SOULS
(TRIPTYCH, PANEL #3)

Céleste held out her palm and warmed a flare into existence before Pierre bumped into one of the seats warping over the rim. The scope of the well was vast and indiscernible. If she slid off Pierre, she might fall forever. She tightened her thighs to his bulk in spite of her irritating wounds and rubbed his head, Pierre walking closer to the wall as the Folies chairs flattened to bedrock. Fine ridges made up the well like threads on a screw, shadowed in her soft light.

The electric fairy, Loïe Fuller, a lampad. Oui, it all made sense. Papa had built Loïe a secret passage from backstage to her apartment so she didn't have to face crowds. Rather, it was so she could sneak off to du Néant and return to the Well of Lost Souls unimpeded. She was guardian of this place. Perhaps it was a dream of hers to dance on the real Folies stage. Though what was the purpose of tempting Nemesis? Quite the gamble to gain immortality.

Why did Hades agree to that? Perhaps in exchange for Loïe guarding the well? Did she have to guard it for a century like Arachne did the Hall of Fabled Objects? If Loïe knew she'd have the chance to become immortal, she could afford to wait, as nymphs had eternal youth, unlike nouvelles nymphes who aged like humans. But the real Folies had opened in 1869. How long had this well been here? As long as demons had been stealing souls, bien sûr.

Perhaps, like Loïe, the Folies had waited for its big break, for its original owner, Albert Boislève, to create the venue from his muse. Pre-1869, the Folies lived in the collective unconscious. But Loïe had a mother and an agent, for the love of God. Who were they? Impostors? Light illusions? Perhaps the agent was real, if there was money to be made. Ten percent was ten percent, but the mother?

Céleste felt Nayla's breath on her neck. Champagne and cigarette breath. How noisome. Céleste was about to tell her to back up when Nayla's cheek rested on Céleste's shoulder. Nayla was tired. She had been flying and fighting and smashing wedding gifts all day. Not to mention, making painful observations.

Was there something fundamentally wrong to be immortal and in search of healing? Nothing said invulnerability and immortality went hand in hand. Why had the gods granted her powers? To aid her in finding immortality? Non. Ridiculous. It was the other way around. Immortality had been applied, and her powers were a bonus, attained after each time she made love. She chose men she fancied. It didn't mean she would fancy them forever or marry each one, but love was there to some degree because of how they made her feel.

Even with Hermes. She gritted her teeth. He was going to pay. It was a good thing being immortal didn't equal invulnerable. If he harmed one hair on Gustave's head, she would hit him where it hurt. Somehow. Some way. She'd start by turning him over to Hades for leading her down here without permission. Knowing Hermes, though, he'd exact the punishment on himself if she gave the word. A tear rolled down her cheek. She should never have gotten involved with him. The tear dripped onto Pierre's neck. She'd rather have wandered the underworld powerless and let her soul-throne hurl her into violent agonies if it meant keeping Gustave safe. If only she'd have known. Why had she not listened to Nayla?

Nayla bobbed along to the slow gait, her hands limp at her sides.

"Nay," Céleste whispered.

"Hä?" she murmured.

"Your grip is loose."

"Ganesha won't drop me."

"Ganesha?"

"Ja, his tusk is missing. Ganesha broke it off when he couldn't find a pen to write the Mahabharata. It's a long Indian epic, like Homer has his epics, though it's much longer than Homer's."

"What's Ganesha doing in Hades?"

"Helping me." Nayla yawned. "Before the god Ganesha was an elephant, he appeared like a man. His mother, Parvati, the goddess of love and motherhood and other things, posted Ganesha to guard her bath. When Ganesha refused his father Shiva entry, Shiva cut off his head. Parvati was so outraged she ordered her warriors to replace it with a new head from the first dead creature they found. It so happened to be an elephant. Am I boring you?"

"Non, Nay, I like your stories. Perhaps that explains his connection to the underworld. His former head and the elephant's body had died."

"Maybe, but I like the idea he's here for me. To pacify Parvati, Brahma, the four-faced creator god—not to be confused with Brahman, which is the unchanging, ultimate reality I wish to reunite with—made it so that Ganesha must be worshipped first before any other gods. If Ganesha is forgotten, calamities occur. If Ganesha is honored, he grants success. And so he is here to help and will not drop me."

"You hear that, Pierre?" Céleste rubbed his crown. "You're the god of success."

"Ja, I'm going back to sleep."

Céleste tipped the flare into her other hand and shook the stiffness out of her arm. She inhaled mildew. The walls were damp. There was water in this well. She peered over and cast down a second flare. The shadows gave way to green water as the flare landed on a stone pathway leading out to a circular platform in the center. It was so far away that the breadth of the well made her feel small.

Where she expected her ramp to lead to the stone path on the water, it stopped half a kilometer from the bottom instead, leading to a wide doorway plastered with ghoulish faces. She gazed down the well from her new vantage point and espied yellow, membranous sacks floating at varying depths beneath the surface. There were lights in them. Souls.

"Nay, wake up." Céleste nudged her.

Nayla yawned and stretched. "Are we at your soul?"

"Close. A spooky doorway."

Nayla rubbed her eyes. "That is spooky. Let's fly the rest of the way."

Pierre's trunk fell upon Céleste's lap.

"Um," said Céleste.

"I think Ganesha wants us to take the scenic route," said Nayla.

Pierre lifted his trunk and nodded.

Céleste noted he could fit through the doorway. "Care to join us on our adventure?"

Pierre shook his head no.

"All right. Didn't want to offend you." She kissed the elephant and pollinated onto solid ground.

Nayla slid off, wall-side, and hit the ground hard. "Ah!"

"What happened?" asked Céleste. "Are you still tight?"

Nayla was on her knees, her arms out on the rough stone. Her face was bent in pain. Something was wrong.

"Ah-ya." She broke the silence.

"You all right?" asked Céleste.

"My arm... I broke my arm..."

Céleste helped her out from the narrow space between Pierre and the wall. "So much for success."

"It's not Ganesha's fault." She winced, upper lip curled, her face a concertina. "He couldn't reach, and he got us this far."

453

"Where does it hurt?"

"My left forearm."

"I don't see any bones poking out. We can use the strap to your flask for a sling, but we need something to brace it."

Pierre pointed his trunk at the foreboding doorway.

"Wait here." Céleste shoved the flare into the dark, illuminating a hallway filled with bones. Femurs, skulls, ribs, discs—all were neatly stacked from the floor to the arched ceiling. The skulls at the top functioned as keystones. Céleste plucked a radius from a slot and ducked back, fearing the whole thing may crumble. When it didn't, she measured the radius against her forearm. It ought to do the trick.

She walked to Nayla and presented the splint.

Nayla looked sideways.

"I can tie it on with my skirt petals," said Céleste.

Nayla held her heart. "For a moment, I thought you were going to poof inside me and swap out the bones."

Céleste tore off two petals at the stitching and secured the splint to Nayla's arm. "Tight?"

"Ja."

"Bien." Céleste took the flask and adjusted the sling. "Ready?"

"Almost." Nayla caressed Pierre on his cheek. "Danke, Ganesha. Do not abandon us. We shall return." She looked at Céleste. "Now I'm ready."

Céleste led the way into the necropolis, her flare held high.

Nayla took her first gander at the tunnel. "Are there catacombs under the Folies?"

"Non."

With trepidation, Céleste crept deep into the hallway, one sandaled footstep at a time. Shadows played on eye sockets and nose holes, on the indentations of cheekbones and tessellated femurs. The voice in the void awakened from dormancy.

I am nothing, I am nothing, I am nothing.

"Luckily it is a tunnel, not a maze," whispered Nayla.

"Oui." Céleste glanced at Nayla's injury to take her mind off the voice. "Thank you for helping me. I'm sorry about your arm."

"You're not going to blame me for drinking?"

"No more than you can blame me for losing my soul."

"It wasn't lost. It was stolen," Nayla corrected.

"It was because I was too weak to hold onto it."

Céleste thought back to Suzon's mirror when it was located in the promenoir, before her soul was stolen. Her image had always flickered looking into that mirror. She'd thought it was cigar smoke and poor lighting. Now she was sure. It was because she was a half-person. Her image was strobing so fast like one of Monsieur Edison's bulbs that she hadn't realized it at the time and not chanced a closer look.

She moved her flare to the other hand and made a turn.

What else had she failed to see? She'd always thought trauma created half-people. What trauma had she suffered before the Incident? Papa was furniture and Berthe was a... a terror. That was it. Céleste wrinkled her brow. Traumatized by her own parents. To have thought she was normal. Anything but. The equation for half-people still held true—trauma had occurred—though it had occurred so far back she could not remember when, which meant... What if she was born a half-person like Nayla? What if she was born unlovable and she was the one who traumatized her parents?

Pelvises cast jagged shadows across the tunnel with their hips as she turned again.

Non, that couldn't have been true. Théo had said Berthe was always a terror. Did the chaos then originate with Céleste or with Berthe? Maman did not have her soul stolen—Céleste had checked—but Maman was certainly a half-person. So was Papa. Did half-people not give birth to whole-people? Berthe's reign started so long ago—calling Céleste names, raging at her, blaming her—the merge so intense, that Céleste could not determine where Berthe stopped and she began. Being unlovable may as well have been in her blood.

Tears rolled down her face in the yellow light, making a third turn.

Unlovable people did not love themselves. They hated themselves. Was that why she had agreed with Charon when he said that she was nothing? She had affirmed the voice in the void. She gave it credence. She had never done that out loud. Perhaps she didn't hate herself as an extension of Charon. Perhaps she hated herself without his help, and he reflected back her own self-loathing. Non, that wasn't quite right. They were two mirrors set before each other and their mutual self-loathing amplified the loathing they had for each other. She knew this to be so, because when she had merged with Antoine, she hated him as an extension of her.

I am nothing, I am nothing, I am nothing.

"Céleste, you're crying."

"I know." She wheezed. "I know."

Nayla touched the back of her arm. "Talk to me."

"I just want to feel complete. I just wanted a loving family."

"You'll have one."

Céleste shook her head. "When my soul stops the voice in the void, I'll be out of things to chase, out of options. That will be it. I was a half-person before and I'll be a half-person after. A sniveling excuse for a nymph, trapped in irreparable despair."

Nayla held Céleste's hand. "When I felt Brahman in Hades museum, for those few seconds, it was only light and love. I was complete. Complete, Cél. For the first time in my life. And I was born a half-person. A Shudra. The soul is divine. God let me merge with him. Let him merge with you."

Céleste nodded uncertain. It was God's fault her soul was stolen and God's fault she was unlovable. She was born like this. Who else to blame was there?

Clicking sounds came out of the dark. Céleste and Nayla froze to the floor. It sounded like a squirrel chipping away at a nut.

Nayla grabbed Céleste's arm. She gulped and opened her mouth in a whisper, "That is a room ahead."

"Flare on or off?"

"On."

Céleste raised her free hand and traversed the floor. In a matter of paces, she was hit by a stench so foul that it took all of her discipline to keep her hand extended and not bring it to her nose. Nayla sneered, fighting the same instinct, her one good hand balled into a fist for any lurking danger.

The hall of bones receded behind Céleste as she entered this new chamber. She lifted her light. Perched behind a pile of rotting corpses slouched an anorexic figure chomping on a leg. The flare showed the blue sheen of his back. Céleste didn't want to judge a book by its cover. He might've been friendly like the owl.

"What's that Hindu god with blue skin?" she asked.

Nayla examined her, eyes full of fear. "That is not them."

The figure leaned back and poked up his head.

Céleste tensed. It was a vulture head, the appendage red and black, his neck hooked like a stove pipe. The bird jerked its neck, setting a yellow eye upon her, frosted over by cataracts. He opened his bloody beak and screamed like a banshee.

"Roast it," said Céleste.

Flame pulsed out of Nayla's fist at the bird. Bipedal, he sprinted into the corner. Céleste dispensed with the flare and opened fire with both palms. Nova after nova exploded around the room. Bones jangled from the walls and rained from the ceiling in the flickering, flashing yellow lights.

Nayla let her flame die out.

Céleste kept up the projectiles for sake of Nayla, so she could see where to aim next.

"Eurynomos," said Nayla. "His name is Eurynomos."

"What does he do?"

"Pecks the flesh off your bone. He's a demon."

Céleste stopped shooting, and let darkness blanket the room. She listened for a pitter-patter of feet or the nut-cracking sound. Nothing came. Nisco. She relit a flare. The yellow orb infused the crypt with warm rays.

Terrified, Nayla turned, eyes tall, the vulture attached to her back. His humanoid legs wrapped her abdomen. His arms groped her collar. His vulture beak leveled above her eyes, ready to strike.

Céleste raised her palm in surrender. A protostar would blow his head off, but her finger gun could miss. His neck was a stick. She could use her barrier—her noxious pollen. Non. It would throw Nayla into a coughing fit and crush her lungs. If Nayla sprang her wings, it might knock him loose. Or she could do that explosive thing she did earlier. Oui.

"Nay, Venus flytrap in three."

"Eins. Zwei. Drei!"

Paper lantern.

Nayla blinked. A bomb went off at her navel, emitting swirls of painted light. The heat vaporized the bird and rattled the bones on the ceiling, causing a collapse. Bones and rubble buried Nayla and dusted the room.

Park bench.

"Nay! Can you hear me?"

Céleste threw a flare and began plucking femurs off the mound and casting them aside. She used both hands, doggedly shoveling bits to the floor. It would take her a day to dig through this heap. Nayla must've known it would make a cave-in, yet she'd done it anyway. *Stupid vulture. Stupid demon bird. Think, Céleste.* Her shooting stars could incinerate some of the rubble, but it might also hit Nayla. Céleste kept digging. God of success, indeed.

That was it. Pierre. Céleste abandoned her work and took off running into the tunnel the way she'd come. In three turns, she saw the great elephant peering curiously into the catacombs from the end of the hall.

"Pierre, Nayla is in trouble! She needs your help!"

Pierre hesitated.

She couldn't believe she was saying this. "Please, Ganesha! This is no time to be shy."

He let out a trumpet shout and stampeded into the hall, his weight rumbling kneecaps and pelvises.

Céleste pollinated on top of him. "Hu', dia! Hop là! Hop là!"

His thundering feet shook the bones free of their stacks, causing a trail of cave-ins behind them as he charged to the first intersection.

She helped him negotiate his large body through the turn, her flare out for them to see, ducking her head at the doorways. Two more turns, and he plowed into the crypt and planted himself at the bone pile. He squirmed his trunk into the criss-crossing rods and lifted Nayla from the debris by her good arm, her headpiece askew.

Céleste pollinated to her side, removed the costuming, and combed her fingers through Nayla's hair, checking for bumps. Checking, checking, found. There was a welt on her head. Céleste patted Nayla's cheek.

Nayla roused. "My sides hurt... Ganesha?"

Pierre helped her onto her feet and gave her a hug.

Céleste allowed a smile despite their predicament.

"I hope there are no more of those bird things," said Nayla, feeling the lump on her head.

Céleste fetched the headpiece for her. "There's no escape if there are. Pierre caused a cave-in to save you. I'm guessing that's why he didn't come in before."

Nayla hugged Céleste. "Danke."

"The explosion was my idea," she replied, reluctant.

"Ja, but the creature is gone, I am not blind, and my skin is where I left it."

Céleste accepted the gesture and hugged Nayla back.

"We have a soul to find," said Nayla, climbing up to Pierre.

He helped her on.

Céleste pollinated in front, unsure of how they were going to retrace their steps or return Pierre to his home. It didn't seem to bother him. He lumbered out of the crypt and into the next hall, away from the horrendous smell. Another three turns and several ramps later, they emerged onto the straight path she had seen from above. The egg-like sacks glowed yellow in the green-watered pool of the well, the brightest spot, their yokes.

I am nothing, I am nothing, I am nothing.

"Céleste, the walls."

Cacodemons slithered up and down the exterior, their black reptilian skin blending into the stone. Higher still, at the top of the well, the harvest moon-hole was eclipsed by darkness. The hole waning, waning, gone. Something or someone slid the cover on. A ball of light rose from the swampy water and flashed into Loïe the Lampad, her toes skimming the surface.

"Bonjour, Starflower. I see you've made it."

Céleste, mounted on Pierre, turned to Nayla. "She speaks a lot, eh?"

Loïe rose to meet Céleste at eye level. "There is no need for me to say a thing. I prefer to show you."

An incorporeal vision of a little girl misted on the water. The little girl, she was dancing. Her figure glowed white, though her pale hair had shades of blonde. She was but five years old. Smiling, dimpled, she skipped and twinkled her toes, and fell.

A new specter rushed in to assist. Mariquita. She stood by and demonstrated a brisé, slapping her legs together midair.

"Is that girl you?" asked Nayla.

"Non." Céleste dismounted for a closer look. "I never had dimples."

Nayla followed suit, this time by aid of Pierre.

"Mariquita has gone gray and she has more wrinkles," said Céleste, viewing the water show.

The girl performed the brisé correctly. She ran to a ghostly man in a mustache.

"Papa," Céleste whispered.

"Did you see me, grand-père?" said the little girl with glee.

He folded his arms around her. "I did, princesse."

The girl ran next to a little boy, another vapor on the water. "Did you see me, Étienne?"

Tears streamed in Céleste's eyes. Her babies.

"Oui. I can do it too. See, Eulalie?" He jumped up and down, kicking.

"That's not it," she said. "Is it, Maman?"

"It's a good try." A matured woman of thirty smoked into being. Blonde hair was tied back. Her face had slightly deeper creases, her body more size.

"That's me," said Céleste in disbelief, a lifetime away.

"It's like this," said the matured Céleste, leaping on the stage with a twinkle in her feet. She did a lot more than that. She lunged, danced an arabesque, pirouetted six times and fell into a Russian split. What bravura! Now *that* was a style of her own.

"Show off." A man walked onto the scene in a white buttoned shirt and black pants. He had dimples and cropped blonde hair, long on top and messy. A square face. Tender eyes. Pointed nose. Céleste absorbed his every detail, from his gold-laced boots to his pale skin. He had the physique of a dancer. He *was* a dancer, leaping and bounding. He joined his Céleste in a grand pas de deux. Its five parts encapsulated their lives in a few short measures, dancing their entrée as children, the adagio as young adults, their variations as grown-ups, and their coda in their twilight years, aging together, smiling like they were kids. She ran at his brawny arms for a lift and together they spun and spun and... evaporated into the ether.

I am nothing, I am nothing, I am nothing.

Céleste reached out as if to capture the mist.

"Is that the future?" asked Nayla.

Loïe floated around the platform, her robes furrowed, blinding in white splendor. "It is her future if she can merge psyche and soma."

"Cél," said Nayla, "when Loïe performed at the Folies, I felt Hestia's presence in the flames. She shows you only what you want to see."

"And you can have what you see," said Loïe. "The first step is to visualize it. The second is to trust your intuition—that you may realize your vision. Listen to it. What does it say?"

"Find my soul," said Céleste.

"Where?"

Céleste roamed the platform, darting from one egg to another. The dense atmosphere blunted her senses. But, in such close proximity to salvation, she trusted herself to detect the right one. On her second pass around Pierre, a pang went up her spine. She walked to the edge and selected a distant egg, in hiding, peeking out from a closer one at the surface.

"There." She pointed. "Do you see it?"

Nayla tilted her body, on one foot. "Ja, it must be twenty meters deep. That is twelve times your body height. If you're going to do this, you need to high dive."

"From what height?"

"Into plain water, a six-meter height should do."

"Plain water?"

"I don't know viscosity—how dense the water is. You could sink like a rock."

"What about higher?"

Nayla shook her head. "The human body can dive no deeper than five meters from any greater height."

"You have pools in the desert?"

"Stepwells."

If the human body could dive no deeper than five meters, she would have to swim the additional fifteen. That was a long way. Wet pollen would be useless to escape.

"What happens if it's not her soul?" Nayla asked Loïe.

"If she chooses correctly, she receives an air bubble from the egg. Incorrectly, she drowns."

"Joke's on you. I'm immortal." Céleste looked down at the shining egg and muttered, "No more demi-personne."

Flower pollen.

The well dispersed in brushstrokes. Greens, yellows, and blacks. She flutter-kicked out over the water, high up in the air. Six meters. *Better make it ten. This should be high enough.*

I am nothing, I am nothing, I am nothing.

Like hell I'm nothing. I am the kingfisher. Be a kingfisher. Anchors away.

The well crystalized beneath her feet. Pierre looked up. Nayla, Loïe. She eyed her egg. The water raced at her and shattered on impact. *Kerploosh*. The force pushed her down. When it carried her no lower, she dipped forward and swam. Bright lights burned all around, a flame inside each egg she passed. Fires. Souls made of fire. She kicked hard, moving her arms as though parting curtains, peeling away the time she'd spent away from her true self. She could do it. Her dancing gave her stamina, had taught her breathing exercises. A little further.

Based on her depth of field, the egg grew from a beachball to the size of a carriage. Her air depleted with every stroke as she drew up to the pod. She placed her hand on its squishy shell and broke the bloom. Steam discharged from the breakage. She stuck her head in so as not to miss the air bubble. Though she need not have done so, she wished not to go unconscious. The egg sucked her through to sweet oxygen and resealed. Succès.

She inhaled deeply while the egg cut away from its viny tether and floated upward. The bubble was clear and reminded her of amniotic fluid. At the heart burned a brilliant white flame. She reached out and held it in her palms. She felt its delicate light with her fingers. Five years, and not a minute longer. She pressed the white flame to her chest. It disappeared through her skin. There.

What?

It fell out.

She picked it off the bottom of the surfacing orb and tried again.

Same result.

Was it not accepting her? Was she not accepting it? Why wasn't it working?

I am nothing, I am nothing, I am nothing.

Ferme la bouche!

Green waters beaded off the bubble as it broke surface, revealing the stone island atop which Nayla blasted powerful orange flames. Cacodemons were swarming her. Why now? Céleste's soul would have to wait. She shoved her flat palm through the sack and pollinated through. A dozen demons soared, skittered all around, harassing Nayla. Pierre had pulled back to the catacombs for refuge. Céleste reappeared in the center of the madness at Nayla's back, her soul in hand.

"You're alive!" Nayla shouted. She pumped a flame, single handed, across a row of demons, and gave the whip a shake. Energy cruised the troughs and crests of the homespun flag and exploded at its tail on the next demon's collar. She eyed the soul. "Doesn't that go in you?"

Shooting stars blasted furiously from Céleste's palm. "It won't stay." She slid the white fire into her bosom, balancing it amid her skin and her bodice to free up her hands. Out came her six-shooters.

The demons flew around them like buzzards, making independent dives.

Ghostly forms appeared on the water. A teenage boy drinking in the gutter. A young woman her age selling herself on the streets of Athens. A thirty-year-old blonde woman reposed in a chair, overweight, chowing down on teacakes. Hermes gave her a foot massage while Charon slammed the door to go out.

"How do you like your future?" Loïe floated overhead, a prism of light refracting beams throughout the well. "You thought you'd claim it so easily? Poor child. Maybe daddy's love will put it back. That's right. He never loved you. He couldn't. You weren't meant for it, or he'd have said the words. Je t'aime. So easy, so difficult."

One of Loïe's beam swept across the platform and blinded Céleste in one eye.

"Nay!" she cried. "Don't look at her light!"

"Maman said she loved you," said Loïe, "while coaxing you back into the womb. How confusing?"

Céleste aimed her finger gun at the nymph. "I can't kill you, but I can stop you." She fired.

The starlit bullet cruised the short distant between them and struck the lampad in the eye. The concussive pebble exploded, potting the nymph unceremoniously into the well. Her long white gown and silk wings fanned the water in a grotesque doily.

Céleste's finger was smoking. "What did I do?" She turned to Nayla, battling the onslaught of demons. "Take to the skies. I'll loose my barrier."

Nayla pitched out her wings and took off, leaving the platform free for noxious pollen to mist out of Céleste like Saturn's rings, sending the half-dozen lizards into coughing fits, then dying fits. It wasn't them Céleste cared about.

"Loïe!"

Céleste dove into the water, vision blurred, and swam for Loïe, hoping it wasn't a trick. When Céleste reached her, Loïe was limp. She swam behind the lampad's neck, hugged her diaphragm, and flutter-kicked back to the platform. There, she pollinated, standing on stone, the scab on her foot burning in her sandal. With all her strength, she heaved Loïe from the water.

Céleste listened for a heartbeat, aware that Loïe might up to life and blind her. No heartbeat. No breath. No rising and falling of her chest. Only one scorched head wound. Had the gods lied to Loïe? Lied to her? Could none of them live forever? Céleste fell onto her scabby butt. Her legs went numb.

Her soul dropped into her lap, burning bright.

The world imploded.

"I'm not immortal," she said. "I'm not immortal."

I am nothing, I am nothing, I am nothing.

Are you of the mind of Herakleitos? He believed that everything changes. Life. The world. You and me. According to him, we cannot set foot in the same river twice. The water will have moved. Everything is in flux. Even this painting on three panels. Perhaps Céleste would've agreed with the philosopher as a means to cope. The soul she parted with in 1887 was not the same one she held in her lap in 1893. Therefore, she could accept she was searching for something impossible to possess. Herakleitos did think a person's soul appeared as white flame, which may lend weight to his camp, non?

The other camp is Parmenides. He said that nothing changes. There is no binary of good and evil. Change is an illusion. Appearances change, while the essence of things remains immutable. Everything is made of the same stuff. Maybe Céleste would approve. It would mean she and her soul never really parted. They are of one universe.

Of course, there was a middle ground.

Empedokles thought two constant forces make up reality—love and strife—along with four constant elements: earth, wind, water, and fire. These forces and the elements are unchanging. But, when the elements are mingled together under the influence of love and strife in endless combination, they create living creatures. Some things change, some things stay the same.

Empedokles believed it was the soul's highest duty to free itself from the unhallowed union with the body and the elements of this world and become reincarnated. Was Céleste fighting nature under this pretext? Was her soul trying to escape her? Was there not enough love in her to attract it and too much strife? You should know, my friend, that to Empedokles, love brought things together and strife pulled them apart.

Maybe we shall take the approach of the atomist Democritus, for he said, *We know nothing certainly, as truth lies at the bottom of a well.*

Stunning altarpiece, n'est-ce pas?

STILL LIFE
OF A SOUL

A nouvelle nymphe of five years might confuse supernatural powers for immortality—but the old nymphs were ancient. Wouldn't they know better? Perhaps Hades had lied to Loïe, and she believed the lie. She had known what Céleste was capable of and fought her anyway. Did that mean Psyche had lied to Céleste about finding love to become immortal? Were all nymphs, nouvelles and anciennes, chasing air castles?

Looking at Loïe's sopping wet dress on the platform and the unforgiveable crater in her skull, it was hard for Céleste to latch onto something that said she was wrong. All signs pointed down, as she fell into a canyon of oblivion.

The only saving grace was that she found her soul. But she wasn't chasing her soul to become immortal. She desired to be whole. Immortality had nothing to do with it. Unless it were a side effect of completeness, perhaps, but that was doubtful. Loïe was lied to, just like she was. Loïe the Lampad. She was no cacodemon Céleste could pick off without remorse. Céleste had murdered a nymph. She tried to stop her thoughts—mortality—her soul—but they stared her in the face. She couldn't help it.

"Céleste!" Nayla called, arcing the well's rim ten-stories above. "Her death is our ticket home!"

Demons chased her in a circle, corralling her into more demons. Skyborne, they clawed and snapped, pushed back by a sweeping geyser of flame.

"The doorway!" Nayla grunted. "It's directly behind you!"

Doorway? There was a doorway? Bien sûr. Loïe might've been hundreds of years old, but she was still from Earth, and to Earth she would return.

Scores of lizards surrounded Nayla, swooping in from all sides like hawks. A dozen. Two dozen. She inhaled deeply and exhaled flame from her mouth in a kiss of fire. The twin flames spun as she soared under, over, and around the demons, her sling jouncing into her gut.

The catacomb was caved in, the well covered. There was no way out, save for the invisible gate.

Céleste stood up, her vision blurred. She pointed her fingers to the sky and launched hot blue stars into the black mass of pterodactyl wings, iguana throats, and Komodo tails. *Don't hit Nayla. Nothing red.* Céleste's fingers were lethal. Anything that wasn't red, she shot. Demons plunged into the water, screaming. One slapped the stone pathway, dead.

Red feathers drifted into the water from the scuffle and sizzled when they touched the surface.

"Céleste, go! Thanatos is collecting Loïe's body!"

Céleste glanced at her soul, pure white at her feet, making sure the invisible god of death didn't get any ideas. Suddenly, Loïe floated into the air, legs bent and back propped, suspended by the unseen force. Over her shoulder, on the stone path, where Nayla revealed the portal to be, Céleste saw nothing but Pierre in the distance hugging the blocked catacomb.

The moment Céleste stopped shooting, the demons would overwhelm Nayla.

She was not playing martyr on Céleste's watch.

"You fly in first!" Céleste shouted. "Then I'll walk through!"

"Nein, gehen!" Nayla's voice echoed down the shaft. "Go!"

"You have to save yourself before you can save others!"

"Oho!" Nayla struggled to descend. "Is that what you were doing, rescuing all those would-be victims from these creatures?"

A demon had latched onto Nayla's back, pulling her upward in great flaps.

The floating Loïe labored by.

Nayla had risked her life for Céleste to find her soul. Nayla had tried to warn Céleste about Hermes, waited for Charon's spell to break, rescued her from Persephone's wrath, carried her when she was too frightened and weak to go on. Nayla was there for her. While the demons of her past tormented her from the grave and the ghosts she hadn't met enticed her from the future, Nayla was there at her side.

Mortal, soulless, if Céleste stepped through that door, the shattered vase of her existence would have ground to powder. Nayla had given so much from a place of nothing. Every gram of energy she could have spent on herself, she exhausted trying to bring Céleste the object of her desire. The white fire that was her soul glowed apart from her, but to no fault of Nayla's. She had come through, a true friend.

Céleste blinked hard trying to restore vision. "Mon Dieu." It was as though Loïe had smudged petroleum jelly on the lens of her eye. There was still time.

She used her thumb as an iron sight and aimed a roving her finger at Nayla's clinging demon. *Up. Left. Side. Down.* Céleste waited for the crest of her exhale. *Fire.*

The star cannoned through the well and popped the demon in the back, who, in turn, peeled off Nayla's. His body struck the water with a hard slap. Relief swelled in Céleste's heart.

Nayla flew closer, clear of obstacles. Nine stories away. Seven. Five.

Loïe's wet robes trailed into thin air.

A flock of demons alighted off their perch in the wall two stories up and ambushed Nayla. They seized her wings with their gouging claws, trying to establish a firm hold.

"Nee-ya!" she cried in pain.

Flame expelled from her feathers in a burst of light to repel them.

Momentarily stunned, they fell and attacked again.

"Hurry!" shouted Céleste. "Loïe's gone. I think the portal's closing!"

Nayla retracted her wings into her spine and fell into a nosedive. The demons did not care. The second she plunged into the water, they dogpiled.

Céleste abandoned her soul on the deck and dove into the green soup. She swam, her arms moving in wide sweeping windmills close to where Nayla had landed. Céleste sucked in a large breath and went under. Several meters down bubbled a blurry orange flame silhouetting a gaggle of black reptiles, their surroundings yellow from the light cast by the uterine souls. Céleste raised her hands at the plucky demons at close range. The targets were bigger and so were her blasters. A vanilla glow thrummed beneath her palms. Brighter and brighter, they burned till she felt overloaded. Ejection.

Her comets shot forth. Their tails illuminated the well, hitting the demons in bouquets of burning confetti. The impacts rattled and incapacitated each one, stealing garbled squeals from their throats as they fell limp as driftwood. She swam through their maze of arms and legs—*Please, no one wake up!*—and reached out for Nayla's steaming hand. They clasped. It was warm, but it did not burn.

Little jets bubbled at Nayla's feet, propelling them upward. Three meters, two meters. Surface.

Céleste gasped for breath.

Demons galore beat their wings and dove at them from all sides.

She raised a trembling hand.

"Children, enough!" boomed a voice, venomous and familiar.

The command shook the mildew off the walls. The lizards hissed and scattered into their nooks and crannies throughout the well.

Looming over Céleste's soul on the platform, in his bathrobe and slippers, was the portly god of the underworld himself, Hades. "All right, you little chits. Out of the water."

Flanking Hades were the recognizable black and white, top-hatted harlequin, Melinoë, and the dapper, irredeemable, mussy-haired Hermes.

"Let me do the talking." Nayla breathed into Céleste's ear.

"You're drunk," Céleste whispered, splashing.

"Not a word about Gustave." Nayla squeezed her hand.

The heat from Nayla's footsoles warmed Céleste's legs as they cruised lamely to shore.

"Bonjour, macchabées," Melinoë cooed down. "Enjoy your visit?"

"What did you put in our drinks?" Nayla shouted.

"I have brought you communion with the unseen," said Melinoë, fanning her arms at the well. "Be thankful."

Hermes offered Céleste a sour grin.

She ought to blast his head off where he stood. Who knew? Maybe immortality was a myth for all parties concerned.

Hermes pressed a finger to his lips as Hades stooped to pick up her soul.

He tossed it in the air like an apple. "So, this is what all the fuss is about?"

Céleste failed to answer. Clearly, it was.

Hades wriggled his hand in the water, grasped Céleste by her wrist with an icy hand, and hoisted her onto solid ground. "Does it not fit? What's the problem?" He stuffed the white flame into her chest. It tipped back out. "Non, doesn't fit. All right."

"What's wrong with it?" she asked, as if he was a medical doctor.

"Nothing. It's a perfectly good soul. The problem is on your end. Bad reception."

The words cut Céleste deep. What could that mean? She had no idea where to turn.

Hades handed the soul fire to Melinoë. "Remove this from my kingdom."

"Wait," said Céleste. "I need it to live."

"Correction," said Hades. "You *want* it to live. You're alive now. Partly."

Melinoë helped Nayla from the water.

"What are you going to do with us?" Nayla asked.

"Hermes will escort you back to the land of the living."

"Can't I take my soul with me?" asked Céleste.

"And roam the surface carrying it in a handbag?"

"Please, I've come so far."

"People are dumb," said Hades, "but they're not that dumb. Nemesis will slice and dice. Unless, you plan to use it for a new act."

"Like Loïe used her powers?" said Céleste, glum. "Non."

"How did she die?" asked Hades.

"I shot her. I didn't mean to kill her. I thought she was immortal."

"She was under that illusion, yes," said Hades.

The question on the tip of Céleste's tongue scared the life out of her, but she had to know. "Am I immortal?" She stepped back as if the answer would bite.

"Did you drink ambrosia?"

"Non."

"Then no."

The last molecule of doubt drained from her mind—and the color from her face. She buried it in her hands. "Why didn't you tell me?" She raised her head. "Why did you let me go on boasting like an idiot?"

"How many truth arrows would your thick head have liked to deflect?" He tapped his foot.

Céleste opened her mouth to dispute the point, but he was right. Nayla had told her time and again she wasn't immortal, and she hadn't listened. Perhaps the truth would have carried more weight coming from the Lord of the Underworld. Or perhaps not. Perhaps she had to see for herself that another nymph made the same claim and got it wrong.

"Did Loïe drink ambrosia?" asked Céleste.

"I gave her a vial of milky nectar and told her it was ambrosia. She had done so well pushing the envelope in exposing the pantheon to humanity, I wanted to see how far she could go. Call it a dose of self-belief."

"It got her killed," said Nayla.

Céleste looked at the floor. It could have easily been her.

"You're lucky I blame myself," said Hades, "and not you two."

Céleste was glad. To him, they were a couple of nymphs causing mischief in the underworld, given that he couldn't be bothered to put pants on.

"What prevented Loïe," said Nayla, "from not exposing everything in her illusioned state?"

"The safety of her loved ones," said Hades.

"Bien sûr," said Céleste. It was the same reason Céleste had stayed bound to secrecy. "Loïe's mother."

"Granddaughter," said Hades. "A descendant." He turned to Melinoë. "The offspring would make a poor replacement. Who was Loïe musing for?"

"One Maybelle Stuart," replied Melinoë.

La vache! Loïe was Maybelle's muse? Apparently, Maybelle did not perform the serpentine dance to Loïe's liking. She had to come up here and do it herself. Poor Maybelle. Upstaged by her own muse.

"She chokes," said Melinoë.

"Keep looking," said Hades. "And find another guard for the well. They need not be one in the same." Hades looked at Céleste. "Pardon the administrative work. It's a dream of ours to surface one day and coexist alongside humanity." He shot his hand at the elephant. "What is Duncan doing here? After you relocate that soul," he said to Melinoë, "return Duncan to his pen and clear the pathway." He whirled on Hermes. "And you. Take these nymphs to the surface before Persephone finds them. She thinks they stole her beauty ointment. You can see why." He gestured at Céleste's bloody appearance and Nayla's broken arm. "Borrowed from the hall, mind you. Once Persephone realizes there's no cause for alarm, she can return to her witch mother, and spring can commence."

"Yes, my lord," said Hermes.

"Report back after you've cleaned up the mess you made."

"Yes, my lord."

Hades and Melinoë vanished in a wave of black smoke.

Were they gone?

They were gone.

Céleste slapped Hermes hard. "Where is Gustave?"

"Ow. Is that how you say salut, ma fleur?"

"Is Gustave dead?" *Céleste held her palm on his forehead.* "Speak."

"No."

"Do you know what you've done?" Her fingers brushed his Balkan features as she lowered her palm.

"I can take you to him."

Nemesis would never stand for this. "You condemned him to die."

"Not yet."

Hermes outstretched his arms like a scarecrow. Wind rushed under his suit and out through his sleeves, forming ripples in the water. The platform rose off its foundation, separated from the path. Nayla held a fighting stance as the platform levitated skyward. The lid to the well uncovered, the eclipse ending.

"Where is Gustave?" asked Céleste, catching her bearings.

"Alive in Erebus."

"Where is my soul?"

"Lost in transit."

Wherever Melinoë was taking it, it was clear Hermes had no intention of returning her to the surface.

STUDY OF A SOUL

Céleste followed Hermes down the glowworm path of boulevard de Sébastopol. She expected Hermes to lead her
to Gustave through an apartment or the storefront of a
tree, but he kept silent on his whereabouts. Evidently, it
was a surprise. Hermes was unafraid of them running off
or attacking him. He knew she wanted to see Gustave and she
knew where this road led. Back to the Styx.

Her hands grew clammy. She rubbed them together, her
bones a chemical blue and green. Amid the chaos of her soul
and Gustave fluttering in her mind, she turned to Nayla to think
of something else. Nayla's glowing skull fluctuating pink and
purple still made her flesh creep.

"Let me see your arm."

"Ja, good idea." Nayla stopped in her tracks.

Hermes spun around, levitating. "Surely, this can wait."

"She wouldn't have broken her arm if you had retrieved my
soul." Céleste turned and punched him in the thigh. "That's for
locking me in the amphora."

"I do apologize," said Hermes, "but Loïe warned I should
not attempt the dive, or I would rupture the sack and flood your

soul. It is dry, and I did not wish to make it wet. In my defense, it's not as though you stayed put. How did you escape?"

"Trade secret." Céleste dared not say, should he decide to trap her again.

She examined Nayla's arm, glowing pink, and found a gap in the bone. "I see it. There's a break in the middle of the ulna about a centimeter wide."

"You know bone names?" asked Nayla.

"Oui. Dancers break bones all the time."

"I can mend it," said Hermes. "Instantly. Once we arrive at our destination."

"Wunderbar," Nayla said in monotone.

Hermes floated on, passing a girthy tree that towered from the neighboring park. It was a baobab, and the park was the Square de la Tour Saint Jacques. They were close to the Styx. There.

Up ahead, where the Pont au Change should've been, was Charon's Bateau Lavoir docked and ready for boarding. Céleste clung to Nayla's good arm and dry swallowed, a hummingbird having a heart attack. Nayla's eyes spoke of worry. The pump of her hand whispered courage. Charon was on that boat, but so was Gustave. Céleste hoped.

The gangplank flexed as Céleste held the rails like an old lady, one arthritic leg at a time. A hooded man stood at the money box. She hesitated. The wooden boards bowed beneath her sandals.

"It's not Charon," said Nayla.

The man raised his head, his face blown off. Chef Maurice. "Blahp."

Nayla pulled out a coin to deposit. One coin for two demigens, unfortunately.

Hermes set his leatherbound feet upon the deck, landing next to the first mate. "Set a course for the Phlegethon River."

Nayla perked up as the first mate departed upstairs for the bridge.

Hermes waved Céleste to come hither. "Gustave is here. Follow me."

She walked the deck and parted the beaded curtains to the party room to find Gustave bound to a chair, blindfolded. Opposite him sat a man under a shroud. She might've guessed it was Charon were he not standing over the shrouded figure.

Céleste rushed to Gustave and threw her arms around him. He roused from sleep.

"Oh, Gustave, Gustave, it's me. You're all right."

"Quel—Céleri?"

"Oui, I'm here." She cradled his head, glaring at Nayla to keep silent.

"It's a miracle. I prayed everyday I'd see you again." He fidgeted. "I still don't see you. Take off this blindfold."

Céleste looked to Hermes.

"Not yet," said Hermes.

"It's him," said Gustave. "My abductor. Has he hurt you?"

"Only my heart," said Céleste, "by taking you." She glowered at Hermes.

"Broken hearts are why we are gathered here today," said Hermes. "Gustave has a secret he would like to share."

"What are you talking about?" asked Gustave. "I've never met you. Where are we? I heard a paddlewheel, but there are none on the Seine."

Hermes smiled. "It's true. We've never met. But you have met him." He gestured at Charon, who plucked off the shroud.

Théo.

Thumpthumpthumpthumpthumpthumpthumpthump.

Céleste jumped into Gustave's lap, hugging him dearly, her eyes shut tight.

"What is it?" asked Gustave, tense.

Théo, the man who'd reached into her chest and squeezed the thing that made her who she was. The part of her that laughed, cried, bled, and lived. He tore it out, root system and all, from where it had been seeded. Breaths hot, breaths heavy. Breaths fast. She hyperventilated. *I am nothing, I am nothing,*

I am nothing. She could feel her shoulder blades on the hard stone bench. Théo hovered near. Wait, not him. Gustave's barrel fragrance.

She had burrowed into Gustave's neck. She blinked twice and sat up, trying to balance her head on her body and deflate the helium from her brain.

"What do you see?" asked Gustave.

She didn't have to look. Théo was stuck in her mind forever, the living dead. He was there when she woke. He was there when she slept. There was no end to him.

"No one. It's no one," Céleste replied.

She risked another glance. A handsome, heavyset man with jowls and a bowler hat pierced her with his gauzy gaze. Discolored cheeks, he provided no smile, no twinkle from his once jolly demeaner.

It wasn't Théo, not really. It was his greasy-haired corpse. And there was something else. Knife wounds had punctured Théophile's belly under his buttoned shirt. The blood had pooled in black.

Papa had said Théo left town. She didn't know he was dead.

"Go on." Hermes nudged the cadaver. "Reveal yourself for the man."

"Tha—Théophile Deveaux."

Gustave's face turned white. "Impossible." The skin on his neck became splotchy around his open shirt collar, under his miraculous medal.

"How did you die?" Hermes asked her Thief.

"Muh—murder."

"Parlor tricks," said Gustave. "Someone is toying with us. They copied his voice. A wax cylinder hidden in the room."

"Can you identify your killer?" Hermes continued.

Théo raised a bony finger, pointing across from him. "Goo-stave."

Her chest heaved. She slapped it, choking on saliva, her heart palpitating wildly.

Hermes displayed Gustave's Apache revolver in his palms, a brass knuckle handle with a blade in place of a barrel. "The murder weapon," he proclaimed, setting it on the table.

"Whatever they're showing you," said Gustave, "they're lying."

"Gustave." Céleste took shallow breaths. How could she protect him from Nemesis while trying to figure out the truth? "I know it's fake, but... How do you know it's fake? You've never heard Théo speak. You've never met."

Gustave dropped his jaw, groping for words.

Hermes stomped his foot and looked at the ceiling. "Who ordered the murder?"

Théo worked his mouth. "Duh-drink."

"The man's a dipsomaniac," said Gustave. "He can't be trusted."

Chef Maurice offered Théo a bottle on a silver platter.

Théophile bit off the cork and guzzled, driveling fluid down his chin. When he was through, he dropped the bottle to the floor. It rolled to Gustave's feet. Formaldehyde.

"Monsieur Deveaux," said Hermes. "Who ordered the murder?"

"Ayyd-ward Marchand."

Papa? Céleste's lips quivered. *How could he?* He was kind, gentle. Tears flowed through her ducts. He was terrified of conflict.

"Céleri, I can explain." Gustave hesitated. "I killed Théo alone. I swear it. Your father had nothing to do with it."

She quaked in his lap. She forced out two blubbering syllables, "Ex-plain."

Gustave leaned his head on her shoulder. "You came home from the cabaret a nervous wreck. Théo was nowhere to be found. A year ago, Édouard had a chance run in with Théo in Les Halles. He told me, and I quote, *Make sure he leaves town permanently.* Édouard knew my background, but the interpretation was mine. He only wanted Théo to keep away. Théo was still in Athens. By the time I located him, you and

I had become friendly, and I didn't know how anyone could harm such a pure soul."

The words broke her heart. What soul did he see?

"I knocked on his apartment door," said Gustave. "He opened. There was a rocking horse. He'd formed a life. Had a child. I decided to back down, but it was too late. Théo recognized me. He had kept tabs. He was terrified. He attacked." Gustave breathed heavily. "Speak to me, Céleste. Anything."

Céleste swallowed hard. "Does Papa know?"

"Non."

That was some consolation. Perhaps Papa hadn't implied murder, or perhaps he'd said what he did in a fit of rage. He tended to bottle everything up and explode. It may've been one of his outbursts. She tried to put herself in his shoes. He had a daughter with frayed nerves and a missing chaperone that had turned up four years later. Papa wasn't a liar, only Gustave.

"Why did you lie to me?" asked Céleste. "After all we've been through?"

"To protect you."

She wanted to fault him, but she couldn't. She had lied to him too. For the exact same reason. Why else would she conceal her identity? To protect him. It was her fault he was held captive in Erebus on the Styx. It was she who'd attracted Hermes into her life. She brought her cult activities too close to home. The only fault she could find with Gustave was that he'd killed a man. How could she explain it in a way that didn't compromise Gustave's life? *Wait, yes.*

"When he attacked me," said Céleste, "Théo was possessed by a demon."

"Céleri—"

"The demon's name is Gergely."

"How do you know this?"

"It's a hunch. Was he still possessed when you killed him?"

"Are you sure you're not making excuses for what happened? The mind—"

"My mind's not playing tricks. I've seen demonic possessions with my own eyes. Exorcisms."

Gustave tilted his head toward her as if to absorb everything. "Have you seen a demon possess a man or only dispossess him?"

It had never occurred to her. She had never seen one of these lizards take hold of a person and implant themselves.

"Dispossess."

"I became a man of Christ, Céleri. What I did, I now take responsibility for. I've asked forgiveness night and day. What Théo did, on the other hand... What I'm getting at is, if your assertion is correct, maybe his demon was drawn to Théo because of his corrupt nature and the choices he made."

"It was," said Céleste.

She had heard it firsthand in the Well of Lost Souls. Demons were drawn to people weak in will, the feebleminded, poltroons. Apparently, she qualified. Her soul-theft proved it. She didn't know corruption would make a person weak too, but it made sense. The demon in the Erebus Room had said that those who were possessed welcomed their demons in—which meant Théo had welcomed Gergely in. She and Théo were born unlovable—predators and prey—all in the same boat.

"What I'm asking," said Céleste, "is did he have a change of heart? Were his eyes black? Did you by chance see a creature with a lizard tail, a snout of a crocodile, and the wings of a flittermouse?"

"I did not see anything leave his body," said Gustave, "or black eyes, and none of this nightmarish ballet your describing. It may've just been who he was."

"Oui, that is a strong possibility. Did he say anything?"

"His last words were, she'll never find it. I assumed he meant forgiveness."

A chill went up her spine. He was still possessed. Wife, child, no change of heart.

It gave her peace of mind for Gustave's sake.

Even if Théo was free, Céleste could not fault Gustave for killing him in self-defense. She had killed Loïe the Lampad.

Her conscience felt heavy thinking about it. Two wrongs did not make a right.

Hermes coughed.

"Are you happy?" Gustave asked him. "You've extracted my confession."

"Quite. Take the killer to the brig."

"Don't struggle," Céleste whispered close in his ear. "I will get us out of here."

Two crewmen removed Céleste from the safest place in the room and escorted Gustave obediently away. When he was well out of earshot, she turned to Hermes.

"What was the purpose of that demonstration?"

Hermes held his hands behind his back. "To sever your ties with the surface world. One chaperone stole your soul, the next murdered his predecessor, all under the unwatchful eye of neglective old Papa. Mariquita can't teach you original dance, you despise your mother, and your children will despise you. Things are not looking good, soulwise."

"How do you know how I feel about Maman? Do you read my mail?"

Hermes sniggered. "You never mention her."

"What do you recommend?"

"Marriage. Come with me to Olympus. I'll ask Melinoë where she stuck your soul, and I'll let you drink ambrosia to your heart's content."

How to manage the situation? She needed to know everyone's motive, including Charon's. Her soul-throne craved a ray of light even now just looking at him, she was so pathetic.

"What's in it for Charon? Do you intend to share me?"

Charon smiled, mute.

"Funny you should say," said Hermes.

A shiver went up her spine. Ice cold.

"In exchange for digging up this corpse"—Hermes covered it with the shroud—"I offered Charon a choice between Circe's staff and my caduceus. The staff can change anyone into anyone else, anything into anything else. My caduceus can heal his voice. It seems pride won out."

"Why not have both?" Céleste winced at the thought of it.

"I can't check out more than one object at a time, and Charon is not a member. But, to sweeten the deal, I will return Gustave to the surface and mend one broken arm."

"Danke," said Nayla in a flat droll.

The boat stopped. Curtains fell around the deck.

"Flame retardant," Nayla observed.

Fires burned on the distant river adjoining the Styx. The last curtain fell over the scene, and crewmen began tying them down.

More electric bulbs flickered on to balance out the dark.

"What do you say?" asked Hermes.

Nayla looked at Céleste, lips apart, awaiting response.

"I agree under one condition," said Céleste. "It would be unfair if Charon benefits while I receive nothing beforehand."

"What do you desire, ma fleur?"

"The Cap of Hades."

Nayla's eyes bulged.

Hermes stalked the dance floor with a pensive expression on his face.

"Céleste," Nayla said, "I think we're in enough hot water."

"A deal's a deal," said Céleste. "You helped me find my soul, I help you get the cap."

"But running off to Olympus? For me?"

"If I can't save myself, at least I can save others."

"And you called me a martyr?"

"You were overcompensating. Those demons would've killed you. I'll be alive on Olympus. It's the only option where everyone walks away in one piece."

"We'll see about that," Hermes interrupted. "I can't check out more than one object. You two will have to steal them."

"Us?" asked Nayla.

"I need plausible deniability." He turned to Céleste. "Though you are both mortal, so is Arachne. Her defeat is possible. However, if Nayla dies, you are to pollinate to the boat. Since the cap is for Nayla, her death will nullify your end of the bargain, and we are to be wed. With cap or without, it's a win for me."

Hermes offered his hand.

Céleste shook. "Deal."

Hermes called the first mate to his side. "Chart a new course to Tartarus via the River Lethe."

"Understood," said the first mate. He motioned to the crewmen to raise the curtains.

"Not the Phlegethon?" asked Nayla.

"You don't park the getaway car too close to the bank."

Hermes parted the beaded curtain. Charon followed him out, leaving Céleste and Nayla in peace.

"I'm glad Gustave is all right," said Nayla. "I can only wish the same for Captain Beauvais. I hope you know what you are doing." She kicked the formaldehyde bottle on her way to the bar, where she poured herself some whiskey.

Céleste approached the shrouded Théo.

It was scary, the risk of time traveling to a specific point in the past to relive a horror she couldn't do anything about to change. It was unalterable time, cemented into the universe. The present, however, she could alter. She could face her fear.

I am nothing, I am nothing, I am nothing.

Her heart pounded with the voice in her chest, as she reached for the shroud, seeing multiple hands in double vision, trying to blink away the damage from Loïe's beam.

I am nothing, I am nothing, I am nothing.

She winced as she uncovered the shroud and faced the fear head on. Théo's egg-white eyes peered back, glazed over, the man semi-conscious, fracturing the voice in the void as if striking a tuning fork:

I am I am I I am no-no-no-nothing.

For a moment, she could hear multiple voices, before they fell back into concert. What was that? Théo looked at her with a flicker of recognition, but eyes so dead, he did not seem in the position to provide many answers.

The man had been just as broken as she was. Gustave had prayed forgiveness for taking his life and he made it through his days all right. Perhaps asking Jesus to forgive her for Loïe was the answer to clear her conscience—and perhaps cleanse her soul.

Her faith, or lack thereof, could have something to do with it. Théo had ripped the crucifix from her neck as if it granted permission for the demon to attack. And her prayer to Our Lady of the Miraculous Medal—She'd recited the words in her head before expelling the demon in the Wild Garden the night of Loïe's audition. Céleste's intention had been to keep herself present. Perhaps it had done more.

She glanced up. Crewmen hustled across the deck, securing panels to the ship. She looked at the bar. Nayla sipped her drink.

Nayla—she was pursuing moksha with the tools she had to work with. She didn't stop practicing Hinduism in light of the Greek pantheon. Why did Céleste give up the Catholic faith? She knew why. She couldn't see it. What she saw was Psyche telling her to find love. She'd liked to think love and immortality were distinct from her soul, but they were somehow intertwined.

How foolish she'd been. She had done so many reckless things. Letting Hermes smother her with attention, chasing it out of Charon, basking in the light of Hades. It was who she was. Her soul-throne compelled her. She couldn't help it no matter what she did.

Her soul wasn't the problem. She was. If she wasn't, she wouldn't have been born to two half-people. Papa wouldn't have neglected her in childhood. Maman wouldn't have blown so hot and cold. If she were different, she could have retained her soul. If she were loved. Lovable. Complete. But all that was fantasy. She was doomed at birth. Her future with Étienne and Eulalie and a loving husband had been so bright when she first entered Erebus. Now it was so far from her grasp it appeared impossible. She did not ask for this. Any of it.

But she must know why the Incident.

"Théo, it's Céleste," she said as if talking to a moribund patient. "Your demon. Papa trusted you. I trusted you. Why did you let it in?"

Théo slowly lifted his eyes and found their mark, curving what was left of his lips into a swagger, his breath a flesh so rotten it scared her nose into her skull.

"Ka-Ka-Quand même."

After all these years, that was all he had to say? No reflection whatsoever.

She arched her brow, shut her eyes, and veiled the corpse.

Helping Gustave and Nayla was her only consolation. If you cannot get crumb, you had best eat crust.

"Prepare to dive," called the first mate.

If the world had but one religion, there wouldn't be much choice, because it would mean that's all there is. This or nothing. Without variety, there is no doubt, and without room for doubt, there is no room for faith. There is your daily Jacqism. I hope it satisfies, my friend.

Non, I am not Unitarian. I have my beliefs, you have yours. I won't share, because it will sound like I'm converting you. People don't change their viewpoints unless they are at rock bottom, anyway. Most of the time. Are you at rock bottom? Thank goodness, my friend, because what would that say about me associating with the likes of you! I kid, I kid. Jacques is not too good for the company of despairables. I was in despair once. Twice. Three times.

Sometimes, at rock bottom, you only crawl sideways. You're sure you're not there? Like attracts like, after all. Ah, then you must have an inkling of how it feels, an experience of those raw emotions in diluted form. Trust me, the further you are from sorrowful events, the better. Chaos at its most potent is difficult to navigate, especially with a bad therapist like Hermes.

You wind up on the River of Forgetfulness, wondering where it all went wrong, traveling deeper into the unconscious.

Who am I? Why wasn't I born normal? Where was God? Am I cursed? Where do I go from here?

You've been staring at squiggles so long they become straight lines—rigid, precise, mechanical—and the idea of damnation cements and dries. It's too late for me. The mind turns rote. The predictable habit patterns that landed us in a well to begin with are identified as permanent.

It isn't all bad. You learn new words like hamartia, the fatal flaw of the personality. But who can think about Aristotle at a time like this? The messenger god has sanctioned a theft. Stand closer. I can feel the heat radiating off the canvas.

TARTARUS

R iver water rushed alongside the ship, goat-milk white. Nayla stood on her tiptoes and watched it curdle against the porthole. Charon had converted his Bateau Lavoir into a submarine. The floorboards purred. The walls thrummed. Nayla set her heels on the cold planks. Her boot soles had burned away from powering to the surface of the Well of Lost Souls. To remedy this, she increased her body temperature while her braid turned red in the window.

"It's something out of Jules Verne," said Céleste, sitting where Gustave had sat, across from the shrouded Théo.

Jules Verne sounded French. Nayla did not care for clarification. "Whatever you do, don't drink the water. It erases memory so the dead cannot remember their past lives."

"Perhaps Hermes can ingest it this time."

Nayla highly doubted it. Hermes was far more intelligent than Charon. Any smog floating his direction could be fanned back at her by his winds. She would also have had to find a way to reach the water through these white panels and safely collect it for that trick.

"Perhaps," Nayla lied.

Céleste rested her cheek on her fist. "Perhaps not."

"Perhaps not," Nayla confessed. "I'm sorry about Gustave."

Céleste glanced at Théo. "He's alive and unaware of the pantheon. There is still hope."

"How's your eye?"

"Not as bothersome as the voice in the void." Céleste touched her sternum. "Looking into Théo's eyes did something to it. Threw it off balance. For a fraction of a second I can hear some of the voices from the rest of the choir. Dissonant. Like they miss their cue."

"Can you make them out?"

Céleste shook her head. "Not really. Two are altos, one a soprano I think, and one definitely a baritone. They're masked by my own voice running over the lot. How's your arm?"

"Oh, I'll be fine." Nayla waved away the pain.

"Fine to fight a spider?"

Hermes slinked into the party room behind Céleste. Nayla made eye contact with the god, fearing Céleste would say something compromising if she were unaware of his presence.

"The caduceus stick can heal whatever injury we sustain," said Nayla.

Céleste glared at her. "Oui, I suppose it could."

"That's my flower," said Hermes, "using her head. Prepare to surface."

Céleste braced her chair.

Nayla hurried to the bar. Who knew when she'd have another drink on this perilous journey? The floor shook her to her butt. Pain shot through her arm as if it'd been laid on a rail and run over by a train.

"Yahh!"

"What you need is healing," said Hermes, "not spirits." He levitated and offered a hand.

Reluctantly, Nayla took it. "The healing is harder to come by." She walked behind the bar, found a canteen at the bar, and filled it with rum as the river foamed in the portholes.

She missed the canteen and fell back against the shelving, catching herself as the ship broke surface. Milk trickled down the windows in silk beads. Steps appeared outside in the sunlight. They were in a stepwell. *Großartig*. She returned to pouring.

Crewmen arrived on deck to unbolt the panel that led to the gangplank. Hermes helped a begrudging Céleste from her chair and gestured for Nayla to come hither. She screwed the cap on tight and joined the escort. On deck, he positioned her and Céleste at the square opening. The heat was atrocious. Nayla dialed up her temperature and took in the view.

The stepwell was of red sandstone, down which trod a revolving line of women, dunking ewers into the Lethe. As soon as one them filled their vessel, she proceeded up the tiered steps, their destination hidden over the lip of the last stair, set against a magenta sky. There were dozens of these women. Each wore a colorful sari.

"Chaleur!" said Céleste, shaking off Hermes. "Where are we?"

"In a stepwell." Nayla put her hand on the rail. "Boah!"

Muscles splayed across the back of her hand, tightly packed between the bones.

She turned to Céleste. Red striations folded in and out of her skull like jerky. Her eyeballs were spheres, their panicked expression determined by the ribbons of muscle on her brow receding into her noodly hair.

Nayla shied back, bumping into Hermes.

He appeared normal in shadow, until he stepped into the crimson light, exposing the ropy cords of his neck and the red discs around his bulging eyes. The tethers in his chin and cheeks contracted as he spoke.

"Good. You've acclimated." He pointed a sinewy arm over the stepwell. "Arachne's Cave is in the ziggurat." He turned to a frightened and bewildered Céleste. "When you return, stand on the bank and wave the caduceus. I'll see you through the periscope. If Nayla tarries, leave her."

Céleste braced the rail. "You can expect us both."

"We'll see." He nudged them onto the advancing gangplank.

"What do you mean by that?" asked Nayla. "Are we in a reflection of Jacoma?"

"No, you are from a reflection of Tartarus."

Clutching the rail, Nayla dared a glance over the edge, peering into the milky waters below. She jumped. Was that her? She ventured another look. Her eyes glared back, adhered to her skull by tissue and ligament.

This nightmare was nothing like Jacoma. A qanat drew water from the mountains to the stepwells, not the River Lethe. And she did not appreciate Hermes's ominous remarks.

"Stay safe, my flower." He blew Céleste a kiss and lingered behind.

The sliding gangplank touched the shore.

Nayla walked, feeling the gaze of Hermes on her back as she stepped onto dry land. The gangplank began to recede. Hermes waved in a gesture of dismissal, to proceed on their journey, while the crewmen replaced the door. The Lethe bubbled and fizzed as le Bateau Lavoir resubmerged.

"Céleste, I won't lie. It's hard to look at you."

"Unnatural," she concurred, pinching herself. "At least I can still feel my skin."

"Tell me you're not really eloping to Olympus."

"I need an object that can save Gustave. All that comes to mind is a lightning bolt to chuck at Hermes's meaty face." Céleste looked up the stairs. "Are the skies maroon in Jacoma?"

"Nein, and our water isn't white, either." Nayla surveyed the steps. "Nor our stepwells this deep."

"We ought to start climbing." Céleste forged ahead. "The less time Gustave spends with Hermes and Charon, the better."

Nayla crossed the five meters of flat poolside and ascended the first step. After a dozen more, her breathing escalated into a pant. She wiped her sweat. She was about a quarter of the way up. The women in saris carried their ewers at a steadier pace than she was keeping. One in green waved frantically at them from the halfway point.

Céleste halted her advance and looked down. "Who are those women?"

"I don't know."

"Let's learn from my mistakes in Erebus and not get involved."

"Agreed." Nayla lumbered up the next step.

Still, the woman in green waved, setting down her ewer. Nayla felt herself drifting in for a closer look. The woman was shorter than the others, with a round face and a braid like hers. Something glimmered from her forehead. It was made of gold. A maang teeka. They all had one.

"Kameera?" Nayla tripped. She threw out her hand and caught herself. A jolt of pain shot through her broken arm as the sling gave it whiplash. "Kameera is dead?" She rose to her feet and ran diagonally up the steps. "Kameera!" It was impossible. Whatever karmic fate tied Nayla to a life of misery, Kameera deserved none of it. She was going to have a big family and play violin concerts and die of old age. Not carry buckets of water up the steps in Tartarus!

These women. Their skin was not transparent like hers and Céleste's. Céleste! She glanced and spied Céleste hurrying after her.

"It's my friend!" Nayla called.

Kameera stepped out of line and opened her arms. Her skin was brown without a hint of exposed muscles underneath, which meant she was, she was...

"Nayla!" Kameera shouted.

Nayla nearly slammed into her, enveloping her body with a hug. "Kameera, is it really you?"

"Ja, Nay, it's me."

"What happened? You were in Spanish Cairo. Where's Pradeep?"

Kameera dropped her arms and looked into the throat of the ewer. "He died."

"I'm so sorry." Nayla shook her head in tears. "Are you dead too?"

Kameera looked forlornly at the ground. "What are you doing here?"

"I'm a nymph." There was no harm in saying so now. "I'm looking for—"

"Don't say anything," Céleste interrupted. She stood a few meters away, higher on the steps, poised, listening. "This may be your friend, but we don't know who she's with. I can't risk Gustave's life again."

"We can trust Kameera," said Nayla.

Céleste shook her head. She was being ridiculous. Nayla could tell Kameera any secret in the world. What did it matter? The only thing stopping her was an argument from Céleste, so Nayla held her tongue and settled with a vague, "I'm here."

Kameera nodded humbly. "It's all right, Nayla. You don't have to tell me. I only ask for your help."

"Help with what?"

"This."

"How long will it take?"

"Oh, not long." A passing woman handed Kameera a spare ewer. "Follow me to the bottom to fill up."

"All the way back down?" asked Céleste. "Nayla, we're on a time schedule."

"Please, Nay," said Kameera. "It's the least you could do for murdering my father."

The words stung Nayla's flesh and sapped her throat dry. She'd avoided Kameera and Cairo for this very confrontation.

"I—I didn't murder him," said Nayla. "It was an accident."

"It's your fault he's here."

"Ravi uncle is here?" asked Nayla.

"Nayla," muttered Céleste, "this girl is your cousin?"

"Nein, *uncle* is what we call a man who is elder to us. Ravi is—"

"—Doomed to work the Blast till his next reincarnation," said Kameera, "as I am doomed to carry this ewer. If I had more help, I might accomplish the task quicker."

Nayla laid herself bare. She deserved every insult, every punishment. Ravi uncle's death was her fault. Had she not told Ravi uncle where to find Baba, he would still be alive. It was fact.

"What can I do to make it right?" asked Nayla.

"Take this." Kameera offered the spare ewer and picked up her own. "Follow me."

Nayla turned to Céleste. "I'm sorry. I have to. I'm responsible for her father's death."

"Ravi is partly responsible for your father's death." Céleste remained where she was. "You were caught in a chain of events you did not intend to occur."

"What do you French say?" asked Kameera. "The road to hell is paved with good intentions?"

"Evidently," replied Céleste.

It broke Nayla's heart. She'd always thought Kameera and Céleste would be best of friends, were they to ever meet. Attractive, fashionable, students of the arts, from higher castes, hardworking fathers—it was such a shame. They had so much in common.

"I'll wait here." Céleste examined the line of women.

"You won't help?" asked Nayla.

"Unlike you, I can die of heat exhaustion. I'm already sweating, and I can't drink from the Lethe to cool off." She wiped her brow. "I'd rather not spend the energy."

"I'll be right back."

Nayla regrettably turned and descended behind Kameera, mindful of her feet. If she tripped with an ewer in her hand, she'd fall on her face. Or arm.

"Céleste is right about Ravi uncle," Nayla began, laboring down the steps. "He didn't know you pawned the maang teeka for me until he discovered it missing. He wanted the money back. He was going to pawn it himself because he saw Pradeep wasn't doing well financially and you were pregnant."

"My baba had a gambling problem," said Kameera.

"Did you always know?"

"Nein. We figured it out after he died."

"And the baby?" Shiva, let the baby have outlived her.

"Miscarried," revealed Kameera. "The doctor said it was stress from Baba's death."

"I'm so sorry. Nobody told me."

"You didn't write."

Nayla stopped in her tracks. Her eyes were leaky faucets. She couldn't take it. *Please stop. No more.* Had she never borrowed that maang teeka to build the mecha-sleeves, a baby would be alive. No escape from Jacoma was worth that. She had been so selfish.

Orange, yellow, blue fabric grazed her skin. Women in saris brushed past.

"Keep walking," said Kameera. "We cannot stop for long."

"Kameera... your baby."

"I know, my baby. We have to keep walking." She tugged at Nayla's pants.

Nayla tried to control her breathing and soldiered on, one quaking foot at a time.

At the bottom of the stepwell, the Lethe's pulpy surface lay flat as ground. One sip, and she could forget all about Kameera and her baby. *Nein, Nayla.* Self-annihilation was not the answer. She had tried this before. If she drank, she might not feel the regret and disgust that followed, but her karma would tally it against her for the next life. She couldn't pass the mark. It had to stop with her. She had knowledge of the Cap of Hades, the catalyst to become one with Brahman. Her next life might not be so fortunate.

But she had messed up so badly, she would rather collect water for eternity with Kameera than face another existence or merge with Brahman. It would be her rightful punishment.

Kameera dunked in her ewer, saturating the air with the odor of vinegar. Nayla stepped up and submerged her jug, maintaining a grip on the handle, careful not to splash. The spouted container weighed about nine kilograms when full.

She treated the Lethe like an open hearth. *Respect the water. Respect the water. Let the can glug it up. Filling, filling, full. Back away. Back away. Puh!*

Singlehandedly, she lugged the ewer up the steps, her calves burning from the work.

"How did you become a nymph?" asked Kameera.

"I created the mecha-sleeves. It impressed the gods. They offered me a potion. I drank it. Here I am."

"I'm glad my maang teeka allowed you to become a nymph."

"Ja," said Nayla, saddened, not wanting to talk about it. Where was the cheery Kameera? The good-natured friend who would do anything for her? Nayla didn't deserve an apology, but she preferred that Kameera understand what happened. How could Nayla begin to describe the horrors of her life when Kameera was stuck in Tartarus, a thousand times worse than the Sand Pits?

When Nayla had climbed to the halfway point, Céleste walked to her side.

"Why are you doing this?" asked Céleste.

"I feel guilty," Nayla whispered, not wanting Kameera to overhear.

"It was Kameera's choice to lend you the maang teeka," said Céleste, not caring who heard.

Kameera glanced back, irritated.

"Kameera," Nayla explained, "I'm sorry for my friend."

"Why are you trying to please people?" asked Céleste. "Who cares what she thinks? It's the truth. You chose to invent something. She chose to fund it. Those choices may have influenced Ravi, but Ravi chose to approach you. He chose to confront your baba. Baba chose to distill liquor in your tenement."

"I chose to confront Ravi uncle at the Blast."

"He chose not to tuck in the long cords on his pants," Céleste replied. "Against Blast rules. Accidents happen."

"Karma happens," said Nayla. "I'm sorry I shared my life story. I should have said karma and let that be it."

Céleste pretended she heard none of that. "Listen, these women carrying the ewers. There are forty-nine of them. I counted. You know what that means? They are the Danaides. They murdered their husbands."

Nayla's face crumpled. "Nein. Not Kameera. She would never." But Nayla knew where she stood. What task the Danaides did. Her readings of Ovid betrayed her. The game at de L'Enfer.

"Je suis désolée," said Céleste. "I had to tell you before you arrive at the top and see the cauldron with a hole in it for yourself."

"Kameera"—Nayla dragged the ewer up the steps—"tell her she's wrong. You would never harm Pradeep."

"He wanted to leave me." Kameera glanced at Shiva-knew-what expression on Nayla's face. Disbelief? Revulsion? "My baba left, you left, your baba left. My baby. I wasn't going to let Pradeep walk out too."

Nayla let out a cry, stooping to the ground.

Céleste grabbed hold of the ewer, another hand on Nayla's good arm.

"My worst fears come to pass," Nayla whimpered.

"Let's do what we came for," said Céleste, "and leave this horrible situation."

Nayla was on her knees.

"Come on, Nay," Céleste said tactfully, "this is busywork, pointless repetition. You hate busywork."

Nayla unscrewed her canteen and chugged, her tears blurring her vision.

Céleste lowered the drink. "You're at full power. This does nothing."

"It—"

"Distracts you from living, je sais."

Nayla twisted the cap. "I did this to her." She lowered her head to the step. "All because I wanted to have a better life."

"There is nothing wrong with having needs."

"I don't deserve to rise above the Shudras. I am a laborer for life."

"Oui, well, my friend Gustave is in trouble because of me."
Céleste hoisted Nayla to her feet. "At the top of these stairs,
we are going to see a cauldron with a hole, and we are going to
walk past it. Perhaps we can find something to free Kameera
from bondage."

"You think so?" Nayla wiped the snot from her lips.

"Oui. Let's go." Céleste pulled her along, carrying the ewer
for her. "You can even dump the water in to feel you contributed."

Nayla climbed the red stairs, feeling their porous texture
on the soles of her feet. She insisted on taking the ewer from
Céleste. It was her responsibility. She got Kameera into quicksand. She must carry the water. Céleste handed it over as the
red stone, which you could fry an egg on, gave way to stain. The
stain was wet, evaporating.

"It's Lethe water." Céleste pulled Nayla off course. "We
shall take a circuitous route."

"Why do their memories not vanish, inhaling the effluvi-
um?" asked Nayla. The line of women tromped right through it.

"Je ne sais pas. Why does Kameera treat you like this?"

"She's been through a lot."

"So have you. You both lost your fathers," said Céleste,
her face bratwurst. "From your description of her, you'd think
she'd forgive you and want you as far from here as possible."

"Why?"

"I love my friends, and I don't want Gustave anywhere near
the underworld."

"Even if you were assigned a pointless task?"

"A task with no goal? Oui, I'd be *more* inclined to push him
away. These women may as well be carrying water to the sea."

The cauldron loomed at the top, bobbing into view as Nayla
ascended. The vermeil pot shined gold in the red sun. It had
tortoise feet and a tortoise head with water spilling from its
mouth and down the rough steps.

Kameera waved her over. The whole perimeter was surrounded by high walls. Nayla approached the cauldron elliptically from the back and poured the milky water into its shell.

"When it gets to the brim, I may depart," said Kameera.

"The problem is the hole."

"Correct. If we make one more trip, we can fill it."

Nayla backed away so as not to be splashed by the other women. "Kameera, are you sure you want me to stay here with you?"

"Ja, Nayla. My entire family is gone thanks to you. Who else can help me?"

Nayla frowned and looked imploringly at Céleste. "I have to stay."

Céleste shook her head. "It's not her talking."

"You've never met her."

"Friends don't say that." Céleste raised a palm at Kameera.

"Cél, what are you suggesting?" Nayla dropped the ewer. It clanged down the steps. She made a fist but did not raise it.

"Demonic possession." Her cells and atoms burst into pollen and dove into Kameera's mouth.

"Céleste!" Nayla changed her fist to a palm. "Don't move, Kameera. She won't hurt you."

Kameera's eyeball sprang from her head.

Nayla jumped, wincing in horror. "Was zur Hölle!" She craned her neck. The eyeball floated but a ruler's length from Kameera's face. It was attached to a scissor contraption.

Pollen dumped from the eye socket's opening and resculpted into Céleste. "That is no human I've ever seen, dead or alive."

Kameera hunched forward like a wind-up toy that had run out of juice.

Nayla creased her brow. "She's an automaton."

Slowly Kameera lurched back. The eyeball retracted into her silicon face. "Am I to assume you won't help me?"

"What are you?" asked Nayla.

"I'm your friend."

"Nein." Nayla shook her head, hand out, wanting none of that. "Nein." She rested her arm on Céleste's shoulder and retreated. "Danke, Cél. If it weren't for you, I'd be stuck there forever."

"How frightening."

Nayla didn't know if Céleste meant frightening that she would've succumbed to her guilt, or if the monotony itself was frightening, and Nayla didn't want to know. Besides, there was bigger news.

"Do you know what this means?" Tears streamed over her smile. "Kameera isn't dead."

"Non, she's not." Céleste squeezed her and pointed. "Look. The exit. It's an archway. No door."

"They can leave anytime?" Nayla glanced at Kameera, going down for another pail. "Why choose to continue?"

"Why indeed?" Céleste gave Nayla a patient look.

Through the arch, she walked onto a street carved from a rusted quarry. Dynamos whirred on the corners. Skeletal buildings with golden girders stretched into the air. Belts looped over intersections stanchioned on pulleys, between which people bustled to and fro, extraordinary people with mechanical arms, bionic legs, turbans and monocles, some of whom were muleteers with automaton livestock made up of horses, camels, and of course, mules. Thin, silver hoops rotated under glass domes on the walls, riding up the iwans. These gears, so large and slender, their cogs, so tiny.

Fire geysers shot platforms up in the air on vertical tracks, and oil gushed through glass pipes around town.

The atmosphere suffused everything in pink, fading to maroon overhead where German dirigibles cruised the sky. In the distance billowed violet smoke majestically from a blast furnace.

Kameera wasn't in Tartarus, but Ravi uncle might be. Nayla had to speak with him. If she learned how he felt about her, about what had happened, it might rest her guilty conscience.

"Where is the ziggurat?" asked Céleste, covering her chest as she would an ear.

Nayla pointed at the Blast. "It's right beyond there." She sprang open her wings and unscrewed her flask. "Get in. I'll carry you."

Céleste poofed into her ride. She would understand. She was a true friend.

IMPRESSION, MARIQUITA

I am nothing-ing, I am nothing-ing, I am-am nothing-thing.
Oui, she could hear it distinctly now. The voice in the void—one member of this unified group standing out from the rest, cutting through the finish of her own silvery vocals. The voice was female. It spoke in clear, modulated rhapsodies, which sometimes rose into a shrill falsetto; she could recognize the voice anywhere—none other than Mariquita's. Why Mariquita? She was lovingly abrasive at times, but did she truly think Céleste was nothing?

Perhaps Mariquita had given up on her. Five years without drastic improvement might've easily convinced Mariquita that Céleste was nothing. Was Céleste nothing or was her dancing nothing? How could she separate the two? Céleste was her dancing and her dancing was her. Did her muscles not support her toes from collapse and spin her about the floor? Did her lines not grace the stage with her figure? This was all wrong.

Mariquita had protected her from Maman, told Papa he should fire people, and had Mariquita been her mother, the Incident would never have happened. If Mariquita's voice had always contributed to the echo in her soul-cave, she couldn't have thought Céleste's dancing was nothing. Her dancing was

at its peak when the voice first spoke. Was the voice a premonition? Getting louder and louder until the real Mariquita
agreed with it?

Oui, a premonition or something like it. Perhaps Mariquita's
place in the choir was of Céleste's own imaginings—fear that
Mariquita could think Céleste was nothing—and it whittled
Céleste down, until her behavior aligned with its message and
solidified the words into fact. If so, those like Mariquita in the
outside world reflected the assertion. Is that why Céleste couldn't
bind with her soul? She had dwelt too much on the voice?

What had Charon said? What the mind concentrates on, the
universe delivers. She couldn't help it. The Incident had planted
a seed, impossible to ignore, which grew into a self-fulfilling
prophecy that she was nothing. Would that mean that if she
believed she was something, her soul would come home? Easier
said than done. Telling a whirlpool it wasn't a whirlpool. Why
could she only hear the separate voices after looking Théo in
the eyes? This place was shoving her fears in her face, much
like how Kameera showed up.

Nayla, get to the ziggurat already! Take us out of here!

RAVI AT THE BLAST

Gold-hooped gears spun in the walls, reminding Nayla to keep momentum. Everything about Tartarus shouted, *Don't stop moving!* She wished to stop and examine everything. Auto-carriages spewing steam, mechanized camels, antennae on rooftops—it was a peek into humanity's collective unconscious—inventions that nymphs would transport to the surface world and whisper into the minds of inventors through divine inspiration. Scientists would be shown flashes, engineers insights, mechanics voices and visions. One mechanic, she recalled, was recently given the gift of the petrol tractor in its finished form to reverse-engineer and construct in reality.

What about her mecha-sleeves? She designed it based on Baba's schematics and her study of trains. Had he seen a nymph? Was his muse invisible? Did the creature merely sow the seed? There was no time to think. Nayla must get to the Blast. How could she explain to Céleste why they were stopping there? To ask for directions? Geographically, Erebus was almost identical to French Athens, as Tartarus was to Jacoma. Stopping for directions was unconvincing. Once Céleste learned the ziggurat was east and not west, she would figure out Nayla had lied.

Unless, that was, Nayla didn't let her out of the flask. Ja. Céleste would never know they stopped. It was perfekt. Besides, Nayla didn't like people seeing her in such a disgusting emotional state and she was bound to be in one after this detour. Woe is me was not a good look, and she didn't know how Ravi uncle would receive her.

A mustachioed gentleman walked by and tipped his fez hello, his arm a complexity of fans and rotors. What friendly inhabitants. She kicked on her footsoles and fired into the sky, arcing over clay rooves, heading into the sulfur that clouded the Blast.

She landed on the red street in front of the gate. A golden post marked each side, bracing an armillary sphere. What did the heavens have to do with the Blast? A large bang went off. The ground trembled. Nayla latched onto a post. It sounded like a furnace had exploded. Another bang shook the earth, followed by the roar of a large jaguar. Something told her they did not make steel here.

She tucked in her wings as she walked the path to the corridor and wandered in below the ogee arch. The roars increased in volume. She covered her ears. Her feet quailed. Soot rained from the ceiling. Céleste, safe in her bottle, could likely feel the vibrations. Nayla adjusted her headpiece, noted she could see her skin again, and pressed on into the clock-in station. There was only one tab in the wooden pockets, covered in soot. She picked it up and blew. Ravi Iyengar. Clock-in date: August 1891.

The gleam of the hearth flared in the antechamber. She rounded the corner and absorbed the breadth of the charging bay. The walls cried lava. The floor was absent of lime and scrap. In spite of the Blast resembling the interior of a volcano, it was the tidiest she'd seen it. She stepped inside, casting footprints in the soot.

Heat lines emanated from the hearth in flurries before the charging doors. The openings were double in size. Why so big? And where was the pool? The slag? She peeked her head in a centimeter or two. She'd never seen the hearth so deep. It was a large bowl she could not find the bottom of. Might she find Hestia at home? She stuck her head fully inside.

At the base, in a puddle of lava, dwelled five bulky men with muscular builds. One sat on the floor dejected, against the liner. The other four had stacked themselves atop each other in a pyramid. The top man reached a charging door a few meters away and pounded it like a gong.

Nayla, head in the hearth, cupped an ear. The fifth man, the sitting one, shot a finger at her. Rays flickered from it like a filament bulb.

"Cronus," he said, "the first door is open."

Nayla turtled. Cronus?

"Come here, little nymph," echoed the sitting man's voice. "Let us out. We won't hurt you."

These weren't men. These were...

"Titans," Nayla whispered.

She staggered from the hearth, reaching for the pull chain that closed the door. It wasn't there. Neither was the door. Only the square opening. How to stop these gods from climbing up and eating her? The drone of a machine answered her call. An electric crane whizzed overhead on a track and lowered a door in place, held by grooves around the frame.

The door received an earth-shattering thud. The noise resonated in the charging bay. The ground shook. Turbulence. Nayla jumped and turned smack into a tunicked chest.

"Ravi uncle?"

"Oh, Nayla"—He hugged her—"thank heavens you're here."

"You're not angry with me?"

"Angry? I'm ecstatic. I haven't had a break in a year and a half."

"Break from what?"

"Prison guard, warden, bailiff. Whatever you want to call it, I'm all of them." He gestured across the charging bay. "I think of myself as a gatekeeper. Problem is"—he pointed at the first door—"the gate moves."

The door received another violent blow.

Nayla winced.

"You get used to it." Ravi gestured to the hearth. "There are four gateways and one gate. I must use my intuition to foresee what gateway the Titans will try to escape from. They can't see the gateways from the hearth's basin. When they make the climb, all they can see is the one gate—the little hole for sampling steel has been removed so there's no peeking through—which is a good thing, because as far as the Titans know, all the gateways have gates."

"I saw one use electricity," said Nayla. "Why don't they use their powers to bust out?"

"Hyperion." Ravi uncle nodded. "The hearth is insulated with a dampener, a type of forcefield. It reduces their abilities dramatically." He coned his ear to listen. The pounding stopped. "If you'll excuse me."

He mounted the ladder on the opposite wall and climbed to the controls. Unlike Kameera, this Ravi seemed like the genuine article. For one, Nayla knew he was dead. She ought not to tell him about Kameera's impostor by the Lethe. It would upset and confuse him.

The drone of the crane motor captured Nayla's attention as the machine hoisted the door from gateway one and moved it to gateway three.

Nayla approached the ladder. "How do you know what gateway the Titans will choose if you can't see them?"

"Like I said. Intuition." Ravi lowered the gate in place and descended the ladder. "Something I should have listened to all along."

"How do you mean?"

"When dealing with the maang teeka, I should've obeyed my intuition. It's knowledge, Nayla, that comes from the soul, tailored just for us. Can you find it in your heart to forgive me?"

Forgiveness? It was so unexpected. "Ravi uncle. Your death was my fault. It is I who should ask you to forgive me."

"Nein, Nayla. You were like a second daughter, and I should've treated you as such. I didn't have to ask you for the money."

Nayla looked around at something to distract her from the awkwardness she felt. His dhoti. "No tassels."

"Work hazard." Ravi patted his leg. "Are you going to tell me that was your fault too?"

An unseen fist clobbered the door. The metal slab vibrated. Nayla winced.

"I've had a lot of time to reflect," Ravi uncle continued. "I hope my death didn't cause you too much unhappiness."

This wasn't happening. Nayla squatted to the sooty floor and covered her face. Mucus wet her hand.

"Oh, there, there, it's all right," Ravi uncle comforted.

"I blamed myself for so long." Nayla revealed her crinkled chin, her tears forming rivers on her blackened cheeks. She gripped Ravi uncle's leg for support, for proof he was really there. The loss hurt her all over again. The loss of a friend, of a mentor. "Why didn't you practice what you preached, Ravi uncle?"

"I only studied the Vedas because my parents told me to. I never actually absorbed them until it was too late." Ravi uncle rubbed her back. "I was blinded by status. I thought birth was all I needed. Being twice-born pushed me over the edge. You deserved a better teacher."

Nayla whimpered against his leg. "I want you."

"The Titans quit their racket." Ravi uncle observed the door. "Come on. I'll show you how to operate the crane. Come on, child. There is still time for one lesson."

He roused Nayla to her feet. She wiped her face as he ascended the ladder. Following, she grabbed the same rung she did when she had caused the accident and let Ravi uncle show her the controls.

"Side to side. Up and down. The clock is to gauge the Titans' downtime before they build their human pyramid." Ravi uncle lifted the door from gateway three. "My gut tells me they're going back to number one. Why? Because it's connected to the entire universe. Brahman." He moved the crane accordingly. "Do you want to try?"

"I could never. They'd escape. I was only able to connect once."

"You are always connected. You just don't know it." Ravi uncle turned to her. "Please Nayla, I could use some relief."

"I sort of have prior engagements."

"How about for an hour? I'll take any rest you afford me. I would ask Naem, but he's at his flat, and I have no way to reach him."

"Baba is here?" Nayla nearly lost grip.

"Ja, though I believe containing the Titans should take precedence, don't you? If only I had the whole Blast to help me."

She had torn herself to ribbons thinking about Ravi uncle's death. How it could've been avoided. What she could've done differently. Namely, if she'd kept her mouth shut regarding Baba's whereabouts and not confronted Ravi uncle while he was operating heavy machinery. Now, here was Ravi uncle before her, asking for forgiveness and help. She needed forgiveness and help. But he said none of it was her fault. Why did her conscience not believe him? Why must she beat herself up? And what a thrashing! Maybe if she helped, it would lighten the blows.

"I will help," said Nayla. "But I don't trust myself to play a guessing game. I require an assistant."

"Nayla, we're the only ones here."

She unscrewed her cap. The pollen traveled to the floor and went poof.

Céleste looked around, hands on her hips. "This is no ziggurat I've ever seen."

"But you've never seen a ziggurat," Nayla said sheepishly.

"True." Céleste looked at her hand. "Hein? My skin is back. What's going on?"

"We're out of the sun. Remember how I mentioned Ravi uncle? He needs my help for an hour."

Céleste squinted. "For a repetitive task?"

"Ja, but there is some variation and a goal."

"Which is?"

Nayla pointed at the hearth. "Keep the Titans in their cell."

Céleste's mouth fell open. "The Titans? The ones that fought Zeus? The ones he locked in Tartarus? Those Titans?"

"Ja, from the Titanomachy. Those Titans."

Bangs and roars sounded from behind the first door. Céleste hopped to a fighting stance and raised her palms while Nayla explained the situation.

"Are you ready?" asked Ravi uncle.

"Non, she's not ready," said Céleste. "Nay, it's one thing to feel sorry for the role you played in Ravi's death. It's another to take responsibility for his actions and give your life away in the process. He's going to leave us in the lurch just like Atlas did for Hercules when Hercules offered to hold up the heavens."

"I promise I won't leave," said Ravi uncle. "I only wish to lay me down for an hour."

Céleste poofed and raced at him in pollen form.

"Don't hurt him!" said Nayla.

Céleste's molecules entered his mouth and emerged from his nose. Poof. She reappeared below. "He's human. Or close to it. I sensed other energies inside of him."

"Other energies?" asked Ravi uncle, dumbfounded.

"Oui, it was strange. It's all I can describe. I felt no demons."

"See," said Nayla, "we can help him."

"We should be helping you and Gustave!" Céleste shouted over a loud bang.

"Why is it all right that you can help others, and I can't?" asked Nayla.

"I save others because I can't save myself," said Céleste. "I understand the picture. Maybe a part of me thought I never could save myself. My soul was so distant that it felt hopeless at times. Now I *know* it is. Five years to figure out the problem was me, eh?"

"Sadly, you get used to it," said Nayla, "but it does not answer my question."

"You care what others think about you. That's the answer."

"Don't you?"

"The voice in the void is so distracting, I don't have time to care what others think. I'm too busy trying to fill it."

"But if it were not for other people to compare ourselves to, how would we know who we are?"

"Quite right." Céleste wiped her sweat. "It's how I know they are whole-people, and we are half. You are too nice. It's a cheap way to force a connection in hopes they will like you and you'll feel valued. But, daub yourself with honey, you'll be covered with flies."

"Who cares what I do?"

"Me. Because you have a soul, Nayla. Be thankful you have a body to put it in. Why try to lose yourself in Brahman?"

"To make the pain go away!" Nayla shed a tear, fighting the urge to burst into flames.

"Then why are we here?"

"Because I wanted to see if Ravi uncle was all right. He's Kameera's baba, and I thought he was dead because of me. Are you happy?"

"I find," said Ravi uncle, maneuvering out of his chair, "activity is often the best medicine." He traded places with Nayla on the ladder, and she took the controls.

"Great, we're committed." Céleste exhaled, drenched in sweat. "What do you need?"

Nayla pointed at the hearth. "Peek into one of those holes. Tell me where the Titans are assembling." She raised the lever to lift the door from gateway one. "And don't poof down inside. You'll lose your powers."

Céleste stole a glance in gateway four and withdrew to the crane's ladder. "They saw me. They're gathering at four."

"Four, sehr gut." She slid the lever to the right, moving the crane on the overhead track.

Céleste turned to Ravi uncle. "What did you say to guilt trip her into this?"

"No guilt. I asked for a break."

Nayla pulled the lever toward her, lowering the door into the slot. She leaned over the edge of the platform.

Ravi uncle had descended and was observing the goings on from a seated position on the back wall, no different from how she had seen Hyperion.

"He didn't have to guilt me," said Nayla. "The guilt was already there."

Loud bangs broke her string of thought. She waited for them to stop.

"Cél, take another peek."

Hesitantly, Céleste approached gate one and withdrew. "They didn't see me. They're gathering at three."

Nayla raised the gate from four and craned it to three. The door hovered over the gateway. Something felt wrong. The smooth stick on the controls lingered in her hand.

"Ravi uncle, I think they're tricking me. I don't think it's three."

"Coeus is the god of intellect and oracle," said Ravi uncle. "If Céleste can see him when she pokes her head in, he can see her. He can out-predict you with what minuscule powers he retains. However, if you can intuit his attempts, rather than predict them by having Céleste stick her head in, nothing in the material world can throw you off your hunch, and his powers are neutralized."

"Céleste," Nayla ordered, "take another look."

"Wait." Ravi uncle held up his hand. "Let her choose."

"These guys can trash the universe," said Céleste.

"Let her choose."

"I'm scared." Nayla jiggled the stick. "I can't trust my intuition without seeing how it will play out."

Ravi uncle looked up at her. "Your intuition protects you in the future by listening to it now."

Some inner voice screamed in her head like a wounded animal.

"What gate, Nayla?" asked Ravi uncle. "What's that ember buried deep in your gut tell you?"

"It says zwei. Two."

"Listen to it. Fan it into a flame. Something Naem never taught you to do. He was too busy calling you stupid and slapping you around. Setting expectations for you he could never reach himself. That's why Kameera befriended you, that's why she played violin so well, that's why she married the right man. Intuition. I never wanted to send her to violin lessons. It was too expensive. She begged and pleaded. She listened to her intuition to reach the end, while I disobeyed mine to find the means. Her intuition told her to give you the money to invent mecha-sleeves, and I should've let it be. I should've used my intuition to realize Kameera and Pradeep's love for each other would see them through any difficult times, and to rely solely on Brahman. Zwei, Nayla, zwei!"

Nayla's fist cruised the door over to gateway two and let it sink into place.

She stared at the hearth. Céleste held out her palms at the open gates. Ravi uncle shut his eyes, poised.

A Titan pummeled the door, roaring bloody murder, inspiring a sigh of relief.

Céleste lowered her weapons.

Nayla sat back in her chair.

All the times she failed to listen to that little voice pounded in her chest in unison with the door. *Don't drink too much. Dismount Ganesha with two hands. Don't shout compromising things in restaurants. Tell Céleste you're going to the Blast. Tell her not to sleep with Hermes. Accept the maang teeka without being so bashful. Run away from Jacoma. Baba is bad news.*

"You see," said Ravi uncle, "when you don't listen to your intuition, my dear, the Titans will come for us."

"So easy to think, so hard to do."

"It does take some practice." Ravi sat back down. "Would you like to try again?"

"To what end?" asked Céleste. "The system is broken."

"Would you like to give it a whirl?" asked Ravi uncle.

"Where can we get more doors?" Céleste asked.

"There's only the one. Hephaestus built it."

"Céleste," said Nayla, "repetition is good if it works toward improving a skill."

"It gives me anxiety," said Céleste. "There has to be another way." She looked pointedly at Ravi uncle. "You're not responsible for the Titan's prison. Zeus is. When the system fails, he can design a new one. What were you told when they hired you?"

"Intuition is the key to your release," said Ravi uncle.

"Release from what?" asked Nayla.

The pounding stopped.

"It's time to choose again," Nayla continued. "Quick, what do I do?"

"Release from fear," said Céleste. "Intuition is the key to your release from fear."

Nayla hated to ask. "What are you suggesting?"

"Ruh-," said Céleste, tremulous, petting her hands. "release the Titans. Chuh-choose no door."

"Ravi uncle?" asked Nayla, hoping for the voice of reason.

"Um." He licked his lips. "What does your intuition tell you?"

"It tells me the underworld has made you both crazy." Nayla leaned forward. "Céleste, there are five Titans down there."

"I saw."

"If we fight them, we die."

"I know."

"If Zeus shows up, he'll ask what we're doing in Tartarus."

"Vacation."

"This is verrückt," said Nayla. "I know you're a little new to thinking you were born a half-person." She wasn't, as a Vaishya, but that was neither here nor there. "Take it from me, the death wish won't solve your problems." She closed her eyes. *Do it, Nayla. Tell her.* "I tried to kill myself jumping into a hearth. Hestia saved me. That's when I was offered my mixis. She intervened during my suicide. In spite of all my suffering, I am glad she did."

"Why would you try to do that?" asked Céleste.

"To solve my problems. Do you hate me?"

Céleste spluttered her lips. "I don't think less of you, Nay, really. But you said you wanted to help Ravi. Well, I want to help you, and something tells me this is the way. By following intuition and facing our fears." Her voice waivered. "I looked Théo right in his cold dead eyes."

"Focus." Ravi uncle scolded. "What does your intuition tell you, Nayla? Is there an ember?"

Release the Titans...? Let the system fail...? She dragged her hand through the ashes of her mind, layered by karma, and burned herself on something hot. She inspected her palm. The skin was red. A blister formed. In the ashes lay an ember. Ravi uncle had been at this a long time with moderate success. His intuition got the job done, but the system was bare bones. Céleste appeared to be right. Fear kept the Titans in the hearth.

When the prison guard is afraid, it's time to get a new prison. Nayla, you are going to die.

She raised the door from gateway two and let it hang. Her wings eased out, and she sailed to the soot floor.

"Zut alors! This is happening." Céleste raised her palms.

"Get behind us, Ravi uncle." Nayla's heart thundered in her rib cage.

Ravi uncle braced himself against the back wall.

"Nay," said Céleste, "could they be the reason Zeus locked up the fabled objects? To keep the objects from them? Did he fear a jailbreak?"

"With one door on the prison, he should have," said Nayla. "The hall is more secure." She aimed her fist at the openings.

Céleste looked back at Ravi uncle. "Do the Titans have any weak points?"

"Before Atlas was condemned to bear the heavens, they were propped up by the four pillars: Hyperion, god of sun and observation; Iapetus, craftsmanship and mortality; Crius, god of constellations; and Coeus, god of intellect. When they rebelled against their father Ouranos, these Titans held him down while their brother Cronus castrated him with a scythe. Make of that what you will."

Nayla glanced back. Ravi uncle had soiled his pants. Tartarus had inflicted enough pain on this poor man. She hoped she made the right call. Doubts flooded her mind. What if her intuition was wrong?

"Nay," said Céleste, "we can offer Cronus his scythe from the hall for his revenge on Zeus."

"Is that a good idea?"

"He put a single door on a four-door cell."

A bearded man with gold earrings reared his head in the slot. Cronus, Titan god of time.

"Sweet Shiva, help me." Nayla unleashed the heat.

He stepped through the portal shirtless, broad chested and with boulders for deltoids. He moved slowly, with all the time in the world, a being who owned the space he occupied. Nayla hit him full blast.

Céleste sidestepped in the corner of her eye to avoid being scorched, aiming her cannons at the next Titan through the gate. Crius.

He stepped through in a dhoti kurta, a blue dhoti around his waist and a black kurta dotted with sequins that stretched to his knees. These men were as big as houses, twice her height.

Céleste unloaded her shrieking stars at the tall god, a blend of yellow novas and blue zippy protos. Crius laughed as he collected them all in a blue map of light.

"Shooting stars at the god of constellations?" Crius inspected the glowing orbs and turned to his brother. "These look like they are from your daughter Asteria, Coeus."

Coeus climbed from the gate in a Persian tunic and dhoti, layered with a vest scalloped in gems, partially covered by his long, curled beard. "Fascinating." He looked at Céleste. "It's not her."

"Shame." Crius cast the net of stars at her, bombarding her with explosions.

Céleste went poof. The walls rumbled. Bengal fire everywhere.

Nayla struck a firm stance, spraying flame at Cronus. His beefy arm reached through the fires and seized her by the wrist. The flame cut out.

"So young, so delicate," said Cronus.

Something was happening. Her skin wilted like a flower. Her braid turned gray against her leg. She knifed out her wings, spun and slapped him loose. She soared up to the crane scaffolding that bisected the bay and refocused, feeling like she got ran over by a horse.

He had aged her. Bad. Tears ran the gamut of her face. Things that once seemed unimportant or sidelined glittered like diamonds from a life not lived—a Gandharva marriage, inventing new machines, seeing Kameera—and worst of all—Her time to find Brahman was more limited than ever.

Cronus had wasted her life. *He must pay!*

Planting her shoes, she felt the metal with her wrinkled feet through the holes in her boots and aimed her pruny fist at the Titan.

Iapetus made his entrance in a tattered, earth-tone caftan, keffiyeh and shawl.

Hyperion emerged wearing a Baju Melayu—a long-sleeved top, a skirt, and trousers. Black locks of hair twisted down from his fez-like cap. Golden fibers surged across his rippling chest beneath his shirt and outlined his abdomen. His entire body glowed, his silhouette a corona like the sun.

Céleste poofed beside her on the track. "Any sign of Zeus?"

"Nein." Her voice was ground to dust.

"Nay, is that you? It looks like you're seventy years old."

She dared not see a mirror. "Don't let Cronus touch you." She looked down at Ravi uncle, unattended, convulsing on the floor. "Ravi uncle!"

The room flashed white. Hyperion stood between Nayla and Céleste, a hand on each of their wrists. Nayla tried to wrench it loose. Céleste poofed free.

"Fascinating." Coeus studied the pink swirls and took a whiff. "Pollen. She is pollen. I know what attracts pollen. Bees. By use of static electricity. The sun also carries an electric field. Hyperion."

Hyperion snapped his fingers. The electric current shocked Nayla as Céleste's pollen clung to his arm.

Nayla's whole body tingled. Her muscles went rigid. She couldn't move her face, her limbs. She could only look and listen.

"You've caught some live ones," said Iapetus. "They're too good for instant death. Throw them in the hearth and let time run its course."

"Nay—Nayla!" cried Ravi uncle. He lay in the fetal position before the behemoth that was Cronus. "Say you forgive me! For—putting—you through the—pain—of my—death."

"I—" Nayla shook in place. "I—forgive you."

Ravi uncle closed his eyes at peace. His skin turned gray. What was wrong with him? Cronus had not touched him. Suddenly, Ravi uncle exploded in size, growing twice the height and width of the Titans. Dozens of arms surged from his torso, launching them at the gods like darting snakes, forcing their bodies into the hearth. In went Iapetus, Crius, and Coeus. Gate one, gate two, gate three.

"Good Gaia," said Hyperion. "He's a Hecatoncheires."

In a flash of light, Hyperion returned to the floor and climbed back into the hearth of his own free will.

Céleste poofed back onto the scaffold, holding her temples.

Scores of arms shot from Ravi uncle's body. One hundred of them. Heads emerged to keep his head company. Fifty of them in total.

Using four of his limbs, he held each of Cronus's and raised him like a rag doll up to the track. Why did Cronus not age Ravi uncle to free himself?

Oho! Time could not age the dead.

"Turn her back," commanded Ravi uncle, letting one of Cronus's arms free. "Every last year that is owed her."

Cronos begrudgingly reached out and touched Nayla on the arm.

Vitality surged through her body.

She looked to Céleste. "Am I?"

"Twenty. Oui."

Nayla smiled, weeping, patting her smooth face, blessed with opportunity and time to find Brahman. She'd be grateful for a life in a hovel after this, living in oneness.

Ravi uncle grabbed Cronus, plunked him back into the hearth, and lowered the door by hand. "Now it is them who fear choosing the wrong gate."

The other heads, other faces... Nayla recognized one from a daguerreotype. It was Khakhar. *These are the men who died on the job.*

"I wish to grant you a gift." Ravi uncle offered two palms for Nayla and Céleste to step onto. "A trip to see Naem." He popped open a hatch to a large pipe sprawling across the side wall. It was an oil pipe.

"C'est pas vrai! I'm not going in there."

"I don't think we have a choice," said Nayla.

"It would be foolish not to accept a gift of thanks," said Ravi uncle in a guttural voice.

"Danke," said Nayla, unsure.

Ravi uncle plonked her into the dark tunnel of warm liquid, then Céleste, and closed the hatch.

Total darkness.

"I'm very grateful our hunches paid off," said Céleste in the echoey pipe, "but I think that transformation affected his brain."

It reeked of oil.

"Don't light a flare," said Nayla.

"Don't strike a match."

Nayla wanted to see Baba, though she was frightened of what he may have changed into. The scary part would be if he hadn't changed at all.

"You hear that faint rushing sound?" asked Céleste. "What is that?"

"Pressure."

IMPRESSION, THÉO

I am nothing, I am nothing, I am nothing.

Vraiment? Now? Could she not even lie in an oil pipe scared out of her wits in peace? What about glory in a job well done? Releasing the Titans worked and she barely had time to enjoy it. After all she had been through. She was this much closer to Gustave and she wasn't getting in her own way for once! Why did the voice have to ruin everything!? That was it. The voice. It wasn't her getting in her own way. It was the voice!

Something pristine had been marred—and not her skin dyed black from the oil. Merde! It was bad as the Styx. Non— It was she herself, her person marred when her diamond was taken from its vault. Trying to replace it with cheap substitutes had only marred her further. To think she had been immortal, found love as a half-person merely by the act of making love. The voice had put her to it! So much for immortality!

This oil was a lapping blanket. What a fine time to contemplate. The vapors made her stupid! Lost her marbles! A crayfish in the pie! The voice had led her here so she could blame her train of thought on both vapors and voice.

If she didn't find love with Antoine, what had she found? Excitement? Passion? Fun? All fleeting. Replaced by pain. Of being smothered. Of being alone. Of the inability to find a husband that spoke to her soul. If it was not love she found in Antoine, or in Charon, what was this merging? Hate? Fear? Emptiness? All three! Clouded over in a rose-tinted fog. She needed something stable. Everlasting. Her soul. Perhaps it would lead to something more. Divine love, like the kind Nayla had experienced.

I-I am nothing, I-I am-am nothing, I-I am-am no-nothing.

One of the voices slipped. The husky baritone, like honey dripping on sandpaper. Théo! *See, his role in the choir made sense.* He must've thought she was nothing, for him and Gergely to have stolen her soul. The connection was already loose, the vault door ajar, effectively a thief magnet. Is that why looking at Théo had mixed up the choir?

Oh la vache! It stank like rancid eggs.

Perhaps some kind of auditory anamoly. Monsieur Desormes had once demonstrated that he could put his foot on the sustain pedal to open up the strings on a piano, have her strike a key on a second piano, and observe the same string on the first piano resonating without Desormes having touched it. He called it sympathetic vibration.

The river of blurping oil grew louder from behind.

Don't lose that thought!

Théo. He had a soul-cave too, his soul having long departed before he had. Locking eyes must've struck a key. Did his voice in the void fall out of joint like hers? And who made up his voice? His barman? The freckled lady? Perhaps he never got a chance to hear it. Or he listened too well and ushered the demon in to take the voice's place.

Voices in her head, mon Dieu! She really did belong in Salpêtrière. She'd take a white coat over a black drain. *Mother of God. Here it comes!*

CBABA'S VANIIAS

fountain of oil shot Nayla into the piping. Oil rushed at her exposed feet and filled her boots, the flume lubricating her butt and back as it propelled her forward in the dark, soaking her clothes and playing with her senses. The stench was unbearable.

Céleste shouted from behind, her voice echoing in the tunnel. Nayla's feet could slam into a wall or a kink in the system, but she trusted Ravi uncle would not endanger her and hoped Céleste was wrong, and the transformation had not affected his mental faculties.

The tunnel descended into a drop. Nayla's heart lifted. She tried running her hands on the ceiling, but there was nothing to hold onto. The best thing was to keep her hands tucked in. Her body dipped into a trough so fast it felt like flying. Up she rose, high onto a crest. Blood rushed to her brain as her feet functioned like the prow of ship, splashing oil into her nose, eyes, and face.

She spat sour oil as she luged down the next hill. A sudden jerk turned her body to the left. Red sunlight beamed through the flits of a grate on the ceiling. She was sliding on a wall into a whirlpool. Funnel. She was in a funnel as tall as the ziggurat.

Around the drain she fled. She couldn't risk turning without throwing herself out of the current.

"Don't struggle." She coughed. "Or you'll fall."

"Oui!" said Céleste.

Nayla slid faster the closer she got to the drain, keeping perfectly still, a human canoe, until the drainpipe sucked her in.

"Boah!"

She plummeted through all three meters of the funnel's neck, went airborne, and crashed down into a tank. The oil engulfed her. The force siphoned her toward the bottom. Her hands ploughed the black mass in butterfly strokes. Thickly, she surfaced. The stuff was worse than paint. She risked irritating her eyes and stole a peek.

Men in dhotis and tunics awaited her at the tank's rim on a catwalk. She closed her eyes and swam until she reached the edge, where they salvaged her from the unpleasant fuel.

"How did they get in there?" said a voice that pierced her heart. "Get them cleaned up."

Hands proceeded to towel her off. Sight. She could see. Blurry, clear. A man stood with exposed facial muscles transfigured by shafts of sun from the skylight.

"Baba?" she asked.

"Nayla? Is that you?" Baba was neatly trimmed, wearing a white Bandhgala suit.

"Ja, Baba!"

"Nayla!"

Her feet left the ground as Baba lifted her into his arms, his face and hands fibrous.

"It's you? It's really you? Are you dead?"

"Nein, Baba." She hugged him tight, a tear in her smudgy face. "Nein." She stepped back. Her oily clothes had ruined Baba's suit, though he waved away her reaction.

"Do not worry, my daughter." He stepped out of the sun, restoring the appearance of his flesh. "You are more important than fancy threads."

"Listen Baba, it's my fault you're here. I was the one who told Ravi uncle where to find you. Kameera had given me the money to buy parts for the mecha-sleeves, and Ravi uncle wanted it back because Kameera was having a baby and Pradeep's job prospects were not good and Ravi uncle was a gambler, and I'm so sorry. Don't hate me!"

"Hate you?" said Baba. "Nayla binti Azmi. I flicked the lighter. I blew myself up. I chose to continue my homemade distillery in spite of our excellent loan. I didn't believe we could do it, but I was wrong. Look what I have accomplished." He gestured his hand across the railing overlooking the factory.

Lathes spun fast to carve cylinders to build pistons. Seamstresses threaded needles to make tunics. Blacksmiths hammered hot metal into boiler shells. Cobblers stenciled shapes onto lengths of boot leather. Glovemakers sewed on the metal buttons that controlled steam flow and water cooling into each units' thumbs. Pipe fitters, wire makers, glassblowers for goggle lenses—Baba had it all.

He had done it. And he was Old Baba again! Thank Vishnu, he'd returned!

Baba tended to Céleste, who was busy wringing oil from her hair. "And who might you be?"

"Céleste Marchand." She extended a black hand.

"I am Naem bin Azmi."

"Enchanté."

"A French woman," Baba exclaimed, looking at Nayla. "My wife was French. She was a dancer."

"So am I."

"Boah, a belly dancer?"

"Ballet."

"We almost went three for three."

"Have you seen Maman?" asked Nayla.

"Not since she died, Es tut mir Leid." Baba gestured to the chrome steps. "Come. I will show you the production line. I have become a real titan of industry."

"I'd love to," said Nayla, while Céleste scolded her with her eyes.

"Gustave," Céleste muttered.

"We won't stay long," said Nayla. Though she could stay forever.

Baba had realized their dream.

She followed him down the textured metal stairs while Céleste spoke in a low voice.

"I've got a way to save Gustave," she said. "Circe's staff. I will transform him into a nouveau satyre."

Circe. The sorceress who'd transformed Odysseus's men into pigs.

"If a transformation can save Ravi's life," Céleste continued, "why not Gustave's too?"

Nayla didn't think Gustave would approve, but she didn't want to hurt Céleste's feelings, so she said, "Ja, that could work."

A wing of the factory had been allocated for testing. A man in mecha-sleeves and goggles pushed a coal car on a section of rail with a stopper at the end. Another man took notes. Dozens of mecha-sleeves hung on a row of mannequins, ready for packaging. Boxes were raised by crane onto cantilevers for storage.

"Brilliant, is it not?" asked Baba. "I am charging one thousand marks a pair. Orders come in daily from across Europe. But there is no one more deserving of a free pair than you." He snapped his fingers.

Quickly, two attendants were at Nayla's side before she could comment, harnessing her into the device.

"Remove the coal compartment," said Baba. "She doesn't need it."

When the buckles were secured around her torso, one of the men took a ratchet and unbolted the extraneous coal tray, while another strapped the piston drills to her legs. When that was accomplished, the men had her sit and slid on her boots.

"Get a feel of the new and improved gear," said Baba.

Gold and silver, those delicate hoops rotated within the glass chest plate. Her bulky gears were a thing of history.

"It feels amazing. But removing the heat source—Baba, how did you know I'm a nymph?" Nayla lowered her gauntlets.

"Dyaus told me when he loaned me the lost ten thousand marks."

Nayla whispered to a confused Céleste, "It's the Hindu version of Zeus. More or less."

"Ah."

The whistle blew. Workers switched off machines and un-buckled their mecha-sleeves.

"Super," said Baba. "Quitting time."

Céleste's stomach rumbled. They had not eaten since de-parting Charon's boat.

"Baba, my friend and I have traveled a long way. We are hungry."

"Come then." Baba pointed to a door framed by a golden tree. "I have built the factory right into our palace. Tonight, we celebrate."

Baba led the parade to the door. A servant opened it for them into a durbar hall, a court fit for a king, bearing her multifoil arches and a massively long table, spread with steak kabobs and fine wine. Servants in tunics ran about the house. One mammoth door had a Bengal tiger imprinted on it, maybe leading to another part of the palace.

Something metal on four legs darted at her. He threw his paws on her thighs and barked through a phonograph horn within his throat. Gold hoops whirred inside his frame. Fans whizzed. Steam hissed. His tail spring wagged.

"Salut, garçon." Céleste pet the creature. "What's his name?"

"Sparky," Baba supplied.

Nayla picked up a wrench off a table and chucked it across the spacious hall. It clanged off the tile. Sparky skittered off to fetch. The sound launched her back to the time Baba had pushed her against the ice box and the whole set clattered. He'd sold them for whiskey she had thought. But they were here before her on the table with all his other tools. Vise-grips. Screwdrivers. His hand drill. They'd all returned, laid out on display. All the sockets, every wrench size.

"I regret ever having pawned them," said Baba.

Nayla was so occupied by the tools she nearly missed the skull, staring at her from the table's edge.

"Baba, whose skull is that?"

"Mine." Baba touched her on the shoulders. "Come, we shall eat. I am absolutely gluttonous." Eagerly, he moved to the head of the table.

Nayla lingered at the skull, trying to ignore it as it intruded on the reunion, stressing the brevity of life, reigniting the explosion in her mind that rocked her tenement—Baba lying dead on the sidewalk, flames consuming his body in the crematorium. Until this moment, she almost forgot she was in hell. Céleste rubbed Nayla's arm, drawing her back into Baba's hospitality.

Nayla took her place on his right, Céleste on his left.

The servants posted around the room like well-disciplined soldiers.

Baba raised a glass. "I dedicate this feast to you, my long-lost daughter. With you at my side, we can accomplish anything."

Nayla savored every moment, the timbre of Baba's voice, the silky table cloth, the cold stem of wine in her hands.

"Prost!" said Baba.

"Prost!" Nayla smiled and drank.

It tasted heavenly.

Baba brought the wineglass to his lips and tilted the stem. The red liquid receded further into the glass, against the law of gravity. Nayla's head turned sideways. How was that possible? She sipped without a problem and set her glass on the table, unsure of what to make of it. The wine tasted like wine. She did not repel hers.

Baba lowered his glass, coughed nervously, and tried again, tilting it until the bottom was at its zenith. The wine remained in the glass, upside down, defying all reason.

"The dunk tank at de L'Enfer," Céleste whispered.

Baba smashed the cursed glass on the floor.

Nayla jumped at the shatter.

Quickly, Baba picked up a kabob and raised it to his mouth for a bite. The beef tip faded into thin air. When he moved the skewer away, the meat reappeared.

"Tantalus," Nayla whispered.

Baba threw his arms on the table, fell to his knees, and let out an agonizing cry.

"Baba, what's wrong? What's happening?"

"I cannot eat." He bawled. "I cannot drink. I thought if you returned, it would work, that I would slake my thirst and satisfy my hunger." He struggled to his feet and poured her another glass from the bottle. "Drink for me, and I will drink vicariously through you."

She felt his warm hands grab hers and close them over the wine glass. Together, she raised the glass to her lips. He did not release until she sipped. The wine went down as it should.

"I feel nothing," said Baba. "Try again."

Wanting to help, Nayla drained the glass.

"Nothing," said Baba.

"Why have the gods punished you, Baba?"

He threw his arms back on the table and buried himself, whimpering. "Because I fed you to them."

"Fed me to them?" Nayla looked quizzically at Céleste, who shrugged and ate her beef before she starved. Nayla looked back at Baba. "I don't understand."

He raised his head amid his convulsions. "Hephaestus, Hestia, Coronis, Hecate." His nose leaked as he spoke. "My actions drove you into their hands."

"Baba..." How did one tell her own father she had almost ended her life? "...after you died... I didn't have anyone. At the Blast... I was going to pitch myself..."

"I know, Nayla."

"Am I so unlovable, as you often told me?"

"Oh, daughter, I'd take it all back if I could."

If she wasn't a Shudra, he may as well have added.

"Being a nymph isn't so bad." She tried to think positively. "If it weren't for you getting the idea for the mecha-sleeves, I would never have completed them. The gods were impressed with our invention. That's why they saved me from the hearth fires."

"An event that led you to the underworld with me," said Baba. "It appears karma isn't done with us yet. It has forced us into these repetitive tasks."

"Repetitive?" asked Nayla.

"We are in Tartarus. That is what we do. But one day. One day!" Baba rose from the table. "If we work harder tomorrow, really put our noses to the grindstone, I will eat and drink in celebration." He offered his hand. "I ask you as a father. Will you help me?"

Céleste eyed Nayla and mouthed, *Non*.

But how could Nayla abandon Baba? Not again. Never again. Maybe if they tried something like they did for Ravi uncle. Let the factory fall to shambles. Do the opposite. Decide the extreme. She remembered an old mantra that might've explained the predicament, and this one wasn't from the Vedas.

"Baba," said Nayla, "you are what you eat. That is why you cannot eat. You cannot eat like a wealthy man, because you did not become a wealthy man, because you did not think like a wealthy man. You chose to continue the distillery, remember? Zeus has forced you to relive the success of a factory owner over and over without indulging in the fruits of your labor."

She was having serious doubts if Baba could've ever pulled off the achievement in Jacoma—Old Baba or drunk Baba. He was penny wise and pound foolish.

"If we do a bad job at the factory tomorrow," said Nayla, "your wealth will match your labor, and you can eat again."

"Give up all that money?" asked Baba. "Are you verrückt?"

"What good is the money if you can't enjoy it?"

"If I slack off, I will be destitute and go hungry. It is impossible. I cannot." Baba was so enamored by gold, he could not see. "I wish for you to go."

"Nein, Baba, I can help you." Nayla walked to his side.

"You are in Tartarus." Baba slid his chair into the window light. "Look at us." He touched his mask of tissues and cartilage. "You are bound to your own repetitive task as I am mine."

Nayla pondered on this. She and Céleste were not assigned any task other than to retrieve the caduceus and the Cap of Hades. She only helped Kameera get water and Ravi uncle guard the Titans and... *Scheisse!* Was she doomed to the repetitive task of having these encounters? Would she start back at Kameera at the end of this?

"Baba," said Nayla, "come with me. I am trying to get to the ziggurat. We can find an object to rescue you."

"Nay," Céleste interrupted, "you're sweating."

"So I am." Nayla willed her body temperature to increase. The sweat remained. "Are my eyes changing color?"

"Non."

"How about my hair?" Nayla picked up her braid.

"Non."

"Scheisse." Nayla dropped it. "I've burned out."

The revelation frightened her. To be powerless in the underworld, to lose her fire power in the depths of hell of all places. How would she fly to the ziggurat? Fight Arachne? Escape the desert? What was she to do?

"You see, it is you who need rescuing," said Baba. He snapped for an attendant to fetched the missing coal compartment.

When the coveralled man returned, Baba got up and reattached the heat source himself.

"Take the mecha-sleeves, and take Sparky," said Baba. "He will keep you on course. I failed the first lifetime. Do not make me a failure in the second." His lips touched her forehead—a wunderbar feeling, but nowhere near as blissful as samadhi. "Go!"

Sparky barked wildly, choking on bolts, and ran for the Bengal tiger door.

Nayla stared at Baba, hesitating.

Céleste grabbed Nayla's hand and tore after the metal dog.

IMPRESSION, PAPA

Sparky ran into the street, electricity bursting from its tail, past a woman with rubies for eyes selling jewelry, splaying necklaces with her machine hands.

"Little Zwergpinscher is fast," said Nayla. "We'll never catch him."

"Sparky, arrête!" Céleste shouted.

He stopped outside of a tea shop and looked back, waiting. Sparky was more rambunctious than Nougat, and Nayla couldn't run with her clock suit.

I am nothing, I am nothing, I-I am no-nothing.

Even with all the cranks and belts and rotors clanking around, she could still hear the penetrating voice clear as day. Was that last utterance smoke coming out of that donkey's mouth? Non, it was a member of her choir out of rhythm. The voice, light. Faint. Feathery.

I-I am-am noth-no-thing.

Papa?

Was that how Papa felt about her—that she was nothing? She had tried to make him proud with her love for dance, in spite of her soul being gone. It wasn't fair. He rarely spent time at home and when he did, he blended into the scenery, a place where he had no control. The only way she was able to bond with him was to go where he went to escape—The Folies Bergère, a place where he could control everything. He was Harlequin from the commedia dell'arte changing the setting with his magical batte whenever he saw conflict.

I am-am noth-thing-thing.

Was Papa referring to himself—that he was nothing?

He'd thrown her to the wolves—Berthe and Théo—to avoid conflict. Oui, perhaps he felt he was nothing. Was he taking ownership for the Incident? Humbling himself beneath the avalanche of shame that came with that responsibility? Did she want him to take responsibility? The voice was in her head, après tout.

She just wanted Papa to protect her. A man she could count on in times of trouble. A man who knew his worth and loved himself and said I love you.

Papa did not feel worthy of the money he earned, much like Nayla's baba, but he needed something to feed Berthe's gambling addiction and he wasn't going to put his foot down. Too much conflict.

Did he ever stop to ask why he can't enjoy life? Did Papa know he was a half-person? A member of the demi-gens? Did he go into marriage knowing he would father a half-person for a child no matter who Maman gave birth to? Did he not care? Was having a child something he did because he saw others do? He never mentioned the subject, so who was to know? It appeared there was no forethought. As a baby she was a shiny new object cast aside when she grew old enough to speak. When it came to the hard work of parenting, he cared not.

What had he seen in Maman? Did her rage bring out the green in her eyes? Oui, perhaps he liked the way she expressed emotions he was too ashamed to accept in himself. Maman had given him the job of soother, like Céleste had given Antoine, and look how that turned out. Papa could not sooth himself. He swept his problems under a rug until the rug was too lumpy to walk on. Try as he might to neglect his own rage, he could not neglect it indefinitely. Maman had a knack for bringing it out of him.

Poor Papa. All that shouting. Her poor neighbors.

Thinking of this made her angry, sad, and confused.

She didn't come from a healthy family, though she had so wanted a healthy family to come from her.

Sparky coughed up grease as he barked, happy to meet her, and ran ahead again.

XENIA

His joints purred as the pistons carried his legs through the streets of Tartarus.

"Sparky, halt," called Nayla, out of breath. "I can't keep up."

If only she could fly and hadn't drank so much.

"You all right?" asked Nayla. "It looks like you had something on your mind."

"I was thinking about Papa. Forget it." Céleste jogged beside her.

"What about him?"

Céleste eyed her. "Remember how my voice in the void is a group of voices that speak as one?"

"Ja."

"Ever since facing Théo, I can hear them individually. One is Mariquita, one Théo, and one Papa. There is a soprano, likely Berthe. And then there is mine, tying them all together. What do you make of that?"

"People who were supposed to love you saying you are nothing?"

"Mariquita loves me. Papa and Berthe are debatable, Théo is a definite non, but oui, that's the gist."

Nayla thought a moment, slowing to a crawl, keeping sight of the dog.

"They're perceptions of yourself through their eyes."

"False perceptions?" Céleste came to a standstill, hope in her voice.

"Maybe for Mariquita's, but I don't know. If a lie is repeated long enough, it can become true to the mind. In other words, it's your perception of their perceptions of you."

"So, if Mariquita were to say, I am nothing?"

"From the sound of it, she never gave up on you. The statement does not jive with her actions."

"And when Berthe tells me she loves me...?"

"None of it was backed up in deed or spirit." Nayla watched Sparky race around a coffee vendor. "You cannot give love without having it."

Céleste stared at the red dust in her toes and looked up. "How are we going to fight Arachne?"

"You'll have to do it." Nayla picked up the pace. "Go poof, sneak past her and go straight for the hall. I'll hang back in the shadows. Then you come out with Circe's staff and transform her."

"What about the cap?" asked Céleste. "The objects are enchanted. I can only choose one."

"I don't know."

Silvery threads of gears spun in the buildings, powering a conveyor belt on the sidewalk. The dog crossed onto the belt and sat. Nayla stepped onto the free ride and paused to rest.

"Where's the Min Pin taking us?" asked Céleste, close at hand.

"The train station, it appears." Nayla looked down the thoroughfare of pulleys and dynamos and steam valves. "It's at the end of this street in Jacoma. The tracks run into the desert, a kilometer from the ziggurat. We'll hop off there."

"He's barking at something."

Sparky had walked off the conveyor and was yelping at the entrance to a cabaret. Not a cabaret. The cantina.

Nayla followed him under the tent.

"Is the train in there?" Céleste said doubtfully.

"Don't you want to see what he's barking at?" Nayla stepped through the beaded curtain.

"Non, leave him."

Nayla walked in, glancing back to make sure Céleste had not abandoned her. They were covered in filth, but the cantina never judged. A goateed man, with a face half machine and half putty, sucked at the stem on his clear tubing that belonged in a laboratory. A gust of hookah smoke introduced her to an otherworldly version of her favorite haunt, populated by automatons in turbans and hooded figures in burnooses. Piping snaked up and down ceilings, interspaced by pressure gauges, all the way to the kitchen door. A patchwork of steel was riveted around the bar in panels. Chains traveled on sprockets all around the room, as if the whole establishment was pedaled by motors just beyond the walls.

Suddenly, the filament bulbs stole her attention, as they dimmed the atmosphere, and footlights lit up a stage in the corner.

Shirtless men sat in a circle while a set of planetary gears served as the backdrop. A woman in a turquoise burnoose stood in the center. The sun gear spun behind her. The planet gears revolved around the sun, all within the cogs of the outer ring that enclosed them. In front of the woman stood a wicker basket.

Sparky stiffened his tail and stuck out his nose at the performer.

Her hood was drawn over her eyes. Slowly, her hand crept onto her chest from the opening of her cloak, her fingers pointed together. Another hand crept out opposite.

The basket stirred.

One of the shirtless men banged a darbuka, providing rhythm. The dancer sashayed her hips, summoning something from the basket. A king cobra. The snake knocked off the lid as it rose and fanned his neck flaps.

The dancer swayed. The cobra swayed.

In one swift motion, the woman whisked off the cloak, revealing her dark-hair and a set of gears glittering over her groin and breasts. She had an angular chin, snub nose, and eyes like diamonds.

Her pendulous braid halted its swing.

Her costume held its chrome twinkle.

Hookah smoke seemed to freeze, the Tartarus air too thick to let it rise.

Nayla knew the woman immediately.

"Maman?"

She was so radiant and so alive. So full of color.

No consumption to sap her strength.

Céleste touched Nayla's arm. She barely felt it. Numbness had engulfed her.

She was glad the tavern sheltered them from the red sun, so it could not shine onstage to steal Maman's beauty.

"That's your maman?" asked Céleste. "She's so young."

"She died when I was nine."

Maman leapt and landed with her feet apart, clattering the castanets in her hands, harmonizing with the goblet drum. The cobra swayed to Maman's hips while her abdomen plied in and out and her hands slithered overhead in tensile lines.

"Talk to her," said Céleste.

"I'll interrupt the show."

"Et alors?"

"People will get mad."

"This is a once-in-a-lifetime chance." Céleste gestured at Maman, now dancing on her back beneath the snake's roving head.

"She won't recognize me. I'm twenty years old."

"Certainly she'll know her own daughter." Céleste placed a hand on her hip. "Look, I'll entertain the audience while you speak with her backstage."

The darbuka beat faster. The cobra curled around Maman's collar. Her hips rocked side to side, an unseen fulcrum hidden in the flesh of her loins, her thighs a walking oil rig. She revolved her navel around her diaphragm, picked up her turquoise burnoose, and cloaked her body as the drummer struck his final note and the footlights dimmed.

Satisfied grunts and chirruping buzzers emanated from the tables.

"I don't think this crowd likes ballet," said Nayla. "They like props."

"Oui, I see, killer cobras. Lucky for me"—Céleste poofed out of her sandals and repoofed barefoot—"as Fleur d'Étoile, I can improvise."

Maman's cloak swept the floor as she headed backstage.

"Dépêche-toi!" Céleste poofed into the air. Her petunia scent blended with the aromatic spices of tobacco.

Sparky bolted past the round tables and scrambled onto the stage. Nayla apologized to the pipe-smoking patrons as she hurried after him. She lunged to the steel platform and hung a right at the planetary gears, walking into the innards of a clock.

Ticking. The dressing room was ticking.

Maman was hunched over a terrarium, putting the cobra away.

Sparky nibbled at the hem of Maman's cloak.

Maman removed the garment and turned. She looked at the mutt and at Nayla, at her headpiece, then her eyes. She was the same height.

"Nay-Nay?" Her voice was syrup.

"Maman." Nayla opened her arms and fell into Maman's embrace. "What gave me away?"

"Your lovely face, child." Maman glanced at the automaton. "And the dog."

"Sparky?"

"Your baba would call him that."

"Baba said he hasn't seen you."

"He hasn't. But I've seen the dog. My tireless reminder. He was built by Hephaestus to watch over baby Zeus." Maman took Nayla's head into her bosom, perfumed by desert rose.

"How could you wind up here?" said Nayla. "I don't understand."

"Your baba and I have violated Xenia."

"Xenia?"

"Hospitality. What the Ancient Greeks call guest-friendship. It's an obligation for hosts to offer a guest a bath, nourishment, and shelter before questioning them as to who they are and where they are going. For the guest, they are to regale the host with stories and never be a burden. Violators are punished by Zeus."

"But Maman, you fed me and clothed me by working at the cantina. I wasn't a guest. I'm your daughter."

"I know. It's far worse to treat a daughter below a guest. You were a stranger once, you know, and the custom of Xenia extends to family by default."

"How did you mistreat me?"

"Nay-Nay, I was never home. When I was, I was no different from the majlis sofa or the cuckoo clock."

"You worked for our family."

Maman shook her head. "I worked to get away. To always dance. Always be in a state of involution and bliss. I could've made time for you. I avoided it. Naem and I had fallen out of step. We were engaged in our own dance. He got nervous and pulled me in. I grew disgusted and pushed him away. Vice versa. Tug of war. Fear of abandonment, fear of intimacy, here to eternity."

"But I was the burden. I should be punished."

Maman looked at her, concerned. "Are you being punished now? Why are you in Tartarus?"

"To be one with Brahman."

"Brahman is everywhere. You didn't need to come here to look for it."

"I need to feel it. To do that, I need the Cap of Hades."

"What if the cap doesn't work? Are you going to stay invisible and escape reality?"

"Nein," Nayla murmured.

"Tell me you won't. Xenia may extend to those who shirk interaction with others, those who abandon society. Zeus is the patron of guests. He will punish you like he did me."

"I promise I won't."

"Bien." Maman kissed Nayla's cheek. "Everyone was a burden to me back then. I was too caught up with my own emotions to handle yours or Naem's." She tapped Nayla's headpiece. "Did you become a dancer like your friend?"

Nayla peered at the stage from the wing. Flares illuminated Céleste's hands and feet as she gamboled through the air.

"I want to, but people say I'm no good."

"Let's see."

A silver hoop spun off its rod, rolled out of the dressing room, and found its way onto the stage. Céleste stopped dancing as the gear's teeth folded in, converting the gear to a ring.

"My arm is broken."

"You only need one."

Nayla felt Maman take her hand and guide her to the wheel for all to see. There, Maman released her hand and grabbed the prop, letting it spin around her body. She stepped inside and spun like the Vitruvian Man in a wobbly coin.

Céleste backed away. "Nayla, what is that thing?"

"It's a wheel."

"A wheel?" Céleste showed the whites of her eyes. "Remember Gustave's game at de L'Enfer?"

Maman spun so fast it looked as though she was in a cage. "Ixion's wheel. Ja."

"Dance with me," said Maman.

"Do not get in that wheel," Céleste warned.

"You always wanted to be a dancer," said Maman. "Dance with me."

"Nayla, I am telling you. If you step in that wheel, you won't come out."

At last, to be close to Maman. To bask in her warmth for eternity.

Nayla stepped forward.

"Nay," Céleste cried.

"It's the chance of a lifetime." Nayla stepped in, placing her feet by Maman's feet, and clung to the bar with her one good hand.

"Mon Dieu."

Together, they spun, facing each other in the awe of the automatons.

The cobra manifested around the bar, binding Nayla in place with his textured skin.

"Isn't this wonderful?" asked Maman. "To not go anywhere or do anything? To forget all about your loved ones back home? No sleep, no shower, no food or drink. Practice, practice, practice, perfect, perfect, perfect. I am perfection. What do I do with this skill? Too much."

"Nayla isn't a dancer," shouted Céleste. "Let her off."

"Oh, you're not?"

Nayla didn't want to disembark. It would mean separation. To be away from Maman's love. Away from the sun.

"I am," said Nayla.

"To be a dancer means to dance no matter what," said Maman. "To no audience. To a full house. It doesn't matter if the venue makes money. If it goes out of business or falls into decay. Just dance and keep dancing. Nothing else matters. We dance to escape. Not to earn money. If the concept of money disappeared tomorrow, we still must dance."

"Nayla's lying!" rang Céleste's voice. "She's an inventor."

"Like Baba?" asked Maman. "Très bien. Another workhorse escapist. To pound anvils and drain hearths. Do you know that it takes nine days and nine nights for an anvil to fall from Earth to Tartarus?"

The whole world rotated. Nayla was getting dizzy. Worse than hemp and whiskey.

"She's a musician too!" shouted Céleste. "She plays sitar."

"A sitar player? How often do you play?"

Nayla felt queasy. "Baba sold it."

"And you did not buy a new one?"

"I was busy looking for money for parts for mecha-sleeves, for Céleste, for Arachne, for the Cap of Hades, for Brahman."

"For escape?"

"From suffering."

"Then you better step off this wheel."

Nayla grew light headed. Like she was going to pass out. "Nein. I want to be close to you."

"I thought you wanted to dance?" asked Maman.

Nayla lifted her head at the realization. She only wanted to dance to be close to Maman. She had no passion for the art. Only an appreciation for Maman's passion.

"I'm not a dancer," Nayla mumbled.

"What's that?"

"I'm not a dancer."

"Who are you?"

"I want to get off."

"Who are you?"

"I'm an inventor, sitar player, nouvelle nymphe."

"Who are you?"

"I am... Brahman."

"That's my girl."

The cobra vanished. Nayla lost grip.

Maman caught her and stopped the wheel.

"Be those things in moderation for the rest of your life," said Maman, laying Nayla on the stage. "The only dance I want you to dance is Shiva's."

The room spun. She felt herself being dragged down the stage stairs, and she hobbled, following the spring of Sparky's tail into the bright street.

IMPRESSION, BERTHE

Nayla hung off Céleste's shoulder with her red arms like an anchor made of steak tartare, appearing as though she didn't know where she was. The infernal dog barked wildly. Sparks flew out of his mouth as he scampered around them on the sidewalk.

"You're all right, Nay," said Céleste. "I have you."

Nayla's eyelids opened and closed like they were operated by magnets. Sleeping was a bad idea. Céleste had to keep her present...

"What did she mean?" asked Céleste. "What is Shiva's dance?

"Energy," Nayla murmured from her daze.

"Really?" Céleste tightened her grip. "That's vague."

"Ravi uncle will teach you," Nayla mumbled, "but he can't."

"Nay?" Céleste patted Nayla's cheek. "How come, Nay?"

"He only learned the Vedas..." Nayla's head sunk forward "...because his parents told him who he was."

I-I-I-I am-am-am-am noth-noth-noth-nothing.

Maman's voice echoed in Céleste's soul-cave like church bells, while a carillon of voices chimed in her head.

His parents told him who he was.

Could Céleste's parents have done the same thing—told her who she was?

You cannot give love without having it.

What if Nayla was right, and Maman never had love, like how Charon didn't have any?

His reflection is not real, said Nayla. *He does not love himself. He loves an illusion. He sees you as a reflection of him. We are not their reflections. Charon was a liar. He is exactly how my baba was.*

If Charon was lying about me, said Céleste, *perhaps Baba was lying about you.*

Mon Dieu! If Baba was lying about Nayla, had Maman lied about Céleste?

Maman had raged at her for feeling sad, for crying, for getting angry. Taught her these were unwanted emotions to have. Anything offended Maman. Doing wrong things was wrong. Doing right things was wrong. Maman had made her feel like garbage. Like she was nothing. Nothing pleased Maman. And now here Maman was in her head, telling her she was nothing, telling her who she was...

Psyche's voice rang forth—*When a man is capable of evil, he might be possessed by a cacodemon. When a man does good, he might be under the guidance of a eudemon. One can loosen the soul from the body, the other secure the binds.*

A cacodemon can loosen the soul from the body... But whose soul was Psyche referring to? The person under possession, obviously, but what about those around the person who was possessed? The demons at the Folies in Erebus had said her soul was loose before the Incident. She had never been possessed, so who loosened it?

Somebody around her. Théo wasn't always there, but Maman was. She had checked Maman after becoming Starflower, but what if Maman had been possessed at an earlier date and the demon fled her? Or grand-mère and grand-père? Perhaps a family member from before them—a demonic presence in her ancestry? What she was getting at was, oui, not only those possessed by cacodemons, but someone with a loose soul had the ability to loosen other people's, and send chaos hurtling down the generations like a family curse!

Doing bad deeds loosened the binds of one's soul and those around them. Doing good deeds secured the binds of one's soul and those around them...

Non! C'est pas possible! That would mean she was born complete and Maman and Papa were acting in the beginning, when she was very young, loosening the binds to her soul, like how Charon was acting when they'd first met! Obliviously inauthentic. Papa and Maman pretending to love her, showering her with praise, reflecting what she wanted to hear, before she entered girlhood and the masks came off. Not only that, it's how she was acting toward Charon! Idealizing him and being someone she wasn't in order to merge. Dieu aide moi.

She knew enough about her demi-gens tribe to know that half-people were terribly inconsistent. They wore masks before the public and took them off in private. She could see their faces like... like exposed flesh. Zut alors! She could see the marbling. Staring back at her in the glint of Nayla's headpiece.

Her original theory, that trauma created half-people, still held true. Why, she was not born a half-person. She became one shortly thereafter!

Had Maman loved herself, she would have loved Céleste, and Maman's love would have secured the binds of Céleste's soul and protected it from demons. Maman would've smelled one coming an arrondissement away, and Céleste would not have been trapped in 1887 like a frozen clepsydra—a water clock unable to tell time. If only Maman had made Céleste's soul feel at home and not frightened it loose. When Maman combed Céleste's hair too hard, she probably tugged her soul right out with the locks and a jerk.

If her parents told her who she was, why, that would mean they were covering up who she was naturally supposed to be. The real her. Complete. Someone capable of a loving husband and beautiful children.

Céleste lowered Nayla to the sidewalk, cradling her, glad she wasn't alone, even if Nayla was delirious.

It would've been harder to face her fears being alone—to accept facts—that God did not assign her loving parents. To keep her soul, she had to secure the binds herself. To do that, she needed love. But she could not use something she did not have to secure something she did not have, and she couldn't find love by forming connections with disconnected people. That was only lust. What was she to do?

I am nothing, I am nothing, I am nothing.

Nothing. There was nothing.

Nothing, but to help Nayla and Gustave, and take comfort in knowing the voice in the void was not her fault, but a blind acceptance of Berthe telling her who she was, a side effect of Papa not telling her anything, a lie that Théo took advantage of, and a fear that Mariquita viewed her in that light. Berthe and Papa chose not to love her before she was born, by choosing not to love themselves. How they were supposed to wake up to the problem or find the solution, she did not know. They had passed it on to her. How to prove the voice wrong, she did not know.

The struggles of the demi-gens.

CONVERSATION ON THE TARTARUS EXPRESS

Steam hissed from a passing camel with ball bearings for rotator cuffs. It brayed like a heavy door scraping on a deck, scaring Sparky down the street. Nayla lurched forward.

"Céleste—" Nayla willed her legs to stand. "Céleste, I don't want to be a dancer."

"I would agree it's not your calling."

Maman did not want her to obsess, but refusing to dance was oh so hard to do. "I only wanted to be close to her."

"I know. Keep her close in memory." Céleste urged Nayla forward. "Dépêche-toi. We can't lose the dog."

She staggered after him, graduating to a walk, as he darted through the legs of gear merchants and clothing vendors.

Arabic singing echoed from the hall of the train station, accompanied by the stringy twang of an ud. The edifice appeared like a clockface, flanked by galleries of pink arcades. Orange and pink ceramics, gold and silver gears, a sand-blasted machine of rails and concourses, more beautiful than Jacoma's counterpart.

The dog wagged his tail and ran up the steps.

"Will they let us ride for free?" asked Nayla.

"Your baba's money would have been helpful."

"Sparky seems to know what to do."

Nayla followed him into the terminal. Inside, Sufis whirled on horizontal gears, spinning to the melody of the fluty ney, joined by the drumming kudum and that divine ud. The Sufis had tall hats and floaty skirts and spun and spun to be closer with God, serving as a signpost that Nayla was on the right track to pursue Brahman.

Sparky chased his tail and ran outside to the concourse. Parked and ready for boarding was the Orient Express. Rather, the Tartarus Express. Gold lettering shined on the red-painted train, a luxury ride in a blazing inferno, the locomotive pointed at the desert like a shotgun.

Nayla really ought to have brought money.

"Sparky? Here, boy." The conductor whistled. "Looks like you've brought friends."

Sparky yelped and jumped around the conductor's mechanical legs. The man stooped and petted the dog's rump.

"We don't have tickets," Nayla explained.

The man wiggled his wire brush mustache and held out his hand.

"The dog is your ticket." He picked up Sparky. "I'll see he gets back to Naem. You're in compartment nine."

The conductor lowered his head to hear Nayla speak over the steam.

"We wish to stop in the desert at the point where the track hooks north toward the mountains." The ziggurat would be immediately south by one kilometer if Tartarus had the same map as Jacoma.

The conductor stood erect. "I will knock on approach." He raised his hand to the carriage. "Enjoy your ride, Fräulein."

Nayla looked inside. It was a restaurant car with red valor and gold trim, populated by people and automatons. Maybe demi-tons. "Danke." She climbed up and found an empty table.

Céleste sat opposite. A waiter approached, dressed in a white tuxedo with red lapels and sporting an exposed metal jaw.

"Guten Tag."

Nayla ordered coffee. Céleste, tea.

The waiter opened his shirt and pulled a coffee cup from a compartment in his chest. He held the cup under his chin while coffee poured from where the lower half of his face should've been.

"Cream?"

Nayla hesitated. "Ja."

He raised the cup to his nose. Cream spurted from his left nostril. He set the cup on the table and produced a tea set from his chest. He poured the tea from his mouth. Maybe the coffee came from his esophagus and the tea from his trachea, but Nayla could be wrong.

Céleste shifted in her seat.

"Sugar?"

"No, thank you," said Céleste.

Nayla wanted to see by what device he would procure it. "I'll take sugar."

The waiter lifted the coffee cup to hear its heartbeat. A lump of sugar tumbled out of his ear and splashed into the cup. With the beverages served, he swiftly departed. The train blew its whistle and, likewise, departed the station.

"Beurk," said Céleste.

"We need to strategize," said Nayla. "If you can only choose one item, I wonder if it's better to choose the caduceus and free Gustave."

"Trust Hermes that he'll keep his word?"

"I don't trust him, but I trust it may be our best option."

"That option would make me bride of Hermes."

"It's the sacrifice to save Gustave," said Nayla. "A sacrifice where you get to live."

Céleste looked into her teacup. "Je ne sais pas. Live on Olympus?"

"Hermes can get your ambrosia. Your soul, I'm not so sure."

"What if I can open the Hall of Fabled Objects from the inside, eh? I let you in, we choose two objects, and you get the Cap of Hades after all."

"We can't rely on that."

"What if I get you the Cap of Hades alone?"

Nayla shook her head no, wanting so badly to nod ja. She creased her brow and saw her reflection in the coffee. Why did she have to drink so much? Past the point of acquiring powers? She had been at full steam... and drank... and drank. She couldn't help it. She needed whiskey to feel better, to treat her melancholy until she could reach Brahman.

"Oui, the cap will work," Céleste continued, "I could sneak on the boat, put the helmet on Gustave, and distract Hermes and Charon while you sneak him off."

"Without my doorways," said Nayla, "Tartarus is inescapable. We need Charon's Bateau Lavoir." Nayla sniffed the coffee.

"No one's ever escaped?" asked Céleste.

"Not without help from the outside."

"I've cornered us into a trap." Nayla winced, afraid to face Céleste.

Céleste said nothing.

Nayla opened an eye. "You're not going to scold me for drinking?"

"No more than I can scold myself for making love."

"Circe's staff is the object we need." Nayla sighed. "Poof in, take the staff, poof out. Transform Arachne into a spider. Transform me to have all my powers. Transform Gustave into a nouveau satyre."

"Oui, there is one problem. No matter what I grab, I need to fight Arachne."

"She is mortal," said Nayla. "Zap her with the staff."

"How fast can she move?"

Nayla recalled the skittering legs, the speed with which she traveled, how quickly she dispatched the legionnaires. "Fast."

"What does her lair look like?"

"It's a cave with walls made of black rock that shine blue and green. A river of fire runs through the center. Phlegethon. There's a ramp that crosses it. She also has a canopy of webs to hide in." Nayla huffed. "I was planning on torching them." She looked at the Persian carpet, disgusted with herself. "The doors to the hall are across the ramp. It's a monument built into the cave."

"Didn't you say Arachne can mimic reality?"

"Ja, she weaves colored webs that appear like moving paintings. Don't worry, they can't hurt you unless you stick to them. I was going to torch those too."

"Speed, webs, mimicry." Céleste stared into her tea. "I wish I was at full power."

"Ja, if you had wings, you could fly up to the webbing and confront her. If you got stuck, poof free." Nayla scanned the automatons in the restaurant car, men with turbans and tunics and dynamos for hearts. "I don't think there's a suitor close by."

Céleste fidgeted in her seat. "There is someone." She flashed her eyes upon Nayla.

Nayla blushed as fear and anxiety made their rounds through her bloodstream. Was Céleste truly implying what she thought she was?

"Me?" Nayla pointed.

Céleste nodded, uneasy.

She implied that very thing! Nayla wouldn't look at Céleste the same. Their friendship would be ruined. The very idea pushed her to the edge of her comfort zone. When she looked out, she saw a blurry drop—unpredictable, indeterminate. It was much safer not to leap. How would it work? What if she did something wrong? Said something wrong? It would be tense during and embarrassing after.

"You're right," Céleste continued, bashful. "It's verrückt."

"Folle," said Nayla.

"Forget I said it."

Nayla tried to control her breathing and think straight. *Clarity, Nayla, clarity.* It was her fault they were in this mess. The whole reason she trekked across the desert to arrive in French Athens was because one nymph could not defeat Arachne. Now here she was, around the globe, deep in the underworld, back where she started with one nymph about to fight Arachne. This nymph could pollinate, ja, but not fly.

Céleste's dead body flashed in her mind. Strangulated, upside down, spider snack. No different from the deceased nymph strung up on Nayla's first visit to Arachne's Cave. What object did that nymph wish to possess and fail to grasp? Nayla may never know. But that nymph had wings. Céleste needed wings.

Had Nayla refrained from drinking...

"I don't want to pressure you," said Céleste. "Excite your martyr syndrome."

"It's my martyrdom that placed me in this predicament."

"How so?"

"I suppose when there's no one around to be a martyr for, I become a martyr for myself with drink." Nayla sighed. "Would it even work?"

"I don't see why not."

"Have you ever made love to a woman?"

"Non. Have you?"

"Nein," said Nayla, doubting Céleste's answer.

"A man?"

"Once. It didn't go well." Nayla blushed. "I have a hard time trusting people."

"Do you trust me?"

"What would Gustave think?"

"He's not my beau."

"I mean morally."

"I didn't think Hindus cared about that."

"We care about being virtuous, if the action hurts anyone or not. Seeing as I don't plan to marry, it will not hurt my future husband."

"You think *my* future husband will hold it against *me*?"

"Where I come from, sex outside of marriage is taboo. Sex with a woman, also taboo. But, from a spiritual angle, if he loves you deeply, he will accept you as you are."

"Then what's the moral dilemma?"

"Christianity considers it a sin. It's your beliefs I'm asking for."

"Loving you would be a less immoral way to save Gustave than marriage to a pagan god." Céleste nudged her teacup forward, untouched. "It was a dumb idea. Excuse-moi." She rose from the seat. "I have to rest for the heist."

Nayla picked up her face-poured coffee and sipped. To make love to her friend. It would increase their success with Arachne and ensure their survival. Coming to Tartarus was her plan. Like the legionnaires before, the people on her expedition were her responsibility. She cared for Céleste and trusted her with her life. Céleste had disobeyed Nayla in the well, and instead of escaping through the doorway from the swarming demons, she dove in the waters to rescue her.

In many ways, Céleste was her reflection, and Nayla considered Céleste and herself the two closest manifestations of Brahman she had experienced in human form, aside from seeing identical twins. Céleste would not judge her. Nayla's greasy hair, her scars from the Blast, her piercings, her laying sprawled naked, showing all shop. She couldn't see herself in a relationship with Céleste, the source of Cél's powers being what they were, and her dream of an ideal family, but the thought of someone's hands on her body exhilarated her.

Nayla stood up from the table, unsure of how to initiate. With trepidation, she walked the carpeted hall to compartment number nine and slid open the door. There were two beds with Egyptian silk sheets, a down comforter, and afghans folded at the ends. Céleste lay in bed. She had changed out of her oil-stained costume into a nightdress. The rusted desert ambled by, waving its mechanical palm trees in the window overhead. Nayla slid the woodgrain door shut. Céleste did not stir.

Nayla saw her reflection in the ornate wall as she crossed to the bedside. The compartment smelled like pastries and petunias from Céleste's pollen. Céleste looked tired. Nayla ought to let her sleep. Nayla didn't even know what to do. It was a dumm idea.

Céleste's eyes opened like a blooming flower. Did she know what Nayla was here for? She must. Nayla stood so close and was biting her lip. Céleste reached out for Nayla's hand. Nayla placed it in hers. Warm.

"Help me up," said Céleste.

Had she changed her mind? Did she rescind the offer?

Nayla lifted her to her feet.

"You can't very well come to bed wearing a clock." Céleste palmed Nayla's shoulder strap and disappeared into pollen with all of Nayla's clothes, save for her sling.

Céleste reappeared with Nayla's clothes stacked in the corner. She made three paces, took Nayla's hand, and rolled into bed. The touch of Céleste's body against hers electrified her senses.

"I'm nervous," said Nayla. "I want to make sure you get your wings."

"I will," Céleste whispered.

She slid the curtain across the window to restore the sight of their skin and brushed Nayla's hair from her eyes. Nayla moved her face to Céleste's lips to try for a kiss. Soft, wet, aromatic. She tried again. This time for a longer one. Nayla's good arm rested on the pillow. Céleste's hand supported Nayla aloft above the hip. Her hand was silk, unlike Nayla's palms, calloused from gripping shovels and swinging mallets. Céleste rolled Nayla onto her back, sparing her the strain of negotiating her broken arm. The pillows were so soft. Not made of tickseed, but the feathers of some exotic Tartarus bird.

Nayla's chest raised and fell as Céleste honeyed Nayla's mouth with languorous affection. Céleste found Nayla's hand, brought it to the pillow, and traced the callouses with her fingertips. Nayla entwined her foot with Céleste's and found that her toes were calloused too, the toes of a dancer.

"You should have seen me after my first pointe class," Céleste whispered. "My toes were tenderloin."

Nayla gave a little grin, less self-conscious.

Céleste dragged her fingers down to Nayla's palm, her wrist, her forearm, receding beneath the covers and landing on her hips, her thigh, the crease between her leg and her loin, massaging her sensitive... How did those horrible Barrisons phrase it? Ihr Kätzchen.

The first encounter sent a tingle up Nayla's spine, and she fell into a reverie. If she had a motor, it was purring. Nayla's hand followed beneath the sheets and diverted the trail to linger on Cél's breast. Firm. Nayla circled the shape to the center and caressed the nipple, feeling the skin grow hard. She continued down the crest to the trough of Céleste's lissome body, rotating her wrist, probing the muscles. One ridge after another, Nayla traveled the abdominal to the end. Her fingers raked through fuzz and felt inside, centimeters deep, working in hard exhales.

Céleste closed her eyes as a quiet moan escaped her throat. Pink dye saturated her blonde hair in ribbons. A light pulsated behind the silken sheets.

"Céleste," Nayla whispered.

"Shhh. I want to try something. Don't stop."

Nayla continued her smooth rhythm as a ball of warm light emanated between her legs. She thought Céleste was going to blow her up, a notion that aroused and terrified her. In her powerless state, she wouldn't survive the force. Suddenly, the orb vibrated, stimulating her nerve endings into a euphoric frenzy. Trembling, quivering, quavering. The murmurs she had clung to out of fear of saying something wrong burst from her lungs in a raspy groan.

The last vestige of hope to pleasure Céleste died under the overwhelming current of bliss. Céleste wailed, joining Nayla's voice in the air, and broke off as her eyes rolled back in her head, and the light faded.

As Nayla's senses returned, so too did her hopes and fears. Céleste placed her hands on Nayla's chest and squeezed as pink monarch wings exploded from her back, extinguishing all doubt. Nayla lay exposed and serene. The wings launched the sheets across the compartment and fluttered gently. Céleste set her head on Nayla's heart, mindful of her arm.

"How do you feel?" asked Nayla.

"Incroyable. Et toi?"

"Befriedigt."

"I can sense it. In your soul." Céleste touched Nayla's sternum. "It's right here." Céleste's head rose up and down with Nayla's breathing. "Your maman's advice not to overdo it. It makes me think I work myself to death. My style should come effortlessly, you know?"

Nayla relaxed, happy Céleste carried the conversation.

"Ja, I can see how that'd make sense."

Nayla giggled.

"What is it?"

"Your antennae tickled my neck."

"Je suis désolée." Céleste laughed and sat up, astride Nayla. "I was afraid it would be awkward for us after."

"Only if you make it awkward, my pet." Céleste patted Nayla's chest. "Your maman. What was her name?"

"Lucie."

"And this boy of yours. Tell me about him."

The brakes squealed. Lamps and books fell. Céleste drifted backward, using her wings to stop from toppling out of bed. She landed on her feet. Nayla slid forward as the train ground to halt.

"Is this our stop?" asked Céleste, shaken.

"I didn't hear a knock."

Céleste grabbed her Fleur d'Étoile clothes off a hanger in the wardrobe and poofed into them. "Want me to dress you?"

"Ja, bitte."

Céleste bent down for Nayla's clothes in the corner and poofed. She re-poofed hugging Nayla, reattired in her haram pants, shawl top, boots, headpiece, and mecha-sleeves.

Céleste opened their compartment door, her hands raised and glowing white. Nayla followed her down the hall and into the gangway, over the coupling into the restaurant car and out the door onto red sand, their bodies fit to be hung in a butcher shop.

Demi-tons assembled outside, herded together by the bristle-faced conductor.

"Are we at the bend?" Nayla asked the man.

"Nein, there's an obstruction on the tracks."

Céleste kept her hands up and marched. It could be Hades coming to intercept them, or the irate Persephone somehow realizing they had not left the underworld, or Hermes suspecting a double cross. Who knew?

The engineer dismounted the locomotive by ladder. Gilt pipes glinted on the boiler's walls as Nayla skirted the machine, and the obstruction came into view: a rough-hewn boulder, half-square, half-sphere.

"Could it be?" Nayla bypassed Céleste and touched the coarse rock. She turned to Cél. "This boulder was part of the wall protecting Jacoma. I pushed it with my mecha-sleeves in a demonstration so Baba and I could secure the bank loan."

"What's it doing here?" asked Céleste.

"I don't know. What's a well doing under the Folies Bergère?"

"Someone's coming." Céleste dug in her heels.

A lanky figure walked out of the desert in a green caftan, the glare of red sun in his yellow frames.

Nayla motioned at Céleste. "Lower your hands."

"Who is he? Sisyphus?"

The man drew closer, raised his goggles, and removed his hood.

Just as Nayla thought. "Ojas."

"Am I seeing a mirage?" Ojas hugged Nayla tight.

"Careful, my arm."

"Oho."

"Ojas, say it isn't so. Is it really you?"

"I'm afraid my luck ran out."

Nayla turned to Céleste and introduced them. "Ojas, Céleste, my dear friend from Athens. Céleste, Ojas, my friend from the Blast. Ojas helped me test the mecha-sleeves."

"Enchanté." Céleste shook his hand and pointed at the boulder. "Where are you going with this?"

"Up that mountain." He struck a finger at the purple peak.

"Why?" asked Nayla.

"If I don't get this boulder to that summit, the Blast owner wins."

"Blast owner?" Nayla asked. "Herr bin Ramli is here?"

"Pushing his boulder up the other side, ja."

"Ojas, you've done nothing wrong," said Nayla. "What crime matches this punishment?"

"My scrap metal scheme. I'd swipe it at the Blast, sell it to a broker, and they'd sell it back to the Blast to make pig iron."

"Why resort to theft?"

"The Blast nearly took my life. I dodged death twice. Remember my lung infection from inhaling sulfur?" He aired his complaints to Céleste. "The second time, a bolt shot off a boiler and clipped my neck."

"Ojas had worked at the Blast longer than me," Nayla added. "Since he was ten."

"And what do I have to show for it?"

"I don't understand why embezzlement would land you in Tartarus."

"I violated Xenia."

"Why does Zeus care?" said Nayla.

"Because Herr bin Ramli could have been the unknown god," said Ojas. "Zeus in disguise, to make sure hospitality is honored."

"The unknown god," said Nayla, "of course."

Zeus and Hermes once took up a disguise and visited the elderly couple, Philemon and Baucis, during antiquity. The couple was generous. They offered the strangers food, shelter, and wine. When Baucis realized the wine bottle never emptied, she knew she was in the presence of the gods. Zeus rewarded them by converting their home into a temple, then punished the villagers who denied the gods hospitality with a flood.

Nayla turned to Céleste. "If you treat all men as the unknown god, you will never offend Zeus."

Even in the Upanishads, Brahman existed in all beings.

"Unfortunately," Ojas conceded. "I'm glad Herr bin Ramli is paying the price too. Unfair pay, hazardous work conditions. He rolls in marks, and we get squat." Ojas put his hand on Nayla's boiler. "Ah, the mecha-sleeves. Mind giving me a head start?"

Her arm was broken. Could she really move the boulder with one sleeve? She could try. "Ja." She deactivated the piston on the one arm, so as not to further injure the break, and handed Céleste some matches. "Light me up."

"Like this?" She opened the compartment and lit the coal ablaze.

After a few minutes, Nayla took her stance against the boulder.

It had been a while, but the chant for wisdom should still do the trick.

She placed one hand on the stone, her shoulder close to her knuckles.

"*Aum bhur bhuva svah.*" *Screws down. Pistons come out.*

The oddly shaped boulder listed and fell off the tracks.

"*Tat savitur varenyam.*" *Screws come up and pistons in.*

Steam hissed along her legs.

"*Bhargo devasya dhimahi.*" *One step, two steps, the train makes three.*

The boulder rolled again.

"*Dhiyo yo naha prachodayat.*" *Water the boiler every eighth walk.*

The boulder came to rest three lengths from where it began.

"There," she said, backing away. "Ojas, without mecha-sleeves, how can you move this boulder?"

He lifted his caftan and revealed mechanical arms.

"It makes no difference," he said. "Every time I get to the mountaintop, it rolls back down. Same for Herr bin Ramli's."

"Why not quit? Nothing is keeping you here. There's no slavedriver with a whip. You're not in chains."

"Oh, no. If I stop, it means the Blast owner can beat me. I'm better than him, smarter than him." He pointed at Nayla. "With both of us, we can do it."

Steam hissed, though not from the mecha-sleeves. From the train. The cowcatcher's teeth pulled the train's face into a snarl. The big hoop wheels leaned forward, ready to pounce.

"Nay," said Céleste, "the train is leaving."

"Alle einsteigen!" called the engineer.

"Please, Nayla," said Ojas. "I saved you from Jacoma. From a Blast furnace some tycoon built in the middle of the desert. It was a death sentence."

Céleste waited by Nayla's side. "Do you remember what Hermes said? These are distractions. Did you see Ojas die?"

"Nein."

"Might he be alive like Kameera?"

"He might."

"Well, I'm not poofing in this one to find out."

"Please, Nayla," said Ojas, "just to the mountain's base."

Her main function was helping others. But why? What was that thing Céleste had said before in a fit of anger? She'd accused Nayla of getting people to like her so that she would like herself. Her identity was dependent on others. In Ordnung. She could accept that. But where was the balance? The sweet spot? How much to help and when should she, without becoming a martyr?

"Nayla," said Ojas, "it's the real me. My arms were crushed in an accident. It was night. I was robbing scrap from a train car when a crane dropped a load on top of me."

The train lurched forward in chugs of billowing steam.

"Et alors?" Céleste said to Nayla. "You didn't see it. He's lying like an epitaph."

"Who are you going to trust?" asked Ojas. "A Hindu or a French woman?"

Nayla looked at Ojas pleading, the train rolling, and Céleste impatient. The thought of Céleste's fingers on Nayla's body sent a thrill up her spine. The feeling had left her so content, it was like she could feel Céleste still stroking her. She could see why Céleste found it so addicting.

"What about the night we shared in the yakhchāl?" asked Ojas.

"In truth," said Nayla, as the tender past by, "I hoped it would lead to marriage."

"I never knew."

"Because we agreed it was awkward. It was my fault I couldn't get you—" Was it her fault? An ember glowed in her mind, her answer in the soot. She breathed it into a flame. Nein, the awkwardness was not her fault. They were in a yakhchāl, for Shiva's sake. It was freezing. Why had that not dawned on her before? She was too busy blaming herself. Curse Baba for calling her interest in boys female trifles. "We agreed we make better friends."

"A friend would help me push the boulder."

She could not let her senses deceive her. She also could not let herself be a doormat.

"I'm sorry, Ojas."

Nayla walked at an even pace with the red and gold train and climbed onto the footboard of the restaurant car.

"Ojas!" she called. "Help Herr bin Ramli. Push the boulders together one at a time!"

"And let the banker win? Not a chance!"

Céleste spread her wings and fluttered onto the footboard with Nayla.

"You did the right thing," said Céleste.

Herr bin Ramli could easily walk around the mountain to help Ojas too, non? Wishful thinking on my part. Ramli won't be outwitted by a lowly shovel hog, a Shudra boy. Why, the Blast provides for men's families. It established this very town. Without the Blast, there was no Jacoma. What's a few unsafe working conditions when the Blast allows people to live? The wage was meager, oui, but people lived. Ramli and Ojas, they are too prideful. Both afraid to budge in their minds, so they budge a rock in their worlds. All that energy wasted on the physical when the mental can move mountains. That would, however, require facing oneself in the mirror. You will see your best friend and your greatest enemy.

There is much the unconscious hides in our waking hours. It comes out in dreams, on the cusp of sleep, and through art. In the underworld, it simply *is*, fully exposed. If the conscious mind allows the unconscious to absorb guilt, in the underworld, your loved ones will guilt trip you to no end. They speak to the martyr within, because it is how Nayla spoke to herself. Asking her to aid in their repetitions, helping the unhelpable for all eternity. Thank goodness Céleste was there to put the kibosh on that.

Ah, Jacques can see it in your eyes. You wish to talk about a certain Sapphic train romance. What did you expect? Gustave's life is on the line, and Céleste's patron goddess is Aphrodite. A patronage which may explain why Hermes was attracted to Céleste in the first place.

He'd once had an affair with Aphrodite. They had a son. Hermaphroditus, très bien. The nymph, Salmacis, obsessed over him, but he parried her advances. So, she begged the gods to join them together into Hermaphrodite, a literal merge.

I wonder if they started off as two half-people. Oui, demi-gens, like Nayla and Céleste. I cannot verify the claim, but I bet you that in that train compartment, in the heat of passion, for the moment they shared together, they felt whole.

Enjoying the paintings? Orientalism meets steampunk. Oui, something you didn't know you wanted until Jacques gave it to you. De rien. Get a feel for this one. The ziggurat in Tartarus. The blue wall really makes the reds pop.

ARACHNE'S CAVE

Wind riffled through Nayla's hair as the train began to hook north. Specs of sand hit her face, prompting her to lower her goggles. From the inside bend, she could see the rails leading to the mountains, when the conductor poked his head from the restaurant car.

"Fräulein?—butterfly wings, my goodness," he said. "We're at the bend. Should I stop the train or can you manage?"

"We've got it." Céleste unstrapped Nayla from the mecha-sleeves.

The boiler was too hot for Céleste to carry while on Nayla's back, so Nayla settled for holding her invention by one hand and coiled the straps around her arm.

"We got it, right?" asked Céleste.

"Ja."

Céleste scooped her arms under Nayla's, their bodies ground beef.

"Danke, Herr Conductor."

Céleste let her sails capture the sudden increase in wind and arced upward like a kite. Nayla pointed out the ziggurat, leafed in gold, due south in the distance. Céleste pumped her wings, flying deeper into the torrid desert. Dust devils ripped up the landscape. The climate, inhospitable. It must've been fifty degrees centigrade, the worst of climes for the leisurely cruise of a butterfly, compared to that of a phoenix.

Céleste was already complaining of the heat when a large oblong shadow loomed across the desert floor. Nayla peered up at the source, a dirigible heading southwest. More sailed across the atmosphere.

"Cél, fly in the dirigibles' shadows as best you can."

"D'accord."

Céleste stayed under the airship's belly until it veered too far off course from the ziggurat, and she lapsed into the red sun to reach the next shadow.

"You're too heavy with the mecha-sleeves," said Céleste. "Drop them."

She dipped from twenty-five to twenty meters off the ground.

Nayla squinted. On closer inspection of the ziggurat, the entrance was blocked at the top by a golden wall.

"I can't," said Nayla, "we need them to open that door. I think. In the Orient, the door was open and the temple abandoned."

"I can pollinate in and have you wait outside until I retrieve the staff."

Nayla shook her head. "I need to be in the cave with you. If you can't zap Arachne, you can zap me to be at full power, and I'll smoke her out."

"All right," said Céleste, "but I'm not walking up all those steps." She dipped ten meters above the ground. "I'll fly you up first, then the mecha-sleeves separate."

Stairs extended from the ziggurat like a tripod, one set coming out the front, the other two laterally, all converging under a turret at the midpoint into a single stair which led to the citadel at the top.

"Get ready to land," said Céleste.

Nayla maintained a jog, pedaling the air until her feet touched down, dragging the boiler and landing by the base of the front steps.

Céleste undid the mecha-sleeve straps from around Nayla and fluttered over the turret with the machine to the citadel at the tippy-top.

Nayla looked up the incline of steps. Céleste's pink monarch wings disappeared out of view. The silence coated the picture with an ominous finish. What cult had worshipped in this temple in Jacoma? Had they been influenced by what lay beneath in the underworld? More importantly, was Arachne expecting her?

Pink monarch wings curveballed around the turret and down the steps. Sandals landed before Nayla, filled with Céleste's sausage toes.

"All aboard," said Céleste. "Sorry, there's no flask for you to fit in."

"The old-fashioned way is more scenic." Nayla hung off Céleste's neck as Céleste took her around the waist from the front, muscle tissues abound. "Any sign of trouble?"

"Aucun." Céleste fluttered up the tiered structure, over the midpoint pavilion, and landed by the golden door to the citadel, six stories off the desert floor. "What do you make of it, Vidocq?"

The door was rectangular, sitting plumb with the floor on its length. It was so wide it could not be hinged at either side, but possibly by a shaft driven through the middle so that the door functioned like a giant flipper.

Nayla placed her smooth palm onto the warm gilt stone and ran her finger down the crack where the door joined the wall. Was it hermetically sealed? She had no choice. She wasn't going to let another friend sacrifice herself for her desires. It wasn't like the Cap of Hades was in the cards anymore, but she had to be there for Céleste.

"Help me into the sleeves," said Nayla.

Céleste poofed the hot boiler onto Nayla's back.

Nayla drilled her boots to the stone and leaned into the door. The solitary piston forced her shoulder from her hand.

She grunted. "Help me." It was heavier than the boulder.

"What could my strength possibly do?" asked Céleste.

Nayla let up from the door. "Have you ever heard the expression 'the straw that broke the camel's back'?"

"Oui."

"The straw made the load too big to carry. Everything has its limit. You see your French Athenian muscles?"

"Oui, I see them."

"They could be all this door needs to open."

"I have a better idea."

"What?"

"This." Céleste poofed Nayla's sleeves off her body and repoofed standing facing the door, Céleste's back against Nayla's chest. While Nayla's left arm continued to occupy the left sleeve, Céleste had fitted her right arm into the right.

The perfume stirred up visions of her supple body on Nayla's, exciting her senses. She had to resist. If Nayla was intimate again, they'd start to merge, something she didn't trust herself to prevent. She shook her head to focus.

"Ja, this could work. Cél, put your hand on the door. Ja. Bring your shoulder to your hand. Sehr gut. Press the button."

The pistons pushed out. The door budged.

"Hold," Nayla muttered, their arms half extended, struggling to fully lengthen, muscles flexing in the red sun.

Steam hissed from her hips, spooking Céleste.

"Hold," Nayla repeated, under the strain.

The door slid forward, giving way to the other side. As Nayla suspected—hinged in the middle. Though she could not yet fit her body through. The gap was too narrow.

"I'm taking a step forward," said Nayla. "Push the second button." The drills came up. Nayla took the step and replanted. "Push it again. Gut." The drills secured her to the ground. "Now lean in, but don't force. First button."

The pistons forced their shoulders from their hands much easier, revolving the door enough for them to fit.

"We're in," said Nayla.

Céleste poofed out of the sleeve and repoofed it onto Nayla. That flowery scent was dangerous.

"Danke." Nayla unscrewed herself from the ground.

"Are we all right?" asked Céleste.

How could she sense it? *Just come clean, Nayla.*

"Ja. It's that,"—She forced herself to make eye contact—"I know you want to be complete and have babies, and I know your soul's long gone, but I still have hope for you, and I'm afraid if we do that again, we shall merge and hate each other and make things harder to untangle."

"Oui, that would be bad." Céleste looked at the desert over Nayla's shoulder for what seemed like a long time, then back to Nayla. "I wasn't born a half-person, you know?"

Was she trying to talk Nayla out of it? It sounded more like a lament. Or simply stating a fact.

Nayla nodded, realizing that Céleste understood the truth, by whatever road brought her there. "Of course not. You are of the Vaishya caste. Far less karma out of the gate."

"Oui, Vidocq." Céleste smiled. "Oui." She passed into shade.

The lure hard to resist, Nayla followed, though resist she must.

Black gems shined in the walls of the tunnel, reflecting multiple views of her own reflection. The prismatic stones had glints of cerulean at one angle and gassy green at another, displaying her curious face with her skin fully restored in their luster. She closed one eye and saw the blues stand out, then shifted her eye to spy the greens.

"Beautiful," said Céleste, "and bizarre."

"These walls," said Nayla. "It's like what a spider sees."

"You think she's watching us through the walls?"

"I don't know. According to Brahman, everyone is their own environment. I'm the Blast. You're the Folies. Arachne is her cave."

"Like the Folies is part of who I am?"

"In a way, ja. To be more abstract, we can't exist without an environment to live in, therefore we are the environment. But, the environment can't exist without a conscious mind to observe it. Every person, place, and thing is faceted together and reflected in one another like gems. The whole concept is Indra's Net. Everything is interconnected."

"Indra's Net, oui." Céleste put up her hands. "I better go first."

"Cél"—Nayla touched her—"I'm scared."

"So am I. I'm not immortal anymore." She pointed to her head. "Up here, anyway. In the well, even when I thought I was, I was still scared. But some broken part of me knew I had to keep going, in spite of the voice rooting against me." She looked at Nayla. "The cave you fear to enter holds the treasure that you seek."

Nayla clutched her heart, as if she could manually slow it down. She had been here before. It shouldn't have been a total shock. It held the object she needed to escape. But would her karma prevent her from retrieving it? What if Arachne killed her? The cycle of suffering would continue. She would be reborn in the dark to any way out. She'd rather suffer with knowledge of the cap's existence than in ignorance of it. *Nayla, you can either idle forever and let your fears control you, or take the leap, knowing in the back of your mind this is the one true path and that the only way out is through.*

"All right," she said in trepidation. "Let's go."

She lingered behind Céleste as they wandered to the end of the tunnel and stopped at a corner. Nayla poked her head out and peered down the familiar ramp. The Phlegethon's blue flame cut a jagged path across the cave. Beyond it, over the bridge, stood the entrance to the Hall of Fabled Objects right where she'd left it, with its white doors, Greek pillars, Jugendstil lettering, and gilt flower stems borrowed from the fatherland that reminded her of a cemetery gate, the whole frontispiece crowned by a golden cabbage and lit by torches.

Nayla ducked back. "This is it. I'll wait here."

Céleste stepped out in full view. "The Greek-temple looking thing?"

"Ja."

"It's gone."

"What?"

"The façade. It just winked out."

Nayla stole another peek. "Webs."

"If I'm not back in ten minutes, run." Céleste looked straight ahead while she spoke and marched down the ramp.

"I'm not leaving you," Nayla whispered, but Céleste was out of earshot.

Why was Céleste walking there in solid form and not floating in as a nebulous cloud? Didn't she want the element of surprise? Or was she appearing as if she belonged here? Ja, maybe that was it.

Céleste crossed the bridge spanning the blue-flamed ditch and vaguely approached the loom masking the entrance. She grasped the colored strings and pulled apart the tapestry. Behind the aras, the Hall of Fabled Objects shined in all its polished glory.

Céleste faced the doors and shouted, "Odyssey."

Nothing happened.

"Odyssey," she tried again.

Still nothing changed.

"It won't work," echoed Arachne's shrill voice.

She zipped down on a web from her nest on the ceiling and landed on the same battlefield from which she'd fought the legionnaires, cutting a stark and threatening figure: spidery legs, venomous thighs, her abdomen and gothic breasts scantly covered. Wispy black locks framed her silk face, her body appareled in the robes of an odalisque. She folded her arms, laughing, walking, her back to Nayla. "Only a god or demigod can enter the hall. Who are you?"

Céleste launched a flare over Arachne's head. Vertical lines showed on her body. "You're missing your chiaroscuro—the gradients of shadow from my light." Céleste called to the gossamer image. "The question is, where are you?"

The real Arachne hovered right above her.

Nayla tensed up and forced out the words by sheer panic, "She's over your head!"

Webs zipped onto Céleste's shoulders and yanked her like a puppeteer retrieving a marionette. Céleste burst out of shape, into pollen, and sifted through the hard-pressed slot of the hall's doors.

She was in!

Arachne skittered across the ceiling on her canopy of webs, more spider than human, heading to where Nayla stood. Shiva, she was fast. If Nayla ran back into the tunnel, she could be trapped. Who knew if the ziggurat door would be open? If it were, what would stop Arachne from chasing her into the desert? It was safer in the cave. Céleste would return soon. She must've heard Nayla give away her position and should know to hurry.

Face your fears, Nayla. She jogged down the ramp toward the bridge, utterly verrückt. That was her best chance at survival. At the bridge, a struggle could land Arachne in the flames.

If she could only—a thread pinned her foot and yanked her upside down. *So much for that.*

"I've got a little nymph in my web," said Arachne, reeling her up. "I remember you. Persistent, aren't we? No one's gotten away from me like you have. I'm going to savor this."

If Nayla fought, the fall would cause serious injury. The mecha-sleeves were virtually useless. *Wait.* She extended the pistons and retracted them over and over, as many times as possible, as she was slowly drawn up the string. Three stories up. Four stories. This time, like during her trials at the Jacoma yards, she did not water the boiler. Her wrist gauge redlined. The machine rattled. Nayla let out an agonizing shriek, unbuckling the straps on her legs for the piston drills, broken arm and all.

Nerves shot up her elbow, throbbing in pain. The drills dangled from the shaking boiler as she undid her torso next.

Stupid latch. She unbuckled the last one and wriggled free, holding the sleeves by their straps one-handed.

Hanging, she swung violently back and forth and back and forth. On the forward swing, she chucked her invention at the canopy.

The boiler gained height and exploded in a blinding fireball, setting the silk loft aflame. The web on her foot released all slack. She put out her hands as the obsidian floor jumped at her.

"Gotcha." A sudden pressure snatched her body from the air by the waist.

Nayla anxiously clung to Céleste's arms, dripping in blood.

Arachne soared through the cave and stuck to the gem-like wall, upside down and apoplectic.

Céleste fluttered to a running stop. "You're hit."

Nayla examined her bloodied arms and legs, filled with shrapnel. "Where's the staff?"

"I dropped it to catch you."

On the bridge lay a rod made of two strips of gold, one meter in length. It had gold leaves sprouted from top to bottom and a green gem enclosed in its head. Céleste had actually found it. Circe's staff.

"Get it," said Nayla.

Nayla pushed Céleste's hands away. Céleste fluttered to the bridge while two spinnerets came into view over Nayla's chest. *Please, don't let this monster impale her!*

Céleste landed and whirled, staff raised.

"Drop the rhabdos," said Arachne, facing the weapon's ire, bobbing her carapace.

Nayla flexed her stomach, expecting the fork on Arachne's butt to run her through any minute.

"Arachne, don't," said Céleste. "I can give you what you want."

"You don't know what I want."

"Freedom. You want freedom," Céleste repeated. "Us nouvelles nymphes chose to have powers. We drank a mixis. But Athena... She transformed you against your will."

"Zeus will grant me freedom when the unknown threat has passed and the hall no longer needs guarding."

Nayla tilted her head while Arachne spoke. Blood dripped from Arachne's arms and back. The shrapnel had maimed her too.

"You are mortal, Arachne," said Céleste. "I won't let you die guarding these treasures."

"You freeing me changes nothing. The gods can descend at any time and demand favors to preserve the pantheon. They must free me."

The amulet on the staff showered Arachne in emerald light.

Arachne's thorax shined into a torso as she tried to stab Nayla with her receding spinnerets. They receded so fast that she failed to break skin, and her six legs merged to two, straddling Nayla, who was unscathed by the jab.

"What have you done?" Arachne looked at her feet.

"Set you free." Céleste drew the staff behind her neck and rested it there with both hands.

"Uh!" Arachne shouted. "Change me back!" She gritted her teeth. "It's hopeless. You can't."

"She can't?" asked Nayla, catching her breath.

"The staff can only transform something once, and only she can wield it."

"Arachne requires moly if I am to transform her again," Céleste supplied. "It's a white flower with a black root, but you won't be needing that, Arachne. You'll get used to the old you, and the talented weaver you were meant to be."

"How do you know that, Cél?" Nayla hurt to move.

"The curator inside told me. He's a Frenchman. I think he's your lost legionnaire."

"Captain Beauvais." A smile fought through Nayla's pained expression.

Céleste ran to her side. "You're bleeding badly. You need the caduceus." She turned to Arachne. "The curator said I cannot choose another item for twenty-one days. Is there a way for you to save her?"

Arachne shook her head. "I wasn't lying. You need to be a god or demigod to enter the hall. Or so I thought. However, I cannot turn to pollen like you."

Céleste ran to the hall, set down the staff, and postured before the façade. Five meters out, she unloaded her screamers. Shooting stars pummeled the door and exploded, nova after nova, stirring up cave dust, blowing the camouflaged tapestries to tatters. She stuck her hands together and fired a large red sun. A bright light flashed. A concussive blast followed, knocking Céleste off her sandals.

"Arachne," Nayla groaned. "What happened to my soldier friend after he pushed me through Hecate's doorway?"

"When he was the last man standing, four patrons showed up. They offered him a mixis and a job." She pointed carelessly to the hall. "Our latest docent."

"He's shackled to the floor," said Céleste, rising to her feet.

Arachne's hand dropped. "Hades won't stand for this, you know. What did you come here for, anyway?"

"The Cap of Hades," said Nayla.

Arachne snickered. "Whatever for?"

"To escape samsara, the cycle of death and rebirth. To end dukha, all suffering. To become one with Brahman."

Arachne laughed, looking at the holes in Nayla's arms and legs. "You're suffering for a chance to escape suffering?"

"When you laugh, you laugh at yourself. Brahman dwells in everyone."

Arachne's smile faded. "Naïve creature." She grabbed loose strands of webbing and made tourniquets over Nayla's wounds. "I guess you can't negotiate desire."

"I guess not." Nayla grasped one of the webs. "Save some for yourself."

Arachne examined her wounds, nowhere near as deep judging from the amount of blood. She finished tying off Nayla's leg and rose, saying nothing.

Céleste hit the door with another volley. When the smoke cleared, it stood defiantly intact.

"Céleste," Nayla called.

Céleste ceased fire and turned. "Vidocq," she panted, glistening with sweat, leaving the staff behind on the floor, "how do we get out of this?"

"Transform me into Fleur d'Étoile at full power," Nayla said. "I'll poof into the vault for the caduceus."

"I'm not so vain as you are verrückt."

"Folle," said Nayla. "It will still be me. I'll just appear as another manifestation of Brahman."

"Oui, moi."

"Please, Céleste."

Céleste stalked to the staff and picked it up as if to safeguard this alternative route. She hesitated before returning to meet Nayla. "I know what it's like to be without a soul. I don't want you to be without a body."

"If I don't heal now, I'll die and receive a new body anyway."

Céleste's face crumpled. She uplifted the rod. Emerald rays flashed in Nayla's retinas.

When Nayla looked down, she saw pale hands the color of apricot. Her garments had turned from red to pink, pants to skirt, flame retardant to leather. A pink bodice wrapped her breasts, which had increased in size. Her hair roped her shoulders in blonde tendrils.

"Wunderbar," said Nayla, her voice strange—that of Céleste's. "How do I go poof?"

Céleste looked at her kindly, her retroussé nose relaxed, a tinge of sadness in her blue-green eyes—eyes that were now hers. "Think about something light in weight."

"Like a dirigible?"

"Oui, that'll do."

Nayla focused on dirigibles. "When should it work?"

"Now."

Dirigibles. Dirigibles. Dirigibles. "It's not working."

"Something's wrong. Your hair is still blonde. There's no pink. Try a star."

Nayla aimed her hand at the ceiling and willed a shooting star. Still nothing. "I don't understand. If the staff depowered Arachne, why does it not repower me?"

Céleste looked at the floor. "Hermes had said the staff cannot heal. That's why he needs the caduceus for Charon." She looked regretfully at Nayla. "We're nouvelles nymphes. We drank a mixis. Arachne didn't."

Nayla nodded, in tears. "Her original change was a direct transformation. Ours is based on stages."

Céleste glanced at the hall. "Wait here. I'll see if Beauvais can help."

She burst into pollen.

THE
HALL
OF
FABLED OBJECTS

éleste's granular structure poured out of the microscopic gap in the door, floated across the cave, and returned to shape over Nayla's body.

"I told him our situation. He's worried about you, but he's powerless to help. I've already chosen my object."

Arachne placed a fist on her hip and cocked her thumb.

Footsteps sounded in the hallway upstairs leading to the ramp. In a flash, Nayla's eyes were upon the entrance.

Céleste stared, incredulous. "It's Hermes," she whispered.

Nayla motioned for a hand up. After an arduous rise to her feet, Nayla, bleeding out, whispered in Céleste's ear.

"He can heal me."

"What if it's not him?"

"We have to hide." Nayla nodded at the hall. "Behind the colored threads."

Céleste pointed the staff at Arachne. "I've shown you mercy. If you give us away, I will blast you."

Nayla gripped Céleste's collar and let her butterfly wings carry them over the bridge. The landing proved laborious; the bending of knees, contraction of legs, feeling the embedded shrapnel pinch in her tissue. Céleste peeled back the curtain portraying the black-gemmed wall next to the hall's façade. Nayla placed her back against the cold rock, able to see clearly the approaching shadow at the top of the ramp. Céleste retracted her wings and held Nayla in place, Circe's staff crooked in defense.

A man appeared in the cave. He looked like Hermes, though clearly he was not. He had blond hair, a white shirt, black pants with gold-laced boots, a red loincloth, and a purple shawl. As he walked the ramp and crossed the bridge, his features became more distinct. A square head with a slender mouth and eyes shaped like Medjool dates. The man tipped his head at Arachne, showing dimples when he smiled.

Céleste braced Nayla harder to keep her from slouching and nodded at the man. Did Céleste know him?

"Greetings, Arachne," said the god or demigod, glancing at her wounds. "Did you catch a live one?"

"For the time being."

"That'll keep you busy." The deity approached the foot of the steps, meters from Nayla. "Odyssey," he proclaimed.

The doorway expelled dust from its cracks and opened to abundant rays of light. The deity waited patiently and walked in like he owned the place.

"Curator," he said, "I have visited my wife's family in the underworld and wish to leave. I must entrance the dog Cerberus. Where is my lyre?"

"Now," whispered Nayla.

Céleste extricated Nayla from the web curtain. Sharp pain electrified Nayla's legs with each step, but the excitement of the open door and choosing one of those beautiful objects spurred her on. She struggled into the vault as it sealed behind her.

A pattern of gold loops corkscrewed the blue tiles throughout the hall, illuminated by cones of light spaced every five meters. The pools of light on the floor marked out intersections where the hall branched off into chambers filled with treasures of untold powers. Beauvais, in a toga, stood in shackles next to a brazier, one of the many disc-shaped firepits that spanned the hall, smelling of burning oil.

"Castor and Pollux," said the mystery god, "is that you in disguise?"

"Oui," said Beauvais, covering for them, "the Dioscuri, the Gemini. They have been experimenting with Circe's staff." He winked at Nayla.

Céleste had explained their predicament to Beauvais, but how did he know which one was Nayla? Oho, her hair was not mottled pink like Céleste's.

"Castor, Pollux," said the god, "don't you recognize me?"

Who was he? He had wanted a lyre to play for Cerberus and was visiting his wife's family...

"You have a wife?" asked Céleste, confused.

Of course! He was the man in Céleste's vision in the well. The vapors on the water. He was her husband.

"Why, come now, Pollux—or is that you, Castor? You've both met Eurydice."

"Orpheus," Nayla said, short of breath. "How do you do?"

"How do I do? I must return to the Elysian Fields."

"Are you happily married?" asked Céleste.

"Why, yes, ecstatically so." Orpheus creased his brow. "Are you ill?"

"Pardon my brother," said Nayla. "Too much ergotized beer."

Beauvais intervened with magnanimous congeniality and pointed Orpheus down the hall. "Your lyre is on the last door on the left, freshly tuned. I will see to the mental faculties of our twin friends."

Orpheus gave Beauvais a bewildered glance, smiled dubiously, and began his walk to the chamber.

Beauvais came to Nayla's aid.

She hugged him tight. "Capitaine, I'm so glad you're alive."

"I have been initiated." He brushed off the news. "Look at you. What have you done to yourself?"

"Shrapnel. My mechanized sleeves blew up." His golden shackles glimmered in the light. "You're held prisoner. Why don't you escape?"

"I can escape?"

"Oui, you're a nouveau satyre, from what Arachne described. You have powers like me. Well, maybe not fire-related, but something."

"I have experienced no such anomaly."

"What did the gods tell you?" asked Céleste. "The ones who handed you a mixis?"

"When I breathe in life's flora, I will become immortal."

"Maybe he needs to smell flowers." Nayla hobbled forward.

"He's already smelled my perfume while I was breaking and entering," said Céleste. "Surely it can wait." She studied Orpheus's receding figure. "Where is Hermes's caduceus?"

"Second door on the right," said Beauvais.

"These shackles that enchain you"—Nayla felt the cold links—"who forged them?"

"Hephaestus. They are the same chains that bound Prometheus. Only Heracles can free me."

Nayla could not abandon Beauvais again. He'd sacrificed his life for her. She was his muse, and he, her artist. "If the chains were built by Hephaestus, he would've used his hammer. If his hammer built them, his hammer can break them too."

"Not again, Nay," said Céleste. "You're bleeding to death. Think of yourself. If you choose the hammer, you won't survive."

"It won't work anyway, mademoiselles," said Beauvais. "Metallurgy requires heat."

Nayla looked at her white hands. Flameless, powerless, bloody. Her eyes lifted to Céleste and the green eye of her staff. "Cél, if you transform into me, you can produce fire."

"Quoi?" said Céleste. "You've gone mental."

Beauvais rubbed his beard and snapped his fingers. "If you transform into Spuckfeuer, you can free me. I will choose the moly to turn you back. Start walking. Orpheus will return soon. I will stall him to secure our escape."

Céleste dragged Nayla down the polished corridor with its diffused light.

"Where is the hammer?" Nayla asked Beauvais over her shoulder.

"The chamber at the end of the hall."

Nayla limped across the refractory tile.

"Listen to me, Nay, as a friend," said Céleste. "You're over-compensating. Beauvais's life is not in danger. Don't reduce yourself because you feel bad."

"He risked his life to save mine, to get the cap, something I wanted. I've been so selfish."

"Think of the silver lining," said Céleste. "You saved Beauvais's life. From what you tell me, he and the legionnaires would've been killed in Siam. A soldier's life expectancy is short. There it is, the second door on the right. Get the caduceus. I beg you."

Céleste bore her weight on Nayla to urge her to stop. Nayla looked in the archway at the glowing treasures. Was she being a doormat? A subservient martyr? A straw hut, as the French said? She'd made it this far. She could heal herself. This was her life. Did she not love herself? She thought about what Ravi uncle had told her, about listening to her intuition. What did it say? Her thoughts were so loud.

"Do you even have the strength to wield the hammer in my body?" asked Céleste.

"Ja, Hephaestus is my patron god," said Nayla. "Are you afraid of transforming into me?"

Céleste shook her head. "Non, I don't care about that. I care about you and Gustave."

"Then why can't I care about Beauvais?"

"Beauvais is initiated. He is safe. Gustave is at the mercy of a lunatic."

Orpheus walked by, adjusting the strings of his lyre. "Gentlemen."

"Orpheus." Nayla held Céleste steady to stop her from doing something desperate.

Time dwindled in the vault as Orpheus made for the exit. It was possible Nayla would never have an opportunity to free Beauvais again. She raked her hand through the ashes of her mind and felt something hot. An ember. It whispered to her, oh so quiet. Free Beauvais. She fanned the whisper into a flame.

Nayla looked at Céleste. "Up until now, I feared Beauvais was dead. This is my chance at redemption."

Nayla separated from Céleste and struggled on toward the end of the hall for the hammer, not waiting for reply.

Céleste barred her teeth and relaxed. "We'll never make it at this speed." Her butterfly wings fanned out of her spine.

She scooped Nayla up like a bundle of firewood and fluttered down the corridor between the marble walls and coffered ceiling. Nayla could see herself in the tiles, zipping by as Céleste ferried her to the end. Céleste landed under the arch, set Nayla on her feet, and collapsed her wings.

A soft shaft of light beamed in the center of the round room, diffusing light onto the golden objects. Nayla inhaled the scent of oil, processed from pig fat, burning in the torches. Her gaze passed over the Bow of Apollo, Jason's golden fleece, and rested squarely upon—

"The Cap of Hades," she said, her words greasing the air.

It had a black, metallic shine, and a plume of blue flame. She viewed herself in its reflection while the eyeholes gazed back at her. The helmet could frame her face as it did every god and hero who'd come before. Created by the Elder Cyclopses, it was given to Hades to fight the Titans. Given to Athena to help Diomedes fight Ares on the Trojan battlefield. Given to Hermes to fight the giant, Hippolytus. Given to Perseus to escape the Gorgons after defeating Medusa. And now it could be hers.

She licked her lips and put her foot on the single step ringing the pedestal. Why bother to heal physically? The Cap of Hades would lead to moksha, end all suffering in this lifetime, where hereafter she could be one with Brahman. She reached for the cap, as if to feel its warmth.

"I warn you." Céleste stood by the Hammer of Hephaestus. "It will be strange. Me being you. It will be like looking at yourself in the mirror. Hearing your own voice will make you think you're having a conversation in your head out loud—a bizarre feeling, to be sure."

Why did Céleste interrupt? She had wanted Nayla to get the caduceus. What did she care if Nayla chose the cap? Was Céleste afraid it might not bind to Nayla as Céleste's soul had failed to bind to her? Was this cap not the reason the legionnaires had come down here? It would be wrong to let them die in vain.

But one legionnaire was still alive. Her friend, le Capitaine. She promised the deceased legionnaires she would save him.

Look at Céleste. She could not bind to her soul and now all she wanted to do was save her friends. If Nayla chose the cap, she would not get that chance. It was odd. The only reason she had met Beauvais and Céleste was to get the cap, and now their lives felt more important than a mere object. Odder still, had Nayla known Céleste in Jacoma, she would never have tried to kill herself. It would have felt selfish—to have someone who understood her and thrown it away—thrown herself away—depriving Céleste and Kameera of a good friend while making them suffer from the loss.

Had Hestia not been there to stop Nayla from making a huge mistake, Nayla would never have met Céleste. Hestia had stopped Nayla from making a mistake... just like... just like Céleste was now.

But Nayla was so close to death. She could not risk another lifetime to figure out how to become one with Brahman all over, could she? Did she not deserve to have this one need met?

In this moment, the ember in her mind told her what she needed. It sizzled in the ash heap. She breathed life into its fiery glow. Help my friends, it said. If she couldn't escape suffering through moksha, at least she could escape the pain of having failed her friends. Brahman could wait another life.

Nayla returned her foot to the floor and stepped back from the pedestal, from the helmet's magnetic pull. She joined Céleste by the stone shelf and gripped the hammer. The handle was the length of her arm, which hurt to lift.

"Danke for not forcing my choice."

"I elucidated." Céleste took deep breaths, gripping the staff, talking herself up. "D'accord, d'accord. Tout de suite!"

She held it overhead and showered herself in emerald rays. A white sunburst enveloped her body, transforming her from larva to pupa, wherein the light heightened her stature, shrank her breasts, curled her hair, widened her nose, narrowed her lips, fattened her eyebrows, sharpened her chin, darkened her hair, thinned out her frame, and faded her skin until she emerged from her chrysalis a whole other person. Well, maybe not whole.

"Dépêches-toi."

Céleste was right. It was strange for Nayla to hear her own voice, and in such flawless French.

Céleste stepped through the door and sprouted phoenix wings. Nayla got in front of her and felt her boots leave the tile, soaring back to the enchanted doors where Orpheus and Beauvais had assembled.

"Orpheus," said Nayla. "I come clean. We are nymphs, and the curator is my friend." She dragged the hammer to Beauvais. "I must save him. I know your story. The pain of losing your lover, the difficult journey you undertook to save her from the underworld. How Hades and Persephone were moved by your music and your love. How you lost Eurydice all over again when your faith wavered and you looked back to see her. You know what the underworld does to people. I implore you, Orpheus. Let me save my friend as my dying wish."

Orpheus was at a loss for words. He stood back, a sign of permission.

"Nay." Céleste looked at her hands. "How do I raise the temperature?"

Nayla put it in terms Céleste could understand. "Think about squeezing a pair of bellows over an open hearth."

Flame engulfed Céleste's body in spontaneous combustion. She slapped her head.

"Your hair doesn't burn," said Nayla, trying to calm her. "Crank the heat and focus it on this piece of chain." She prodded the links on the floor with the hammer.

"D'accord."

Some biological valve from deep within set Céleste's neck and shoulders on fire. She raised her fist to the chain. Tufts of flame shot at the floor in intervals.

"They're not shooting stars," said Nayla. "Hold a constant stream."

Céleste repositioned, held both fists together and squinted at the chain. The jet turned on like a faucet and gushed forth.

"Ja, like that. Keep it going."

Her arms and legs full of tacks, Nayla picked up the hammer, wound it overhead, and slammed it against the hot links. Céleste was right. Nayla lacked upper body strength. Nayla's new legs were stronger, but she couldn't wield a mallet with her feet. She raised the hammer again and struck. Sparks flew.

"Hold flame."

Nayla circled the hammer up and back down.

"Hold."

The links burned hotter. Blinding white. It hurt to look at, but she had to.

Nayla swung. The hit landed.

The links cracked apart.

"Fantastique," said Beauvais.

"Nay," said Céleste, nervous, cutting off flame, "how do I lower my temperature?"

"Picture a lit candle die to nothing."

Céleste snuffed her flame, reeking of fireplace.

Beauvais pulled the chain loose. Although shackled, he was free.

"Merci, Nayla, I knew you would return for me."

The hammer clanged to the floor. Light-headed, Nayla lowered herself and sat. It was too much exertion, a life of exertion. She was fatigued, drained, spent.

Céleste patted her body to triple check the flame had gone out and approached. Nayla fell back into Céleste's embrace, too weak to talk.

"She's dying," Céleste said to Beauvais.

"Should I choose the moly or the caduceus?" asked Beauvais.

Nayla forced the word, "Moly."

"Chut!" Céleste ordered. "Get the caduceus."

"Nein, you could be like me forever," Nayla murmured. "You're so far away from yourself."

Beauvais ran down the hall, the tail of the chain still hot, and disappeared into the second door on the right. He reemerged with the herald's wand, entwined by snakes, its head crowned by wings and capped by a blue stone. Beauvais raced back and touched the scepter to Nayla's chest. Cyan light emitted from the end, dissolving the pain of her wounds. She reached for the web bandages and ripped them free of her arm. Little pieces of metal sprinkled from her skin. She'd healed instantly.

"I'm... better."

Céleste helped her up.

Nayla extended her broken arm and prodded at the spot it had been swollen. The break had mended. "Look, my arm is healed." She unbandaged the splint. "I feel amazing."

"I could've spellbound you all with my lyre," said Orpheus, "though I am touched by your acts of sacrifice. It is true, I know what it's like to botch a second chance. If you explain to me your plight, I may be of service."

"Hermes," Nayla began, thinking fast, "has made a deal with me. If I retrieve the caduceus, my friend can acquire Circe's staff." She pointed to Céleste. "The caduceus is to heal Charon's voice. He drank from the Styx. In exchange for my friend borrowing the staff, I am to marry Hermes and live on Olympus. Hermes could not come himself because the area is verboten and—"

"—one item per customer," said Orpheus. "Charon and Hermes took me to Hades once upon a time to help me find

Eurydice. I will assist you back to them and pretend I never saw you."

"Danke," said Nayla.

Orpheus approached the enchanted door. "Iliad."

Its hinges creaked as the door, stone on stone, opened.

Arachne was seated on the bridge, her legs dangling over the blue fires. She fixated on their company as Orpheus led the way down the steps armed with his lyre, Beauvais the caduceus, Céleste the staff, and Nayla the hammer. Arachne knew better than to protest or flee into the hot desert alone.

Arachne looked at Céleste. "You're well."

"I see they disarmed you, Arachne," said Orpheus. "I am leading a party to the surface."

"Are you coming with us or not?" asked Nayla.

The Hall of Fabled Objects closed behind them.

"I am not," said Arachne. "All my friends are dead, and Athena will exact her revenge tenfold."

"Speaking of," said Beauvais.

Arachne caught sight of him and rose. "What is he doing free?"

Beauvais raised the caduceus as if to heal her, then swung it across her chin. "This is for Khoumag."

"Beauvais, non!" cried Céleste.

Nayla jumped.

The blow knocked Arachne off the bridge and into the Phlegethon.

Nayla peered over the edge, in disbelief at what had happened.

"Why did you do that?" asked Céleste, searching the fire. "She was mortal and I depowered her. She won't survive."

"She killed my brothers in arms."

"The pantheon gave you a mixis and spared your life."

"Spared my life to enslave me."

Sweet Shiva, what was Orpheus going to think about this? Would he turn them over to Hades? Nayla had to calm Céleste down first.

"Cél, Beauvais is a soldier."

"Et alors? I wanted her to live," said Céleste, "and learn the error of her ways."

"When?" asked Beauvais.

"Never." Céleste said angrily. "Now who is going to guard the hall from the unknown threat?"

The words fell hollow on Nayla's ears, as Céleste had considered helping the Titans break in. Nayla could sense the real issue. What Céleste really cared about was how fragile they all were. Nayla put a hand on Céleste's shoulder to help her cope.

"The door will suit fine," said Beauvais. "Right, Orpheus? What do you say?"

"Are you upset?" Nayla winced.

"Oui," said Céleste, as if the question were directed at her.

"The maenads tore me limb from limb," said Orpheus. "Her death was painless by comparison. I wasn't here. I know nothing."

"Will you still help us?" asked Nayla.

Orpheus looked into their hopeful faces. All looked back at him save Céleste, who stared hopelessly into the flames.

"There's a green ring down there," she said.

Nayla looked, knowing she'd see nothing. "Hecate's doorway."

"I see Thanatos," said Céleste.

"He is taking Arachne's body back to Earth," Nayla supplied.

"Can you fly us down?" Beauvais asked Céleste.

"She could," said Nayla, "but we'd receive third-degree burns." Nayla was doubtful she'd make it through the flames unharmed even if she could achieve pollen form, given how frightened Céleste was against Nayla's fire.

"Point it out, and I'll jump," said Beauvais. "I can heal us after with the caduceus."

"We can't leave." Céleste frowned. "S'il te plait, Beauvais. I need you to heal Charon so I can save Gustave. Nayla, I transformed for you. You have to show my face. You're the only one who—"

"Shh," said Nayla. "I won't leave you."

Céleste exhaled and clung to Beauvais. "Please. If it weren't for me, you'd still be in chains. You are a French soldier, so fight for the French."

"How will we get home after?" asked Beauvais.

"Orpheus can take us. Can't you, Orpheus?"

"I suppose I can drop you off on the way to the Elysian Fields," said Orpheus.

Céleste looked tensely at Beauvais.

Beauvais rubbed his beard and sagged his shoulders. "Je suis avec toi."

"Dieu merci." Céleste relaxed. "Merci, Orpheus. I could kiss you."

"I've heard that song before," said Orpheus. "Follow me."

He led them off the bridge, up the ramp, around the corner, and into the gem-laden hallway where the red sun shone.

"Beauvais," said Nayla. "I must warn you. The red light changes our appearance to salami."

"So I have heard." Beauvais still expressed shock, looking at his hands as they emerged on the pinnacle of the ziggurat overlooking the desert and the mechanical city on the horizon.

"Could be worse." Beauvais dropped his hands. "I never thought I'd be out of there."

"What is your name, curator?" asked Orpheus.

"Capitaine Jacques Beauvais of the French Foreign Legion."

"Orpheus, son of Apollo." Orpheus shook his hand. "Ever flown before?" He tugged on a rope attached to a spike. Above them hovered a pirate ship suspended by a dirigible canvased in beige.

"Sacré bleu."

It appears the jig is up. I am Capitaine Jacques Beauvais of the Légion Étrangère, and I am very thankful the pin on my lapel did not give me away. See here, the seven flamed grenade. That's right, a fossil of a bygone era. But how were you to know that I am one and the same? That I am immortal? Do not be alarmed. It is still good old Jacques. Oui, I have tasted ambrosia, the nectar of the gods. I have lived in the hypogeum inside of the ziggurat. My time as curator has made me a walking encyclopedia.

Take, for instance, the myth of Eros and Psyche. In case you are unfamiliar, let me bring you up to speed. Psyche was the youngest of three daughters to an unnamed king and queen. The townspeople, they shirked their worship of Aphrodite at her temple and grew enamored by Psyche, a living beauty. To retaliate, Aphrodite commanded her son Eros, the god of passion, to make Psyche fall in love with a beast. Eros crept into Psyche's bed chamber, drew his bow over the sleeping princess, and was so stunned by her beauty that, when she turned in her sleep, he accidentally wounded himself. Not wanting to be seen, he fled the room. It appeared Eros had bungled his task, but

Psyche's beauty could not go unpunished. Aphrodite decided that no mortal could ever pursue Psyche as a lover.

And so, while Psyche's two sisters got hitched, Psyche had no suitors. What to do? The family urged her father to seek the oracle. The Oracle of Delphi prophesied that Psyche would marry a beast and therefore must be abandoned on a cliff, lest a terrible curse befall the kingdom. Princess Psyche received a hug from her despondent dad—very heartfelt, oui—then she mounted the cliffside and jumped. Lucky for her, she did not go splat, non—the winds of Zephyrus carried her to Eros's palace in the clouds.

That night, Eros arrived to Psyche's bedroom, shrouded in darkness, where they married and made passionate love. Then he left before dawn, as you do. Wash, rinse, repeat. After months of not knowing her lover's identity, Psyche asked Eros, "Excusez-moi, qui êtes-vous?" Eros assured her she may use the more familiar personal pronoun of "tu" and reasoned the love they shared was enough and that, in the dark, they were equal. She nodded, satisfied with the arrangement.

The satisfaction did not last. Psyche grew homesick. Eros, not one to cling, let Psyche go back to her family. If she were to ever return to him, it would prove her love was real. Her sisters, on the other hand, were jealous of Psyche and her rich husband and convinced her that she had married a monster, hence all the shadow and secrecy. With this seed of doubt planted, Psyche went to the mountain, leapt into Zephyrus's wind, and flew back to the empyrean palace.

Eros was pleased. Psyche's return had proved her love. Or so he thought. When he next fell asleep in the dark, she unsheathed a knife and lit a lamp. As she approached the bed, the lamp revealed his features. Paralyzed by his beauty, Psyche knew deep in her heart that he was a god. Suddenly, oil dripped from the lamp and splashed his chest. He shot up and saw a dumbfounded Psyche wielding a knife. "Es-tu folle, femme? How dare you cross my boundaries? You shall never see me again." Eros fled out the window. Psyche leapt after him and took a nasty spill. But, she survived the fall—as much as one can survive with a broken heart.

Why do I share this tale? Oui, beauty is more than skin deep, that is true. But also, Psyche is soul, and Eros, passion. When the soul demands too much of a lover, passion flees. The object of our love can be experienced but never possessed. That would be merging and not love. With a merge, you cannot tell where one person ends and another begins. Each partner's value is assigned to the other. Emotions overlap. There are no boundaries. The equilibrium of love will have toppled and passion vanished from our beds.

Psyche begged Aphrodite to reunite with her son, Eros, and was ultimately sent on a quest to the underworld. For Persephone's beauty ointment. Très bien. Like Psyche, her patron goddess before her, Céleste too was sent on a quest to the underworld. Are the ointment and Céleste's soul MacGuffins? I beg your pardon, my friend. But their goals were not to obtain beauty ointment and souls in wells. Their goals were to be happily married. And for Céleste to have well-bred children. Think of these objects as stepping stones, or whatever you like. Jacques will not lead the witness. Too much.

You see, the underworld provides opportunity to disentangle oneself from belief systems, like I have done. Forgive me for Arachne's death, my friend. It took me many years to remove the fight of Ares from my blood. Killing was not the source of my powers. Non. Perhaps I am too close to the story to comment further. Let the painting speak for itself. Voilà. Orpheus in the Underworld, and I don't mean Offenbach's opera. Try not to stick your fingers in any moving parts.

ORPHÉE AUX ENFERS

Orpheus wrapped his foot around the mooring rope and cut it loose from the spike. He sheathed his blade, gave the cord a tug, and the airship winched him toward the keel, his purple scarf and red shawl fluttering in the wind. *Take off time.* Nayla grabbed the staff from Céleste and instructed her on how to expel flames through her feet. *Flex your legs and pretend the fire is an unbroken volley of shooting stars.* Céleste gathered Nayla in one arm and Beauvais the other, opened her phoenix wings, and fired on her thrusters, blowing holes in her shoes.

Feathers rippling, she aimed for the bay doors on the keel of the ship, surpassed Orpheus, and fanned out her wings to slow down for arrival. They crash-landed on some crates and recovered their fabled objects.

Gracefully, Orpheus stepped off the spooled rope and bid they follow him up to the main deck. He climbed a ladder through the cargo bay and stepped onto the lacquered planks of the pirate ship. His earrings made him look just like a Barbary corsair. He walked the steps to the quarter deck and took command of the helm. Captain on the bridge.

"Where to?" he asked.

Nayla looked over the railing at the bustling clockwork town. "Where the stepwell empties into the Liver Lethe. It's in the Persian Quarter."

She wasn't aeronautically inclined, but the jib sails and top sails were beautiful. As was the giant balloon stringing the whole works together by net. She waved Beauvais to join her by the mast on the main deck and placed his shackles on a cannon overlooking the rail.

"This will serve as our anvil," said Nayla.

She stationed Céleste close to the iron and told her to point her finger at the shackle's keyhole.

"Gut, Cél," said Nayla. "Now pull your thumb like you're cocking the hammer of a gun."

A blow torch shot on from Céleste's finger.

"It's quite wide," Nayla observed. "Squint to focus the flame."

Céleste did so.

"Nervous?" Nayla asked Beauvais.

"Calm under fire," he said. "Make it quick."

"Cél, lower the flame into the hole."

Céleste hesitated. "Perhaps I don't believe le Capitaine will change his ways and I slip?"

"Then I burn up"—Beauvais glared—"and you wield the caduceus."

Céleste glared back. "Perhaps I use Circe's staff and make my own." She smirked.

"Do it and see."

Céleste's smile faded. "It won't work, will it?"

"Non, mademoiselle, it will not. You cannot transform ordinary objects into fabled objects, nor fabled objects into other fabled objects, or I would have had you turn Hephaestus's chains into pixy dust."

"Why can't I?"

"That's how Circe made it. In case the staff ever wound up in the wrong hands."

"Cél," said Nayla, prodding, "why don't you thank Beauvais for helping us?"

"Merci." Céleste touched her finger to the golden shackles and watched them fade to a fervid white.

"Lift up," said Nayla, happy the conflict was over.

Céleste withdrew her finger.

Nayla picked up a spike, set it in the keyhole, and tapped it with the hammer. The cuffs unclasped. Beauvais pulled back, rubbing his wrists as the shackles clattered to the deck.

"How do I put the torch out?" asked Céleste.

"Pop it in your mouth."

Céleste's face contorted.

"Respect the flame," said Nayla. "You can do it."

Céleste closed her eyes and snuffed the flame on her tongue in a satisfying sizzle.

Beauvais took in his surroundings, the red landscape, the golden-figured Hindu temples, the domed masques. "So, this is what it looks like outside of that cave."

"We're in Tartarus," said Nayla.

"Jacoma from hell."

"Industrial hell," said Nayla, turning to Céleste. "Well, did I martyr myself correctly in saving le capitaine?"

"Non," said Céleste, "you did not martyr yourself at all. I misspoke. On this occasion, you saved your friend, and I saved mine." She side-hugged Nayla. "Are you disappointed you didn't get the cap?"

"I would like to know what it feels like, ja," said Nayla, "but I'd rather have Beauvais."

"What about transforming into me?" asked Céleste. "What does that feel like?"

"Like a reincarnation where I get to keep my mind from a previous life. Almost like I can start over afresh, but I'm aware of all the karma and the cap to remove it. How about you?"

"I feel like I'm wearing a mask," said Céleste. "If I become your facsimile, kindly slap my face."

"Do you think I still get my powers by drinking?"

"Oui. Only our skin has changed."

Nayla pulled out a rolled cigarette. "Do you mind?" She pressed Céleste's thumb to the end and lit up.

"Seeing me smoke looks so odd," said Céleste.

Nayla coughed up a lung. "It feels odd."

"Your body isn't used to it."

"Because it's yours?"

"Because you healed."

"May I?" Beauvais extended his hand.

Nayla gave him a cigarette. Céleste lit Beauvais. He inhaled deeply.

"Mademoiselles," he said, "what is our exit strategy? Are you going to elope with Hermes?"

"Nein," said Nayla. "Beauvais, you and I will meet Hermes and Charon in the stepwell. Their submarine will rise. You heal Charon with the caduceus. They give us Gustave. He is Céleste's good friend."

"Ah, a hostage situation."

"Ja, sad but so. Hermes will ask Céleste to come with him. He will think I am she. When I am safely out of the underworld, I will reveal myself to be Nayla binti Azmi, and he will let me go."

"Are you sure about that?" asked Céleste.

"Why would he marry me? Did you hear his comment to Charon? Hermes offered to transform someone into your lookalike while Hermes would keep the genuine article. He does not want an impostor."

"Where will I find you when he discovers your ruse?"

"French Athens, if I can make it."

"There are no guarantees he will release you to Earth."

"I know."

"This is the stupidest plan," Céleste protested.

"Emotionally, ja," said Nayla. "But it is the most logical."

"I can't lose you."

"Only temporarily. If you can think of something where everyone gets to live, I'm listening, but the ship is on the move, and Orpheus won't wait forever. It has to be this way."

Céleste hugged Nayla close.

"Where will I be during this rendezvous?" asked Céleste. "I, meaning you."

"To Hermes, you successfully heisted the cap and left to some far-off place invisible. Really, you will hide behind the partition at the top of the well with Circe's staff. If the plan fails, transform him."

"And the hammer?"

"I'll keep the hammer. If Hermes asks, I used it to free Beauvais, which I did. He is a fellow Frenchman."

"And Orpheus?"

"Orpheus will wait in the airship for me, Hermes, and Charon to submerge. Then he will guide you and Beauvais out of the underworld with his lyre."

"I wonder if he'll take me to the Elysian Fields to visit," said Céleste.

"I don't think so," said Nayla. "He lives there with *Eurydice*."

"Why do you put it like that? Why say *Eurydice*?"

"I believe Loïe planted him in your vision to toy with you."

"Or I witnessed my own future. There is one way to find out. I'll casually inquire." Céleste walked the steps to the quarter deck.

"Cél, wait," said Nayla.

"I must know for sure. Strike while the iron's hot, eh?"

"I lost the thread." Beauvais exhaled tobacco. "God, it feels good to smoke again."

"Céleste saw Orpheus as her husband in a vision in the Well of Lost Souls."

"Waouh, you went there? Creepy place."

"You're telling me," said Nayla, fearful of how Beauvais would respond to her next revelation. "I also saw Khoumag. And Eugène. And your men on Charon's boat. They wanted me to find you."

"So you have." Beauvais shut his eyes to ruminate. He was not angry, or at least his face did not read anger. He opened his eyes and kissed her hand. "Did they have regrets?"

"Only that they couldn't be with you."

Beauvais nodded, appreciative. Nayla was well aware he was a lone soldier now, a legionnaire without a company.

"They fought bravely," said Beauvais, inhaling his smoke.

"I'm proud of them," Nayla added.

"Do you feel guilty?"

"Ja."

"They died doing what they loved."

"Would you have?"

"Oui. It is part of our esprit de corps. But confidentially, between you and me, my muse, I prefer to die a raconteur."

"You can be your own muse now," said Nayla. "You drank a mixis."

"So I did."

"Do you still have it?"

Beauvais produced the bottle from his robes. "My souvenir."

Nayla inspected it in the red glare. "There is a cloud, a sword, a stylus, and a winged shoe."

"Zephyrus, god of the west wind. Ares, the god of war. Calliope, the muse of epic poetry. And Hermes, god of travel."

"What did you create?"

"My short story."

"I remember you saying. What was it about?"

"Love on the Niger, between a soldier and a Mandinka woman."

"I'll read it when I get back."

"You assume we'll survive... I like that. Me and the boys always spoke of future plans before a tense situation. It gave us confidence we'd live."

"I'm going to Jacoma to eat sheepshead next week." Nayla smiled.

"That's how it's done. How do you feel?"

"Better," said Nayla. "How do you feel?"

"Glad to see another day." Beauvais pointed his cigarette at the helm. "There's always something in this world to entertain me."

Nayla and Beauvais walked closer to the deck to hear.

"S'il te plait," said Céleste, caressing Orpheus's arm. "You are a virtuoso, husband material."

Orpheus shook her off. "It will never work."

"But why?" she groveled.

"Two reasons, darling. Insecure women rear insecure children, and no one holds a candle to my Eurydice. You have forced me to rethink my assistance. Be gone from my sight."

Céleste's lips quivered into a frown as she backed away, distraught.

How horrid. Nayla walked up the steps and consoled her. She had never seen Céleste rejected before, not on first encounter.

"He is my constant source of love," said Céleste. "I know it. If I had my body. If I had my soul. I'd have won him over."

Nayla stroked her hair. "I know. I know." She walked Céleste into Beauvais's charge.

"There goes our ride home," he said.

"Not if I can help it." Nayla returned to the quarter deck for a word. "Orpheus, I must apologize for my friend. She saw you as her husband in the Well of Lost Souls."

Orpheus slowly nodded. "The universal mind may have detected me in her future, blended it in her unconscious with her desires, and projected them upon the water."

"You are aware of Brahman?"

"I have a spiritual side. My music doesn't come from reality." Orpheus looked over the rail.

"Where are you taking us?"

"To the edge of Tartarus."

Nayla looked out onto the city. "I see the stepwell in the distance." She turned to Orpheus. "Please, wait for us. We have to make the exchange and save our friend, Gustave. I'm about to marry Hermes. My friends need a way home."

"Have Hermes take them."

"I don't trust him," said Nayla. "I prefer you take them. I ask you as one musician to another."

Orpheus perked up. "What do you play?"

"Sitar."

"Play for me and I'll consider it."

"I do not have it on me."

"You have a wand that can change anything into anything."
Orpheus handed her a cannonball.

Nayla lugged it down to the main deck where Céleste raised
her muscular face from her hands, crying.

"I am telling her the ways of the world," said Beauvais.
"Kill Arachne. No problem. Take a man from his loving wife.
Big problem. Is our ride secure?"

"Almost."

"I'm sorry I ruined everything," Céleste whimpered.

How many times had Nayla seen her own face in tears?
Such a peculiar out-of-body experience.

"You did not ruin everything," said Nayla.

"How Orpheus acted is exactly how I treated Hermes."
Céleste sniffled. "Now Hermes is obsessed, and I don't know
how not to be."

"By focusing on the task at hand to take your mind off
Orpheus."

Nayla picked up Circe's staff and placed it in Céleste's care.

"Can you change this cannonball into a sitar? Get us our
ride back. I need to play for him if he is to help us."

"Anything for my future husband," she said despairingly.

With an emerald shower, the ball was converted.

Nayla tuned the sitar and returned to Orpheus. She sat and
played him a serenade.

Orpheus closed his eyes. His head bobbed back and forth
to the music, nodding up and down. He removed the lyre from
its pouch on his back and joined her melody.

Their harmony captivated Beauvais and Céleste, who wiped
a tear from her eye.

The music hypnotized, the notes flowed in key with the
universe—playful, joyous, with touches of melancholy to reflect
the sordidness of life. Somehow, up in the airship in Tartarus,

Nayla felt everything would turn out well. She had the plan, the escape, and three fabled objects. It was all coming together. Here came the finale. *Don't choke, Nayla. Don't choke.* She homed in on her intuition and plucked the last cord in unison with Orpheus. The note hummed and died in the air.

"We're here," said Orpheus. "Above the street outside the stepwell. I patiently await your safe return."

The song had pleased him.

CATHARSIS

"A drink for luck?" Orpheus passed Nayla a bottle of rum. The powers of the caduceus had restored her health. Maybe they had reset her burnout. Usually, it took a week to recover after a month-long binge. It would be nice not to face Hermes and Charon totally powerless. Nayla took the bottle and guzzled half of it. The rum burned a river down her esophagus and settled into the reservoir of her stomach. She belched and returned Orpheus the bottle.

Nayla met Céleste and Beauvais on the main deck overlooking the cargo bay. She set down the sitar and picked up the hammer. Her buzz kicked in as she descended the ladder into the hull.

Gears whirred, opening the hatch underneath the ship, revealing Tartarus and its golden towers. A perimeter wall outlined the stepwell. Stains spilled down from the top where the Danaides tried to fill their cauldron with Lethe water. Tiered steps faded into the stepwell's milky center, revealing a shadow of Charon's submerged Bateau Lavoir.

"Are you ready to save Gustave?" Nayla offered a hand.

"Oui." Céleste took it. "Nayla?"

"What?"

"Thank you for leading me to my soul."

Nayla shifted, uneasy around praise. "But you didn't get it."

"Non, but I may never have gotten this far without you. I just wanted to say, you're the best friend a girl could ask for and I hope I have enough love in my heart to mean it when I say, I love you."

Nayla hugged Céleste, smelling her own scent. "It will all work out according to plan."

"That's why I said goodbye."

"For now." Nayla swallowed.

"Wait," said Beauvais. "I'm not about to go charging around in a toga. Can you change some cannonballs into my old uniform? You've seen how the legionnaires dress, haven't you?"

Céleste dried her eyes. "You don't trust me to change your toga?"

"Not with me in it."

She raised the staff. "Too bad."

Emerald light transmuted Beauvais's toga into a rough approximation of his old blues and whites with Tartarus accoutrements.

Beauvais touched his face to make sure it was still his. "Merci."

"Make wide circles south of the gate." Nayla told Céleste as she borrowed her staff for the flight. "We'll land in the street."

Céleste took Beauvais and Nayla under her arms.

Nayla stood at the brink, her sandaled toes edging over Tartarus.

"Un, deux, trois."

Nayla bent her knees and leapt forward with Céleste and Beauvais in a collective jump. Céleste expanded her wings and circled as directed, around a gilt tower, their images reflecting in its glass domes, espying the spinning hoops and their cogs. She approached the ground next to a cypress tree that resembled a pipe cleaner. Nayla pedaled her invisible bicycle as she landed so as not to fall.

She handed Céleste her staff and led them across the street, past a rug merchant with gears in his legs, and touched the wall surrounding the stepwell. Beauvais followed on Nayla's heels, around the corner and through the arch of gears in full view of the stepwell.

"Stay here," said Nayla.

Céleste hugged Nayla once more and released.

Nayla peeked over her shoulder to make sure Céleste hung back, which she did.

"I remember these watering holes from Jacoma," said Beauvais, grasping the caduceus like a club. "Not those strange women, though. They are Danaides."

"I could've used you earlier," said Nayla.

The automatons barely paid them notice, except for the one in green. Kameera eyed her suspiciously and kept on bucketing water to the tortoise pot with her ewer. This time, her eyeballs were fastened in her head. Nayla paid her no mind. It felt so much easier to walk down a set of stairs without her broken arm banging against her chest.

"Tomorrow, I'm drinking wine at the cantina," said Beauvais. "How about you?"

"I'm going to Jacoma to eat kale pache next week."

"Feel better?"

"Slightly." She made it down the last step to the deck, level with the well, and parked her hammer at the edge. "They're underwater."

A periscope plunked into the Lethe. Moments later, the white-paneled Bateau Lavoir bubbled to the surface. Rills of water dripped off its roof as the twin storied boat rose fully from the shallows and extended its gangplank.

Hermes, in a suit and tie, floated over the metal path, while Charon traversed on foot in a sea captain's uniform, leading a blindfolded Gustave by the shoulders, their faces red.

"Céleste," said Gustave, "are you there?"

"I'm here, Gustave," said Nayla. "I got what they wanted."

Hermes stepped onto the stone. "I see a caduceus. That is a good sign, ma fleur. Why the hammer?"

"I freed my French compatriot from servitude."

"Did Nayla retrieve the helmet?"

"She did."

"Good. May she have peace and abundance."

"Curator, my son," said Hermes.

"Dad," Beauvais said, facetiously to his patron.

"Charon can't command without a voice."

Beauvais leveled the entwined snakes at Charon's throat. Cyan glow radiated from the wing-headed staff.

"Merci, captain," said Charon. "Yer men have told me all about ye."

"And?"

Charon chuckled. "They said ye were laconic. You might've been a spartan in yer past life."

"Should we be speaking so explicitly?" Nayla nodded to Gustave.

"He'll be fine," said Hermes. "I keep my word. Curator, you may now heal Céleste. She has slept with Hades, and I wish to have her in mint condition."

"Who told you?" asked Nayla.

"His actions, when he located you in the well."

"What did Hades do to me?"

"Gave you syphilis." Nayla's jaw dropped. She'd slept with Céleste. Did Nayla have syphilis? Nein, Beauvais had healed her, broken arm and everything. Sweet Shiva, Céleste had syphilis. They never healed her!

"He is king of the underworld," said Hermes. "Don't look so shocked." He snapped at Beauvais.

"I have seen men lose their minds from the disease," Beauvais commented.

He aimed the caduceus at Nayla. The soft glow warmed her body. She felt refreshed yet again, and completely sober. Any chance of poofing free might've been shot down in flames.

Hermes stretched his hand. "Come, my bride. Leave the hammer."

"Wait," said Gustave. "This masquerade is wearing thin. I want to know Céleste is not a phonograph recording like Théophile."

Hermes tapped his foot impatiently and sighed. "Go on. Ask her anything."

Nayla gulped silently. The saliva left her mouth. Her throat ran dry. Her heart banged in her chest. She knew Céleste well, but not every detail of her life. What if he asked her a ballet position? Nein, Gustave didn't know ballet.

"Finish the prayer," said Gustave. "O Mary, conceived without sin, pray for us who..."

"Pray for us who..." Nayla hesitated. Her mind blanked. "Pray for us who... love Jesus."

Gustave shook his head in disgust. "It's not her."

Hermes looked incredulous. "Are you sure?"

"Yes, I'm sure," said Gustave. "And her accent is off."

Hermes closed his eyes, deep in thought. He cocked his head back and opened them snidely upon Nayla. "Where is she?"

"Don't be ridiculous," said Nayla. "I'm right here."

Hermes scanned the stepwell. "Does she have the helmet? No, she has Circe's staff." He levitated off the ground and floated the perimeter. "Show yourself, Fleur d'Étoile." His voice boomed far and wide, carried on the winds. "I need to see you're still you. Hades gave you syphilis. My caduceus can heal it."

Nayla made it a point not to look at the archway.

"Charon." Hermes floated midway up the well. "Remove the blindfold."

Charon whisked off Gustave's bandanna and thrust him forward. He rubbed his eyes and opened them in the red glare of the sun.

Céleste stepped into view in the archway, screaming in Nayla's voice.

Beauvais took off at a sprint, up the steps toward Céleste, caduceus in hand. At the halfway point, he raised the wand to heal her.

Hermes snatched it from Beauvais's grip, flying, and turned to Céleste. "My parting gift for your insolence, ma fleur."

"Wait," Céleste cried. "I'll marry you. I'll do anything."

"No soul, no body," said Hermes, "and no mind that knows what's good for you. I'm afraid Theseus's ship has been altered one too many times for my liking. This arrangement is over."

Céleste scowled and raised the staff, firing green showers into the air.

Hermes dodged them easily and sailed back to the Lethe. He smiled at a bewildered Gustave and traveled with Charon on the retracting gangplank back to the boat.

"Where am I?" Gustave measured Nayla up. "Who are you? What the hell's wrong with your skin?"

"It's me, Nayla. Céleste and I switched bodies. We're in Tartarus. The light here has a weird effect that shows our muscular systems. I know it's a lot to take in."

He looked at his arms and recoiled in horror.

"By what devilry... I heard the name Fleur d'Étoile. It's that fairy artists see in French Athens."

Céleste nearly crash-landed at Gustave's side. "Gustave, it's me, Céleri."

"Is it? Is it? O Mary, conceived without sin..." he blathered in disbelief.

"...pray for us who have recourse to thee," she finished.

Gustave enveloped her in his arms. "Tell me I am hallucinating." He fell to his knees. "I was abducted by a statue I pass on Hermes Hill on boulevard de Clichy."

Céleste shook her head, clinging to Gustave. "It's the real Hermes."

"Non, non, something is off. Real Hermes... There is no such thing... Earlier, you said a demon stole your soul..."

"Oui," Céleste lamented.

"Mon Dieu," Gustave looked at her, his eyes roving. "They're all demons. They are Nephilim."

"From pre-flood times?"

"Oui, when the Watchers descended from heaven. They were angels tasked to oversee humanity, but they interbred with our women and gave birth to abominations. Giants, gnomes, fairies."

"Am I Nephilim?"

"Non, you are pure. Born human. Somehow they roped you into their cult."

Nayla hadn't heard of the Nephilim before, though it all sounded very plausible on paper, but the deities were Hindu. There was no mistaking it.

"Are you sure?" asked Céleste. "Are you sure God didn't abandon me at birth?"

"Why would you say that?"

"If God was there for me, He wouldn't have given me parents who do not love me and He wouldn't have let Théo attack. I asked God for His protection the day it happened and He wasn't there."

"Céleri, listen to me." He held her hands. "We were born with original sin and freedom to choose. Théo made a choice to allow evil into his heart. His desires were not brought to him out of love, but taken by force. When you ask for God's protection, you must know you have it as fact. Not hope. Fact. Seeing the future as fact equals faith. Édouard drew Théo into your life and he must bear that burden."

Nayla was taken aback. Here Gustave was, spirited into the underworld and comforting Céleste, not overly concerned with his surroundings, when it should've been the other way around.

"What about having Papa and Berthe for parents?"

"I don't have all the answers. What I can tell you is, perhaps it's God's way of preparing you for something."

"Like Jeanne d'Arc?"

"The greater your conflict, the greater your calling."

Céleste nodded, wiping her tears.

Nayla looked up at the sun and saw a bird flying toward them. She pointed.

"Cél, what is that?"

Céleste brimmed her eyes with her hand.

Gustave splayed his fingers to shadow his face. "That is a fallen angel."

"Nemesis!" Céleste squealed. "Gustave, listen to me. She maintains the secrecy of the cult. She's coming to kill you."

"Then I will die defending your life."

"I can change you, Gustave." Céleste gripped the staff. "Into an initiate. She won't kill you if you're one of us."

"He may need a mixis," said Nayla.

"Then I will make a mixis. I can save you."

"I have been saved. Jesus is the Truth, the Light, and the Way."

"Non," Céleste whimpered. "You'll die."

"If it is my time, it's my time. Promise me you won't dwell on my death. Do not look back."

"Non. Don't speak like that."

"Promise me you won't look back."

"Like Orpheus looked back at Eurydice?"

"Like Lot's wife looked back at Sodom as it burned." Gustave placed his hand over Céleste's lips. "Céleri, it is a miracle I found you. All those nights alone at the bar at the Folies." He shook his head. "I prayed for this chance, that I would gladly give my life to let you be safe, and God has granted it to me."

Céleste removed his hand, tears streaming from her eyes. "Not without a fight."

"Cél," Nayla warned, "Nemesis is immortal."

"Et alors?"

Nayla thought about dirigibles and failed to go poof. She had either not recovered from the burnout, or the caduceus had healed her of her poisonous libations.

"I have no weapon," said Beauvais.

"What would you like?" Céleste grabbed an empty ewer from one of the Danaides approaching the Lethe and threw it to the ground.

"A Gras-Vetterli repeating rifle."

The emerald light reconfigured the can into a gun with a bayonet. Beauvais picked it up and cocked the action.

She grabbed an ewer coming away from the Lethe and transformed the white liquid crimson right in the automaton's hands. "Pour toi." Céleste gave the container to Nayla.

Nayla smelled it. "Wine." She held the spout to her mouth and guzzled, letting it pour down her bodice.

Céleste threw another ewer to the ground and changed it into an Apache revolver with a blade for a barrel. She took the gun and handed it to Gustave.

Gustave clasped her hands over the staff as the figure of Nemesis grew larger and larger, her bandeau fluttering on her head.

"Pray with me, Céleri."

She looked up at Nemesis approaching and back at Gustave. "D'accord."

"Saint Michael the Archangel, defend us in battle. Be our protection against the wickedness and snares of the devil. May God rebuke him, we humbly pray. And do Thou, O Prince of the Heavenly Host, by the Power of God, cast into hell Satan and all the evil spirits, who prowl through the world seeking the ruin of souls." Gustave looked into Céleste's eyes. "Amen."

"Amen," she repeated.

"I must warn." Nayla gripped the hammer. "Her appearance is disturbing. Don't let it throw you."

Beauvais took aim and fired. He ejected the brass. Fired. Ejected. Fired.

Nemesis flew in hot, her sword raring to claim someone's head. She sliced the rifle clean in half. Beauvais turned and kept firing through the damaged barrel. A shot rang off her cuffs. More shots from Gustave. Céleste pointed the staff. Green rays beamed upon the spot where Nemesis stood. She ducked under and sliced at the object. Unable to break, the force ripped it from Céleste's grip, and it flew into the Lethe.

Céleste wound back her fists and let flame shoot forth in geysers, scorching Nemesis's garments, burning the bandeau right off her face, singeing her feathers. While Nemesis was distracted, Nayla dashed in, mallet raised. She thunked it down hard.

Nemesis, agile, swept clear, though not her sword, which clanked into shards under the hammer's weight. The goddess frowned at Nayla, the pupils furious through her enclosed eyelids. Céleste's heat was unbearable.

Nayla backed away. Nemesis swiped the broken sword at Nayla's abdomen.

Weather balloon.

The stepwell burst into wavy lines along with the cloying image of Nemesis. The movement. It was like swimming. That's what Céleste had to do. Swim for the staff. It was the only way to stop this madwoman. If Céleste held her breath, she could make it easily in Spuckfeuer's body.

Anvil.

Nayla reappeared behind Nemesis, hammer in hand.

"Cél, you have to get the staff."

Céleste traded her geysers for volleys of flame. She chucked fireball after fireball at the shying Nemesis, who struck them with her broken sword.

"Create a firewall to contain her," Nayla shouted. "Think of an overturned bowl."

The fireballs ceased. Céleste raised her hands to the skies, summoning trees of fire around Nemesis which folded over her into a dome.

The goddess swiveled around, taking them all in, the sword ready to hack, though she made no move to escape.

"Use the jets on your feet to swim," Nayla instructed.

Céleste ran to the stepwell's edge and dove into the Lethe with a hair-raising splash.

"She won't make it," said Nemesis. "It's too deep. By the time she returns, she'll have no recollection of what transpired."

"What do you want, demon?" Gustave demanded.

"To maintain the pantheon's integrity. However, I will spare your life, mortal." Nemesis eyed the milky waters. "Drink and be purified."

Gustave cocked his revolver, Beauvais his sawed-off rifle.

Nayla sidestepped to Nemesis's flank, should one of the bullets pierce the firewall and strike her.

The licking flames gradually lowered their tongues. The firewall was dying, Nemesis growing more smug. How deep was that stepwell?

"Time's up." Nemesis walked through the fires straight for Gustave.

Beauvais stepped in front and pulled his trigger. The round deflected off her breastplate. Nemesis delved her sword through his gut and into Gustave.

Nayla let out a shriek. Her friends were her responsibility. The plan was her idea. She could not stomach the guilt.

Gustave swung out his arm, jabbed Nemesis in the stomach with his blade, and fired.

Nemesis pulled out the sword and backed away, groping her wound. Gustave fell to the stone. Beauvais stood, feeling his midsection where the sword had penetrated. Smoke wisped from his robes. The sides of his hair had gone white, and parts of his beard.

How could he...? He had triggered his powers... breathed flora... the cigarette. *Hold on, Gustave.*

Nayla rushed the injured goddess, hammer raised. Nemesis turned abruptly, swatted Nayla aside with her wings, and took flight.

The blow sent Nayla teetering close to the Lethe. Beauvais grabbed her arm to regain balance.

Phoenix wings exploded from the well like cannon fire. Céleste arced into the air and landed on the stone border by Gustave, choking for breath, Circe's staff glowing green.

She looked down at him with a vacant stare.

Nayla clung to Beauvais, looking on, helpless.

"Céleri," Gustave sputtered, blood running from the corners of his lips, "to find your soul, ask God what you desire. In recognizing Him, He will place the event you seek on your path." He struggled to speak, but determinedly forced the words out. "He already knows what you seek, but you have to take action in the asking and recognition of Him. Ask, and you shall receive. Seek, and you shall find. Before ye call, I shall answer. It's how I found you." He ripped off his necklace and handed it to her, choking. "May she bless you with a grace." His hands fell limp on his shirt.

A cry escaped Céleste's throat and cleaved the air. She choked as her expression of anguish faded to oblivion with the staff's emerald light.

"Cél." Nayla jostled her arm.

Céleste looked at her, hostile, like they'd never met. "Who are you?"

"It's me, Cél. It's Nayla."

"The waters," said Beauvais. "She swallowed them."

Céleste looked at where Gustave had stood.

"What is she looking at?" asked Beauvais. "A ghost?"

"It's an electric ring," Céleste answered, "hanging on the air like a Christmas wreath."

"A doorway," said Nayla.

"There is a man in a turban," said Céleste.

Gustave's body rose from the stone and receded into an unseen portal.

"He is taking that man," said Céleste.

"What's in the doorway?" asked Nayla. "What do you see?"

"I see an alley with curly rain gutters and snow on the ground."

"Home," said Beauvais.

Nemesis flew into the red sun on the horizon high above the wall. Orpheus had cast off. Nayla lowered her gaze.

What bloodshed need further be spilled on her account? "I could have done something different, learned the Virgin Mary's prayer, told Céleste not to jump in the Lethe. I could've..."

"Predicted the future?" asked Beauvais. "Played God? Brahman is in us, but we are not him."

Beauvais was right. These were impossibilities. She couldn't blame herself for things outside her control. It was so hard not to, though.

Nayla took the staff from Céleste and passed it to Beauvais, who abandoned his gun to receive it. She nudged him on the back to step through first, took Céleste by the hand, and headed into the wintery night.

"Are we going home?" asked Céleste.

"Ja." Nayla could not control her tears. "We are going home."

"Do I have children waiting for me?" asked Céleste.

"You will someday."

Tragedy. According to Aristotle, the audience experiences fear and pity harmlessly through the characters so it may purge them of emotions. I am too close to confirm on this occasion, but Jacques will leave that for you to experience. For me, there is no comfort, as I am not a bystander looking in. My relief is that we escaped Tartarus at all. One cannot live in the unconscious indefinitely without a conscious mind to delineate order. The underworld is too stuffy. Too abstract. Insubstantial. It drives one berserk.

But we need it. We, homo narrans—story-telling humans— value the act of creation through our imagination. The nymphs of poets, painters, philosophers, inventors, dancers, and musicians dive into the depths and emerge with something to show us about ourselves. We need it. Man cannot live on bread alone. And we need our unconscious for more than that. We need it to restructure our beliefs. Or to not. The brave thing is that we took the stance sharply before the mirror and made the attempt. The benefit would have been for us all. The failure, of us all. I salute any effort to find harmony.

Look at the time. I have been spinning yarn for hours. The museum closes in five minutes. It is already dusk. Keep going?

We'll be burning the midnight oil into next afternoon. You wish to hear more? Are you in Athens long? Tomorrow, 9 a.m. Père Lachaise Cemetery. Perhaps we'll find Céleste. Perhaps Nayla. In the flesh? Who is to say? It won't hurt my feelings if you don't show up. I must warn you, it has a different appearance now than before the city was de-Guimardized. I love art nouveau as well. So glad you were paying attention. You have made my day. I will tell you more about caps and souls. Tomorrow, tomorrow. Your friends are waiting for you at the hotel. Oui, I consider you my friend too. So nice to have made your acquaintance. Until we meet again.

Au revoir.

ACKNOWLEDGMENTS

First and foremost, thank you to Diane Callahan of Quotidian Writer for being my alpha reader/dev editor. Your detailed notes and funny comments helped me to springboard Spitfire to the next level. I went deeper, not wider.

Thank you to Angela Traficante of Lambda Editing for polishing my prose and checking my German. Danke. Bérénice Hamza, thank you for checking my French. Merci.

For helping me with all things Indian culture and Hinduism—caste, karma, mantras and more—thank you to Casey Kaiser and Ritika. Ritika, your reactions made my day, and you both gave Nayla's world the extra kick it needed.

Josie Baron and Ana Flávia Hantt, your comments were delightful and encouraging. They helped me rethink the opening and add Céleste's origin story. So happy I did!

Sarah Gutsche-Miller, your book, Parisian Music-Hall Ballet 1871-1913, is one of a kind. I wouldn't have been able to recreate the Folies Bergère without it.

Liz Heinecke, your dive into Loïe Fuller in your book, Radiant, helped me sharpen her image in mine. For that, I appreciate you.

Sylvia Sagona, your lectures on Napoleon and France are wonderful and inspiring. I'm a fan.

Dosha of Rabbitwood & Reason, thank you for creating that beautiful steampunk Mata Hari headpiece for Nayla. I say you did Miriam Haskell proud.

Neha Shreshta of TOABH Talent Management, I'm forever grateful to you for organizing the photoshoot, working with FedEx, and standing up to Indian Customs.

Thank you Sagar Pawar for photography, Monisha for hair and makeup, and Ujasna for modeling. You made a great Nayla.

Kira Rubenthaler and James T. Egan of Bookfly Design, thank you for arranging and creating this amazing cover!

Patrick Taylor, thank you for fattening up the font on my chapter titles.

Lastly, thank you to my subscribers on Write Like for supporting the book. You know I'm about to do a doc on some of the authors Jacques mentioned now. Pierre Loti comes to mind.

I love you all.

Printed in the USA
CPSIA information can be obtained
at www.ICGtesting.com
JSHW081250230624
65220JS00001B/1